G000141572

SIGN FOR THE SACRED

SIGN FOR THE SACRED

Storm Constantine

HEADLINE

First published in 1993
by HEADLINE BOOK PUBLISHING PLC

10 9 8 7 6 5 4 3 2 1

British Library Cataloguing in Publication Data

Constantine, Storm
Sign for the Sacred
I. Title
823.914 [F]

Hardback ISBN 0–7472–0693–7

Royal Paperback ISBN 0 7472 7908 X

Phototypeset by Intype, London

Printed and bound in Great Britain by
Clays Ltd, St Ives Plc

HEADLINE BOOK PUBLISHING PLC
Headline House
79 Great Titchfield Street
London W1P 7FN

ACKNOWLEDGEMENTS

With thanks to my editor, Caroline Oakley, for – as ever – a thorough job on grooming the manuscript for this book; Mark, for putting up with my creative blocks and offering uncomplaining support; Ruth Oakley and Paula Wakefield for their invaluable help during the shaping-time; Andy and Lisa for the loan of their incomparable personalities; Trev, Tony, Stuart and Bones Ghost, and Helen, for the same; Jill Strong for her ideas for the chapter headings, Dave Horton for their execution; Amanda Billington for the cover art; Sal Bryant and Skez for critical appraisal of early drafts and poetic inspiration accordingly; Vikki Lee France and Steve Jeffrey, of course, for their continuing hard work on the Information Service; the Wolvey mafia – Flo, Ben, Mary, Michael, Oliver, Juliet and Vi – for providing a fascinating big old house for me to write about; Neil Flinn and Mark Haines for the impromptu readings late at night; and, last but not least, Debs, Tigger, Ash and Shep for their shoulders and their patience throughout all.

Sign for the Sacred

Saturated, sense-numbed, by the luxuriant spill of winesong,
Deluded by passions riot, the eyes conspire
With avarice, to strike the carnal forge.
For others, hostage to Promethean shadows, images beguile;
Vagabonds at erudition's bound, inventions to furnish minds,
Feed flames, fire dreams.

From eyes of angered hue leaks the essence of despite,
Ill-directed on heedless winds; faint whisperings of distant malevolence,
Hinting at blasphemy, yet sparing the body of faith.
Hatred's focus, pulsating, drumming with influence.
A pulse-beat of rumour, feeding the fated pursuers,
Marching upon the orchestrated upheaval of conscience.

To regain this lost daughter of self,
Breached must be the skin to unhindered country;
Bereft of companionship – the endless rope of adversity -
Pinned forever, at both ends, to oblivion,
Where time sides with reflection, and discovery
lights the taper of fulfilment,
Begins the cycle of regenesis,
Exhales the last breath of pain.

SKEZ

Introduction

Today, heretics would be hanged in the Ambustiary yard. The accusations had been made, the evidence presented, the official papers sealed. There was no chance of repeal.

The Ambustiary was an old site. The Archimagery had grown up around it over the two centuries that Ixmarity had been the principal religion in Gleberune. At one time, enemies of the god Ixmar had burned there regularly, and in some places the ground was still black with the memories of those immolations. Some said that on quiet moonless nights, the high, buttressed walls still rang with the ghosts of ancient screams. No pyre had been built there for many years.

Perpetuis Sleeve, the current Archimage of the Church of Ixmarity, did not condone the burning of heretics. It caused him discomfort. Such a barbaric practice. Wayward souls had to be culled, or at least silenced, but why inflict unnecessary agony upon the accused? In Sleeve's opinion, the expedient killings should be clean and noiseless. When he'd first accepted the office of Archimage the inevitable stench that had drifted up from the Ambustiary yard during executions had offended him greatly. His quarters were only a few storeys above the yard, and one balcony actually overlooked it. As soon as he'd felt secure in his new position, he'd amended the law concerning heretics. He'd argued that hanging was a far more preferable method of dispatch for miscreants, since it generated no unpleasant odours and no distressing noise; these were irritants which could easily intrude upon or spoil an afternoon's devotions. Also, the Church must be seen to progress in its methods. He'd found no real opposition to his suggestions.

Sleeve walked out onto his balcony and glanced down at the jumble of ornate buildings. The final preparations for the hanging were being conducted in the yard below. The smell of newly cut spruce filled the air with a pleasing perfume. It was a fresh spring day, and even though the air was cool, men worked without their shirts. A group of spectators, all of them aristocrats, had already gathered in the yard and were being directed into seats by a church official. Soon, the heretics would be brought from the pressyard into the Ambustiary and Sleeve would raise his hand to initiate

1

the execution. Already his fingers tingled, as if aware of their own power of life and death.

At no time would Sleeve admit, even to himself, that the concept of execution itself appalled him. After all, it was his signature that sealed the fates of those unfortunate enough to annoy the Church, but then he signed many papers every day. Requisitions for stationery, sentences of death. It made little difference, for he rarely read what was presented before him. He had so little time, or so he told himself. The Sacred Books of Ixmar said that heretics should die, and who was Sleeve, Ixmar's representative on earth, to argue? They were not real people that died, but symbols. Dark stains upon the surface of life. Sleeve could not allow himself to think that the accused had histories, feelings, grieving loved ones.

Sleeve had occupied the position of Archimage, and the accompanying palace in the city of Gallimaufry, for nearly five years. He was a graceful man of middle age; his frame was spare but lent itself well to the hanging of splendid robes. He saw himself as an innovator within the Church, building upon the sound foundations of his predecessors. He liked to think he exhaled a breath of vitality into the dustiest corners of Ixmarity's creed. His detractors considered him a liberal, and potentially spineless. Sleeve would have been dismayed if he'd known that his careful, probing questions during ecclesiarchical meetings had been interpreted as lack of faith. As a person of lower status he might have been a hazard. As Archimage, the highest position within the Church, he was, paradoxically, contained. A figurehead in splendid robes.

As a young man, he'd been a zealous ascetic, hungry to immerse himself within the rigid structure of the Church. His enthusiasm had done much to expedite his career; his mentors had considered him a prodigy. But now, as he settled into his middle years, Sleeve liked to think of himself as a tranquil and wry individual. He did not deny himself a few simple pleasures, and indeed saw the need for them in any man's life.

A young male acolyte, with shaved head and silver-grey robes, glided noiselessly from the inner apartment and presented himself at Sleeve's side. He carried a plate of sugared almonds. Sleeve took a sweet and sucked it thoughtfully.

'Has Lord Implexion arrived yet, Marmick?'

The youth shook his head. 'He has yet to present himself at your door, Your Sacredness.'

Sleeve recognised the ambivalence of that answer. Whenever his duties permitted it, the ecclesiarch, Implexion, came to Sleeve's chambers in order to view the executions from the excellent vantage point offered by the Archimage's balcony. Sleeve was aware that whenever Implexion visited the Archimagery, he always spent half an hour gossiping with Sleeve's amanuensis in the office downstairs, hoping, no doubt, to glean any tantalising morsels of information Sleeve might have withheld from him. Sleeve tolerated this prying habit, knowing that Implexion's thirst for hidden knowledge, to demystify every enigma he came across, was what made him so adept in his duties. But today, if he didn't arrive soon, he might miss the hanging, and Sleeve knew Implexion had a particular interest in this execution.

Today, two Jeopardites would swing from the gibbet in the yard below, next to the old cinder pit, still blackened from a thousand burnings. The day before, they had been arrested in one of the city plazas, following an appearance by their prophet who had, as was his habit, verbally abused the Church of Ixmar and called for its destruction, and then slithered out of the city to safety. What was Resenence Jeopardy thinking now? Did he feel remorse that others would swing in his place?

Beyond the walls of the Ambustiary, trees were putting forth young shoots and the air vibrated with the promise of perfume to come, seeping from seams in the sealed buds of blossom. Gallimaufry, principal city of Gleberune, was spread out below the Archimagery. It was a place Sleeve loved with deep sincerity. Every day, he spent at least an hour on his balcony, studying the outline of the city. Now, he felt he could draw it in his sleep; the graceful yet imposing silhouettes of the governmental buildings, the convoluted whorls and towers of the king's palace, the ragged muddle of the markets and the precise geometric lines of the harbours and jetties. This was Sleeve's province. Though ignorant people beyond the city might believe King Aristocete and his councillors ruled the land, Sleeve knew better. He knew Gleberune belonged wholly to Ixmar and His Church, and as Ixmar's principal representative on earth, Sleeve was the shadow king of the entire country.

As if to underline this glad fact, one of King Aristocete's aides came striding into the Ambustiary. He was dressed in ceremonial robes and carried a scroll, which would presently be read out to the accused. No lofty balcony seat for the representative of the king! Sleeve, standing against the balustrade, smiled and raised his hand in scornful greeting to the royal official. He did not like the man particularly; he had a woolly brain.

The sound of voices in the room behind announced that Wilfish Implexion had arrived. Sleeve straightened up. Half of him was always pleased to see Implexion, the other half put on edge by his presence. Sleeve looked upon the man as a staunch ally, even a sword hand, but knew in his heart that it would take very little for Implexion to transform into a powerful adversary. There was an underlying sense of unpredictability in Implexion's nature, a look in his eye occasionally that spoke of unconstrained ferocity. Sleeve wondered whether this was only his imagination at work. Why should he feel that way about the ecclesiarch? He was the Archimage, beyond reproach. The heavy tocking of hammers from the yard below sounded suddenly sinister making him shudder. Sleeve turned his back on the yard and walked slowly into his room.

Ten ecclesiarchs administered the Church, but Implexion was a man apart from his colleagues. Sleeve knew Implexion should really have opted for a military career. Only his elevated position within the Church, and the existence of an Ixmaritian militia, allowed him to exercise his caprices. If Implexion was a thinker, he thought only of strategies and plots and conspiracies. Sleeve doubted he ever contemplated the mysteries of existence or the complexities of Ixmar's ineffable being. Still, despite the ecclesiarch's obsessions, Sleeve generally enjoyed his company. He at least had a sense of humour, a trait which sat bizarrely among his other attributes.

'Sorry, I would have got here earlier,' Implexion said, handing his stiff black coat to Sleeve's acolyte. He grimaced. 'Had business to attend to.' Implexion was not an overly tall man, but had the knack of being able to appear tall. Sleeve was amused to see the ecclesiarch had pinned a spring flower to his lapel, reinforcing his view that Implexion was indeed a creature

3

of contradictions. He waved the ecclesiarch's apology aside.

'No matter. You are still in time.' He gestured towards the balcony. 'Shall we?'

Wilfish Implexion followed him outside, and leaned on the balustrade. He took a few deep breaths. 'What a glorious day!' he said. 'Aah! I love this season!'

'You seem in good humour today,' Sleeve remarked.

Implexion twisted his ropy features into a wry expression. 'It always gladdens me to see Jeopardites kicking air!'

'You are in danger of making this a personal issue,' Sleeve said lightly, and directed his attention to the scene below. Implexion made no response, but Sleeve could tell he had something to say on the matter. No doubt it would be revealed at what Implexion believed to be the right moment.

The accused were being led into the Ambustiary; a man and a woman. They appeared to be little more than drab peasants, but Sleeve knew that many sons and daughters of rich houses had joined the Cult of Jeopardy over the last year or so, much to the chagrin of their families who had complained in bitter terms to the Church. Sleeve knew their grievances were based more upon the loss of funds which their wayward children had taken with them when they'd fled their homes, rather than a concern that their offspring were turning away from the true god and facing a life of affliction and punishment. Powerful voices were clamouring to have something done about the prophet and his following. They stole money and children from the rich. In Sleeve's opinion, Jeopardy was nothing more than a crazed megalomaniac, too addled to be of real threat to the Church. Others, Implexion especially, disagreed, but whenever the Ixmarite militia rode forth to deal with the problem, the Jeopardites scattered quickly like ants into the hilly wildernesses of northern Gleberune. But as long as Implexion continued to catch a sackful of Jeopardite ringleaders now and again, and the embittered parents could watch them hang, it appeared that Ixmarity had the situation under control.

Sleeve examined the two standing in the yard between their guards. As true martyrs should be, they were unbowed and far from begging for mercy. Their eyes were raised above the walls.

'I wonder what they're thinking,' he said to Implexion.

The ecclesiarch made a scornful sound. 'No doubt Jeopardy has convinced them that hanging is a noble death, so that they now believe they are in some way promoting the cult. They are probably welcoming a beatific afterlife!'

'You think so? I understand Jeopardy believes in no gods other than those he creates himself. What kind of afterlife do the Jeopardites believe in?' Sleeve knew the answer but wanted to hear Implexion's response. He was quite fascinated by the effect the Cult of Jeopardy appeared to have on the ecclesiarch.

'They believe they create their own afterlife, as they do their gods. No doubt those two are busily imagining the paradise they'll be inhabiting within the hour.' Implexion laughed in a cruel manner. 'Let's hope our beloved Lord Ixmar will instruct His Divine Sons to boot them down the steps of His Celestial Mansion when they present themselves at His door! Thus will heretic souls learn the folly of their weak and passive tendency to be led by men with loud voices!'

'In that case, it's perhaps unfortunate no Jeopardite ghosts have ever

4

returned from death to advise their comrades of their foolishness,' Sleeve remarked drily. 'Would you care for a sweet?'

The king's aide had begun to read the charges in a bored, monotonous voice. An Ixmaritian high priest stood two paces behind him, waiting for his cue to step forward and entreat the heretics to recant their mistaken beliefs. The priest also looked bored. He'd performed this task many times and had come to learn its futility.

Presently, all the official requirements fulfilled, the Jeopardites were nudged up the steps of the scaffold, nooses placed about their necks. Sleeve raised his hand at the appointed time and was back inside his chamber before the Jeopardites had even begun to kick. Implexion joined him a few moments later.

'Your executioners must regard you kindly,' he said.

Sleeve raised his brows in enquiry, and dropped gracefully into a tapestried chair.

'Well.' Implexion continued, 'you obviously trust them implicitly, because I've never seen you supervise the most crucial moment of their work.' Implexion appeared amused.

'This is not a duty I relish,' Sleeve replied candidly, recognising the implied criticism in Implexion's remark but choosing to ignore it, 'I am a man of imagination, and greatly fear the thought of being sentenced to death. The hours before his final dawn must be the longest in a condemned man's life. It hurts me to contemplate how they must feel at that time. The grinding inevitability of it all. The frustration, the desire for freedom, the sight of blue sky beyond the prison window.'

Implexion nodded. 'I agree. A wise man, like yourself, would consider these things before he committed heresy, treason or murder.'

Sleeve sighed. 'Of course. Still, it is sad that we are forced to pass such grim sentences so regularly.'

Implexion tapped his lips thoughtfully with steepled fingers for a moment or two, then crossed the room and sat down opposite the Archimage. 'Of course, should the Church embark upon a full-scale purge of the Jeopardites, seize Jeopardy himself and rid Gleberune of his ranting presence, it might serve as an example to others and discourage them from mimicking his ways, thus relieving you of the distress you feel today.'

Sleeve narrowed his eyes. 'Implexion, never mistake compassion for weakness. Do not speak to me as if I were a fool!'

Implexion sat upright. 'I had no intention—'

Sleeve flapped his hand at the ecclesiarch to stem the torrent of excuses. 'Wilf, you are becoming obsessed with Jeopardy. Every time I see you, there is another tale to relate concerning how he has affronted you personally, and, I might add, the tales are always told to me in a loud voice emanating from a purple face!'

'I can't deny it,' Implexion said. 'The Jeopardites are like rats running over a laden dinner table, intent on stealing food in full sight of the diners. They have the same audacity!'

'They do not, however, go for the throat when they are cornered.'

Implexion made a hurried gesture. 'The analogy was not meant to be precise. Only yesterday the impudent rabble was crawling over the walls of the Archimagery itself, scrawling slogans and draping flags. Have you forgotten your outrage so quickly, Perpetuis? Jeopardy demeans both you and the Church with his irreverent acts.'

5

'They are the taunts of a naughty child.'

'Church soldiers have been murdered in the Swinkback hills! If a child kills, do we condone its behaviour because of its youth, or do we address the problem and remove that child from its environment, so that it may no longer harm others?'

Sleeve stared at Implexion thoughtfully. 'I cannot help feeling your metaphor is in bad taste, considering certain actions concerning Jeopardy's offspring you induced me to condone in the past,' he said.

'That action was expedient,' Implexion said gruffly. 'As distasteful to myself as to you.'

Sleeve shook his head. 'What's done is done,' he said. 'I know what you are trying to convince me to do now.'

Implexion smiled. 'But?'

Sleeve raised his hands in a languid gesture of sufferance. 'My instincts advise me not to act overtly at this time. Not in the manner you'd counsel. You must trust me, Wilf. Action has already been taken – caution prevents my saying more. I have received reports.'

'Such as that from the house of Salaquin Mandru?' Implexion said.

Sleeve grinned. 'I won't ask how you discovered that.'

Implexion continued, 'A report concerning a runaway Ixmaritian vibrancer, once connected to the House of Mandru, whose name coincidentally is Resenence Jeopardy?'

'That might well be the report I'm thinking of.'

Implexion flung himself back in his chair. 'And how does that help my men when they are attacked by Jeopardite berserkers in the hills?'

'Not at all. It would help your men more if you refrained from ordering them to hound Jeopardites into that territory. Perhaps your analogy with the rats is more precise than you think, and I was in error. The Jeopardites fight and kill because you are trying to capture them. No man or woman submits willingly to the prospect of being hanged. Left to their own devices, the Jeopardites merely dance about in public while their prophet makes nonsensical poetic speeches. Our people are bemused, but I do not see thousands flocking to Jeopardy's side.' This was an argument they'd had often.

Implexion raised his hands abruptly. Sleeve could tell he was trying desperately to control his temper. 'Perpetuis, you have not seen them!' he said. 'I myself witnessed one brute of a man, Jeopardite to his bones, kill ten of my people without using a weapon. How many more like him are there concealed in the Swinkbacks? I say we send a full commission up there immediately, request reinforcements from the king's army in Shanariah and the royal barracks at Thworn. If we flooded the Swinkbacks with men, the Jeopardites could not hide and mock us from their lairs. We should flush them out. Now!'

Sleeve and Implexion stared at one another in silence for a few moments, Sleeve directing the full force of his disapproval at the ecclesiarch. Eventually, Implexion dropped his eyes.

'Your advice is noted,' Sleeve said. 'You know I value your counsel but as I have already said, the action you suggest is inappropriate at this time. I do not wish to involve the state in what is ultimately a sacerdotal matter. The king's councillors will leap on this issue with a nauseous zeal comparable only with famished dogs offered a fresh carcass, and the whole thing will exceed any sensible proportion. Also, it is hardly politic for them to think

6

we cannot control this situation ourselves.'

'Well, it grieves me to say this, but I don't think we can.'

'And it grieves me to say this too,' Sleeve said, 'but I fear the only thing we cannot control is your overwhelming interest in Resenence Jeopardy! Leave it, Wilf. Let the local clergy deal with local matters as they arise. If we are called upon for assistance, we shall offer it in prudent measure. But I do not want Jeopardy, his sympathisers or any ambitious councillor thinking we are deeply concerned about this matter. We should manifest a sublime disregard as a general rule, acting swiftly and justly only when the occasion merits it. That is all I will say.'

Implexion stood up, and bowed formally. 'I cannot pretend I'm not disappointed, and I shall make a report of my displeasure to the Chamber of Ten.'

'You will not find support there,' Sleeve said in an even voice. 'Nine of the ten ecclesiarchs share my view.'

'I have a foreboding you will all come to regret that unity.' Without further comment, Implexion left the room.

Sleeve sighed and lay back in his chair. This particular disagreement with Implexion had been intensifying for nearly three years, ever since Jeopardy had first appeared in public. Sleeve could not share the ecclesiarch's dire apprehensions. In his opinion the Cult of Jeopardy was not a serious threat to Ixmarity. He believed the human mind to be an organism that adored variety and change. He also knew that it was easily attracted to new belief systems and ideas, which could be discarded just as quickly in favour of something else. Many sects and cults had come and gone since Perpetuis Sleeve had joined the Church. Many existed still in the northern territories – pagan religions of peasants and gypsies. But none of them had ever threatened the stately immensity of Ixmarity, simply because of the Church's size and fixed state. Also, Ixmarity had political power, which none of the smaller cults had. Ixmarite officials sat on the King's Council and all the regional bodies. Neither Jeopardy nor anybody else was a threat to that. Self-styled priests, prophets and wizards could rant and inspire people as much as they liked, but the clean, inexorable force of Ixmar, which without fuss or room for explanation built the gibbets and hung example heretics high, could not be beaten.

Despite Implexion's anxieties, Sleeve did not believe Jeopardy would ever raise an army, and that was the only threat the Archimage and the majority of the ecclesiarchs could take seriously. To kill the prophet now would be a mistake. It would swell his movement rather than diminish it, for his minions would spring up out of the very rocks of Gleberune and joyfully spread the word of the martyr. Sleeve believed Jeopardy to be mad. He had observed his career with patient interest and he intended to discredit the prophet in his followers' eyes. The time for that was close, but not yet imminent. Sleeve would rather have the half-wits, poseurs and fanatics that seemed attracted to the Jeopardite cult safely under the prophet's wing, where the harm they could do was minimal. The majority of Glebish people were entertained by the prophet, and flocked to his talks and performances out of casual interest, but even though they might throw him a few coins for his efforts, few joined his cult with any conviction.

Sleeve possessed a passionate adherence to his beliefs, but was not a cruel man. Like many before him, he was largely unaware of the atrocities those beneath him committed in Ixmar's name. But the previous year, Implexion had infected him with a certain measure of paranoia concerning the prophet, and he'd endorsed a plan which had resulted in seven children under the age of five being killed, simply because Jeopardy had been their father.

Sleeve remembered their conversation well. Implexion had joined him in his garden, where he liked to walk each evening. The air was balmy and relaxing, full of the voluptuous perfume of rare flowers.

'My agents have brought interesting information about Jeopardy to my attention, which I feel we cannot ignore,' Implexion had informed him eagerly.

Sleeve paused before a voracious wasp-orchid bush and bent to pluck out a few venomous, tongue-like stamens with his gloved fingers. 'Such beauty,' he said, 'such potential for destruction.'

'Your Sacredness,' Implexion went on, his voice tight, 'did you realise that Jeopardy not only steals the daughters of noble families, but also fills them with his loathsome seed?' Implexion strove to inject a full measure of repugnance into his voice.

'His followers carry his children,' Sleeve said in a flat tone. 'That does not surprise me. Should nubile young women flock to any common man's side, it would not be unusual for him to take advantage of the situation.'

'Ah, but there is more to it than that,' Implexion said. 'As you know, several families have hired professional kidnappers from Ixibatae in order to steal back their wayward children from Jeopardy's side. In many cases daughters have returned carrying babes. Naturally, my staff have interviewed these females and have also examined their children. All of them bear a peculiar mark on the forehead, which certain of my employees declare resembles the mage's speck.'

'The mage's speck!' Sleeve interrupted. 'Wilf, what are you saying? Only characters in fairy tales carry such a mark. It does not exist!'

'I have examined the evidence myself,' Implexion continued, keeping calm, 'and there is little doubt. The mark has the appearance of a clawed eye. It is uncanny, and unless I'd seen it myself, I would not have believed it.'

'Yes, well, this is all very intriguing,' Sleeve said, 'but during your interrogations, you didn't think to extract information concerning the prophet's whereabouts, did you? I cannot help feeling that in view of the many lectures you have given me on the subject, such facts as the size of Jeopardy's following and whether they have weapons would be of greater use to us than details of the deformities of his children.'

'Of course, those matters were looked into,' Implexion replied stiffly. 'But I beg you to consider the implications of what I have told you. Jeopardy is seeding the noble houses of Gleberune with his spawn. Those children will inherit the wealth of our realm. What if they should one day rise up and adopt their father's creed?'

'So, what do you think I should do about it?'

Implexion failed to notice the dry tone of the question. 'It is obvious. The children must be weeded out and destroyed!'

'My dear Wilfish, the Ixmarite militia cannot burst into respectable households across the land and slaughter their infant relatives! That would provoke an uprising, not forestall it.'

'Not if those respectable families are already uneasy about having the infants under their roofs,' Implexion pointed out hastily.

Sleeve straightened up and folded his arms, eyeing the ecclesiarch with a keen eye. 'Can you honestly tell me that that is the case?'

'Your Sacredness, I cannot lie to you. That is indeed the case.'

Sleeve shivered, as if touched by a presentiment. It seemed there was a sudden chill to the air. Had he been wrong to dismiss Implexion's concern about the prophet? Was it possible Jeopardy's power was growing, spreading throughout Gleberune like a fungal spore beneath the land?

'I cannot have families of prominence and influence offended,' he said.

The two men eyed each other, conveying sentiments without words. Implexion bowed, and took the Archimage's right hand in his own, pressing the seal of Ixmar, which Sleeve wore over his glove, to his brow.

'Your Sacredness, I implore you to trust my discretion in this matter.'

Sleeve withdrew his hand. 'Very well. Do as you see fit, but I want no complaints. If, in some cases, compensation seems in order, then offer it generously.'

'I had already anticipated such a palliative.'

'Good.' Sleeve sighed. 'There is a foul breath in the air this evening,' he said, rubbing his gloved hands together. 'Some of my orchids may have succumbed early to a blight.'

'Then you should have your gardeners uproot them,' Implexion said smoothly, 'before they pollute the rest of your lovely garden.'

Sleeve stared at him with steady eyes. 'There is some merit in what you say,' he said, 'but, metaphors aside, I am unhappy with this necessity. The hanging of heretics is one thing, but I have always believed children to be innocent.'

'These Jeopardite offspring cannot be viewed as ordinary children,' Implexion said. 'I too have had to harden my heart to come to this decision.'

Since that time, Sleeve had vowed not to let the ecclesiarch's obsession overwhelm him. He was still unconvinced Implexion had been right about the children. Still, it was too late now and mercifully there had been little or no backlash concerning the infant deaths.

'This matter must be kept in proportion,' Sleeve said aloud to himself. The plate of sugared almonds was at his right side. He reached out, took one, examined its smooth, perfect surface, before popping it into his mouth. He rolled his tongue round the hard, spiced sugar skin and then bit down hard.

Sleeve nearly gagged. He spat into his hand. The almond was bitter as bile.

TRAVELLER

Some time during the night, the surface of the path beneath his feet had changed from dried yellow mud to flaking black ashes. Lucien Earthlight had walked all night, and for half the day before that, with barely a pause to drink from his water leather. Fortunately, exhaustion had been kept at bay, following a lucrative session of augury at the last hostelry he'd stayed in at Weastraw, further down the coast. The spirit of clear sight had been with him that day, and predictions had fallen effortlessly from his lips, to the delight of the inn's clientele, who'd paid him generously. Before continuing his journey, he'd purchased an ample wad of sleepbane from Master Meticulus, a local apothecary, and had been using it ever since. Now, Lucien's jaw ached from constantly chewing the fibrous pulp. The sleepbane tasted of over-ripe cheese, a flavour that did not diminish, however long it was chewed. Lucien was also suffering from several side effects of the drug; his perceptions had become warped, thrusting him into a surreal world, where sight had become sound and hearing become taste, and travel was becoming increasingly difficult. Lucien strove to ignore these discomforts, however, because he was sure that if he refused to rest, he would finally catch up with the prophet, Resenence Jeopardy.

For nearly four years Lucien had been following Jeopardy's elusive trail, until the search seemed to have become the sole reason for his existence and, at the same time, to have lost all meaning. For nearly four years, Resenence Jeopardy and his band of close followers had kept just ahead of Lucien, almost as if they were aware of his pursuit, and had decided to tease him. So many times Lucien had been on the verge of abandoning the chase. He'd arrive, yet again, at another town or village where the Jeopardites had appeared in public, only to discover his quarry had vanished scant hours before. Drinking ale, late into the night, to numb the crushing disappointment that never dulled, no matter how many times he experienced it, Lucien would drunkenly resolve to end his journey, turn back to Shanariah, return to the house of Cartesian Blink, his erstwhile employer, and admit defeat. Then the morning light would kindle his compulsion once more. *Today, I shall find them. Today, they will let me find them.* Also, it seemed that when

11

frustration waxed strongest within him, significant portents would manifest along the way; as tangible as scraps of rag beside the road or crumpled leaflets advertising a Jeopardy appearance, or else as evanescent as a ghost of music in the air, an indefinable smell of success. Then, returning to Shanariah would seem an impossible and ludicrous idea. Lucien would laugh at the feelings of futility he'd experienced the night before, which were surely nothing but imps of delay conjured by the liquor.

In Weastraw, the last town Lucien had visited, he had been given what appeared to be reliable information concerning the Jeopardites. Usually, upon entering a town, it was fairly easy for Lucien to discover where Jeopardy had appeared and what display he had devised for the benefit of the crowd that always gathered round him. More often than not, Jeopardy's followers would put on a show in the town square, dancing in coloured rags to the music of fiddles, hand-drums and flutes, or else moving slowly in harmony to the accompaniment of eerie choral singing. On these occasions, Jeopardy might, if the mood took him, join in the performance towards its end, but generally he was content to observe from the sidelines, tapping his toes to the music and collecting money from the crowd. These affairs, however, were not the highlight of the Jeopardites' repertoire. Sometimes, they would erect a podium in a public place, and then there would be no light entertainment at all. When enough people had assembled, curious as to why the podium had been built and who would use it, Jeopardy would leap up, as if from nowhere, and assault the crowd with his own charismatic oratory. His favourite topics of admonishment included a diatribe against Ixmarity, and a condition he referred to as the Inner Sleep. He would speak out in forthright terms against the Church of Ixmar and its leaders. He would make dire prophecies in a disturbingly convincing manner and attempt to goad his audience into taking action against what he saw as their oppressors.

Jeopardy, as Lucien well knew, had very personal reasons for this apparent hatred of Ixmarity. Lucien also knew the people of Gleberune did not lend themselves easily to innovative ideas, especially if it involved inconvenience and discomfort, as mutiny against the Ixmarites surely would. To the majority, adherence to Ixmar's creed was but a small price to pay for a tranquil life. If a person was judicious enough to keep their behaviour correct, and their opinions free of unorthodox beliefs, then the heretic's gibbet remained nothing more than a distant threat. Occasionally, however, someone would be inspired enough by Jeopardy's exhortations to join his following. As the group that actually travelled with Jeopardy numbered only thirty or so individuals, Lucien presumed that converts made their way to the eastern range of hills known as the Swinkbacks, presumably to enter the Jeopardite community that was rumoured to have sprung up there. It appeared that Jeopardy himself hardly ever visited the place for, as far as Lucien had ever discovered, the prophet had kept on the move between the cities of Shanariah and Gallimaufry ever since Lucien had begun his search. There was the possibility, of course, that a lot of the information he uncovered was deliberately falsified. However, in Weastraw, the apothecary's daughter had been eager to talk about the Jeopardites, whom she'd seen a few evenings before.

The apothecary's shop was a dark and dusty establishment that reeked of the various essences and powders Master Meticulus used in his work. While he put together Lucien's order, his daughter Virtuine had chatted happily to Lucien, casting him lash-veiled glances from her wide green eyes that signified a more than casual interest in his person.

'I'd heard from my cousin in Hemping that the Jeopardites give a hearty show,' she said, and then frowned. 'However, there was little merriment the other night.'

'What do you expect?' her father had called from further down the counter where he was kneading Lucien's order of sleepbane into a dense lump. 'Prophets are by necessity quite mad. In one town, his crazy devotees trip their toes in a madcap dance and grin like imbeciles at the crowds. In another, they wear sacking and tear their hair while their master utters curses and maledictions. Both performances, I hear, provide a robust income for the cult. Jeopardy is a charlatan! I hope you did not throw good money into his mouth.'

The girl pulled a sour face at Lucien to indicate she objected to her father's criticism. 'The prophet was indeed in a dour mood.' she conceded, in a lower voice, 'and was quite curt with the crowd who had given him their time. However, his delivery was impeccable and he was a pleasure to look at.'

Lucien smiled thinly. 'You were not, I take it, convinced to become Jeopardite yourself.'

Virtuine shook her head, rolling her eyes upwards and tossing her abundant red curls. 'I should say not! The Ixmarites hang them, don't they? Anyway, if Jeopardy speaks to his followers in the manner he addressed the crowd last night, I wouldn't last two minutes in his company, no matter how comely his appearance.'

Lucien was familiar with Jeopardy's bad-tempered and hectoring aspect. He had heard many accounts similar to Virtuine's in other towns. It seemed the prophet was often frustrated with people's apathy concerning the Ixmarites. He was impatient with authority, and clearly expected everyone else to feel the same, although events suggested he was not averse to wielding it himself. 'Whatever your feelings, Jeopardy at least made you ask yourself questions,' Lucien said.

Virtuine narrowed her eyes and stared at him intently for a few moments. 'Did he now! What do you mean by that?'

Lucien shrugged. 'Some of what he said rang true with you. Today, although you will not show it, you are thinking deeply about what he said. Tomorrow, these thoughts will have diluted somewhat, and by the next day they will have disappeared completely from your conscious mind. But they have left a mark that will inevitably, in the future, influence your decisions.'

The girl laughed. 'Aha! So now it becomes clear why you are talking to me,' she said. 'You have the gift yourself, don't you? I thought you found me interesting, but in truth you are only trying to uncover information about your rival.'

'I do not class myself a prophet,' Lucien said, with a smile. 'Neither do I consider myself in competition with Jeopardy. My gift, as you put it, is a fleeting presence, and therefore unreliable. Did the Jeopardites give any indication where they were travelling to next?'

Lucien did not expect a clear answer, but the girl replied with certainty. 'Gallimaufry,' she said.

Lucien could not help sounding abrupt. 'Did they tell you that?'

She nodded. 'At the end of his oratory, Jeopardy talked about soiling the robes of the Archimage. He said he intended to speak in Gallimaufry itself, the seat of Ixmar's representatives.'

'That seems unlikely,' Lucien said. 'Why would he advertise his forth-coming activities when it's well known the Ixmarites would very much like to end his career?'

The girl shrugged. 'I can't answer that, other than to suggest he really is mad.' She grinned and leaned forward onto the counter, displaying a generous amount of bosom. 'Well now, will you tell my fortune for me?'

'No need,' Lucien replied. 'It is obvious to me you will get what you want in life.'

After he'd left the apothecary's shop, Lucien contemplated what the girl had told him. He hadn't lied to her about his clear sight: it was a sporadic faculty. Indeed, he wished it was more reliable because then he'd be able to foresee the culmination of his search for the prophet. Unfortunately, all he ever divined was trivia, which more than pleased anyone who consulted him but was of very little benefit to himself.

He took the sleepbane from its wrapping of waxed paper and broke off a small, gluey chunk. A strong smell of cheese surrounded him. For a few moments he closed his eyes and summoned his fractious inner voice. It spoke: faintly, but with certainty. His guts flexed in anticipation; Virtuine's information had been correct. Lucien put the sleepbane into his mouth and began to chew. Almost instantly, the nagging weariness he'd experienced over the last few days began to abate.

The cold night was drawing back her skirts, and the herald of dawn had brought a grey haze to the undulating landscape through which Lucien travelled. Weastraw was far behind him. Indistinct pale shapes revealed themselves to be sheep by the tocking of the bells round their necks, their bewildered bleating. They could just have easily been memories floating by. The memories of Lucien, former Vibrancer of the Church of Ixmarity, often assumed unusual physical manifestations. Since leaving Shanariah two years before he had perceived stringent messages from the past in the contour of black tree branches against the sky, in the curve of a herdswoman's smile as she'd passed him on a moorland trail, in the exact and meaningful position and shape of clouds overhead at dusk. Lucien knew that the whole world was comprised of such messages. He was the centre of the world and it spoke to him in symbols, some of them perversely obscure.

Over the past few weeks, the messages had become more direct and urgent. Standing on a bare, black rock, high above the world, looking down at a distant sea port, Lucien had suddenly been transported back to his childhood. He'd not seen his family since he was seven years old, and could not remember having thought of his original home since he'd left the Ixmaritian academy of Por Tanssie at the age of seventeen, ten years ago. Yet suddenly it was as if he was inside a small body, standing on tiptoe, straining to peer out of his bedroom window. The windows of the Earthlight house had all been set too high in the walls for a child to see out of. Still, he was aware of the beckoning smells of sea and tar that rose from the private beach below the house, and felt secure in the certain knowledge that his aunt was in the room behind him.

This complete sensual recollection had assaulted Lucien so suddenly, it had stolen his breath. The vision was brief and, even as if faded, he'd wondered whether he'd really seen, smelled and touched that room, those forgotten feelings.

He had walked quickly down to Hemanny, scolding himself that he must be hallucinating from hunger. When had he last eaten? He couldn't remember. He had been smothered by an onslaught of melancholy over the previous few days. Jeopardite clues had been nonexistent, and Lucien had feared he'd lost the trail. Still, if he dropped dead from starvation in his tracks, he would never achieve his objective. Luckily, there were still a few coins in his money pouch. He'd earned them a couple of weeks before, when his clear sight had been vivid and energetic.

Hoisting his backpack into a more comfortable position, he'd followed the signs for the market place, intent on buying something to eat. There, among the canopied stalls, he had seen a tall, mature woman, in a rose-coloured stole, holding a kerchief to her nose. For a moment, he'd been convinced it was his mother. Until that moment, he'd been unable to recall her features, yet the woman's face before him was as familiar as his own. Her expression was pinched and anxious, her thin mouth pursed, as if she disapproved of life's coarse intrusion on her tranquil thoughts. Tiberia, his mother, had looked that way. Lucien had made some small yet frantic move to attract her attention. Then, without noticing him, the woman had emitted a couple of dry sniffs, and put away her kerchief in some secret pocket of her gown. Her image had shifted in Lucien's sight, revealing her to be a stranger. She did not resemble his mother at all. She was not the person who had surrendered her son to a life of servitude and confinement.

Following this unnerving incident, Lucien had hurried towards the nearest stall and squandered nearly all his coins on fruit and bread, which he gorged in a fever of anxiety. Later, his body had complained emphatically by vomiting all the food back, but not before he'd experienced another hallucinatory recollection. Walking out of the town, through a residential district, he had heard the distant sound of children's laughter coming from a walled garden, and in an instant had been transported back to the statue-lined garden of Cadarusus the Diplomat, a friend of his father's. Once again, he'd felt as if he was a shadow on the border of light, a light that was other children playing freely. He had actually sensed the quality of the day as being summer leaning towards autumn, despite the fact it was springtime in Hemanny. And, although he knew the time to be just past midday, it had felt like late afternoon to him. Something warm and yellow had flashed past his eyes – the flounced dresses of little girls, their bouncing curls. He'd felt as if he'd stood within a circle of hands, of circling bodies, of spiralling laughter.

Retching into a gutter, his eyes screwed tightly shut, Lucien had hazily considered the message being given to him. He had never experienced hallucinations like these before. Could it mean he was at last approaching his goal, his destiny? Was the man he had followed for the last two years just ahead of him, the ground still vibrant with the passage of his feet, the air still disturbed? Jeopardy's face appeared before his mind's eye. He could almost believe that if he opened his eyes, the man would be there before him. The past was coming back.

Now, feeling closer to the Cult of Jeopardy than he had ever been, Lucien climbed the cliff path beyond Weastraw, buffeted by the arms of a sea-scented wind, towards the brow of a hill. He knew he was very close to Gallimaufry. Under normal circumstances, Lucien would have given the city a wide berth, for he was justifiably nervous of entering an Ixmarite stronghold. Born into an Ixmaritian family in Shanariah, given by his parents to a Church academy at the age of seven, Lucien had since wriggled free of the iron grip of faith, as well as a more physical bondage. However, as a child, hardy seeds had been sown in his soul, and even though he might have felled the heavy tree they had generated, its deep roots still persisted inside him. He no longer respected Ixmar and, on confident days, even denied His existence, but the ingrained fear of the god would resurrect itself whenever he was vulnerable.

His dread of the Ixmarites themselves was perhaps more well-founded. He knew that Gallimaufry was the headquarters of the Church militia, and that Wilfish Implexion resided there. He justifiably felt afraid of the ecclesiarch. It was well known throughout the land that Implexion had a keen nose for heresy, and a particular hatred for Resenence Jeopardy. Lucien was nervous of being within the same city walls as Implexion, almost as if he feared the ecclesiarch would somehow become aware of a lingering smell of Jeopardy around him, and come sniffing him out. If Lucien's identity should be discovered, his punishment would be the most severe Implexion could devise. Although his Ixmaritian brand was hidden from casual inspection, Lucien could not help feeling that his appearance, even the way he moved, identified him as an Ixmaritian vibrancer. As vibrancers were never seen abroad in the land unless accompanied by owners or Church officials, he was taking a very real risk in entering Gallimaufry. It was nearly six years since he'd fled the noble house to which he'd been sold by the Church, and in that time he knew he'd changed a great deal, but the intrinsic caution of the runaway gripped his spirit. If an Ixmarite official looked at him, he was sure he'd be recognised for what he was.

Ashes from the path fretted up around his body in a black and white flickering pattern. The hushed sounds of their whispering dance snagged in his throat, and he gagged, thinking of cindered flesh. perhaps there were hooves and bones in the ash. Standing in the dawn, his back to the rising sun, Lucien pulled his coat more firmly round his angular body. He felt taller than usual. Below him, the road to Gallimaufry was a ribbon of perfect white slabs that brought a taste of sugar to his mouth, which was bizarre for they were surely salt-scoured. To the left, held in a cup of sheer white cliffs, the towers of the city smouldered against the sky, their pale grey stone dyed the colour of unripe peaches by the awakening light. Covered wooden jetties fingered their way into the bay and many ships lolled in the low tide against the harbour. Perhaps he should turn round now, retrace his steps towards the east. Perhaps it was best not to invoke the past. Lucien stooped and gathered up a handful of ashes from the path. He stood up straight, breathed deep of the hissing air, and leaned his body out over the hilltop towards the wrinkling sea, and spat out the wad of sleepbane.

'Paradouze,' he said, in a low voice, and allowed the wind to strip the ashes from his open palm. 'Paradouze.'

The word could be spoken softly, to sound like a sigh of endearment, an avowal of love. Such was the way Lucien had pronounced it when he'd lived in the academy of Por Tanssie. it was the name of a god, one of Ixmar's sons, who was the patron spirit of all the arts, the Vibrancy especially. Even though he was able to turn his back on Ixmar, Lucien could never abandon Paradouze, whom he now refused to associate with His Divine Father's cult. Lucien supposed that in his formative years as a novice in Por Tanssie, he must have sung Paradouze's name many thousand times. *Paradouze, hear my steps, taste my balance, see my intention. Paradouze, make me exceptional.* Since that time, Lucien had learned a new pronunciation for the name of the god that he'd invented himself and now used as a ritual of personal protection. He had become adept at spitting the word out like a curse, holding his voice so tight in his throat it sounded like a hag's croak, using his breath to make the sounds rather than his vocal chords. He did not use this pronunciation now. The occasion did not merit it. Yet.

Ixmaritian officials on duty at the city gates presided over a complicated wooden entrance run, through which all travellers were required to pass in order to gain access to the city. The contraption was like a huge child's puzzle, for its slats and gates could be manoeuvred and swung aside in certain sequences so as to allow the largest vehicle to pass through comfortably. This thorough inspection of all new arrivals inevitably caused a pile-up at the gates, mainly of provincial traders and merchants, many laden down with produce. Expensive carriages, on the other hand, appeared to have little trouble gaining entrance.

Despite the early hour, enterprising traders had established booths along the roadside selling refreshment, and there were several pawnbrokers sitting cross-legged in a row, waiting to trade coin for belongings with those who lacked the gateway toll. Some people – farmers, merchants, inhabitants of the city – waved tattered paper passes aloft, and were allowed through the corral more swiftly. Lucien assessed the crowd queueing at the toll gate with a sinking heart. He knew he should have anticipated something like this, and chided himself for his lack of preparation. Now, he would have to improvise, and trust that Paradouze would aid him. Was it possible Resenence Jeopardy and his followers had passed this way and been allowed ingress? It seemed unlikely, and yet Lucien's instincts did not tell him he should turn back. Take the risk: go forward. Jeopardy *must* be in the city.

Now that he'd stopped walking and had found himself in the stressful situation of a bustling crowd, the full impact of the sleepbane made itself known to Lucien's senses. Barely able to stand, he shivered as his perceptions ran riot. Hoping his deranged state was not obvious to casual observers, Lucien slumped inside his long, high-collared coat, and wound his facenetting firmly over his head, leaving only his eyes exposed. Very soon, he would be at the gate himself. He was desperate to enter the city, if only to find a quiet corner in which to recover. This need for respite overcame any fear of discovery. He did not know how much longer he could retain control of himself, terrified he would lose his grip on reality completely, and run amok among the crowd, gibbering absurdities.

Infuriatingly, the queue ahead shuffled to a halt. A robust middle-aged woman, surrounded by several children, was arguing with the officials on duty. She wore a bright red shawl over a heavy long coat and her thick dark hair was held up by an array of bead-encrusted pins which were coming adrift. Through a haze of strident colours, Lucien watched the spaces in the air carved by the woman's wildly gesturing arms. Addled as he was by the effects of the sleepbane, it seemed as if her words smelled of bile.

People nearby began to grumble at the delay; some quietly cursed the rigid procedure of toll-paying, others complained at the woman's persistence. From her loud remarks, it was obvious to everyone nearby that she had no money to pay the toll. In resounding tones she informed the officials, and anyone else who cared to pay attention, that she'd left both her money pouch and her pass inside the city. The pass was newly acquired, because she'd only recently come to live in Gallimaufry, and it was hardly surprising

17

the officials could find no mention of her on their census sheets. The supervising official, stony-faced, would not move from his position of denying her entrance. Two of the youngest children, hardly more than babes, clung to the woman's coat, whimpering and wet-faced. Lucien had to close his eyes for a moment, overwhelmed by the odour of sour milk and faeces that the sight of them invoked.

'And how am I to get back inside, then?' the woman asked, hands on hips, having realised her pleas were falling on deaf ears. 'Fly over the walls?'

The official folded his arms. 'Get the money. Beg. Sell your children.' His response was delivered in a flat monotone. Under other circumstances, in another voice, it might have sounded like an attempt at humour.

'Look, I have a man in the city,' the woman pleaded. 'He works for the aromanauts. He is well thought of. He will pay for me and the children. Could someone not fetch him?'

Lucien noticed the official's face become slightly animated by an expression of extreme scepticism. He huffed impatiently. 'Move aside, madam, you are holding up the queue.' He gestured for the next in line to move forward.

Throwing up her arms in frustration, the woman turned aside for a moment, desperately scanning the crowd behind her. Lucien could taste the red smoke of her thoughts, the confusion there. She approached a man, who turned his back on her. She grabbed hold of a woman's shawl. 'Will you . . .' The only response was a nervous smile and a shake of the head. Perhaps nobody believed her story. Then, one of her older children, a boy who appeared to be in his early teens, grabbed hold of her arm. She bent down as he whispered something to her. Lucien felt strangely unnerved; the air vibrated with presentiment. The woman frowned, and then turned directly to Lucien. Their eyes met in a brief, intense contact. Purposefully, she took a few steps towards him. 'Sir,' she said, 'I am having difficulty, as you probably noticed. Would you be so kind as to take a message to the aromadule for me?'

Up close, her face loomed large and round like a child's painting of the moon. Lucien did not speak, but neither did he turn away. He was aware of the boy standing motionless behind his mother, watching him intently. The woman reached out a wide, damp hand and clutched Lucien's robe. His body shivered with cold, reacting to her heat. 'Please!' she said. 'What else can I do? I can't walk back to Tempaly, the children are hungry and tired. Take a message for me to Edgebone. Edgebone Anywhither. He is indentured to the studio of Orocete. Tell him Bessie waits at the gates, tell him I need the toll. He'll pay you for your help, I'll see to it that he does. Oh, please, sir, have heart for me!'

Lucien pulled gently away from her grip. He made no sound, but inclined his head and let one long hand hover over the woman's arm for a second. She backed away, staring at him, wide-eyed. An unsure smile hovered at the corners of her mouth. She gathered her children to her with strong arms. The queue moved forwards.

When Lucien reached the official, he was greeted by an abrupt demand. 'Your coin?'

Lucien had no money left. His coin pouch, tied to his inner belt, felt momentarily heavy, as if to emphasise its absolute emptiness. The official stared at him with ox-like patience from heavy-lidded eyes. Lucien was conscious that this was not a vindictive man, but simply someone who had become inured to human imprecations and desperate excuses, having been a gateway official for several years. He had blinded himself to entreaty.

'If you do not have the coin, please move aside,' said the official. 'The queue is building behind you, sir.'

Lucien straightened himself a little and initiated eye contact. 'Your fears concerning your colleague Omprint are well founded,' he said in a low voice. 'You are quite correct in assuming he covets your position and is seeking ways to undermine it in order to acquire the status himself. However, he is engaged in certain illegal activities concerning the supplies depot of your parish, and should you be vigilant in this respect, you will be able to obtain evidence to rid yourself of this unwelcome adversary.'

The official narrowed his eyes and blinked once, clearly taken aback, although he strove not to show it. 'How do you know these things?' he hissed, leaning forward so that others might not hear him. Naturally, the people queuing behind Lucien strained to listen to the whispered exchange.

Lucien did not move and spoke gently. 'There is something under the grain bin, the one with the oblique scratched markings. Look there. Now, will you let me in?' He took one of the man's hands in his own as if to press a coin there.

The official blinked once more. There was a moment's stillness, and then he pushed the slats aside. No further words were exchanged. Lucien passed into the city. Later, the official would remember the message and act upon it, but he would never remember the messenger.

In contrast with the bulk of the city, which was spacious and airy, the area between the outer and inner walls of Gallimaufry was a dark green, damp and eerie cavity. Its floor was concave and a runnel of slime-cuffed water leaked down its centre. Officials hurried travellers across the entry gap, as if to discourage anyone glancing to either side down the dark tunnel. Great iron rings were thrust into the lichened walls, as if the cavity should be half full of water with boats moored to the rings.

Keeping with the crowd of incoming travellers, Lucien followed the main thoroughfare that would pass through the outer market quarter. A clutter of untidy stalls stood there, from which lower-caste individuals sold ironware, cutlery, stoneware, and domestic tools. It reminded Lucien of a relic market; to his reeling senses the items on sale seemed to carry a patina of ancient dust, as if they'd recently been dug up from the site of a fallen city. Nothing appeared newly forged or crafted. As Lucien approached, he could see that traders were already loading their carts and sledges for a day's work. They were talking in hushed voices, and the clank of iron was muted.

Weariness was creeping back into Lucien's body, and the effects of the sleepbane were becoming muted, so that he walked in a dreamy haze. Paradouze had indeed been with him at the gate. Now, he would be able to replenish his exhausted funds by carrying out the task given to him by Bessie Anywhither. In some areas of Gleberune, notably the more rural parts, Lucien had discovered that money was not always a necessity, as many people lived by bartering and he had been able to exchange divination sittings for food and shelter. Such conditions did not exist in the cities, where the worth of every person was measured by the weight of their purse. He needed money quickly.

The aromadule was situated on the northern edge of the outer market. Here were blended all the fabulous incenses and perfumes that were used in Church rituals throughout Gleberune. As well as the expensive incenses that

19

swung in the high chambers of the Ixmaritian churches and cathedrals, other inferior blends were manufactured that every household was required by Church law to burn at certain times. A vast array of perfumes was made, from those that adorned the brows of the Archimage and his staff to those that were rubbed upon the exposed breasts of condemned heretics. As the court of Orocete was one of the largest studios in the area, Lucien only had to make a single enquiry before he found it. He walked under an archway, through tall open gates and emerged into a wide cobbled yard. The far side was invisible from the gate, owing to the festoons of coarse rusty-brown netting that were strung out on bound wooden frames, into which unskilled workers wove aromatic roots to dry in the sun. The frames were all on wheels so that they could be moved out of the shadows as the sun moved overhead, and even taken indoors during bad weather. To Lucien, the air was pulsing with a thousand colourful odours, redolent of the sharp creak of the flower presses in the workshops that ringed the yard. Workers flitted back and forth among the frames, shadowy as ghosts through the netting. A girl came to examine a plait of black roots on one of the frames, giving Lucien a suspicious glance as she passed. Lucien approached her and enquired where he might find Edgebone Anywhither. The girl, heavily cloaked, was obviously a resin eater. Lucien recognised the bird-like sounds and the earthy reek of resin in her breath, even though the scars of blood-letting, an unavoidable requirement of her vocation, were hidden from view.

'What is your business?' she wheezed.

'It is of a personal nature,' Lucien replied.

At first sight, Anywhither did not seem the kind of person with whom the homely Bessie would be likely to share a hearth. His body was small and wiry, and he had the kind of eyes that could not conceal his innate tendency to deceive. Lucien half expected him to ignore Bessie's request, but apart from a few moments' nose-rubbing and sighing owing to the fact he would have to take time off work, the man made no complaint.

'We have this trouble occasionally,' he told Lucien. 'Bessie is so obviously a countrywoman and the officials are never lenient with her kind. I must have told her a dozen times to make sure she takes all her papers with her when she leaves the city.' He sighed again, and shook his head.

Lucien wondered whether he should offer to take the necessary funds back to the gate, but on reflection decided against it. His ephemeral influence over the gate official might not work for him twice. 'I myself suffered difficulty at the gate,' he said.

Anywhither nodded sympathetically. 'It was good of you to come,' he said. 'Many wouldn't.'

Lucien shrugged awkwardly. 'Forgive me, but the lady Bessie did mention you might recompense me for my errand. Normally, I would not press the matter, but I have been travelling and find myself temporarily in financial woe.'

Anywhither grinned. 'Of course. But please don't think me impolite if I ask you to wait here until I am assured of Bessie's safety.'

'Not at all. I have plenty of time.'

Arriving at Orocete's court on the arm of her husband, her children straggling behind, Bessie Anywhither insisted that Lucien should not only be paid in coin, but should be offered the hospitality of the Anywhither residence into the bargain. From her manner, and the way she described the abundant contents of her pantry, Lucien supposed she was anxious to show off her home, perhaps to prove that despite appearances and the humiliating treatment she had recently endured, she occupied quite a desirable niche in Gallimaufry.

'Look at you!' she cried, when Lucien made lame excuses as to why he couldn't take advantage of her offer. 'Your arms are but sticks! You need an Anywhither casserole to help cushion your bones!' She would hear no more excuses and, leaving her spouse to conclude his day's work, took hold of Lucien's arm and dragged him out of the courtyard.

The Anywhithers rented a house in a residential district near to the aromadule, where many of the aromanauts, resin eaters and unskilled workers associated with the industry made their homes. The outer area, where the aromatics magnates lived was beautifully landscaped. Bessie and Lucien walked down a wide avenue where, behind high walls that were festooned with decorative creepers in spring bud and crowned with elaborate iron spikes, graceful manses regarded the coarser outside world with aloof countenances. Bessie pointed out an imposing grey-walled villa, approached by a curving driveway lined with statues of historic aromanauts, where the Orocete family resided.

'Orocete is the most famous aromatics court in the whole of Gallimaufry,' Bessie explained. 'Its incenses are exported all over the world, and the Archimage himself wears a perfume specially blended for his use. If Edge-bone continues to stir his essences with imagination and flair – he is well thought of by Gregaric Orocete and his sons – one day he will be appointed to the rank of master blender, and we too could own a house like that.'

Lucien could not help feeling this was an unrealistic aspiration. From his limited experience of Shanariah, houses like the Orocete villa tended to be inherited rather than earned.

Soon, Bessie turned off the wide avenue and she and Lucien entered a more modest district where the buildings clustered together and opened onto the street. There was a shrine to Ixmar's daughter, Panphyla, on the street corner. As they passed it, Bessie withdrew a corked vial of perfumed oil from her purse and flicked a few drops onto the greasy altar. The robed shrine attendant nodded in approval and wiped the altar with a palm branch.

'Fortunately, we get our votive oils for free.' Bessie murmured in a conspiratorial tone as they moved on. 'It can cost a pretty penny otherwise.'

Lucien smiled politely. The cities of Gleberune were thronged with such shrines, and in order to acquire the favour of Ixmar and His Family, citizens had to anoint at least three altars a day with sacred oils. There was no way the Ixmarites could police such rituals, but fear of Ixmar's displeasure did more than enough to ensure the populace obeyed the law. In Shanariah, when his faith had first wavered. Lucien had learned the trick of carrying common cooking oil in a coloured bottle. He had smiled at the shrine attendants and flicked the cheap oil without flinching. Cartesian Blink had taught him that. It had saved him a good deal of money.

'When he was first apprenticed to Master Orocete, Edgebone rented a room nearer the city centre,' Bessie said. 'He shared it with three others, so they worked shifts in order to avoid mutual irritation. Now, he rents a whole house, and has taken himself a wife – that is me – and is clearly moving up the ladder of society.' Bessie preened her thick dark hair and then scowled at one of her children who had plunged one of his shoes into a dollop of dog faeces in the gutter. Lucien caught the eye of the older boy who had apparently coaxed his mother to approach Lucien for help. The boy's face had a sullen, mulish expression. What had inspired him to single Lucien out from the crowd?

'Next year,' Bessie said, 'Edgebone will have enough money to educate two of the children. They shall wear blue smocks and attend the Ixmaritian school in the next street. Then let anyone accuse him of not being a man of ambition and thrust!' She smiled. 'You look tired, sir. Not to worry, we're nearly there.'

It seemed to Lucien that the high buildings lining the street were clutching desperately at the sky, an effect that made the street seem narrower and darker, enhancing the retention of old ghosts. Lucien believed that ghosts lived in stone and that only by destroying it could people be free of hauntings. Bessie noticed Lucien's furtive glances down each side alley.

'You know people here?' she asked.

'No,' he replied. 'That is, I'm not yet sure.'

'A strange answer,' she said, with an admonishing smile.

He shrugged. 'I am looking for someone.'

'Oh!' said Bessie, and then laughed. 'You're only a boy aren't you, but a boy who's seen much, I'll wager.'

'I have travelled a lot,' Lucien said. 'In the countryside beyond the southern cities, I've discovered that people's lives can be very different. It is almost magical.'

'Then you must tell us tales after you've eaten!' Bess cried.

The Anywhither house stood next to a shop that sold wind chimes, straw body brushes and other implements of exorcism. Although the house was not grand, it was built at the brow of the hill and boasted a good view of the harbour. Its roof was flat, edged by a wooden fence, painted red. Wooden steps led down from the roof to a small yard at the side of the building. Bessie took Lucien in through the front door which she unlocked with two keys hanging on a string attached to her coat pocket. They entered a dark lobby and proceeded into the kitchen at the back of the house, which Lucien later discovered was the largest room. The house seemed stuffed with children, undoubtedly fathered by someone other than Edgebone, all of whom regarded Lucien with hostile or disinterested stares.

'You're so thin,' Bessie cooed as she tried to drag Lucien's coat from his body. 'I dare say you've been neglecting yourself. Edgebone is the same. If I didn't shove a plate in front of him every night, he'd forget to eat.' Lucien was reluctant to be parted from his coat, and even more reluctant to unveil more of his face. Bessie, however, would not let go of him and ignored his obvious displeasure, so eventually Lucien relented, for the sake of politeness.

'Sit next to the hearth,' Bessie said. 'I'll get a fire going.' She barked a few orders at her brood, who'd all followed them into the kitchen. Sulkily the tribe retreated behind a curtain which clearly led to another room. After hanging Lucien's coat on a hook on the back door. Bessie knelt down before the hearth and began arranging tinder in the grate.

'So, who are you looking for?' she asked, and then before Lucien could answer, 'I've not been here long, but I know a lot of people, oh, ever such a lot. I make friends easily, you know. I have the kind of face that says "talk to me", so people do.'

Lucien was about to make a carefully worded enquiry about Resenence

22

Jeopardy when the older boy came back into the room. He was a wily-faced brat, who possessed a disquieting expression of scornful wisdom. After assessing his mother's visitor for a few moments, he walked purposefully across the room and kicked Lucien sharply on the leg.

'Out, Walterkin!' shrieked Bessie. 'And apologise to the gentleman! I'm so sorry, Mr . . .'

'Lucien.'

'Mr Lucien. I really am. You are a brat, Walterkin!'

'He's got funny eyes,' accused the boy.

Lucien narrowed his 'funny eyes' in a meaningful way. The boy stood his ground for a second or two and then backed off.

'Don't make personal remarks, Walterkin,' Bessie chided. 'Haven't I told you about that? Now, make yourself useful. While I see to Mr Lucien, go and help your sister Ellyann feed the babies.'

'Feed them?' sang the boy. 'I'll kill them!'

'Do as you're told!' Bessie yelled and began to lumber to her feet. Sticking his tongue out at Lucien, the boy ran from the room.

'A blessing and a bane,' Bessie declared. 'But they bring love into your life.'

'Do they?' Lucien found it hard to see how. 'I must admit I'm curious why your son suggested you speak to me at the gate.'

Bessie frowned. 'Did he?'

'Well, yes. It appeared that way.'

Bessie shook her head. 'I really can't remember.'

'Then why did you approach me?'

'I'd approached several people. I'd have asked everyone eventually.'

Lucien shrugged, and decided to let the matter lie. It was of little consequence, after all.

'Now, where were we?' Bessie was working furiously with her tinder. 'Oh yes, who are you looking for – that was it. Well?'

'Have you heard of the Cult of Jeopardy?' Lucien began. Over the months he had evolved a painstaking routine for his enquiries that led very delicately to the vital question.

Bessie let out a groan and rolled her eyes. 'Them? Them!' she cried. 'Oh dear me, Mr Lucien. I do hope the friend you're looking for isn't mixed up with that rabble. Oh dear me, no.' Bessie was squatting, hands on hips, before the hearth. Behind her, a feeble flame was struggling to take hold of the tinder. 'The Jeopardites! You should have seen them!' she roared. 'There must have been a thousand of them, wailing and leaping all over the place. It was a sight, believe me.'

'You saw them?'

'Well, yes. My friend Moura came to fetch me, you see. When there was all that to-do outside the Archimage's palace. You could hear them all over the city, you really could. Calling for Perpetuis Sleeve – Ixmar bless his name – they were, singing and carrying on. Unbelievable! Well, Moura and I, we just had to take a look, because Sylvia next door to Moura had seen them all trooping up the Dovesway Boulevard, you see. This girl came skipping up to me and gave me a leaflet. What a gypsy! I was just standing there, minding my own business and she comes up to me, calls me 'sister', gives me a leaflet. Edgebone told me to throw it away because we don't want anyone thinking we're involved in anything like that, you see.'

'Where are the Jeopardites now?' Lucien asked.

'Oooh!' Bessie got to her feet and glanced behind her. 'Now, wouldn't you know it, the flame won't catch. I tell Edgebone to fetch me quality tinder, and this is what happens. Course, he's never here to see it because he's out at work when I light the fire, but—'

'The Jeopardites,' Lucien interrupted gently. 'Where are they now?'

'Hammered and scattered!' Bessie said. 'The Archimage handed the business over to the ecclesiarch, Wilfish Implexion. He's a man who takes no nonsense, believe me. He led a veritable army of church militia to the place where Jeopardy was speaking, but those Jeopardites, they're quick as eels! Scarpered quick, they did, but not before Implexion caught a good many of them. Threw nets over them.' Bessie risked a smile. 'It was a sight, I believe, though of course I wasn't there myself. Couple of my kids were on a church roof nearby and saw it all.' She frowned. 'In truth, Walterkin has not been the same since. He's not usually a rude child, but I've found him fractious and awkward since that day. Perhaps it upset him badly.'

'Were the Jeopardites hanged?' Lucien asked, in dread, although in his heart he knew Jeopardy was not among the captured.

'Implexion strung two of them up, who he announced were true Jeopardites. The rest were hangers-on and they got away with a branding on the buttock, before being driven out of the city in their underwear.'

'When did all this happen?'

'Two days ago. Oh dear.' Bessie's face crumpled in sympathy. 'You *did* have a friend with them, didn't you!'

'Yes,' Lucien admitted. 'An old friend whom I haven't seen for a while and I'm worried.'

'Worry well-founded,' Bessie said. 'Oh, I am sorry, Mr Lucien. I hope it's not your intention to follow them now.'

'Where did they go?'

'Who knows? If that information was known. Implexion would follow it.' Bessie lowered her voice confidentially. 'If you ask me, the Jeopardites don't have much time left to them. Mr Lucien. It's no secret that Implexion has a particular hatred for the cult and, as you know, the Ixmarites do not tolerate defiance or heresy as a general rule. And they have the power to destroy anything that threatens them. People say the Archimage and his ecclesiarchs have only endured this much from Jeopardy and his band because they know the Jeopardites are lunatics. One has to feel a measure of pity for lunatics, after all. But a time is approaching when the Ixmarites' patience will expire. Then the foot of Ixmar will crush the Jeopardites flat! And that time's not far off now. I heard that Perpetuis Sleeve was quite purple in the face when he came out on to his balcony and found it draped with Jeopardite flags, and he is famous for his equanimity. In your position, I'd try to get my friend away from the Jeopardites before it's too late.'

Lucien rubbed his face wearily. It was already too late. How could he have felt so sure that this time he'd catch up with Jeopardy? His instincts had been so emphatic. It must be another cruel taunt. And yet, even though Bessie's evidence appeared exact, he could not abandon hope. His mind had crumpled in defeat, but his heart was not yet convinced this was another disappointment. 'Yes,' he said. 'I will do as you suggest, Mistress Anywhither. I shall attempt to find my friend, if he is still in Gallimaufry.'

'But not tonight,' Bessie said.

Lucien looked up at her. She seemed to shine with the intense and genuine light of kindness. It smelled of childhood, of candles and warm bread.

'There's an empty bed in one of the children's rooms,' Bessie said. 'You must stay with us tonight. Half a day won't make much difference to your journey.'

II

MADNESS

It was the madman who brought the plague to Samberdell. He brought it with his swinging axe, his twisted, blackened face, his snarls. At first, the people believed that his lunatic violence was the only sickness he carried, but they soon found out it was more than that.

The Ixmarite priest in the village declared the madman was a messenger from Ixmar, come to display the god's displeasure with His followers on Earth. Whenever he paused in the street to discuss the topic with those who questioned him about it, the Ixmarite's eyes filled with meaningful glances. He spoke of how Ixmar might have noticed that, despite the dutiful payment of Church tithes, the people of Samberdell held little love in their hearts for the true god and still pranced about at night in praise of false deities. He cited as evidence the fact that the lunatic's first victim had been the monotheistic Domino priest. Ixmar was offended by the Dominish faith, even though its adherents, like those of several other small, unimportant cults, currently paid double tithes to Ixmarity in order to continue in their worship. How long this situation would endure before Ixmarity decided to outlaw every other belief system was a matter for debate.

The Ixmarite's smug proclamations were cut short when his tongue turned black and swelled to fill his throat. He was the first victim of the plague. During his last moments he even forsook his faith in order to take advantage of the services of a witch healer. She could not save him.

Delilah Latterkin was not in the village when the madman came. She was sitting dream-catching in the clear air above Bethany's Knoll watching the summer colts sizzle over the grass. The only sounds in that enchanted place were those of insect and bird. She did not hear the cries from Samberdell, perhaps because they were muffled by the skirt of thick trees that shadowed the base of the hill. Or perhaps she did hear the cries but interpreted them as figments of her maidenly fantasy, the lament of willowy ladies drooping from high bowers over the wax-pale corpses of beautiful boys.

Delilah savoured these moments when she could escape from the mundane life below and position herself in the depression in the centre of the knoll. Bethany's seat, it was called, a place where a girl had once been

26

impregnated by the tongue of the earth. In some places, the people regarded the earth as male, although Delilah's kin took the path of the humpbacked Mother Moistfoot, an early goddess who still held gentle sway in certain hidden corners of the hills. Delilah knew that things were changing. Since her great-grandmother's day, stern priests of Ixmar had edged into the hill communities. When her mother had been a child, Ixmarity had come to Samberdell. A stark new church had been erected, which had been rebuilt several times since, each new incarnation being grander than the last. A clutch of Ixmaritian priests had come to educate the villagers; any effigies of older gods had been removed by the militia who accompanied the priests, and residents were firmly requested to remove all pagan artefacts from their homes.

Mother Moistfoot had no church. All her rites were conducted in the open air. Her religious trappings were the trees, the hills, the sky. How could they be removed? The Ixmarites knew they could do little about that. Although they told everybody that Mother Moistfoot, and all the other old gods, did not exist and never had, it was clear they had little real hope of converting the hearts and souls of the hill people. They spoke at length of the god Ixmar and His Family and how He was made quite miserable by the fact that so many people, to whom He had given the lovely land of Gleberune, denied His existence. In fact, it appeared His divine patience was wearing out and soon, unless they mended their ways, He would visit all manner of catastrophes on His erring children. In order to appease the god, it was necessary for the villagers to sit in His brand new Church once a week and also pay over a certain amount of income, whether in goods or coin, to the Ixmarite priests. If this was not carried out, the priest would send a pigeon flying down to Gallimaufry with a message, and presently an army of Ixmar's soldiers would come and take prisoners in lieu of the taxes. These prisoners would be forced to work in Ixmar's ore mines, and thus pay off the debt of their community.

The crusade into the north was more to do with accruing income for the already wealthy church then accruing devout souls.

The northern villagers were descendants of the ancient Runic race. They were fundamentally different from the southerners, who were pure Glebish stock. The Runes had once been the sole occupants of the island realm now known as Gleberune. They had always espoused a more magical view of life than the Glebish, who had come across the sea from the south, bringing Ixmarity with them. A host of Runic barbarian chieftains had been battling to control the country. One of the most civilised had appealed to the King of Glebe for help. Aid had been offered in the form of soldiers and political advisers, but the cost had been high. A unifying Runic throne had been built, and a little Runic king placed upon it, but the inexorable power behind that throne was Glebish, and the ruling force of the Glebes was their Church.

Glebes had come across the sea to populate the new cities that sprang up along the southern coast. Native Runes had been absorbed into the new society, or pushed north into the hills. The land there was less suitable for intensive farming, and the threshing northern sea, with its fanged cliffs and reefs, was more difficult to negotiate. The Glebish liked to get their own way and despised traditions outside their own culture. The Runes had known in their hearts that one day Ixmarity would venture forth forcibly to convert the remaining pagan population. The Church thought nothing of breaking heads and bones to achieve its aims and there were not enough people to fight against the might of Ixmarity. So the taxes were paid and the churches were full. For the time being, people continued to pursue their own religious traditions in private, and were virtually unmolested. If Ixmar existed, the northerners did not believe He could possibly be interested in them, and they were certainly not His children. The tangible power of His representatives, however, was respected.

Delilah, held in the womb of the land, could not conceive a petty, jealous god such as Ixmar. If there was doom to come for religious transgressions, it was the heritage of people other than herself, those that lived in the cities further south, who travelled the seas to other lands. Delilah disliked the Ixmarite priest, especially so since he'd forced her friend Saphia to marry him and had cut off all her hair. She was fearful, too, of the four men who lived behind the Church, who looked like cutthroats. The Ixmarite priest called them 'deacons'.

Delilah closed her eyes and leaned back on stiff arms, letting the sun soak into her skin. She felt light-headed and was aware of a strange sensation in her chest, as if her heart was beating erratically. She opened her eyes, leaning forward to hug her knees. It seemed the landscape had become watchful, as if every blade of grass was waiting for something to happen. Delilah took a few gulping breaths. She wanted to run away, but felt transfixed. It was as if a huge figure was looming behind her. She dared not look round. In her mind, this figure was both threatening and attractive, dangerous but somehow protective. Could it be Mother Moistfoot herself? Many people had spoken of having strange experiences on the knoll. Delilah herself had often caught glimpses of what she thought had been spirits, but they'd never bothered her unduly.

As the extraordinary impression of being watched settled around her, Delilah suddenly realised, in completeness, that the thing behind her somehow belonged to her. It possessed the potential to carry her far away from Samberdell. What could it be?

Slowly, Delilah got to her feet. The skin between her shoulders prickled unbearably. She turned round swiftly, but there was nothing there. She decided to hurry home and tell her mother what had happened. As she scurried down the grassy slope, she could see clearly past the ragged foliage of the trees below. Someone was running along the hedge-bordered lane, away from the village. The figure seemed to stagger from one side of the lane to the other and back again, as if drunk. But surely no drunk could move so quickly? The limbs flailed wildly as if the runner was caught in a nightmare, unable to move forward fast enough. Delilah paused and watched. Perhaps the person had been stung by an insect or bitten by a snake. But if so, why run *away* from the village? The distant figure crumpled to its knees. As far as Delilah could see, nobody else had come out of the village. I must go and help, she thought, but she suddenly became reluctant to move. Some part of her wanted to remain on the knoll for ever, despite what she'd just experienced. Only by lingering within the circle of the trees would she be safe. This feeling was so strong, she almost sat down again. It was as if unseen hands were pulling at her dress and her hair, begging her to stay. Then she saw the face of the Ixmarite priest looking up at her from behind an oak, his features full of scornful censure. She often saw faces in the trees. Sometimes they were real, sometimes not, but whether the priest

28

was vision or otherwise, she had no desire to spend any time in his presence.

Shaking out her skirt, and ignoring the faint inner voices that begged her to stay, she scampered down into the cool shadows, her tough bare feet hardly pricked by the sharp stones and nuts that littered the brown mulch. Every moment seemed hard and clear. She perceived detail in every veined leaf. She felt as if she was casting something away, that part of her would for ever abide on Bethany's Knoll. A strange numbness stole through her, like clouds rolling across the sun.

Delilah emerged from the trees and ran over the shadowed ground to the hedge, over which she scrambled. The runner now lay face down and motionless on the grass verge. Approaching closer, Delilah saw that it was a woman and also that she lay in a pool of bright blood. Delilah instantly recognised the fringed green shawl that lay a short distance up the lane. It belonged to Merryann, the blacksmith's wife. Delilah hurried over to the injured woman and quickly established that it was indeed Merryann. She had dreadful wounds to her shoulder and neck, which looked as if they had been made with a cruel cutting weapon. Her left arm was nearly severed from her body. How she had managed to run so far and with such spirit, Delilah could not guess. And how had she come by such appalling injuries? Delilah knelt beside her on the compacted mud, and pressed her fingers against her lips in confusion. She knew she had to fetch help. Her healing skills were good, but Merryann's wounds were beyond her expertise.

Despite a glum conviction that Merryann was beyond help, Delilah jumped to her feet and ran back up the lane. Rosalie Bluegarter, a local witch and accomplished healer, lived in a cottage just outside the circular wooden enclosure of the village. If anyone could save Merryann, she could. Delilah hoped desperately she would be at home.

As she drew nearer to the village, running through the dappling shadows of the trees, Delilah became aware of some very odd noises from beyond the wooden palings of Samberdell's wall. They reminded her of the terrible cries the cows made at night when the big, blood-coloured bull was let into their field. She could hear men shouting too, and the shouts had a high, desperate note.

After knocking on Rosalie Bluegarter's door for a few seconds, and even daring to venture inside the cottage to call the witch's name, Delilah established Rosalie wasn't in. The gateway to the village was only a few yards from the cottage. Samberdell was covered by a roof of woven withes in wooden frames, which could be removed in summer to admit more light and secured in the colder season to keep the streets free from snow. The outer ring of the village was often kept covered on hot days so that dairy produce could be kept cool.

Delilah ran on to the slatted wooden pathway that led beneath the gate. She ran under the arch, into the rusty shadow of the covered outer circle. Crooked stripes of sunlight came down through the weave of the overhead matting; dust motes danced in the beams. She was aware of the utter stillness, of the dimness to either side. Ahead of her, a straight radial pathway led towards a hot bright confusion. Delilah could see right down it to the central open area of the village, known as the Gather Patch, where a small market was held once a week and communal leisure activities took place.

People were running everywhere, back and forth across her field of vision.

There were shouts and cries and wet crimson in the afternoon. Delilah could smell blood. Whatever had happened here, she must find someone to help Merryann.

Advancing slowly down the narrow street, she passed the open door of the Dominish shrine, and a claw of unease stroked her spine. The interior was dark and silent, but she felt strongly that it contained something terrible. A cat scampered across her path, glancing up at her furtively, its belly low to the ground. The wooden buildings of Samberdell creaked gently in the afternoon around her, exuding a rich smell of pine and sealant resin. Something was happening up ahead, something bad, something that couldn't possibly belong in the quiet daily life of Samberdell, where troubles were few.

We are simple people, Delilah thought clearly. The sentence seemed to hang in her mind as she moved along. Hadn't she made this journey only a short time before? Hadn't she seen the cat and smelled the wood just a few moments ago? Her body seemed huge and heavy, she felt full of inexplicable rage and despair.

When she reached the edge of the Gather Patch, Delilah surveyed the scene of carnage with a numb brain. All the trestles, which had been in the process of being erected for tomorrow morning's market, had been overturned or broken. People lay everywhere among the splintered wood and torn canopies. Women were crying and groaning, children were screaming. There was also a dark core of activity that she didn't want to look at just yet, even though she knew the hideous blot was spiralling towards her. It had no form to her, but she could sense it clearly; a ball of mindless energy. She looked down. A ribbon of blood crawled towards her feet, and in the shadows of a nearby dwelling, a skinny brindled hound with distended nipples nervously flicked out her tongue to taste it. On the ground, at the corner of a house, Delilah could see an arm, which she supposed was still attached to a body hidden by the walls. The fingers were curled; the hand did not look very big. Whatever had passed this way had left its mark here. And now, almost as if she was calling it to her, she could feel it coming back.

The shadow fell over her before she raised her eyes. A huge figure was lunging towards her, its forearms soaked in blood, its face black with rage and a matted beard. All Delilah could focus on was the wet red mouth, foam flecking the filthy beard, manic eyes. Enormous hands reached out to her, a heavy short-handled axe held in one, the other flexing its fingers which were reddened with gore. Delilah froze. She knew that this was the formless thing she had imagined looming behind her on Bethany's Knoll. This, the creature that belonged to her, that could carry her away. She also knew that the maddened eyes hanging over her could not truly see her, could not recognise her for what she was; a weirdly reluctant ally.

Am I about to die? she thought, and a fleeting image of sundered flesh, a thud, a spray of blood, shot through her mind. How could she make this fearsome creature really see her? She felt sure he'd know her if she could only *reach* him.

Someone called her name. 'Delilah! *Delilah!* Run!'

Run? Delilah thought. Run where? 'Here I am,' she said, the words coming unbidden to her lips. 'You are mine.'

As she spoke, the terrible eyes above her seemed to glaze over, become unfocused. She sensed the hesitation, and also a sense of recognition. The axe never fell.

That was when a neighbour, Mr Antrim, threw the piking rod which pierced the intruder between the shoulder blades. The huge maniac staggered forward and then toppled past Delilah with a soft grunt, whereupon the men of the village hurried forth, threw themselves upon him before he could attempt to rise, and constrained his writhing body with ropes. Delilah felt utterly detached from the situation. She stared at the defiant shaft of the rod protruding from the lunatic's back. Mr Antrim was the brother of Merryann, who without a doubt now lay dead upon the road outside Samberdell. The rod was decorated with an embroidered grip that Delilah knew Merryann had crafted herself. There seemed a wry justice in that.

Seven people died in the warm afternoon, and twice that number were injured. Blood steamed on the packed earth. Villagers moved slowly through the mess left in the wake of the lunatic's killing orgy, their faces bewildered. And yet there was a resigned feeling that life must go on. Wounds were tended, bodies removed. Delilah saw her mother standing with limp, hanging arms on the other side of the Gather Patch, at the entrance to the pathway that led to their house and workshops. They looked at one another. Then Delilah crossed the space and followed her mother home.

Where had the madman come from? Nobody knew. He had simply entered the village and set about killing the unsuspecting inhabitants. He had not been killed by the piking rod. In fact, because of his size and bulk, the sharp tip of the rod had simply become embedded in his muscles. Many of the villages thought that the madman should be executed outright, by the grieving relatives of those he had murdered. More moderate voices stated that the matter should be adjudged by the Cabal of Three, a group of philosopher mystics whose traditional function was to act as judges for Samberdell and the surrounding communities. A messenger was sent to the secluded dwelling, six ridges north, where the Three meditated upon the complexities of life and attempted to discern a pattern within them.

Meanwhile, the felled lunatic was confined within the cellars of the Ixmaritian church, where the priest supervised his incarceration and ordered other people to test the strength of the chains that confined him. It was reported by onlookers that the madman glowered and ground his teeth continually, and seemed quite oblivious of the injury he had received. The Ixmarite priest, who had prudently locked himself in the attic of his church during the carnage, began to speak smugly of divine vengeance. The people of Samberdell built funeral pyres, danced sad cotillions to their goddess and with heavy hearts awaited the arrival of the Three.

The following day, nobody was particularly concerned when the Ixmarite priest fell sick. Certainly, his illness was not associated with the growling prisoner held in the church cellar. The symptoms were comparatively slight at first, and did not cause anyone to suspect plague. The priest complained of feeling weary, and was forced to cut short his morning circuit of the village. By the end of the day, he could do no more than slump in a chair; he put up very little argument when one of his deacons suggested a witch healer should be summoned. As the evening slipped down over the hills, the priest sat blinking at his window, weakly sipping the tisanes that the witch had brought him. By morning, his tongue had changed colour and swelled to such a size that, by lunchtime, it had choked him. The death was almost polite in its swiftness. The witch healer, who had been standing at the kitchen tap, heard only a restrained cough coming from the priest's bedroom. By the afternoon, she too succumbed to a great weariness and, despite the efforts of her colleagues, quickly followed the path of the priest.

The sickness spread silently, rapidly throughout the community. Its touch was soft; it was named the Doomsigh, but not even naming this particular demon lessened its power.

Without knowing why or how, Delilah Latterkin knew she had nothing to fear from this mysterious disease. Neither was it chance that she had been spared from the madman's axe. In some way she had yet to fathom, she and the murderer were connected. Despite the atrocities he'd committed, she could not find it in her heart to hate him. He fascinated her, and she could feel his presence in the Ixmarite's cellar every moment of the day, wherever she was. She knew she would have to confront him eventually, but the time was not yet right. She waited patiently, in a daze of private reverie, imagining how the meeting would proceed when it occurred.

While her mother painted the door and window frames of their home with an infusion of nettles and bark to repel unsavoury humours that might be floating on the air. Delilah worked steadily at her needlepoint, humming tunelessly beneath her breath, sometimes making an appropriate response to the rasping imprecations of her desperate parent.

'Take these pods, Lilah,' her mother said, and Delilah popped them obediently into her mouth. 'Rub your skin with this tonic.' Delilah knew that none of these precautions were needed. She could not explain why, but the knowledge was a hard, dark feeling deep in her belly.

While the plague crawled relentlessly through the village, Delilah felt as if she inhabited a cloud hanging above the world. She felt removed and tranquil. When her mother died, following the path of her father who had expired from heartrot several years before, Delilah felt she should at least shed a few tears, and did so. And yet it was hard for her to imagine that the bloated corpse lying on its back on the parlour couch had once been her mother. She felt very little affinity with it.

What is happening to me? Delilah wondered. She had suffered tragedy, the pattern of her life had been destroyed, yet she felt no emotion; neither grief nor anger. She had not been outside the cottage for five days, obeying her mother's instruction and latterly administering to her parent's last needs. She supposed someone would come round in the evening, politely knock on the door and discreetly enquire as to the health of the householders. Then she remembered that these regular visits from the representatives of the town elders had ceased at least three days ago. Still, she waited.

By the following afternoon, no one had come to ask for her mother's body, so Delilah steeled herself to wrap it in several large sheets. She felt numb as she dragged it out through the back door, to the patch behind their workshops which now stood silent, as if aware they would never harbour industry again. The vegetables growing at the back of the patch looked sick and parched – no one had bothered watering them for days. It was then Delilah noticed how quiet Samberdell had become.

Taking her father's old spade, she dug a shallow grave among the dying vegetables and rolled her mother's shrouded body into it. The sheets had become stained by liquids emanating from the corpse. Delilah wished she could summon nausea, but experienced only a flat kind of resignation. She had no doubt that every subtle essence that had comprised her mother had already departed this world, but she uttered a few toneless words of prayer, nevertheless, to wish her mother's spirit speed into the Garden of the Mother. Then she covered the body with soil. Several heavy wooden pallets were ranged against the fence of the yard; Delilah hauled two over to the grave and placed them on top, to prevent stray animals from excavating it. Then she went back into the cottage.

All was silent. She walked through the three lower rooms, touching the things she had used every day with her mother: the cutlery, the pots and pans, the broom, the fire poker. All seemed alien and cold. Her embroidery, and some of the tapestried coats her mother had been working on, lay folded beside a work basket in the back parlour, next to the couch where the corpse had lain. Delilah picked up her work and peered at it closely. She could not remember having made any of the stitches herself. The stiff cloth did not feel familiar. Delilah dropped the piece of embroidery carelessly back into the basket. She glanced up into the mirror hanging over the fireplace. It was tarnished, cloudy. The room seemed so dark.

Delilah walked up the rough wooden stairs to the sleeping gallery. The sheets and quilts felt damp to the touch, as if brushed by the dankness of the grave. There was an unused, musty smell. Delilah realised that the house had died with her mother. It was an empty shell. She could not stay.

I must go outside, she thought. She put on her woollen coat, even though it was a warm day, and stepped out of the front door. She considered locking it and leaving the key in the eaves of the porch, but decided against it. What would it matter if anyone entered the house? She did not feel that anything left inside belonged to her any more.

So where do I go? What do I do?

Delilah had no other relatives in Samberdell. Her mother had come there as a girl to marry her father. He had been a travelling man who'd had the gift of charming water. The village elders had persuaded him to settle there – they'd been having a great deal of trouble with the irrigation pumps and plumbing of the village. Delilah's grandparents, aunts and uncles, on her mother's side, all lived a day's walk away in Tackspinny, another village further north. Delilah wondered whether she should go to them. But wouldn't she risk taking the spores of the plague with her? Though they didn't harm her, they might harm others.

She realised that she was trying to avoid confronting the obvious thing she should do. It was time to seek out the madman. He too might have succumbed to the plague, but she doubted it strongly. She could only remember his size, nothing more. What would she say to him? Perhaps she'd been deluding herself about the sense of connection she'd felt. No, the feeling had been real, no matter how unlikely.

Unable to decide whether to head straight for the Ixmaritian church or not Delilah began to walk round the village. All was deathly quiet and, as she wound further into the spiral of the community, dreadful smells grabbed her by the throat. Animals had been spared, for she saw dogs and cats relaxing in the heat, having a mysteriously bloated and contented appearance, but every rose vine crawling up the trellises and walls of the village carried black buds, rotted on the stem.

An unexpected sound broke the silence and cracked the path of her wandering thoughts. It was the sound of a lusty male voice raised in song, a sound distinctly alien in the death hush of Samberdell. Delilah instinctively followed the song. It led her to the grey stone walls of the Ixmaritian church, and appeared to be coming from a grille set into the ground at her feet. She realised at once, with both relief and dread, that the madman must still be alive. Her feet had led her to him; she could no longer avoid confronting him.

Delilah hesitated for a moment in the shadow of the porch. The song of the lunatic seemed to fill the space within, thrown from wall to wall. The sound held such an intensity of life, she was powerless to resist being drawn by it. Am I risking death again? she wondered, knowing the answer even before she accepted the question. Nothing in Samberdell, alive or dead, had the ability to harm her. She was meant to be here.

The church smelled of old incense and mouse droppings, tinged with the sweet corruption of sickness emitted from the bodies of those who had died there, prostrate bundles of rags before the altar. The stern, somewhat bewildered face of Ixmar stared out over their bodies at the open door. Delilah felt that it was the first time she had ever truly looked upon His face, and it too was dead. An empty idol, a hollow thought. He has no power, she thought. He never had. She had only come to the church once a month, just often enough to appease the priest. Then, she had always sat with her parents, and latterly only her mother, day-dreaming while the priest told tales of Ixmar and His divine family. She had never really examined the building in detail, but now, walking slowly down the central aisle, she observed its austere grace. The church was the only stone building in Samberdell, and Delilah felt it lacked character. She had always preferred the rites of Mother Moistfoot, held in the groves beyond the village in the open air, beneath the radiance of the moon.

The voice of the madman had fallen silent, but suddenly it broke once again into lively song. 'Ma-arching, ma-arching, on the road, the road!' There was a rattle of chains from below. 'Free-eedom is our only lord!'

Delilah knew that under normal circumstances the man should have been dead by now. The plague did not tease its victims unnecessarily, but took their lives swiftly and without fuss, and once the first few victims had succumbed, people had deduced that the prisoner must have brought the sickness with him to Samberdell. Delilah wondered why he had not expired from it. Was it something to do with her? His voice sounded huge and vibrant as it rang around the silent church.

Behind the altar, a huge metal grille which usually covered the cellar opening was lying on the stone flags beside a gaping hole. Delilah crept to the edge and peered down. She and the lunatic might be the only people left alive in Samberdell. Was it possible he'd come to the village specifically to meet her? If so, why had everyone else had to die? Was there some sort of price to be paid for their coming together? The sound of the prisoner's voice somehow penetrated the daze that had gripped Delilah during the past few days. It jolted her back to reality and the realisation that she had to carry on living, feed and clothe herself, survive. I am alone, she thought, and the flimsy weight of her youth seemed too fragile a thing to support her for the future. She remembered how her mother's feet had protruded from the makeshift shroud she had sewn round the body. She recalled the chickens scurrying away from her as she dragged her mother's remains to the inadequate grave. Delilah began to shiver. What could she possibly do now? Could her future really rest in the hands of the man below?

34

'There is joy in my heart, in my heart!' sang the lunatic. He sounded as if he meant it.

Holding her breath, Delilah took a few steps down to the cellar. It was gloomier than the white painted hall above, but dim yellow light came into it from a basement grille set high in the wall. She could not see the lunatic until she had walked halfway down.

The prisoner was sitting on a stone bench, chained to the wall, singing fiercely. He looked even larger in the relatively confined space of the cellar, like a huge, hairy bull. His great head was maned in a grey-streaked thatch of black hair, most of his face in a beard of similar constitution. His lips were very red and moist, stretched into a smile. His eyes were extremely deepset.

'And the great one said, "Freedom is my name, my name, my name. Freedom!" ' he sang, banging his fists against the bench and stamping his bare feet against the floor. For someone who had taken a piking rod between the shoulders, Delilah felt that he appeared alarmingly healthy, although the front of his rough-spun tunic was stained with handprints of dried blood. Delilah stood at the bottom of the steps and watched him. She did not feel as if she knew him now. The idea of announcing her feelings, her experience on the knoll, seemed preposterous. The madman seemed oblivious of her presence, his eyes fixed on the grilled window. He also seemed very different from the lumbering ogre who had towered over her only a few days before, with an axe held in his bloodied hand. At the moment he did not look at all violent in nature. She wondered whether it would be safe to speak to him. It might invoke his violence. Even as she was debating this, the prisoner's eyes flicked in her direction and he changed the tone of his song into a softer melody and murmured, in a sweet, mellow voice. 'And then the angels came, led by the child of beauty, came to lead me to the starlight . . .' He stopped singing and grinned at her, his hands braced on his knees.

'Everyone's dead,' Delilah said. 'They died from the plague you brought here.'

The prisoner's smile crumpled into a frown. 'Dead?'

Delilah nodded. 'Yes. You killed everyone.'

The prisoner slumped visibly and put his hands against his eyes. 'Such as he spoke, it has occurred!' he declared. 'Such is my curse! My absurdity!'

Calculating how far the chains might reach, should the man decide to lunge at her, Delilah timidly took a few steps forward.

'Why did you come?' she asked. 'Why the axe, the killing?'

The man looked at her mournfully from beneath heavy black brows, his head lowered. 'I am a demon,' he said, shaking his hair. 'As you have seen. If you value your life, stand back, or better still, finish what the rod thrower started.'

Delilah wrinkled her nose and forced herself to walk forward in a purposeful manner. 'You don't sound like a demon when you're singing,' she said. 'Anyway, you've had the chance to kill me twice and both times failed to do so.'

The man raised his head a little. 'Oh? How is that?'

'Quite simple,' Delilah replied. 'You stood over me with an axe, with nothing but murder on your mind, yet something stayed your hand. Neither have I fallen victim to the sickness.' She decided not to mention her experience on the knoll just yet.

35

The man shook his head thoughtfully. 'This is omenic indeed,' he said. 'Perhaps I should look at you.'

Nervously, Delilah walked to the place on the floor where the dim yellow spears of light fell in through the window. The prisoner peered at her.

'Your name?' he asked.

'Delilah Latterkin. I am fifteen years old.'

The man nodded. 'It is plain you are eldritch,' he said. 'There is a turn to your mouth, a tilt to your chin that speaks of it.'

'I don't know about that,' Delilah said carefully, 'but why did you kill everyone? I think I have seen demons before, among the trees of Bethany's Knoll on moonless nights. They don't look like you. They are naked and warty, or else creatures of smoke and perfume. You are not a demon, but you may be a madman. Why didn't the plague kill you?'

The man sighed. 'I am a follower of the Cult of Jeopardy,' he said. 'And if I am not a demon, then I am certainly cursed by a demonic grain. The sickness and the madness are both aspects of my curse. They condemn me to a life of solitude, and if not that, then one of being loathed and repulsed by my fellow beings.'

'Why not have the curse lifted?' Delilah asked. 'There must be a hundred magi in these parts who could do the job.'

The madman shook his head. 'If it was so simple, I would long ago have freed myself. The nature of the curse is this. If the pull of the moon does not twist my spirit to murderous rage, the heat of the sun broils my filthy violence into a spore of death that infects anyone who comes near. Only Resenence Jeopardy can hold the curse at bay, and in the company of Jeopardites I was always safe. But tragedy occurred. An Ixmarite force attacked us and I became separated from my group. Since then, I have been dragged by the curse throughout the land, spreading a stain of death wherever I pass.' He paused. 'I strove to avoid my fellow beings, but on the afternoon I came across the smoke of your village, the moon was visible in the daytime sky. I was possessed by both aspects of the curse at once, and all ability to make conscious decisions was eclipsed within me. You must believe me when I saw this is the only time I've destroyed an entire community, the first time I have killed so many. Not that that absolves me.' He sighed and rubbed his face with his huge hands.

'Did you . . . did you feel there was anything different about Samberdell?' Delilah asked hopefully. 'Did you feel something was waiting for you here?' It seemed unlikely now, but she felt she had to ask.

The madman frowned and shook his head. 'I felt . . . nothing,' he said.

'Oh.' Delilah hid her disappointment. She'd been so sure he'd say 'yes'. Then she could have told him everything. Now, he'd think she was as mad as he was himself.

'Can't you return to this . . . Jeopardy thing?' she asked. She realised coolly that she still could not hate the madman for what he'd done, although she was wary of him. Half of her still believed he belonged to her in some way, and her other more sceptical half seemed devoid of emotion or the ability to judge. He seemed contrite and polite. 'What is it, this Jeopardy, anyway?'

The madman's sad face crinkled into a weary smile. 'Jeopardy is not an "it", but a man, the greatest man alive,' he said with passion, leaning forward and emphasising his words with his great hands. The chains that

36

confined him clanked as he talked. 'He is the kindest, wisest creature ever to tread the Earth. One day, the grandeur of his spirit will hold sway completely, and everyone will enjoy the freedom that follows.'

'I've never heard of him,' Delilah said.

'You will,' said the prisoner, and then sighed deeply. 'More than anything I yearn to return to him, yet because of what I am and what I have done, I should die.'

'Oh no, you should not!' Delilah blurted out heatedly. She must tell him now, she must. He must not die before she could find out what linked them.

Before she could summon the right words, the madman spoke again. 'It is a weak human selfishness for me to want to sustain this miserable life, when it is so dangerous to others.' He paused and extended his hands. 'Sweet Delilah, do you think you could kill me?'

Delilah looked at him hard. She supposed that, rationally, he did deserve to die for the despicable things he had done. Yet the conviction in her heart spoke against such an idea. Was killing him the only interpretation of the feeling she'd experienced on the knoll? No, she couldn't believe that. Nor did she believe this man was solely responsible for what had happened. Everything that had occurred in Samberdell had been preordained, part of some unknown pattern, she was sure of it. Yet how could she explain that to him? He had not recognised her when he'd seen her, and obviously had not been thinking about her during the past few days, as she'd imagined.

'Would you like something to eat or drink?' she asked abruptly.

The prisoner looked at her warily. She recognised hope in his eyes, but whether that was the hope she would poison him shortly or the hope she might let him live, she could not tell. He nodded. 'I am thirsty,' he said.

Delilah went back into the church, her heart beating wildly. She raided the ambry in the priest's office for the remains of his sacramental mead and cakes. She was feeling rather hungry herself. The prisoner fell on the generous heap of cakes with gusto and swigged half of the mead in one gulp. Delilah feasted more delicately.

'What of your injury?' she asked. 'Are you in pain?'

The man wiped his lips. 'No. Resenence Jeopardy taught me the ways of using the mind to heal the flesh. I heal quickly.'

'You could be a healer then, if you weren't a killer,' Delilah observed.

The man frowned. 'The curse would not let me heal others,' he said. 'I stumbled into your village with the ghost of the gravid lady moon sailing up the afternoon sky. She provoked me to madness. She always does. She laughs at the notion that I could be a man of healing.'

Delilah could not credit that the Lady of the Moon, a sister of Mother Moistfoot, could be so cruel. Perhaps this man had offended her at some time. She decided that once they'd finished eating, she would risk setting him free.

The man was fastidiously wiping his hands on his trousers. Delilah knelt on the ground in front of him, her hands folded in her lap. 'What is your name?' she asked him.

'Trajan Sacripent,' he replied.

She took a deep breath, hoping her words wouldn't falter. 'Well, Trajan, what would you do should I unlock your chains?'

He narrowed his eyes at her. 'Only a fool would do that,' he said, and then added, 'Anyway, how would you find the keys?'

'Oh, there are hundreds of keys hanging in the priest's office,' she said, her eyes flicking away from his gaze. 'One of them must be the right one to unlock the chains.' She held her breath.

'But why should you want to do that? I have killed all your people!'

Delilah shrugged. 'I don't know exactly.' It was an honest answer.

Trajan sighed. 'I had believed my torment would end in this place,' he said, glancing round the walls and raising his hands wearily. 'Now you come as a temptress to offer me more life. I wanted only to die.'

'Then why were you singing?' Delilah accused.

'For comfort. To invoke pleasant memories.'

Delilah took another deep breath. 'Trajan, I can't explain how or why, but I strongly believe I was *meant* to meet you.'

He frowned. Delilah thought she saw disbelief in his expression. 'No,' he said. 'That can't be so.'

'Why not?' Delilah said impulsively. She gabbled out the story of what she'd felt on the knoll, and how Trajan had been in her mind ever since. 'Do you see?' Her hands curled into fists in her lap. 'Do you *see*?' She doubted her powers of persuasion.

Trajan nodded and laughed gently, which made Delilah blush. 'Many men would happily accept such a theory,' he said. 'And I wish it could be true. But you don't realise the dangers of my acquaintance. If I left this place with you, you'd be condemned to isolation from the world. I could take you into a wilderness, but not a new life.'

'But there must be something we could do to control your madness,' Delilah insisted. She'd noticed he wasn't wholly against the idea of leaving with her. 'What does this Jeopardy person do to help you?'

'He lays his hands upon my brow and the fevers of moon and sun depart. You are not Jeopardy.'

'No . . .' Delilah frowned in concentration. 'But I am immune to the plague and safe from your violent urges.'

'You have no real proof of that.'

'I think I do,' Delilah continued. 'I know we belong together . . .' She hesitated, and blushed again, her glance veering away from his gaze once more. 'Not in the way it sounds, that is. Something else. Companions . . . No, more than that. Something will happen. Oh, I can't explain!'

Trajan Sacripent smiled at her. 'Do you know,' he said gently, 'I think I do remember you now. I remember seeing someone standing before me like a blade of light in the afternoon sun. I could not kill that person then, because the power to do so was taken from my hands. I believed you to be an advocate of my own death. Then the rod took me. Now, I find that you are that person, and you are real.' He shook his head. 'There is something strange about you, Delilah Latterkin. I saw that from the moment you came in here. You should hate and fear me, yet you don't. You have your own convictions and obsessions that seem to match mine in madness. What kind of pair would we make?' He laughed sadly and then added, as if to himself, 'And what kind of protection am I for such an innocent girl?'

'I don't want to stay alone in Samberdell another night,' Delilah said, in a determined voice. 'For the last few days I have walked in a dream, but now I feel different. I don't want to share the night with so much death. I have to leave, and because I'm so young and know nothing of the world beyond the village, I need protection. Who else is here to help me? My family and friends are all dead.'

38

'For which I am responsible..'

'Precisely,' Delilah concluded primly. 'I am asking you to be my companion, as I shall be yours.' She looked up at him earnestly. 'Trajan, I have the world before me now. I don't just want to go to my relatives and continue the life I was once destined to lead. A life of nothing! There is something more for me now, I'm sure of it.'

Enlightenment bloomed on Trajan's face. 'Yes,' he murmured wonderingly. 'Yes, perhaps . . .'

'Perhaps what?'

Trajan held out his hands and, hesitantly, Delilah placed her own small fingers in them. It gave her a strange thrill to do that. She felt the connection between them then as real and tangible.

'Perhaps,' Trajan said, 'there is some good to come out of these dark months of insanity. Perhaps you are meant for Jeopardy himself, which is why I came here to find you.'

Delilah frowned. Was that the answer? It was possible. She smiled. 'Well, I would like to meet the man who can hold curses at bay with the touch of his hands. Perhaps, together, we could find him.'

Trajan had tears in his eyes. He grinned and thumped his knees with his hands, which made Delilah squeal in pain for he still had firm hold of her own hands. 'Oh, to find him again! Is that possible?' He glanced down at her, blinking away his tears. 'With you? Have you been sent to me, an angel of deliverance?' His joy seemed almost as frightening as his earlier murdering lunacy.

'I don't know,' Delilah answered. 'I am sure there is something waiting for me, out in the world. Whether that thing is your Jeopardy person or not, I don't know. I only know I want to leave here with you.'

Trajan leaned forward and hugged her, his chains digging painfully into her arms. 'It must be the reason,' he boomed, shaking her joyfully. 'It must!'

Delilah collected what she believed would be an ample amount of food from the shops near the church. Flies buzzed around the rotting hams, so she helped herself to fruit, cheese, bread and eggs. She had no desire to return to her old home, so she also stole a few clothes from another shop. All of this she packed into a large tapestry bag, appropriated from the priest's quarters. On the wall behind the priest's desk, bundles of keys were hanging on a wooden board. Delilah lifted them all down and then, out of curiosity, tried some of the smaller keys on the locked drawers of the priest's desk. In one of the drawers, she discovered a metal cash box. A search of the other drawers produced another key, taped to the base of an upper drawer, which opened the box. The money Delilah found inside was not an awesome amount but, she felt, adequate for her needs. The silver coins all bore the face of King Aristocete and had a Gallimaufric seal. She put them all into a cloth purse which had been stuffed into the back of the drawer, and secreted it among the clothes in the tapestry bag.

She carried all the larger keys down to the cellar where she and Trajan tested them on the locks of his chains. As she had predicted, the correct key was among them. Trajan removed his bonds and neatly arranged them on the bench beside him. Then he rubbed his wrists, neck and belly where the iron had chafed him. Delilah was poised to flee should his madness return, but he appeared so sane and ordinary, the very idea seemed absurd.

* * *

39

It was the middle of afternoon when Delilah climbed through the trees to Bethany's Knoll, with Trajan Sacripent lumbering behind her. Waiting for him, she turned to gaze down on Samberdell. Perhaps she should have put it to the flame. For a moment, she considered going back and doing so. Then she turned round and looked out across the gently swelling buttocks of the Thurible Ridge. Silver water threaded serenely through the valleys – the River Tickpike. All was peaceful and serene. Delilah sensed the immensity of the landscape ahead of her, its insistent beckoning, the wideness demanding to be trodden. Behind her, Samberdell would be left in the hands of Mother Moistfoot. Someone would come along soon and wonder what had happened there. Let them wonder. She felt as if a part of her had been cut away, but it was a part that had become too heavy. She felt lighter, more buoyant, without it.

'Hurry up, Trajan!' she called. Perhaps his wound was still bothering him, after all. I must learn to become something else, Delilah thought, something powerful. She took the first step down the hill.

Two days later, the Cabal of Three arrived in Samberdell, with an entourage of five acolytes and the messenger who had summoned them. Fortunately, the spores of Trajan Sacripent's plague, which existed only while there were people around to believe in them, had vanished completely, so the infection was not passed on. The grief-stricken messenger entreated the Three to explain why everyone had died. In swift response, the mystics took a sample of the air and a sample of the sounds of the village. Later, mystified themselves, they gave their hypothesis. It seemed to them that Samberdell had died of disbelief.

III

MASKS

A clear morning light brought the scent of the sea high over the upper quarters of Gallimaufry. Lucien awoke, immediately conscious of being at the heart of Bessie's nest. The whole room was filled with a soft scent of infant breathing, a murmur of bees. Lucien was lying on a pallet near the door, beneath a window whose curtain was too short. He blinked for a few moments at the hand's-width band of morning coming into the room. Soon, he would lift himself, shake out the sleep from his bones, and leave this house. Soon, he would begin his search once more. The never-ending search. Sighing, he turned his head upon the pillow – a thin, two-dimensional article, barely deserving the name – and found the face of Walterkin Anywhither staring at him intently. The face of a minor demon, thought Lucien.

'What's in your eyes?' the boy demanded. He was sitting on the edge of the bed next to Lucien's, wearing only a nightshirt, threadbare and worn, kicking the legs of the bed with grubby naked feet.

Lucien returned the stare. 'History,' he answered, 'probably.'

Walterkin nodded thoughtfully. 'Are you very old?'

'Sometimes.'

'When?'

'First thing in the morning mostly.' Lucien sat up and shook his head vigorously. The child reached out and snatched at a handful of his hair.

'It's like the Jeopardite flags,' he said, and his voice sounded eerily mature.

'How?' Lucien asked, his head yanked to the side.

'Black rags. Long black rags.' With a final pull, Walterkin released Lucien's hair and sauntered in a rolling walk to the door.

'And what do you know of Jeopardites?' Lucien asked him.

'More than I know of you,' replied the boy. 'Come with me to my mother's garden.'

There was a ladder against the back of the house, half obscured by a feral ivy vine, a route used by children who scorned the easier access by steps at the side of the house. Having paused only to pull on his shirt and trousers, Lucien followed the boy up the ladder onto the flat roof, where miniature

41

trees stood in tubs around a few collapsing wooden chairs. Behind the house, Gallimaufry reared in a series of increasingly affluent residences, while in front it dropped in terraces towards the ocean. It was very early and the city was only just beginning to awaken. There was a lovely sleepy ambience in the air, and also a promise of activity to come. Shading his eyes to gaze out to sea, Lucien felt optimism rise within him.

'It is beautiful here,' he said.

Walterkin ignored the remark, and sat down upon an ancient, faded rug between the chairs. He had brought a pitcher of milk with him and a bowl of grapes. 'Eat,' he ordered.

Lucien squatted down in front of him. 'I'm not hungry.' He rarely ate before midday.

The boy shrugged and began nibbling one of the grapes, spitting the pips over the edge of the roof. 'I know two of their songs,' he said.

'Whose?'

'The Jeopardites. Do you want to hear them?'

Lucien smiled. 'No. But tell me what you saw of them when they came to the city.'

The boy shrugged. 'There's little to tell. We climbed the weather vane in Eastbale Park to watch them pass, and a girl threw us a black dove.'

'Did you see Jeopardy himself?'

The boy frowned. 'I don't know.' Then, he shook his head vigorously. 'No, Jeopardy wasn't with them. Of course he wasn't with them. Would he risk being branded on the buttock and thrown from the city? Would he risk being hanged?'

'I don't know. How come you know this much?'

'News travels in the stone,' the boy replied and took a gulp from the pitcher of milk, which he offered to Lucien.

Lucien shook his head, raised a hand. 'You have a harking gift then?'

Walterkin narrowed his eyes. The boy was eldritch of course. Lucien could see that now. He suspected Bessie Anywhither had never noticed. Beneath the grime, and a rather rough homely appearance, there was a shine in the flesh, a beauty contained, held back. 'Tell me,' Lucien said.

Walterkin shook his head. 'No, you tell me.'

'What?'

The boy leaned forward. His eyes were a very deep blue, almost unnaturally so. Lucien shuddered at a memory he couldn't formulate. 'Everything,' Walterkin said. 'I have to hear it from you.'

'Hear what? I don't know what you mean?' Lucien suddenly felt cold and wrapped his arms about himself. He should have brought his coat with him.

The boy sucked on another grape. 'Your life. Your history.'

Lucien laughed, although the knowing look in the boy's eyes was disquieting. It was almost as if he knew everything about Lucien already. 'You are a cheeky child,' he said. 'Why should I tell you anything about myself?' Despite his scornful tone, he felt intimidated; a feeling he hadn't experienced for years.

Walterkin screwed up his face into a lopsided grin. 'We could trade stories,' he said.

'I doubt you have any I want to know.'

'I know lots of things. Would you like to know where Resenence Jeopardy goes to meditate alone?'

Lucien glanced at him sharply. 'Of course. Do you know?'

42

Walterkin grinned widely and drank from the milk pitcher. 'No, I don't.'

Lucien made a noise of disgust. 'Why are you so interested in me?'

'I like stories.'

'It's more than that, boy. You told your mother to approach me at the gate to the city. I saw you do it. Why?'

Walterkin pulled a mournful face, his intelligent eyes sparkling in amusement. It was not an expression that sat happily upon the face of one who appeared so young. 'Lucien, you needed help as much as Ma did. Are you complaining?'

'I didn't need help.'

'You were dead on your feet. You needed to talk to someone. Anyone with an ounce of sense could see that. Your stories are bursting out of you, splitting your skin. You need to talk.'

'To you? I could go to a shrine of Paradouze and unburden myself to a priestess.'

Walterkin laughed. 'No, you couldn't. You couldn't say anything about yourself to an Ixmarite.'

Lucien shivered with dread. He knew there was truth in Walterkin's words, he did need to speak to someone. He had been alone for so long, and no words concerning his true feelings for Jeopardy had passed his lips since he'd left the House of Mandru. Those feelings burned him from the inside sometimes. What would it be like to unleash those words, to purge himself of them? Would it be an exorcism or an invocation of deeper pain? 'You seem to have already decided what half my history is,' Lucien said. At that moment, he knew that very soon he would begin to tell the boy everything. There was no harm in talking to a child, surely? Such an intelligent child, obviously sensitive, even if he was a mite bizarre. Lucien needed to release the contents of his soul, be free of it, and now that the suggestion had been made, he longed to talk about the past.

Walterkin shrugged. 'Your history is written in your eyes, and in the things you don't say, the spaces between your words.' He narrowed his eyes and smiled, an expression that was almost lascivious. 'Tell me, Lucien. Tell me everything.'

Lucien almost shied away. It was as if Walterkin was no longer a young boy, but something older, and more cunning, wearing the flesh of a child. 'What are you?' Lucien asked, in a low voice, and then added, in a sudden panic, 'An Ixmarite spy?'

The boy uttered a low, gravelly, adult laugh. 'You know I'm not that,' he said. 'Come on, speak! Be rid of it. Make it a black dove.' He threw back his head and this time the laugh that escaped his throat was a ringing child's laugh. Lucien glanced upwards and a black bird flickered across his vision. When the boy had finished laughing, he began to speak.

'My first memory of Por Tanssie Academy in Shanariah is this: a smell of incense, cool, stone corridors, a swish of cloth across the floor, the tinkling of a far bell, a faint, distant call.

'The first thing they did to me there was pierce the skin of my throat with a silver ring. The second thing they did to me was inlay one of my front teeth with the sign of Paradouze, the Son of Ixmar. The sign was metal, very small; a triangle over a bar. When it fell out, I had it put into a medal, which I used to wear about my neck, but I have lost it now. Some of us had jewels in the bar, but these were always inlaid at a later date, when we had earned them. I was about seven years old then.

'The academy was always silent, at least in the passageways. Without the silence, we could not perform. We danced, but not to music. I was holy then.'

'What makes you think you are no longer holy?' Walterkin asked.

Lucien looked at the sky. There were no birds in it, black or otherwise, and only a hint of cloud. 'I transgressed,' he said.

The boy laughed. 'Transgressed? By running away?'

'No, before then. I lifted the lid of one of our teachings and found a black lie within.'

'But that was not at the beginning,' Walterkin said. 'Tell me about that. The beginning.'

'I remember blinking up at the white sky and seeing these slow, stately forms gliding along the walls of the academy,' Lucien said. As he recalled this, his head filled with the scent of hot dust.

In those days, Por Tanssie was administered by Caringolat, known also as the Master of the Form. He was thirty-two when Lucien's aunt Pershti took him to the academy gates, but looked far younger. Caringolat was an austere individual, who took Ixmarity very seriously. Two years or so after Lucien left the academy, he surrendered his position in order to join a secret sub-sect of the Church, whose members were rumoured to live in underground caves and do nothing but study holy books.

It was a very hot day when Lucien left the house of his family. Having been starved for three days, he was unsteady on his feet. The walls of the academy seemed impossibly high and smooth; the walls of a fortress, continually patrolled by members of the sacristine, young men in their early twenties who had not been released into the service of the noble households. Lucien recalled the dirty lilies wilting in the shadow of the walls, sacrificing themselves to the advent of summer. 'No one looked down from the wall at us. My aunt had wrenched on a bell pull but we had heard no chime. Her cheeks were very red, and she kept mopping her brow with a square of silk. She complained about the heat and said it was not the sort of weather to be kept waiting in.'

'How did you feel?' Walterkin asked.

Lucien shrugged. 'I think I was beyond caring. You see, to me, arriving at those gates signalled the end of my life. Ever since I could understand the most basic concepts, it had been drummed into me that I would end up there. As to what would happen to me afterwards, no one would say, so I could only imagine a great nothingness. My birth configuration decreed I should be given to the Vibrancy. There could be no argument about that.'

Walterkin leaned forward on the rug and gripped his toes. 'Your family just gave you away?' He pulled a face of disbelief. 'In Gallimaufry, no rich people ever do what they don't want to. Neither would the Church ask it of them.'

Lucien smiled wryly. 'Have I said I came from a rich family?'

Walterkin shrugged. 'No. But it is obvious you did. The way you move, your voice . . .'

'Then I shan't deny it,' Lucien said. 'In Shanariah things are different. Rich families pay a toll for the services the Church bestows on them, although they look upon it as a privilege to offer one of their children to Ixmar.'

Walterkin frowned. 'You must have felt very angry about it.'

Lucien shook his head. 'I could not imagine a world where my fate could

44

be otherwise. At the time I couldn't think properly. For five days, my aunt had been feeding me poppy juice, just in case I got upset. I was very young.'

So young. Lucien remembered. His childhood had been a hollow until then. He'd had no proper friends, other than the children of his parents' friends, who all thought him peculiar because he did not attend the public college like them and had little idea about how to behave with people his own age. He knew that many of them believed him to be an invalid. On rest days and festivals, he had been forced into their reluctant company, which had been like a waking nightmare. Their games were incomprehensible to him, noisy and fast. He could not understand their animal cruelty, or the way that they conducted themselves so differently once away from the eyes of their parents. He could barely understand their language, and found it difficult to laugh.

He was never allowed to run anywhere, because his feet were sacred, the first part of him to be dedicated to the Vibrancy. As other children untied their shoes and scampered over the hot prickly summer lawns of the various villas he visited, Lucien stood uncertainly to the side, his toes curling in discomfort. Several of the girls tried to like him, dragging him into their make-believe, garlanding him in flowers, treating him like a doll. Perhaps this was because they were more sensitive, and understood a little of what his life was, and would be, but eventually they abandoned him, another discarded toy by the poolside, as they ran on to more adventurous fantasies. Lucien, like a doll, was autistic in their company, alone in the circle of their hands, the circle of their chanting voices.

Now, as he related these things to Walterkin, he wondered how much the boy could possibly understand. Shanariah had its own culture, it was apart from other Gleberunic cities. The customs and traditions of the noble families there, who were all of pure Glebish stock and jealous of their heritage, were no longer sustained anywhere else in Gleberune. There were no other academies quite like Por Tanssie. How could he convey what it had really felt like, now that memory was dulled by years of experience in the outside world? He paused in his narrative and said, 'I was a very different person then.'

'Only younger,' Walterkin said.

'No. More than that.' Lucien steepled his fingers and tapped them against his lips. 'I shall tell you about the evening when my parents bade me farewell. I'd been summoned to their crepuscularium, where my mother used to spend an hour or two with my father after dinner every day. She was sitting, as usual, beneath the nighted lilies, dabbing her eyes with a scrap of lace. Her face was grave. My father sat nearby and mumbled a few words about duty, sacrifice and honour, how their pain was tempered by pride. But their sadness was simply ritual, nothing more. We were strangers to each other.'

Later, in his teens stripped of much ignorance by life in the House of Mandru, Lucien had once felt angry about that. Other Ixmaritians of the Household had been talking about when they'd left their homes, the parties that had been thrown in their honour, the tearful families. In some cases, parents had attempted to resist giving their children away, and there had been traumatic scenes. Only in Shanariah was the sacrifice made willingly. In other places, families were well-paid for their loss, and in some, children were taken as a penalty, a fine for religious transgression or the inability to pay church tithes. Lucien had been surrendered without argument or reward. He had felt humiliated by that, unable to confess it to his companions, and resented his parents' apparent cold indifference to his fate. Now, he could understand them better. They had no choice, yoked as they were by the harness of tradition. Their distance had been a defence against grief. They had never let themselves love him; they knew he was already lost to them.

'The following morning, I was dressed in new clothes and bundled into the family carriage, accompanied by my aunt. My parents did not show themselves. I remember the long drive down the straight road to the academy walls. From a distance, you can see the sprawling college complex itself, the shrines, the dormitories, the kitchen garden, the exercise lawns. Then the valley swallows you, all you can see are the walls, rising up, glistering rough yellow stone. I did not have a thought in my head as we approached, no thought as we alighted from the carriage, no thought as my aunt pulled the bell. Civilian carriages were not allowed inside the gates, and I did not even wonder about whether I'd have to walk the final league to the main buildings. You see, I was blank. Completely blank. A new page waiting for a pen. A life waiting to begin.'

He knew that was not entirely true because when, finally, someone had opened the spy hole in the gates, he'd begun to shiver uncontrollably. His aunt had explained who they were and the gates had opened like vertical jaws.

'She bundled me through them with almost indecent haste. She did not kiss me, or even say goodbye. When the gates closed I was in a new life, alone.'

Walterkin made no comment. His eyes were round. He held a grape in one still hand. Lucien was finding it easier to talk. He realised he did not really need a listener.

'Caringolat greeted all new arrivals in person. It was the only occasion when he was anything less than strictly formal. I believe a sacristine escorted me from the gates to the reception area, but I cannot be sure, for my memory of that short journey in the sun is hazy now. Some of the past is vivid; some is cloudy.'

Lucien's belly suddenly contracted, and he remembered how weak from hunger he'd been back then, how mindlessly dazed by poppy juice. Nevertheless, his first meeting with the Master Adept had been such a profound experience that the feelings it had invoked within him, rather than the actual memory, had remained with him always.

Passing from sunlight into the shadow of the academy reception area had brought him back to his senses a little, for the perfume of polished wood and smouldering myrrh had come at him like a lance. Caringolat had not been waiting for him; someone had to fetch him. Lucien had sat on a wooden bench for several minutes, listening to the hush of the new world around him. The light in Por Tanssie seemed brown. Everything was made of highly polished wood, paintings on the wall were ancient and dim, all the flower arrangements consisted of dried autumn leaves and seed pods. There were no other students around. Presently, a door opened with a sigh further down the corridor and a tall figure glided towards Lucien's bench, seemingly without the agency of feet.

Lucien stopped speaking for a moment. He could almost feel Caringolat's presence in front of him on the roof, gliding down a memory towards him.

'Go on,' said Walterkin. 'What happened?'

46

Lucien realised he had closed his eyes and opened them. 'Are you really that interested?'

The boy shrugged. 'Perhaps I'm more interested in what comes later, but I have to hear it all.'

'Why?'

'I want to picture you in your world.'

Lucien narrowed his eyes at the boy. Should he refuse to carry on? Do I really want to relive this? he wondered. Caringolat's face was still hanging in his mind; the long nose, the slanting eyes and the mouth that perpetually smiled at nothing.

'Caringolat's presence was so overbearing, I stood up and then sank to my knees,' Lucien said. 'Nobody stopped me, but then maybe I was alone anyway. All I can remember is Caringolat. He leaned down and raised me to my feet. It was a perfect metaphor for all that he did to me, a raising up from the common crowd. "Welcome," he said, or maybe not. He might have said, "Stand straight, Lucien Earthlight. We do not tolerate weakness here." Or he might have simply held me in his arms. All three of these memories ring true, and I have no way of knowing which is the right one; perhaps they are all true. From the first though, as every other boy who made that journey in the sunlight felt, I'm sure, I knew I had met my standard, my template. I wanted to be like him, because I wanted that power, that charisma.'

After this introduction, Lucien had been taken deep into the heart of Por Tanssie and left alone in a bare room. His clothes were taken from him and he was given a thin knee-length shirt of cheap grey material to wear. There was nothing to eat or drink, nothing in the room but a sense of imminence. It was a waiting room, in all senses of the word. Lucien lay shuddering upon the floor until midnight. Then a double line of sacristines, holding long white candles, came to escort him through the moonlight to the novitiate's court. It was an awesome high-ceilinged hall, its walls virtually covered in more old paintings of past Vibrancy adepts, the only windows small and of dark stained glass, high up, so no one could see out or in. There was very little light, just a few bowls of wax burning on pedestals around the edges of the hall.

The academy tutors had gathered in rows before a raised dais supporting Caringolat's ceremonial throne. The Master himself entered the room after everyone else had taken their places. All the students had been roused from sleep and were arranged in ranks down the side walls, dressed in long, saffron-coloured robes. Some were still yawning discreetly, getting away with this breach of manners because the tutors and Caringolat's staff were more concerned with observing the preparation of the initiation instruments. Standing alone, shivering in the thin shirt, Lucien saw the table, the chair with leather straps, the instruments of torture laid out in gleaming lines.

He fainted during the throat-ringing and only regained consciousness at intervals during the dental work. All he could remember was the faces hanging over him, enormous fingers coming towards him, dull pain, passionless eyes. Eventually, the proceedings were concluded by a bitter taste of poppy juice and Lucien was dragged off to one of the novitiate's dormitories and put to bed. At dawn, the bells woke him, and he opened his eyes to a crowd of boys tumbling out of bed, scratching themselves, calling to each other in muted tones. One of the tutors marched into the room and ordered someone to help Lucien out of bed. Surprisingly, he did not feel too ill, although hunger had become an agony. Later, they would let him eat, after morning devotions at Paradouze's shrine.

'Didn't you cry?' Walterkin asked.

Lucien shrugged. 'I have no recollection of it, but perhaps I cried in my sleep.' Wouldn't a child do that, far from home among strangers? He smiled. 'In Mandru's House I often woke up in the middle of the night feeling desolate. My face would be wet with tears, but then it was the dreams that upset me, dreams of the future maybe, or of the distant past. I know I used to feel embarrassed about it, but I don't think anyone ever saw me do it.'

'Were you kept drugged all the time in Por Tanssie?'

Lucien found he resented that question. 'No. There was no more poppy juice after the first day, although later I was given elixirs to help augment my strength. I could feel my mind waking up again. I suppose it was like being born, or reborn, for my world had changed entirely, and I needed to learn the names of its objects and abstracts. Memories of my old home were not discouraged, but gradually they faded away – so little had happened to me there.' Lucien frowned.

'What is it?' Walterkin asked. 'What have you remembered?'

Lucien shook his head and sighed. 'Nothing in particular. I was just thinking how the past is so fragmented. I can remember the disciplines I learned in Por Tanssie, but not the order of my learning them. I know that I made friends with the other boys quite easily – it must have been a relief to find there were other monstrosities in the world like myself – but I have a feeling that those friendships were somehow stilted; mere performances that were extensions of the Vibrancy. It is strange, but I can remember only a few of their faces, a few of their names.'

'Perhaps the Ixmarites were very strict with you there.'

'Perhaps. I remember we were taught to respect ourselves, to remain aloof. I was totally unprepared for reality when I was released into it, wholly unaware of life beyond the academy walls.' Lucien laughed. 'All I knew, or needed to know, was that Gleberune consisted of Ixmarity. True, I knew the names of King Aristocete and his young queen, Shumah, but little else. We were subtly indoctrinated with the belief that royalty was somehow less than priesthood.'

Once a year, the king and queen came to their palace in Shanariah, to celebrate the autumnal religious festival of Duomass, the birthday of two of Ixmar's sons. Their duties during this time included a visit to Por Tanssie, when the students demonstrated their art. On these occasions, the king would present a diadem to the most accomplished vibrancer, who had been chosen in advance by Caringolat and his assistants. Lucien remembered Aristocete as a sad-faced, heavy man, who always looked tired. Shumah had been a slight, pale figure, whose small mouth did not stretch on the rare occasions she smiled but only turned into a little up-curving line. He had never been presented with a diadem by the king.

'Did you enjoy your life in the academy?' Walterkin wanted to know. 'Or was it terrible?'

Lucien considered this question. 'I existed in a strict routine, which had its comforts, I suppose. Of course there must have been times when I was miserable, disciplined harshly when I made mistakes, but I cannot remember them. I learned and accumulated knowledge. I understood the secrets of my body and mind, how to empty myself of purpose and distraction. I learned to attune myself to the inner music that no one but we

48

vibrancers could hear, and to dance to it. It seems so easy in retrospect, but I cannot truly believe that it was.'

'Lucien,' said Walterkin, interrupting again, 'what was the purpose of the vibrancers? What are they for?'

Lucien smiled tightly. 'Sometimes I wonder that myself. We were an indulgence, I suppose, part of the regalia of religion. Also, we were sold like pets or slaves to rich families.'

'Are vibrancers always boys?'

Lucien shook his head. 'No, although I did not discover that until I left the academy. There were no girls at Por Tanssie, and all the staff were male. I knew there were other academies dotted about the country, where other religious disciplines were taught. At first, I thought Por Tanssie was the only Vibrancy academy, which of course it is not. We were encouraged to believe it was, which was simply a part of the indoctrination to make us somehow inhuman. We believed that most of the other academies were concerned solely with the training of priests and how to manage money, but there were others that educated choristers, absolvers and scourgers.'

'What happens when a vibrancer grows up, then?'

Lucien realised Walterkin must surely know the answer to that. There were vibrancers everywhere, male and female ones. Still, he was prepared to play the game for the time being. He just wished he could convince himself it was only a child's game.

'Once qualified in the Vibrancy, most of us were sent to outside appointments, such as public churches and official institutions, or else to the houses of the nobles, all of whom kept a full staff of Ixmaritians in their households. It is simply another cost Ixmarity imposes upon the rich, similar to how people are required to buy sacred oils to anoint public shrines. Sometimes, some of us would be shipped abroad to augment the households of expatriate families.'

'How did the Ixmarites know when you were ready to leave? Was it when you reached a certain age?'

Lucien shook his head and explained that as students, the vibrancers were arranged into grades, according to accomplishments. Examinations were held at regular intervals, and on passing them, students were elevated to a higher grade. At each grade, they were awarded an additional throat ring. Thus, neophytes were known as First Ringers. For his first examination, Lucien had to compose a dance to the rhythm of his name, twisting his body to an inner resonance of the syllables. This was seen as a devotion of the self to the authority of Paradouze; the name itself became an act of worship. Students were not allowed to concern themselves with trivia, which inevitably resulted in a lively underworld of gossip and intrigue among the cloisters.

'You were an exceptional student, weren't you?' Walterkin said.

Lucien shook his head. 'Not at all. In the world outside. I would be regarded as a superb dancer, no doubt, but within Por Tanssie, my ability was competent but unremarkable. I can remember sitting at the edge of one of the dance courts, watching one of the most gifted vibrancers, Corocante, leaping across the floor through the dust-laden sunlight. I felt sick to my stomach, knowing I could never emulate that precision of movement, that subtle humour, that moving pathos.'

For the students, excursions beyond the academy gates were rare, but on those occasions when they did venture outside, their ankles were tied together by a black cord, permitting them to take steps only of a certain, measured size. This stricture was designed to remind them, and anyone who saw them, that the fluid grace of the Vibrancy was reserved for the academy courts alone. Paradouze was jealous of his creatures. Beyond the academy, vibrancers were required to wear long, grey, hooded robes, their faces concealed by veils which were sewn to the edges of the hoods. They were not permitted to eat in public, but could take liquid refreshment, as long as they did not remove their veils.

'I can conjure up the taste of the silk gauze even now,' Lucien said. 'It was a faint mustiness mingled with watered fruit cordial. I can recall the way the wet veil stuck to my mouth, and its sticky stiffness once the juice had dried. Our hands remained gloved and we walked among the bright living souls like ceremant-bound, animated corpses. Still we regarded it as a treat to go outside.'

'What did you go outside for?' Walterkin asked.

'Sometimes we had to visit churches in outer parishes of the city to perform a Vibrancy. Lower grades were always sent out to do that. Only the cathedral in Flogging Square and the three major churches commanded the services of the adepts and the sacristines.'

Walterkin frowned. 'I can't understand why they didn't just make you travel in covered carriages,' he said. 'If they wanted to keep you hidden.'

'It was deliberate,' Lucien said. 'We were pets, actors, puppets. We had to be part of the scenery. Also, our lives had to mirror certain myths of Ixmar's family and celestial followers. Ixmar's servants, for example, can never be perfect enough to deserve the honour of waiting upon the gods. Although they enjoy many privileges, they are constantly punished and humiliated. It was like that with us. We were treated as special beings, but occasionally abused. Many of the initiation rituals and rites of passage involved physical pain.'

'Why didn't you run away then?' Walterkin demanded. Lucien detected a note of scorn.

'We were never alone. Members of the Church militia always accompanied us. They wore masks of beaten brass that portrayed the bland face of Paradouze. The god owned us utterly and, strangely, we did not protest. Now, having roamed the world, and fought for my life with tooth and nail, having tasted all the fruits of life to the full, I could not accept such treatment. Then, it was a perverse kind of security. Also, we had no knowledge of the forbidden fruits existing beyond our enclosed world. Instead, we thought that we were special, elevated above the ignorant people of the civil world. Rather than feeling humiliated or hard done by as we walked the city streets in our shrouds or had our bodies pierced by decorative spikes before we performed important ceremonies, or suffered the degradation of auction day, we felt important, aloof, mysterious. I can honestly say I never had an urge to experience greater freedom, to cast off my veils and run from the guard at my side. I was quite content.'

Lucien realised he had sounded defensive, and then wondered why he had admitted his feelings. Walterkin was smiling at him.

'How you've changed,' he said, his smile widening.

Lucien did not admit that after a visit to the city, he'd always found it a comfortable relief to return to the tranquillity of the academy. He and his peers would be unhobbled once the gates had closed out the world and then link arms to walk the final league up the path. They would be welcomed in the refectory with muted yet excited whispers and would talk importantly of all that they had seen.

Lucien felt he must have been a smugly loathsome creature then. He'd been too pious and had wanted to excel, absorbing without question every irrational detail of Paradouze's doctrine.

His tutors had told him that he would walk through life for ever alone, that he was elevated above the common desires of humanity and would never need love other than Paradouze's distant regard. Lucien had believed this and had not objected, even to himself. Later, in the House of Mandru, he discovered it to be a lie, yet in Por Tanssie he'd been grateful to be a sacrosanct little vessel for Paradouze's indifferent concern. He could remember praying earnestly before Paradouze's idol: 'Make me perfect, make me pure, make me worthy.' As he prayed, he was always filled with a vast energy; it was like white light behind his clenched eyelids and an oceanic thrumming in his ears. He breathed too quickly and too shallow, and once fell unconscious during a prayer. Later, he'd convinced himself he'd experienced a religious vision and had walked in an ecstatic daze for over a week afterwards.

'You are telling me a lot about your life in the academy, but not much about the Vibrancy itself,' Walterkin said. 'What did you learn? What was it like?'

Lucien flinched at the boy's intensity. Then, he nodded. 'You are right, but you must understand the Vibrancy is a very private thing. You are taught not to discuss the art with outsiders.' He sighed. 'Sometimes I still feel guilt . . .'

'You still perform then, regularly?'

Lucien shook his head. 'No. Since I lost my faith and saw through the bulk of lies that comprises Ixmar's worship, the Vibrancy has lost its magic for me. Sometimes I regret that, for it played such an important part in my life, perhaps too much so.'

'You speak from your heart,' Walterkin said. 'Have you ever said any of this to anyone before?'

Lucien shook his head and smiled. 'Not even to myself,' he said.

Walterkin stretched his arms up over his head and wriggled his toes. It seemed to be a signal that their conversation was over. Silence reigned on the flat roof. Lucien closed his eyes and tilted his head back, listening to the sounds of the city as it flexed its limbs around him. He did feel better, lighter and refreshed. Had he been indiscreet to reveal so much of his inner self to a stranger? At the moment, he could not care about it.

A few moments later, Bessie Anywhither heaved herself up onto the roof. 'Edgebone's gone off to work,' she said, 'but there's still a panful of fried bread and smoked fish downstairs. I suggest you come and eat before the kids polish it off.'

Lucien stood up and shook out his limbs. He felt quite stiff, and also extremely hungry. As if on cue, an aroma of frying food wafted up from the kitchen. 'Yes, the air of Gallimaufry gives one an appetite!' he said. 'You have a lovely view here, Mistress Anywhither.'

Bessie smiled at the compliment. 'It's not a bad spot,' she said, and then flicked her hand in the direction of Walterkin who was concentrating hard on his bowl of grapes.

51

'I hope that boy of mine hasn't been bothering you,' she said.

Lucien shook his head. 'No. He showed me your roof garden, kept me company. I've enjoyed talking to him.'

Walterkin jumped up. 'We'll talk again later,' he said and darted over the ladder, swinging himself down the side of the house.

Bessie beamed after him. 'I have great hopes for that one,' she said. 'He's bright.'

IV

WASP ORCHID

Cleo Sinister wanted to be somebody's goddess, but not necessarily that of the man she had married. In appearance, she was striking, which had perhaps inspired her husband Wakelate to take her as a wife. Cleo would not have chosen the melancholy Wakelate for herself, had she been in a position to make a choice. True, he did not treat her badly and she was assured of his devotion and adoration, but physically he had little to attract her. He always smelled of the tools of his trade. He was a poisoner.

She had wanted to leave him for a long time but, as her friend Dame Kleetie said, unless you are being brutalised, abused, or have met someone better, you are more likely to stick with a marriage than not. The incident with the child, however, changed. It took place almost a year before Lucien Earthlight set foot in Gallimaufry, and it gave Cleo the impetus to do something about the situation.

Wakelate's was a time-honoured profession and like all other gentlemen of his persuasion, he lived beyond the law. Cleo herself was the daughter of a forger and had been sold to Wakelate at the age of fourteen, or more accurately had been swapped for a discreet killing. She had grown up among the gutters and alleys of the Burrows, a dark sprawling extension of the great city of Scaraby. A dark and eye-catching child, she had already assumed by the time she was nine years old that she was a changeling who did not belong in the Burrows. She had a vivid imagination and existed within a cloud of elaborate lies and fictions. She wore red skirts and painted patterns on her feet and ankles with charcoal, because she believed the fenniks did that. Fenniks were Cleo's own particular invention. They were mostly invisible people, but when they did manifest themselves they were either very small or very tall. They were thin, black, stick-like creatures, who did not like human beings very much and took delight in perpetrating small cruelties on children. Many of Cleo's friends had lived in fear of the fenniks for many years, bewitched by Cleo's gruesome tales. Cleo believed herself to be a princess of fenniks, a half-breed of human and fennik stock. After all, didn't she have the fennik eyes, so black and slanty? And weren't her hands

53

unnaturally long? 'Do wrong by me and your skin will be pinched in the night,' she told adversaries. 'You will go rotten and die.'

Cleo's large family lived in a run of cellars beneath the pawn shops of Gamespick Row. They shared this accommodation with three other families. Sometimes people got lost in the warren of tunnels and arched passages. Sometimes there were mysterious falls of rock and masonry that buried people alive, and Cleo was quite convinced the cellars were also home to many ghosts and goblins, who were perhaps responsible for most of the tragedies that occurred.

When she was told she was to be given in marriage to Wakelate Sinister the poisoner, she was excited. Her sisters told her that Wakelate lived in the upper parts of a tall house on Blackback Street, which was certainly a more salubrious area of the Burrows, if such distinctions could be made in such a place. Cleo looked forward to becoming mistress of this establishment. Wakelate Sinister must mix in better company than the Groudies, her own family. Lords, politicians and celebrities from the city proper sought his services and, because it was sometimes necessary for him to mingle in genteel society, he had a number of aliases that pretended aristocratic birth.

At first, all of Cleo's fantasies were realised. The house was perhaps more rickety than she had imagined and it was certainly darker, but there was magic in the curtained workrooms at the top of the house, a sort of potent grandeur, which she liked and respected immediately. The living rooms were spacious, if rather draughty, and Wakelate, indulging his pretty little minx of a bride, was happy to let her bring a feminine touch to his abode. Cleo had never imagined being able to spend so much money. She became light-headed on the experience of it, even though most of what she bought was necessarily stolen, and therefore her purchases lacked some of the cachet of ordering goods from the city. Still, Wakelate let her have whatever she wanted and by the time the giddy intoxication of abandoned spending had left her, the house was packed chaotically, decorated wildly; it was a palace fit for fenniks. Wakelate didn't notice. He was never concerned with his environment.

As Cleo lay on a couch in a room strewn with sixty-two exotic rugs, a room without echo, her toes burrowing into a wealth of fleecy fringes, she realised she had finished. There was nothing more to be done now except live in the place. She was fifteen and a half years old.

For a further fifteen and half years, Cleo remained mistress of the poisoner's house. Sometimes she wondered where her life had slipped away to; days ran like fluid through the fingers of her experience, and at the age of thirty-one she could not imagine how she could possibly have used up so much time. Dissatisfaction had clawed her bones for some years. As a young woman, Wakelate had taken her into the city where she had pretended to be foreign, smiling behind a veil. She had even conducted one or two discreet affairs with the willowy, fragile boys who hovered on the precincts of noble society. When she was twenty-one, she'd decided to learn some of the secrets of her husband's trade, although in reality it proved to be far less exciting than she'd imagined. So much weighing and measuring, so little scraping of arcane materials from tombs or enchanted forests.

Wakelate was flattered by her interest. In truth, the ease with which she could flatter this melancholy man annoyed her. But he was not a gifted teacher, and Cleo often found herself yawning as he strolled up and down the shelves in his workroom, she sitting on a stool before him, telling her the properties of various chemicals, roots and powders. The poisonings seemed too neat and tidy to be of interest. Where was the black-tongued, writing agony of the unfaithful lover, wife or husband? Where the consumptive wasting of the obstructive heir? From what Wakelate told her, most of his victims simply fell asleep and never woke up, their relatives believing them to have suffered from some heart affliction. How disappointing.

In her naiveté, Cleo had believed the art of the poisoner to be a romantic profession, of visitations from black-veiled ladies in the middle of the night, curt requests for certain annihilations written on creamy paper in thick waxed envelopes with a seal. Sadly, only the long-nosed servants of rich businessmen seemed to frequent the stairs of the poisoner's house. After Cleo had let them in, they would scurry into Wakelate's office and speak quickly in low, furtive voices, pitched so low, in fact, that Cleo could never discern what was being said, even when she had her ear pressed right up against the door. Still, it was bound to be dull – concerning the extinction of some fat old man or another. The most exciting occasion had been when an Ixmarite priest had sidled up the narrow stairs – her heart had leapt in anticipation – but Wakelate would never tell her what he'd petitioned for. She imagined a slender Vibrancer, one of the Ixmaritian dancing boys whom she'd seen perform at various functions in the city, might have incurred displeasure; he would die as he danced. She sighed. Unlikely. The priest would only be seeking the riddance of some fusty official, some barrier to career or status. In her humdrum life, she had learned, there was no doorway for intrigue of a fatal nature.

Dame Kleetie occupied the two lower storeys of the house. She managed a couple of thin, wasp-natured girls who patrolled the streets of the markets selling their bodies. Sometimes, the girls kept Cleo awake at night, arguing with each other in harsh, high-pitched voices; arguments that always ended in lewd laughter. Cleo thought the girls were repulsive and was not surprised that Dame Kleetie's apartments lacked some of the more opulent appointments that Wakelate's earnings could provide upstairs. Still, Cleo liked the older woman and, as the years progressed, spent more and more time in her company. One day, Kleetie said to Cleo. 'Where's your mind, girl? What's bothering you?'

'Nothing,' Cleo replied. 'Why?'

They were sitting in the early afternoon sun in the little yard Kleetie had outside her kitchen. It was filled with potted palm trees, most of which were half dead owing to the fact that Kleetie's cats urinated in the pots. The girls were out, slithering through the streets somewhere, resembling undernourished alley cats themselves. Cleo thought Kleetie's cats were more attractive than the girls, being sleeker and glossier by half.

Kleetie narrowed her eyes at Cleo, rocking a few times in her chair. 'Oh, I've an idea you're rattling around in your life like it's a big house. I've watched you for a while.'

Cleo shrugged. 'Sometimes I get bored.' She sighed. It was true. At one time, she'd have sought out an ephemeral love affair, but she had to admit she'd seen little to interest her for a long time in the way of men.

'What you need is a child,' Kleetie said.

Cleo smiled broadly, thinking this was a joke, but she quickly saw that Dame Kleetie was quite serious in her suggestion. 'What for?' she asked. She could remember the state of her sisters, aunts and mother when they were pregnant, the slow draining of their life-force after the births. It had never attracted her as a prospect for the future, but she was sensible enough to realise the conditions her family lived in might have contributed more unpleasantness to the procedure than was usually, or naturally, the case.

'It stops a married woman getting bored,' Kleetie said. 'What else is there to do when a man holds the key to your life?'

Cleo thought this was an odd philosophy. She'd never considered that Wakelate held the key to her life. She wondered whether now would be the right time to confess to her friend just how she habitually relieved her boredom. But Kleetie had known Wakelate for so long, she might not approve.

'Believe me, I know,' Kleetie intoned darkly.

Cleo pulled a face. 'I've never thought about it,' she said. She had no intention of acting upon such a suggestion.

Still, events conspired to bring a kind of synchronicity to her life, and although this did not occur in the way Dame Kleetie might have imagined it, it did involve a child.

Wakelate often didn't come to bed until dawn. He espoused certain Ixmaritian customs, if not all of them, and so did not actually share a room with his wife, but they were situated next to one another and were connected by a door that was locked only when Cleo was engaged in toiletry activities she considered ungainly or unsuitable for the eyes of a man. Still, Cleo always woke up, if only for a few minutes, when Wakelate stumbled into his bedroom. Generally, he walked back and forth across the creaky floor-board that lay between his bed and his washstand. He would wash his hands, causing the unreliable plumbing arrangements of the house to groan and shudder. The springs of his bed would cry out, as if in weary despair, as he sat down upon it to remove his boots. Two hollow thuds would follow. Cleo derived a certain feeling of security from these regular sounds, although she would never admit it, even to herself.

One morning she awoke to realise she had slept the entire night through. This meant either Wakelate had not come home at all, or else he had not come to bed. As she knew him to be a creature of obsessive habit, Cleo was alerted at once to the fact that something unusual must have occurred. For some moments, she sat before her dressing mirror, idly contemplating whether or not to brush her hair. Wicked thoughts streaked through this mundane consideration. Was it possible something dreadful had happened to Wakelate? Could he possibly be dead? A series of tantalising images presented themselves to her mind: Wakelate caught red-handed in an act of toxification by appalled relatives of the victim; Wakelate shambling home, locked in his habitual post-venom depression, and knocked to the road by a passing carriage driven at breakneck speed by one of the city's young bravos, who'd been out whoring and drinking until the dawn. Or perhaps Wakelate had been the victim of a pounce attack in one of the outer alleys of the Burrows, and at this moment lay bloodless and cold upon the stones, stepped over by the hard-bitten slatterns of the streets, who believed him simply to be a worthless drunkard.

What would happen to her if he was dead? Cleo supposed she would inherit the house and its contents, for all the natives of the Burrows were meticulous in the matters of wills and legacies, perhaps because death was a not uncommon hazard of their professions. There would be a period of mourning, of course, during which Dame Kleetie would support and protect her from invasion; Cleo felt she could perform the role of young widow quite effectively. Following that, she could resurrect Wakelate's business, only this time catering for a clientèle more to her taste. A dreamy smile had spread across her face as she sat before her mirror, the silver-backed brush drooping from one hand.

She experienced a sensation that felt almost like being physically crushed when there was a sharp knock on her bedroom door and Wakelate's hesitant voice called, 'Cleo, Cleo, could you come to the parlour, my love?' Cleo pulled a sour face at herself in the mirror and then reached for the flounced robe of black and red lace that she usually wore to breakfast.

There was a stranger in the dining room. Belting her robe more tightly, Cleo stalked through the door in time to see a portly, well-dressed, middle-aged man make a frantic gesture at Wakelate, to which he responded, 'Don't worry, she's my wife.'

'Is something afoot?' Cleo asked.

The middle-aged man put his head into his hands.

'My dear one, there is a small matter with which I feel you could assist us,' Wakelate said. He looked even less happy than usual, Cleo thought, if that was possible.

'Oh?'

'In the small workroom,' Wakelate said. He escorted her up the stairs, after equipping his guest with a large measure of liquor and leaving him to bemoan an as yet undisclosed calamity.

The child was divinely beautiful. It lay upon a leather couch in Wakelate's smallest workroom, covered by a flimsy golden shawl with silken fringes. Cleo's eyes went quite round as she stood in the doorway. 'What is this?' she asked in a breathless voice.

'Oh, I know, I know,' Wakelate responded, which was hardly a satisfactory answer. 'I was quite against the idea from the start but Sir – I mean my *client* begged me to assist.'

Cleo padded into the room. Her fingers itched to touch the flawless creamy skin, to smooth the dark curls from the perfect face. She leaned over the couch, in a froth of black and blood-red ruffles, but the child did not wake up. 'And where do I come into this, husband dear?' she enquired.

Wakelate made the uncomfortable huffing noises of a male helpless in female territory. 'Someone has to care for the little thing . . . someone.'

Cleo cracked her knuckles. 'Ah yes, of course.' She glanced round at her husband. 'Who is this child? Am I permitted to know, or is this yet another of your secrets?'

Wakelate closed the door, and Cleo recognised the signs that he was truly perplexed, for only in that condition did he ever completely confide in her.

'It is purportedly the son of Resenence Jeopardy,' Wakelate whispered loudly.

'Resenence who?' Cleo supposed she ought to know.

'Jeopardy. He is a religious man.'

Cleo grimaced. 'Oh.'

'You do not understand. The Cult of Jeopardy could possibly have great power one day. Some say it could rival the Church of Ixmarity itself.'

'So what is that to me?' Cleo asked. 'One religion is very much the same as another. They all have rules, for one thing. It makes no difference to me who has the most power, as long as I don't have to put up with it.'

Wakelate smiled and reached out to touch his wife's black hair. 'Listen,

57

my lovely love. The man downstairs is the child's uncle. His younger sister was seduced away from home by the lure of the Jeopardites some years ago. The Cult had little power then, and few followers.'

'I have never heard of it,' Cleo said, 'which leads me to conclude it has little power now.'

Wakelate raised one eyebrow. 'My dear, it is said that Resenence Jeopardy deliberately impregnates the sisters and daughters – even wives in some instances – of powerful men. He is an enchanter, a sorcerer, of great puissance, and one day he will command all his children to rise up and take control of their families. Thus, it has become expedient to the Ixmarites to weed out these bastard offspring and destroy them.'

Cleo hissed at her husband, her hand flying to her lips. Were these children all as beautiful as this one?

'The Church has sniffed this boy out,' Wakelate went on.

'It is said the children are tortured to death. His uncle wants a more honourable, a less painful, fate for his nephew.'

'You can't!' Cleo said.

Wakelate nodded and sighed. 'There are . . . difficulties,' he agreed. 'At the last moment, the uncle collapsed into tears and changed his mind. I am not a hard man, and the child is indeed beautiful. Now, I am unsure how to proceed.'

'It is obvious,' Cleo said. 'We shall keep it here. I want it.'

'My dove, I would accord you your every desire,' Wakelate said sorrowfully, 'but sadly, I feel that on this occasion—'

'*I want it!*' Cleo said.

Wakelate sighed, shook his head, gestured helplessly with his hands and stomped out of the room. Cleo closed the door behind him, and listened to him groaning his way downstairs to the dining room. She looked back at the sleeping child. 'Such a pet, such a dear,' she thought.

After a few moment's further appraisal, she whisked back the shawl and pinched the boy sharply on the leg to wake him up. The child gave a panicked cry and opened his eyes, drawing up his limbs in an instinctive attitude of protection. The eyes were black as charcoal, as wide and full of potential as a distant horizon. Cleo was pleasurably entranced.

'Do not be afraid, little pretty,' she said. 'Cleo is here to look after you.'

The following two days were a dream of falling in love, for that is exactly what Cleo did, in her own particular fashion. She named the boy Inky and dressed him in some of her clothes – her wedding dress, her tortoiseshell comb. She fed him plates of beetles fried in garlic butter, gave him glasses of wine mulled over the cooking range. She found, to her surprise, it was quite fulfilling to be looking after so helpless a creature. Also, she regaled him with lurid tales of the fenniks, to which he responded most favourably, his lovely dark eyes becoming larger and darker as she spoke, shadowed with a satisfying fear. Looking at his haunted face, with its promise of later blossoming, the faint traces of exquisite bones beneath the skin, Cleo found herself wondering about the man who had sired the child. Had the looks come from him or the mother? Cleo could not stop pondering the matter.

At nightfall the following day, the boy's uncle reappeared at the house. Eyeing his corpulent figure and chinless face with scorn, Cleo doubted whether Inky's looks could be inherited from his mother's side of the family, but she had to be sure. As she led the man up the stairs to Wakelate's study, she turned on him sharply, nearly causing him to fall backwards in alarm.

'Does he favour his mother?' she snapped.

'I beg your pardon?' The man raised one heavily ringed hand to his flabby neck.

'The child, which of his parents would you say he most resembles?'

The man made a sad Ixmaritian gesture, two fingers patted on each side of the mouth. 'That is a fateful question,' he said. 'Ixmar preserve us, but my sister claims the poor mite is the image of his father, a legacy that untied the sword of doom above his head.'

'Your sister, then, is fair like yourself?'

The man pulled a face to indicate Cleo's interrogation was not at all welcome. 'She has a pale colouring,' he admitted grudgingly. 'Er, Mistress Sinister, your husband is at home, I take it?'

Cleo smiled sweetly and continued to lead the man upstairs. 'Forgive my questions,' she said, over her shoulder, her gown held up daintily in one hand, 'but I confess to being intrigued by the child. He is unusual.'

Her tone seemed to mollify the man, and he offered more information without pause. 'Indeed, he is that. My dear sister is demented to have lost him, but she was already quite mad when she returned to us three months ago.'

'How tragic!'

'I would like to blame the prophet, madman that he is, but in honesty my poor sister was unfit for the life of a vagabond. The dirt of the road got into her hair and skin so much, it drove her insane.'

'Why did she join the cult then?' Cleo asked.

The man sighed. They had come to Wakelate's door. 'A question her family have asked themselves often,' he said. 'She was out shopping in one of the common markets when she came upon Jeopardy addressing a crowd. When she returned home, she amused us with the story of how he insulted those who stood to listen, but the next morning she became restless and perplexed. By evening, she had fled the house with our mother's jewels, and we did not see her again for years. Only when she returned were we able to discover what had happened to her. At the time, we believed she'd run off with a lover. She was always a lively, capricious creature. Alas, no more.' He shook his head.

Cleo had her hand upon the door knob. She nodded thoughtfully and then tossed back her head. 'Why have you come here again?' she demanded in a harsh voice. 'The child is dead to you, dead to the Ixmarites, swallowed by the Burrows. Why have you come? Is it to pay us?'

The man visibly jumped at her verbal assault. 'That is the business of your husband and myself alone,' he said pompously, inserting a thick finger between the folds of his neck and his collar.

'Wakelate's business is mine,' Cleo said. 'What have you to say to him?'

'Plans have to be made for the future,' the man replied.

'What plans? What need is there of plans?' Cleo raised her arms in an aggressive manner, causing the man to flinch away. 'I say to you, wash your hands of this business. It is not your problem any more.'

The man tried to edge round Cleo to the door, perhaps hoping Wakelate might make an appearance to rescue him. 'Where is your husband?' he demanded in a brave yet quavering voice. 'Stand aside, woman. This is not your concern.'

'Worm!' Cleo hissed, but allowed him to sidle past her.

Later, Wakelate came to her bedroom, causing Cleo to think with some annoyance that one of his rare conjugal visits was presaged. However, it soon became clear he had come to give her orders.

She had brought Inky into her bed and had dosed him with a sedative, because he had been whimpering all evening; a sound she found quite irritating. Wakelate lumbered into the room and glanced mournfully at the child. 'Beloved, my client is grieved by what you said to him this evening,' he began.

'Grieved, is he?' Cleo said. 'I'll give him grieved! What was he doing here? What business is the boy of his now? Didn't he surrender the child into our hands?'

'My dove, the situation is not quite as simple as you perceive it,' Wakelate said. 'The Ixmarites are far from satisfied, seeing as they have no Jeopardite progeny to expunge. They are persecuting the family of my client, and it is causing untold distress. They do not wish to offend the Church. Between you and me, their current level of taxation is all that they can bear. The Ixmarites do not believe the boy's mother is ignorant of her son's where-abouts. A body is needed.'

'Then for Ixmar's sake, provide one!' Cleo yelled, standing up. 'I cannot believe that, for you, such a project would be difficult.'

'Unfortunately, Jeopardy's children carry marks,' Wakelate said. 'You must have noticed the smudge beneath the child's hair, on his forehead. It is said to resemble the legendary mage's speck.'

'And the Burrows is full of surgeons and cosmeticians who are undoubt-edly very capable of emulating that mark,' Cleo argued.

'Why is this child so precious to you?' Wakelate demanded. 'You are telling me to go out and murder another child to save this one! I cannot understand the difference. If you want children, there are many ways we could have them. You could have a baby of your own, for Ixmar's sake!'

Cleo realised a change of tack was required. She had tested the limit of Wakelate's patience several times during the early days of their marriage and had learned, through bitter experience, that he could become quite unmanageable once the boundary was breached. 'I want this child,' she said, in a soft, tearful voice. 'I love him. I want this one.'

'I don't know,' Wakelate said sorrowfully. 'I don't know.'

He left the room.

Nothing more was said for another two days, during which time Cleo amused herself by smothering the child with her inimitable devotion. Although he had been scared of her to begin with, he was gradually starting to get used to her company, and even appeared to enjoy getting drunk with her in the afternoons. Cleo obeyed the restriction Wakelate had placed upon her, whereby she could not inform Dame Kleetie of the child's existence. One afternoon, Wakelate told her that Kleetie might become suspicious about her absence, and that she should go down that afternoon, as was her habit, to spend a few hours in the yard with her friend. Cleo agreed this might be a good idea.

All the time she was in Kleetie's company, Cleo cherished the secret of her darling child, hidden in the rooms above. Kleetie commented that Cleo's mood had changed and that the incubation of her recent illness, which had kept her confined to her bed for the last few days, had obviously been the cause of her discontent. 'I am quite happy,' Cleo confessed.

'Wakelate is treating you well?' Kleetie said, with a knowing gleam in her wrinkle-wrapped eyes.

'Oh yes.'

'You have thought about our conversation the other day, then.'

'Most certainly.' Cleo smiled and squinted up at the windows overlooking the yard. 'Most certainly.'

Before she began to prepare the evening meal, Cleo decided to look in on Inky and see how he was. She'd left him playing in one of her lounges, a small angel among the fleeces and fringes. He was not, however, in the place she had left him. She searched all the floors of the house, and could find no sign of him. Had Wakelate taken him away? Surely not! Although Cleo knew her husband was working on a particularly difficult toxin and had told her not to disturb him on any account, she galloped up the stairs to his workroom and burst inside. He was hunched over a bench, apparently lost in his work.

'Where is Inky?' Cleo demanded.

Wakelate looked up. At first, he said nothing.

Alerted by a thrill of female instinct, Cleo fled into the smallest room. As her guts had anticipated, Inky lay upon the leather couch, covered by a silk-fringed shawl. She cried out and whisked the shawl away from the boy, pinching his leg sharply in order to wake him. The moment she touched him, Cleo knew that no amount of pinching would have any effect. Inky was dead.

She did not scream, did not cry. She hugged herself tightly and stared at the dead child, aware that her husband had followed her into the room. She knew she was looking at a broken human being, the most broken thing she had ever seen. It could not be mended. In a way, there was wonder in that.

'I am so sorry,' Wakelate said, reaching with huge, timorous hands to touch the shoulders of his wife.

Cleo shrugged him off. 'It's all right,' she said. 'It doesn't matter.' With no further words, she walked from the room.

Downstairs, she drained the bottle of cooking sherry she kept in the larder and then sat in a daze at the kitchen table. She was thinking off Inky's beautiful face, no less beautiful in death than it had been in life. Wakelate kept away from her, and the sun sank. In the darkness, someone came. Someone rang the door chime, but Cleo did not answer it. She listened to Wakelate's ponderous tread coming down the stairs. She listened to the furtive voices, the steps going upstairs, Wakelate's door opening and closing. For a while, there was silence, and then she heard the door upstairs open once more, and the slow, uneven steps of people coming down.

So, they had their body now. The family, whoever they were, were safe. Safe with a mad daughter. Stupid bitch! Why had she gone back to them?

Cleo stood up and went to look out of the window at the moonlight shining down into Kleetie's yard. Two cats were swapping insults in the shadows, a sincere, hateful sound. Somewhere out in that beautiful night, being touched by the radiance of that same beautiful moon, was a man who sired beautiful children. Cleo knew he was a religious man, but that did not matter. She would leave this house. She would find him. She would become his goddess.

V

PAIN

After his breakfast, Lucien put on his coat and went out into the city. Bessie had extended her offer of hospitality and Lucien was happy to accept it. He was curious about Walterkin and wanted to speak with him again. It was strange, the way he'd been able to open up to the boy and tell him things he'd not told a living soul before. Then he remembered that Chasteless, whom he'd encountered in the house of Cartesian Blink, had often been a silent recipient of his outpourings. Chasteless, however, could hardly be termed a living soul. Lucien sighed at the recollection. Poor Chasteless! At the beginning she had played a significant role in his search for Jeopardy. Did she still exist? He realised he had not thought of her for months. Would he tell Walterkin all about her eventually too? She had played an important part in his life, after all. What was it about the boy that impelled him to confide in him? Would he be disappointed if today Walterkin had tired of the game and was no longer interested in hearing his story?

As he walked through the wider streets to Gallimaufry's city centre, Lucien was surprised at how buoyant he felt. True, he had to remain alert for interested Ixmarite eyes, but he no longer felt hunted or vulnerable. It was as if by telling Walterkin a little of his history, he had somehow cut himself loose from a heavy part of his past. It was a process he wished to continue.

There was no sign of the Jeopardites in the places he visited that day; not even a scrap of graffiti. Lucien bought a cerulean blue flower from a pair of old women squatting in one of the market areas. He had seen Jeopardy's eyes that colour. By lunchtime, as noon bells began to toll in the Ixmarite churches, Lucien was back at Bessie's house.

She seemed surprised to see him home so quickly. 'How did your search go?' she asked.

Lucien blithely offered her the flower, which she accepted with an embarrassed giggle. 'Not too well,' he admitted. 'I was thinking of enjoying the sun this afternoon, on your roof, if you don't mind.'

'Not at all,' Bessie said. 'I might join you myself later, when the housework is done.'

'Is there anything I can do to help?' he asked.

She waved him away. 'No. You've been travelling hard. You need the rest. Be off with you.'

Lucien hesitated before going out into the yard. 'Is Walterkin around?'

'Somewhere,' Bessie answered.

Lucien was reluctant to question her further.

There was no sign of Walterkin on the roof, which disappointed Lucien, who'd thought the boy might be waiting for him. He settled himself on the rugs and lay down, putting a cushion beneath his head. He felt dizzy staring up at the eternal empty sky. It would be terrible if Walterkin did not want to hear any more about his life. He needed to talk about it now. Closing his eyes, he dreamily began to continue the narrative in his head, imagining that Walterkin sat before him. It would serve the same purpose.

Lucien's day had begun at dawn, when the academy bells were rung in sequence. Each bell symbolised a member if Ixmar's family, and their tolling mimicked the gods talking to one another. Soon afterwards, the Caller came along the corridor outside Lucien's dormitory, knocking once on each door and making a sound which might once have been a word but which had mutated through decades of repetition into a sort of braying. This signified that the students must get out of bed. As one, hands would reach out behind heads, drawing the modesty curtains round the beds. They would put on their robes which, for the initiated students, were in beautiful pale colours, of the finest fabrics that caressed the skin, made it feel supple and graceful inside the softly swaying folds. It was not a feminine grace, but that of the gods themselves; genderless. The students were never, under any circumstances, encouraged to think of themselves as effeminate.

Once clothed, they would each shake a tiny hand bell that stood on the small cupboards next to their beds in which copies of the texts they were currently working with were kept. Nothing else. All their clothes were looked after by the Linen Master, and they owned no personal effects.

Once all the bells had been shaken, the boys could draw back the curtains and look at one another. Thus, the day began.

Before eating, the students made their way to the morning shrine, which was situated underneath the bell tower. Here, a couple of sacristines conducted a ceremony, intended to focus the students' intentions for the day. The sacristines were regarded with both suspicion and awe by the younger students. Their years of training and dedication had tempered them into a new substance, something barely human, and their faces were devoid of outward expression. They only came alive as they danced, when they would put aside their robes and release the energy of muscle and bone. They were the Vibrancy; nothing else. Later, when Lucien became a sacristine himself, he realised their behaviour was artificial, designed to impress the lower grades. Among themselves, they were fiercely competitive and no less interested in gossip than the rest of the academy. They believed themselves to be superior beings; it was a lie that everyone was taught.

At the shrine, with the morning coming in faintly behind the altar, one of them read from the sacred texts.

'Here now my feet, the doves of Paradouze. Here, they fly . . .'

Such pretty words. The students performed group hand movements, each grade assigned a different sequence. They would try to outdo each other, subtly improvising the traditional gestures, adding embellishments of their own. The sacristines watched sternly, their faces as still as if they were wearing their masks of brass. Sometimes one of them might get annoyed and call for stillness, clapping his hands sharply into the flock of moving hands. The sound was usually discipline enough.

After the morning devotions, everyone filed out to breakfast in the refectory, where they were permitted to talk. Breakfast consisted of warmed milk and hot sugar-bread in winter, cold milk and fruit in summer. They were also given a large spoonful of Bloom Oil by an elderly priest, who came round the table with a pot on a wire, which contained the oil. It was said that the oil was only to help them grow strong and fit, but it probably also induced tractability and killed libido. By sixth grade, students were allowed the dignity of taking the oil themselves in private. Small privileges for maturity.

After breakfast, lessons commenced: religious history, symbolism and languages, the last because some of the students might be sent abroad. They were also given options for other subjects. Lucien chose writing, because his aunt, in a rare moment of candour, had once advised him to do so.

Afternoons were always given over to the Vibrancy. As a neophyte, Lucien did not exercise his first movement until after he'd been in the academy for several months, but he attended lectures on Vibrancy theory from the second day. There were two thousand, five hundred and twenty-five set routines, all of which symbolised various Ixmaritian myths, which in turn were fables about human behaviour and morals. New pieces were invented all the time, but they had to be exceptional to be added to the Books of Paradouze. Most of the performances created by the students were performed only a few times and then forgotten, but the set routines all had to be memorised. This was made easier by the fact that the required steps and elaborations were abbreviated in the title of the piece. If the student could remember the name of the routine, he could remember the movements.

Lying on Bessie Anywhither's roof garden, Lucien opened his eyes and raised his hands. They were outlined against the impossibly blue sky. He twisted them into a configuration that invoked the name of Paradouze. He felt a thrumming in his veins, a tingling in his flesh. He wanted to dance.

'Lucien!'

Abruptly, the feeling fled. Lucien sat up quickly, turned, and saw Walterkin's head poking over the top of the ladder behind him.

'Were you dreaming?' Walterkin asked, leaping up onto the roof and skipping over to the rugs.

'No, I was awake.'

Walterkin dropped down beside him. 'I've brought you a cake,' he said.

'Must you always force food on me?' Lucien took the cake.

'My mother made it. She says you've been out looking for Jeopardites.' The boy grinned widely. He seemed just like an ordinary child. Lucien wondered what had possessed him earlier to think otherwise.

'I was only looking round the city,' he said.

'Can I sit with you now?' Walterkin asked eagerly. 'Will you tell me more stories?'

Lucien shrugged, inwardly delighted. 'If you like.'

'I don't want to hear any more about that academy place,' Walterkin said, screwing up his face. 'Tell me about where you went afterwards.'

Where I had a fateful meeting, Lucien thought. He smiled affably. 'Very well.' How much could he tell a young boy?

Lucien was eighteen when he left the academy, a devout and disciplined sacristine in a pale yellow robe. He did not see the agent who bought him, because the sun was in his eyes. Those sacristines who'd been elected for sale had been summoned from their beds before dawn, taken to the morning shrine empty of younger presences, where one of the tutors had led them through a brief ritual. The sun had not yet risen; it was quite dark, and the candles smoked and sizzled like burning fat. The sacristines were reminded of how they were to be the academy's representatives out in the world, how they should remain true to their devotions, free from impurity and taint. 'Though you will have none of the supervision you have become accustomed to, rest assured that Paradouze will be watching over you constantly.' A chalice was passed round; all took a mouthful. The wine within the cup was fortified; it dampened any excitement, numbed the mind. After that, the sacristines sat down upon the floor, and locked themselves into silent contemplation until the rest of the academy came to the gates of the shrine. Then they were led out of a rear door, so as not to pass by the ones who would remain behind. The traders did not arrive until mid-morning, but the wait did not seem very long.

Business took place in a hall reserved solely for that use. Benches were set up at one end, on which the agents of the noble house sat, clutching parchment catalogues describing what was on offer. Houses that had contacts within the academy would already have been notified of which vibrancers were considered the best buys that day. Throughout the last year of their training, the sacristines had been indoctrinated with the idea that the humiliation of the auction day was a sacred part of their duties. There was a legend that spoke of how Paradouze had once been kidnapped by his evil aunt, Atavenom, who was Ixmar's dark female counterpart. He had been kept as a slave in her flame-lined, subterranean halls for many years. Atavenom had made him dance for her every evening and, becoming bored of the performance, had eventually convened a panel of pimps and auctioned her nephew off as a joke. Ixmar had refused to help His son, because Paradouze had become arrogant and proud, believing himself to be as splendid and powerful as his father. The legend implied that even Paradouze, as the son of the highest god, was not beyond degradation for his audacity. Only at the last minute had his Divine Father stepped in to save him. Chastened, Paradouze had gratefully accepted his lower status within the Ixmaritian pantheon. Throughout their lives in the academy, the sacristines had been taught that they were superior beings. Now, they were impressed with the fact that the privilege of being sacred could be withdrawn by those with greater power at any time.

The sacristines filed in through a doorway at the other end of the hall, wearing a cloud of incense and their masks of brass. Sunlight streamed in through high windows behind the traders, obscuring them from sight, filling the eyes of the dazed sacristines. Offices of the domestic staff arranged them into a line. A memory of winter came rising up through the stones of the floor, a chill that stabbed right through the thin fabric of their sandals. The Domicilitor, in charge of all students, came into the hall, wearing his keys, and attended by two lesser acolytes. He walked up and down behind the sacristines, murmuring, 'Stand straight now. Give a good show.' When he tapped them on the shoulder, they had to remove their masks and tuck them beneath their right arm. They were not asked to dance. Then, the bidding began.

Those agents who had already received recommendations from the academy purser, of sacristines that might be especially suitable to their employers' establishments concluded their bidding swiftly. One by one, the sacristines were taken from the line.

Lucien had not been recommended to anyone. He stood there, mindless as a goat, mask beneath his arm, staring into the sunlight, feeling serenely important. Money changed hands via imperceptible signals from the agents. The flesh was auctioned, although the flesh believed itself to be spirit, or something of rarer value. There were no tutors present at this soulless event, not even Caringolat, only the Domicilitor and his staff. The bidders made barely a move to indicate whom they wished to purchase; the sacristines could not determine when and by whom they'd been acquired. Then, the inevitable moment came when Lucien felt the Domicilitor's hand on his shoulder, a slight shove. One of the servant boys, who had been running backwards and forwards all morning, ushering the sacristines out of the hall, took hold of Lucien's sleeve and led him away.

Now, he belonged somewhere and to someone. His life had reached the Harvest Time. Another lie.

Prior to dispatch to their various destinations, the sacristines were confined in a small room near the outer kitchens and laundry. Benches lined the walls and they sat there in silence. Once business had been concluded in the hall, the Domicilitor came to supervise the next stage of dispersal. This was the insignment, another symbolic ritual; the holy books declared that Paradouze himself still bore the seal of his aunt, which she'd had burned into the flesh of his thigh during his captivity.

The sacristines were led out of the room in threes, to a place outside where a brazier had been heating since early morning. Irons glowed in the fire, the flesh seals of Ixmar and Paradouze. Now, the sold sacristines would receive their insignment; they would be branded. The insignment had been mentioned briefly several times during the final course of their instruction. They had been taught to regard it as being a small part of the academy for them to carry out into the world. It was a holy, precious thing, and not to be feared or shunned. Paradouze had endured a similar indignity, and the sacristines should strive to emulate his courage humbly.

The procedure was quite simple and conducted without undue fuss. Standing in line by the brazier, each sacristine was required to raise his robe to thigh level on the left side. This experience alone was strange to them, because the only time their flesh had been displayed previously was when they danced. The morning air felt cool on the skin. The Domicilitor and the Insignateur (who was generally only a blacksmith), stood beside the fire, the Domicilitor holding a list of all the allocations. Then the emblems of the gods were applied to the flesh. The meat was marked for transfer. The heavily greased and blackened hand of the Insignateur steadied each leg, and then came the smoke, the smell of it, the jerk of the body. A servant boy with a pot of pain-killing and antiseptic salve came and slapped a palmful of unguent onto each thigh. The sacristines, passive to the end, believing themselves to be undergoing tests of religious significance, uttered not a sound. One of them, however, could not stop himself vomiting, even though he bravely attempted to swallow it. This prompted the Domicilitor to sigh, and call for a boy to clear up the mess. One or two other sacristines fainted when they smelled their own flesh burning, but these events occasioned no more than minor delays.

The House of Salaquin Mandru was in the Scarcement Chase district, which lay north-east of the city, a few hours' drive away by carriage. Ancient, sprawling demesnes clung to a great, granite backbone poking out of the earth, surrounded by cultivated forests and artful follies. In legend, this area was the spine of the Serpent Mipstang, servant of Ixmar's wife, Aufiria, lady of fertility and death. Here the most venerable families had their estates; courtiers of the king, retired generals, cathedral deacons, viniculture magnates. Terraces of grape claimed every crust of soil that was not appropriated as garden or pleasaunce lawn.

All the noble houses were required by law to keep a troupe of Ixmaritians in residence for their personal absolution and agency of worship. In a large household, this could encompass half a dozen vibrancers, several priests and priestesses, plus choristers and absolvers. There was an official scale which decreed that each household should have one Ixmaritian per three servants. The larger the establishment, the more Ixmaritians were in residence. Lucien's own family had owned only two Ixmaritians, and neither of them had been a vibrancer, who were the most expensive to buy. Lucien did not associate the sour-faced, middle-aged priestess and the thin, pallid boy chorister who'd lived in the Earthlight manse with himself.

The students of Por Tanssie were all well aware of the arrangement Ixmarity had with the rich, but they were wholly unaware of what life could be like in their households. Horses, chickens and goats are similarly uninformed; when purchased by a rich man, their destination could be the stable or the slaughterhouse. A hound might be purchased for companionship or the fighting ring. It is doubtful whether these beasts consider the slaughterhouse or the fighting ring to be real possibilities because to an animal they are unimaginable. Likewise, dumb and ignorant as the beasts, the sacristines of Por Tanssie had faith in the benevolence of their mentors. They believed themselves to be artists, not slaves.

After having raised his brow, scratched his face, or whatever other esoteric gesture had marked the sale of Lucien to the House of Mandru, the agent did not bother to inspect his new property further. He and the other agents left Por Tanssie as soon as the auction was concluded. Transport, however, was provided to ferry the sacristines to their new home or, in the case of those who had been bought by foreigners, to the harbour.

A plain, covered cart, its bare wood embossed with the seal of Mandru, waited in the academy guest yard. It was the sort of vehicle used by lower servants when purchasing potatoes from the city markets or large consignments of fish from the harbour. It was not a passenger vehicle. Other carts, from other houses, waited nearby; all the drivers were talking together, drinking the refreshment that the academy domestics had provided for them. The sacristines were led out to the yard, some limping badly, some barely conscious, and were unceremoniously matched with the correct carts. At the gates, phantom new boys were ringing the bell as the carts rumbled past. The sun curved downwards in the sky. The day continued.

Mandru's cart, drawn by two ponies, was covered by a thin awning and packed with old cushions for comfort. The cushions supported the body of a vibrancer, just a body, because there was no mind at all. The body did not

67

think. It did not care that it had left the academy, and was unconcerned about its destination. It felt neither uncomfortable nor distressed. It had a name – Lucien – but in essence it was only a property.

The sacristines had made no fond farewells to each other, even though it was likely they would never see each other again. The potioned wine they had drunk at the morning rite had clouded their minds, but finer human emotion rarely enlivened the cloisters of Por Tanssie anyway. There was no grief inside them, and no excitement. The sacristines were nothing but ciphers of acceptance. After all, they had surrendered themselves to the academy at the age of seven and nothing bad had happened to them. The rites of the auction and the insignment had not really been any worse than some of the other rituals they had endured, those of fasting and body piercing, over the years. Their lives would now continue as they always had. They were subject to a change of location but would still have no responsibility for their own lives. No decisions would have to be made, no real existence withstood. They did not want, could not imagine, life any other way.

Their masks of brass had been surrendered at the academy gates, but the sacristines had been given veils with which to cover their faces. They believed they would have to wear these veils always, out in the world. It would be necessary to remove them when they performed, of course, but they also believed that the noble houses would, like the academy, have their own private dance courts, where they could uncover themselves with dignity. Looking out through the back of the cart belonging to Mandru, out through a veil, Lucien could see the city and the sparkling sea below. Ixibatabian ships were in port, their cloth-of-gold flags trembling in the breeze. The cushions in the cart smelled of old fluff and body powder. They supported a body that believed it was a rare treasure being carried to its place of installation, where it would be admired by and displayed only to its privileged owner. The deep pain in this property's thigh, which was observed but not felt, was a badge of excellence; the body, devoid of awareness, was ignorant of its implications.

The gates to the House of Mandru, set in walls of pale, warm stone, were made of dark, lacquered wood. They were not as impressive as the academy gates, because they lacked the significant carvings, but they were much larger and grander than the gates to the Earthlight estate in Racervine Park, within the city walls. Guards wearing Mandru's livery stood to attention on either side. Every time the cart driver went through those gates, he would call out the same greeting. Beyond was a steep, upcurving driveway which led under an arch and into the main kitchen and stable yard.

The estate had no name other than the House of Mandru. The house itself crawled up and away from the yard, like a low, grey lizard, in and around the rocks of the cliff. It crawled round gnarled ancient trees and skirted outcroppings of bare stone, enclosing them utterly, incorporating them into its Self. Some of the rooms had walls made entirely of ginger-coloured glass, others were but dank stone cells. It had high-ceilinged, airy rooms, rooms that seemed bigger than the outer structure, and small, secret rooms, with light-bowls that gave off a blood-red glow. There were many stone passages that seemed incredibly ancient, passages with expensive polished marble floors and skylights overhead; in the upper quarters where the servants and the Ixmaritians lived, the passages were wide and well-lit, with bare wooden floors, waxed to a silky sheen and always fragrant-smelling. Despite all this Presence, the house itself seemed like an illusion; from beyond the gates it appeared as if nothing was there but the wild, wind-torn cliffs. A house of ghosts or dreams.

The property that carried the name Lucien Earthlight, but little of Lucien's spirit, had to be helped out of the cart because its leg was injured. The driver was obviously used to this. Whistling through his teeth, perhaps thinking of his dinner, the condition of his ponies, the weather, the gambling den below the kitchens which he might visit later, he undid the bolts that held up the plank at the back of the cart, lowered it and pushed aside the curtain. The property within had two eyes of glass, set in a face that was serene but blank. The cart driver murmured a few words as if he was speaking to an animal; a low, coaxing sound. As he had no doubt done many times before, he held out his hand, an offering of support. The property looked at this appendage steadily. To the driver, it must have seemed as if this idiot boy had never seen a hand before. He waggled the fingers. Come on, now. Down. Out. Was he paid to be patient? Probably not, but he was used to handling animals. He might have interpreted the lack of response as fear, but it was more likely puzzlement. The sacristines had little contact with servants, and were certainly never touched by them. When Lucien saw the hand stretching towards him through the back of the cart, he thought, 'How dare he!'

Walterkin was staring at Lucien very intently, so much so that Lucien became a little unnerved. He'd impressed himself with his narrative, but the expression on the boy's face suggested he was not affected in quite the way Lucien had hoped.

'Why are you lying to yourself?' Walterkin asked.

'What?' Lucien felt suddenly hot, then cold. Clouds had drifted in from somewhere and the afternoon light had become dull. A breeze plucked at Walterkin's hair. His eyes were hideously knowing, his smile mocking. He is not a child, Lucien thought, and then chided himself for being too imaginative again. 'What do you mean?'

The boy shrugged. 'What possible good will it do if you lie? Are you trying to present the Ixmarites in a more favourable light, or is your memory genuinely faulty? Is your lying conscious or unconscious? I know that you are not telling the truth, Lucien. I really do.'

Lucien began to shiver. He felt slightly sick. 'I am not lying. Why should I?'

'You tell me.' Walterkin reached forward abruptly and put one small, grubby hand on Lucien's left thigh. Lucien yelped and shuddered. It hurt. It burned. 'You tell me.'

'You don't want to know.' Lucien didn't know why he said that. It was as if a stranger was speaking from inside his head.

'I do. But, more to the point, so do you.'

'No!'

'They betrayed you. They fooled you. They turned you into an animal!'

'That's not true!'

'It is. Speak it. Tell me.'

Lucien covered his face with his hands. His fingers smelled of burning flesh. 'All right,' he said softly, looking up. 'All right.' He gave a deep shuddering sigh. His skin felt uncomfortable now; too small for what it contained. His eyes felt dry and hot. He took a breath and it scorched his lungs.

'You realise from the first moment you see those faces at the end of the hall exactly what you are. Even through the fog in your mind, you realise that. The wine was bitter, the drug strong, but you still know. The hall is full of incense to mask the stink of fear, the stink of the sweat of fear. That morning, you wake up and you are treated differently. It is as if you are already sold, or already dead. The pretty myths, the convenient legends, the *lies*, don't matter any more. They are not essential to keep the animals in line. The branding is intentional because it tells you your value. Why give it an honourable name? It is humiliating and painful. You are not serene; you vomit, soil yourself in fear. You struggle, but your cries might as well be the bleating of a sheep. You realise the utter senselessness of all your training. What was the point of it when the end result is this? What is the point? Why do they have to do this to you? It doesn't make sense. It never has. Who cares what Paradouze once went through? It's not relevant: happened too long ago, happened to a god. You are only a boy of flesh and blood. The word "Mandru!" is shouted in the yard, and a man raises his hand, puts down his drink with a final laugh to his companions: "See you in the market, the tavern, perhaps here next year . . ."

'He does not look you in the eye. You probably smell unpleasant. In the cart, you weep with confusion and terror. The pain in body and mind is so intense, you do not even think of death to end it. Then you reach your destination, and the man says to you, "It's all right. Come on. It's over. You'll be all right now." And the voice is low, like that of a man speaking to a frightened animal, and the hand is offered, but you are afraid that it will be like the last hands that touched you. You will be afraid of hands for a long time. You are eighteen but, because of all they did to you, you have the mind of a child: naive, innocent, ignorant. Some women come to you, because they have always found that women handle the situation better. They have to pull you from the cart. You claw at the wood to stay inside, among the cushions. Your bladder has emptied over your robe. Urine has got into the burn, which later will become infected, causing fever. You cannot think of dying because only humans have the intellect for that, and you are no longer human. You want to hide, not die.

'That is how it was, Walterkin. You wanted to know.'

The boy had tears on his cheeks. He was a child, nothing more. He was silent.

'I'm sorry I told you, but you did ask. It was you who turned the key, you who let the truth out. Now, it is yours to keep.'

70

DROWNED MAN

Full of youthful zest and vigour, striding out into the unexplored world beyond Samberdell, Delilah had blithely assumed it would not take long to find Trajan's prophet. All they would have to do was retrace Trajan's steps. But Trajan's memory of his deranged journey to the village was fragmented at best. He could remember few landmarks, and could only recall that he had travelled beside a river. Delilah at first assumed this must be the Tickpike, to the west of the village. And yet it was not impossible Trajan was referring to the Lallyflow, which was a narrower and younger stream that flowed down past the east side of Samberdell, in a westerly direction, before veering east once more and disappearing underground. After some debate, the pair decided to follow the River Tickpike downstream. Trying to establish some kind of timescale, Delilah grilled Trajan about how long he'd been estranged from his cult. 'Too long, too long!' was all he would say. He seemed equally reluctant to discuss the circumstances which had caused the separation.

Still, Delilah soon discovered that Trajan was happy to talk at length about the prophet himself. So much so, and with such adoring vigour, that she began to question whether this paragon of masculine virtue actually existed, or whether Resenence Jeopardy was just a phantom conjured by Trajan's undeniably sick mind. The madman's vision of Jeopardy seemed to change from day to day. During one account, Jeopardy would be described as a simple sage, while in another as a powerful magician. He was called a prophet, yet seemed to make few prophecies. Perhaps Trajan had forgotten them.

'What does he look like?' she asked.

'Like an angel, an angel!'

'And what does an angel look like, Trajan?'

At these words, Trajan turned his head towards the sky. In those first few days of their journey, the moon was coming to her fullness, and the white light would pick out the grey in Trajan's beard; feminine moon-thread in such a mat of maleness. 'He has the height of a tall woman and his flesh is spare, but in his power he towers over taller men.'

71

'A magician, then.'

Trajan frowned. 'No, no. His hands speak.'

'How?'

'Like this.' And Trajan wove his fingers clumsily in the air, then shook his head and groaned. He could not emulate the dancing hands of the great man.

'What colour are his eyes?'

'They change.'

'With the moon?'

'Most certainly. At the Hunter's light, they are yellow, and then should his gaze fall upon a man who has beaten his wife, the man burns, his flesh shrivels; he falls smoking to the ground.'

'Oh!' Delilah hoped that one day she would witness the trick herself. 'What other colours, Trajan?'

'The moon's blue, the doe's brown, sometimes silver when the gods speak through him.'

'I want to meet this man.'

'You will.'

There was a silence. 'Trajan?'

'Yes?'

'If Resenence Jeopardy is a religious man, and his religion is not Ixmarity, does he pay tithes to the Ixmarites like the Dominish do?'

Trajan shook his head with a smile. 'No, lovely. He does not.'

Delilah frowned. 'Then one day he'll be shut away or killed, like the villagers from Soarcrest, further north, who tried to stop the Ixmarites entering their territory.'

Trajan nodded contemplatively at her observation. 'It is always a possibility, but because Jeopardy and his group move around so much, they are in less danger than if they kept to one place.'

'The Ixmarites will root out every other religion one day,' Delilah said. 'My mother said so. I often heard her talking with her friends about it. They said the Mother would be driven beneath the hills.'

'Jeopardy's cult will not be rooted out,' Trajan said firmly. 'Every day it grows larger, its influence spreads. One day . . .' He curled one of his hands into a fist, and then smiled and shook his head. 'Let's hope we can find Jeopardy in the meantime.'

Trajan sometimes mentioned names other than Jeopardy's, which Delilah deduced must belong to erstwhile Jeopardite companions, but he refused to elaborate upon them. Sometimes he seemed confused and frightened about the past. Delilah resigned herself to being patient.

Their route along the Tickpike took them over rolling heathland in a south-westerly direction. They kept away from the lanes and roads in order to avoid coming across any other travellers or patrolling units of Ixmarite militia. Plumes of smoke were similarly avoided, although Delilah sometimes thought wistfully about seeking shelter in a village or lonely farmstead. Luckily, the weather remained clear; Delilah scanned the sky daily with dread. She had never liked getting wet. At night, she curled up against Trajan's massive side, and slept soundly.

At first, striding out over the hills, breathing in the fragrance of Mother Moistfoot's kingdom, Delilah had felt excited and optimistic. After two days of this, however, the novelty palled, and she questioned the wisdom of condemning herself to Trajan's company. Since leaving Samberdell he had manifested no symptoms of a violent nature. She felt under no threat from him, yet dared not feel so confident about his reaction to strangers. He spoke gloomily about his afflictions. He told her how, despite the precautions he'd taken in avoiding other people, he had sometimes come across them accidentally. Powerless to resist the urges that possessed him, he had torn them limb from limb and bitten off their fingers and noses. Strangely, Delilah found it hard to be horrified by Trajan's tales. Some part of her, she realised, did not wholly believe them. The only way she could keep the vision of Trajan as murderer alive in her mind was by concentrating on the carnage she had witnessed in Samberdell, the image of his enormous bulk hanging over her with an axe. Sometimes she found herself thinking that his afflictions might be as fictitious as his beloved Jeopardy. Perhaps there was no curse, he was simply a lunatic.

Gradually, as the days of their journey lengthened into weeks, the country-side changed and Delilah no longer recognised the landmarks. As a young child, she had often accompanied her father on his journeys to other settle-ments where he would place strictures on the water spirits and see to the plumbing arrangements. She could remember riding his broad shoulders, nestled comfortably on the backpack he carried. They had never left the hills then. When he went further afield, he left his daughter behind, telling her there were dangers beyond Mother Moistfoot's realm. Now, the gentle landscape, with its feminine, undulating curves and feathering of trees was becoming more masculine; spiky and rocky. The trees were taller and darker: evergreens with a pungent smell; dead forest floors covered with old, rusty pine needles.

They continued to follow the course of the Tickpike, but now it seemed to possess a more energetic and youthful flow, tossing out white foam so that the rocks it gushed between were perpetually wet. Luminous moss and flat white flowers with round waxy leaves grew in the dampness. Hopping hordes of shiny green amphibians fled from their heavy human feet. The light was always twilight. Delilah was not sure whether she liked this new landscape. It did not seem more powerful than Mother Moistfoot's realm, but its energy was certainly different, and perhaps less benevolent. She caught glimpses of an unfamiliar type of spirit. Sharp faces like foxes or cats peered from the shadows. Sometimes she caught a glimpse of paw-like hands on the bark of a tree, which vanished before she could look at them properly. Eventually, she told Trajan about them. She expected him to humour her, pat her head and mention something about her childish imagination, but he only nodded at her insistent remarks.

'Hewkins,' he said.

'What are they?'

'An old race,' Trajan explained. 'They're not goblins or fairies or ghosts, but people like us.'

Delilah looked at him dubiously. 'They don't look like us.'

Trajan grinned. 'Well, perhaps they're not quite human. They're very shy. Don't worry, they won't hurt you.'

She was not sure whether to believe what Trajan said.

Delilah had brought what she thought would be enough food to last them for several weeks, but she had forgotten that much of it went rotten after a while. She should have gathered more dried food and root vegetables, instead of the plump loaves and soft, creamy cheese. Many of the eggs were broken, and fruit alone did not seem to satisfy her hunger. The supplies ran out very quickly and the only sustenance they could find growing wild were tart turtle-berries. The hills were otherwise covered in grass or heather, and all the crop fields of the farmsteads they had passed had been protected by dogs to prevent stealing. There were plenty of rabbits about, but they had proved impossible to catch. Trajan, despite his size, seemed to exist on air; he was rarely hungry. Delilah, however, felt the acid gnawing in her belly continually, and cursed her lack of foresight. When she complained to Trajan and told him she was going to approach the next homestead they came across to buy food, he'd replied that he would not wait for her.

'Turtle-berries are the traveller's friend,' he said. 'You can live on them for weeks.'

'They taste horrible!'

'You'll get used to it. You've enough puppy fat to last you a season anyway.'

'I want proper food,' Delilah whined. 'I'll not have the strength to travel otherwise.'

Trajan remained adamant. 'Turtle-berries contain all the nourishment you need,' he said firmly. 'Save your little collection of coins until we really have to use them.'

One morning they came to a place where the river plunged downwards in a riotous, fern-girdled spume between dark, wet crags, and the path all but disappeared. Distorted trees with long, trembling leaves clung doggedly to the rock, leaning out over both canyon and travellers, showering them with a soft misty rain. Trajan managed to discern a narrow walkway along the edge of the chasm, almost hidden by the ferns. Delilah was very frightened walking along it. Below her, the water fell away and shouted in a dangerous, thundering voice, as if demanding her life. She dared not look down in case she was compelled to obey the wordless instruction and fall to her death. Spray soaked her and her feet were unsteady on the slippery wet rocks. She held on tightly to the back of Trajan's coat. Despite his bigger feet and less agile body, he trod confidently along the path, whistling carelessly between his teeth.

Suddenly he stopped moving, and Delilah skidded into him, falling painfully onto her backside.

'Hmmm,' Trajan murmured.

'What?' Delilah scrambled to her feet and peered round Trajan's bulk. A totem was set into the rock. A long pole of carved pine topped by a manikin with red woollen hair.

'Whose property are we about to violate, I wonder?' Trajan said.

'I think I know,' Delilah replied. She remembered tales that her father had told her concerning a group of women known as the wheel-maidens. They were, apparently, one of the dangers that a child should be protected against, although from what Delilah could recall of the legends, children had less to worry about than adults. The wheel-maidens were reputed to live in an ancient, dusty mill beside a bottomless pool. Here they ground corn between enormous slow-moving stones. According to the tales, they also ground the bones of men who strayed unaware into their territory. They sold cakes made from this grisly meal to women who wanted to become pregnant, or who desired the power to kill a rival. Delilah related this legend to Trajan.

'My father said the wheel-maidens mark the boundaries of their territory

74

with dolls of themselves to warn men away,' she said. 'The maidens are supposed to have long red hair.'

Trajan stroked his beard contemplatively. 'We have come a long way,' he said. 'It would be a pity to turn back. Anyway, I expect these so-called wheel-maidens are just a bunch of old crones who don't want to be molested. I think we should press on and if necessary pay them a toll for passing over their territory.'

Delilah did not feel comfortable with Trajan's plan. As far as she could remember, only men and boys were threatened by the wheel-maidens. She did not want her lumbering companion to be put at risk, but nor did she want anyone else exposed to the hazards of Trajan's unpredictable temperament.

'I think I should go on alone and find out how the land lies,' she said.

Trajan made a predictable protest.

'Have you forgotten the curse?' Delilah said.

Trajan sighed. 'You are right. The truth is, I had forgotten the curse. Being in your company has eased my heart, Delilah. Still, I cannot help worrying about you venturing on alone. Whether the stories your father told you were fairy tales or not, you are still very young and vulnerable. Witches aside, there could be bears or wolves ahead, even bandits.'

'I will be quite all right,' Delilah insisted with more confidence than she felt. 'I can run very fast, and I can smell out danger before it even knows I'm there. Give me one of your knives.'

'Perhaps we should turn back.'

Delilah shook her head. 'I don't want to,' she said. 'Anyway, we need food, and where are the turtle-berries here? Hidden beneath the rocks, perhaps?'

Trajan made no comment.

'Corn is surely to be found at the mill,' Delilah continued. 'Perhaps I could even buy bread.'

Trajan pondered her words for a moment and then gave a short, reluctant nod. 'I will come a short way with you,' he said.

Presently, the path widened out once more, and at Delilah's insistence Trajan climbed up the rocks to the side where he could secrete himself in some bracken. 'Stay here until I come for you,' Delilah said, feeling important, and then added, 'If I don't come for you, well . . .' She shrugged.

'You have until sundown,' Trajan told her. 'Then I shall come looking for you.'

Gripping the knife in one hand and listening as hard as she could for any noises that might be concealed beneath the racket of the cataracting river, Delilah advanced cautiously down the path. The ground dropped rapidly and soon the river began to organise itself into a smoother flow. Grass now grew among the rocks above her head and herb-covered banks flanked the water. Elderly willow trees dipped their tresses among the reeds and pewter-grey waterfowl paddled up and down the languid flow, uttering harsh cries of warning when they noticed Delilah creeping along the path. She sensed no hint of danger; all was placid. Eventually, the round, spired roof of a mill could be seen through the trees ahead. Delilah thought she heard a trill of female laughter. She tucked her knife into the belt of her skirt so as not to appear aggressive and walked forward with a more purposeful stride.

The first thing she saw was two old women sitting on flat rocks beside the river, with their stockinged feet dipped into the water. They were combing out a hank of yarn between them, russet yarn that looked just like a thick switch of auburn hair. Could these be the wheel-maidens? If so, it seemed Trajan had been right to call them crones. They wore layers of stiff, faded green skirts, tight bodices festooned with brooches made from dried flowers and beetles' wings, and enormous black woollen shawls. Their long grey hair was coiled in plaits about their heads.

The path had now turned into crudely hewn steps and as Delilah descended them she could see that the crones were not alone. Waist-deep in the black water of the mill pool were three young women, apparently naked, who were rinsing out their long hair which was the colour of old blood.

As Delilah reached the bottom of the steps, the two hags looked up from their work and appraised her with suspicious eyes. Delilah made a gesture that, in Samberdell, implied respect, and greeted the women.

'A glad day of pleasant air to one so pretty as yourself,' announced one of the hags, stirring the river water with her heels. Delilah smiled at the woman, although she was discomfited by the way the hag's eyes looked in completely different directions.

'Madam, I thank you,' she replied, bobbing a brief curtsy.

The younger women had now all swum to the edge of the pool and were blinking up at Delilah from a floating mat of hair.

'Corn, is it?' said one.

'Little money,' added another.

'A hopeful heart,' murmured the third.

Delilah shrugged awkwardly and crouched down beside the two hags. They gave off a strong smell of burning moss. She noticed one of them had a black rat curled round her neck, while the throat of the other was adorned with ancient symbols of goddess worship, worked in iron and bone. It seemed obvious to Delilah that none of these women had any truck with Ixmarity.

'What you say is true,' she told them. 'I have been forced to travel from my home, and have now run out of food. I was living on turtle-berries further back, but can find no more. I do not know which plants can be eaten around here. Hence, I am hungry.' Delilah sighed. 'I admit my predicament is mainly my own fault, but the Mother's realm is not as fertile as I imagined.'

One of the hags cackled and reached up to poke Delilah's ribs with a twig-like finger. 'She is fertile, pretty, you're simply walking on her and not through her.'

'There is a difference,' agreed the other. 'What is your name, girl?'

'Delilah Latterkin.'

'And we are the Nitgrass sisters,' said the first hag. 'She's Menace and I'm Measle.'

'Pleased to meet you.' Delilah sensed the privilege being bestowed upon her by this introduction.

'And these are the Saltcats,' Measle Nitgrass said, jerking her head in the direction of the three maidens who were staring silently up at Delilah from the water. 'Rakehelly, Waxen and Upanker.'

'You will not stay long,' said one of the maidens, twisting her hair into a rope, and wringing it out.

'Not as long as we'd like,' said another, leaning forward onto the bank and putting her chin in her hands.

'In fact, you are already on your way,' added the third, raising her arms over her head and scratching her scalp.

Delilah grinned weakly. She felt so hungry. She had to sit down.

Measle Nitgrass put her arm round Delilah's shoulder. 'Your journey is over, for a while,' she said. 'This is women's territory.'

The maidens emerged from the pool in single file, gesturing for Delilah to follow them into the mill. They were clad only in their soaking hair, which stuck to their thighs like weed. The mill was huge; it resembled a castle with a single turret. Lower buildings were attached to it on the side that did not face the river. All were constructed of a pale yellow stone. As the maidens passed under the door lintel, a scrawny bird of prey fell off its perch just inside the building. It hung flapping and squawking in a cloud of shedding feathers as the maidens glided by. Delilah edged past it warily, conscious of the flailing claws and yellow murderous eyes. Yellow eyes. A man beats his wife. He burns. He falls.

Inside, the mill was very dark, but the air was hot and full of sound and smells. Delilah could not only hear the great machinery of the mill grinding and turning, she could feel it in her flesh and blood. The dusty aroma of meal and corn enfolded her. The door behind her was open to light, but it was simultaneously closed by the dense atmosphere of the mill.

Leaving damp footsteps, the Saltcats walked silently up a floury wooden stair, Delilah following behind. The higher they climbed, the more the air was filled with the powder of the grain, until it swirled around them like smoke. Delilah could hear a great sucking sound coming from within the walls. She could not imagine what it might be.

Eventually, they emerged into a wide round room that the Saltcats and their attendant Nitgrasses obviously used as both kitchen and living space. The floor was thick with flour dust which had drifted towards the walls like snow. Delilah could not identify all the items lying on the floor because of this coating. Some of them might even be animals, motionless or dead. Delilah was so interested in looking around herself, she barely noticed the Saltcats' departure from the room. There was no compulsion to follow. She knew this was where she must stay. After a few moments, a door opened beside the great hearth and Measle Nitgrass came through it. She now wore a splendid green shawl with a long silk fringe over her faded elderly garments.

'Sit down, sit down,' she said, waving a hand at the huge table in the middle of the room. Delilah attempted to wipe away the dust on the bench beside the table but, realising the futility of such an act, resigned herself to sitting in it instead.

Should I be here? Am I in danger? she wondered. Her thoughts sounded very loud in her brain, echoing like a voice in an empty room.

Measle Nitgrass produced a small metal pot, seemingly from some corner of her apparel. She brushed away a patina of flour with her shawl and removed the lid. The room was immediately filled with an aroma of chicken broth. Delilah could hear the pot bubbling. 'A spot of soup, ducky?' Measle asked.

Should I? Delilah wondered, and then nodded. She was too hungry not to. Measle poured the thick golden liquid into a cracked pewter bowl which she took from a pocket of her gown; it was covered in sticky fingerprints. She placed it before Delilah and handed her a wooden spoon. Delilah began to eat. Never has she tasted such a savoury broth. As she swallowed she could smell newly mown hay, and a vision flashed before her eyes of larks flying through an aching blue sky, over a shivering yellow field. There was redness among the corn. Poppies, perhaps, or the blood of a man. She took another mouthful. What did it matter?

Once the meal was finished, Delilah was overtaken by an irresistible compulsion to fall asleep. Throughout the meal Measle had been a softly rustling presence behind her at the hearth but now she appeared to have left the room. Or perhaps that dust-shrouded shape leaning against the wall was not a jumble of old coats hanging from a hook. Perhaps. Slowly, Delilah pushed her bowl away from her, making a wide track through the dust on the table. She folded her arms and let her head drift gently down to rest upon them. She felt as if she had become dust herself; it was a dreamy, glistening feeling.

Trajan Sacripent fought against an overwhelming lethargy. The sun was slowly sinking behind the trees, staining the river to gleaming copper. A few minutes before, he had begun to walk down towards the mill, because Delilah had not come back to him. Sinister murmurings whispered in his brain. Occasional flushes of fury summoned blood to his face. The sound of the crashing water further upstream was becoming muffled. Trajan could barely move his legs. Each step took more effort until eventually, even before the tower of the mill was in sight, he toppled forwards with a sigh to land in a plush nest of fern. The fronds furled round him gently and covered him completely. He descended instantly into a deep sleep, his limbs shivering like the paws of a dreaming dog. In his dreams, he tore at flesh, but the ferns held him fast. He did not wake.

Midnight and the moon rides high. She draws her skirts of darkness behind her, splintered with stars. And the Saltcats come slithering down their stairs from the high reaches of the groaning mill, naked as guilt. They pour like a stream of milk through the door to the kitchen, and a ghost of dust rises up around their bare feet. Their toes grip the wooden floor. They comb their hair with their long, agile fingers. They are caressed by a smoke of flour, a powder of shed skin, of age, of memory.

'Such a young heart, such an old heart,' purrs Upanker Saltcat. She stoops through a veil of hair and prowls towards the table, leaving a trail of delicate footprints that appear wet.

'Heart is flesh. I speak of souls,' says Waxen, edging closer behind her sister.

'I speak only of desire,' murmurs Rakehelly. She covers her face with her hair, but she is the one who touches the sleeping girl. She climbs onto the table and crouches before Delilah. The fingernails of her left hand reach out to Delilah's cheek.

'Wake now, pretty,' says Rakehelly Saltcat. 'Wake.'

Delilah has been dreaming of water; the black water of the mill pool that is dark as an unknown path yet clear as polished crystal. She can taste its mineral essence in the back of her mouth. Knows at once where she is and who she is.

'Come with us,' Rakehelly says.

And they go down to the mill pool, a line of women, down the stairs where small, unseen things are skittering through the dust. Down the stairs with their high, narrow windows, webbed and fly-blown, filtering moonlight. Out into the clear, breathless night, where duskflies skim the river water.

Delilah wonders what the Saltcats want with her. Is she to be privy to their mysteries? And won't there be a cost for that? Her mind passes briefly to Trajan Sacripent, whom she presumes still waits among the bracken thickets upriver. It seems so long ago since she last saw him, as if the mill and its maidens have possessed her for a hundred years. Waxen and Upanker slide into the water like white fish, submerging completely but for their hair. They are a glimmer of silver beneath the still, fly-kissed surface. They are the tough white tubers of river-floor plants, sprouting a foliage of russet fronds. Hydra-women.

'There is something for you to see in the heart's mirror,' Rakehelly says, standing beside Delilah at the edge of the pool. She is not much taller than the girl.

'The heart's mirror?' Delilah whispers.

Rakehelly extends one arm and gestures at the pool. 'Lean forward, come see,' she says. Her other arm snakes gently round Delilah's shoulders, applies a gentle pressure. 'Look. One day, this image will be of use to you.'

What am I to see? Delilah wonders. My future? A bitter past? Will she push me in, drown me, tangle me in her sisters' hair? An owl screams from high in the mill house. Bats fly low, flirting with the river surface. What will I see?

The surface is so smooth, like glass. The moon is there, pale and vigilant, the Mother's sister. Delilah stares into the water. She is looking for a cloud, a mistiness, a change. What she sees is a man beneath the water. When she sees his face, she cries out, tries to draw back. A man, a drowned man! But Rakehelly's hand has become a bony claw; she will not let go.

'Look at him, Delilah Latterkin,' she hisses. 'Learn his face. When the time comes, you must open his eyes.'

He is lying there like a dead king, eyes closed. His hair falls back from a noble brow that carries the magician's mark. He is a spare thing, a thing of bone, of torment, but he is beautiful. 'Drowned?' asks Delilah.

'No. Unaware,' Rakehelly responds, and makes a small sniffing sound. She lets go of Delilah's shoulder and leans forward to muddle the water with her hands. The image of the man is lost, he is broken up, yet Delilah feels she can still see him. She is sure that his eyes, had he opened them, would have been silver.

'Who is it?' she murmurs, realising even as she speaks that she knows the answer.

'Resenence Jeopardy,' says Rakehelly Saltcat. 'The prophet.'

In the morning, Delilah woke up with her head in her hands, still sitting in her chair, but sprawled across the kitchen table of the mill. Her arms, her hair, her shoulders were covered with a fine powder that glistened faintly in the dim light. She felt completely alone. The mill was silent around her, holding its breath. The hush was so vast, Delilah became unnerved and leapt to her feet in a shower of sparkling dust. She ran to the window, looked out. Below, the river was blanketed in mist. Delilah could not see the trees on the far bank of the pool. Where were the Saltcats and the Nitgrasses? Could it be possible she'd dreamed them?

Around her, it appeared the kitchen had not been touched for many years.

There was no sign of life. Delilah ran over to the table, intending to look for the bowl she had eaten from the previous day. It was not there, not even as a dust-entombed lump. The only thing on the table, apart from its mantle, was a roughly drawn symbol. Delilah stared at it. Perhaps she had accidentally drawn it herself as she'd jumped up. It looked like the letter R. Delilah stretched out her hand. She wrote the rest of his name, and heard a bird call from the trees outside, heard a noise behind her, felt the mill flex its stone bones, heard the groan of waking timbers, and turned to see Menace and Measle Nitgrass coming into the room, smiling their peg-toothed witches' smiles.

Delilah spent another day at the mill and, later, the memory of that place would be fragmented, remembered only as a series of pictures: steam in the kitchen, the kitchen being clean and then dusty, the moon in the mill pond, a single duskfly hanging over the water, early moonlight caught in its filmy wings. She would remember the face of Rakehelly Saltcat reflected next to the countenance of a drowned king. She would remember nothing.

Physically, it was very difficult to tell the Saltcats apart, although Delilah quickly learned to recognise a certain flavour to each sister's company. Rakehelly always made her feel excited, as if a secret was about to be revealed. Upanker made her feel languorous; it was a watery feeling. Waxen, on the other hand, made Delilah feel very much awake. She seemed to comb unruly thoughts into order.

In the morning, while she was eating a bowl of porridge the Nitgrasses had given her, Delilah began to worry about Trajan. Hadn't he promised he would come to find her if she hadn't returned to him by sundown? Where was he? Had the Saltcats *done* anything to him? She eyed the floury porridge with misgiving.

'If you're looking for the face of your hulking companion in the curds, then look again,' Menace Nitgrass said suddenly, behind her. 'You'll find no sign of him there.'

Delilah felt her face flush. Had the Nitgrass read her mind?

The old witch chuckled then, and put a claw-like hand on Delilah's shoulder. 'Not all the stories you've heard are true,' she said, but there was a certain note to her remark that implied that many were.

'Trajan, the man I was with, told me he would come looking for me,' Delilah said, a slight tone of interrogation in her voice.

'He sleeps,' Menace replied sharply. 'By the Lady, he needs the rest!' She laughed and shuffled out of the room, her long gown dragging through the flour dust.

Far from being shunned by the local populace, it seemed the wheel-maidens had a thriving business. The day Delilah arrived at the mill had been a weekly holiday in that part of the land, a day sacred to the local goddess, Famnuwe. Upanker Saltcat told Delilah that the people had changed Famnuwe's name to Panphyla, who was a daughter of Ixmar. It meant they could still worship her without fear. Because of the holiday, there had been no visitors to the mill the day before, other than Delilah herself. The following day, however, carts started arriving around mid-morning, laden down with sacks of corn and bales of wool.

One of the buildings attached to the mill was a carding parlour, where the Nitgrasses prepared wool for spinning by combing out the fibres. Other buildings housed a spinning parlour, where yarn was spun, and a dye house, where the Nitgrasses coloured the yarn in deep, autumnal shades. Delilah was fascinated by these processes and especially liked the wooden shed where all the dye weeds, mosses and woods were hung up to dry.

Men and women alike came to the mill, travelling the uphill path from the south. Nobody seemed to come from the north, down the steep, shadowed path that Delilah had used. She was quickly caught up in the daily activity of the mill and the wool shop, and spared barely a thought for Trajan Sacripent.

In the afternoon, Upanker Saltcat asked Delilah if she'd like to accompany her across the river to a patch of woodland where specific dyeing weeds could be picked. Delilah readily accepted the invitation; she was curious about how a Saltcat would behave separated from her sisters.

Further downstream, an arched rickety bridge spanned the river. Several planks were missing halfway across, and Delilah could look down onto the dreaming water below. She noticed that many dark-brown catfish lurked in the shadow of the bridge, which Upanker told her should not be caught and eaten on any account as they were the messengers of certain water spirits, who would object to their creatures being harmed.

It was a warm, scented day, and the woodland beyond the river was a web of sunbeams and floating seeds. Here, growing alongside brightly coloured fungi, were bushes of bloated ice-berries, their dull black skins filled with a sweet watery pulp, mellowed by the winter frosts. Upanker directed Delilah to collect some of the fruit, while she ferreted among the undergrowth, seeking the roots she needed. After an hour or so, they sat down together beneath a spreading oak to eat the ice-berries. Delilah sucked at the fragrant pulp, eyeing Upanker with a sideways glance. The maiden leaned back against the tree trunk, exposing her white throat to a ray of light coming down through the foliage. She exuded an atmosphere of tranquillity that was almost soporific. Delilah, encouraged by Upanker's dreamy smile, risked a question.

'Upanker, what is this man, Resenence Jeopardy, to me?'

Upanker, who'd had her eyes closed, opened them and blinked slowly up at the sun. 'What is he to you?' She sounded as if she hadn't understood the question.

Delilah wriggled uncomfortably, unsure now whether she should have spoken. Some things, she knew, belonged only to the night. 'Well, I know there must be a pattern to what has happened to me. Last night, your sister showed me an image of Jeopardy in the mill pond. She told me I'd have to open his eyes, or something. Is he, or will he be, important to me?'

Upanker chuckled. 'Sometimes it is better to interpret messages in a literal sense. And it seems to me the question you are really asking is, "What am I to him?" '

Delilah's face grew hot. 'It can't be a coincidence you know about him,' she said, rather abruptly because she was embarrassed. 'And this morning, his initial was written in the dust on the kitchen table.'

'Was it?' Upanker stretched languorously. 'This man means nothing to us. He is, like most things beyond the Mother's realm, an ephemeral creature. He is hot and sudden, he is filled with himself, with his own beauty, like a splendid male butterfly. Without the colours and the wing span, he would be quite a plain little insect. And yet, even here, we can sense the movement in the air caused by the flutter of his wings. We are *aware* of him.'

'Am I meant to find him?' Delilah asked.

For the first time since they'd begun the conversation, Upanker turned her head to look at Delilah. She smiled and reached out to squeeze Delilah's shoulder. 'You will find him,' she said, 'but whether that is *meant* or not is subject to a philosophy other than mine. 'You saw his image in the mill pool because he was in your head, not ours. You wrote his name in the dust because the letter "R" made you think of him. Someone else might have written "Run!" and fled the mill. Another might have written "Reality" and stayed. You wrote Resenence Jeopardy because he has fascinated you through the agency of his follower.

'My sisters and I, we see things, we know things, we even predict things, but we shrink from creating things. Creation, in your life, is your privilege. When you leave this place, you might think Jeopardy is an important phenomenon because we spoke of him. It might be that he is important, and that our part in your journey is indeed significant. Or it might all mean nothing, just be part of the random disorder that comprises your life. It all depends on how you view the situation yourself, I suppose.' Upanker stood up, and brushed down her long, russet skirts. Delilah stared up at her, unsure of what she'd heard.

'Is Trajan all right?' she asked.

Upanker frowned and shook out her hair. 'He sleeps,' she said, 'but not for much longer. When the constellations shiver, he will wake. Then, you must leave us.'

'I wish I could stay with you for a long time,' Delilah said. 'I feel there is so much I could learn here.'

'You can learn it anywhere,' Upanker replied. 'Come along. Menace wrung the neck of a plump fowl this morning. It will be roasting for our supper presently. How's your appetite?'

'I'm famished,' Delilah said. She jumped to her feet and followed Upanker back to the mill.

As the sun slipped down below the horizon, Trajan Sacripent woke up in his nest of ferns. He blinked up through the nodding fronds and stared into the cold, passive face of the rising moon. A fury stirred within him, turned over in his heart and came alive. He saw Delilah's face hanging before his eyes. Where was she? Moonlight burned his eyes. He was mindless with hunger and a sense of desertion. He stood up, tearing ferns up by the roots as he stumbled onto the pathway. He began to lumber towards the mill.

Delilah had already eaten her supper on the flat rocks beside the river in the company of the wheel-maidens and the Nitgrasses. It had been a lazy, relaxing meal and now Delilah was helping the Nitgrasses to carry dirty plates back into the mill house. The maidens had preceded them into the building, in order to prepare themselves, in some upper chamber, for their evening's devotions at the pool. Delilah was in the kitchen, rinsing plates at the sink, when Trajan arrived. She had been aware of an alien sound for several minutes, a kind of low howling. She had wondered what kind of animal made a sound like that. Then, with a sick thrill, she recognised the howling was coming from human lungs. She knew immediately that it was the cry of an enraged man, a lunatic. She knew this because she had heard it before, in Samberdell, on the day Trajan Sacripent had brought ruin to the village.

Delilah was alone in the kitchen. The Nitgrasses had a habit of disappearing inexplicably. Had they heard the noise? Perhaps she could get outside and control Trajan before something terrible happened.

She ran down the dusty stairs, her feet barely touching the wooden treads. She ran past the flapping, squawking bird and into the moonlight. She was surprised to see that the Saltcats were already beside the pool, because they had certainly not passed through the kitchen. Perhaps there was another exit to the mill house. The wheel-maidens were dressed in long, pleated gowns of thin white muslin. They stood as still as trees on the rocks beside the river, their arms straight by their sides, their faces expressionless. Beyond their pale shapes, the apparition of Trajan Sacripent could be seen, stumbling violently down the hewn steps to the mill. His mouth was a screaming black hole, his eyes were virtually popping from his head, and his hair and beard appeared to be bristling with fury.

He doest not see any of us, Delilah thought. It is something else he sees.

The Saltcats manifested no immediate concern for the insane creature crashing towards them. Trajan juddered to a halt upon the flat rocks beside the pool and threw up his arms to the moon. Delilah could see that his beard was wet with maniac foam. It was almost as if his eyes were glowing silver. With a final roaring complaint at the sky, he threw himself towards the maidens, his hands curved into murderous claws. He needed no weapons; his meat would be strong enough to rip flesh from flesh. Delilah wanted to run forward, she wanted to prevent what she perceived would be a hideous, bloody massacre, but she felt gripped by a useless torpor. Her limbs resisted all attempts to move.

The maidens did not stir. They stood, slightly stooping, like vague blades of light. Why didn't they run? Behind them, the pool was dark as a witch's glass; there were no faces beneath the water. Trajan was broken up into a series of flickering images in Delilah's eyes. His moon shadow seemed to blot out the Saltcats. He towered over them, irrepressibly male, irresistibly strong. And then, it was as if the surface of the water shivered, as if light was reflected from a thousand diamonds. The air around the dark shape of the man was filled with flashing light. Delilah saw the Saltcats shiver round Trajan Sacripent in a gossamer whirl. She heard him growl and roar. Saw his arms flailing. He was caught in a net of light.

The Saltcats stepped backwards, and one of the Nitgrasses came scurrying out of the mill carrying a lantern. The net holding Trajan looked like strands of shining silk. He couldn't escape them. After a few futile struggles, he fell to his knees and began to sob. Delilah found she could move again, and hurried after the old witch with the lamp. Waxen Saltcat brushed back her hair. She was panting in the moonlight, the only evidence of fear or action. She looked at Delilah with narrowed eyes, and the girl was afraid she'd identify reproach in that gaze, but there was only fierce triumph.

'A quarrel with the lady moon,' said Menace Nitgrass shaking her head as she held the lantern over Trajan's moaning body.

'No quarrel,' said Upanker Saltcat. She prodded Trajan through the strands of the net with a long finger. He shuddered at her touch and fell quiet.

Rakehelly Saltcat was also breathing hard. She twisted her long hair into a rope and knotted it loosely at the nape of her neck. 'Come here!' she said to Delilah.

'I'm sorry . . .' Delilah began, but Rakehelly shook her head to silence her.

'No apologies.' She reached out and, putting a strong slim hand on each of Delilah's shoulders, pulled her close. 'Look at me,' she said.

For the first time since she'd found the mill, Delilah felt frightened. She could hardly breathe. The wheel-maidens no longer seemed like vague and wispy elemental beings, but creatures of solid power, women of flesh and blood.

'I will give you a tool of control,' said Rakehelly. 'Use it wisely, for your companion, though a strong guardian, is a senseless danger to all.'

'If I keep him away from people, he's all right,' Delilah said breathlessly. 'I should not have left him so long. I—'

'Hush!' Rakehelly leaned down and kissed Delilah on the mouth. It seemed to Delilah as if something fluttered through her lips that she could only describe as an invisible bird, or a song.

'When you need the lunatic, whistle for him,' Rakehelly said. 'When you need to control him, whistle.'

'The song will not stay with you for ever,' said Upanker. 'It has a limited life, so use it carefully.'

'It is the best we can do,' said Waxen. 'It is not our task to heal him.'

'Then whose? Mine?' Delilah asked. 'Can anyone heal him?'

The maidens looked at one another.

Rakehelly nodded. 'If you follow the right roads,' she said.

Then, all three of the Saltcats embraced Delilah in turn. She knew, in her heart, she was being dismissed.

'It is time for you to go, Delilah Latterkin,' said Rakehelly Saltcat. 'Keep travelling south. Seek the face you have learned.'

'But what do I do when I've found it?' Delilah asked. 'What then?'

'Stir the pool,' said Waxen.

'Look to the sky,' said Upanker.

'Harness his eyes,' said Rakehelly.

They handed her a silver leash which was attached to the net binding Trajan Sacripent. Measle Nitgrass gave her a sack containing food. And in the moonlight, Delilah led the silent, humbled Trajan Sacripent away from the mill. They went down the lane that led away from the mill, a lane that was hugged by ancient, stooping trees. Moonlight dappled the path.

They walked all night, following the scintillant train of the Queen's Robe, a southern constellation hanging like a veil in the sky above them. In the morning, they fell exhausted into a bracken bed beside the road. When Delilah woke at noon, she reached for the silver leash and could not find it. Trajan slumbered beside her, his brow unlined. He was no longer bound, but his clothes were soaked with water, his fingers laced with river weed. Eventually, the sun dried him, and he awoke. He could remember nothing of the night before, and Delilah did not tell him.

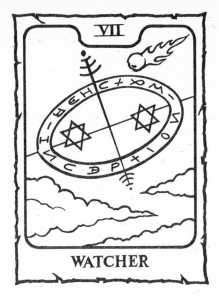

VII

WATCHER

In the evening, Lucien again sought out the roof garden of the Anywhither residence. To his disappointment, Bessie and Edgebone were already sitting there enjoying the night air. An enormous jug of Edgebone's home-brewed ale sat on the floor between their chairs. Bessie poured Lucien a generous tankard-full. Neither Walterkin, nor any of the other children, were anywhere to be seen.

Bessie sighed contentedly and leaned back in her heavily cushioned chair, pulling her red shawl more tightly round her shoulders against the evening chill.

'This is the best time of the day,' she said, taking a mouthful of ale.

Edgebone nodded and smiled, reaching out to squeeze his wife's plump knee. She patted his hand.

'The stars are so clear,' Lucien said. He sat down on the rug in front of the Anywhithers and leaned back on straight arms, gazing up at the sky.

'You've an interest in the constellations?' Edgebone asked.

'I know very little,' Lucien said, and was about to add, 'it was not part of the Vibrancy studies', but remembered in time that that was a remark suitable only for Walterkin's ears.

'I studied the stars as a boy,' Edgebone said. 'I can still name many.' He pointed. 'The Queen's Robe, the Crouching Hound, the Slaughtered One.'

'I can only remember the Maid's Hook,' said Bessie, 'because it stands all on its own in the heavens and has such a definite shape.'

'Where is that, then?' Lucien asked, entering into the spirit of the Anywhithers' conversation. He was enjoying their company.

Bessie pointed. 'There,' she said. 'What is that one, Edge, the one that looks a bit like a crown?'

There was some pointing and explaining as Bessie indicated the cluster of stars she meant. Edgebone rubbed his face. 'It's not a crown, it's a cat's head,' he said. 'It's called the Night Watcher, I think.' He laughed. 'When I was a kiddie, we were told that if its eyes ever turned red, the world would die.'

Both Bessie and Lucien stared intently at the constellation. Lucien

85

narrowed his eyes, until the shape of the stars truly resembled the watchful countenance of a cat. It seemed to be staring right at him. He blinked and looked away.

'Don't some of those batty Jeppy folk call their prophet the Night Watcher?' Edgebone remarked.

Once the ale was finished, Bessie and Edgebone went back into the house to go to bed. Edgebone had to get up early for work in the morning. Lucien remained alone on the roof, gazing out over the shimmering city. 'Somewhere,' he thought. 'Somewhere . . .' His thoughts became no more definite than this, a wistful longing with no proper form. Presently, he heard the foliage rustling behind him, and turned to see Walterkin coming over the edge of the roof. He was not surprised to see the boy.

'Shouldn't you be in bed?' he asked.

Walterkin made no comment. He sat down silently on the floor against one of the chairs. Lucien felt distinctly uncomfortable. Walterkin emanated a powerful brooding air that seemed peculiar in one so young. His face looked pale and waxy in the starlight, his hair, freshly washed, was white as bleached silk.

'Lucien,' he said.

Lucien's flesh crawled. The voice sounded different, older. He had to move suddenly to dispel the grip of fear.

'What?'

'You are so . . .' Walterkin's voice faded away. He knelt up and leaned towards Lucien. His hands reached to touch Lucien's face. 'Will you forget me?' he asked in an adult's voice.

'Stop it!' Lucien hissed, and slapped the boy's hands away.

Walterkin moved away and sat down with raised knees. He put his hands over his mouth and giggled. At the sound, the strange atmosphere seemed to rise from the roof garden like a vast bird soaring up into the sky.

'What were you thinking of?' Lucien asked, aghast.

'I don't know,' Walterkin said with a shrug. 'I wasn't thinking anything. Something made me want to touch you. Are you angry?'

'No. Yes. I should be,' Lucien answered in confusion. 'I don't want your parents suspecting I'm trying to seduce you. You're so young.'

'Nobody saw us.'

'That doesn't matter. It was a silly thing to do.'

'I know. It's so strange. Sometimes I feel so strongly I want to do that – touch you – and yet it doesn't seem like my idea. Does that make sense?'

Lucien grimaced. 'Sounds like growing up to me. But I don't want to be part of that, Walterkin. I can't be. Please respect that.'

'I do. I said I'm sorry.'

'Then we'll forget it.'

'Good.' Walterkin grinned with apparent innocence. 'So, what happened next in your life? What was the House of Mandru like?'

Lucien wondered whether it was a good idea to continue telling his story to the boy, given the direction it was heading in. What happened next . . . Perhaps he should omit the details. Wouldn't it be encouraging Walterkin's obvious attraction to him if he didn't? 'Aren't you sick of hearing about me yet?' His smile, he knew, was unconvincing.

'Of course not. It's another world.'

'I don't know.' Lucien shook his head and sighed. 'I don't think we should continue these talks.'

'Lucien!' Walterkin cried, sounding hurt. 'You said you'd forget what just happened. Don't you trust me now? I'm not a child.'

Lucien didn't answer. Contesting that remark would only provoke an angry response from the boy.

Walterkin narrowed his eyes. 'Why fool yourself? You know you need to tell me.'

Lucien put his head into his hands. The boy was right. He could not stop now, even though his common sense told him he should. The release inspired by the telling was too sweet.

Lucien had had little experience of female-kind in his life, and it was the women of Mandru's household who were the most kind to him during the first traumatic days of his life there. It was the women to whom he turned for comfort. Their first instinct, upon seeing someone in distress, was to touch, to hug and hold. Lucien could sink into their arms and escape his anxieties. Closing his eyes against a warm breast, he became a child again, he felt safe. This made him aware of how much he'd been missing before in the cold, masculine environment of the academy. He swiftly chided himself for such thoughts; he'd been taught to shun physical contact, even on a platonic level. But he was so fevered and bewildered, he could not refuse the comfort offered. He felt too weak to think rationally. Because the women were so strange to him, it was as if he could sense the warmth of their spirits as a palpable force in the house. He was aware of their presence, their smell, their power, even when he was alone.

The Ixmaritians in Mandru's household did not have to share rooms as they had in Por Tanssie. Each had a comfortable, good-sized room of their own in which to live. It was the first private space Lucien had ever occupied and, until he got used to it, made him feel edgy and a little frightened.

After he'd been coaxed out of the cart in the yard, three serving women had carried him into the house. He'd lolled half-conscious in their arms as they carried him along corridors and up stairs. They seemed to him to be nothing more than soft, huge shapes. They were like friendly bears. Behind his closed lids, light flickered orange, pink and then black. Sometimes, the women stopped to talk to somebody, but he could not understand their words. Eventually, they laid him on the bed in his own room, and undressed him. Later, when lucidity returned to him, the recollection of that made him blush and cringe, but at the time he did not care. The women bathed his body where he lay, gently turning him, wiping his limbs and face with soft, scented cloths. Then they peeled back the bedcovers and laid him on a crisp sheet, covering him from the waist down with another sheet. They gave him fortified water to drink.

After this, a female healer had come into the room, dressed in an Ixmaritian robe but with a colourful blanket thrown over her shoulders. She was much younger than the serving women and her aura was rather more severe. After she'd attended to Lucien's wound, which was hurting so much he could not tell when she was touching it, she lit a bowl of tamara weed and other herbs to induce sleep. Bitter-sweet smoke filled the room, and the women held their shawls over their mouths and noses, backing away.

'I don't know how long I slept for,' Lucien said to Walterkin. 'Perhaps it was for days. I only know that, at some point, I awoke into a noontime heat although the sun did not fall directly into my room. The curtains were long and gauzy, fluttering in a slight breeze. My throat felt dry, my eyes heavy and painful to move. The air beyond my room was full of alien sounds – voices calling, laughter, clattering, animal noises.'

'What was your first thought?' Walterkin asked.

Lucien frowned and considered the question. 'My first thought? It was probably "I am alive".'

'And the second?'

Lucien shrugged. 'It is difficult to recall exactly. I was wary though, I do remember that. At some point I did wonder whether I had more humiliation and torture to look forward to. Then I met Azmaveth, and many of my fears were eased.'

'Azmaveth?'

Lucien detected a sharp note in Walterkin's question. 'She became my friend,' he explained.

'You're awake?' A young woman moved into Lucien's line of sight. Lucien had never seen an Ixmaritian priestess in the flesh before, but he recognised her robes from illustrations in the sacred texts of Paradouze: a long green gown of soft linen covered by a darker green tunic of embroidered, stiffened cotton. Her eyebrows met over the bridge of her nose. Her lips were large. Crossing to the bed, she put a hand behind Lucien's head, raised it, and offered him a few sips of water from a rough ceramic bowl. Lucien gulped the water greedily. She put the bowl down on top of a chest of drawers standing next to the bed and folded her arms. For a few moments, she regarded Lucien gravely, and then shook her head.

'You are not the first, you will not be the last,' she said, and then smiled at him. Lucien felt so dazed he could not remember what a smile was supposed to mean; to him, it looked vaguely threatening. 'You should thank your Lord Paradouze you came to Mandru,' she said. 'It is not too bad here.'

Mandru was a nonconformist. Unlike the more staid and less affluent families of Racervine Park, residents of Scarcement Chase did not adhere so strictly to Ixmaritian law. Distance from Shanariah, coupled with enormous tithes to the Church and the fact that many of the Ixmarite hierarchy owned estates in the district and were therefore friends and neighbours, guaranteed the residents a certain freedom of belief. As long as they paid their dues, they did not suffer interference from the Ixmarites. Later, Lucien realised just how fortunate he'd been when Mandru's agent had made a bid for him at Por Tanssie. From other Ixmaritians in the house, he learned that certain estates, even in Scarcement Chase itself, tended to adopt a more stringent Ixmaritian code for their vibrancers and priests. Life in such places could be very hard.

'How long did it take you to realise that?' Walterkin asked. 'It must have all seemed very strange.'

Lucien nodded. 'It was. I had to accept what had happened to me in the past before I could even begin to accept the changes in my life. More than anything, I wanted Paradouze to help me understand why I had suffered.'

Walterkin frowned. 'You mean that even after what had happened to you, you never questioned your faith?'

Lucien nodded again, gesturing with stiff fingers. 'Of course not. Paradouze was the only person to whom I'd ever felt close. I saw Him as my only friend. Therefore, there had to be a reason for all that had happened. I was convinced it would eventually be revealed to me.'

'And was it?' Walterkin risked a nervous grin.

Lucien pulled a sour face. 'Perhaps I'm still looking for it.'

The men and women of Mandru's household interacted rather more freely than was common among the upper class of Shanariah. In Lucien's family, they had only come together at the times appointed by the Church: meals, various holidays, family councils and those mysterious, Church-nominated occasions when children were conceived. At the Earthlight manse, women had been attended only by female servants, and men by male servants. Under normal circumstances, Lucien would have been reared by his uncle, Enkhari, who was not a blood relative but the lover of his father. It was a common practice in noble Shannish society for married couples to have lovers of their own sex. This followed the pattern of an obscure Ixmaritian legend concerning Ixmar and his female aspect, Atavenom. However, Enkhari had died young, a year before Lucien had left home. Because it would only be for a short time, Lucien's parents had decided it would not be a religious transgression for his aunt Pershti, his mother's lover, to look after him.

At Mandru, the Lady Nehushtah, Mandru's exotic Ixibatabian wife, had male as well as female attendants, and all the Ixmaritians lived together in the same building, regardless of their gender. At first, this made Lucien nervous, especially the first time he came across a half-clad female sauntering along the sky-lit corridor outside his room on her way to the bathrooms. He never found the proximity of women offensive or objectionable, which was probably due to Pershti's gentle influence (she had not been Shannish), but it took Lucien a while to overcome a feeling of discomfort, having so many of them around him. They intrigued him immeasurably, almost as if they were rare and unusual animals or birds, although at first he was often too shy to speak in their company. They made a great fuss of him, because he was new and had come from Por Tanssie which had a bad reputation.

After he'd been at Mandru for a while, Lucien learned that Mandru had refused to have any more boys from Por Tanssie after his last purchase from that academy had committed suicide. The only reason he'd changed his mind was because he'd received advance notification that there would be a choice morsel on offer that day – a boy named Garimel. Mandru's agent had been outbid, however, and he'd been reluctant to return home empty-handed. Lucien wasn't quite sure how he felt about being a second choice, but comforted himself with the knowledge that Garimel had undoubtedly been bought by a less lenient household. If he had to be a slave, it was better to have a fair master.

The priestess introduced herself as Azmaveth. 'Mandru will want to see you,' she said. 'But only when you're well. How do you feel?'

In response Lucien could only blink, but he turned his head to examine his surroundings. The floor was of pale, unpolished wood and there was a brightly coloured rug on it, with a pattern of stripes and a fringe at either end. The bed was low but wide, and made of the same pale wood. He was propped up on three pillows, which felt strange to him. In Por Tanssie, the students had always slept flat on their beds. On either side of the bed, ornate brass oil lamps were attached to the wall, and there were two more on the opposite wall of the room.

'The rooms aren't bad,' Azmaveth said, folding her arms. She smiled at him. 'Come on. Say something.'

Lucien croaked.

'Almost!' Azmaveth said. 'Here, have another drink.'

Azmaveth came from the north and spoke with a strange accent. After Lucien got to know her better, she told him shocking things. Apparently, she had been taken by an Ixmaritian academy as part of a tax levied against her family, whose crops had suffered a blight one year and who were in severe financial hardship. She told Lucien how much the northerners resented the Ixmaritian tithes, and how in some cases people had shed their blood to resist them, a course of action that had been doomed to failure.

'We learn in the academies,' she said, 'but not what they think they teach us. We learn to keep silent, to keep faith in ourselves. On the surface, we obey, but inside we wait. One day, we will reap the harvest of this silence.'

Lucien had no idea what she meant by this. He could find no comparison between Azmaveth's simmering endurance during her training and his own obedient years at Por Tanssie.

'But what of Ixmar?' he asked her. 'If we suffer in life, it is only to earn our way into His Celestial Mansion when we die.'

He recoiled in horror as Azmaveth spat on the floor.

'Ixmar! Pah!' she snarled, and then regarded Lucien with a wary eye. 'If you are lucky, you will learn. You might wake up.'

Her remarks confused Lucien, but at the same time he was very interested in what she had to say. She spoke scathingly of Por Tanssie and said it was a place where rich men paid for position and status with sons. This made no sense to Lucien. He knew it was a person's natal chart that decreed whether he should become an Ixmaritian, and where he would be educated. Yet Azmaveth seemed so passionately sure about what she said.

'A natal chart is like a portrait,' she said. 'Certain features can be enhanced, others suppressed. Think about it.'

Lucien experienced the first inklings of how the Ixmarites might possibly manipulate their own rules for their convenience. There had been no quietly sprouting seeds of rebellion at Por Tanssie; of that he was sure. The vibrancers had truly believed what they'd been taught and had never questioned anything. Now, Azmaveth had told him that in other academies, conditions were very different. The students harboured hidden resentment and committed deceit. Lucien found it hard to doubt Azmaveth's words because of the zeal with which she spoke, but he still had difficulty believing her. Azmaveth only laughed at Lucien's perplexity. She told the other girls about it and they found his ignorance quaint and charming.

'He will wake up once his body is drained of all their noxious potions,' one of them said, with a grin.

'What do you mean?' Lucien demanded.

'They kept you asleep there,' Azmaveth said. 'They fed you poison. In some cases, it rots the brain. We've seen it. We've seen what happens to some of them. They can't cope with real life and kill themselves. You were lucky.' She grinned. 'Believe me, you have many awakenings to look forward to.'

Salaquin Mandru sent word that he wanted to see his new Ixmaritian vibrancer a week or so after Lucien had recovered from his fever. During this time he'd settled with ease into the household, which had surprised the girls who looked after him; they had anticipated difficulty. It was they who showed him where everything was – the Ixmaritian refectory, the exercise courts, the recreation room, the chapel. The male Ixmaritians paid him little heed and seemed to look at him as if he was a freak, but two girls, who occupied the rooms next to his own, became his especial friends. They were named Ketura and Sydel, both of them vibrancers themselves. This alone was enough to intrigue Lucien: female vibrancers. From them he learned that his arrival had increased the number of Mandru's vibrancers to eleven. Five of these were women, the youngest of whom was Sydel, who was nineteen. The oldest was a woman of thirty-eight, whose name was Sabraxis. She supervised all the other vibrancers, both male and female, and choreographed performances.

When Mandru was in residence, he commanded a performance at least once a day as part of his Ixmaritian devotions, which were rumoured to be half-hearted at best. Sometimes, when there were guests in the house Mandru liked to have a vibrancy performed after supper, or during the afternoon, purely for entertainment. Vibrancy as entertainment was a new concept for Lucien to grasp. In his eyes, it seemed to demean the art. Nehushtah, Mandru's wife, also liked to watch vibrancy performances, although she had no grasp whatsoever of their religious significance. It was considered a treat to perform in Nehushtah's chambers, despite her peculiar foreign ways, because she always showered the Ixmaritians with gifts and gave them delicious food and wine for refreshment.

Once his leg healed, Lucien quickly found that he would be kept busy. He spent more time on the Vibrancy at Mandru than he ever had in Por Tanssie. Sabraxis was a stern mistress, but she was very imaginative and continually updated the traditional pieces. New ideas from the other vibrancers were always welcomed and experimented with.

From a Vibrancy point of view, Lucien could not have been happier. He was expected to practise for several hours a day, but was entrusted to supervise his own timetable. There were two large exercise courts in the house, where he could either practise alone or with others, depending on his schedule for forthcoming performances. Discipline was only introduced in the event of a vibrancer becoming visibly sloppy in their work. Then, Sabraxis would make the individual concerned practise with her five hours a day for a week. That was generally punishment enough for any offender. Sabraxis had the stamina of a horse.

Sabraxis had come to visit Lucien in his room as soon as he was well enough to converse. She was a tall, muscly woman, of handsome countenance, her faded blonde hair held up with an array of jewelled combs. Like all the other vibrancers in the house, she wore loose trousers and a shirt of pale colours, but also affected a bright red embroidered waistcoat to denote her superiority in status. She instructed Lucien to be careful with his leg, and to exercise the rest of his body only while lying or sitting down for a while. She did not want him to exercise his leg until the infected burn had healed completely. The brands were something all Ixmaritians received before being sent out into the world, but only Por Tanssie conducted the procedure without anaesthetic and proper medical care. Sabraxis, like Azmaveth, made no secret of what she thought about Por Tanssie. She even called Caringolat a pervert, who derived pleasure from making boys suffer.

Lucien was horrified by her remarks but said nothing in Caringolat's defence. In only a few days, he had learned it was better to keep silent in that respect.

As soon as he was able, Lucien began to exercise every day before going down to the refectory for breakfast with Ketura and Sydel. He knew he should obey what Sabraxis had said, but was concerned he might lose condition if he remained inactive. Consequently, he endured the pain as he went through a few simple movements. One morning, he was struggling bravely through a particularly agonising sequence when there was a knock at the door. At first, he didn't respond. He thought it was Ketura who generally came to call for him before breakfast. She always knocked and then walked in without waiting for a response. That too had taken a little getting used to. In Por Tanssie, no one would have marched into a room uninvited in case the person inside was in a state of undress. The knock came again, and Lucien called, 'Yes?'

The door opened and a young priest came into the room, a wiry man of middle height. He was the first male to visit Lucien since his arrival.

'I am Tavalouze,' said the priest. 'I've been sent to fetch you.'

'For what?' Lucien asked. He had seen the priest in the refectory before, but had never spoken to him.

'The master of the house has requested your presence.'

Lucien experienced a thrill of dread. 'But I've not yet eaten,' he said.

'Lord Mandru is taking breakfast presently,' the priest said with a wry grin. 'I have no doubt you will be fed in his salon.' He indicated the way with one hand. 'If you are ready?'

Lucien's first instinct was for disguise. Until that moment he had not felt uncomfortable exposing his face, or even certain parts of his body, in the company of the other Ixmaritians in the house. But it was inconceivable that he should meet the lord of the house inadequately dressed. His sacristine robe had been disposed of, being totally ruined, and his veil had disappeared with it. Lucien could not endure the thought of appearing barefaced in front of a stranger, especially a person of great status. He hesitated in confusion, while the priest rolled his eyes.

'Lord Mandru will not eat you for breakfast!' he said. 'There is nothing to fear. Please, hurry up. It is not proper to keep our beloved master waiting.'

'I am not suitably attired,' Lucien said.

The priest folded his arms and subjected Lucien to a slow head to foot inspection. 'You look fine to me. Still, your feet are bare. Why not put your slippers on?'

Lucien's hands flew to his face. 'I have no veil.'

'You do not need one here. Come along.'

'Wait!' Lucien hurried to the wardrobe where several garments were hanging up for his use. He sorted through them in a numb panic. Shirts. Trousers. Woollen tunics. Nothing else. No gloves, no veil. In desperation, Lucien shrouded himself in an outdoor cloak, and wrapped a thin, fringed shawl, which had been left as decoration over a table under the window, round his head and face, tucking its corners carefully beneath the cloak's hood. The priest Tavalouze stood looking at Lucien with a faint smile on his face, but said nothing. Lucien found his insouciant manner both insulting and offensive, hardly correct behaviour for a priest of Ixmar.

Tavalouze led the way to Mandru's morning salon. The family lived in the eastern side of the house, separated from the kitchens, laundry and servants quarters by a covered walkway that bridged the gardens. Lucien could not see very far in front of himself because of the tablecloth hanging over his face unaware of the bewildered and amused glances he received from passing house staff. Tavalouze said nothing but strode ahead of Lucien, his worn sandals slapping loudly against his feet and the marble flags of the corridor. Lucien, keeping close behind, noticed that Tavalouze's robe was a little stained, and his hair was as unshaped and straggling as a beggar's. He was surprised that the Mage Initiate, an elderly man who supervised the clerics of the household, had not chastised Tavalouze for his appearance. The priests who'd officiated at Por Tanssie had been as neat as soldiers.

When Tavalouze and Lucien entered Mandru's salon, a Vibrancy was in progress. Every morning, Mandru liked to indulge himself in religious spectacle, although the Ixmaritians all doubted whether this was inspired by faith and devotion. His morning room overlooked a terrace, where foamy-plumed wading birds with long beaks stood proudly, if mindlessly, in a wide pool. The room itself owed much to Ixibatabian fashion, being decorated in deep reds, terra cotta, and ochre yellow. Brass lamps hung from the roof, which were unlit. Light came through the stained-glass skylights, which were predominantly green and blue, and through a wall of windows of clear glass that held the faintest hint of turquoise. The room was permeated by a fresh bitter odour of crushed fern, which combined pleasingly with a heady floral scent being exuded by fragranced fountains at the far end of the room. The odours, the colour and quality of the light, the sound of falling water, combined to create an atmosphere of tranquillity and space. In comparison, the human presences were bulky and intrusive.

To Lucien, the Vibrancy performance was a perverse travesty because the dance was accompanied by music – a flute and a couple of hand drums played by two young musicians sitting next to the windows. Lucien immediately recognised the movements of the dance as being those of a classical piece: Paradouze being taught the sequences of the Vibrancy by His uncle, the cat-headed snake Smoobillow, a body of knowledge which Paradouze would later pass on to humankind. Here, however, all similarity between the piece Lucien was familiar with and what he saw being performed before him ended. In Por Tanssie, the vibrancers had always been instructed to keep a certain distance between them. Sometimes, allusions to physical proximity were unavoidable, but it was never, on any occasion, represented literally. Here, however, the vibrancer taking the part of Smoobillow held Paradouze, who was being played by a girl, close against his body, shaping the young limbs into the correct movements. Caringolat and the other tutors at Por Tanssie would surely have been stupefied by such a lewd spectacle. Was Caringolat aware how the precise and fastidious sequences of the Vibrancy were being corrupted beyond Por Tanssie? It still hadn't occurred to Lucien that more than likely Caringolat didn't care.

Reclining on the couch beside the long, gauze-veiled windows, Salaquin Mandru was watching the performance from heavy-lidded eyes. Two servants were arranging his breakfast on a table to one side, while two other vibrancers sat on cushions in front of Mandru's couch, apparently discussing, or criticising, the performance. Lucien was appalled by their indecency, their uncovered faces, their indecorous sprawling, their undisciplined laughter. They were both male; Lucien recognised neither of them. He only realised they were vibrancers by their costume, for their postures were lax and their hair, unlike the tidy short haircuts of Por Tanssie students, very long. They appeared to be extremely familiar with the master of the house, for they demonstrated no obvious signs of respect for his person. To Lucien, they were an insult to the Vibrancy; common and coarse. Prim and disapproving inside his cloak and makeshift veil, Lucien directed his attention to Mandru himself.

Salaquin Mandru was an exhausted-looking man of early middle age, who had the kind of craggy face that becomes more attractive upon closer acquaintance. He wore a heavy velvet robe of deepest crimson and indigo, trimmed with black fur. Beneath it he wore black velvet leggings, and his feet were encased in black slippers, decorated with gold embroidery. Lucien had already questioned his new friends extensively about the master. He'd been told various stories that had supplied small but interesting details about Mandru's personality and private life. Apparently, he never wore much jewellery, unlike the majority of nobles that visited him, but that which he did wear was of fabulously high value. He'd sent both his children abroad to Ixibatae for their education, in order to please his wife. Rumours suggested his marriage was not the most harmonious. Once Mandru had even been frank enough to remark to one of the vibrancers that the sound of Nehushtah's voice gave him a headache. Lucien had also been warned that Mandru's liberal attitude towards his Ixmaritians was misleading; his demesne ran like a well-oiled machine, and he abhorred waste. Laziness was punished, and persistent laziness prompted expulsion. Mandru expected the best from his Ixmaritians and would sell one without a thought if they did not live up to his requirements. Many of his acquisitions had eventually bored him and had been disposed of by auction, but the most accomplished and entertaining individuals were rewarded, once they became too old or unattractive to perform their requisite duties, by unconditional liberation from the household and a generous pension. Even in his ignorance, Lucien saw at once that it was essential he make a favourable impression upon this man.

Lucien and Tavalouze remained near the door of the room until the Vibrancy was concluded. Then, as the final genuflexions were being made, Mandru clapped his hands together once, and the vibrancers bowed to him in a solemn fashion, before running from his presence through a curtained doorway behind his couch. The girl exited the room in a series of flamboyant somersaults, and the musicians stood up to follow her, their instruments tucked beneath their arms. At this point, Tavalouze cleared his throat and announced in a clear voice, 'My Lord Mandru. May I present Lucien Earthlight, the new vibrancer from Por Tanssie.' With a firm hand, he propelled Lucien forward.

The room had fallen uncomfortably silent except for the tinkling of the fountains. Lucien kept his eyes lowered behind his substitute veil, striving to maintain a straight spine, but with his head bent forwards. It was a posture of submission and respect. He could feel the attention of strangers' eyes fixed upon him, and was glad of the veil. Through a grille of lace, he studied the marquetry of the wooden floor. A face, worked in subtle blocks, seemed to stare back at him. There were lilies sprouting from its mouth. It looked like someone being suffocated by flowers. Was it supposed to represent that? At least it provided somewhere for Lucien to anchor his attention.

Several muffled sounds came from Mandru's corner of the room, which could have been stifled laughter or exclamations of surprise.

'Tavalouze.' The voice was deep and stern, but held a note of humour. 'Is this a prank? What is this shuffling ghoul you present to me? Do you desire to bring laughter to my breakfast table?'

Tavalouze's light voice came from behind Lucien's back. 'By no means, my lord. Laughter at breakfast is bad for the digestion. I collected the boy from his room as you directed, and he saw fit to equip himself in a . . . *presentable* manner.'

Mandru laughed. 'I see. Boy, come closer!'

Tavalouze again pushed Lucien further into the room. Lucien dared to raise his head. Mandru was staring right at him, a wide smile stretching his face into ropes of muscle. One of his teeth was silver.

'Well, boy,' he said, gesturing. 'Show me. Reveal to me the great secret. It must be worth the revelation!' One of the vibrancers at his feet uttered a faint laugh.

Lucien was unsure what Mandru meant by these remarks. Was he supposed to perform a Vibrancy now? Would it be incorrect to plead disability? He wanted to do his best the first time he performed, and knew he was not in peak condition. Also, the robe would be cumbersome. Tavalouze sidled up behind him and said in a low voice, 'Remove your hood, the veil. Take it off. He wants to see your face.'

'But that's not possible,' Lucien hissed back in alarm, as quietly as he could.

Tavalouze leaned closer to whisper cruelly in Lucien's ear, 'Nothing that Mandru asks is impossible. You'd best remember that, or it'll be the auction block for you pretty swiftly.'

Lucien made an anguished sound, prompting the priest to sigh. He pinched Lucien's arm through his cloak. 'Listen, you either do it yourself and preserve your precious dignity, or someone else will do it for you. Take that ridiculous cloth off your head!'

'A problem, Tavalouze?' Mandru enquired delicately.

'No, my lord,' the priest answered. 'The boy is coy. Allow me to persuade him.' He again whispered to Lucien alone. 'Now, or I'll do it for you!' He put his hand on the back of Lucien's neck in a threatening manner.

Ducking away from the contact, Lucien fumbled awkwardly with the fastenings to his hood. He had never felt so ashamed. In Por Tanssie, he had felt privileged, superior to the common herd of humanity. In the presence of people who had not undergone religious training, his face, his body were sacred and should be revealed only during the course of the Vibrancy. Now, he was having to unveil himself for nothing more than curious inspection. He shook himself free of the hood and pulled the shawl off his head, his face burning in humiliation. He dared not look Mandru in the eye. He felt exposed and puny. His head felt cold.

Mandru made a pronouncement. 'Too pallid. Have him taken into the sun at least once a day.' Then, he turned aside and said to one of the vibrancers lounging against the legs of his couch, 'Who purchased this one?'

'Dorian,' was the bored reply.

'There could not have been much of a selection this time, then. It's a pity the recommended individual commanded too high a price. I should have anticipated it and upped my limit.'

'If you are displeased, perhaps you could have this one sent back,' the vibrancer said. 'He is far from a beauty.'

Mandru laughed. 'I could not be so cruel. If they're not irretrievably addled, the puppies from Por Tanssie cut a sharp caper. We'll give him a chance.'

During this exchange, Lucien decided Mandru's inspection must be over, and began to pull the hood over his head once more. The remarks that had been made about him were confusing. He wondered how he could have displeased the man as he'd yet to perform for him. Before he could conceal himself again, Mandru's voice came across the space between them.

'Make it known we have no shrouded corpses in this house!' The remark was presumably addressed to Tavalouze.

Lucien lowered his hands. Was Mandru disappointed with him because of his face, his appearance? What was wrong with it? How could it possibly be important? Lucien had never before considered how much appearances could mean. He had never been encouraged to think about the way he looked, other than to keep his body fit for the Vibrancy. His vanity had been trained only in certain directions. He was desperate to escape this appalling interview. None of the women he had met in Mandru's house had made him feel ugly. They liked him, they fussed over him. What had he done wrong here?

One of the vibrancers stood up and sauntered behind Mandru's couch. 'Is it worth seeing the rest, do you suppose?' He had an abundant mane of yellow hair and a face and body of classical proportions. Lucien presumed he was looking at something deemed beautiful. He had to admit there was very little similarity between himself and this splendid creature.

'Who can tell?' Mandru replied.

'If you want him disrobed, you should instruct him to move,' said the vibrancer still sitting on the cushions. 'Otherwise he will die of shame.' His voice was deep but perfectly modulated; a voice of music, a chorister's voice. His skin had an olive hue, signifying foreign blood, and his indecently long hair was very black, worn in a multitude of thin braids and confined at the back of his neck. He leaned casually backwards against the couch, his knees raised. His expression was calculating, perhaps cruel. Under his gaze, Lucien no longer felt even faintly human.

Mandru made a short gesture in his direction. 'I've no time for that now,' he said.

'I want to see him,' said the vibrancer standing behind the couch.

Mandru turned to look at him. 'Are you requesting a favour?'

The yellow-haired vibrancer shrugged. 'I was thinking of your entertainment alone, my lord.'

Mandru grinned, and tapped the seated vibrancer on the shoulder. '*You* show us,' he said.

The dark vibrancer turned his head. 'Me? Whatever for?'

'Are you questioning my order?' Mandru asked.

The vibrancer stood up. 'That, as you are aware, is beyond me.' He made a silky genuflexion at the couch. 'For your pleasure,' he said.

The yellow-haired vibrancer leaned forward. 'As the brat will be touched by your hands, Res, the pleasure can only be his.'

Mandru made a sound of irritation. 'Don't torture the lad.'

Terrible dread rose up within Lucien. He knew these people planned something terrible, although in his ignorance and confusion he had not grasped entirely what. The dark-haired vibrancer strode lightly across the intervening space, pausing before Lucien and shaking his head. He looked

Lucien in the eyes only once. There was no expression of reassurance in his gaze; it was utterly cold.

Lucien had unconsciously drawn up his hands to his chest. He could only whisper one word. 'Don't.'

The vibrancer ignored the word. He took hold of the collar of Lucien's shirt and pulled hard so that the soft fabric ripped like parchment. Lucien cringed. He could not bear this violation. Some harsh, agonised sounds must have come out of him. The dark-haired vibrancer pulled the shirt down past Lucien's shoulders and stepped back, gazing at a point beyond Lucien's shoulder, perhaps at the priest behind.

'Is that all?' called the yellow-haired vibrancer, with a laugh.

'Yes. That's all,' the other replied.

'Stand straight, boy!' Mandru snapped at Lucien. 'Let me have a look at you.'

Tears had come to Lucien's eyes. Showing emotion in such a way doubled his shame. He could not believe what was happening to him. Tavalouze poked him between the shoulder blades until he straightened up. There was no further admonishment.

'Actually he has a good neck,' Mandru said. 'Yes, the lines are clean. Perhaps even pleasing. Shame about the hair. Do they have to hack them about like that?'

The dark-haired vibrancer moved back to the couch and sat down on the floor again. 'You called me a dog the first time you saw me,' he said. 'Don't you remember? A partly shaved dog!'

'This one does not look like a dog,' Mandru said.

'No,' agreed the yellow-haired vibrancer. 'A mouse perhaps?'

Mandru waved a finger at Lucien. 'Mind you, like this they are a challenge. I like to see them bloom.' He smiled. 'Cover yourself, boy, don't stand there so wretchedly. No one's going to hurt you.'

Lucien found the torn edges of his shirt and with trembling fingers pulled it up over his shoulders.

'Come here,' Mandru said, beckoning Lucien over to the couch. 'Are you really afraid?'

Lucien felt he should not answer in the affirmative. He shook his head.

'I'm glad of that.' Mandru leaned back on his couch and made an expansive gesture to include his vibrancers. 'They have teased you,' he said. 'Don't mind it. They do it to everyone.'

'I don't mind, my lord,' Lucien said in a small voice. Despite his humiliation, he was desperate to earn some measure of approval.

'See, it can speak,' Mandru said. He indicated the table of food beside the couch. 'Now, the ordeal is over, and you can share breakfast with us.'

Lucien could imagine nothing worse than trying to eat in front of these people. He knew he'd be sick. He wished one of his female friends were here. He had no allies in this room.

'Tavalouze, you are always hungry,' Mandru said. 'Come and join us. I want to hear about your trip to Gallimaufry. Did you catch a glimpse of the venerable Archimage?'

Tavalouze marched forward and gracelessly threw himself down on the cushions. He immediately began to help himself to the food. 'No, I'm afraid not,' he said. 'Although I did watch the Ten in session from the visitors' gallery.'

'Fascinating!' Mandru said, and everyone laughed.

Lucien felt he had been forgotten. A serving girl gave him a plate of fish and eggs, which he stirred with a fork, but did not eat. No one noticed. Far from calming down, his heart had begun to beat faster. When could he escape? It seemed inconceivable that he was of the same race as the two vibrancers sitting near him; inconceivable, too, that they shared his art. And their appearance must be what was considered beautiful. Could he ever be like that? Was it even necessary? The dark-haired vibrancer caught him staring and gave him a withering look. He oozed an air of power and confidence. 'You are not a slave,' Lucien thought. 'You never have been.'

Eventually, the meal was concluded and Mandru stood up, prompting everyone else to do the same. He touched the shoulder of the yellow-haired vibrancer and directed a short glance at Lucien. 'I look forward to seeing you perform,' he said.

'I will do my best for you,' Lucien said. He could see that this remark pleased Mandru. It seemed speaking when you felt like it was a way to gain approval. Mandru smiled and nodded, and preceded his entourage from the room. Only Tavalouze and Lucien remained.

'Can you find your own way back?' Tavalouze asked, and then answered his own question. 'Oh, probably not. Come along. I'll take you.'

Lucien hesitated. 'The one who touched me, who was he?'

'Don't think about that,' the priest replied. 'Mandru's favourites like to let everybody know their position, that's all. I've seen them do that many times. You were lucky though. They didn't strip you naked. I've seen that, too.'

'What was his name?' Lucien asked. Now that the experience was over, he felt dazed and light-headed.

The priest shrugged. 'Resenence,' he said. 'Resenence Jeopardy.'

'Did you fall in love with him then?' Walterkin asked.

'With who?' Lucien stood up and walked to the front edge of the roof. His leg pained him, a memory of pain. It was nearly daylight. A low pall of smoke hung over the nearby buildings; there had been a dawn funeral, a burning. Lucien could smell only incense.

'Resenence Jeopardy,' said the boy.

Lucien shook his head. 'No. He held a prominent position in the household. It was suspected he serviced both the master and the mistress in their chambers. It was probably true.' He limped to the side of the roof and looked down into the yard.

'Was he already a prophet then?'

Lucien turned round. Walterkin had a mischievous expression on his face. Sometimes, it seemed as if he knew every detail of this story already. A startling realisation came to Lucien.

'You've met him, haven't you?'

'Was he already a prophet then?' Walterkin repeated, ignoring Lucien's question.

Lucien made an impatient gesture. 'The gift of prophecy is not generally something you simply acquire. You either have it or you don't. Jeopardy was an actor then, I suppose. He scorned religion.'

'What changed him?'

Lucien wanted to say, 'I did,' but he knew that wouldn't be, couldn't be, true. He shrugged. 'The potential for what he became must have been in him all the time.' He paused. 'Walterkin, you must tell me. Have you met him?'

Walterkin dropped his gaze. He shrugged. 'I have seen him,' he said. 'Lots of people in Gallimaufry have.'

'That's not what I mean. You know it isn't.'

'I'm sorry,' Walterkin said. 'I have nothing to tell you. Nothing to give in return. I'm sorry.'

Lucien walked to the front edge of the roof again, looked down into the street. 'I did not expect it,' he said.

POISON

It is a dolorous thing for a paladin to lose his faith, for it is his faith, more than his physical strength, which sustains such a man. It is the solid tower into which he can flee at any time for sanctuary. To lose it is to become homeless in a world that is suddenly alien and hostile.

Dauntless Javelot, paladin of the Order of True Valiance, had been trying to deny that his faith was dying. 'It is only a passing melancholy,' he told himself. 'A delusion, a distraction, a temptation, a lie.' He rode through an ancient forest alone. There was no one to contradict him.

At one time, the Order of True Valiance had been a strong and powerful body of men, slaves to no one and nothing. But that had been a long time ago. Now it was simply a staggering movement, paying lip service to Ixmarity, cravenly begging permission to exist, and then buying that permission. Their god was not the god of Ixmarity, or any of his relatives. Their god was True Valiance, a splendid celibate of noble brow and sturdy limb, whose destiny was to seek out injustice in the world and restore what was lawful and proper.

In the past, when warring factions had been rife on the island, families of breeding had automatically sent at least one son to train in the Halls of Valiance in the western region of Gleberune and, as a consequence, generous donations had showered into the Valiance coffers. Then the Glebes had come to the island, the petty tribal squabbles had been quelled, and Ixmarity established as the major religion. Valiance did not belong in Ixmar's pantheon. Although its voluntary recruits diminished, the order had managed to limp on for nearly two centuries under Ixmarity's watchful eye. The Church viewed it with derision rather than suspicion. But then, nearly twelve years ago, a young and ambitious deacon in the Church militia had decided to further his career by carrying out a survey of all small cults in Gleberune. The name of that deacon was Wilfish Implexion. Dauntless had been a young boy then, newly recruited into the order and eager to prove himself worthy. He could remember Implexion coming to the Valiance Redoubt, a sardonic and mocking personality. It was known that Implexion had been responsible for the dissolution of many sects in Gleberune, and

100

that he would resort to violence if his injunctions were not obeyed. The Grand Masters of Valiance argued long into the night with Implexion and his staff, claiming that Valiance should not be viewed as a rival religion, but simply as a fellowship that promoted justice for the weak and helpless. Implexion eventually gave in to the Grand Masters' begging and pleading and, for a fee, agreed to present Valiance's case to the Chamber of Ten.

The outcome of this magnanimity was that True Valiance was allowed a doubtful annex to Ixmar's pantheon, instated as a squire to one of Ixmar's sons. This concession cost the order ten per cent of its yearly income. The income itself was not grand by any standard. Donations had foundered. Nowadays, the only noble families who sent sons to the Valiance Redoubt were those who had formerly exposed faiths other than Ixmarity and were now, under the ever-expanding rule of the Church, so impoverished by Ixmaritian tithes they were desperate to offload children in any direction.

Most income came from the hiring out of paladins as mercenaries in territorial disputes. It was an ignoble end to a once splendid venture. Dauntless found it hard to maintain his belief, or indeed suspend his disbelief, in what he was doing.

And what was he doing anyway? At the direction of his lance master, he had been patrolling the ancient forest of Haling Heart, south of Scaraby, for three seasons and had found no quests with which to occupy himself, never mind accrue funds for the order. Before he could return to the Redoubt, he would have to earn an income deemed acceptable to the lance master and his treasurer. Dauntless cursed the ballot through which he had been burdened with this particular region to patrol. Nobody lived in the forest but hewkins, charcoal-burners, gypsies and deranged vagabonds, who were probably discarded bastards. None of these could afford to hire him, even had they needed his services. Dauntless had been forced to live off berries and the flesh of rabbits. His horse, formerly a destrier of statuesque proportions, had become a spindly nag beneath him, undernourished, and in need of corn. He himself had acquired a cadaverous appearance; a shrinking manikin within his leather and steel-scale carapace.

Sometimes, the leering face of Wilfish Implexion came back to haunt him. Dauntless blamed Implexion for his circumstances. A heartless, power-hungry dolt who had no grasp whatsoever of what chivalry meant had brought the order to its knees, reduced its paladins to figures of ridicule. How Dauntless hated that man. When, three years ago, news of Implexion's investiture into the Chamber of Ten had come to the Redoubt, Dauntless had locked himself in one of the private chapels for two days. He had fasted and prayed, desperately seeking the answer to why men such as Implexion succeeded in life, at the expense of others, and noble men such as Dauntless's peers and superiors were doomed to failure. Eventually coaxed from his seclusion by his lance master, Dauntless confessed his doubts and disillusionment. The lance master had replied that success or failure in life had little to do with whether people were good or bad. It had to do with determination and persistence. He also added drily that religion could be used as a tool of control if sufficient political and financial power was behind it. Dauntless's faith had begun to founder then. No matter how long the lance master lectured him about truth to oneself, inner nobility and purity, the words seemed hollow in the light of his first remarks. Those were the words that stuck in Dauntless's brain.

Now, Dauntless had no hope. Maybe he would continue to ride pointlessly around the forest of Haling Heart until he died in the saddle, and maybe even then he would still ride pointlessly around. Sometimes, he wondered whether he might have died already and not realised it.

Perhaps the only thing that kept Dauntless Javelot from perishing of dreariness and despair was the fact that no matter how long he rode through the forest, he never seemed to visit the same place twice. The rational part of his mind knew this could not be the case, and that it was most likely he'd been travelling in circles. Sometimes, he would catch glimpses of wonderful things through the trees: silver wolves slipping like fluid between the gnarled trunks, their eyes the blue of an early autumn sky; hewkin maidens of astounding loveliness dancing in a spotlight of moonbeams, curling their slim green hands towards him in bird-like gestures; ghost children with berry-red faces and tomb-black eyes, laughing down at him from high branches. These revelations never failed to lift his spirits, if only temporarily. In optimistic moments, he liked to think the forest itself was concerned for him and keeping him alive.

When he saw the black-haired woman sitting beside the stream, he thought at first she was simply another ephemeral vision transmitted by the trees. He was sure that as he approached her image would waver and fade. He had been following the narrow forest path downhill for some leagues, the trees soaring ever taller overhead, so that the sunlight came down in muted bars between the leaves. The calls of the birds seemed very far away, high above the gloom of the forest floor. Here, nothing grew except needle-like blades of sparse grass, which made Dauntless's horse curl back his lips and roll his eyes when he'd tried to eat it. Pale, bulbous knobs of fungi clinging to the tree trunks exuded a sticky scent and a faint suggestion of phosphorescence. Dauntless had seen nothing remotely intriguing for hours; this was not one of the most attractive areas he'd travelled through. Then, he had become aware of a gout of light pouring down through the trees, and an ache of green against his eyes. The forest path had widened into a grassy glade, a fairy haunt no doubt, and probably dangerous to lone travellers. A silvery thread of water cut through the forest lawn, a gambolling secret between high narrow banks. And sitting on the edge of this stream, embraced by the mellow light, was a female creature, who could have been human or fairy or perhaps neither.

As the paladin approached, however, the woman appeared undeniably solid and real. She was sitting with her back to him, and did not turn round even though she must have heard the sound of horse's hooves on the hard pebbled path behind her. An old rusty-coloured wool coat, a pair of battered black boots, ragged black woollen stockings and a worn leather bag lay on the ground beside her. Matted black hair covered her back like a shawl. Her feet were plunged into the water.

Dauntless Javelot was no callow youth and had learned, through sour experience, that it was not always prudent to approach strangers found in desolate spots. However, he cared little about his life at this time, and it was possible that this lone female might be in need of courteous assistance. He did not think about how certain dreadful fates do not encompass death, though death would be a welcome release from such destinies.

His horse, Contralto, was dazedly looking around himself, as if wondering whether the grass covering his fetlocks was real or illusory. Dauntless dismounted and loosened the saddle. Still the woman did not turn round. Dauntless shambled over to the edge of the stream and threw himself face down on the grass, cupping handfuls of water and throwing it over his head, gulping it greedily.

'Sir,' said a voice, 'in your place, I would have refreshed myself some inches upstream from my feet, for I have been walking in these boots for months, and the juice flowing away from me cannot be sweet. Or is it your intention to drink my soil?'

Dauntless's dark wet hair was hanging over his eyes. He looked at the woman through a shimmering haze. She was twisting a hank of hair between the fingers of her hands, her stained and torn crimson skirts hoiked up over her knees. She had the face of a cat or a witch, but although she was smiling at him in a queerly macabre way, she looked exhausted and forlorn. Dauntless found he was having trouble remembering how to speak.

The woman sighed. 'Am I to expect ravishment now, or something similar? Please don't kill me, for I have things to do.'

At these words, Dauntless was driven to spring to his feet, his body automatically recalling how to sweep a magnificent bow. 'Madam, I am a paladin of True Valiance. You have nothing to fear from me, in any respect. My life is dedicated to honour and justice.'

'I am relieved to hear it,' said the woman. 'Have you anything to eat?'

Dauntless shook his head. 'No, but perhaps in this spot I might find wildlife to slay.'

'Hmm.' The woman twisted her mouth to the side in an expression of some scepticism, and glanced narrowly at the horse that was gratefully cropping the grass around them. 'I never expected travelling on foot to be so arduous,' she said. 'So comfortless, so time-consuming, so fruitless. How big the world is! I feel as if I have been wandering through this forest for an eternity, and it is some days since I have found anything to eat. Hunger, I find, is not a condition to relish, and there was me thinking I had a *small* appetite. Forgive me, sir paladin, but at this point I am contemplating eating your animal alive.'

'A pointless exercise. He carries little meat.'

'Neither do you, it seems.' She smiled again, a fierce, desperate expression.

Dauntless reviewed his feelings about imminent death. Perhaps it would be a release to suffer extinction at the teeth of this woman. She was not beautiful, and hardly fey as he had come to expect from the fair sex, but there was something undeniably compelling about her. Perhaps she had been dropped onto his path on purpose. Perhaps this was a test. 'So where are you travelling to?' he asked. Did her unkempt condition preclude making a quest out of her? It was doubtful she carried much money, but even so, could he possibly ignore a lady needing assistance?

The woman shrugged. 'I am trying to reach the city of Gallimaufry. I am looking for someone – at least, that was the original intention. Now . . .' She sighed. 'It seems impossible I'll ever find who I'm looking for. Too many corners, too many paths. And I am convinced this forest is enchanted; it leads a person in circles.'

Dauntless drew himself up to his full height, causing the woman to squint up at him. 'Madam, I too have been a wanderer in these woods for some time. However, perhaps if I were to concentrate my efforts on finding an emergent path for your good self, I would be successful. My aim in life is to serve. Therefore, I would be honoured to offer you my assistance, my sword arm and a seat on the back of my horse.'

103

The woman stared at him for a few moments as she mulled over his offer. Then, she nodded. 'I suppose that will be all right.'

Dauntless felt a little chagrined she wasn't more impressed and grateful, but then he supposed he looked little other than a lunatic scrap himself at that moment. 'I am Dauntless Javelot,' he said, with another short bow. 'It is beyond me to ignore a lady in distress.'

The woman took her feet out of the stream and dangled her arms between her upraised knees. 'I am Cleo Sinister,' she said. 'Your offer is charitable; at least I hope so. I cannot afford to pay you.'

Cleo wished now that she hadn't visited the mad woman. It had seemed an expedient course of action at the time, as she'd waited there in her kitchen, in the late afternoon dark, for Wakelate and his client to return to the house. The child's corpse must have been loaded onto some form of transport that had been waiting beyond the yard. Soon, Cleo thought, Wakelate and his client would return so that their business could be concluded, and a measure of liquor shared, as was the custom in Wakelate's house. Presently, she was alerted by the sound of hushed male voices in the yard below. She heard someone blow their nose loudly, and a wheedling complaint followed. She could not make out the words, but knew instinctively they'd been uttered by the uncle of *her* child.

Wakelate came into the kitchen and Cleo, still standing stiffly by the sink, watched him turn on the gas of one of the wall lamps. 'It is dark,' he said, needlessly. Cleo said nothing, only hugged herself tighter. Wakelate applied a sizzle stick to the sibilant huffing of the gas. Funereal light bloomed in the room. Wakelate examined Cleo's tense posture with apparent embarrassment, and then blew out the sizzle stick with as mournful expression. He shrugged at her.

'Where is that man?' she demanded. 'Bring him in! He needs attention.'

Wakelate did not bother to conceal his surprise at this request. Normally Cleo avoided his customers after her first inspection.

'He is using the privy,' he said.

Cleo sighed heavily and turned to face the window. Wakelate left the room, and Cleo heard him making gruff remarks through the privy door on the landing outside. Shortly, he accompanied the dead child's uncle back into the kitchen. The man had to be supported by Wakelate's arm; he appeared almost witless with grief, turning a wide-brimmed hat in his hands. Cleo narrowed her eyes at him in approximation of a sympathetic glance, although in her heart she felt no pity at all. She found the man's weakness incomprehensible. Should Ixmarity have demanded a relative of hers to torture and kill, she'd have hidden them, helped them run away. No one could tell her what to do! And yet, despite his obvious distress, this man had not even tried to save his nephew other than, through his lamentable dithering, allowing the poor child a few more days of life. This same dithering had also damaged Cleo irrevocably. It had allowed her to form an attachment to the child, an attachment doomed to ruin; she could never forgive that.

Wakelate settled the man into a chair and brought out a dusty bottle of valerian wine. It was mind-numbingly potent and generally only used by the Sinisters to calm hysterics. 'You cannot give him that,' Cleo said sharply. 'How will he get home tonight?'

'My dove, we can offer him accommodation,' Wakelate responded. He

104

was not often prone to unbusinesslike displays of compassion, but when the spirit of charity took hold of his heart, he became unsuitably ferocious in his generosity. Sometimes Cleo wondered how he'd ever managed to make such a lucrative living as a poisoner.

'Stay here?' Cleo cried. 'Totally inappropriate! This poor creature should be back with his family who undoubtedly need him at this dreadful time.'

'I should, I should,' the man agreed, raising his head from his hands. His grief was undeniably genuine.

'There, you see? Bring out the brandy. That will do.'

Wakelate nodded glumly and made a new excursion into the pantry.

'You are kind, madam, kind,' said the grieving uncle, wiping his eyes and blowing his nose into a huge silk handkerchief. 'I know you cared for the boy yourself.'

'What was his name?' Cleo asked. 'I called him Inky, but now I would like to know his real name.'

'She called him Aspirant,' said the man, shaking his head and stuffing his handkerchief back into the pocket of his coat. 'She always had hope.'

Cleo sat down opposite the man and laced her hands neatly on the table. She watched him carefully as Wakelate brought in the brandy and poured out a generous measure. The man appeared to have regained a certain amount of composure. He nodded politely to Wakelate and took the glass of brandy with a crooked little finger. He drained the measure in one gulp.

'So, what will you do now, Mr . . . ?' Cleo hesitated and smiled widely. 'Please, give me a name. We have shared much together these last few days. I would like to address you personally.'

The man flicked a glance at Wakelate, who stood behind Cleo's chair. He must have made some assuaging gesture. 'You may call me Banyon,' he said.

Cleo nodded. 'Thank you. Be assured of my discretion. However, to my question: will your family be safe from the Church once you have given them Inky's – Aspirant's – body?'

The man did not respond for a while, but pressed his fingers firmly into his eye sockets.

'Well?' Cleo prompted.

Banyon sighed and raised his head. 'We can only hope that Implexion's agents will be appeased by our offer, although it is likely we will still be penalised for failing to furnish them with a living child.' He shook his head dismally and held out his glass for Wakelate to refill it. 'Yet, oh sweet Ixmar, no penalty will be too high! I could not let the boy suffer.'

'What of the mother?' Cleo asked. She envisaged a spoiled, pampered woman, whose sole concerns were those connected with her own safety. There would be tears, yes, but how many for the child?

Banyon shrugged, his body shuddering with another dismal sigh. 'It is hard to tell,' he said. 'Alas, it will always be hard to tell.'

Cleo frowned. 'What do you mean?'

Banyon pulled a face to indicate distaste. 'She has not been . . . *with us*, in the proper sense, since she returned to Scaraby. Her mind is still with Jeopardy. It always will be.'

'Then why did she come back at all?' Cleo demanded.

The man's face hardened. 'We do not know! She cannot tell us! By Ixmar, if I knew the scoundrel's whereabouts, I'd have his guts! It is clear to all of us that he must have discarded poor Lina . . .' He hesitated, realising he had unwittingly released another name. Cleo stared at him blandly. 'He must have used her,' Banyon continued. 'What a scoundrel!' He glanced at Wakelate. 'The Church should arrest him. I made my displeasure on that score quite clear to the ecclesiarch's agent. If the wretch wasn't free to have his way with helpless women, then tragedies such as ours would not occur. Who is it that takes the burden of grief? Him? Most certainly not!' Banyon shook his head in weary disbelief.

'Surely your sister must know where Jeopardy is,' Cleo suggested.

Banyon eyed her fiercely. Obviously that had occurred to him too. 'If she does, she cannot, or will not say.'

'Perhaps she feels loyal to the man,' Cleo said.

Her remark seemed to agitate her guest. 'She is quite beyond any such feeling,' he said. 'Jeopardy has ruined her.'

'How has he ruined her?' Cleo insisted. 'It was her choice to run away with him, and her choice to return here.'

'She was bewitched!' Banyon declared. Behind Cleo's chair, Wakelate made a few pitiful noises of social discomfort that Cleo ignored.

'Have you evidence of that?' She shook her head. 'No, I don't think you have. You said yourself you don't know what happened to her. It could be anything.' She sat up straight. 'I would like to meet her myself. Perhaps she would talk to me.'

'Impossible!' Banyon pushed his glass away from him so sharply, it fell over and spilt a small pool of brandy on the table.

'Cleo, my dove, you know that is impractical,' Wakelate said in a low voice.

'Why?' Cleo demanded. 'Because we live in the Burrows and are not fit company for the rich people uptown? Because this man here does not want to admit he knows the likes of us?' Her eyes had become very dark. 'Your sister's son spent his last days with me. Have you no thought of her feelings? She might *want* to speak to me!'

Banyon stood up so hastily his chair fell over behind him. 'I no longer wish to discuss this matter with you,' he said. 'Come, Mr Sinister, we must conclude our business. I am anxious to return home. What is the balance of your account?'

Wakelate turned away. 'None. Take your leave, sir. There is no further charge.'

Banyon made an anguished sound and, after burrowing in his coat pocket, threw a handful of coins onto the table. 'You are generous, sir, but I have no wish to be in your debt.' He glanced at Cleo coldly and pulled on his hat. 'Good night to you both.'

After he'd left the room, it filled up with a stressful silence. Cleo stared at the scattering of coins. They gleamed gold in the lamplight.

'My dear,' Wakelate said, after a few minutes, 'I know you are stricken with grief, but I fear you overstepped propriety just then.' He had obviously been searching for appropriate words of censure during the silence.

Cleo hissed in reply, stood up quickly and marched up to her bedroom, slamming the door behind her. The blood in her veins seemed to be singing in fury. She would not be denied her wishes.

Lying in bed, wearing most of her clothes, Cleo listened to Wakelate activating his squeaking floorboard. They had both retired to their rooms very early. A mindless litany repeated itself endlessly in her mind: 'Find Jeopardy, find Jeopardy.' Despite the almost annoying quality of their

106

persistence, the words had a certain romantic ring that appealed to her. She wished she could fulfil her search for this singular man from her bed, by the power of her mind alone. If she concentrated hard enough, would she *feel* his presence out there in the world? Her own world did not extend far beyond the boundaries of the Burrows; central Scaraby was still largely alien territory to her. However, because of what had happened during the last few days, she knew she could not simply let this matter fade from her mind. With the death of the child, she felt that a cycle of her life had rolled to its conclusion, yet she was unsure of how to address the new beginning. In such a short time, she had become obsessed with the idea of Resenence Jeopardy. Was it possible she'd somehow inherited mad Lina's dementia through the beautiful eyes of her child?

This unseen woman was almost as fascinating to Cleo as Jeopardy himself. Was she a rare and special creature, some fabulous beauty, of whom Jeopardy had been fond, or had she simply been a vessel for his seed? What exactly *was* this Cult of Jeopardy? Cleo was convinced her search for the holy man should begin with the mad woman who had borne his child. First, of course, Cleo had to find her. Supposing that Banyon had given his real first name, and that of his sister, a few enquiries should produce results. Cleo could perhaps use one of her old contacts in the city, one of the young men whose ardour she had inflamed.

Eventually, Cleo heard the sound of Wakelate's boots hitting the floor, followed by a complaint from his bedsprings. He cleared his throat a few times and groaned like an aged dog in pain. No other sounds were forthcoming. Presently, Cleo was able to discern the rattle of gentle snoring coming from the adjoining room. She eased herself slowly from the bed.

Over the years, she'd kept back a portion, every week, of the money Wakelate gave her to buy food at the market. This small act of concealment had partly stemmed from the fact that she herself had never had money. The knowledge that a fat bag of coins was hidden among her stockings in the top drawer of her dresser gave her a cosy feeling of security. She also had an irresistible urge to deceive Wakelate and get away with it whenever she could, even though such deceptions were very easy to accomplish. In matters concerning his domestic life, Wakelate was notoriously sightless. Cleo had never really thought about how she might spend the money, other than considering it to be insurance against the unlikely events of Wakelate either casting her off or dying and leaving her penniless.

There was another collection of pilfered items secreted in Cleo's stocking drawer, of which Wakelate was unaware. These were a dozen or so stoppered glass bottles containing a selection of Wakelate's most virulent and inventive poisons. He never kept a catalogue of his stock, so it had been easy for Cleo to pour out a generous measure from each flagon on the upper shelf in Wakelate's workroom. She kept them in a black velvet bag and would occasionally take them out, when Wakelate was busy, to stand them in the sunlight. She liked to look at the dreadful toxins through the jewelled prison of their coloured glass bottles: ruby red, peridot green, indigo blue. Sometimes she had to fight an urge to unstopper one of the bottles and press the deadly lip of glass to her mouth. It was the same feeling as that experienced when standing at the edge of an enormous drop and the desire to jump seems overpowering.

Cleo took the velvet poison bag and the money pouch out of her drawer, together with a handful of stockings, and stuffed them into an old leather holdall in which she'd formerly kept a collection of limbs, torsos and heads from broken porcelain dolls. Tonight, she would leave her husband and the tall house in the Burrows. Tonight, she would begin her search for Resenence Jeopardy. She was not frightened by the enormity of her plan. Despite her relative inexperience of the world, she was prepared to face its terrors alone. Anyway, she had long been bored. It was time for a change.

As she crept from her room and edged slowly down the stairs – avoiding the most creaky – she put from her mind any thought that Wakelate might follow her. He would miss her when she'd gone, certainly, and it was not impossible that he might be driven to drink away his grief, resulting in one of his rare fits of violent temper. She preferred not to consider what might occur should he find her again during one of these fits.

Creeping past Dame Kleetie's door and fleeing like a shadow across the yard, Cleo opened the gate and stepped out into the alley beyond. As it was night, the Burrows was rustling with clandestine life. As Cleo hurried down the alley, she was aware of furtive whisperings in the shadows, the grate of metal, panting breath, and once the sound of bare flesh being slapped. There was a smell of burning fat in the air and, in the distance, the bray of raucous singing.

There was one particular youth whom she thought she might approach for information. Lorimer De Belving was the youngest son of a family that considered the very finest blood of Scaraby coursed through their venerable veins. She'd enjoyed a brief dalliance with Lorimer a few years earlier, after she'd met him at one of the receptions Wakelate had attended, incognito, on business. Wakelate had been invited to the De Belving residence in order to inspect a potential candidate for poisoning – some obstructive colleague of the De Belving patriarch.

The nature of Wakelate's business necessitated that he and his wife should blend in with the other guests. This was not a requirement that rested easily with Cleo, who liked to show off, and while obeying Wakelate's orders to a certain degree, she always took pleasure in singling out a male at these dull gatherings, on whom to focus the power of her charms. At the De Belvings', she'd levelled smouldering, smoky gazes at young Lorimer over a black feather fan, until he obeyed her wordless summons and approached her. Then she pretended to be a mute – she always invented some oddness about herself when consorting with the preening rich boys of the city.

While her husband occupied himself with making mental notes as to his proposed victim's physical constitution and disposition of character, Cleo amused herself with Lorimer, communicating with him by pulling delightful impish faces and fluttering her hands. Lorimer had been enchanted by her apparent demure silence and, later, following a particularly emphatic hand gesture on Cleo's part, had escorted her outside. While Wakelate Sinister furtively discussed business with Lorimer's father in an inner office, Lorimer had gratefully coupled with Cleo up against one of the cold, marble statues that lined a colonnaded walk along the back of the house.

Cleo had subsequently met the young De Belving several times at a squalid inn on the outskirts of the Burrows in order to have sex with him on a greasy, flea-invested bed in an upper room. As a lover, he had bored her, but she liked the idea of his having to steel himself to visit her in the filthy venue she had chosen for their affair. She had ended their relationship by rediscovering the ability to speak and berating his sexual performance. With flaming face and wilting manhood, Lorimer had furiously thrown money at

Cleo where she lay upon the bed, her skirts up round her waist. He'd called her a Burrows whore, a soulless hag. But Cleo had only laughed at his insults, and later added the scornfully thrown coins to her collection in the stocking drawer. She did not care that he'd called her a whore. One thing that particularly attracted her to seeking his assistance now was that he, more than any of the other lily-skinned boys she'd seduced, had been terrified of his family discovering his stealthy dalliance with the poisoner's wife. Cleo knew where the De Belving residence was. She had an audacious plan in mind.

She left the rancid air of the Burrows behind and crossed the Hempelier Bridge of the River Utmost, which served as a boundary between the Burrows and Inner Scaraby. Passing the imposing façade of Ixmar's wife Aufiria's fane, she hurried up the wide paved road that led to Candlegate, a rich area where she would find the De Belving estate. Eventually, after walking along many avenues flanked by big houses and grand, white, marble wayside shrines, keeping her direction heading uphill, Cleo came to another wide bridge which was decorated with gilded wrought-iron curlicues. This was Ladyfoot Span. It crossed the River Carrow and led directly to the estates of the rich. As she walked across it, Cleo gazed at the blaze of lights shining out from the imposing architectural piles that dominated the hills ahead. This was a world that shunned her. She crept through it like a cat, keeping to the shadows, avoiding anybody who might ask what her business was in this place.

The De Belving manse was more like a palace than a house, having an ostentatious spire at each corner from which flags bearing the family seals declared their status on the wind. A heavily embroidered Ixmarite flag hung virtually lifeless from a pole in the centre of the roof, weighed down with gold thread. This advertised the De Belving's favour-currying with the Church. Cleo knew their sedate yet sumptuous soirees were always peppered with gourmand bishops. The gardens surrounding the building were fussy and characterless, the statues of the colonnade representing dour-faced De Belving ancestors in shapeless robes.

As she approached the back entrance to the place, Cleo reflected that, even if she'd had the money, she would never want to live in a building like this. There was nowhere, either inside or out, where a person could sprawl in comfort. Every room was supervised by hideous paintings of humourless De Belvings and all the furniture seemed designed to inflict an ache upon the muscles of the human body. It was no wonder, on reflection, that Lorimer had been so eager to spend time in Cleo's irreverent company. It had undoubtedly been the only time he'd been able to relax.

Cleo marched up to the butler's door, which was slightly more grandiose than the servants' and tradesmen's entrances situated to either side, as it boasted the added splendour of being reached by a flight of steps. The bell pull had a brass handle polished lovingly to lustre. The steps were neatly blacked, the wood of the door polished to a satin finish. It advertised a character of fastidious and correct nature, someone whose collars would be uncomfortably starched. Cleo mounted the steps and pulled smartly on the bell.

Very shortly, the door was opened by a maid whose uniform was as severe and stiff as the habit of a nun. Her expression was pinched and tired. Cleo asked to speak to the butler. Her mission, she explained, was of the greatest delicacy and while she was loathe to broach the matter with the matriarch of the De Belvings, it was too serious to be discussed with anyone but the most trusted member of the household staff. Reluctantly, the maid consented to request an audience for Cleo with the butler, Master Jobbernole. From her expression, it appeared she had little faith that this august personage would oblige. However, it seemed the news that a low-class woman had presented herself at the back door alerted Master Jobbernole to the possible reason for her presence and its consequences. He responded to Cleo's summons with haste.

The man was as sleek as a seal, much as Cleo had expected. Like many of his kind, he was cadaverous and nasal-voiced. His long face was set in a lugubrious expression, and he had a slight squint owing to the length of his nose, which, to Cleo's eyes, was a veritable proboscis. He invited her into one of his lesser parlours. The house smelled of cooking meat. Dinner would recently have been served. Cleo knew that most of the noble families took their evening meal late.

Seeing no point in beating about the bush, she spoke directly. 'My visit concerns Master Lorimer De Belving,' she said.

The butler inserted a hooked finger into his collar, grimaced and huffed. He obviously anticipated what was coming next. 'In what manner, young woman?'

Cleo patted her belly. 'I'm carrying his child,' she said. 'A circumstance which I doubt that his mother, the Lady Claudia, will greet warmly.'

'I find it hard to believe Master Lorimer could be responsible for your condition,' droned the butler. 'Are you quite sure you are . . . *accosting* the right person?'

'Quite sure,' Cleo replied. 'Ah, come on now, Master Jobbernole, you know what these young noblemen are like. A quick fumble in a downtown tavern while they're drunk, with no thought about consequences.' She then went on to describe certain physical attributes of Lorimer De Belving that would be known only to an intimate.

Jobbernole listened painfully to her remarks, but did not bother to make further enquiries. Cleo concluded it was probably not the first time he'd had to deal with a situation like this. 'You are asking for money, I suppose,' he said frostily.

Cleo shook her head. 'No, all I'm asking you for is a few moments of Master Lorimer's time. If I have any further requests, I prefer to make them to him personally. He will know me instantly. Tell him that Cleo, the poisoner's wife, wishes to see him.'

Jobbernole could not prevent the raising of his eyebrows at that point. Cleo could almost hear him thinking, 'A *poisoner's* wife?'

'I will see whether Master Lorimer is at home,' he said. 'Of course you must appreciate I cannot guarantee he will see you.'

'Then, if that should be the case, perhaps you'd better mention my predicament to Lady Claudia,' Cleo said.

The butler sniffed once and retreated, despising etched into every feature of his face.

After he'd gone, Cleo giggled to herself, and examined the room. She stole a white porcelain cup, edged with gold, which was standing on a table beneath the window. She did not bother stealing the saucer. She was not sure what she would do if Lorimer refused to see her. It was doubtful that Lady Claudia would furnish her with the information she needed, no matter how much the family reputation was at stake. This was where an element of danger lurked. Cleo had seen Lady Claudia on her previous visit and had recognised the woman instantly as a merciless tyrant to whom prestige and dignity meant more than legal rectitude. Cleo knew it was not beyond Lady Claudia to have her neck wrung in order to remove any threat to the De Belving honour. She would simply have to trust in Lorimer's dread of his mother.

The minutes passed, and Cleo began to feel edgy. Would Jobbernole return with a brace of male servitors, throw her into a sack and thereafter into the River Carrow? Would she be taken out into the slaughter yard behind the servants' quarters and have her throat cut? Horrible images assailed her mind. She was on the point of fleeing from the building, and was in fact pressed up against the door, listening intently for any sounds outside, when footsteps approached rapidly. Cleo only had time to jump backwards before the door opened. There, looking older and puffier about the face than she remembered, was Lorimer De Belving. He was alone.

'Oh!' Cleo exclaimed, and then managed to smile.

Lorimer did not return the expression. He shut the door and stood with folded arms in front of her, a young man of handsome countenance, although already in the early stages of dissipated decay. 'What is this, you filthy witch?' he hissed. 'You cannot possibly be pregnant with my child. I haven't laid eyes on you in an age. What do you really want?'

'Very little,' Cleo said. 'Don't look so scared.' She grinned. 'I'm sure my presence is distressing for you, so I will keep this meeting brief. I need to know where I can find a woman who has recently returned to her family after having run away with a man called Resenence Jeopardy.'

Lorimer barked an unconvincing laugh. 'How, by Ixmar's eyes, should I know the answer to that? How dare you come here like this! If I give you money, will you go away?'

'Lorimer, please listen,' Cleo said patiently. 'This woman is named Lina. She is from a noble family. She has a brother named Banyon, a middle-aged man, fat and fair-haired. They've recently had trouble with the Ixmariters, concerning a child.' Cleo saw a stealthy expression of recognition cross Lorimer's face.

'I've never heard of these people,' he said with feeble conviction.

'You are lying,' Cleo replied. 'Come now, Lorimer, you don't want unpleasantness. Just tell me what I need to know. Where does Lina live?'

Lorimer clawed his hair. 'I cannot tell you. It's obvious you mean them harm.'

Cleo shook her head. 'No, you are absolutely wrong. It is vital I speak to Lina. It was I who cared for her murdered child through his last days.'

'You?' Realisation dawned and his mouth stretched into an unpleasant smile. 'You mean the Salamancas had their nephew *poisoned*?'

'You don't need to know about that,' Cleo said, but she could see she'd caught his interest. This was clearly interesting gossip. 'Salamancas . . . Where is their estate?'

Lorimer sauntered across the room and sat down on a chair by the butler's fire. He was still grinning like a fox. 'You tell me what you know about them, and I'll return the favour,' he said.

'Lorimer, I'm in a hurry!'

He shrugged. 'Play fair, Mistress Sinister.'

'All right.' She knew she was violating Wakelate's code of practice in the worst possible way, but absolved herself by remembering that her need was great. Lorimer listened avidly to all she said. He laughed out loud at the end of her story.

'What a tragedy!' he exclaimed, gleefully rubbing his hands together. 'We'd heard of Lina's return, of course, although they tried to keep it quiet. And there was rumour of a child and Ixmarite interest. Well! This is news indeed!'

'Where are they?' Cleo asked.

Lorimer pointed behind him with his thumb, out of the window. 'Their estate lies next to ours,' he said. 'You have only to hop over the wall to reach them, supposing their dogs don't get you.'

'Take me to her,' Cleo commanded. She was not unaware that Lorimer had warmed to her during her disclosures.

Lorimer laughed. 'Me? I think not, Mistress Sinister. It would cause a scandal. Come now, I've obliged your request. Shall I give you coins as well? The story was worth it!'

Cleo adopted an expression of appeal. She brushed back her long black hair. 'Lorimer, please! Lina's family will not want her to see me, but I am quite convinced she herself would welcome my presence. She has been treated sorely, Lorimer. Her child has been taken from her and killed! I had an affection for that child myself. As a woman, I *need* to see her. I'm sure she will feel the same.'

Lorimer guffawed loudly. 'What is this? Compassion from the stone-heart whore? I must be dreaming.'

'I have learned much since I last saw you,' Cleo said, in a small, contrite voice. 'Perhaps I am not the person you remember.'

Lorimer eyed her intently for a few moments. 'You are still a handsome minx, Cleo Sinister, I'll say that for you. But you broke my heart once, crushed me into the dirt. Can I ever forgive you that?'

Cleo blinked her huge dark eyes slowly. She said nothing.

Lorimer sighed and slapped his knees. 'Oh, I must be a madman!' he declared. 'But this might be an adventure, and further revelations from the lips of the Lady Lina would not be without reward! Can you climb, Mistress Sinister?'

'I can do whatever is necessary,' she replied. The meaning was not lost on Lorimer De Belving.

Lorimer and Cleo left the De Belving manse by the butler's door. Lorimer had thrown a dark coat, belonging to Jobbernole, over his splendid indoor clothes in order to affect a certain measure of disguise. He led Cleo through the kitchen gardens to the wall that separated the two estates. Here, there was a door which was of course locked. But because the servants of both households often had business with one another, Jobbernole possessed a key. Lorimer had taken charge of this before he'd left the house.

The Salamanca estate was much more to Cleo's liking. The gardens consisted of tree-lined walkways, and the statues gleaming pallidly in little grottoes along the way represented mythological figures, naked and half bestial.

'What about the dogs?' Cleo whispered.

'They know me,' Lorimer responded.

'You are a frequent visitor, then?' Cleo asked.

Lorimer shrugged. 'I have . . . friends . . . among the staff here.'

'Of course!'

By this time, the hour was getting late, and few lights burned in the windows of the Salamanca household. It was a beautiful building, quite plain in design, but constructed of snowy-white stone. It was approached by a shallow flight of steps on all sides, as if standing on a plinth. Lorimer took Cleo round to the left side of the house, which was thickly covered in ancient ivy. Balconies poked out through the burgeoning leaves. Cleo was alert for any patrolling servant, but Lorimer seemed oblivious to such hazards. A trio of enormous hounds came bounding round the building, causing Cleo to gasp in alarm. They barked loudly a few times, but Lorimer ran swiftly towards them. 'Plato, Vesta, Rouen!' he called, in a hissing voice. In moments, they were snuffling at his thighs, jumping up with gleeful whines to lick his face. Cleo hung back doubtfully. She was always wary of dogs.

After placating the hounds, Lorimer jumped up onto the wall of the house with surprising agility and began to climb the ivy.

'Lorimer!' Cleo hissed.

He glanced down. 'I said we would have to climb,' he replied in a low voice. 'Follow me!'

Cleo cast a dubious glance at the dogs who were all looking up at Lorimer with smiling, gaping mouths and wagging tails. 'Won't we be heard?'

Lorimer uttered a disparaging sound, leaning down to talk to her, hanging onto the ivy with one hand. 'Salamanca has cut back on its staff,' he said. 'Its mines are failing. Inside this place, half the valuables have been sold. There is little security. Also, should someone come across me, they would remember how the De Belving coffers have assisted Salamanca in its affliction. Eyes, I feel, would become mysteriously blind. We are good neighbours. Still, that is no reason for me to advertise my acquaintance with such as yourself. We must be cautious and surprise Lady Lina in her chamber. Come!'

With one last glance at the dogs, who mercifully ignored her, Cleo began to scramble up behind him. She was cynically amused by the fact that Lorimer seemed so familiar with this form of ingress into the Salamanca manse. The climb was intensely disagreeable. Her ankles were scratched by the brittle ancient stems, her fingers scored. Birds, nesting in the ivy, squeaked as she disrupted them. Large spiders and segmented insects streamed ahead of her through the leaves, as if to escape attack. Presently, Lorimer climbed over the edge of one of the balconies. He stood looking down at Cleo, rubbing his sore hands. 'I believe this is our destination,' he said.

'It is fortunate you are so intimate with the geography of this house,' Cleo grunted, hauling herself up beside him.

Lorimer grinned and beckoned her over to the long windows. The drapes were partly closed and a dim light could be seen burning within. The windows were opened slightly to admit fresh air into the room. Lorimer poked his head inside and then boldly opened the windows further and stepped over the threshold. Cleo, more cautiously, followed. It was immediately apparent they were in a lady's room. All the decorations were white and festoons of snowy lace gushed from every appropriate appointment. A large white bed dominated the room, and within it lay a porcelain-pale figure, propped up by banks of pillows, its shadowy eyes wide open. This figure did not move as Cleo and Lorimer approached the bed. The eyes did not even blink.

'Lina?' Lorimer murmured. 'It is I, Lori. Do you remember me?'

Cleo appraised the woman in the bed. Her skin, like nearly everything else in the room, was ghostly white, yet strangely bruised along one cheekbone and about the neck. Her hair, braided into a long plait which fell over one shoulder, looked dusty and lustreless. Her lips, which were almost as pale as the rest of her face, were cracked and papery. She wore a high-necked white nightdress. In age, she was perhaps in her late twenties or early thirties, although as she was so thin and haggard, it was difficult to estimate with any certainty.

Lorimer took one of the motionless hands that lay outside the coverlet. 'Oh, but Lina, you are ill,' he said. Cleo assumed he was shocked by the woman's appearance.

At his words, Lina Salamanca's body shuddered in the spasm of a monstrous sigh. Her eyelids flickered, although she did not train their stare upon her visitors. 'Who is that?' she asked in a faint voice. 'Is there someone there this time?'

Lorimer repeated his introduction, which provoked only a groan from the woman in the bed. Cleo pushed her way forward.

'Lina, my name is Cleo Sinister,' she said in a businesslike tone. 'Perhaps you have heard of me?'

Lina Salamanca frowned. 'Who's there?' she murmured, and her head turned restlessly upon the pillows. 'Oh, is that a voice?'

'Yes, Lina, it is,' Cleo said baldly. 'I've come to see you about your son, Aspirant.'

Lina gasped. 'Aspirant!'

'Yes, that's right. I looked after him for a few days before he died.'

Lina uttered a faint wail. 'Ah, dead, dead!' she groaned.

'Cleo,' Lorimer interrupted, 'perhaps it would be better to proceed more delicately.'

Cleo directed a hiss over her shoulder, and sat down on the bed. 'Lina, listen to me. I want you to tell me about Aspirant's father.'

'Dead! Dead! I too am dead!' the frail woman gasped.

'No, you are not,' Cleo corrected. 'I know you can talk to me. Tell me about Resenence Jeopardy.'

The sound of his name seemed to work like magic. Lina turned her head to look at Cleo and a cunning intelligence stole into her eyes. 'What about him?' she snapped.

'Where can I find him?'

The woman laughed. 'Find him? You can't. No one can. You'll never take him. None of you! Oh, put away your leather bar. You'll not beat it from me.'

Cleo glanced round at Lorimer. 'They beat her,' she said.

'Perhaps we should leave,' he answered.

Cleo shook her head. Pursing her mouth, she lifted Lina's limp hand in her own strong brown fingers. 'Lina, I am not an Ixmarite. Listen to me, listen. My husband was the man commissioned by your brother, Banyon, to poison your son. I did everything I could to save the boy's life, but to no avail. Now, I am discarding my former life. Like you, I am fleeing Scaraby. Like you, I intend to seek sanctuary with Resenence Jeopardy. You must tell me how to find him.'

Lina's mouth stretched into a sneer. 'You? You think you can have him? No one can! No woman alive! He'll not want you!'

'Where is he?' Cleo insisted, ignoring her remarks.

Lina sighed. 'If I knew that I would not be here,' she said, in the most lucid tone Cleo had yet heard her utter.

'Lina, are you mad?' Cleo asked.

The woman narrowed her eyes at her. 'Mad? I don't know. Sometimes, I forget things. Sometimes all I can remember is his eyes, Resenence's eyes, and how he looked at me once. What am I doing here? What happened? Oh yes, I know. He sent us back. All of us. He sent us back to have our children killed!'

'Why?'

Lina's face crumpled into a grimace. Tears gathered in her eyes. 'I don't know. He spoke to me. He inspired me to return. I can't remember what he said to convince me, but I obeyed his request. I had no choice. I could never deny him.' Her body shuddered in another racking sigh. She swallowed as if it caused her pain, her face screwed up. 'Perhaps I dreamed it. Perhaps he said nothing, and I came back here in a dream . . .' Her eyes flicked wide open. She pulled her hand from Cleo's grip and grabbed her wrists. 'Find him!' she hissed. 'Find him! Kill him! Kill him for me and my dead son.' Then she fell back on the pillows.

'How do I find him?' Cleo asked in an even voice.

Lina blinked twice. 'I came into the city through the water tunnels. I came north-west, therefore you should travel south-east. There is a forest called Haling Heart that covers the land to Gallimaufry. He'll end up there sooner or later. His destiny lies in that city. He always said so. One day, if you wait, if you look, if you listen, you will find him there.' Lina sighed again and closed her eyes. 'I can tell you nothing more.'

'Not even how you came to follow such a man?'

Lina opened her eyes once more. She looked infinitely tired, infinitely ancient, infinitely sane. 'Not even that,' she said. Her eyes strayed to where Lorimer De Belving was standing in agonised embarrassment behind where Cleo sat. 'Visit me,' Lina said to him. 'On one day or another, I might be allowed to recognise you.'

'Lina, what must be done?' Lorimer asked. 'What is wrong with you?'

'I loved him,' she replied. 'And love of the man twisted my heart into a dry rope. His image, his strength, occludes my mind. Sometimes, he leaves no room inside me for reality.' She licked her lips and looked once more at Cleo. 'The boy, did he . . .'

'He knew nothing,' Cleo said gently. 'Nothing. I did all that I could.'

Lina nodded. 'Banyon promised me that,' she said. 'Now, both of you, go away, go away, go away . . .' Her voice lapsed into a whisper. Lorimer touched Cleo on the shoulder. Cleo glanced up at him and then rose from the bed. Together they went to the window.

As they walked back through the haunted lanes of the Salamanca gardens, Cleo voiced her thoughts to Lorimer. 'There was so much I wanted to ask her,' she said, stabbing the air with her hands. 'So much. If only I'd had more time. A day in her company, a week.'

Lorimer had apparently been so affected by what he'd seen and heard in Lina's room, he could barely speak. At the door between the two estates, he turned to Cleo and touched her arm.

'I know little of what you women were speaking of,' he said, 'but I feel I should counsel you against seeking this man Jeopardy yourself.'

Cleo shook her head. 'Don't bother,' she said. 'What else can I do? Stay here with you? Oh, don't look so afraid. I was joking.'

'At least let me—'

'I want nothing from you,' Cleo said. 'Nothing. Thank you for taking me to see Lina.'

With no further words, she set off across the wide lawns of the De Belving gardens, scattering a couple of sleepy peacocks as she went. Once, she turned to wave. Lorimer watched her as the shadows swallowed her small, defiant shape. He watched the empty darkness for some time afterwards.

SCRYING

Wilfish Implexion woke up with Jeopardy's name on his lips. He woke gasping, the heavy bedclothes twisted round his legs. He'd been fighting the prophet, but every time he'd laid hands on the man, he'd changed shape, become a cloud, a venomous snake, a wildcat, a mad woman.

'What is it?' The woman lying next to Implexion had woken up too. She was a shadow beneath the huge, swaying canopy of the bed.

'Dream,' Implexion said shortly, rubbing his face. 'Nothing.'

'You said his name again,' the woman said. 'It woke me.' She sighed and, pushing aside the canopy curtains, got out of the bed and shrugged on a green muslin bathrobe. Implexion stared at her. She went to stand next to the long windows at the end of the room. The curtains were open; she was a shadow in a pool of moonlight. He was confident she wouldn't say anything further about the dream. She never did. She knew her place. A man like himself needed a woman like her. Discreet, mature. Inanna Grisaille; she supervised the clerks in the Chamber of Ten's office. She and Implexion had been conducting a casual affair for years; she knew him better than anyone. She had learned more things from his silences than others had from his most garrulous speeches. True, she was getting a belly on her now, her neck had started to sag, but her attractions had always gone beyond the merely physical. She pressed her forehead against the glass of the window, a flag of thick dark-brown hair hanging down her back. Was she feeling ill?

'Nana, come back to bed,' Implexion said gruffly. 'I can't sleep with you pacing about.'

Inanna wheeled round quickly, her robe flying open, revealing the pale length of her body. 'How long is this ridiculous charade going to continue?' she demanded.

'I beg your pardon?' For a moment, Implexion thought she meant their affair and was attempting to push it into the realms of firm commitment.

'This business with Jeopardy,' she said baldly.

Implexion groaned and covered his face with one arm.

'Night after night, I hear you complaining in your sleep,' Inanna continued, prowling back towards the bed. 'Night after night, that name, that damned name on your lips! You are obsessed, Wilf, obsessed!'

Implexion sprang up in the bed. 'Hold your tongue, woman! Church business should not be discussed in the bedroom.'

'Look at you!' Inanna made a bitter sound and sat down on the tapestried coverlet. 'It will be the death of you. It's eating your life away.'

'I will not discuss this with you.'

'Why not? What are you afraid of?'

Implexion realised the argument could become ugly and he might be provoked into making remarks he'd regret. 'Nana, you must understand,' he said gently. 'This is a difficult time for everyone. I am not obsessed with Jeopardy, but simply concerned about the effect he could have on our society.'

'Rot!' Inanna declared. 'He is one man, just one man! If he's such a threat, I can't understand why you haven't dealt with him before now. It's absurd.'

'I know,' Implexion said quietly.

Inanna made a growling sound, threw off her robe, and crawled back between the bedcovers. 'I'll say no more,' she said. 'If there's one thing I pride myself upon it's my disgust of prying women. But I don't want to hear that name uttered in this room again!' She turned her back on Implexion and pulled the covers over her head. He could feel her seething with suppressed anger.

Implexion lay in the darkness, his arms behind his head. You *are* obsessed, he told himself. That is the power of the man, that is where the danger lies. He fascinates you, lures you into the chase. Then why give in to him? he asked himself. Why not turn your back? You know, in your heart, it is the last thing that charlatan wants.

The ecclesiarch had tried so hard to penetrate the mystery of Resenence Jeopardy, to understand the mechanics of his attraction. How many Jeopardites had he interrogated, even tortured, to learn the truth of exactly why they were compelled to follow the man? He remembered when he had led a regiment of Church militia into the Swinkbacks, driving a ragged group of Jeopardites before them. Rain had lashed the bare rocks, turned the narrow gully beneath the horses' hooves to mud, stripped the spare trees of their flimsy leaves. They had cornered the Jeopardites in a canyon where a few makeshift tents indicated a Jeopardite camp had been discovered.

'Bring me the women first,' Implexion had said, striding into the largest tent and making it his temporary headquarters.

They'd not been drabs either, those women. Daughters of good houses, tattered as gypsy whores but still with a plum in their mouths.

'Tell me,' he'd said to the first. 'What made you give up your privileged life to join this man?'

She'd stood there, shivering with the cold, her already ragged clothes ripped further by the rough handling she'd endured at the hands of the militia. Her chin had gone up straightaway. He could tell she'd been used to ordering people about at one time.

'I think you already know,' she said in a clear, ringing voice. He sensed the accusation, even the scorn, behind her words.

'I asked you a question. Be so kind as to answer me. To be blunt, you can be a sensible young woman and be escorted back to your family, or carried out of this wilderness in a sack. The choice is yours.'

118

The woman folded her arms, flared her nostrils. She was not afraid of him or his threats.

What was that flame that burned inside her and sustained her? Implexion was sure she was nothing more than a spoiled and pampered daughter of a rich house, as ill-prepared for privation as it was possible to be. Something had changed her. Someone.

She seemed to sense his thoughts. She smiled. 'You want to know about Jeopardy? He is a god.'

Implexion laughed politely. 'I think not. Try again.'

'Meet him, then you will see,' the woman said. 'Once you have had contact with Jeopardy, you can never be the same again. But perhaps you are already aware of that.'

Implexion looked at his hands. 'Take her away,' he ordered the nearest guard.

The others had revealed little more. They would have endured the worst torment he could have devised rather than betray Resenence Jeopardy.

It was not the Church's policy to execute the members of noble families retrieved from Jeopardy's clutches. The Ten would not hear of it. They were always sent home; their families could deal with them as they wished.

Implexion had stood in the mud of the canyon, the pathetic tents being demolished around him by his militia. He had watched Jeopardy's high-born women being bundled into an open cart. Proud creatures with the rain dripping off their straggling hair, their bare, muddy shoulders. They'd hugged one another. They had not wept. Five males, who had accompanied them and who were of lower stock, had been hobbled together to follow the cart. They would be impaled by the roadside as an example.

If I could only interrogate him, Implexion had thought. Just an hour – less than that, minutes. If only I could . . .

The cart had trundled out of the canyon, an equerry brought Implexion's steed to him. He'd mounted, turned the animal in a circle, gazing up at the sheer, wet cliffs. Was anything of Jeopardy left in this place? Was he watching at this present moment from some hiding place high in the rocks?

As with all his dealings with the Jeopardites, Implexion could recall the event in detail even now; the chill squall of the weather, the earthy smell, the quality of the light in the metal-grey sky. Jeopardy *had* been watching him. He was sure of that.

If we could only learn his secret, Implexion thought, staring into the moonlit darkness of Inanna's bedroom. Ixmarity would know no bounds, if we could only learn his secret.

Lucien had slept too long. An hour after noon he wandered out of the room he shared with Bessie's children and went into the kitchen, where he splashed water on his face. It seemed no one else was at home. The house was full of a sleepy afternoon quiet. From the street, the yodel of a sulphur blender could be heard, extolling the virtues of his ointments. On the wall next to the sink, a V-shaped formation of peacock-blue cheese beetles, each the size of a man's fingernail, arrowed towards the floor. Their metallic carapaces flashed, as if someone was shining a light on them. They reminded Lucien of something that had happened a long time ago, but he couldn't remember what.

He sighed. He felt drained, as if he'd been drunk the night before. His head felt packed with damp sacking. Trickles of water ran down inside his collar. He felt strangely angry.

At dawn he'd woken up briefly, plagued by the vanishing wisps of a vague and irritating dream. He knew it had featured Resenence Jeopardy, but the details were indistinct. One thing he could remember, however, was that in the dream Jeopardy had been communicative, Jeopardy had listened to him. Lucien couldn't remember what he'd said to the prophet. Now, in the afternoon, he was haunted by Jeopardy's presence. As always, Lucien's dreams had invented a happier history for him. He knew the man he dreamed of did not exist.

After making a foray into Bessie's pantry, Lucien helped himself to a quick meal of bread and meat. Then, throwing on his coat, he ventured out again. Perhaps, this time, there would be some hint, some clue, as to where the Jeopardites had fled. Gallimaufry itself seemed lethargic that day. Hawkers in the street yawned as they advertised their wares. Lucien saw a street juggler drop one of her multicoloured balls; it was glass and smashed instantly on the pavement.

Eventually, his wanderings led him to the ornate frontage of a steamhouse. These establishments could be found in every district in Gallimaufry; places where citizens could relax in the vapours of restorative perfumes. An advertisement upon the outer wall advised Lucien of the advantages of an ennubelation in lively-sprig essence. Feeling that anything was worth the price if it removed the torpor from his brain, Lucien handed over a coin at the reception booth and went inside.

Attendants in stiff, white robes swooped forward as soon as he entered (indicating tips would have to be paid), offering to show him to the changing rooms. The roof of the foyer consisted of an enormous green glass dome. It cast an unflattering light upon the skin, it made voices echo. Reluctantly, Lucien handed over another coin to one of the attendants and was conducted through a maze of corridors to an enormous room, where Gallimaufrians disrobed behind screens. The attendants folded the clothes and exchanged them for a token, before placing them upon tiers of racks. Customers were given long, belted robes to wear on their way to the baths.

Having paid for a private room, Lucien was escorted by a young vaporeuse through another labyrinth of corridors to a row of cubicles. On the wall outside each of them was an array of brass knobs and gauges, with which the staff of the establishment set the jet speed and volume of the essences. Steam hung heavily in the air, a thousand battling perfumes. The girl asked Lucien if he would like his steam bath to be followed by an aromatic rub. He declined, conscious of the mark on his leg that advertised his truancy from Ixmarity, although the thought of being massaged with perfume appealed to him greatly. The girl pulled a face of annoyed disappointment to show Lucien that by not taking full advantage of her services he was really wasting her time. Then, with a shrug, she opened one of the cubicle doors and ushered him inside.

The room was made of unpainted white stones. There were no windows. Lucien settled himself upon the only piece of furniture – a bench – and leaned back against the wall. The vaporeuse asked him what level he preferred the steam to be set at. He told her he was unfamiliar with the process, and that he would trust her judgment. She shrugged and closed the door, with the final remark that she would come back once his paid time was up. Presently, steam began to hiss from ducts overhead. Lucien breathed deeply

120

and closed his eyes. Far from invoking a sense of wakeful alertness, the essence seemed only to induce further drowsiness. Lucien could feel a cloud of sleep stealing through his limbs. He took off the hired robe and lay down naked on the bench. The wood was pleasingly warm and aromatic; the hot steam washed over him in tingling waves. Then, just as it seemed that sleep was a compulsion he could no longer resist, Lucien heard a noise in the room. It sounded like footsteps, followed by a sliding noise, as of someone pressing themselves against the wall and sitting down. Immediately, Lucien sprang upright and threw the robe round his shoulders. He knew he should be alone. He had not heard the door open. The cubicle was thick with fragranced fog but he could just make out a dark hunched shape on the floor near the door.

'This is a private room!' Lucien cried, aware of a tremor of fear in his voice. The shape shifted in front of him.

'Lucien, I did not think you'd mind sharing with me.'

It was Walterkin Anywhither.

'You followed me!' Lucien said.

'Don't be angry. I wanted to surprise you.'

'This is not a surprise, but a shock,' Lucien said. 'How dare you creep up on me like that!' Lucien felt vulnerable and threatened. If Walterkin could sneak in on him so easily, anybody could. He should have remained alert.

'I want to hear more stories,' Walterkin said.

'Here?' Lucien laughed. 'I don't think so. You should have waited until I returned to your mother's house.'

'But here is the right place,' Walterkin argued in an even voice, 'for the next part of your history.'

Lucien could not see the boy's face through the steam. Perhaps I am dreaming, he thought, perhaps I have simply conjured him up. He might not really be here. I'm sure the door didn't open. And yet, I am relieved he is here. Why? Because I need to purge myself of the past more than anything. And will this next part be painful? No. More painful to hide it inside.

It seemed as if Walterkin's request for more information had become a subliminal trigger which Lucien could not, or did not want to, ignore. He lay down once more upon the bench and, his lungs filled with a crush of flower essence, began to speak.

Resenence Jeopardy had a lover. Her name was Amber Epipheny, and she was a female vibrancer. Amber was a fiery, independent creature; very beautiful. She stalked around the House of Mandru as if she was always in a rage about something. Her hair was dyed an incredible brutal red. In sunlight, it appeared transparent like flames. By lamplight it was a smouldering fire, a smoke around her shoulders, from which her dark green eyes sparked like chips of precious emerald. Like Jeopardy, she walked with the confidence of royalty. Anything positioned beneath the tilt of her chin seemed to escape her notice.

Every morning, at an early hour, Amber and Resenence practised movements together in one of the dance courts. Few other Ixmaritians of the household used the court at this time, as most of them preferred to begin their exercises once breakfast had been digested. Lucien, however, liked the comparative privacy of the court and, once he'd become familiar with the routines of the household and felt confident enough to venture around alone, went there often to limber up for an hour before his own breakfast.

Also, although he would have denied it had any influence at all, Ketura had told him Jeopardy used that court, and that he always practised early.

The first time Lucien went there, it was out of curiosity. Ketura had neglected to include the information that Amber would also be present, and he had felt strangely disappointed when he realised Jeopardy was not alone. The pair whirled round one another like columns of fluid. They practised, as Lucien always had, without music, scorning even the metronomic hand drums that other Ixmaritians favoured. At first, Lucien had watched them in awed fascination, hardly daring to practise any movements himself for fear of ridicule. After only two visits, however, the novelty wore off, and it was patently obvious that Jeopardy and his partner were oblivious of his presence; it became easy to ignore theirs. Lucien knew that, to them, he was a nobody. From their lofty height of existence, it was as if they could not even see him. Lucien had had no social contact with Resenence Jeopardy since his interview with Mandru, but had thought about him often. He had questioned Sydel and Ketura about him, and they were happy to gossip. They were quite convinced that if Jeopardy had not been quite so stunning to look at, most people would not like him at all because he was arrogant and cold. Lucien told them that he believed Jeopardy to be a shallow individual, an offence to the art of Vibrancy. Both Ketura and Sydel had strongly contested this.

'His work is the only thing that sustains him,' Ketura said. 'Certainly not for the religious significance of it, but for the dance itself. He takes it very seriously.'

Lucien found he had not wanted to hear that.

Sydel told him that when Jeopardy argued with Amber, it was never about love, but always about the Vibrancy. 'He does not see her as a woman,' Sydel said. 'True, she is his partner, she helps him, and when his body calls for lust, she is there for him, but I would not say she is a prime concern in his life.'

'Nobody is,' Ketura added, 'which is perhaps why he is so fascinating. There is an element of challenge involved in his acquaintance. Is this why you are asking all these questions?'

Lucien had flushed at that. He did not want the girls to know that Jeopardy interested him. After hearing what they had to say, Lucien told himself he disliked Jeopardy. Nor was he much impressed by Amber Epipheny. The pair of them seemed pompous, arrogant and vain to the point of caricature. Lucien grudgingly had to admit that they were first-class vibrancers, but to him they still seemed an insult to the art. He knew they abused their bodies with liquor and narcotic essences. He knew they soiled themselves with one another. They must have little self-respect. And surely their behaviour was an offence to Paradouze.

One morning, Azmaveth came running down the corridor outside Lucien's room to intercept him before he went to his practice. She told him that she and some others were being escorted by the household guard on an expedition to the country that day. Nehushtah, Mandru's wife, had decided upon it the previous night.

'Come with us,' Azmaveth said.

Lucien wrinkled his nose. 'Oh, I don't know . . . I don't really feel like it. There's something I'm working on today.'

Azmaveth made an exasperated noise. 'Who wants to work when you've been offered a holiday?' she asked. 'Come on, Lucien, you'd enjoy it.'

'I've got to perform for Sabraxis tomorrow,' he said. 'She wants to judge my development. I want to make sure my movements are perfect.'

'Oh, Lucien, you can work this evening,' Azmaveth insisted. 'Listen, you should take the trouble to ingratiate yourself with Nehushtah. Her favour incurs many privileges.'

Lucien secretly disapproved of the way his colleagues fawned over the lady of the house. To him, it seemed that the privileges of Nehushtah's acquaintance consisted only of the opportunity to get intoxicated in her chambers. He had seen Nehushtah only once as she'd weaved her way, in a froth of acolytes, across the gardens. He hadn't liked what he'd seen. She was too tall and sensual of feature, too voluptuously loose in her movements to command his respect. He sensed that the touch of her attention engendered immoderation, and also that, should she meet him, she would not like him either. He shook his head. 'Thanks for asking me, Veth, but I can't. Another time maybe. I feel like I'm on trial at the moment. I don't want to disappoint Sabraxis.'

Azmaveth wouldn't give up easily. 'You can practise any time,' she said. 'Trips out only happen now and again.'

Lucien shrugged. 'I take my work seriously,' he said. The implied criticism hung in the air between them for a few moments. Then Azmaveth made a dismissive gesture with her arms.

'You should have stayed in Por Tanssie and become a tutor,' she said scornfully. 'Or they should have sold you to some terrible household where you'd have been treated like a dog. Someone else should have been allowed to come here. Someone who'd have appreciated what's on offer! You can be such a bore, Lucien.'

Lucien shrugged again, awkwardly. He suspected she might be right.

Exercising his body slowly and with care in the practise court, Lucien was aware that, despite the cross words he'd just had with Azmaveth, he was actually content in his new surroundings. He'd been in the house for nearly six weeks now and although he had not yet been called upon to take part in a Vibrancy performance, he had all the time in the world to practise. Sabraxis had given him a schedule to work through, most of which he knew already as it was based upon traditional pieces. She had also made one or two favourable remarks on the occasions she'd seen him working out, and had assured him that, once he'd attained the standards she'd set for him, he could look forward to being given a fairly prominent role in the next major presentation. Mandru had been away on business for much of the time since Lucien had arrived, so performances had been few. Nehushtah generally commanded only the talents of her favourites. However, Lucien knew that once autumn took hold of the land, Mandru would remain in residence in order to supervise the harvest. Then, there would be at least two presentations a day, perhaps more when guests were in the house.

So far, Lucien had not sullied his art by performing to music, but he was aware that as soon as Sabraxis had approved his ability, that would be the next thing he'd have to learn. He was unsure about whether he'd be able to do this, and was also uncomfortable knowing that soon he'd be performing merely to provide entertainment for Mandru and his guests. The thought of this not only made him feel uneasy, but embarrassed. At least Mandru did not expect his Ixmaritians to perform naked, as was the traditional custom.

Still, judging from Sabraxis' remarks and the fact that, despite its defects, Por Tanssie did provide incomparable training, Lucien felt sure his new master would acclaim his talents.

Lucien happily fantasised as he practised. He saw an awed and grateful Mandru, wiping tears from his eyes after Lucien had completed a performance. He heard Mandru tell all the other Ixmaritians that never had he seen such eloquence of posture, such moving pathos. Lucien accepted this praise with downcast eyes, aware that the most accomplished of Mandru's vibrancers were biting their knuckles in shame, because they had not practised diligently enough to emulate Lucien's glowing performance. Transported in such blissful reverie, Lucien raised his arm into a graceful curve, a black swan against the faintly orange glass of the floor-length windows of the court. He poised motionless on his toes, caught in a timeless stance.

Raised voices intruded coarsely into his meditations. The argument must have been going on for some time, although Lucien had been hardly aware of it. As usual, he had blanked out any other presence in the court in order to concentrate on his movements.

'One day, you son of a whore, I will kill you!' The abuse was uttered by a female throat.

Jolted from his daydreams, Lucien had time only to feel a rush of air as Amber Epipheny swept past him. She was in such a hurry to leave the court, she almost knocked him over. Lucien made a small, indignant sound, his arms flailing before he recovered his poise. Amber was forced to notice him, but instead of apologising, she curled her lips into an ugly snarl. Lucien was astonished. He had never suffered such vulgar treatment from another vibrancer before. In Por Tanssie, interruption of a student's practice was prohibited, whatever the reason. Wilful impediment of the sacred moves was not only ill-mannered, but the worst form of blasphemy. Amber, however, seemed to have little consideration for Lucien or what was considered sacred. Her face set in a mask of intense fury, she slammed the doors hard as she left the court. The echo of her exit filled the high-ceilinged room for some seconds afterwards.

'Bitch!' Behind Lucien, Resenence Jeopardy punched the wood-panelled wall of the court, causing one of the tapestries to swing ominously.

Lucien was shaken to the core by all this rude conduct. It was unthinkable that two vibrancers could behave in such a manner. Uncertainly, he turned his back on the prowling form of Jeopardy and attempted to curl his body into the movement Amber had disrupted. He closed his eyes and two images entered his mind. One was of Azmaveth and her friends bundled into a comfortable carriage, being taken to some silvan retreat to eat, drink, sing and dance. He experienced a sudden pang of regret he'd rejected her offer. The other image was of the person behind him, Jeopardy, with his hair unplaited and his eyes fierce, pacing like a caged animal along the wall. Lucien broke out of his movement and stood perfectly still, staring through the orange light. He sensed this moment was of prime importance. Something had happened.

'What happened, Lucien?' The boy was invisible in the steam. It hissed malevolently into the tiny cubicle, its herby bitter odour masking a certain taste of earthiness.

Lucien sighed. 'Something happened in my mind, Walterkin. It was like a door opening.'

124

'Was there light beyond the door? Was there a garden full of flowers?'

Lucien rolled his head from side to side upon the wooden bench. The steam was burning his lungs. 'No. It was dark, dark and frightening. But fascinating too.'

'And this door had Resenence Jeopardy behind it?'

Lucien could not answer.

After a few moments, Walterkin said, 'Perhaps it was the same for him.'

Lucien shook his head. 'No, it wasn't. It couldn't have been.'

'But he must have noticed you then. He must have. Or did he leave the court without speaking?'

Lucien closed his eyes. 'In one reality, perhaps he did. In another, he called to me and asked – no, demanded – I finish his practice with him. Jeopardy and Amber had been working on a piece which they intended to perform when Mandru returned home. Their argument had been about that; some minor point or another. Something unimportant.'

'He was very young then?'

'We both were. And yet he seemed so . . . not wise, that isn't the right word, aware of life, I suppose. He seemed older.'

'What was it like when you touched him?'

Lucien looked sharply at the boy. 'I don't think I did, not then.'

'You must have. You were performing together. What did he smell like? What colour were his eyes?'

'You are very interested in Resenence Jeopardy,' Lucien said. He heard the suspicion in his own voice.

'You make him come alive in a way that none of his fancy speeches can,' Walterkin said. 'Tell me how you felt.'

Lucien sighed. Behind his closed eyelids, he was back at the House of Mandru, surrounded by the dusky orange light of the exercise court. Before him was the heat of another soul.

'You!' Jeopardy yelled. 'You're from Por Tanssie, aren't you?'

Lucien shrugged. 'Yes.'

Jeopardy made a curt gesture with his arms. 'Then you should be good enough to work with me. Nearly. Come over here! Do you know the Denouncement of Atavenom sequence?'

'Of course.'

'Well, I've modified it in this way. Can you follow?'

He performed a few precise movements. Lucien could see the adjustments. In some ways, they improved the sequence, introduced a more fluid element. He copied the movements well enough for Jeopardy to smile.

'Almost!' he said.

Lucien knew his imitation had been perfect. He performed the movements again, adding an embellishment of his own.

'Don't get clever,' Jeopardy said sharply. 'It corrupts the pure lines.'

Over the few weeks he had been in Mandru's house, Lucien had acknowledged Jeopardy's beauty and talent, but had also despised him. He would never admit to himself that this was because Jeopardy seemed beyond him; Lucien was convinced he could never be included in Jeopardy's elite circle of friends, and so it was easier to dislike him, to pick fault and criticise. Now, everything had changed, and their bodies were moving round each other in the orange light of the dance court. Jeopardy was close enough for Lucien to touch. He could see the colour of Jeopardy's eyes – brown, but tinged amber by the light. When he looked at Lucien, there seemed to be a shadow of amusement in his eyes, a sureness. Later, Lucien told himself that this shadow had been of the future. Jeopardy had always known the future, or had perhaps chosen it himself that day.

They had practised together for only an hour, yet it seemed like an eternity. Lucien knew that Jeopardy had worked him hard, tested his limits. He felt sure he had exceeded Jeopardy's expectations. He himself had enjoyed the practice immensely. He felt that Jeopardy coaxed the best out of him.

When they'd finished, Jeopardy said, 'You're not bad. How would you like to continue that piece with me?'

Lucien hesitated. 'What about—'

Jeopardy cut his question short with a grimace and an angry gesture. 'I'm asking you. Yes or no? There are no other considerations.'

'I've yet to pass Sabraxis' tests,' Lucien said, eager to accept, but afraid of doing so. 'Perhaps I should get her permission.'

'Don't be stupid,' Jeopardy said. 'Just tell her. Same time tomorrow?' He'd left the court before Lucien could stutter an assent.

Lucien had sought Sabraxis out right after breakfast. She did not seem surprised at Lucien's news. 'You're talented,' she said. 'Res will want to use that.'

'You don't mind if I work with him, then?' Lucien asked.

Sabraxis smiled. 'Why should I? Just don't let him swamp you. And that doesn't mean you get out of your test tomorrow. I want to see you before lunch.'

Lucien couldn't help asking her what his position would be should he fail her test.

'You won't fail,' Sabraxis said. 'You know that already.'

All day, his mind swam in a dreamy haze. He confessed to no one but Sabraxis what had happened in the exercise court that morning. During the afternoon, he accompanied a clutch of lazy Ixmaritians out to the gardens where they sat in the sun and gossiped. Sydel commented on Lucien's preoccupation. 'You look smug today,' she said. 'What's on your mind?'

'Nothing,' Lucien replied.

The girl narrowed her eyes at him. 'You are so hard to read,' she said. 'I get the feeling you're hiding something, yet what can you possibly hide?' She shook her head. 'You have ambitions, Lucien, don't you?'

'Sydel,' he said, 'there is something, but if I tell you about it, it might not happen.'

She looked at him askance and opened her mouth to ask a question. Lucien looked away. She said nothing.

Lucien feared that if he told the other vibrancers he was working with Jeopardy, it would excite resentment among them. After all, Jeopardy commanded high status within the house and Lucien was only a newcomer. He was also afraid that when he turned up for the next practice, Amber and Jeopardy's argument would be resolved, and he would no longer be required. Everyone knew that the couple argued constantly.

The argument turned out to be of longer duration than normal, and Lucien practised with Jeopardy for seven consecutive days. They worked well together. Jeopardy was pleased, even to the point of suggesting they should perform the piece for Mandru together when the time came. Lucien dared not believe this might happen.

126

Far from resenting Lucien's new-found favour, the other vibrancers in the house began to treat him with a new respect once his alliance with Jeopardy became common knowledge. Suddenly, he was one of them. At first, he'd worried that Amber Epipheny would be jealous of him, and wondered whether she'd confront him about the matter. But she simply ignored him as she always had and began to practise with the yellow-haired vibrancer who'd been with Jeopardy in Mandru's salon on the morning Lucien had met the master. His name was Marist. They prudently used the exercise court that Jeopardy never frequented. The only gossip which came back to Lucien was that Amber thought him too plain in appearance to work well with Jeopardy, and considered him merely a tool that her lover was using in an attempt to provoke her. She obviously saw no threat in Lucien.

Other Ixmaritians commented on Lucien's practise sessions with Jeopardy; they made jokes about Jeopardy's difficult nature, which Lucien found very funny. He laughed, and made jokes back. In his heart he felt he was betraying something very new and delicate, but he could not stop himself. He was bemused by his sudden close proximity to such a powerful individual and enjoyed the attention this brought him from others.

The more time he spent with Jeopardy, the more he realised Jeopardy only ever saw people as extensions of his work. Lucien had believed commitment to the Vibrancy involved a strict and pious discipline. Now, he knew otherwise. In some ways, Jeopardy was more committed to the Vibrancy than he was himself, but there was little discipline as far as his private life was concerned. To Lucien, he was a hedonist. When Jeopardy was not working, he was often intoxicated. He and Lucien never talked about anything but their work. Lucien was never invited to participate in recreational activities. Jeopardy was not interested in house gossip. Other people's lives bored him and he became sharp and irritable on the one occasion Lucien tried to impart some interesting snippet of information Azmaveth had told him. Jeopardy was selfish and self-centred, but irresistibly compelling. When he smiled, the warmth in his eyes, so stunning for being so unexpected, made up for his cranky disposition, his overwhelming pomposity. Lucien enjoyed spending time in his company, but anticipated the day when this flimsy alliance would end. He could sense nothing permanent, nothing significant, in their relationship.

Then one night, the dream came.

As he dreamed, Lucien was wandering through a vast network of halls and chambers, which were crammed full of people, all talking loudly. He eventually came to a kind of theatre, which he also knew was Mandru's morning room, expanded to vast proportion. There was a stage at one end, where the fountains usually were, over which water was pouring in a frothing cataract. Everyone from the house was in the room, sitting in a spacious balcony seat high above the stage. Lucien knew that a performance was about to be enacted, a performance by Resenence Jeopardy. He was about to join his companions on the balcony when someone whom he could not see touched his arm and told him he was needed somewhere else. 'Where?' Lucien asked. There was no reply. Then he was walking round the building once more, searching for something. He knew he had very little time before the performance began. It was very dark, the lights yellow and dim. People milled everywhere, dressed in black, murmuring in anticipation. Lucien walked down endless dark corridors. His search, the place where he was

127

needed, had now become the auditorium, the balcony where his friends were waiting for him. He was trying to find his way back, but the building was so large, so labyrinthine, he kept getting lost, seeing the same blank faces, the same corners, the same stairs. Then Jeopardy was there, coming from nowhere as people do in dreams. He took hold of Lucien's hand.

'Come with me.'

They mounted a wide staircase, more brightly lit than any place Lucien had yet visited. People walking up and down the stairs paused to watch them pass. I am with Resenence Jeopardy, Lucien thought in his dream. He is the greatest of all vibrancers. He is about to perform for the Archimage himself.

At the top of the stairs, somewhere beyond a short, misty journey, Jeopardy led Lucien into a room where a handful of musicians were preparing themselves for the coming performance. It seemed as if the instruments they held – long pipes and hand drums – were somehow becoming part of their bodies. They ignored the newcomers. Lucien and Jeopardy sat down upon rough wooden boxes that had presumably once held the instruments. Lucien could feel sharp splinters digging into his skin through his clothes.

'Look at me,' said Jeopardy.

Lucien did so, and behind him he felt a kindling of curious scrutiny from the musicians. Their conversations were slowing down. They were listening. Jeopardy's eyes were almost black; an unwavering stare. His hair was loose round his shoulders, a wild mane. He took both of Lucien's hands in his own.

'I want you. I need you,' he said.

Lucien felt a dreadful thrill, dreadful in its literal sense, full of dread. He was conscious of the silence behind him, a strong sense of disapproval.

'No,' he said.

'I want you. I need you.'

'Stop!' Lucien pulled his hands out of Jeopardy's grasp and put them over his ears, his eyes. 'You mustn't!'

'I can't stop. I have to tell you.'

'What about Amber?' Lucien said. 'Don't say these things to me. She'll hate me.'

'I don't care.'

Lucien stood up, tried to back away. 'I care,' he said.

'Lucien, I love you.'

'You don't! Be quiet!' He was staring at the wall, a cold, white wall. 'I don't want this. I don't!'

'Lucien, don't deny me.' Jeopardy was weeping; tears of desperation, of need. Even as it terrified him, Lucien was triumphant. Even as he denied it, he knew he wanted it.

'I won't listen to this!' He ran out of the room, down the stairs, back into the auditorium. He ran to his seat, sat down among his friends, said nothing. In another balcony, opposite where he sat, a grand figure in the golden robes of the Archimage was being conducted to his seat, accompanied by ten faceless men in black cloaks. Then the room went dark.

A strange glow was emitted by the water on the stage, which gradually increased in brilliance until it revealed a vibrancer performing the opening sequence of a presentation. But it was not Resenence Jeopardy who danced. It was an older man, with a beard. A large, lumbering man, who fumbled through the ankle-deep water without grace. The room filled with angry

128

consternation. What has happened? Where is the one we have come to see?

The man on the stage raised an accusing finger and pointed right up at Lucien. Everyone turned to look.

'You did this,' said the man. 'You destroyed him. You did this!'

Lucien stood up, shouted back. 'I did not. I didn't ask for it. It's not my fault. I don't want it!'

Lucien woke up with a racing heart. He could not believe what he had just lived through. It was the first of many dreams.

'It was a torment to see him again after that.'

'You woke up to yourself.' The steam seemed to have cleared a little and Lucien could see that Walterkin sat up straight against the far wall, his knees raised, his hands dangling between them. 'Lucien, do you believe in the power of dreams? Do you believe dreams reflect reality or that they are real?'

Lucien shook his head. 'No . . .' He shrugged. 'I don't know. I strongly felt that Resenence had come to me in the dream and yet, when I awoke, when the morning came, I told myself I had created it myself. It was my secret longing. He had nothing to do with it, and yet, even now, it seems so powerful, so strong, so clear. I remember his face as he spoke. I remember his grief, his agony.'

'Was he different with you after the dream?'

Lucien sighed. 'I don't know. I was looking for signs afterwards. I read omens in everything, significance in everything. It might have been a lie. I noticed his concern for me, and I know he was concerned, but that might have been there all along. I don't know. It's impossible to tell now. All I do know for sure is that I woke up loving him. A fruitless, pointless love. He couldn't see people. He was blind to them. Maybe he sent me the dream. I don't know. I have to ask him, I think. I never told him about it.'

Lucien was so disturbed by the dream that the following morning he considered staying in his room and not going down to the exercise court to practice with Resenence. He was afraid the events of his dream would be clearly written in his eyes. However, the need to confront this new-found object of desire overcame his trepidation. He had to see. Would there be a change?

There wasn't. Resenence Jeopardy still expected him to work hard, was still friendly and attentive, but hadn't he been like that the day before? In desperation, Lucien cornered Azmaveth at breakfast.

'I have to speak to you,' he said.

'You look disturbed, Lucien,' she observed. 'Yes, I can see you do need to speak to me.'

She took him to her room where they could have privacy. 'What has happened?'

Now that he had the opportunity, Lucien was too embarrassed to speak.

Azmaveth sighed and folded her arms. 'Who is it?' she asked in a resigned tone.

Lucien sat down on her bed, wringing his hands in despair. 'I dare not say,' he said.

'Are you afraid I'll tell people?'

He looked up at her, studied her face for a moment. 'No.'

She smiled and shook her head. 'I know, Lucien.'

He glanced away. 'Do you?'

'It's Jeopardy, isn't it?'

Lucien cringed beneath her appraisal. He dug the heels of his hands into his eyes.

'I knew before you did,' she continued. 'I have an instinct for these things, Lucien. I could sense what you felt inside. It shone from you.'

'I hate this,' Lucien said. 'I don't know what to do.'

Azmaveth sat down beside him. 'There are several things you could do,' she said.

Lucien looked at her with utter wretchedness. 'What? He is oblivious of other people. They mean nothing to him. And yet . . .' He shook his head.

'And yet?'

Lucien told her about the dream.

'Azmaveth, in my heart, I feel the dream spoke truly to me, yet the evidence of reality tells me otherwise. I feel so confused. What is real?'

Azmaveth rose from the bed and crossed to a chest of drawers. She opened the top drawer and withdrew an object wrapped in purple silk. 'May I consult my sticks about this matter for you?'

'Sticks?'

Azmaveth unwrapped the silk. Within, tied together with a red ribbon, were about three dozen etched and painted wooden sticks of varying length, the longest being the size of a grown man's finger, the shortest the size of a child's. 'Karipo sticks,' she said. 'They're Ixibatabian.'

Lucien frowned. 'Isn't their use prohibited under Ixmaritian law?'

Azmaveth sighed. 'Of course. Do you want some insight into Jeopardy's head or not?'

'I don't know.' Lucien eyed the sticks, which Azmaveth was still holding out for his inspection, with suspicion. 'Only senior officers of the Church can attempt divination. You know that as well as I. We are too young, too inexperienced. We might invite catastrophe.'

'Oh, don't talk such nonsense, Lucien!' Azmaveth cried. 'Do you believe everything you're told?'

Lucien flinched away from the scorn in her voice. She had said those words to him many times, reminding him of his indoctrination at the hands of Por Tanssie's officials. 'Oh, very well,' he said. 'But I doubt you'll learn anything.'

Azmaveth did not argue but knelt down on the floor by the bed and laid out the silk square in front of her. She untied the sticks and rubbed them together between her palms. After a few moments of apparent concentration, she handed the sticks to Lucien. 'Do as I did,' she instructed. 'Rub them together.'

Lucien took the sticks from her. They felt warm to the touch, slightly damp from Azmaveth's palms. He let them roll between his hands. Could Jeopardy's thoughts and intentions really be intimated by a bunch of coloured twigs? It seemed unlikely. Still, he had little to lose.

'Now, let them fall over the cloth,' Azmaveth said, 'from a height of two handspans.'

Lucien obeyed this instruction and waited while Azmaveth leaned over the cloth, making small sounds of recognition, surprise and consternation.

'Well, what do you see?' Lucien demanded.

'There is no doubt,' she said, shaking her head.

'No doubt of what?'

She looked up at Lucien, and he saw immediately that her eyes were troubled. 'I would not have believed it,' she said, 'but the fall of the sticks is emphatic.'

'What? What?'

'He loves you,' she said. 'Look.'

Lucien's heart seemed to turn over within his ribs. He felt slightly sick, there was a humming in his ears. 'Look at what?' he snapped. 'It's just a jumble of sticks!'

'No, really. Examine the juxtaposition of these three here, the ones that form a triangle.' Azmaveth indicated the significant sticks. 'Love, concealment and – this one – the emblem of the sacred dancer. It's too much of a coincidence.'

'That could just refer to me,' Lucien said.

Azmaveth shook her head. 'I did not ask them about you, I asked about Jeopardy.'

Lucien hugged himself. He had begun to tremble. 'Did he send the dream to me, Veth?'

'Yes,' she answered, 'but he might not know it.'

Lucien rubbed his face. 'Oh, this doesn't help!' he cried. 'I don't want to feel like this. I've no idea what to do about it.'

Azmaveth considered something for a few moments and then nodded to herself, as if she'd made a decision. 'There are options,' she said. 'I believe Jeopardy is interested in you, but is not consciously aware of it. Therefore, he has to be made aware of his hidden thoughts. Once this happens, events should take a natural course.'

Lucien looked at her in alarm. 'I can't tell him!' he cried.

Azmaveth shook her head quickly. 'No, no, I'm not suggesting you do. You have to send a dream back to him. You have to remove any obstacles.'

'How?'

She shrugged. 'Well, I could do that for you. I have the ability, Lucien. I'm a northerner. Ixmarity is not my native religion. You know what is.'

'Profanity.' He hugged himself tighter. All he knew of the northern religions was that they embraced demonology and witchcraft. 'Azmaveth, you are talking about heresy against Ixmar! Only the Archimage and his ecclesiarchs have the ability to influence reality. If anyone else attempts it, it is a delusion, a blasphemy, an incursion into Ixmar's realm.'

'Oh, you would say that, wouldn't you!' Azmaveth exclaimed. 'Lucien, you look wretched. You have never loved before. How long do you want to suffer?'

'I want this feeling to go away, that's all,' he said primly. 'I didn't say I wanted to do anything else about it.'

Azmaveth uttered an exasperated snort. 'You have to start living one day. Why not begin now, with the best?'

'You are not a priestess, you are a demoness!' Lucien said. 'A temptress! I should denounce you.'

'Yes, perhaps I am all the things you say,' Azmaveth replied, 'but you won't denounce me. I am your friend, after all.'

Lucien watched her as she gathered up the sticks. He sensed that despite her words, his outburst had hurt her. He sighed deeply. 'All right, all right,' he said. 'Do whatever you can. Make something happen.'

'Are you sure?' she asked in a cold voice. 'As you suspect, it would be witchcraft, a crime in Ixmarity's eyes.'

'Yes,' he said. 'I'm sure. The moment I set foot in this house, my world turned upside down. I might as well complete the process.'

Azmaveth nodded, but made no further comment. She tied up her sticks and wrapped them in the silk again. She went back to the chest and opened another drawer. Lucien watched in silence as she removed a brass censer and a black veil.

'Are you going to do it now?' he asked.

She did not turn round but busied herself with placing a palmful of incense into the censer and lighting it. 'It is the best time,' she said. 'Your emotions are strong at this moment.'

She carried the censer carefully over to the bed and placed it on the floor. Then she covered her head with the black veil. 'Breathe the smoke, Lucien.'

Lucien leaned forward a little way. The perfume of the incense was sharp yet voluptuous. Even after the first inhalation, he felt a little dizzy. Why am I doing this? he wondered. Why can't I stop? It was against all he believed in and yet some inner part of him would stop at nothing to attract Jeopardy's notice. He told himself he was not looking for a lover, but simply the opportunity to tell Resenence about the dream. He did not want to pollute his body; he wanted a purely cerebral affair.

'You must really want this to happen,' Azmaveth murmured. 'Really, really want it. Because it will happen once we've finished here. It will happen.' She began to chant in a low, eerie voice, words in a language foreign to Lucien. He heard the power in her voice, the confidence. He knew then that she spoke the truth.

'You practised magic, Lucien!' Walterkin was laughing.

'There was no other way. I could not wait.'

Walterkin shook his head. The steam had almost completely cleared now. Soon, the attendant would come to tell Lucien his session was over. 'I confess I feel shocked,' Walterkin said. 'I didn't think you would have used magic.'

'Why not?' Lucien felt faintly insulted. He sat up on the bench and pulled on the robe.

'Because of your faith, your love of Paradouze. Didn't you think of Him at all?'

Lucien smiled grimly. 'The truth is, no one was further from my mind at the time than my god. Already I had been corrupted by Mandru's household.'

The boy shrugged. 'I know too little of you, yet I know too much. I have learned a lot from our conversations.'

Not for the first time, Lucien wondered exactly what it was this peculiar boy hoped to gain from dragging his history out of him.

As if she'd been waiting outside for a convenient pause in their conversation, the vaporeuse knocked on the door and opened it. She asked whether Lucien required a further session. He declined. His skin felt scorched enough as it was, although he had to admit his head felt clearer. The girl made no comment about Walterkin being there, but seemed to know him vaguely, judging from the way they spoke to one another on the way back to the changing rooms. Lucien wondered whether Walterkin had bribed her to let him into the cubicle.

Outside, the city seemed to have become livelier, although Lucien realised that earlier he must have projected his own lethargy onto his surroundings.

'I shall take you to Hartshorn Park,' Walterkin announced. 'We can continue our conversation there.'

'Aren't I keeping you from something?' Lucien asked. 'Shouldn't you be working for your mother?'

Walterkin did not answer the questions. He led Lucien onto a narrow street lined by tiny, dark shops. All of them seemed to be toy shops.

'Do you know what magic is, Lucien?' The tone of Walterkin's voice implied he would dispute whatever answer Lucien gave him. Consequently, the answer was delivered stiffly.

'Yes. You invoke the spirits of the incense to make them work for you. You ask for something and, if they feel disposed, they will aid you.'

Walterkin grinned widely and stared at the ground as he strode along. 'You know so little! Magic is the ability to shape reality through the strength of your own belief. If there are spirits at work at the time, they come only from yourself, not from the fume of the incense. Why should spirits aid living beings? What arrogance is it that drives people to believe they can have power over them? The perfume helps focus your will, but it is your will alone that weaves the spell.'

'Who told you that?' Lucien's voice was sharp.

Walterkin looked up at him, his face beatific. 'The park gates are just down here. It's not far.'

The effect of Azmaveth's magical working was almost immediate. The following morning, Lucien nearly retched in horror when he walked into the practise court and saw Amber Epipheny conversing with Resenence Jeopardy. Her gestures were emphatic but, from a distance, did not appear threatening or abusive. Jeopardy was leaning against the wall, his head thrown back, arms folded, looking down at Amber with inscrutable eyes. Lucien hovered by the door. Had he visualised his desires to Azmaveth inaccurately when he'd breathed the fume? Amber should not figure in this design. What was she doing here?

Jeopardy's eyes slid to the left and he caught sight of Lucien. He raised a hand and beckoned him over. Lucien had the direst of forebodings about obeying that summons, but was powerless to resist it. Amber swung round on him in a flash of red hair.

'It seems we've found a prodigy,' she said. Her tone was not exactly friendly, but its harshness was of bemused disbelief rather than jealous suspicion. She looked him up and down.

'Grow your hair,' she said. 'Your features are fine, but on the whole indistinct. I think hair would improve that.' She turned to Jeopardy. 'Of course, you must make him wear a wig or some kind of decoration for the performance itself.'

Jeopardy grinned. 'You have a delicate touch, my lovely,' he said, 'your tongue is a feather. Ignore her, Lucien. As a vibrancer, you are superb. Dance your best, and I will be happy. If you cut off your nose and ears before we perform, I shall not complain, so long as it does not mar your ability to dance.'

Lucien shrugged awkwardly.

'I don't mean to insult you,' Amber said. 'But it is the truth. What is wrong in telling someone how to make the best of themselves?' She smiled, and Lucien was surprised to discover that, like Jeopardy, Amber became a different person when she smiled. 'Res has no appreciation of beauty,' she said. 'They did wicked things to you at Por Tanssie, boy. The place is run by a lunatic. I've heard about it. Has anyone advised you yet to unlearn all the rubbish they taught you there?'

'Yes,' Lucien said. 'But it was not all rubbish.'

Amber looked faintly surprised he had contested her remark. 'But of course not. You wouldn't be a prodigy otherwise, would you?' She reached out to touch Jeopardy on the cheek, her hand gliding to rest on Lucien's shoulder as she prepared to leave. 'He speaks highly of you,' she said. 'In some ways, I regret losing my opportunity to perform this piece, but I don't begrudge you yours.'

She swept magnificently from the hall, clearly aware of, and gratified by, her own gracious magnanimity. Lucien watched her go, thinking, 'Oh, Paradouze, I am nothing, a puny scrap. A good vibrancer, but an unattractive scrap. What was I thinking of yesterday?' The shame of believing he could initiate any intimacy with Resenence Jeopardy made him flush.

Jeopardy pushed himself away from the wall, his arms still folded. He wandered towards the windows on light feet, a panther's tread. Lucien turned his back and began flexing his limbs. This was too horrible. He felt guilty thoughts were written all over his face.

'She is quite wrong.'

Lucien turned round. Jeopardy still had his back to him. 'What?'

'About you. You look fine.' He spun round and smiled, effortlessly dropping into a series of forward flips to land at Lucien's feet. 'Are you ready?'

Lucien could not look into Jeopardy's eyes after that, and the practice went badly. He felt dazed and confused because he could not decide what Jeopardy had meant by his remark. His limbs seemed out of his control; he fumbled and slipped. He missed his cues. This ineptitude infuriated Jeopardy. Never a person to hold back criticism when he felt it was needed, he lashed Lucien mercilessly with harsh words, and threw up his hands in despair when Lucien fouled yet another movement. Eventually, after an hour of torment, Jeopardy swung out of a configuration with the words, 'It is clear we will accomplish little today.'

Lucien slunk from the court a tortured thing. He was convinced Jeopardy would hate him for ever, change his mind about the performance, change his mind about his prowess. For the rest of the day, Lucien could not stop thinking about Jeopardy. He analysed every moment of the morning practice, haunted by the echo of Jeopardy's voice, the image of his smile, the even teeth inside that smile. Lucien was convinced his feelings were based on more than physical desire. He believed that Resenence Jeopardy had penetrated deeper into his soul than that.

The following day's practise session began no better. Attempting to execute a difficult move, paralysed in the core of his muscles by nervousness, Lucien lost his footing and ruined the sequence. Jeopardy stumbled and nearly fell. Lucien thought Jeopardy would strike him and cowered backwards, stooping down.

'What is wrong with you!' Jeopardy demanded. His hands were curved into claws.

Do not let me wince, Lucien prayed, wincing.

'Well?' Jeopardy grabbed hold of Lucien's wrist. He felt the bones twist within his flesh. 'Been at the liquor, have you. The silly weed?'

'No!' Lucien's voice could be nothing but indignant. Such substances were Jeopardy's weaknesses, not his. 'I did not sleep well, that's all.'

Jeopardy made a scornful sound. 'That should make no difference. Don't whine at me!'

Lucian tried to pull away. 'I'll do the movement again. Let me go!'

Jeopardy's lips curved into a snarl. He released Lucien's wrist and turned his back, lifting his arms over his head, reaching behind him for his shoulders. He leaned backwards, his hair hanging down until it nearly touched the floor. 'Then dance,' he said. 'And get it right this time.'

You are enjoying this, Lucien thought. What is it you want from me? He performed the movement faultlessly.

'Strange how a feeling of inadequacy can be changed by anger into indignation,' Walterkin said. 'Angry, you performed well.' They were sitting together on the grass of Hartshorn Park, some distance away from a gravel path where tourists wandered up and down, pointing towards the follies and monuments around them.

'A state of affairs Resenence Jeopardy used often to extract the best performances from his colleagues,' Lucien said drily.

Walterkin nodded and put his hand into his trouser pocket, taking out a small mirror in a gilded frame. 'And did he use the same formula in his intimate relationships?' He held the mirror up so that Lucien could see into it.

I look old, Lucien thought, so old. There are lines round my eyes and my hair has become a hag's rope. He would not recognise me now. Is my body the same? What was once muscle has become plaited wood, frayed and plaited wood. I am too thin. 'I cannot name, or articulate, the formula Resenence used in his personal relationships,' Lucien said. 'It is too complex, beyond words. I could never understand it.'

'Why should you have wanted understanding? What would that have gained for you?'

'Something,' Lucien said. 'Something.'

'You were obsessed by him,' Walterkin observed, laying the mirror flat in his palm. 'You still are.'

Lucien could not summon an objection to this observation. 'It would seem so. I seek to exorcise it, although in many ways my obsession has become my life. What will be left for me if I wriggle out of its skin? Life would become dull. I would need to discover new obsessions.'

'Life itself is an obsession.'

Lucien nodded and sighed. 'That might be true.' He pressed his fingertips against his brow. 'You have to understand part of what caused the obsession. In Por Tanssie we were fed toxins that killed our desires. No doubt in some houses, Ixmaritians were forced to continue this practice. Mandru did not insist on it because he was a sensualist. He enjoyed observing the affairs of his staff; it intrigued him. I had nothing inside me to dampen my blood; it caught fire.'

'And did this fire become a conflagration, did it burn itself out or was it doused by water?' Walterkin laughed.

'It became white-hot. It blinded me.' Lucien rested his chin in his hands. 'He touched me that day. We had performed the movement so many times, our bodies slipping past each other into a new configuration. That day, he caught hold of me. Looked at me strangely. I could not interpret it. He said. "I am not what you think I am," and I asked him what he thought I

135

believed him to be. "Cold," he said. Then what are you? I asked, but it was only in my head. "I have great fears," he replied. "You will never understand." At that point, I did not want to. I was beyond appreciating the proximity of his flesh. I could not feel it. Confusion numbed me utterly. I regret that. Now, I remember, and I put sensation to the memory, but it is only a fantasy. I felt nothing.'

'It was your magic coming true then, but there was a cost.'

Lucien nodded thoughtfully. 'I should have known that.'

THE HAUNT

Dauntless Javelot had never imagined a woman could be such abrasive company. In his mind, he had believed the female breed to be compliant, sighing creatures. Cleo Sinister possessed neither of these qualities, nor did she appear to be familiar with other desirable attributes such as obedience, silence and the possession of gentle manners.

Dauntless tired of her voice, tired of her bony fingers digging into the cracks of his leather carapace as she clutched for balance astride the horse behind him. Her hair blew forward like a dusty web and stuck to the corners of his mouth. He knew that she carried a pouch of poisons. The fact that this singular, somewhat oppressive female was seeking out a religious man seemed absurd. Dauntless doubted whether she could direct her attention upon anything long enough to sustain a sense of faith. Travelling, which had once been such a bore to him, was now a continual nightmare. And yet it seemed her annoying presence somehow energised him. For so long, he'd felt like a phantom. Now, in the company of Cleo Sinister, his senses seemed to be waking up. Sounds, sights and smells were more vibrant. Could it be that unpleasant experiences were necessary to make a person feel real in the world, or was it caused simply by proximity to another living soul?

Whatever the reason, Dauntless bit his tongue and resolved to put up with Cleo Sinister. If he was to be a martyr to this strange woman's caprices, then so be it. Valiance had surely put her in his path. Perhaps this vexing quest was the proof he needed that Valiance existed. If Cleo represented a hair shirt, he would wear it, and withstand the chafing. He would carry out the quest he had appointed himself; take her to her holy man.

'Have you not heard of Resenence Jeopardy?' she'd asked him on the first day of their acquaintance.

He'd frowned. 'No. What is it?'

'It is not an it, but a he,' she'd replied. 'A man of great power. I knew his son before my husband killed him.'

'Oh.'

'My husband is a poisoner. I never loved him,' she'd explained airily, pulling leaves from a tree overhead and showering Contralto's head with

137

annoyed insects. Dauntless hoped they would not sting. 'But despite his faults – which I confess were many – he was adept at killing. He taught me well. I know much about the human constitution and what it takes to stop it working.'

Dauntless felt distinctly uncomfortable with this blithe confession.

'I'm sure we will find many uses for my skills upon our journey,' Cleo said.

Dauntless began to dread the future. He wondered how long they could travel before they met anyone Cleo felt inspired to poison, and whether he would change his mind about his commitment to her before then.

At night, he courteously surrendered his domed leather tent to Cleo's use. Far from being grateful, she complained of the smell within and declared that sleeping in the open air had its merits. She did not decline the offer, however, which forced the paladin to sleep on the ground, with his head on Contralto's saddle, beneath the trees outside.

Each evening, before they slept, Dauntless attempted conversation with his new companion. She was not reluctant to talk about herself, and described with glee how she had left Scaraby through the sewers, emerging on the northern verges of Haling Heart. She asked no questions in return, however, and when Dauntless volunteered information about himself, appeared bored in the extreme. Still, it appeared her advent had summoned a little luck into his life, for suddenly they began to discover plentiful growths of grass potatoes, forest leeks and turtle-berries, a welcome change from the stringy little rabbits and bitter roots they had eaten until then.

Gradually, their surroundings changed, and they emerged into an unfamiliar area of Haling Heart, which while being more lush, was also wilder and difficult to negotiate. What paths existed were mostly overgrown. One afternoon, after they had been travelling together for several days, Cleo ordered Dauntless to pull Contralto to a halt.

'What is it?' he asked irritably. The previous day, she had demanded halts at least a dozen times, claiming they were being followed by something in the undergrowth, to the left of their narrow path. Dauntless had patiently examined the foliage every time, but had found nothing to suggest pursuit.

'I can hear something,' Cleo said. 'I can hear voices.'

Dauntless could hear nothing but the chomping of Contralto's teeth against his bit and the distant scream of birds high above.

'There's nothing—'

'Wait!' Cleo interrupted. 'It came again as you were speaking! Go forward!'

Sighing, Dauntless urged Contralto up the path. Presently, he too heard the faint ghost of a sound, almost too muted to identify. It was the laughter of children.

Ignoring the paladin's complaints, Cleo kicked Contralto's flanks to make him trot, and presently they came to place where the path widened. Tree branches met high overhead, creating a wavering green canopy through which sunlight fell in shadows and coins of light. Sitting in a rough circle on the grassy mud path were three children. Dauntless was instantly suspicious because there had been no sign of human habitation for days. Cleo, however, leapt from Contralto's back and, paying no attention to Dauntless's warnings, walked smartly to where the children played.

They were not very old, perhaps as young as four or five. There were two girls and a boy, all of them dressed in sparkling white clothes. The girls had long ringlets of the deepest black that cascaded down their backs, while the boy's hair, similarly black and lustrous, was tied in a ponytail at his neck. Their skins were as pale and smooth as cream, their eyes wide and slanted. They seemed to glow in the flickering green-gold light, as if embraced by a holy nimbus. Cleo felt an overwhelming sense of familiarity. It was like stepping backwards in time.

'Hello!' she said brightly. The children ignored her approach, but now turned their heads towards her. None of them returned her smile. All looked at her with wary distrust. Cleo entered their halo of light and squatted down among them. Close to, the illusion of glowing feyness dissipated. They appeared to be ordinary children, their white clothes a little soiled by mud and grass stains. The boy's face was grubby around the mouth. 'What are you doing here?' Cleo asked them. She looked into the circle of their cabal, and saw what had occupied them. 'A doll's tea party!' she exclaimed. 'What fun!' Her voice, however, wavered.

Dauntless dismounted from Contralto and led the horse forward. He looked down over Cleo's shoulder to see what the children were doing. There were about half a dozen porcelain dolls sitting among them, the kind with which his sisters had played as children. He had been intensely frightened of those dolls as a young boy. They'd been too lifelike, while too still. Their glass eyes had been horribly knowing. The dolls he was looking at now were old and battered, their clothes colourless and torn. One was blind, having no eyes. Another, whose face was made of wax, had been hideously disfigured, as if the victim of a conflagration. Others were missing limbs, or hair. In the centre of the circle of dolls and children was a metal cauldron, the size of a milk pan. In a soup of pond water, twigs and shredded leaves, small china limbs and glass eyes floated with eerie realism: dolls' limbs, dolls' eyes. A huge wooden spoon protruded from the cauldron. Observing his scrutiny, one of the little girls solemnly lifted the spoon out of the grisly soup and offered it to Dauntless. He took a step backwards; the horse snorted and shifted restlessly behind him.

'My name is Cleo Sinister and this is Dauntless Javelot,' Cleo said. She gestured behind her. 'Our horse is called Contralto.' She took the spoon from the girl and pretended to drink from it. 'Mmm!' she murmured appreciatively. 'What are your names?'

'I am called Hope,' said the larger of the two girls, tossing back her hair. 'This is my brother and sister, Sanguin and Eternia.'

'Where do you live?' Cleo asked.

The children exchanged a glance, passing it round their circle like a secret. 'In a big tree,' said the boy. The two girls giggled.

'What fun!' Cleo said. 'I would like to live in a tree too. I don't live anywhere at the moment. This forest is my home. I would like to see where you live, perhaps talk to your parents.'

'Cleo,' Dauntless said warningly, 'you know nothing of these children. They could be the progeny of bandits or gypsies!'

'Give us a fingernail and we'll show you,' said Hope.

Cleo extended her hands. 'Alas, as you can see, my lovely nails are all broken down. I couldn't even bite off a sliver.'

Hope frowned. 'No, we meant from the root. A whole fingernail.' She picked up a little knife which had been lying in the lap of one of the dolls. Its handle was the carved wooden figure of a mermaid with huge painted eyes. 'I can cut it out.'

139

Cleo withdrew her hands swiftly. 'The price is too great,' she said. 'But I have poisons.'

'Cleo!' Javelot cried in exasperation. Cleo and the children ignored him.

Hope shook her head. 'Oh, we have plenty of those. We have everything we need. Everything. Except living things.'

'What are you?' Cleo asked.

The boy threw out his arm at astounding speed and touched her face. Cleo could see that where the sleeve of his shirt was drawn back, his skin was a greenish colour, like chicken meat that was beginning to rot. She put up her hand to her face and found it wet. When she examined her fingers, they were red with blood. 'We are fenniks!' Sanguin cried.

Uttering a cry of disgust, Dauntless leapt forward and dragged Cleo up by the arm. She did not resist, but narrowed her eyes at the children. 'You are too light in colour for fenniks. I think you are something else.'

'Cleo, we must go,' Dauntless pleaded. 'These brats are ghouls. Look at them!'

The children had got to their feet and stood in a line across the path, observing the two adults with passive faces. They had gathered up the dolls in their arms, some of which were nearly as big as they were. Their eyes looked dark in faces too pale. The green light surrounding them now seemed to be imparting a sick lifeless pallor. Dauntless helped Cleo up onto Contralto's back, swiftly following her. The horse appeared reluctant to pass the children, so Dauntless drew his sword and waved it in their direction in a threatening manner. The children moved reluctantly to the side. Contralto, eyes rolling, ears flat, skittishly began to mince past them. The smallest girl, Eternia, suddenly jumped forward and grabbed Cleo's foot.

'We are your friends!' she cried, her small white face screwed up in an expression of bewilderment. 'Your friends! We want to see your wedding dress, your coloured combs!' She tugged earnestly on Cleo's boot. Cleo made a sound of distress, and Dauntless applied his heels to Contralto's shuddering flanks. The horse jumped forward a few paces with his limbs bunched up and then, holding himself for a brief moment in a static rear, galloped off in sheer terror down the path.

Cleo looked back once. As she expected the children had vanished perhaps into the trees.

'This forest is full of very peculiar things,' Dauntless said. He was attempting to comfort Cleo, who had been uncharacteristically silent since their encounter with the children. He could feel her trembling against him.

'I've seen nothing like that,' she said.

'Haven't you? Well, I've seen strange children aplenty,' Dauntless replied with contrived joviality. 'Funny little faces peering down at me through the branches overhead. Who knows what they are? They are certainly not human. Don't let it upset you, Cleo.'

'I'm not upset,' Cleo retorted. 'Not in the way you mean. It's just that they reminded me so much of the poor child my husband killed. I loved that child. They could have been his siblings.'

'Perhaps that was deliberate,' Dauntless said in a sturdy voice. 'If they were spirits, or rogue hewkin babes, they could have plucked an image from your mind, like a berry from a bush. You must put them from your thoughts now.'

Cleo sighed heavily. 'My face hurts,' she said. 'That boy scratched me deeply.'

'You must put something on it.' 'Who knows what venoms lurk in those creatures' claws.' Dauntless kept an eye on the tree trunks to the side of the path and eventually spotted a growth of swage mushroom, just above head height. He pulled Contralto to the side and stood up in his stirrups to gouge a handful of fungus from the bark. This he kneaded into a pulp and then gave to Cleo to hold against her scratched cheek. She complained of how it stung, but eventually her lamenting subsided and she rested her head against his shoulders.

For an hour or so they continued to travel through the sighing trees, Cleo slumped against Dauntless's back. The pathway had virtually disappeared and now Contralto pushed through breast-high bracken. The hissing of the leaves overhead had become soporific. Dauntless himself was fighting an urge to doze. Cleo suddenly became alert behind him and pulled herself upright.

'Look!' she cried excitedly, pointing past his face. 'Through the trees! The walls of a house!'

Dauntless cringed as she bellowed in his ear. 'It's only a ruin,' he said.

'I don't think so. There's smoke.'

Dauntless sighed. 'But who would live here? There are no paths, no sign of life at all.'

'Then surely a very interesting person must live here,' Cleo said.

Dauntless uttered a caustic laugh. 'As interesting as the monsters who scratched your face and wanted to cut out your fingernails, hmm?'

The trees thinned to reveal what once might have been a clearing but which now resembled only a poisonous-looking wilderness. The black walls of an enormous sprawling house rose menacingly from the rank weeds and thorns and, as Cleo had noticed, a thin reed of smoke was seeping from one of the many narrow chimneys. Dauntless regarded this imposing edifice with dismay. The roof was full of holes, all of which sprouted grass and moss. Most of the windows were broken, and those that weren't were boarded over. Judging from its appearance, he doubted that whoever lived there could be of a benign character.

Cleo did not seem to share his forebodings. 'How wonderful,' she exclaimed. 'It's so big!' She began to wriggle down off Contralto's back.

'No!' Dauntless thundered. 'We are riding past!' But his order was ignored.

Cleo scampered to the edge of the clearing and looked back. 'There is a pathway here,' she cried.

'Cleo, come back,' the paladin shouted, without much confidence of being obeyed. He watched with the direst of misgivings as Cleo began slapping a path for herself through the wilderness ahead. Fetid muscle-grass sagged against giant stands of thorn-apple, elephant rhubarb and halo thistle. Nettles with leaves the size of dinner plates fought a battle for possession of the clearing with garrotte vines, which sought to strangle the nettles with tendrils that sprouted vivid scarlet trumpet flowers.

Sighing, Dauntless urged Contralto to follow Cleo into this prickly, toxic jungle. He was relieved somewhat by the fact that the horse did not balk at approaching the house. By the time Contralto had won free of the nettles, Cleo had already reached the door. Lifting a huge door-knocker in the shape of a retching demon, Cleo advertised their presence to whomever was concealed within.

Taut with nervous expectation upon the horse, Dauntless expected one of two scenarios to ensue: something maddened and destructive would erupt at the signal of Cleo's knock, or else there would be utter silence and no response at all. He considered what action he should take concerning both of these possibilities. If the former should occur (presuming whatever came out of the house did not destroy Cleo immediately, and he was not without hope that this might happen), he would draw his sword and attack. If the foe seemed too large or numerous to deal with, he would withdraw discreetly and leave the witless Cleo to her fate. He'd had more than enough of her reckless approach to potentially lethal situations. Under these circumstances not even Valiance could blame him for abandoning his quest. However, should Cleo's entreaty elicit no response, he might consider investigating the building with her. It might possibly be occupied only by a raddled ancient, of no threat.

At first there was no response to Cleo's knock, at which Dauntless was greatly relieved. She looked back over her shoulder at him and pulled a sour face. Then, squaring her shoulders, she lifted the knocker again and pounded it repeatedly against the door. Almost immediately, frenzied barking erupted beyond the door, which to Dauntless sounded like a pack of hellhounds released from sorcerous slumber. Cleo took a single step backwards down the short flight of steps that led to the door. Dauntless leapt down from Contralto's back. There was a crash, as of heavy, well-muscled animal bodies being hurled against the door, and Dauntless was sure he perceived the wood shaking on its hinges.

'Cleo,' he said, 'come here. Now!'

She looked back at him once, her fingers clasping her face, but she did not stir. The cacophony within the house seemed to last for several minutes, but was perhaps only of seconds' duration. Then the door creaked open an inch or two. There was a sound of chains rattling, and the fervid snarling of the beasts increased. Dauntless took down his sword from its saddle sheath. Contralto huffed and pulled in his chin with foreboding at the angry growls.

Cleo did not feel at all frightened. Her childhood in the Burrows had well-acquainted her with fearsome beasts of all shapes and sizes. As whoever stood beyond the door fought with its security measures, she considered her own plan of action. It sounded as if there were several animals waiting to launch themselves upon her. She knew how to blind mad dogs with her bare hands, and also how to break their jaws, but she was also very proficient at a less violent form of defence, which her father had taught her. She knew that if she stood very still and sent forth quiet animal-soothing thoughts, it was often enough to discourage attack. As a young girl in the Burrows' this method had saved her on more than one occasion from a corner of adversity. It was not a technique she was comfortable using, however.

The door opened a few more inches and a pair of wide dark snouts pushed through, snuffling noisily.

'Good day,' Cleo said in a loud, clear voice. Another smaller snout, quite white, appeared at the bottom of the door. 'We are travellers, and though we are not lost in the true sense of the word, we perhaps lack direction.'

While she had been speaking, the dogs had been struggling to get through the narrow crack of open door. Cleo stood on tiptoe, trying to see who hid behind the door. The animals managed to push their heads through the gap, which were quickly followed by powerful shoulders, massive bodies and, mercifully, a pair of wagging tails. A third animal, which was a small, short-legged creature, weaved out between the prancing legs of his companions, barking in a high-pitched voice. Cleo staggered back from the loving assault being bestowed upon her by the two larger animals. She put her hands against their huge hard heads, and the warm power of them gave her confidence a strange boost. This surprised her, for generally she did not like dogs. She remembered the hounds at the Salamanca estate. In what ways were these animals different from them? Or was it she who was different now? She drew herself up to her full height. 'I am Cleo Sinister,' she announced.

In the open doorway stood an unkempt though not unattractive young man who was dark of hair and eye. He appraised Cleo with an expression of suspicious enquiry. 'What do you want?' he demanded, looking past her at the paladin, who was brandishing his sword. The small dog was sniffing round Contralto's heels, causing the horse to skip nervously from side to side.

Cleo smiled and smoothed her skirts, finding them quite wet with dog spittle. 'Well, we are seeking hospitality,' she said. 'We saw the smoke from your chimney through the trees.'

'Visitors are few to these parts,' the young man responded with distrust, 'on account of the isolation and, to be sure, the condition of our estate.'

'It is a wonderful estate,' Cleo exclaimed. 'It is like a house I dreamed of once, where I wandered through its rooms for an eternity.'

The young man glanced behind himself dubiously, into the interior. 'Have you any money?' he asked abruptly.

'Yes,' Cleo replied boldly.

'Hmmm.' The young man stroked his chin, and then apparently came to a decision. 'Very well, you are welcome to enter and partake of our hospitality. What there is of it. I hope you're not expecting anything too grand.'

'I expect nothing,' said Cleo. 'That way, I am rarely disappointed by life.' She turned to Dauntless and summoned him peremptorily. 'Paladin, tether Contralto to that tree. We are to be guests of this house.'

The dilapidation and solitude of the house effectively concealed the commerce that was conducted within its walls. Cleo and Javelot soon discovered that it was occupied by five individuals, who were stowed away in far chambers like ideas in a vast empty brain. The young man who had let them in introduced himself as Malengin Fole. 'We are a scientific community,' he said as he led them into a dismal cavernous hall, 'and also a spiritual one.'

'In what way scientific?' Cleo asked.

'One of our number, Master Dratslinger, harnesses ghosts by means of vibration. We assist him in this task and some might, because of that, categorise us as musicians.'

'Indeed,' Cleo exclaimed. 'Is it by music, then, that you seek to tame the spirits?'

Malengin Fole frowned a little. 'Yes, I suppose so, but our creations are perhaps not accessible to a trivial mind.'

'I am intrigued,' Cleo declared. 'So what is the spiritual aspect of your community?'

'As I said, we work with ghosts.'

They crossed the dark hallway, which smelled strongly of damp and dog, the animals themselves charging gleefully back and forth across the floor. There was no matting underfoot, and hardly any light because the windows, high up over a ponderous staircase, were all begrimed. 'No woman lives here,' Cleo thought.

Malengin Fole led them through several apartments, all of them apparently abandoned. Evidence of decay and neglect were manifest. Wallpaper and plaster were parting company with the walls and high ceilings, and decomposing furniture lay everywhere, as if hacked apart by axes. Cleo hoped that some upper part of the building was more habitable.

'It seems the scientific mind precludes the accumulation of more tangible comforts,' Dauntless observed quietly to Cleo. Malengin, however, overheard him.

'We have to attract the ghosts,' he said, as if that were explanation enough for the dissolution.

Eventually they arrived at an enormous kitchen. Here, it seemed, some labour had been applied to physical comforts, although there was little evidence of efficient housekeeping. Ropes of onions and garlic hung from ancient rafters, and sacks of rice and potatoes were crammed beneath a huge stained table. Boxes of apples, which filled the air with a sickly sweet perfume, were stacked beside a cracked sink that was flanked by warped wooden draining boards. The floor was of cracked tiles, and in several places pale weeds grew from the cracks. Above the sink, ivy had burrowed its way through the walls and was now spreading in profusion towards the ceiling. A row of curtainless windows punctuated the wall behind the sink, all of them opaque with ancient grime. Cleo wanted to see outside. She had to rub the filthy glass in order to see anything. There was a wide, cobbled enclosure, flanked on all sides by sagging black buildings. Numerous poles were set into the mossy cobbles of the yard, connected at a height of six feet or so by thin cords. They resembled washing lines, although instead of clothes, several dozen peculiar wooden and metal contraptions were pegged out. They resembled musical instruments, though remarkably different from any Cleo had seen before.

'What strange laundry you have,' she remarked.

'New devices,' Malengin explained. 'They have been varnished and are hanging out to dry.'

'But the wind is blowing dust and leaves up from the ground,' Cleo said. 'Won't that spoil the varnish?'

'On the contrary,' Malengin said, attempting, with difficulty, to turn one of the three taps over the sink. 'It imparts a certain voice of earth into each instrument. Would you care for tisane?' His efforts were rewarded by an agonised groan from the plumbing, a shudder, and a thin trickle of water.

'Very much so,' Cleo said. 'I am parched. How about you, Dauntless?'

'A small cup,' the paladin said, eyeing with misgiving the black grease-encrusted cooking range that squatted in a corner like an enormous metal dragon. Thick pipes sprouted from several places in the range, some disappearing through holes in the ceiling, others through the floor, while one snaked along the skirting board before vanishing through a door.

Malengin set about preparing the beverage. He opened a door on the range and was rewarded by a cough of brilliant flame which gusted briefly into the room. He shovelled a small amount of coal inside, and then placed a kettle on one of the hotplates. He directed Cleo and Dauntless to seat

144

themselves on a bench at the table. It creaked and wobbled ominously under their weight.

'So, where are you travelling to?' Malengin asked. 'You say you are not lost, yet it seems unusual for someone to come across this spot.'

'We are on a quest,' Cleo said, pre-empting Dauntless's explanation.

'For what?' Malengin leaned against the sink with his arms folded. The idea appeared to amuse him.

'A man,' Cleo said importantly. 'A great man. His name is Resenence Jeopardy.'

Melangin pulled a sour face. 'Ah yes, I have heard of him.'

'Out here?' Dauntless said. 'How surprising!'

Malengin went back to the range and peered at the kettle. 'Not really. You forget we entertain spirits. Many have died in Jeopardy's train.'

Cleo sighed and rested her chin in her hands. 'I would have expected it,' she said dreamily. 'The mere idea of the man is romantic.'

Malengin smiled at Cleo's observation. 'He is more of an idea than a man,' he said.

'How so?' Cleo asked.

Malengin, however, did not answer, but offered Cleo and Dauntless two stained cracked mugs filled with something that appeared to be heated pond water. Cleo stared at the contents with dismay.

'Don't worry,' Malengin said, 'the water here looks acrid, but tastes well enough. It has an earthy tang. However, you might find it unusual. This might help.'

He took down a large earthenware flask from a shelf above the range, unstoppered it, and poured a measure of golden liquid into Cleo's mug. An inviting smell of liquor rose on the steam. Cleo sipped. She could taste fire; little else.

Dauntless declined the offer of liquor, and sipped with evident distaste at the tisane. 'You think this Jeopardy character doesn't exist, then?' he asked.

'We have not researched the phenomenon extensively,' Malengin replied ponderously, 'but there are certain aspects that speak of legend rather than fact.'

'Such as?' the paladin enquired.

Malengin shrugged. 'Miracles are ascribed to him, which I find hard to believe. They say he can be in several places at once, can work magic, hypnotise with his eyes, cause death, resuscitate corpses, make women pregnant with a glance. Surely, if such a puissant individual existed, he would enjoy greater fame and also far greater power and influence than he does.'

'But not all the legends can be lies,' Cleo protested. 'I met a woman who'd borne Jeopardy's child. I cared for that child myself.'

'His children are all dead,' Malengin said, and then smiled. 'Well, so the stories would have us believe.'

'It's true I saw one die,' Cleo said, and her wistful words invoked an uncomfortable silence in the room.

Dauntless was discomfited by the way Cleo was so open with Malengin Fole, a man he had instantly distrusted. He had, in Dauntless's opinion, a murderer's brow. For someone who appeared so gleefully wicked and amoral, Cleo seemed surprisingly dim when it came to character judgment. Dauntless wondered again what he was doing in her company. Had she

145

really been sent to him by the spirit of True Valiance himself, to test his chivalry and honour? He dared not conjecture, but the possibility of that was the only thing that prevented him from abandoning her.

He observed with simmering rancour as she began to tell Malengin about her life in the poisoner's house in Scaraby. Had she no sense of discretion? Then, as if drawn by the presence of strangers, another of the household came into the kitchen. Alerted by an ominous creaking sound coming from near his feet, Dauntless glanced down to see a trapdoor in the floor being opened from beneath. A peculiar head slowly rose from the hole and peered into the room with patient animal scrutiny. Dauntless flinched away in distaste. At first glance, the head seemed to consist solely of a long nose protruding from a tangle of hair, thereby resembling the countenance of a maned vole, though considerably larger in size.

'Ah, Flittern,' said Malengin, bestirring himself from beside the cooking range. 'We have guests.'

'I smelled as much!' declared the newcomer, a remark which served only to inflame Dauntless's discomfort. 'Are they here to buy?'

'Buy what?' Cleo asked.

'Our merchandise,' Flittern said, and with a jerk of long, spidery limbs, he leapt up out of the hole. Cleo's jaw dropped open in surprise.

'You are looking at Flittern Rattletrap!' announced the man, extending a limb to shake Cleo's hand. He was an alarmingly tall and thin individual, whose long, bedraggled dark hair fell nearly to his waist. He brought a pungent, earthy scent of cellars with him, which was not wholly unpleasant.

'Pleased to meet you,' Cleo said, 'but I don't want to buy any ghosts.'

Flittern Rattletrap rippled his attenuated fingers on the air. 'Ghosts? Oh, you do not understand. We have more than mere ghosts on offer: wights, visitants, creep-haunts, duppies, spooks both gaseous and plasmic, bogles, lych-folk and ghouls.'

Cleo's face did not register any enthusiasm.

'On the other hand,' Flittern said, folding himself onto the bench beside her, 'we could perhaps tempt you with a bottled rogue amorous thought, distilled at the first quarter of the moon, and salted with a spark of starlight. Such a pretty sight. The bottles are first-class and blown on the premises to your explicit specifications.'

Cleo shook her head. 'No thank you.'

Flittern Rattletrap frowned. 'Oh, then perhaps—'

'These are not customers, Flit, they are paying guests,' Malengin interrupted.

'Oh.' Flittern's face fell. Then he grinned and opened his mouth, as if to list further commodities produced on the premises, when a further member of the household came into the room, this time through the doorway above ground. This young man had orange hair that fell in tangled plaits from the crown of his head. Cleo thought he had a trickster's face, like that of a malevolent clown. Like Flittern Rattletrap and Malengin Fole, he wore dark-coloured garments that had nearly fallen into rags.

'This is Tumblejack,' Malengin informed his guests. 'He is an evocator of unsurpassable skill.'

'Indeed,' said Tumblejack, bowing extravagantly to Cleo. 'For as little as a copper coin, I will utter a howl guaranteed to wake the dead.'

'Perhaps now is not the right moment,' Flittern suggested.

Tumblejack shrugged. 'People have said that no moment in the existence

146

of the universe is propitious for the ejaculation of one of my howls. If that is the case, and bearing in mind I intend to ignore such advice, then surely all moments are of equal suitability.' He opened his mouth and emitted a short mournful squall, which set Cleo's teeth on edge.

Dauntless felt his skin crawl. He mistrusted all of these bizarre individuals with equal zeal. According the the lore of True Valiance, necromancy in any form was an abomination. He was soiling himself simply through his proximity to these sorcerers. It was not impossible they planned to work some malign mischief upon himself and the gullible Mistress Sinister. Cleo, as perhaps he should have anticipated, seemed delighted by this motley collection of ghost-trussers. She was grinning from ear to ear, her eyes sparkling in excited anticipation, like a child watching magicians at a carnival. Dauntless decided to take a firm stand in the matter.

He cleared his throat and spoke loudly. 'We had best be on our way soon, Cleo, before dark falls.'

Cleo directed a glance of extreme malevolence in his direction. 'What, to sleep in that disgusting tent of yours again?' she exclaimed angrily. 'What a happy prospect!'

'You are welcome to stay here awhile,' said Malengin in a silky voice. 'At least overnight.'

'That is kind of you,' Dauntless said firmly, 'but time presses—'

'Thank you very much,' Cleo interrupted. 'I need a rest from travelling. I have decided the horse is an inclement beast, and this land is hardly friendly to travellers.'

Dauntless was aghast. Was she mad? Could she really countenance spending a night of long dark hours in this ruin, a ruin whose sole purpose was the gathering of ghosts? He shuddered. Discomfort in the open air was far preferable to him. He stood up. 'I think perhaps we should confer in private on this matter,' he said.

'Whatever for?' she replied. 'I have made up my mind. Come along now, paladin, be flexible.' She grinned. 'Or is it you're scared of ghosts?'

'I,' Dauntless declared, 'am a paladin of True Valiance. I am afraid of nothing.' Simply by reminding himself of this fact, he felt inspired by a new confidence and was just about to lift Cleo physically from her seat when yet another resident of the house made an appearance. She came in through the yard door, and from the moment he saw her, Dauntless could tell she was a sorceress of deftness and strength. Her arrival effectively stemmed any action he was about to take. She was not a tall woman, being a hand's width shorter than Cleo, but her small frame was crammed with energy. She was dressed in a long white robe of finely pleated linen, which was belted loosely at the waist. Her teased black hair surrounded her like a storm cloud. All the men in the room seemed cowed by her presence.

'Fole, what is this?' she demanded. 'I did not realise we had guests.'

'May I introduce Apanage, the mistress of Drago Dratslinger,' said Malengin. He turned to the lady and executed a nervous bow. She inclined her head with derision.

'Actually,' said Tumblejack, 'whether these people are guests or not is a moot point. They were just arguing about whether they should leave.'

'I am hardly surprised,' Apanage declared. 'Look at the state of this place! What are you thinking of, entertaining guests here in your revolting lair? You should have summoned me at once.' Without waiting for an explanation from the men, who had all assumed sheepish expressions, the lady gracefully

147

turned towards Cleo and Javelot, her arms extended. Poisonous-looking talons embellished the end of each delicate finger. 'I am not in the least amazed you have been discouraged by the noisome ambience of these apartments,' she said, darting an evil glance towards her colleagues, 'but I assure you we have more appealing accommodation elsewhere in our little establishment.'

'We really should be on our way, madam,' Dauntless said, with a stiff bow. 'Although we are grateful for your kind offer.'

'Dauntless!' Cleo cried. 'Why are you so intent on making me miserable? I yearn for a night beneath a sound roof, without insects crawling in my hair and vermin nibbling my toes.' She rubbed the painful scratch on her face as she spoke.

Dauntless directed a glance at Cleo to convey it was unlikely she'd be free of such nuisances anywhere in this place.

Apanage glided forward and intervened. 'Please, you cannot be in such a rush. At least let me take you to the rooms I share with Master Dratslinger. You must be hungry. Let me feed you and provide soothing balm for the lady's wound. I am sure my lord will be most interested in meeting you. Variety is too infrequent in these parts.' She reached out and touched Dauntless's arm, apparently unaware of the shudder that convulsed his flesh. 'I can see you are distressed by the business conducted here, but I can put your mind at rest. You could be no further from danger than in our apartments above the stables. We do not allow the least whiff of spiritual curd or coagulum to cross our threshold. Come there with me now.'

'My companion is a paladin,' Cleo explained to Apanage. 'He is mistrustful of matters arcane and weird. You must forgive his apparent rude conduct.'

Together, the women led a vaguely protesting Dauntless from the house and out into the yard.

Outside, they dodged and ducked between the lines of drying instruments. A gentle breeze was investigating the cavities and strings of each device, which produced an eerie yet subtle cacophony; an accidental music. Cleo turned and craned her neck to take in the massive black pile rising behind them. The house seemed to watch her with a calculating eye. She smiled at its brick countenance. 'A house like this should have a name,' she said, 'but I saw no inscription at the front.'

'We call it The Haunt,' Apanage told her, with a shrug. 'It is simple, while precise.'

'The Haunt,' Cleo repeated. 'Yes, I like that.' In fact, she liked everything about the dismal house with its strange air of disuse. She liked the moss-covered cobbles of the yard, and appreciated the random design of the shaggy tufts of grass hanging down from the eaves of the ancient stable blocks ahead. Fan-tailed doves, which evidently roosted in the haylofts above the outbuildings, complemented the wind-music with a rhythmic cooing. Cleo could not understand why Dauntless was not similarly enchanted by the place. Once they'd come out of the house, he'd shaken himself free of the women and had now adopted a surly silence. He'd made no move to leave, however, and scuffed along behind them.

Apanage glided forward beside Cleo, her robe trailing along the ground. One of the monstrous hounds had followed her out of the main house and now pressed close to her legs. Apanage laid her hand upon its broad head. 'Drago has renovated sections of the loft area,' she said. 'It is where he

148

formulates his experiments and conceives designs for new instruments. Fole and the others help him complete his designs, and subsequently assist in invoking the spirits. Sometimes, I regret, there is a frightful racket, but occasionally the discordant melds into harmony and a new resonance is reached. It is at these times that the ghosts flock most cordially to our summons.'

'What do you do with the ghosts when you've got them?' Cleo asked.

'Generally, we bottle and sell them,' Apanage replied. 'Fole and Rattletrap go to the Crypticole Market – it is held infrequently and its location must of necessity change often, owing to its nature. All manner of exotic produce is bought and sold there. We barter the bottled ghosts for the things we need: provisions, new materials and suchlike.'

Dauntless was impelled to break his silence. 'Isn't bottling rather a cruel thing to do to a spirit?' His voice sounded gruff.

'Oh dear, you have awoken his sense of decency!' Cleo exclaimed.

Dauntless frowned at her. 'Well, after my travails upon this sad world are done, the last thing I would want is to view eternity from the inside of a bottle.'

Cleo shrugged.

'The spirits we invoke are never trapped for eternity,' Apanage said, smiling sweetly at Dauntless. 'At the most, they are confined only for a century or two. After that the bottle will undoubtedly have broken or some fool will have accidentally released the spirit. What are a couple of centuries in comparison with eternity? I imagine it must seem like the blink of an eye to a ghost, don't you?'

'I have no way of knowing,' Dauntless replied, pointedly.

Apanage's smile assumed a more acid cast. 'I am having difficulty appreciating why the fate of these ghosts, who were unknown to you in life, mean so much to you,' she said.

'Dauntless is a paladin,' Cleo reminded her, 'and therefore believes himself to be pious and true. His mission is to assure that everyone he comes across has a happy life. I presume he must also want them to have a happy death. Isn't that right, Dauntless?'

'Oh dear!' said Apanage.

Dauntless merely uttered a gibbering sound and abandoned the argument.

The living area and workrooms inhabited by Apanage and Drago Dratslinger were certainly more comfortable than those of the main house. A sprawling area of loft, still retaining a pleasant aroma of musty hay, had been transformed into a spacious apartment. Coloured rugs covered most of the ancient dusty floor and the walls were of bare brick, but hung with decorations constructed from skulls, feathers and tapestry, which Apanage announced she had contrived herself. Cleo exclaimed over the rooms and their appointments with delight. Dauntless remained sour of countenance.

After applying balm to Cleo's face. Apanage took them to Dratslinger's workroom. It was a small chamber, with a single round window. Light from outside fell meagrely into the room; illumination was chiefly provided by scores of candles which were stuck onto every available surface and adorned wrought-iron candelabra hanging from the ceiling.

Dratslinger looked up when Apanage led her guests into the room, an expression of irritation on his face. His workbench held an array of half-finished instruments and the air smelled heavily of varnish. In appearance he was a tall and forbidding character, whom Cleo thought at first was rather too grim of face. However, once his mistress had informed him they had guests, his dour features brightened up considerably. He was eager to show them the instrument he was constructing.

'Look at this,' he said to Cleo, and handed her the delicate instrument, which was a web of vanes and strings. Cleo ran her fingers over the strings and a frail sound came out. What ghost would this summon? she wondered. Could it call Inky's shade to me?

'You have a wistful look about you,' Drago said. 'I knew a girl once who had such a look. She had seen a massacre. She looked as you do, hungry for ghosts.'

Cleo put the instrument down. 'I am not looking for a ghost. I am looking for a man.'

While Drago and Apanage went into the small kitchen next to Drago's workroom to prepare a meal, Cleo and Dauntless sat in a cosy parlour where a log fire warmed the stones of an enormous chimney breast. The floor was covered in woven, woollen rugs coloured purple and blue. The visitors were joined by the monstrous dog who'd come from the main house: her name, Apanage had told them, was Fawn. Now, she lay panting by the fire, warming her flanks and apparently listening to the humans' conversation.

'These people are so funny,' Cleo hissed, smiling.

'Funny? Insane, more like,' Dauntless answered. Although his instincts could pick up no sense of immediate threat in these rooms, he still felt far from at ease.

'I like it here. It's cheering me up.'

'Cleo,' Dauntless said firmly, 'has it occurred to you that the business they're involved in is very dangerous? These people seem like halfwits unaware of the hazards. Although they're full of droll talk and amusing mannerisms, they are still necromancers. Don't forget that.'

Cleo pulled a sour face. 'You always have to spoil everything,' she said bitterly, and lapsed into silence, her buoyant mood crushed.

Dauntless watched Cleo carefully as she sat on the rugs beside the dog, stroking its short, dense fur. Sometimes she seemed such a gullible innocent, sometimes she was an infuriating harridan, sometimes a malevolent witch. Now, she appeared simply as she really was: a woman who was tired and drawn, and far from home. It was as if she'd let the qualities of courage and daring, which were only masks she wore to protect herself, slip from her face. She looked lost. Dauntless wondered what went on in her head. She talked of quests, of finding this absurd religious character, but he was unsure of her conviction. Relaxing before the fire in the warm room, he felt he could view Cleo Sinister with unprecedented clarity. He suspected that, inside herself, she was totally bewildered and perhaps despaired of ever finding Resenence Jeopardy. Over the years, Dauntless had become used to loneliness, but he suspected that for Cleo it was a new condition which she was having trouble getting used to. He knew that she thought him to be a stiff and unimaginative person. Sometimes her caprices made him behave as if he was. Sometimes, he really wanted to abandon her, yet looking at her now he could not imagine why he ever felt that way. She seemed so fragile; her bravado was an act. It was his duty to protect her.

'Cleo, have you asked yourself whether you are doing the right thing?' he asked.

'What do you mean, paladin?' Cleo said. 'I have escaped marriage to a poisoner who killed someone dear to me. I am driven to seek the man who sired that dear child. How could I ever question what I'm doing?'

Dauntless sighed. 'But the man is a dream. Didn't that character Fole virtually say so? "He is more an idea than a man." Somehow the feeling in my bones agrees with that statement.'

'I cannot believe he is not real,' Cleo said. 'How can an idea father a child?'

'He may be dead. The Ixmarites would not tolerate such a man for long, I am sure.'

'You don't *know* that.'

Cleo lay down beside the dog, resting her cheek on one hand. She continued to stroke the animal, but her movements had become less languid. 'I have to find him, Daunt. As to why, I cannot truly say. I can only remember listening as a child's body was carried down the stairs of my husband's house, and the way the moon came into my kitchen as I listened. I can taste the liquor in my throat, which I drank to still the pain in my heart.' She looked directly into Dauntless's eyes. 'I have never loved, Dauntless Javelot. Never.'

Dauntless had to drop his gaze. He felt embarrassed, yet cursed himself for feeling that way.

Cleo sighed. 'I wonder whether I ever can or ever will be able to love. All I am sure of is that in the face of that child, as he lay dead upon the couch, I saw something of my own future. Something which was destined to influence me. A sick obsession overcame me. I projected the child's face into his own vanished future and attempted to see the man he would have become, the man I intend to find.' She paused and shook her head. 'This makes no sense even to me. What hope have I of making sense to you?'

Dauntless reached out and touched her shoulder.

'And what will you do if you find your dream?'

She turned round and smiled at him, in a watery fashion, because her eyes were near to tears. 'I don't know,' she said. 'What can I possibly do?'

Dauntless shrugged and squeezed the flesh and bone of her shoulder through the worn cloth of her dress. 'Follow him, I suppose,' he said. 'Isn't that what he would expect and want?'

Cleo turned away and rubbed her nose, sniffling loudly. 'I have made this search my life,' she said. 'But if I'm honest, I must admit that I regret it now.'

Dauntless leaned towards her earnestly. 'Then return to Scaraby! I will take you there if I can.'

Cleo shook her head. 'No.' She frowned. 'I do not miss Wakelate at all. I barely remember him . . .' Then she sat upright on the rug, and the dog opened her jaws to let her tongue hang from her mouth. It looked as if she was grinning.

'Daunt,' Cleo said, 'I can never go backwards. I see that so clearly. It is as if the path is closed to me. Neither can I deviate from the path I have chosen. Is this a sacred thing, that I can only go forward? Is it a true dream, or am I deceiving myself? Will Resenence Jeopardy give me some kind of knowledge? Is that what I'm seeking?'

'You are clutching at down-seeds in an autumn wind,' Dauntless said.

Cleo sighed, and opened her mouth to speak, but at that moment the door to the parlour creaked and Drago Dratslinger and his mistress brought in the meal they had prepared for their guests, and the talk turned to that of wood and spirits, of how to trap a wandering soul.

151

After the meal, Drago told them that he had recently completed a new instrument and that at midnight he and his colleagues were planning to play together, in order to invoke some ghosts. Apanage's task during the operation was to bottle the spirits while they swayed deliriously to the music.

Dauntless looked far from happy that a ghost-bottling session would be conducted while he was staying at the house. He had been uncharacteristically relaxed and jovial during the meal, which had both surprised and pleased Cleo who'd anticipated having to apologise for him all the time. Now, his mouth clamped into the grim line she was familiar with. It presaged difficulty.

'Perhaps you and Cleo would like to participate in our little experiment,' Drago said to Dauntless.

'I think I must decline that offer,' he replied with strained laughter.

'What would we have to do?' Cleo asked. 'Is it dangerous?'

'Not at all,' Apanage replied. 'The ghosts are driven quite stupid by the music.'

Cleo's face assumed a calculating expression. 'Can you conjure *particular* ghosts?' she asked.

Dauntless glared at her. 'You are thinking of the child!' he said harshly. 'You are mad.'

Apanage and Drago looked surprised, although they said nothing.

'You are a cruel, heartless beast!' Cleo yelled at Dauntless. 'Have you no understanding?'

'I understand only that you intend to meddle in things you know nothing about,' he said.

The Dratslingers now looked embarrassed. 'There is no danger,' Apanage repeated lamely.

'I cannot participate in necromancy,' Dauntless said in a tone of voice indicating that he would not be persuaded otherwise. 'It is against the lore of True Valiance, and as your protector, Cleo, I must insist you don't take part yourself.'

'I'll do what I want!' Cleo spat, and turned earnestly to Apanage. 'Please, I'd like to join in.'

'No!' Dauntless cried, which prompted an angry wail from Cleo.

Apanage's measured voice interrupted them. 'We don't want to cause an argument,' she said, and turned to Dauntless. 'Look, neither of you have to participate in the conjurations if you don't want to. If Cleo wants to be present, she can simply watch from outside the circle. It is quite safe, I promise you. And sometimes the ghosts are so pretty to look at. It would be a shame if you missed seeing them while you are here.'

'Oh, Daunt, don't be such a bore! Let's go and see them,' Cleo said firmly.

'I can't,' he insisted.

Cleo pulled an aggrieved face. 'Then you must wait here,' she said. 'I'm not going to miss it.'

With glum weariness, Dauntless realised that, in order to keep to his quest, he would either have to restrain Cleo physically, which the Dratslingers might prevent, or else accompany her to whatever eldrich ceremony was about to be performed. Some instinct told him he should not let Cleo out of his sight.

'If I come with Cleo, you must allow me to draw my own circle of

152

protection,' he said to the Dratslingers. 'Would the symbols of Valiance interfere with your procedures?'

'That is very unlikely,' Drago said drily. 'Do whatever makes you feel happy.'

About an hour before midnight, Cleo and Javelot were taken across the yard and up a rickety stair on the outside of the main house. The moon was full, the sky clear; it seemed an ideal time for the manifestation of ghosts. Apanage led the company, carrying a large glass lantern; her pale, tiny shape made her appear like a spirit herself. Drago unlocked the door at the top of the stairs, and led the way into a high narrow storeroom. Using the lantern, Apanage lit candles set in sconces on the wall. The candlelight revealed that the room was packed with old iron bathtubs which were full of wooden rocking horses. Their painted eyes seemed to be full of a malignant resentment, as if they'd once been living horses that had been turned to wood by an enchantment. Cleo ran her hands through their manes and tails, which were made of real horsehair, exclaiming in wonder.

'An earlier experiment,' Drago explained, frowning at the tubs. He indicated at the end of the room. 'If you'd care to come this way.'

After scrambling along a series of dark and dusty corridors which were lit only by Apanage's lantern and the feeble light of the moon fighting its way through filthy skylights, Cleo and Dauntless were eventually led into a spacious attic. Malengin Fole, Flittern Rattletrap and Tumblejack, having used a stairway inside the house, were already there, preparing their equipment.

Under Dauntless's watchful eye, Cleo prowled around the attic, exploring. There was very little floorspace as every available area was covered with materials that might have been rubbish, or else discarded and half-completed instruments. Perhaps the jumble of wood, cloth, metal and coal were even items of importance for the ghost-bottlers' art. Complicated paraphernalia composed of long, delicate wooden struts and gossamer silk hung from the roof, as well as various instruments that seemed astronomical or alchemical in design.

Cleo wondered whether the rapid fluttering sensation she could feel in her chest was inspired by fear or excitement. In some ways, she shared Dauntless's misgivings about the forthcoming event. Cleo had never, to her knowledge, seen a ghost, although she had often sensed their presence in the shadowed, tragedy-haunted alleys of the Burrows. She had heard that the sight of some spirits was so terrifying, it could drive a person insane, never to recover their wits. The occupants of The Haunt were all rather peculiar. Was that conclusive evidence that insanity was the salary of meddling with necromancy? What would the ghosts look like? Perhaps there would be nothing to see, and their manifestation would simply be advertised by an intense cold in the room or a sparkling plasma. Perhaps they'd be malevolent, ugly and aggressive.

Cleo realised she was frightened, but if there was the slightest possibility she could catch sight of Inky's shade, she was prepared to risk whatever might happen over the next few hours. Wouldn't her presence in this house summon him here? The business with the children in the wood and the subsequent discovery of this place was too much of a coincidence, surely.

Cleo glanced at Dauntless. He was sitting near the far wall, as far from

153

everyone else as possible and, having cleared a space in the rubbish around him, had drawn a crude circle on the floor with a sliver of chalk he had begged from Apanage. Cleo noticed he had left the circle incomplete; she knew he expected her to join him within its protection before he sealed it. She was not sure whether she wanted to sit within the circle; it might seem more like a restriction than protection. She might not be able to run away should she feel the need.

Drago Dratslinger seemed to perceive her unease. He strode to her side and placed a paternal hand upon her shoulder. 'There is very little risk associated with our processes,' he said.

'What do ghosts look like?' Cleo asked hurriedly. 'Are they like floating bedsheets with eyes, or glowing skeletons, or banks of mist? I've never seen one.'

Drago shrugged. 'Ghosts assume many guises,' he replied. 'Sometimes, it is impossible to tell the entity is discarnate; they can look just like a living person.'

'But can they be horrible?' Cleo demanded. 'Can they be so hideous in appearance the mere sight of them drives you mad?'

Drago chuckled and with a sweeping gesture indicated his companions. 'Are any of my friends drooling and witless? No. That should be evidence enough.'

Cleo eyed the manic grin of Tumblejack, the cadaverous sway of Rattletrap and the imp-like perversity of Malengin's countenance with qualms. 'In truth, sir, it is very difficult for me to judge,' she said, 'owing to the fact I have never met any people like you before.'

Drago laughed indulgently. 'I take that as a compliment, whether it was meant or not. Now, I suggest you go and sit with your friend inside his circular drawing. I think he needs your company.' He propelled her to where Dauntless was sitting, in wide-eyed tension, upon a pile of sacking. He had now drawn several arcane symbols round the boundary of the circle in a shaky hand.

'Could we not take some part in your work?' Cleo asked impulsively, unsure whether or not she really wanted to.

Drago rubbed his jaw. 'Hmm, this circle might interfere with any melodious resonances, but I suppose I could give you a rattle each to shake.'

'Wouldn't that summon the ghosts directly to us?' Dauntless rasped. 'Wouldn't they stamp upon the chalk of my circle and break through the protective insinuati?' He shuddered and directed a baleful glance at Cleo.

Drago shook his head. 'No, the spirits are drawn, irresistibly to the acid strains of my six-vaned lamentarion. They jerk in surrender to the pulse of Fole's hammerskins, the tremulous yodelling of Tumblejack's voice. They gyrate in perplexity as Rattletrap confounds them with scales upon his chasmochord. The contribution of rattles would merely provide a backdrop.'

This information did not appear to inspire Dauntless with confidence. He spoke to Cleo in a prim voice. 'Despite these assurances, I am far from happy with the idea of arcana being present within the circle. Cleo, as you insist on being here, please indulge me by being content simply to watch the proceedings.'

Cleo sighed. 'Oh, very well.' She scuffed through the gap in the chalk circle and threw herself down on the sacks. Privately she was relieved Dauntless had refused to let Drago give them rattles. Sometimes she exasperated herself with the stupid ideas she had.

While Cleo and Dauntless tried to arrange themselves comfortably upon the sacking – which smelled malodorous in the extreme, as if the dogs had been using it as a toilet – Apanage busied herself with the ghost-bagging equipment. She employed a series of nets in her art that seemed so insubstantial, Cleo could not imagine how anything as ephemeral as a spirit – which surely lacked substance in a material sense – could be entrapped within them. The shimmering folds of the nets were arranged in a looping canopy above where the musicians played, and effected a startling, glowing paleness in the untidy gloom of the attic. Thin silk cords and silver chains hung down from the nets, which Apanage adjusting by pulling and tweaking them. With a final attunement, she nodded to Drago. 'All is prepared.'

Drago lifted a huge stringed instrument and slung it round his neck. To Cleo it appeared to consist of a jutting arrangement of elephant tusks, stretched membranes and taut strings. Drago applied his fingers to some of the strings and adjusted a turnkey on the end of one of the tusks. The instrument emitted a doleful exclamation, at which Drago winced and scowled, before making more improvements. Finally, satisfied with the tuning of the machine, he signalled to the others.

Malengin Fole stationed himself behind a series of upright drums. Some were as high as his chest, while others came only to his knees. He began to beat out a rhythm on them, using a pair of long bones – perhaps the thighs of an ox, Cleo thought – as drumsticks. Flittern Rattletrap hammered the strings of a low-throated stringed instrument, his feet stamping time. The sound was not unpleasing, and Cleo began to tap her foot. She noticed Dauntless tapping his fingers against his raised knees. Then Dratslinger's howling lamentation screamed out a few chords, Tumblejack began to give tongue like an animal in severe affliction, and the true invocation began.

The cacophony all around her was enough to numb Cleo's senses to any supernatural phenomena. She put her hands against her face, thinking, 'I shall stand this for only a few seconds more, then I shall leave.' She glanced at Dauntless beside her. He, too, seemed horribly distressed by the raucous din. His face had become very white, his eyes almost sunken in their sockets. 'Well, at least it is not affecting me that badly,' Cleo thought, and pinched him sharply on the arm to get his attention. It was as if he did not even feel it, for there was no response. 'I do believe this music, if music it is, is making him ill,' Cleo thought. 'Spineless creature!' Not for the first time, she began to wonder just how much protection the paladin afforded her. He had assured her he would be able to lead her out of the forest, but so far they seemed only to have become tangled further in its mazy pathways. Perhaps she should steal Contralto and gallop off alone to find the edge of Haling Heart.

As if summoned by the music, a pang assaulted her heart. She felt a renewed desire to seek out the prophet Resenence Jeopardy. She was wasting time here. Tumblejack's howling voice rose to a final ascension around her; her heart leapt in hope and renewed faith. She felt reborn. Cleo leapt to her feet within the circle, submitting to the ear-splitting climax of the music.

Then the manifestation occurred.

It began as a faint glowing cloudiness that hung in the rafters of the attic, which was exactly the sort of phenomenon Cleo's mother had described in the ghost stories she'd told her daughter as a child. It gradually descended and changed in colour, until it became a blue-grey mist seething over the

155

heads of the musicians, almost as if the sweat generated by their exertions was steaming in cold air above them. The air in the attic, however, was far from chill, and the sweat of men had never smelled so strange. 'It is like stale flowers,' Cleo thought, 'or musty sugar.' Her heart began to beat faster, her body filled with energy and she jumped up and down on the spot. Was it Inky coming to her? Was it? Dauntless grabbed hold of her skirt.

'Sit down!' he hissed. 'You will attract attention.'

Cleo ignored him. The mist slowly condensed into a whiter substance, which continued to swirl and roil beneath the nets.

'My, this one's a strapping brute!' Apanage yelled, adjusting the tension of her cords and chains.

'But not too strapping for your nets?' Cleo called back, straining to be heard above the din.

Apanage did not reply. She was darting back and forth across the clutter on the floor, tweaking the cords and muttering beneath her breath. The ghostly cloud hung beneath the nets, tumbling and churning in time to the pulsing rhythm of the music.

'Play harder!' Apanage urged. 'The apparition yet resists!'

Drago tore tortured notes from the lamentarion, Tumblejack pranced and roared, Flittern made his instrument groan and thunder, while Malengin was a blur behind the drums, chips of bone flying off his skin-hammers.

'Oh my,' Cleo thought, putting her hands over her ears. 'The roof will fall in, the rafters will crumble.' In fact, a shower of dust, cobwebs, bat droppings and lathe had indeed begun to splatter down upon the musicians and their small audience.

'Nearly!' Apanage cried, her sepulchral gown a flying mist about her scampering limbs, the spectral mist a flying tantrum above her.

The warm air in the attic suddenly turned cold. Cleo's breath steamed before her face. A shrill whistle could be discerned, audible above the scrape and screech of the music. It was a sound that seemed to plunge needles into the roots of Cleo's teeth and through the backs of her eyes. Beside her, Dauntless had become rigid, sounds of torment squeezing from between his clenched jaws. His eyes were round and staring, and a thin, bloodied foam seeped from the corners of his distorted lips.

'He's having a fit!' Cleo cried out, but nobody took any notice of her. Stretched out against the nets was the solidifying form of a ghost. Cleo could see clawing limbs and the suggestion of a malevolent face. She could not imagine how Apanage's flimsy nets could ever contain such a monster.

'Now!' Apanage cried, and the music reached a deafening crescendo, which made Cleo realise just why these people had elected to live out in the middle of nowhere. Neighbours would surely have objected in the strongest terms to such a racket. The creature writhed and grimaced in the most horrible manner, malignance imprinted in its every contour. It most definitely was not Inky.

'It deserves to be bottled,' Cleo thought. 'It's terrible. It deserves to be trapped!'

Suddenly, Apanage tweaked a sequence of cords and chains, and the net lifted in a momentary puff of silk before floating down to consume the apparition. Cleo thought at first that the net would only drift right through the spirit, but it swiftly formed a sparkling ball round its prey, and Apanage lost no time in drawing the opening of the silk tightly together. Then she produced a large green glass vase, which she attached to the closed orifice of

156

the net. As the music sobbed and sighed to a conclusion, she breathed upon both the bottle-neck and the opening of the net, gradually releasing the tension on the cords as she did so. Now that the music had died down, Cleo wanted to ask a hundred questions, but fear of somehow affecting the efficacy of the operation held her tongue. She sat down again beside Dauntless, casting him nervous glances. His fit seemed to have abated, but he appeared to be only half conscious.

'Daunt!' Cleo whispered, prodding him in the ribs. 'Are you all right?'

Slowly, he turned his head and blinked at her. His skin was damp and pallid. Cleo felt a stab of guilt for having forced him to suffer the ghost-bagging. Then she absolved herself by remembering it was he who'd insisted on accompanying her. She shook his arm. 'It's over now.' He did not appear reassured.

Impatiently, Cleo turned away from him and directed her attention back to Apanage's machinations. She was still breathing evenly upon both bottle and net, when suddenly the net expanded and then deflated with an abrupt whooshing sound. The outside of the green bottle became crusted with frost. Apanage deftly drew the bottle away from the empty net and inserted a magical cork into its neck. She held out her trophy to Cleo and Dauntless. 'Ha! held fast!' she said. 'Attracted by the warmth of human breath and the possibility of escape, and trapped by such.'

'Well done,' said Cleo feebly.

Apanage tossed the bottle into the air and caught it again. 'Catch!' she said. 'We have other morsels to bag tonight!' She threw the bottle over towards Cleo's lap. Cleo instinctively cringed, not wishing to have any contact with the vessel, but before the bottle reached its target, it exploded. Glass flew everywhere in a treacherous emerald shower. Cleo screamed and ducked. She felt an icy wind howl over her, a graveyard stench enter her throat, a chill finger touch her cheek. Dauntless whined and twisted his body beside her. She grabbed hold of him in terror. And then everything became still.

Dauntless panted in worldless terror. His limbs felt paralysed, his vision obscured. A child, a dreadful child! It had loomed over him out of the spectral mist, more horrible by far than the ghoul brats he and Cleo had encountered in the forest. As Apanage and her friends had cavorted about, gleefully operating their equipment, Dauntless had quailed beneath the smoky glance of the dead child's spirit. He knew then that the occupants of The Haunt were aware exactly of how dangerous their business was, and also that it was the thrill of that danger which sustained them. They were touched by it, in more than obvious ways. Awarded a vast and sudden insight, as if Valiance himself had spoken the words, Dauntless knew that the ghosts were more than mere spirits of dead people. They were all the thwarted ambitions, evil intentions, bitter memories, crushed hopes and suppressed lusts that had emanated from human hearts since life began, and which now invisibly thronged the air. The Dratslingers and their troupe plucked these impulses from the ether, made them coagulate, gave them form. What they sold in bottles was not a collection of spooks, but the wordless cry of frustration and despair that was the dark side of the collective human soul. Exactly what the contents of those bottles were used for by whoever bought them Dauntless dared not imagine.

And the child, who was a sad memory from Cleo's heart, had looked at him. It had pointed insubstantial fingers in his direction. It had grinned. It had spoken. 'You will die, Dauntless Javelot. You will die upon the road. Very soon.'

And then the nets had smothered it, the glass had contained it, but not for long. What flew forth from the shattered bottle was not the ghost memory of a child, but something else. Something that had grown from it. It was attached to Cleo and Dauntless in some way, and it was still with them.

SMOKE

One evening, Lucien asked Walterkin Anywhither if there were any shrines dedicated to Paradouze in the vicinity. Walterkin had smiled slyly and muttered something about 'foul weather faith'.

'Are you in need of spiritual sustenance, Lucien? Is your hope running thin?'

'I have never abandoned my trust in Paradouze,' Lucien said stiffly. 'At least not as a symbol. If I have abandoned the tenets of the Ixmarite Church, I have at least the imagination to fuel my own beliefs.'

'Aha! A reinterpretation of Ixmarity!'

Lucien took offence at Walterkin's amused expression. 'Not at all. My beliefs bear no resemblance whatsoever to Ixmarity. Now, is there a shrine nearby or not?'

The shrine was very old and of modest size, but was attended by a regular priest who kept the votive lamps burning and the incense cones replenished. Entering into the perfumed shadows, Lucien was transported back to his childhood. The incense of Paradouze had pervaded all his training: the scent of roses and aromatic gums. He asked Walterkin if he'd mind waiting at the door of the shrine, as he wanted to meditate alone for a few minutes.

Behind a curtain in the small lobby was a darkened chamber of worship, presided over by a statue of the god, who stood on one foot, the other leg raised with the foot tucked up behind, one arm held out in a Vibrancy gesture, the hand of the other pressed against the statue's lips in an entreaty for silence, both on an outer and inner level.

Lucien knelt before the statue. It was surrounded by a sea of candles. He found he had little to say to his god. Dare he ask for Paradouze's assistance in finding Jeopardy, when the god supposedly enjoined his vibrancers to chastity? Had Lucien not broken that rule a thousand times?

Did you watch me, Lord Paradouze? Lucien thought. Were you there?

Perhaps he should pray for release from his obsession.

And die before I see Jeopardy again? Could I ask for that?

He heard Walterkin cough beyond the curtain, and raised his eyes hurriedly to the stone countenance of the god. 'I could never believe in your

159

father's laws,' he murmured. 'To this day, I am convinced they are the laws of men, not gods.' He sighed. What point was there in repeating aloud thoughts he had directed to Paradouze since the day he'd left the House of Mandru? He did not feel guilt or remorse for anything he'd done in his life, so why kneel here now, paying lip service to a creed he'd effectively abandoned? The Paradouze of his heart lived only in his own mind. There was no point trying to communicate with Him in a shrine built by other men.

Outside, Walterkin was waiting to be facetious. 'Were your devotions fulfilling?' he chirped.

Lucien ignored the question. 'Take me to Hartshorn Park,' he said. 'There is more to tell.'

At the estate of Salaquin Mandru, the harvest was over, the grapes trodden and fermenting successfully in enormous vats which were lodged in barns behind the house. The olive and walnut trees had been stripped of their fruit. The onion terraces lay empty. Mellow autumn was winding down into one of the mild and innocuous winters common to southern Gleberune. The kitchens of the House of Mandru were busy with the processes of bottling and pickling. Tempting odours filled the air from dawn till dusk.

Lucien's performance with Resenence Jeopardy of the Denouncement of Atavenom had been greeted with acclaim and delight by Mandru and the four noble guests who had been in residence at the time. Sabraxis had already watched the piece and given her approbation. She also ordered new costumes to be run up, so that older garments from the wardrobe would not have to be used.

On the evening of the performance, Lucien's limbs were rubbed with oil and sprinkled with sparkling dust. As Amber had suggested, he was equipped with an elaborate wig, decorated with brightly coloured clay serpents, and his face was painted to resemble the traditional harlot's face of Atavenom. After these ministrations, as senseless with intoxicated fear as a virgin facing his first lover, he was virtually carried by his dressers into the splendid hall where Mandru was entertaining. The low tables had been cleared of dishes, fresh oil was burning in the censers and servants glided smoothly and unobtrusively among the guests' couches dispensing wine. Even Nehushtah was in attendance, which was unusual. Some suspected she must harbour a fancy for one of the guests, for she generally avoided Mandru's friends.

Once he stepped onto the polished floor where he would perform, Lucien's nervousness abated. Now, the Vibrancy was all that mattered. Resenence Jeopardy appeared across the hall, his skin darkened to symbolise Ixmar's displeasure, his long hair waxed into ringlets. His face had been painted into a snarl. It had been agreed that they would perform the Vibrancy to the accompaniment of drums only, because Lucien still felt uncomfortable having the din of musical instruments cluttering up his head while he performed.

That night, Jeopardy moved with the unconscious litheness of a puma. As Ixmar, he conjured forth his female element, played by Lucien. They slid along each other's bodies, their skin gleaming in the dim light of the floor lamps. To Lucien, even though he had run through the presentation with Jeopardy so many times, it was as if he was performing it for the first time. He felt more aware of his partner, his body attuned to the symbolic undercurrents of the piece. He felt as if his soul was tearing.

At the completion of the Vibrancy, there had been resounding applause. Mandru himself had stood up and taken the floor in order to introduce the performers to his guests. He took Lucien's hand and said, 'My newest acquisition! As you will have noticed, he is quite a find!'

Lucien, panting and shaking on his feet, had wanted to weep with joy. Even the most audacious of his secret fantasies had not fulfilled him as much. Mandru insisted that Lucien should sit on the dais beside himself and his wife. Nehushtah eyed Lucien narrowly as he sank down with gracious ease onto a cushion by her couch.

'You're good,' she said. 'How come I have not seen you before?'

'Thank you, my lady,' Lucien had replied. He did not know what else to say.

Nehushtah nodded. 'You will come to my rooms some time,' she announced. 'Yes.'

'I am honoured,' Lucien said. He realised he had just been promoted.

The compliments were sweet, but Lucien would gladly have escaped the adoring company if only he could have talked to Resenence Jeopardy about their performance. Jeopardy had been summoned to the couch of one of the guests, and was now engaged in conversation. He did not look in Lucien's direction once. Lucien's heart, however, was so full of the golden warmth of success, he was quite happy to wait. He watched Jeopardy with patience, embraced by the certainty that their friendship was strongly forged. Soon, the party would end and the guests would depart to their chambers. Soon, the Ixmaritians would be dismissed. Then, Lucien and Jeopardy would talk again. They would touch.

In the event, Jeopardy left the hall before anyone else, but by that time Lucien had consumed several large goblets of opiated wine, so was deliriously beyond caring. He ended up staggering to his room, with a few other Ixmaritians, just before dawn, where he collapsed onto his bed, without removing his wig or his make-up. Nothing could mar his happiness, not even the excruciating headache he was destined to wake up with in the morning.

The few days that followed were a giddy, ecstatically happy time for Lucien. He was congratulated daily for his talents, and discovered that everyone suddenly wanted to know him. He was invited to small gatherings in people's chambers in the evenings, when the Ixmaritians liked to drink together, share food and gossip. His free time, when once he used to sit alone daydreaming in the small shrine of Paradouze in the gardens, was no longer his own. He had feared the other Ixmaritians might resent his rise in status, but the opposite seemed to be the case. One thing, however, blighted Lucien's pleasure. From the moment when their performance had ended, Jeopardy just seemed to fade out of his life. Had Azmaveth's magic faded so quickly? They never seemed to get the chance to talk together alone.

The events of that delirious night became history, and although Lucien lost none of the status he'd earned, new presentations and episodes of domestic drama occupied the tongues and attentions of the household. Jeopardy had not asked Lucien to work on a new piece with him, and Lucien had once again resorted to practising his movements alone. Even though he continued to visit the exercise court before breakfast, he never found Jeopardy there. Was Jeopardy avoiding him? Surely not. Their performance had been perfect. Why then hadn't Jeopardy suggested they should attempt some other, perhaps more ambitious piece?

Lucien felt wary of approaching the subject himself, for fear of appearing importunate or too eager. He could not understand how his relationship with Jeopardy could have changed overnight, especially as Azmaveth had intimated Lucien's feelings were returned. As they worked together, Lucien had felt as if Jeopardy was a friend. Now, he enjoyed no more intimacy with the man than the exchange of brief greetings when their paths accidentally crossed in some corner of the house. It also appeared that Jeopardy's relationship with Amber had mended, even though she was still working with Marist, because Amber made it known she and Jeopardy were spending every evening together, shut away in Jeopardy's room. Lucien, continually plagued by dreams of his erstwhile partner, tortured by thoughts of Jeopardy directing all his attention towards someone else, chided Azmaveth that her magic had been weak and of short duration.

'What more did you want?' she'd responded waspishly. 'I seem to recall you spoke of platonic friendship and an amiable working relationship. Isn't that what you achieved?'

'I am not working with Jeopardy now,' Lucien said.

Azmaveth shrugged. 'You made no overtures to him once the Denouncement was performed. If anything, you seemed to distance yourself from him. He probably believes you wish to address yourself to your own presentations now.'

'What do you mean, I distanced myself from him?' Lucien snapped. 'He made no overtures to me either!'

Azmaveth seemed bored by the matter. 'So you have an impasse,' she replied. 'That is not the fault of my magic, but the reticence of your tongue. Approach Jeopardy now and suggest a new collaboration.'

Lucien shrank from such action; he feared rebuff.

The Ixmaritians were working on light-hearted pieces for the forthcoming midwinter festival, which commemorated Ixmar's marriage to his redoubtable wife, Aufiria. Salaquin and Nehushtah were leaving home for a month or so, on a rare trip abroad together. Nehushtah claimed she was pining for her children, and had insisted that her husband should accompany her on a visit to the land of Ixibatae, where their son and daughter were being educated in the house of Nehushtah's parents. Nehushtah never travelled light, and a huge entourage, comprising servants, Ixmaritians and favourites from home, would be in attendance during the journey and for the duration of her stay in Ixibatae.

In the absence of the master and his wife, the running of Mandru's house would be placed in the hands of his housekeeper, Lucrezia Tine. Lucien had had few dealings with this formidable female, but feared her regime, for she seemed a sharp and unbending creature. All his friends, however, assured him that once Mandru's support had been physically withdrawn from the house, Lucrezia's obsession with detail and trivia would make her an easy target for ridicule. From previous experience, the household staff had learned Lucrezia did not possess the authority to correct any behaviour she considered to be insubordinate. Servants and Ixmaritians alike looked forward to the Mandrus' absence with glee. The vibrancers were perhaps alone in not feeling so optimistic. After all, they fell under the management of Sabraxis, who was not easily fooled and retaliated against sloth with zeal and swiftness.

On the day when the Mandrus' entourage made ready to leave, the entire household gathered in the long sloping courtyard of the house in order to utter prayers that would ensure the travellers enjoyed a safe journey, free from the nuisances of bad weather, cutthroats and disease. Ten carriages would carry the party and their luggage to Ixibatae. Passage would be taken, by sea, from the harbour at Shanariah.

Lucien had suffered a particularly restless night, and slouched down to the yard alone, shunning even the company of Ketura, Sydel and Azmaveth. The dreams that had assailed him had been blissful. He and Jeopardy had conversed freely in sunlight, close to one another but not touching, their minds in perfect accord. Lucien had awoken to reality, feeling the wrench of loss as sorely as someone suffering a bereavement. Now, he was surrounded by annoying noise and bustle, which was a situation greatly at odds with his melancholy mood. A few vibrancers were performing a high-kicking piece – When Paradouze Sailed the Heavenly Sea – and several groups of people were chanting different prayers. Men loaded cases and chests onto the backs of the carriages, and the horses, made nervous by the clamour and activity, were backed into their traces. Lucien leaned against the wall of the laundry and looked on glumly. He felt utterly apart from the event, as if he were a ghost, invisible. The gestures he saw and the remarks he heard around him meant nothing; as impenetrable as the clucking of hens. He felt faintly sick.

Amber Epipheny was among the Ixmaritians whom the Mandrus had elected to take with them to the villa of Nehushtah's parents. Lucien saw her flounce down the steps from the upper house, wearing a long, flowing coat of black velvet edged with fluffy purple feathers. Her hair looked very red. Two companions held her arms, and all three of them were singing a repetitive travelling benison, pausing only to giggle and pull faces at one another. A household official holding a noteboard directed Amber and her friends to one of the carriages. Those who were staying behind called out to her; wishes of good luck, cries of envy, requests for presents. Amber smiled and waved at everyone as she was helped into her carriage. Then, once all were aboard, she leaned out of the window to scan the crowd, as if searching for someone. Lucien knew who she was looking for. He also knew her search would be unproductive. Resenence Jeopardy was not in the yard. Lucien had already examined every face in order to determine that. After a while, Amber pulled a small frown and ducked back inside the carriage.

Lucien leaned against the wall between the wash-house and one of the kitchens. He hugged the shadows to him. Soon, I must surely die, he thought, mulling over his dream. He hugged his arms and for a moment imagined it was Jeopardy who held him. The illusion was too painful. He dismissed it.

Once all their party were safely stowed inside their respective carriages, Nehushtah and Mandru made their entrance into the yard. Nehushtah was muffled in sable furs, her black hair arranged in coils atop her head and confined with jet beads. Mandru, who intended to ride ahead of the carriages with his valet, once the house was out of sight, was dressed plainly in green and tan breeches, boots and a grey overcoat. His only concession to vanity was a black peaked hat, decorated with long viridian feathers and rosettes. After a brief speech, in which he bade farewell to his household and instructed them to apply themselves diligently to their duties during his absence, he conducted Nehushtah into the leading carriage and climbed in behind her. Mandru was an impatient man, he hated to be kept waiting.

163

The carriages began to move forward instantly, the creaking of the wheels muttering promises of the strange lands to come. Feeling lonely and sorry for himself, Lucien wished he was going with them. There would be new sights to experience, new sounds, new smells. There would be distance. The household surged forward to follow the procession to the gates. Lucien saw a white hand waving from the back of one of the carriages. He saw smiling faces in shadow. He saw a glint of red hair.

Lucien raised a hand in half-hearted farewell. His limbs felt heavy. People surged past him, flowed away from him, running, skipping towards the gates. Presently, the last of the carriages was swallowed up by the shadow of the gateway. People tried to run out onto the steeply sloping road, but the gateway guards pushed them back. Pigeons lifted in a whirring, crooing flock from the walls of the yard.

'Goodbye,' Lucien said aloud in a forlorn voice.

He did not hear footsteps approaching in the narrow alley behind him. His first awareness of someone being near was when he was gripped round the waist by a pair of arms. He said, 'Azmaveth!' for the arms felt strong. Ketura and Sydel were more delicate. The moment he had spoken, however, he knew it was not Azmaveth. The arms were male. He froze. He felt breath in his hair. He could not speak.

'Lucien . . .'

It did not sound like Jeopardy's voice, but he knew it was.

'You missed them,' Lucien said. His voice sounded appallingly squeaky in his ears.

Jeopardy ignored the remark. His words came out in a tumble, as if he had to speak urgently, as if there was too little time in which to voice his thoughts. 'You are unique, do you know that? There is no one in the world like you. No one. You are pure spirit. You wear your flesh like a temporary garment, yet it fits you so well.'

Lucien tried to wriggle away. Jeopardy had held him a hundred times when they had practised together, yet he knew this was different. There was a faint reek of tamara weed in the air; Jeopardy had been smoking.

'People will see,' Lucien hissed. But nobody was looking. Everyone was still crammed into the gateway, peering out at the steep road that was dappled with the long winter shadows of poplar trees, and clouded with dust from the carriages' passage. Jeopardy leaned forward and put his mouth against Lucien's neck.

'Lucien, when I look at you, I feel safe, I can taste your healing properties. I need to be healed.'

'Of what?' Lucien couldn't help saying. The first thought that came to him was of Amber.

'The future,' Jeopardy said. He nipped Lucien's neck.

'Don't do that!' Lucien succeeded in pulling out of Jeopardy's hold. He took a single pace forward and rubbed his neck.

'Look at me!' Jeopardy ordered.

Lucien shook his head, hugged himself. 'No.'

'Are you afraid of me?' Jeopardy's voice held a taint of mockery.

Lucien shivered. 'No.'

Jeopardy crept forward and put his hands on Lucien's shoulders. 'Do you dislike me, then?'

'No, of course not.'

'Then why won't you look at me?'

164

Lucien sighed. He could say nothing but the truth. 'Because your eyes will swallow me whole.' He wanted to blurt out something about the dreams. He wanted to ask questions, reveal further truths, but it was as if his tongue was bound. He felt awkward, stupid.

'Don't you want to be swallowed by my eyes?' Jeopardy whispered. 'Isn't that something we've both dreamed of.' The words he used could have been metaphorical, nothing more. Lucien dared not think it was anything more.

'Why are you doing this?' Lucien asked. 'We've barely spoken for two weeks. I've been down to the exercise court every morning, but you are never there.'

Jeopardy sighed and leaned his head against Lucien's hair. 'I had to think,' he said. 'There are consequences for the way I feel. Now, I have made up my mind, and there is no point in dissembling. We have to move to the next performance.'

Lucien's heart leapt. 'Another Vibrancy? Which one?' He offered a swift, silent prayer of thanks to Azmaveth.

Jeopardy chuckled. 'I was not referring to the Vibrancy,' he said. 'I was referring to our friendship. You know that it has to move on. The Denouncement was an agony. It felt as if I was expelling half of myself. Now, I want it back.'

'I don't know what you mean,' Lucien said. He was suddenly filled with dread. It was as if he'd been playing with a dangerous animal that had seemed so sweet and tame, but which had now turned on him with ferocity.

'You do know,' Jeopardy replied. 'You will have heard, at least. They try to geld you in Por Tanssie, but thankfully they do not use a knife. Wake up to me, Lucien. I know you've been thinking of it.'

Lucien could not answer.

Jeopardy sighed. He was clearly trying to be patient, but it was not a quality he possessed. 'Look, you must realise that some things are simply meant to be. Obstinacy and pretended coyness will only serve to delay the inevitable.'

Lucien cringed. He heard Azmaveth's voice in his head, and she sounded harsh: 'Well, what else did you want, Lucien?' Why couldn't he speak now, defend himself? Why couldn't he say, 'Yes, this is what I want?' He felt dumb and mindless. How could Jeopardy want him?

Jeopardy squeezed his shoulders. 'I'm sorry, I'm too blunt, perhaps. I have to talk to you, Lucien. I feel that is your function in my life, an important function. Don't ask me why. But first we have to address the appetites that make us human.'

Lucien shuddered. He found his voice. 'What you are implying is against the code of Paradouze.' It sounded hatefully prim and smug, even to his own ears.

Jeopardy made a disparaging sound. 'You mean it is against the code you've been indoctrinated with. Face it, Lucien, you are ashamed of your body and its desires, but that's only because you are unfamiliar with both.'

Lucien turned round. 'How many times have you said this? Does Amber leave here regularly?' The mention of human appetites was shocking. In his fantasies, Lucien had never envisaged Resenence was even capable of being so direct.

'I have already told you that you are unique,' Jeopardy said and, taking Lucien's face in both of his hands, kissed him on the mouth. They staggered back into the shadows of the alley, Jeopardy pushing Lucien hard against the wall. To Lucien, it was like being drowned, being forcibly held under water. He wanted air, but he also wanted to suffocate. He had fantasised a thousand times about how he and Jeopardy might become close, but he had never imagined anything like this. It felt brutal and obscene, this panting and mouthing and clawing at flesh. It was as if Atavenom had really been invoked. Now, she demanded her sacrifice.

Jeopardy gasped and jerked his head backwards, breathing hard.

'Do not let go of me!' Lucien cried.

'I won't,' Jeopardy replied and pulled him close with a soft cry of affection. 'I'll never let you go.'

Shortly, they crept down the alley to a door that led into the house.

'Did anyone see us?' Lucien asked.

Jeopardy shook his head. 'No. Come.' He held out his hand. Lucien took it.

Using the less frequented stairways and corridors, Jeopardy led Lucien to his private chamber. Here, his ardour seemed to cool a little. His approach became less direct, more subtle. Lucien sat down on the end of Jeopardy's bed and looked around himself. The chamber was like any other occupied by the Ixmaritians; there was little sign of Jeopardy's personality, no embellishments or decorations that might give away some clue to his character. The only indication of the way his mind worked was that he had set an earthenware flagon of wine to cool in a bowl of iced water. Obviously, he hadn't doubted Lucien would accompany him here. Lucien accepted the cup of wine which Jeopardy gave to him. He laughed nervously.

'What are you going to do to me?' he asked. The enquiry was crass, and Lucien regretted it the moment he'd voiced it, but he could think of nothing else to say.

Jeopardy seemed not to have heard the question. He sat down in a chair some distance away, crossed his legs. 'Lucien, I am changing,' he said. His face was creased into a frown.

'Changing in what way?' Lucien asked. He experienced a sudden mixture of relief and dread that Jeopardy would not touch him again.

Jeopardy leaned forward in his seat, and gestured emphatically with outstretched fingers. 'There is a voice trying to speak to me, but it's not loud enough. Not yet.'

'A voice?' Lucien hesitated. 'What kind of voice?'

Jeopardy made an angry sound and leaned back again. 'You would not understand. Still . . .' He rubbed his face. 'I need a catalyst. I believe you are part of it.'

Lucien shrugged awkwardly. 'If I can help . . .' he began weakly.

'You can't help. I have to help myself,' Jeopardy said. He stared at Lucien with cold eyes. 'You are beginning to unfold like a flower. You will be beautiful.'

'You are beautiful now,' Lucien blurted.

Jeopardy made an impatient gesture and grimaced. 'No, I don't want to hear that. I don't want flattery.'

'I wasn't—'

'Hush!' Jeopardy stood up. He sauntered over to where Lucien sat and put one hand beneath Lucien's chin, forcing his head up. 'Such innocence! Am I right to defame it?' He shook his head. 'No, it is an elixir, nothing more. I am going to use you, Lucien, do you realise that? But I shall teach you too.'

Lucien tried to swallow, which was difficult with his head tilted backwards. Jeopardy leaned forward to kiss him again, causing him to drop the clay cup he was holding in numb fingers. Wine spilled over the floor, but Jeopardy took no notice other than to kick the cup away. He assumed the role of the lover and began to perform it faultlessly. Lucien dared not let himself be fooled, but he did allow himself to pretend.

Jeopardy was neither impatient nor aggressive in his attentions. He seemed sensitive to Lucien's inexperience and uncertainty, and did not attempt to push him beyond the limit of what he felt comfortable with. 'In Por Tanssie, Caringolat and the others want to deny us this,' Lucien said. 'Do they deny it to themselves, do you think?' It was the first time such a thought had occurred to him.

Jeopardy shrugged. 'I neither know nor care. Neither should you. It's behind you.' He smiled. 'Mind you, I remember the case of Mercante, who came here from Por Tanssie a year or so ago. Once the effect of the drugs they'd used on him had worn off, he was plagued by a constant need to relieve himself – in a sexual sense. Being of a more pious, perhaps less intelligent, nature than yourself, he denied himself. It resulted in him attempting to rape one of the girls, who beat him senseless. Everyone laughed about it. Thought it was a joke.' He frowned. 'Then the poor sot hanged himself. He couldn't cope. You're lucky, Luce. You're not like that. I recognised it in you the moment I saw you. I knew the veneer of that false piety was thin.'

Lucien had not been aware of that himself, and doubted its veracity. 'I do have faith in Paradouze,' he said.

Jeopardy snorted. 'Oh? In that case why are you lying here on my bed?'

Lucien wriggled uncomfortably. 'This does not seem . . . it does not seem wrong to me. I can't explain.' He sighed. 'I know I've betrayed my faith a dozen times since I've been here.'

'In what way?' Jeopardy asked. He was grinning, leaning over Lucien and stroking his chest.

Lucien nearly mentioned the incident with Azmaveth, but stopped himself in time. 'Well, I've imbibed intoxicating substances, for a start. I haven't been as assiduous in my worship as I used to be. I've used the names of Ixmar and his family in oaths. Now . . .' He smiled weakly. 'Now, I'm here, with you.'

'Heinous crimes, all of them!' Jeopardy declared. 'Soon you will no doubt be committing rape and murder!'

'Don't laugh at me,' Lucien said. 'I was being honest with you.'

In response, Jeopardy leapt up from the bed and took a small hand mirror from the top of his chest of drawers. He lay down again, and forced Lucien to look into the glass. 'What do you see?'

Lucien closed his eyes, tried to turn away. He felt dazed, full of unshed tears. 'Something insubstantial,' he said. 'I've had no life. It shows.'

Jeopardy laughed. 'You will become great. You are special. You have talents. Pain will make them manifest.'

'You can't foretell the future,' Lucien said.

'Can't I?' Jeopardy said, with a grin.

Lucien stared at him and sighed. 'I think you would like other people to think you can.'

Jeopardy laughed. 'How harshly you judge me,' he said. 'You shape me into a selfish creature.'

167

Lucien sat up and put his head into his hands. He suddenly felt wretched. 'That is because you are a selfish creature,' he said. He wanted affection from Jeopardy now. He wanted to be looked at in adoration. Instead, it was as if they'd never touched, or if their intimacy had meant nothing more to Jeopardy than when they'd danced together.

'Mmm,' Jeopardy murmured, as if considering Lucien's remark. 'That is an interesting observation, though entirely false.'

'It is true,' Lucien said, turning round. 'I think you are self-obsessed.'

Jeopardy was lying on his back with his arms behind his head. He looked sated and content. 'You puzzle me,' he said. 'I sincerely thought you were a shy and timid soul, yet now you speak your mind with aplomb. Astounding. I am rarely wrong.' Lucien knew that, in some way, his remarks had pleased Jeopardy. He had unwittingly passed a test.

During the weeks that followed, Lucien went to Jeopardy's room whenever he got the chance, mentioning nothing to his friends about where he went or what he was doing. With so many of the household absent, he was rarely questioned about his movements. A lethargy seemed to have fallen over the house. It seemed empty.

One day, Jeopardy said to Lucien, 'You have never really questioned your faith, have you.' It was not an enquiry.

'How can I question what simply is?' Lucien responded. 'Paradouze has always been a part of my life.'

Jeopardy made an exasperated sound. 'I'm not talking about Paradouze, pretty concoction though He is! I'm talking about the whole concept of Ixmarity. Why can't people see it for what it is?'

'Isn't it the truth?' Lucien asked warily, expecting the consequent outburst.

'Truth? Pah! It's a tool of control which the Glebes brought with them from the south. A senseless set of rules about how to live your life. But if you examine them carefully, they are empty. The only rule is that the Church must continue to bleed the country, or rather the people, of riches. The laws might well have been made up by a committee of bored priests one afternoon when they had nothing better to do.' He mimicked smug, ancient voices.

' "Let's make everyone spend stupid amounts of money on sacred oils." '

' "I know, here's a good one: if you're a rich man, you can't sleep in the same room as your wife." '

' "But we mustn't let people have any other beliefs. We must make them think such things are wicked. I know, let's invent a few more gods, relatives of Ixmar, so everyone can be satisfied." '

Lucien laughed at this imaginary conversation, although Jeopardy's words made him feel uncomfortable. 'So, who made us up?' he said, trying to join in with the spirit of what he hoped was a game. 'Who invented the Ixmaritians?'

'Some perverted ghoul,' Jeopardy answered bitterly. 'What compelled our mindless parents to obey them? Do I want this for my life? No. I don't believe in any of it.'

'Res, don't!' Lucien could almost feel the clouds of Ixmar's wrath forming above the house. It was bad enough when Azmaveth came out with blasphemous remarks, but this was worse because of Lucien's feelings for Jeopardy.

'Are you afraid, Luce?' Jeopardy laughed. 'Listen, Ixmar has no power to hurt you, not if you don't believe in Him. He was only invented by people. Ixmar is a dead rat's testicle, Ixmar eats dead babies! See, has anything struck me down?'

'Your punishment will come after you're dead.'

'I don't think so. I think it's as simple to design your own afterlife as it is your own gods. Whatever you believe in exists. And if that's Ixmar and his charming relatives, more fool you.'

'Res, you mustn't . . .' Lucien felt near to tears. It was as if Jeopardy was sentencing himself to death.

'Tell me, why do you believe in it all? Why? What proof have you that any of it is real?' Before Lucien could answer, he continued, 'Because you were brought up in Por Tanssie, dedicated to a god? Because of the Books of Paradouze, which were written, incidentally, by men? Lucien, take the freedom. Cut yourself loose from the restrictions of those crazy ideas. It's as simple as opening your eyes.'

'The laws of Ixmar are good laws,' Lucien said in a small voice. 'They guide people to live good lives.'

Jeopardy laughed loudly. 'Good lives? Burning heretics is good, is it? Spending more money than you can afford on oils and holy artefacts is good? Don't be stupid!'

'I don't mean that. Paradouze – Ixmar – tells us to be pure in spirit, and noble. Not to pollute our selves or our thoughts. To be spiritual.'

'To be mindless,' Jeopardy amended. 'So we cause no trouble for the Church, which continues to reap the benefits. They make us fear punishment in the afterlife – the door of the Celestial Mansion slammed in our faces – so we'll do as they tell us while we're alive. It's all rubbish!'

'How do you know that? Surely your beliefs are as much an act of faith as . . . mine?'

Jeopardy hesitated. He had no immediate answer. 'If neither of us can be proved right, then neither of us can be proved wrong, which in my opinion means we're both right. Happily, I have a more sensible belief system than you.' He grinned. 'But I'm generous, I'll share it. When you have the sense to join me.'

Spending so much time in Jeopardy's presence, surrendering his body to Jeopardy's touch, Lucien fell deeply in love. However, these sentiments made him feel angry rather than joyful. As he became more familiar with Jeopardy's personality, he realised his first impressions had been quite accurate. Jeopardy's inability to sense other people's feelings and needs bordered on being a disorder of character. When he wasn't expounding his heretical philosophies, he talked continually about himself and how he'd taken the Vibrancy into new, more challenging, realms. Whenever Lucien tried to talk about his own feelings, or about his past, Jeopardy simply yawned, or interrupted him in the middle of a sentence. Lucien realised it was pointless to complain. Jeopardy would simply look blank and fail to understand what he'd done wrong.

What do I love about him? Lucien wondered, daily. There is nothing in him to love, other than his physical beauty. For a while, he told himself his obsession was based purely upon lust, but even in his darkest moments, he knew this was a lie. Within Resenence Jeopardy was an elusive quality that was irresistible. He was utterly fascinating, even at his most exasperating. There was a seed of great potential within him, an indefinable presence that reeked of magic. Jeopardy, Lucien was quite sure, could make things happen. It was no coincidence that no one had noticed how much time they spent together.

'Have you ever wondered what is beyond this place, Lucien?' Jeopardy was lying flat on his back on his bed, in the yellow afternoon. Two plumes of smoke seeped lazily from his nostrils.

Lucien was lying on a woollen rug at the foot of the bed, examining some notes Jeopardy had made concerning a new Vibrancy he was working on. He rolled over on the rug, letting the sunlight stripe him with shadow from the window blinds. 'Beyond this place, the hill slopes down towards the city. The city is very white, like a blind eye or a monstrous child's tooth.' Being with Jeopardy had affected him in more ways than one. At one time, he'd never have spoken like this. Even as he uttered the words, he was aware that, to a degree, he was speaking with Jeopardy's voice. 'Above us, the vineyards rustle towards the sky. I listen to them at night. Some say that vine-hewkins walk between the frames. They can grant you a wish or a curse. I have asked for wishes.'

'Haven't you just!' Jeopardy laughed. His laughter, as always, was private. 'However, I was referring to time rather than space in this instance. You will not be here in the House of Mandru for ever, Lucien. Neither of us will.'

'I have never thought of it,' Lucien said. He sat up and grasped his knees.

'I have.' Jeopardy sat up more slowly. 'I am still young,' he said, 'but I will not accept the authority of others for much longer.'

'You cannot run away,' Lucien said hurriedly. 'They will fetch you back, punish you, sell you.'

Jeopardy took no notice. 'I intend to take on a mantle of insanity,' he announced. 'That will be my escape, or at least the beginning of it.'

'You are already mad!' Lucien said with a laugh, but Jeopardy's words worried him.

'They cannot keep me here,' Jeopardy said, nodding to himself. 'My destiny lies in other places, another life.'

'You mustn't go!' Lucien knew that Jeopardy either could not, or would not, hear his words. At that moment, Jeopardy was alone in his room, speaking his thoughts aloud.

'I look forward to the day of betrayal,' he went on, in a faint voice.

'What are you talking about?' Lucien asked. 'Are you practising madness already?'

Jeopardy continued to ignore him. His eyes had become unfocused, his mouth slack. 'The pain will release me.'

Lucien wriggled uncomfortably on the rug. 'You are too concerned with pain, Res,' he said, and picked up the sheaf of papers lying on the floor. 'This promises to be a brilliant piece.' He waved the papers.

Jeopardy continued to stare blankly ahead. He drew in his breath sharply and winced. 'I shall be wounded,' he said, 'several times.'

'Res, stop this!' Lucien cried. 'What are you doing?'

Jeopardy seemed to come back to reality. He blinked at Lucien, almost in perplexity, as if he'd forgotten who he was. 'Telling you things,' he said frostily. 'Things that will happen.'

'Why think of the future?' Lucien said. 'You could make bad things happen.'

Jeopardy shrugged. 'You don't understand. I have little choice. The future haunts me.'

Lucien smiled weakly. 'Future ghosts?'

Jeopardy nodded, and briefly narrowed his eyes. 'Yes,' he said.

'So tell me my future, then,' Lucien said.

Jeopardy glanced at him coldly. 'I have already told you enough.' He hesitated. 'One thing I have not told, which I will relate now, is that our lives will diverge. But one day we shall meet again.'

'When will we part?' Lucien demanded sharply. 'When Mandru returns?' He dared not speak Amber's name.

Jeopardy smiled gently and shook his head. 'It's not how you think,' he said. 'Neither of us will live in this house for long.'

'The world's too big for us out there,' Lucien said, attempting to make light of the horrifying thought. 'I wouldn't know how to survive in it, I'm sure. All I can do is dance.'

'Rubbish!' Jeopardy said. 'The world is an infinity of different realities. Some people live in a kind of fairyland, and it is real to them. They create their own myths and live them. Others live in a humdrum, boring world, and it never changes. Routine is the order of the day. There is no magic in their lives, no possible space for it. But, despite these different views, everyone lives in the same world. Fairies and magic exist for one person, but not for another. Both are right, because they have created their world that way. How individuals perceive the world makes the only difference. Do you see?'

Lucien frowned. 'I think so.' He wasn't sure.

Jeopardy became impatient, his hand gestures more emphatic. 'Look at it this way. Some see the world as treacherous, and consequently find danger. Their lives are lived in fear or seclusion. On the other hand, people who are brave and fearless look forward to the challenges in their lives. Danger, to them, is an adventure.'

'I don't think I'm one of the brave ones,' Lucien said. All he could envisage of escaping the House of Mandru was a spear in the back, or a heretic's gibbet.

'You're weak at the moment, Luce, that's the trouble,' Jeopardy said. 'But it's only because you believe you are.'

Lucien wanted to ask, 'Am I important to you? Are you happy to be with me?' But he dared not. Each moment in Jeopardy's company was gilded; he was never bored. He did not really believe that Jeopardy would run away. Punishment for absconding Ixmaritians was too severe, despite Jeopardy's fancy words about belief and creating his own world. Mandru would be incensed enough by truancy to do all in his power to bring an abscondee back. Azmaveth had once said to Lucien, 'We are privileged, but we are slaves. If we overstepped the boundary of freedom we are allowed, which admittedly is indistinct here at Mandru, we would quickly discover just how enslaved we are.' It was the truth.

'I wish I was strong enough to protect you from yourself,' Lucien said bitterly.

'You are,' Jeopardy replied, 'but I won't let you do it.'

When the Mandrus returned home, Jeopardy made it clear to Amber he no longer wanted her in his life. Lucien had not expected that, but in no way deceived himself he was the sole cause. The dissolution of the affair was

171

very public; Amber would have it no other way. She raved, she stalked, she swore and complained. She cornered everyone and demanded to know what had occurred while she'd been away. Jeopardy remained tight-lipped, and Lucien hid himself from Amber's wrath, afraid his face would betray his secret. For some reason, it didn't occur to her to question him.

No one knew that he had been visiting Jeopardy in his room. No one even suspected. Although Lucien was relieved by this, some part of him longed for people to discover his relationship with Jeopardy. Occasionally, he even dropped hints in company, but nobody picked up on them, which was unusual considering their love of intrigue and scandal. Sometimes he found himself wondering whether his alliance with Jeopardy was real at all, or whether it was some bizarre hallucination invoked by his desire. Could he be dreaming it all? Lucien ached to speak openly with someone about it, if only to give himself proof he wasn't insane, but he knew that Jeopardy prized the secrecy of this affair above the relationship itself. If he revealed the truth to anyone, Lucien was convinced that Jeopardy would have nothing more to do with him. It was possible that Azmaveth was aware of the truth, but she asked no questions.

Some nights, but never with any regularity, Jeopardy would climb in through Lucien's window. Occasionally, they would have sex in the moon-light or the starlight. Lucien never allowed himself to term their activities making love. Most times, however, Jeopardy came to talk. He would whis-per urgently into the shadows of Lucien's neck, where his black, lengthening hair curved like fledgeling wings against the flesh.

'Why have you turned away from Amber Epipheny?' Lucien once had the courage to ask. He cherished the tiny hope that the answer might have something to do with himself.

'It is part of my preparation,' Jeopardy replied. It was all he would say, and hardly encouraging.

One night, Jeopardy said, 'In the future, you will look very much like me.'

'Have you made me that way?' Lucien asked.

Jeopardy shook his head. 'No. I simply recognised you. You are an unformed part of myself, I think. Perhaps a lost, innocent part I discarded a long time ago. You will outlive me.'

'Don't say those things!'

'But it is true. Why should I keep silent?'

'Because I love you,' Lucien said. Jeopardy frowned and moved away.

'Don't,' he said. 'It's pointless. A waste. I don't deserve it.'

'I can't help it,' Lucien said mournfully. 'I wish I could. I will carry you to my grave.'

Jeopardy laughed nervously. 'Lucien, you may well have to carry me to mine.'

In the afternoons, the Lady Nehushtah commanded her favourite Ixmariti-ans to attend her. Once everyone had gathered in her afternoon salon, the Lady always directed her maid to light the smoking pipes. Dreamily sucking intoxicating fumes through a golden tube, she would command distractions from her Ixmaritian favourites. Since Lucien had attracted the Lady's notice, his presence was often requested. Nehushtah, appreciative of his skill, if unable to comprehend its nuances exactly, liked him to perform solo Vibrancies for her entertainment. In the Ixmaritian way, which was a welcome relief to Lucien, she did not expect her vibrancers to move to music. She claimed she could hear the body music while she was smoking and was more than capable of appreciating the performances without the clamour of pipes and bells.

There were always at least a dozen other people present, Ixmaritians and members of Nehushtah's personal staff. Her body servants and close retainers were all of Ixibatabian stock like herself. Her maid Kamariah was a slant-eyed shifty-looking girl, attractive at certain times of day, sometimes malevolently ugly. Lucien had a sneaking admiration for her. Pathra, an acolyte of the Ixibatabian goddess Throon, was Nehushtah's personal priestess. She dressed in dark-brown robes edged with gold thread. Her head was shaved and her neck was uncommonly long. Netofer and Oholah were Nehushtah's body servants, youths that could have been twins, and perhaps were, though they were obviously lovers. Netofer, upon meeting Lucien informally, had taken it upon himself to change Lucien's appearance, and had plaited several copious hanks of false black hair into Lucien's own. After this operation had been completed, Lucien realised Amber had been right about him. An abundance of hair did seem to improve his looks, somehow realigning his features into a new shape. Jeopardy, however, had passed no comment on the change, even though it had been quite dramatic.

One day, shortly after the Mandrus had returned from Ixibatae, Lucien received a summons from Nehushtah as he was eating lunch in the refectory with several other Ixmaritians. Kamariah handed him a note scrawled in red ink on thick, creamy parchment; a torn scrap. 'Today, I want you,' it said. Nehushtah usually worded her notes like that; a lascivious hint. It was a common affectation of hers. Lucien kept his lunch light, eating only lettuce and radishes so as not to affect his performance. He enjoyed dancing for Nehushtah because she seemed to appreciate his art, even though she was always rather delirious while he performed. His opinion of her had improved, although he still thought her a very strange and overpowering individual. She was affectionate with her staff, and never deliberately cruel, although she could be forgetful and was therefore occasionally cruel by omission. Lucien at first considered her to be of low intelligence, a false impression which later he gladly revised. She was hardly a beauty, being too heavy of feature, too tall and too large, but she was incredibly striking in appearance, and undeniably sensual. All her movements were slow and graceful, her laughter low and husky. Her black eyes brimmed with secrets and the promise of delights. Her sense of humour was as sharp as broken glass.

The passageway to Nehushtah's chambers was long and high-ceilinged, a covered causeway leading from the main wing of the family quarters to a cluster of rooms higher among the rocks of the estate. Its entire, windowless length was draped in thick curtains of dark velvet; sable browns, dull golds, deep crimson. The curtains always seemed to swallow the sound of approach, and to Lucien, walking along it was like entering a vast womb. Globes of burning oil hung from the roof to provide illumination, but the light was dim.

At the end of the corridor was a doorway that led directly into Nehushtah's afternoon salon. The doorway itself was at least thirty feet high, and was screened by long curtains, of Ixibatabian crushed velvet, which fell down in black folds to pool like glistening ink on the tiled floor. When he'd first seen these prodigious drapes, Lucien had wondered how they were ever cleaned,

173

until Azmaveth had informed him that, once they were musty with smoke and incense fumes, Nehushtah simply ordered new ones from her home land. As far as Nehushtah was concerned, the old curtains were burned. In reality, however, they were cut up and made into dresses and trousers for the lower staff. Nehushtah never noticed them.

Lucien was fighting his way through the heavy folds of the curtains, which were never tied back, when the sound of an anguished voice coming from within the room made him pause. Nehushtah was prone to outbursts of temper when her husband had disappointed her in some way, which Lucien always found very embarrassing to witness. He hoped the Lady wasn't upset today, and peered cautiously through a narrow gap in the curtains. It quickly became evident that Nehushtah was not the source of the complaints. Sitting on the couch beside her was Amber Epipheny. Her red hair was hanging over her face, her features distorted by grief, and her shoulders heaved in wrenching sobs. Nehushtah, with hooded eyes and a gold pipe in her mouth, had draped her free arm about Amber's shoulders.

'You must forget him,' Nehushtah advised in her strong accent, removing the pipe from her mouth. 'Why weep for someone who cares not whether you live or die?'

'I can't!' cried Amber Epipheny. 'It would be easier for me to forget how to breathe!'

'Ah, but he is only a man,' observed the Lady, once more inserting the tube between her lips and taking a sip of smoke.

Amber shook her head. 'No, he is more than that. I cannot explain.'

'There will be others.'

'Not like him.'

'No,' said the Lady, drily.

Having observed this exchange, Lucien slipped back noiselessly through the curtains. This was women's business. It was not his place to be there. He wondered whether he should abandon his visit, but was wary of disappointing Nehushtah. After a few moments' consideration, he retraced his steps a short way back up the corridor and then renewed his approach, making a great deal of noise by coughing and slapping his sandals against the floor. When he reached the curtains once more, he pulled them so hard, the heavy gold rings they were suspended from clattered together with satisfying volume. By the time he entered the chamber, Amber Epipheny, as he'd hoped, had composed herself and now sat some distance apart from the Lady Nehushtah. She pretended to be greatly interested in a selection of cosmetics pots that were lying on an adjacent table.

'Lucien, welcome!' cried the Lady. 'Look, Amber. Look who is here. Is he not lovely, a gentle ointment for your grieving eyes?'

Amber looked up briefly, her expression grim. She grunted in assent.

'We need diversions,' announced Nehushtah. 'We need them now.'

'Am I too early?' Lucien enquired. 'As you are alone . . .'

'Ah, no, the others were dismissed. I requested a moment's privacy.'

'Would you prefer me to return later?'

Nehushtah waved away his question. 'Nah! Here, take a lungful of this smoke and dance for us. Vibrance our souls. Amber needs a diversion!' She laughed, in a manner that suggested she had been puffing at her pipe for some time.

'As you wish, my lady,' Lucien said, with a grave bow. 'Although if you will excuse me, I will forgo the pipe until later.' He was conscious of Amber's

174

eyes upon him, but dared not look up to read their expression. He was frightened of discovering hate or envy there.

Turning away from the women, Lucien prepared to dance. He flexed his body, moving without conscious thought. Thin bars of sunlight fell upon the tiled floor of the chamber, and Lucien stood utterly still for a moment with open arms, his face turned up to the bleaching rays. As a golden inner peace descended, he became aware of his body, every cell. He became aware of the tide of his blood. He became aware of his breath; slow, deep, a summoning. Time ceased its forward progress and his hands curled into a preliminary configuration. Aligned to the Earth, his spine became a rod, an axis round which his limbs revolved. The torrent of blood became music. Very faintly at first, he heard it in the distance, the distance that is beyond time and space as they are known by humankind. So faint. The music was familiar to him; it dictated the form of the dance. He knew which sequence was coming to him.

What inner impulse moved him to perform that piece, he could not tell, but it was to Amber Epipheny that his presentation was directed. It was not a heavy piece, just an introduction to a more potent religious description. A frippery, a dance of light touch, an entertainment, but its symbolism was pertinent. The daughter of Ixmar, Panphyla, mourns the loss of her lover, who has been turned into a stone by her jealous father. The movements speak of loss and grief, the movements are tears, yet within the lament is the seed of hope. The colour of life, of her own spirit, invades her melancholy. The dance itself energises her soul. Panphyla finishes her dance by whirling away from the stone. She has exorcised her grief. She carries the love, and always will, but the dance of life has called her, she has heard its secret tune, and the veil of grief is left upon the stone.

Lucien finished the piece at Amber's feet. At the beginning of his dance she had been leaning back moodily among the cushions, but she had clearly recognised the message Lucien was giving her and now sat upright, her hands knitted on her knees. Lucien looked into her eyes and she was smiling through a haze of tears. She held out her hands, waggled her fingers. Lucien offered her his own.

'Thank you,' Amber said thickly. 'Thank you.'

'You have excelled yourself today, Lucien,' the Lady said huskily, exhaling a silver plume and exposing her gem-studded teeth in a smile.

'You are a romantic creature, Lucien,' Walterkin said. It was midnight, and they had only recently departed Hartshorn Park in order to take supper on Bessie's roof garden. Above them, the sky was like a velvet, stone-crusted cloth, and the moon was skirted with thin, luminous cloud.

Lucien was cold. He took a shawl from the back of one of the chairs, which Bessie must have left there in the afternoon, and wrapped himself in it. Its fabric was faintly damp and fragrant with dew. It did not warm him. 'I used to be romantic, I suppose,' he said.

'I think you are still,' the boy continued. 'Why did you perform that dance for Amber? Did you care about her situation?'

Lucien frowned. 'I didn't think I did, but in retrospect it is clear that I must have done.' He shook his head. 'It was a mistake, a terrible, irrevocable mistake.'

'Why? Is it a mistake to show compassion?'

'Sometimes. It brings responsibilities. My relationship with Resenence was like a dream, or an hallucination. Most of the time I could not believe in it. Every time he came to me, it was a shock. I don't know what he gained from our alliance.' Lucien cupped his face with his hands. 'Oh Walterkin, what I did was a dreadful thing, because it caused what happened next.'

'Which was?'

'Because I had performed that piece for her, Amber became attached to me. In her mind, I was a true friend, an empathiser. From that moment forward, I could not be rid of her.'

Walterkin pulled a wry face. 'Was that so bad? She seems, from your description, an interesting creature.'

'She was. But can you imagine how it seemed? Resenence kept our affair private, so we were never together in front of others. Amber, on the other hand, wanted to be with me continually. I enjoyed her company, I cannot deny it, but I was for ever conscious of Resenence's eyes upon us.'

'You think he was jealous?'

'I don't know. He never mentioned it when he came to visit me. But then . . .' Lucien covered his eyes with his hands.

'Then?'

'He visited me no longer. It just stopped. And I wasn't invited to his room again. There was no explanation. Nothing. I was devastated, but had no outlet for my grief. Azmaveth did not want to know about it, and I could not talk to Amber. Resenence avoided me. He would not even look at me.'

'Did you attempt to speak to him?'

'Of course. Twice, he snubbed me in public. People said it was because Amber and I had become friendly. They did not know the other side of it. He must have thought I was betraying him.'

One morning an excursion was announced. The Ixmaritians would accompany Nehushtah out onto the hillside for a picnic. They would travel in a pair of covered carriages, escorted by mounted officers of the household guard. The invitation was inevitably extended to Lucien, of whom Nehushtah had clearly become fond. When the Lady summoned, no one could decline, so Lucien had no choice but to attend the party.

As the carriages trundled up the hill road towards the high meadows, Lucien sat glumly among his more cheerful companions. His mind felt dead, not just because he was confused about Jeopardy's abandoning him and was missing him greatly, but also because he had recently suffered a further traumatic event, connected with the moribund affair.

That morning he had entered the dance court as usual to practise, and Jeopardy had been there. Lucien had not expected to come across him; he had not seen him in the court or spoken to him for nearly two weeks now: Jeopardy had deftly avoided him, and had excited comment from others because he'd not left his room for any length of time for days. Even Sabraxis had been concerned, and had apparently confronted him about it. Reports conflicted as to what had transpired at the interview. Some said that Jeopardy had refused to open his door to her, while others suggested he had bared his heart to her, confessing that he missed Amber's company and was jealous of Lucien having her attention. Lucien was sure that neither of these reports were true. When Sabraxis had approached him, Jeopardy would doubtless have offered some blithe excuse for his current isolation.

Was he jealous? Lucien wondered, standing by the door. Jeopardy was practising with his back to him, apparently oblivious of Lucien's entrance, although Lucien was not deceived. Jeopardy would have known he'd find him here at this hour. Watching that lissom body twist and curl before him, Lucien suffered a tremendous pang of sorrow. Jeopardy looked so beautiful, exercising there in the orange light. He also looked terribly alone.

Lucien realised that this might be his only chance to explain to Jeopardy about Amber. If only he could convince himself Jeopardy was concerned about that. Some part of him, an instinctual part, was sure that Jeopardy's aloofness was due to something other than Amber regarding him with favour. Others in the house were not so convinced. 'Look how violently he has reacted,' they said. 'He fears you have taken his mistress, Lucien.' One thing Lucien was convinced of was that Jeopardy had no feelings whatsoever for Amber. But if the household commentators were correct in their assessment and Jeopardy's behaviour was indeed inspired by jealousy, then Jeopardy must have at least some measure of feeling for him.

If only I could read your mind, Lucien thought. If only I knew.

Leaving his dignity by the door, he mustered his courage and walked steadily towards Jeopardy.

'Res, will you talk to me?'

Jeopardy stopped moving and after a moment turned round, his face a cold, inscrutable mask.

'What have I done?' Lucien asked harshly. 'Tell me! Have you turned away from me because of Amber?'

Jeopardy snorted, folded his arms and pressed himself against the window.

'Why won't you answer me?' Lucien cried. 'Silence is not the answer! I won't let you chill me with silence!'

Jeopardy did not move. Lucien could feel emotion churning inside him. If Jeopardy did not speak soon, he'd lash out at him uncontrollably. He couldn't bear this silence.

'Why are you here if you won't talk?' Lucien said. 'What are you trying to do to me? Please, tell, me what's wrong!'

Jeopardy turned away from the window. 'I can't,' he said, and then walked past Lucien to the middle of the floor, where he stretched his body into a Vibrancy configuration.

'Damn you, then!' Lucien yelled. 'Damn you!' He ran out of the court, hoping, praying, that Jeopardy would call him back. The call never came.

Out on the hillside meadows, high above the house, Nehushtah and her favourite Ixmaritians drank wine together and bit salty olives. The atmosphere was that of relaxed gaiety. Occasionally, one of the revellers would stand up to perform a Vibrancy, an uneven, tipsy frolic among the starry flowers. Sometimes, two or three people would break into a song that was taken up by the rest of the company. Others lay beneath the spreading branches of the trees and caressed one another through slippery silk and webby gauze.

Lucien, estranged from the convivial company, sat alone with his back against a massive oak. He had drunk two cups of wine quickly, but was disappointed that he did not feel drunk. He felt as if his blood was boiling. The heat of it was desiccating his flesh. He wanted to cry, but his eyes felt too hot, too dry.

'Lucien! Hoi!'

He realised, without pleasure, that Amber had spotted him and was now striding up the meadow towards him. Her bright hair hung loose round her shoulders, and her soft green gown, which hung to her knees, revealed the smooth curves of her body as it swung in time with her strides. Lucien raised his hand half-heartedly in greeting. At that moment, he hated Amber Epipheny. He did not want to be at her disposal. He felt as if she'd somehow trapped him, dragged him into a life he did not want.

She sat down beside him and shook out her hair, raising her face to the sun. Then she narrowed her eyes and smiled at Lucien mischievously. 'Lucien, what is wrong with you?' she demanded, reaching out to pat his hand. 'You seem so glum.'

He shrugged. 'Nothing much.'

Amber rolled her eyes. 'Oh, I believe you!' She frowned earnestly, to show her concern. 'Truly, Lucien, tell me what's on your mind. It's such a beautiful day, and we're all having a wonderful time. You should be happy! What is there to mope about?'

'I don't feel in the right mood for this, that's all.'

Amber laughed. 'By Ixmar, you look as if you're in love!' she exclaimed. 'Is that the case, Lucien? Are you lusting for someone?'

It was with considerable effort that Lucien refrained from a bitter response. 'I am not lusting, as you put it, no.'

Amber leaned back on her elbows. She plucked a stem of grass and chewed it thoughtfully. It seemed she found the silence between them restful; to Lucien it was fraught and strained. Eventually, she rolled onto her side, supporting her head on one hand. 'Lucien, I know you find it difficult to speak about such things, because of where you came from, but I think I understand what you're going through.'

Lucien glared at her. 'I don't think so.'

Amber did not take offence. 'I can help you,' she said. 'In fact, I would count it as both a pleasure and an honour.'

Lucien sighed. 'You cannot help me, Amber. No one can.'

Amber reached out and took hold of one of his hands, shook it. She rolled across the grass and leaned closed to him, whispered in his ear. 'Come with me.'

Lucien tried to pull away. 'Where?' he demanded suspiciously.

Amber stood up and dusted down her skirt. 'I want to talk to you in private, that's all. We can go into one of the carriages. They're empty.'

'Amber, there is nothing to say.'

'Then don't speak,' she retorted. 'I intend to do the talking actually. Come along. I won't take no for an answer. If you don't come, I'll drag you there, and then everyone will notice and make fun of you.'

Sighing, Lucien heaved himself to his feet. He felt dizzy. Amber hooked her arm through his and led him down the meadow. There was a smell about her, a strange, compelling smell. It reminded him of a distant horizon seen at dawn.

Lucien was not blind to the expressions on the faces of those they passed on the way to the carriage. Nehushtah, sprawled out on a bed of cushions covered with shawls, grinned at him, her eyelids half lowered.

Once they'd climbed up into the carriage, Amber drew the curtains across all the windows. The seats had been removed, and banks of cushions installed in their place, so that more people could be accommodated. Amber sat down heavily in the cushions and patted those beside her. 'Sit here, Lucien.'

He complied, hugging his knees in an attitude of defence. Amber sighed. 'How prickly you are today. How unapproachable.' She reached out and ran her fingers over his thigh. 'Relax!'

Lucien rested his chin on his arms and stared at her. She stared back in a confident, assured manner. 'Lucien, you can have me. You can do whatever you want with me.'

'What?'

'It's what you need. At least . . .' She broke off and moved towards him. He allowed her to press him backwards into the cushions, feeling nothing but a deep lethargy. She ran her hands over his body, taking care not to be too invasive, but exclaiming in delight over his shape, his muscles. 'You are lovely, Lucien,' she said, and rolled on top of him, fastening her mouth over his. Lucien had never kissed a woman before. Her face felt alien against his own, strangely smooth. Resenence had only kissed him upon the mouth eleven times; long kisses, but few enough to count. Lucien could remember the night-time rasp of Resenence's unshaven chin. This was nothing like that. Amber's tongue was like a grub coming out of a hot, over-ripe fruit, but he found, to his surprise, that it was not unpleasant.

'It is springtime,' Amber murmured. 'In Shanariah, your parents will be coming together at this time for the sacred rites. Man to woman, flesh to flesh, upon the marriage bed.' Her body stirred against him. 'Do you want me, Lucien? Can I be the one to take the chains from your heart and body?' Gently, her hand stole between his legs. She squeezed him softly. 'Well?'

Lucien could not speak. His body instinctively reacted to her touch. In order to keep the silence, he pulled her head down to kiss her again. Perhaps that would be answer enough.

'You are a virgin,' Amber whispered reverently, her breath hot against Lucien's neck. 'Oh, but you are eager not to be, I can tell!' She pulled away from him, and with lowered eyelids, her eyes a mere gleaming slit, slowly pulled her skirt up over her hips. Beneath, she wore loose drawers with a laced crutch. With one hand, she unfastened the lace. Lucien could see a hint of pink flesh inside. She took his hand in hers and together they explored her secret territory. She threw back her head and moaned in delight. Never had Jeopardy been so demonstrative in his pleasure. Even before Lucien had finished unlacing his trousers, she'd pulled him into her. Outside, he could hear people singing. The carriage was full of the sound of Amber's groans and sighs. A single refrain rang through Lucien's head as he moved upon her body. 'Why you? Why you? Why you?'

FUTURE GHOSTS

After the ghost-invocation ceremony had ended so abruptly and so dramatically, Dauntless fell into a manic stupor. He appeared to have been driven, catatonic by the manifestation of the ghost, or was it perhaps by the crazy, warped music of Dratslinger's troupe? Drago had thrown down his instrument and had run across the room to where Apanage stood rigidly amid the fragments of glass, her arms badly lacerated. Blood dripped from her outstretched fingers onto the floor, but her eyes were glittering with a weird excitement. Cleo had the distinct impression what had just happened had satisfied Apanage in some way. Drago fluttered round her in consternation, but Apanage waved away his attentions, pointing to where Cleo was trying to shake Dauntless back to his senses upon the sacking.

'She mustn't touch him!' Apanage said.

'Daunt! Daunt!' Cleo was deaf to Apanage's advice, and shook the paladin's rigid body violently. Drago approached cautiously and leaned down wordlessly to detach Cleo from her companion.

Behind Drago, Tumblejack went to put his arms round Apanage and tried to help her from the room, down into the main house. At first, she resisted his offer, but then relented and allowed him to lead her from the room. She appeared to be limping. As she reached the door that led the stairway, she pulled from Tumblejack's hold and said harshly, 'Search the room, search this floor. If there is any remaining spiritual effluvia, find it!'

Malengin Fole and Flittern Rattletrap made signals of assent to her, and began to poke around the rubbish with Malengin's bone drumsticks. Cleo could hear them muttering to one another; their voices sounded excited. Occasionally, they laughed together.

'What's happened to Dauntless?' Cleo asked Drago in a high voice. 'Look at him!' He was sitting upright, as rigid as a pole. The only movement in his body was the chattering of his teeth. The pupil of each eye was as small as the point of a pin.

Drago squatted down to examine the paladin, inspected his eyes, moved his limbs. 'Hmmm,' he said, after a while. 'He appears to be in shock.' He stood up. 'Malengin, come here a moment, if you please.'

He clambered over the clutter and approached. 'There's no sign . . .' he began, grinning, but Drago interrupted him with a shake of his head.

'I thought not. Take Master Javelot down to the house now. Give him a posset of suitable herbs and spores.'

Malengin nodded and called to Flittern to assist him. Cleo watched in consternation as the pair of them manhandled Dauntless from the room.

'I must go with him!' she cried, leaping to her feet.

'Fole and Rattletrap will attend to him,' Drago replied firmly, catching hold of her arm. 'They know what to do.' His words suggested it was not the first time this had happened.

'You said there was no danger!' Cleo shouted. 'You promised! You lied!'

'It was no lie,' Drago said. 'I truly believed you would be safe.'

'Do things like this happen often?' Cleo asked.

Drago shrugged. 'Spirits can be unpredictable, a handful. Usually, it's nothing we can't contain.' He pulled a mournful face that reminded Cleo strongly of Apanage's dog; the same crinkling and folding of skin. He glanced speculatively at Cleo. 'Perhaps it was your companion's circle that caused the escape. Perhaps something else . . .'

'It was nothing to do with me,' Cleo snapped. She remembered, with a shudder, the bottle shattering in mid-air. She glanced around the attic, which was now empty but for herself and Drago. She shivered. 'Where has that monstrous thing gone to? Is it still here?'

Drago put an arm round her shoulders and began to lead her from the room. 'Oh, it's undoubtedly gone,' he replied with forced joviality. 'Fole and Rattletrap found no trace of it, and that should be assurance enough. They have a nose for such things.'

'Get me out of here,' Cleo said, with feeling. She couldn't stop trembling.

Drago took her to an ancient bathroom in an upper corridor adjoining the main attic, which must have been used by servants when the house had been in its prime. Regarding her reflection in a bleary mirror, Cleo could see that she too had suffered cuts. There was a diamond-shaped wound on her forehead, right between the eyes. As soon as she became aware of it, the cut started to hurt. Drago wet a rather grubby piece of cloth and wiped the blood from her face. There were some very minor cuts on her cheek and neck, which also began to sting as Drago bathed them.

'There,' he said. 'That will suffice. Tomorrow, we shall give you an ointment.'

'Drago, what happened tonight?' Cleo asked. 'Why did the spirit escape? Was it different from the ones you usually try to bottle?'

Drago made a dismissive gesture with his hands. 'Something out of the ordinary perhaps. Unexpected. I'm sorry it had to happen while you were present.'

Cleo peered at her face in the mirror and fingered the scratch she'd received at the hand of the boy in the forest. 'I seem to be collecting injuries,' she mumbled dolefully.

'Nothing serious,' Drago said cheerfully. 'Now, let's find you some accommodation. We've all had an exhausting night. You'll need some sleep.'

'No,' said Cleo, 'I'm not tired.'

'All the same,' Drago responded. 'This way.'

'I'd rather not be alone.'

'The rest of us have things to do,' Drago replied shortly.

Glumly, Cleo followed him along the corridor which had a round window at the end, and down a short flight of stairs to the right. They emerged into another corridor, lined by closed doors. Drago paused by one of these and removed a bunch of keys from his pocket. Cleo couldn't stop thinking of what might have happened if the broken glass had flown into her eyes. She would have been blinded! How would they have removed the cruel slivers?

'Will Apanage be all right?' Cleo asked, as Drago unlocked the door.

He narrowed his eyes at Cleo suspiciously for a moment, and then nodded. 'Oh yes, I'm quite sure her injuries are of a superficial nature.'

'And Dauntless. Will he be all right?'

Drago paused for a moment, and then pushed the door open with his hand. It creaked loudly. 'His hurts, unfortunately, are more tangible.'

'What do you mean?' Cleo followed him into the room.

'Shock, fright. I'm sure he'll be all right by morning. A good sleep can do wonders for a nervous mind.'

'I hope you're right,' Cleo said. 'I think he is easily scared.'

'A condition I trust you do not share,' Drago said with a smile.

'Oh no,' Cleo confirmed. She glanced around the room. It was small, a servant's bedroom. The only furniture was a narrow bed and a couple of broken wicker chairs. A small, dirty rug covered the bare floor next to the bed.

Drago cleared his throat. 'Well, Cleo, I hope you won't mind staying here until the morning.'

'Do I have a choice?' Cleo asked.

'Unfortunately, I have business to attend to,' Drago said hurriedly.

'Can't I stay with Dauntless?'

'He should be allowed to sleep.'

'But I could sit with him, watch him, make sure he's all right.' For the first time since she'd met him, she and Dauntless were apart. It made her realise how much she relied on his company.

'I think you should stay here,' Drago said. 'It would be . . . safer.'

'You said there was no danger.'

'It's been a strange night. Please, trust me.'

Cleo sighed dismally. There was little in this room with which to occupy herself. She hoped the window would at least give a good view of the forest beyond the house.

Before Drago left her, he lit a fire in the small iron grate, which thankfully had been stocked with kindling. 'I suggest you sleep now and forget this unhappy evening,' he said.

Cleo sat down on the edge of the bed which was tucked beneath the uncurtained window. 'Yes,' she said miserably. 'I will.' She had never felt less like sleeping.

'I will fetch you tomorrow morning. Good night to you.' He exited the room swiftly, and Cleo heard the key turn in the lock. He'd locked her in! She sprang up immediately and turned the door handle. 'Drago!' She banged on the door. 'Drago, let me out! I won't be locked in! I won't!'

There was no reply. Cleo rested her cheek against the door. There was no sound from the corridor beyond. She might be alone in this house of ghosts. There was no telling where, or whether, the others were in this enormous building.

Sighing, Cleo went to kneel upon the bed so that she could watch the moon through the tiny, grimy panes of glass above her. The blankets under her hands were gritty and greasy and smelled of dog. She wondered why

Drago had been so insistent in hurrying her away from the others. Why had he locked her in this room alone? Surely, in view of the traumatic event they'd all just experienced, they should have sat up together for the rest of the night, discussing what had happened. And yet she couldn't help feeling that Drago and his troupe had somehow enjoyed the horrible episode. Cleo didn't believe they were in control of the procedure as much as they made out, and she suspected that Drago believed she, or Dauntless, was in some way responsible for the accident. Was it possible he was right?

'What am I doing here.' she wondered, 'sitting on this bed, in a ruined house, with crazy people all around me, in the middle of an endless forest? Am I glad I left the city? Do I miss my husband?' She closed her eyes for a moment and, in her mind, fancied she could hear the familiar tread of Wakelate's feet as he trod the squeaking floorboards of his room, far away in Scaraby. 'What madness possessed me?' Cleo asked herself aloud. 'What madness possesses me now?'

'The madness of desire which some might say is the need to grasp the lost half of a sundered soul. All souls are sundered in life.'

She had not expected an answer.

Cleo turned quickly. She had heard no one enter the room. A figure was sitting on the torn wicker seat opposite the end of the bed. Such a pale and bloodless creature it was; bleached by the moonlight perhaps, but she didn't think so.

'Who are you? Have you been here all the time?' It was possible. The moon had sailed across the sky while she'd been sitting here. Perhaps this stranger had been in shadow only a short time before.

'All the time?' responded the vigilant. Its face was as white as if covered in actor's paint, the eye sockets dark as if shadowed with fresh charcoal powder.

'Yes, you heard! Who are you?' It would be typical of this household, she felt, for them to have mad friends or relatives locked away somewhere. Perhaps this was an insane dependant who had escaped restraint, its chains or locks shaken free by the thunderous music earlier in the night. She could not tell immediately whether it was male or female; the voice was sibilant, almost a whisper, and yet indescribably penetrating too.

'I am . . .' began the visitor, and then it frowned and sighed. 'We wear the form of an abandoned persona, but the name of that persona is neither relevant nor pertinent to our situation. We *are*. That is, we are pure being, a mote of information in the cosmic scale of relevances.'

'We?' Cleo murmured, confused.

'We are a memory; our own, and of those who once knew us.'

It was a ghost. Cleo knew this as surely as if the creature had told her in plain language. Nothing else could be so grave-gripped in its appearance or tone. She was disappointed she could not see *through* the visitor, because she'd expected that as standard in the haunting kind, but then she had never actually seen a ghost before this night. It was a relief to discover she was not frightened. Should she be frightened?

'If you cannot tell me who you are, then where have you come from?' Cleo asked.

The ghost shrugged, its expression one of mournful perplexity. It appeared to be wearing a long, heavy coat, such as a traveller would wear, which was covered in dust or mould – perhaps grave-mould. Its hair hung lank upon its breast, its hands were long, the fingers like gnarled pale roots.

'Why are you sitting here?' Cleo asked. 'Can you at least tell me that?'

'The entrapped ones, in their mortal ignorance, attempt to call and bind. Many thoughts and essences are delayed in their destiny by such folly. We are able to address such abuse with disdain. We are part of history; essential. We are beyond their thrill-seeking games.'

'You escaped the bottling process because you are stronger than most?' Cleo attempted to translate its strange remarks.

The ghost again shrugged, making an elegant gesture with one spectral hand. 'Indeed. There was a perfume that drew us to you, a perfume we recognised; one that we wore ourselves in life. We wore it with pride and honour, that special miasma. We perceived it floating around you like your black, black hair.'

'I'm not wearing any perfume,' Cleo said. 'I wish I were. I adore it. I smell so bad, after weeks on that wretched horse.'

'The perfume is not a smell associated with the nasal sense,' said the ghost drily. 'On the contrary, it is an inner mystical fragrance, an expulsion of hallowed essences, which speak to us of a like soul – even if it is shackled in meat at the present time.'

'You are referring to me?' Cleo asked with a nervous laugh. She failed to appreciate how she could have much in common with the ghost. 'What were you in life?'

'Followers,' it replied, 'of a great and singular man. No, man is not the word we seek, for it implies a puny transience. Spirit is the word. We were the followers of a great spirit.' If the ghost had had any blood in it, Cleo felt that its face would now be red with passion. She drew back from its vehemence, although the spectre seemed oblivious of her reaction. 'A true visionary, who could strip the world of its false power structures that impede and bind the human soul,' it cried, black eyes glowing with an eerie fire.

'Resenence Jeopardy!' Cleo exclaimed. She could not think who else could link her to the ghost. 'But I am not a follower of his.'

'You are,' the ghost asserted, pointing at her with a stiff finger, 'for you smell of him.'

'I once held his child in my arms,' Cleo said. 'Could that be what you smell?'

'A child,' said the ghost, and then frowned in concentration. 'Were we children once? Did we have fathers? Children, yes, children upon the road. Is that what you seek?' It shook its head. 'No, maybe not, but that is what you will find.'

Cleo leapt up from the bed. 'But I already have,' she cried excitedly. 'I met three children yesterday. They were very strange.'

'Death, like life, means many things to many people,' the ghost said unhelpfully. 'Your life is linked with a child.'

'*Another* child?' Cleo asked. 'Or do you mean Inky? Your words are confusing me. Are you speaking my future to me or my past?'

'Future? Past? What conceits are they?' demanded the ghost. 'There is no such thing as finite time. We already exist as a hundred concurrent reincarnations of ourselves.'

'Tell me what you mean. I can't understand you.' Cleo was thrilled by the thought that this unearthly visitor might be able to reveal hidden knowledge.

The ghost wiped shaking fingers across its brow. 'Such rude, untrammelled energy,' it remarked. 'So uncontrolled, so vulgar. Listen to us: you

184

will meet a child on the road and be moved to murder, but the bane will be remedy in the event.'

'What do you mean?' Cleo squealed. 'What do you mean?' She stamped on the floor and waved clenched fists at the ghost.

The ghost made a languid gesture. 'That is all we can impart. Is it our fault you lack the power of interpretation?'

'Will I find Resenence Jeopardy?' Cleo demanded. 'Will I ever see him?'

Now the ghost assumed a calm expression, all animation falling from its face. 'Find him? He is all around you, so adept is he. He watches you now, no doubt. Seek the child within yourself and you might find it on the road of life. Jeopardy can only be found by the whole, and there are sundered parts to fix. Only you can accomplish that, Cleo Sinister.'

'You know my name,' Cleo said.

The ghost shrugged. 'No great feat. Your soul is shouting it constantly, for it is fond of itself.'

'Why am I looking for Resenence Jeopardy?' Cleo asked. 'I don't understand that. I gave up my life for this search. It makes no sense to me.'

'Once he's touched you, there is no going back,' said the ghost. 'You may find him or you may not. You may follow him or you may not. You may let him possess your soul or you may kill him, if you can. He is no mean force, Cleo Sinister.'

Cleo opened her mouth to ask more questions, but found herself staring at an empty chair. There was an after-smell in the room, as of burning flowers covering a faint reek of carrion. I will never remember all that, Cleo thought, and searched the room in a frenzy to find charcoal, chalk, or a quill and ink. She found nothing. So she turned what the ghost had told her into a song to a familiar tune, and memorised it that way.

At length, she lay down, fully clothed, upon the gritty bedclothes, the song swirling in her head, like water through a narrow, twisty concourse. She was sure she would never sleep that night, but found herself being awoken in daylight by the sound of someone turning a key in the door to her room. She jumped to her feet immediately, which made her head spin. If Drago Dratslinger walked through the door, Cleo decided she would slap him. How cold she felt, and how her limbs ached from the lumpy bed. What sort of hospitality was it that involved a guest being left alone without proper bedclothes in a draughty closet? Her mouth brimming with complaints, Cleo was surprised into silence when Dauntless walked into the room. He looked sheepish and pallid of face, but otherwise none the worse for his peculiar turn.

'They locked me in,' Cleo exclaimed needlessly and then rushed over to touch him gingerly on the arm. 'Daunt, are you all right?'

He nodded wearily at her and then looked away. 'Nothing that distance from this establishment won't cure.'

Cleo thought she could see censure and recriminations lurking in his eyes. 'I'm sorry,' she said contritely. 'Perhaps you were right. We shouldn't have attended their ceremony.'

Dauntless shrugged. 'What's done is done,' he said stiffly. 'I woke up this morning wondering whether I was dead, and found myself alive. One of Dratslinger's disgusting goblin assistants gave me the key to this delightful room of yours, and told me how to find you. Apparently, there is breakfast downstairs for us, though whether I have the stomach for it is another matter.'

'This is my fault,' Cleo began, but Dauntless silenced her.

'I won't dispute that. All I can suggest is that we put this place behind us as soon as possible. I'd be grateful if you would refrain from interfering when the terms of our account are brought up.' He wrinkled his nose in distaste and glanced around the room. 'Personally, I cannot see how they would dare to charge us for this accommodation.'

Cleo walked past him into the corridor. 'I suppose your room was no better.'

'Well,' Dauntless said, indicating the way to a staircase further down the passage, 'as it happens, my chamber was not quite so . . . basic. However, despite the ample quilts, warming possets and roaring fire, it was situated over an old dairy and consequently suffered from draughts. I intend to voice my displeasure to Master Dratslinger at the earliest opportunity.'

'Hmph!' Cleo grumbled. She eyed Dauntless narrowly. 'My adventures did not end after you'd left me last night.'

He returned the narrow stare. 'Knowing you, Mistress Sinister, that does not surprise me.'

They had reached the bottom of the stairs and were now proceeding along a wider corridor. 'I saw a ghost,' she said. 'In fact it was *the* ghost, the one Apanage caught in the bottle.'

Dauntless's eyes widened, his face paled. 'What?'

'Yes, it was a horrible man who looked like he'd just crawled out of a grave.'

Dauntless uttered a sigh which, to Cleo, sounded bizarrely like a sigh of relief. He pulled a scornful face. 'You were dreaming.'

Cleo shook her head. 'No, I wasn't. The ghost was attracted to me, Daunt. It was the shade of one of Resenence Jeopardy's followers. It told me things.'

Dauntless increased his pace. 'This place is dank,' he said. 'We should leave at once. Ah, down these stairs, I think, and the insalubrious kitchen should be nearby.'

'Don't you want to know what the ghost said?' Cleo trotted to keep up with him.

'No!' he replied emphatically. 'It is all arcane, and suspect. It is against both the creeds of True Valiance, who abhors supernatural caprices, and the Ixmarites, who hound those unlucky enough to witness or participate in them.'

Cleo was stung by his response. Just when she decided to like him, he repulsed her with his boring piety. I am glad he was ill, she thought, he deserves it!

'The ghost told me my destiny,' she continued blithely, in spite of Dauntless's spluttered protests.

'You should have shut your ears to it!' he urged loudly. His voice echoed like a howl. Then he visibly collected himself and said, 'You would be wise to forget it, whatever happened.'

'Do you give this advice as my protector,' Cleo enquired coyly, 'or in order to protect yourself?'

Dauntless lowered his eyes. 'It is common sense,' he said gravely. He stopped walking. 'Perhaps, under the circumstances, we should vacate this house immediately.'

'What, without breakfast?' Cleo cried. 'And without hearing Master Dratslinger's explanation for locking me in what amounts to a cupboard? I won't hear of it!' She flounced off ahead of Dauntless, following the aroma of frying bacon, until she found the kitchen.

Apanage was busy at the cooking range. She wore a green pinafore over her gown, and her arms were bandaged to the elbows. She smiled brightly at Cleo as she entered the room. 'What a night!' she exclaimed. 'I am mortified such events occurred when we had guests. I must apologise for the brouhaha.'

'Never mind that,' Cleo snapped. 'How about apologising for locking me in that dreadful room? It was woefully lacking in comforts.'

Apanage turned away from Cleo to poke the bacon with a fork. 'Securing you safely in your room was considered the safest course,' she said. 'It would have been unwise for you to wander about the house alone last night. It was possible that spectral essences might have been lingering, and that could have frightened you. I agree that room is dreadful. I myself would not have chosen it for you.' She looked up and smiled. 'Drago lacks a woman's sensitivity. I doubt whether it even occurred to him you would prefer more sumptuous surroundings. You must forgive him. He never notices his environment, and would sleep on bare boards if wasn't for my looking after him. How many eggs can you eat?'

Cleo decided not to pursue the matter. After all, everyone must have been upset by the violent behaviour of the wayward ghost. She also decided to keep the story of her spectral visitor to herself for the time being. Perhaps the Dratslingers already suspected it, and would prompt her for information in due course. 'I will take two eggs, poached,' Cleo said and sat down at the table. 'Where are your colleagues?' She jerked her head at Dauntless to induce him to take a seat beside her.

Apanage forked bacon onto enamelled tin plates. 'They are working,' she replied, 'but Drago will be along soon. Would you care for a pancake, Master Javelot?'

Eating the abundant breakfast soothed Cleo's spirits. She noticed that Dauntless did not share her appetite, but was merely pushing his food around on his plate.

'Eat, Daunt,' Cleo encouraged. 'Who knows when we'll be eating as well as this again?'

He shook his head, and pushed his plate away from him. 'I feel nauseous,' he said.

'No doubt it's because of your . . . spasm, last night.' Apanage said. 'Have some tisane.'

She had just sat down at the table with her guests when Drago came in from the yard. He greeted Cleo and Dauntless with an almost overpowering effusiveness, and apologised in a lavish manner for the inconveniences of the night before. Cleo and Dauntless eyed each other speculatively. Both could tell that Drago was nervous and perhaps feared their questions. Neither felt moved to voice their complaints.

Drago sat down in a seat opposite them, while Apanage went to remove a laden plate for him from a warming oven at the bottom of the range. Cleo waited patiently until Drago had almost finished his meal before embarking upon a gentle interrogation.

'Master Dratslinger, what do you think of my quest?'

Drago observed Cleo with a keen, meditative eye. '*Think* of it? What do you mean exactly?'

'I am just interested in your opinion of the prophet, Resenence Jeopardy,'

Cleo said. 'Your colleague, Malengin Fole, believes the tales of his miracles are largely figments.'

'Well, we've heard many extraordinary, and frankly incredible, accounts of this Jeopardy character,' Drago answered carefully, dabbing his mouth with a napkin and fastidiously pushing his empty plate away from him. 'It is said that multitudes flock to Jeopardy's side, but the reports are bound to have been exaggerated.' He paused and frowned. 'Personally, I find the whole business disagreeable. I would never adhere to another man's beliefs, preferring my own entirely. But then, I am perhaps fortunate in that I have the wit to invent my own.'

Cleo sensed disapproval. 'Do you think I am wasting my time?' she asked acidly. 'Or am I just being stupid?'

Drago shrugged cautiously. 'It is hardly my place either to judge how you spend your time or to classify your intelligence. It struck me as soon as I met you that you are a singular woman driven by uncanny passions. I perceived a strangeness about you, a desperate odour of obsession and zeal. And your companion . . .' He glanced at Dauntless, who stared back with an unreadable expression on his face. 'There is more to you, sir paladin, than meets the eye.'

Dauntless raised his eyebrows. 'I suppose I should be flattered.'

Drago shook his head. 'Neither flattery nor insult was intended, but I sense it was no accident you met Mistress Sinister in the wood.'

'I am a paladin of True Valiance,' Dauntless said coldly. 'The antics of false prophets can have no influence over me.'

Drago displayed his palms and gave an elegant shrug. 'As you will. However, I feel impelled to advise you to be cautious. If this Resenence Jeopardy still exists, then he will undoubtedly be gifted with great eloquence, but his words might well be hollow.' Drago sighed. 'I don't know why the thought of this man makes me feel so uncomfortable, but I can only speak what burdens my mind. Take my advice: suspect any feeling or idea that does not spring wholly from your inner heart. Do not act against your instinct, even when the reason proffered might seem noble or correct. Observe with a detached eye. These are policies I would adopt, should I find myself in a situation similar to yours.'

'It is not a weakness in my character that makes me want to find Jeopardy,' Cleo said abruptly. Her voice sounded anguished.

'I did not say that,' Drago replied. He smiled. 'Neither should you think it.'

Cleo made an embarrassed, exasperated gesture. 'I cannot help feeling it has been implied,' she exclaimed. 'Why did you lock me away last night?'

Drago regarded her gravely. 'You were not, as you put it, *locked away* last night. The security precautions were for your own safety. There was every possibility of a malign presence being about.'

'Indeed there was!' Cleo cried triumphantly. 'In fact, you locked it in the room with me!'

Drago looked astounded. 'What?' he said.

'You heard,' Cleo replied. 'Your escaped ghost was in my room, and I could not get out! I was trapped!'

'I find this hard to believe,' Drago said.

'It is true,' Cleo insisted. 'It spoke to me.'

'And, er, what did it say?' Drago enquired.

Cleo sighed. 'Well, it tried to impart some kind of message to me, but I confess I understood little of what was said.'

'Perhaps you had better relate this information to me.'

Cleo was about to speak, but suddenly Dauntless lurched to his feet. 'Enough of this talk!' he bellowed. 'It is dangerous and unwholesome. Cleo, you are influenced by the ambience of this house of necromancers. We must leave immediately.'

'But you can't,' Drago said. 'If Mistress Sinister experienced an unearthly episode last night, then she must tell me about it at once.'

'No!' Dauntless thundered. 'Cleo, on your feet, gather your belongings. We are leaving.' He sneered at Drago. 'I trust my horse is where I left him?'

Drago appeared speechless with surprise. 'I really think—'

'Daunt, how could you be so rude?' Cleo cried. 'Master Dratslinger has shown us every courtesy.'

'Those grateful sentiments hardly resemble the words that were on your lips when I unlocked your room this morning,' Dauntless retorted.

Cleo shrugged. 'Well, naturally, I was angry at the time, but I am now satisfied with Master Dratslinger's explanation. He is also the only person who could possibly shed some light on the ghost's meanderings. The information might well be important to our wellbeing.'

Dauntless attempted to stare Cleo out, but she held his gaze until he lowered his eyes with a grumble, and reluctantly threw himself back into his seat. 'Bah, you obstreperous viper! Don't blame me if you hear something you wish you hadn't.'

Cleo scowled at him and then turned to Drago and related all she could remember of what the ghost had told her, and also what she and Dauntless had experienced with the strange children they'd come across the previous day. 'All this talk of children disturbs me,' Cleo said. 'It seems too pertinent, considering what induced me to begin my search for Jeopardy.'

Drago rubbed his chin thoughtfully. 'Your meeting with the children and your consequent visitation from the spectre would seem to be connected,' he said. 'There are many peculiar phenomena to be found in Haling Heart, but these particular manifestations are new to me.' He shrugged. 'Your friend, Master Javelot, might have been right. They could have been brigands' brats.'

'But you do not think so.'

Drago shrugged again. 'No, I don't. I would not be surprised if you were to have further experiences of a similar kind.'

Cleo stared at Drago with unflinching eyes. 'All Jeopardy's children are dead,' she said. 'Malengin Fole said so, and I know the Ixmarites were trying to kill them. Were the babes on the road the shades of Jeopardy's progeny? Is that possible? Will Inky rise up before me on the path before my journey is done?' She shuddered. 'I'm not sure I could bear that.'

Drago reached out in a reassuring manner to pat her hands, which were knotted together on the table top. 'All I can do is remind you of my warning,' he said. 'When you leave here, keep heading south. The trail from here is defined by cantrips, small spells of protection, that Malengin and Tumblejack have placed at regular intervals. Consequently, the path stays true and does not lead the traveller on wild jaunts. From what we've heard, if you're destined to find this prophet at all, it will be in the vicinity of Gallimaufry. His activities have lately been confined to this area. However, I suggest you hasten your journey. The Ixmarites will not tolerate his rambunctious defamation of their creed for ever.'

'It might already be too late,' Dauntless added in a doom-laden voice.

Cleo snarled at him. 'It isn't! I know it isn't! Wouldn't the shade have known if it were?' She rubbed her arms as if she were cold and turned back to Drago. 'Why do people follow the prophet? Do you know what it is about him that makes him so compelling?'

Drago laughed. 'You will be able to answer that once you've met the man. I doubt if I can tell you anything you don't already know: the sons and daughters of rich families have shunned lives of prosperity and comfort in order to run around the country in Jeopardy's following. They steal from their families to bring wealth to the movement. They prostrate themselves at the prophet's feet. From what I can gather, paupers are few and far between among his cult. He attracts the rich, or if his people are not rich, they are skilled in some way. He must be a man of great charisma, and I am always suspicious of such men.'

'I am not rich,' Cleo said.

Drago smiled. 'No, you are not,' he agreed. 'Not in a material sense. But I think you must have some talent Master Jeopardy would find useful.'

'I am a poisoner,' Cleo said. 'Is that what he wants from me?'

Drago gestured with one hand. 'Who can tell?'

XIII

OMENS

The night had filled with the swelling voice of a choir. It sounded like angels singing, somewhere far below where Walterkin and Lucien sat on the Anywhither roof. It was the middle of the night and some secret Ixmarite ceremony was taking place in an adjacent district. The Ixmarites always conducted their private rituals at the darkest hour, when the public were less likely to intrude. 'Listen to them, Walterkin,' Lucien said. 'It sounds like they're baying for blood.' He and the boy had been silent for some minutes, thinking about the latest anguished words that had spilled from Lucien's heart.

Walterkin wrinkled up his nose and squinted into the darkness. 'Can you feel the imminence?' he murmured.

Lucien shivered. 'Yes,' he whispered back, and felt tears grow hot behind his eyes.

Walterkin drew in a shuddering breath and straightened his spine, his arms gripping the ankles of his crossed legs. 'You have scars upon your body, Lucien, I can tell,' he said. 'How did you come by those scars?'

Lucien found he had to wipe moisture from his face. A tear had escaped. 'It was after I left the House of Mandru. An inheritance of fate.'

Jeopardy had begun to neglect his duties and spent most of his time visibly intoxicated. Lucien did not flatter himself he was the cause of this debauch, even though he sometimes indulged himself in fantasies to the contrary. Sabraxis had confronted Jeopardy on several occasions. Lucien heard on the grapevine that she had subsequently been summoned to private interviews with Salaquin Mandru himself in order to explain Jeopardy's behaviour. She had told the master that Jeopardy was suffering from a nervous illness, and that treatment had been prescribed.

'It's a lie,' Sydel said. 'She's covering for Jeopardy. She's fond of him.'

'But how long can she keep Mandru satisfied?' Ketura said. 'Eventually Jeopardy will be confronted by the master himself, and his excuses had better be believable.' She'd glanced worriedly at Lucien. 'It's because of Amber. It has to be.'

191

Lucien shook his head. 'I don't think so,' he replied. 'Their relationship has never been that deep.' Now, his words on the subject were given credence, because in the eyes of the household he and Amber were an item. Wearily, he went along with this, bonelessly caught up in the slipstream of Amber's enthusiasm and passions. Her strong personality, her genuine liking for him, eased the soreness of his heart concerning Jeopardy. She sometimes talked about her previous lover and while Lucien felt he could not contribute to the conversation, he could at least listen.

'You are a good listener,' Amber had said to him, on more than one occasion. 'It helps me to talk to you.'

People were very interested in Amber's healing process and were eager for details of her relationship with Jeopardy. Gradually, she felt comfortable enough to offer more information. Lucien envied her that release. Marist once said to her, in Lucien's hearing, 'You must feel avenged, now that Res is so obviously regretting losing you.'

Amber had laughed in a coquettish manner. 'Do not doubt it,' she'd replied. But later she had confessed to Lucien she didn't really think she was the cause of Jeopardy's melancholy.

'I sensed it coming on for a long time,' she said. 'I never reached Res's heart, no matter how hard I tried. There was a part of him that always seemed dangerously unstable, just below the surface. I sensed a black wave approaching. I don't think it would have made any difference if we'd remained lovers, this decline would still have happened.'

One afternoon, Amber and Lucien were in Nehushtah's salon, and the Lady herself had commented on Jeopardy's mood. Although she had never said so directly, Lucien had worked out that Nehushtah had little liking for Jeopardy. Whenever his name was mentioned, her movements became abrupt, as if she was annoyed. She would make a hissing sound between her teeth and laugh. Also, she had never invited Jeopardy to her private rooms.

'Only an imbecile would deny that he is a fine-looking creature,' she said, clicking her teeth against the end of her pipe and frowning up into the smoke trickling from its lip. 'But he is perverse, so perverse. Sometimes, I believe he deceives us all. He is an actor; cunning. I have watched him with Salaquin. One moment, he fawns at my husband's feet like a faithful hound, the next, he's casting him dark, resentful glances and being insubordinate. Salaquin humours him. I think he is a fool. I'd have the creature flogged! Amber, I don't know how you tolerated his selfish tempers.' It was the first time the Lady had ever voiced her true feelings for Jeopardy.

Amber, sitting at Nehushtah's feet with Lucien's fingers touching the ends of her own, threw back her head and grinned. 'I did not tolerate it,' she said. 'I always spoke my mind.'

'Yet his coldness hurt you, and you grieved when you lost him.'

Amber shook her head. 'No, I was only angry at myself. I despised the weakness of my emotions.'

Lucien knew that wasn't true. Strengthened by the presence of a new lover, Amber felt able to alter the past.

Nehushtah shrugged. 'Still, he must have possessed finer points as well. I dare say he was a frisky buck in the summer fields.' Nehushtah was given to using metaphors from her own lands, badly translated.

'As a lover, he was diffident,' Amber said frankly. 'I believe he has little interest in love-making. To him, it was a need to satisfy his body, in the same manner as emptying his bowels or filling his stomach.'

Lucien longed to contest this; he had, on rare occasions, known Jeopardy to exhibit passion. He wanted to explain that Jeopardy restricted himself on purpose. That he did not want people to love him because he knew he could not fulfil them, but that in his heart he wanted to be loved. Lucien realised it would be rather too revealing if he should say such things and gazed at the rugs beneath him.

'What do you think, Lucien?' Nehushtah asked. 'You are male. Give us insight into Jeopardy's mind.'

Lucien shrugged awkwardly. 'It would take more than sharing his gender to be able to do that' he said. 'Resenence is a law unto himself.'

Nehushtah pointed her pipe at him. 'Do you know,' she said, 'I hadn't realised it before but you remind me of him very much. You are a younger, saner, more sociable version of the man.'

Lucien looked up abruptly into her smoke-wreathed stare. Nehushtah grinned, displaying her gems. She glanced at Amber and winked at Lucien. Lucien felt absurdly shamed. Blood rose to his face.

'The shyer ones are more adept in the ways of love by far,' Nehushtah said.

That evening, after dinner and a group practice for a forthcoming Vibrancy, Lucien was again summoned to Nehushtah's chamber. Netofer delivered the request on this occasion, which was unusual.

'Shall I bring Amber with me?' Lucien asked. It was rare they went anywhere separately nowadays.

Netofer hesitated. 'No,' he said at last. 'The summons is solely for you.'

Lucien expected to join an evening gathering in Nehushtah's salon, but when Kamariah met him in the outer chamber, the Lady was already in her boudoir.

'She will see you there,' Kamariah said.

'What is this about?' Lucien asked as he accompanied Nehushtah's maid along corridors he'd never seen before.

The girl shrugged. 'Who can tell with the Lady?'

'Does it concern Resenence?'

Kamariah gave him a strange look. 'I very much doubt it. What interest has she in him?' She shook her head. 'Nehushtah's behaviour is impossible to predict. She could want you for anything.'

Nehushtah's bedchamber was not as large as Lucien had imagined it would be, and seemed ridiculously cluttered. He stood awkwardly against the doorway drapes as servants scurried back and forth with folded clothes, pans of steaming, herb-fragranced water, and flagons of hot, spiced milk. After an initial curt acknowledgement of Lucien's presence, Nehushtah ignored him. She sat before her mirror while Netofer and Oholah brushed out her thick black hair. Her statuesque body was swathed in a bronze-coloured robe and she chewed opiate pastilles from a small Ixibatabian pottery dish on her dressing table. Eventually, she languidly slapped her boys away and ordered everyone else to leave the room. Alarmed by her harsh tone, Lucien also made a move to depart.

'Not you!' Nehushtah snapped, her reflection looking at him fiercely from the mirror.

Lucien froze in dread. He had a presentiment of why he might have been summoned. Nehushtah yawned and stretched, flexing her fingers into claws high over her head. Her robe gaped at the chest, revealing her large, olive-skinned breasts.

'Some things it is pointless to take hold of because you know you will be disappointed,' she said. 'Other things provide adequate substitutes.'

'My lady?'

Nehushtah smiled at herself in the mirror, picked something up from her table, and swung round on her stool. Affording Lucien only a single, bland glance, she lifted her robe, spread her legs wide and inserted a dripping wad of contraceptive moss into her body. 'Now strip,' she said to Lucien. 'I want to see your body.'

'I beg your pardon?' Lucien squeaked although he had heard her perfectly.

'Take off your clothes,' Nehushtah said with a slight frown. 'I said I want to see your body. Do not keep me waiting, Lucien. My time is precious.' Her tone brooked no argument.

Shrinking in mortified embarrassment, Lucien self-consciously removed his clothing. He knew what was about to happen, but could think of no way to escape.

Nehushtah inspected him expressionlessly and then nodded to herself. 'Come here' she ordered. Lucien limped nervously across the room. Close to, Nehushtah seemed enormous like some voluptuous fertility goddess. Her skin was poreless, like yellow marble. She ran her hand down Lucien's chest and belly, and then lifted his penis in a cold hand. She handled the organ for a few moments with a wooden expression, before frowning and nodding to herself again. 'That will do. Get yourself hard.'

Lucien's jaw dropped in horrified dismay. He felt it would have been easier to produce a diamond from thin air.

Nehushtah, apparently oblivious of the effect her words had had, or hadn't had, upon him, threw off her robe and lay down on the bed. 'Hurry up' she said and, opening her smooth meaty thighs, began to masturbate in a ponderous fashion. After a minute or so, she commanded, 'Now!'

Lucien frantically tried to comply with Nehushtah's request. He attempted to conjure erotic fantasies of Amber, who in her sweet airy way never failed to arouse him when she wanted to. The ghost of Amber, however, was faint in his heart, and it seemed he would be unable to fulfil Nehushtah's request. What would she do to him?

'Lucien, I'm waiting,' the Lady said in a silky voice. It held more than an edge of impatience.

Lucien closed his eyes and imagined it was Resenence Jeopardy lying on that bed, Jeopardy who would never allow him anything but a passive role in their communion. This thought kindled a spark of lust. Wary of missing the moment, Lucien lunged at Nehushtah and desperately attempted to comply with her wishes. After a few minutes, she shrieked and convulsed, seemingly ignorant of the fact that Lucien was having extreme difficulty maintaining an erection. At the earliest possible moment, he disengaged himself and knelt up on the bed between Nehushtah's knees.

'Do you want to talk?' Nehushtah asked.

'No,' Lucien replied.

'Good,' Nehushtah said. 'Then go.'

Lucien barely paused to drag on his clothes, and was still fastening them as he hastened away down the corridor. He attempted to banish all memory of what had just occurred from his mind. Never had he experienced sex so sordid or passionless. The woman must be mad! And yet he knew so little about women. Was it possible such behaviour was more common than he believed? What if she should summon him again? How would he face her when others were present in the afternoons? Should he tell Amber about it?

'Paradouze, is this your revenge for my intemperance?' he asked his god bitterly. He broke into a run once he reached the long, curtained passage that led back to the main house. Armed guards standing at the farther doors proffered him stony glances as he scampered past them. Lucien didn't stop running until he reached the skylit corridors that led to his own room. Here, he slowed to a walk, panting breathlessly. The radiance of a full moon cast a wan light down through the glass. In this black and white kingdom, dull yellow oil lamps burned low along the walls.

Opening the door on his little sanctuary, Lucien realised it was the first time he had found the room truly welcoming. For the first time, it felt like home: safe. However, even though he'd left a fire burning in the hearth, the air was chill. After a quick look round, he saw that his window was open. When he'd left the room, it had been closed. Who'd been in here? When he crossed the room to close it, he discovered the window was not only hanging open, but that the lock had been forced. A hostile intruder? Lucien wheeled round in alarm, half expecting some attacker to lunge from the shadows, but he quickly realised the room was empty. With cold fingers, he struck his tinder and lit every lamp in the room. Sullen coals gave off a faint red glow from the grate. Lucien knelt down and placed a few sticks of kindling on the dying fire, blowing into the crimson glow. He was still so dazed by what had happened with Nehushtah, it wasn't until he'd been mindlessly blowing onto the flames for some minutes that he realised he should go to Sabraxis immediately and inform her of the forced entry into his room. He knelt upright, rubbing splinters from his fingers. It was then that he noticed the paper lying on the rug, just in front of the chair he habitually relaxed in. The torn scrap was held down by a stone, one of those rare stones called a cat's egg, which when split in two revealed a nest of crystal whiskers. Lucien stared at the paper for a few moments, before pulling it from beneath the stone and reading it. It was a message from Jeopardy, and yet he felt no surprise. From the moment he'd noticed the paper, he'd known where it had come from. The lines were stark and unemotional and at the end urged the reader to destroy the paper. Resenence Jeopardy had fled the House of Mandru.

'He came for you one last time, then,' Walterkin said. 'If you hadn't been servicing the Lady Nehushtah, he might have taken you with him.'

Lucien shook his head. 'I doubt that very much. If I'd been there, he would have slid the letter through a crack in my windowframe. Once he saw my room was empty, his arrogance impelled him to climb in and leave the message under a stone. He probably had to go back to his room to fetch it. He liked to appear mysterious.'

Walterkin shook his head. 'You judge him harshly, yet you love him,' he said. 'So what were his reasons for leaving?'

Lucien shrugged. 'I have a hundred theories. Unfortunately, his last words to me were, as usual, opaque in the extreme.'

'You can remember every word?'

'No, I'm afraid not. It shocked me so much the first time I read it, I tossed it into the flames immediately.'

'But what did it say?'

'I told you, I can't remember,' Lucien snapped. 'He just said he was leaving.'

Walterkin looked sceptical. 'Were you sad?'

Lucien shook his head. 'Emotionally, I felt nothing. I don't think Resenence expected me to, which was why he left the message with me. I also believe he trusted me to keep the information secret. To give him time, I suppose.'

'That doesn't make sense,' Walterkin argued. 'You'd already told him your feelings for him. Why should he expect you to feel nothing?'

Lucien sighed. 'You don't understand,' he said. 'Resenence knew we had a bond, I'm sure, but he thought I was more like him than I actually was.'

Jeopardy's departure naturally caused an uproar in the house, although it was not noticed until the evening of the following day. Jeopardy's behaviour had been so erratic over the past few weeks, it was not considered unusual for him to stay in his room for days at a time. Sabraxis, however, had become concerned when, upon the questioning the staff, she learned that Jeopardy hadn't eaten anything for over twenty-four hours. Fearing an acceleration of what she supposed was his depression, she hastened up to his room, accompanied by a servant bearing a tray of food. After their repeated entreaties for entry elicited no response, and an attempt to walk in had been thwarted by a locked door, Sabraxis battered the door down with her own shoulders. Lucien tried to imagine what must have been going through Sabraxis' mind as she threw the strength of her body against the wood. Had she dreaded finding Jeopardy dead inside the room? It was empty, of course, and after a hurried inspection Sabraxis discovered that all of Jeopardy's belongings had vanished. Most of them were later found, partially burned, in a badly constructed fire at the far end of the gardens. The news, taken first to Mandru, spread quickly.

That night, Lucien had retired early, plagued by a headache. The day had been almost impossible to bear; Amber had nagged him incessantly to tell her what was wrong with him.

'Lucien, you look like you've been given a death sentence,' she said. 'Has something happened?'

He could not tell her the truth.

Eventually, gossip had filtered through concerning his late-night visit to Nehushtah, which provided Lucien with a welcome excuse for his apparent distracted state. Amber had been stoically loyal.

'Don't worry,' she'd said, hugging him in reassurance. 'I'm not jealous. Nehushtah orders every beautiful man in the house to her room. It's not your fault.'

Lucien had smiled weakly. He wanted to say, 'Not *every* beautiful man,' but held his tongue. He'd been waiting with dread for someone to discover the true cause of his preoccupation: that Jeopardy had fled the house. He had little fear his mood would be connected with the revelation, but still felt he had to steel himself against the hurricane of emotion, outcry and retaliation that was sure to follow.

He sat up in bed, dosed with a pain-killing posset, and attempted to read a book. It was after he'd read the same page at least a dozen times that he realised the futility of the attempt. Shortly after that, the storm broke, and Amber came bursting into his room. The moment he saw her face, Lucien knew the news was out. She was distraught to the point of hysteria, a condition she tried to conceal with harsh laughter and sarcasm.

'He's gone,' she said, her face aflame, striding up and down at the end of Lucien's bed.

He had to ask: 'Who?'

'Resenence,' she replied. 'He has evidently become bored with his life here. He is clearly bored with sanity!'

Lucien listened painfully while Amber related all she knew: Sabraxis' concern, her subsequent discoveries.

'Imagine the gall of it!' she exclaimed. 'He ups and offs like a wild bird. And why has he done that? Like all of us, he has led a pampered life. Does he think he can survive out there in the world?'

'Amber,' Lucien began tactfully, 'have you ever considered there might be a side to Resenence that none of us know.'

Amber made an angry gesture. 'By Ixmar's eyes, I hope he dies!' Then she turned to Lucien, her face a mask of desperation. 'Has he run away because of us, do you think? Is that possible, Lucien? I never would have believed it. He seemed so cold, so callous, he never loved me, but, oh Lucien, was it possible he was jealous of my relationship with you? Even hurt?'

Lucien shrugged helplessly. 'It's . . . it's possible, I suppose,' he said lamely.

Amber sighed and sat down on the end of the bed. 'Mandru is furious. He will send out the house guard and bring Resenence back. He will punish him severely.' She put her head in her hands. 'Dear Ixmar, they might kill him!'

Lucien knew that Jeopardy would not be caught. How he knew this, he could not say, but the knowledge was sure and certain in his heart. Perhaps, in the end, he had come to believe Jeopardy's predictions about himself.

He watched Amber's heaving shoulders for a moment or two; her grief was silent. He felt absurdly responsible for that grief. He should not have shut her out. In their relationship, too much was left unsaid. He realised he had shown little respect for her. It was unfair; were her feelings any less valuable than his? They had a common bond.

Lucien climbed out of bed and sat down beside her. Tentatively, he wrapped an arm round her shaking shoulders. 'Amber, there's something you should know,' he said gently. 'Res left a note in my room last night.'

Amber looked up, stunned. She rubbed her eyes. 'Here? Why here?'

Lucien decided not to confess too much. He shrugged and looked away. 'Who can tell?'

Amber pulled away from his arm. She leapt up. 'You knew?' she screeched. 'You knew last night that he'd gone?'

Lucien made an awkward gesture. 'I'm sorry. In the note, he asked for my silence. I couldn't tell anybody. I probably shouldn't be telling you now.'

'Why would he leave notes with you, though?' she demanded. 'You were nothing to him. He danced with you once! That *was* all, wasn't it?'

Lucien filled the awkward silence with a jerky shrug. 'Yes. You know it was.'

'Then why should he tell you and not me? I loved him!'

Lucien realised he might have made an error of judgment in confiding in Amber. The information should have brought them closer. He had not expected blind jealousy. 'Perhaps it was because of your love for him that he dared not tell you.' Lucien said, desperately trying to extricate himself from this volatile situation. 'He did not want to hurt you. He knew you'd be upset. He knows we are lovers. Perhaps leaving the note with me seemed the best way to reach you.'

'Where is this note?' Amber yelled. 'Show it to me!'

'I can't,' Lucien said. 'I burned it.'

'Burned it?' Amber released a whoop of nervous laughter, and clawed the air above her head with hooked fingers. 'You fool! How could you do such a thing? It was *my* note. You had no right.'

'He told me to,' Lucien said hurriedly. 'He didn't want anyone else to see it, not even you.'

'I can't believe that.' she cried. 'There would have been some message that only I could have understood. He would not have gone without saying goodbye. I know he wouldn't.'

Lucien shook his head emphatically. 'No, there were no messages. All he said was that he was leaving. He gave no reason.'

'Tell me the exact words.'

'I can't remember them.'

Amber snorted wildly, sat down upon Lucien's bed, put her head in her hands, snorted again, sat upright, stood up and paced the room. Eventually, she sank down against the wall, beneath the window, and began to weep in racking, convulsive sobs. Lucien watched her with dispassion. He was no longer moved to comfort her. Her dramatic displays of emotion would have appalled Jeopardy. It seemed inconceivable she'd ever had a relationship with him. At that moment, Lucien despised her. She hadn't deserved Jeopardy's attention.

'I can't believe he's gone,' she said. 'I'll never see him again.'

'No, you won't,' Lucien replied. 'None of us will.'

A troop of men on horseback were sent out from the house that very night to scour the countryside for signs of the fugitive, but no sign of Jeopardy was found. The escape was unprecedented. Never before had an Ixmaritian tried to abscond; the penalties were too severe, and the benefits of good behaviour too great to risk losing. People said that Jeopardy had run away because of love, had fled in order to kill himself. Others only shrugged and voiced the opinion that sanity and Jeopardy had only ever enjoyed a tenuous relationship. Mandru informed his Church friends on Scarcement Chase of what had happened, and several high-ranking clerics came to the house, not just to glean information but to console Mandru in his loss. After all, Jeopardy was a product of theirs, and had proved faulty. Good money had changed hands with the guarantee that Jeopardy would fulfil his duties to the letter.

When Mandru's guards returned to the house, rumours began to spring up concerning phenomena of an uncanny nature. One man spoke of how he'd been resting apart from his fellows beneath the shade of a tree. 'I opened my eyes and a vivid green serpent was hanging down from the branches,' he said. 'Hung right over my face, it did. Naturally I froze, because I feared its bite, but then it spoke to me. I swear I heard it speak. "Go home," it said. "Your search is fruitless." I swear to Ixmar, the snake spoke in Jeopardy's voice.' The household were thrilled by this tale, but even so they thought the man must have been dreaming.

Then, in Mandru's salon, the hands of a clock began to move backwards. One afternoon, ten birds fell dead from the sky into the stable yard, and several of the kitchen staff became subject to strange dreams that frightened them during the daylight hours. Sometimes, someone would come running into a room, claiming they had just seen Jeopardy in an upper corridor, or practising the Vibrancy in some secluded corner of the garden, but upon investigation by the guard no trace of Jeopardy could be found.

'Is he dead?' Amber asked Lucien one day. 'Do all these things mean that Res is dead?'

Lucien felt numb. Now that Jeopardy had utterly departed from his life, it was as if a picture had been taken down from his wall; a picture of someone he half loved and half feared. In many ways, he was relieved Jeopardy had gone. It had been agony to live under the same roof and not be able to touch him. Amber was not relieved. She became jumpy and given to violent fits of temper. She could be found often on the roof gazing out over the mountain walls, the distant sea, the sky. It made Lucien realise just how much Amber must have given to her relationship with Jeopardy. Despite her cheerfulness, her apparent happiness in Lucien's company, she had obviously never ceased to mourn Jeopardy's loss. Lucien wanted to ask her exactly what their life together had been like, even though he had deliberately refrained from questioning her before. She'd talked about Jeopardy all the time, but she'd kept the important details to herself: how it had felt when she and Jeopardy had been silent together, not even touching.

One afternoon, about a week after Jeopardy's escape, Amber and Lucien were sitting in the gardens together, in the shade of a crumbled wall festooned with ivy. Lucien held Amber's hand and did not invade her brooding silence. She squeezed his fingers now and again to show she appreciated his company.

'It is *not* over!' Amber blurted out apropos of nothing.

'What isn't?' Lucien felt a sudden thrill of apprehension. Amber's voice had sounded hollow, almost prophetic.

'This mess in our lives called Resenence Jeopardy.' She drew in her breath, her face taut and white, and fixed Lucien with an unflinching eye. 'I might as well broach the subject, seeing as you never will: how long were you sleeping with him, Luce?'

Lucien, upon hearing these words, expected to feel nauseous. He felt nothing. Should he deny it? He looked away. 'I don't want to talk about it.'

'Neither did I,' Amber replied. 'Not to you. Why do you think I made a point of befriending you, Lucien? I always knew about you.' She laughed harshly; a desperate, miserable sound. 'By Ixmar, you must have thought I was so stupid. Still, I was amazed you were so easy. I thought you'd put up a fight, resist. It hurt me the first day we made love, Lucien, because I knew how little respect you must have had for me. You didn't even argue. You had my lover, you smugly kept it secret, and then you just casually took me, as if I was a common whore!'

'It wasn't like that,' Lucien said. 'Don't insult yourself, Amber.'

She began to cry. 'Why did you never tell me, Lucien? I should never have touched you.' She grabbed fistfuls of her hair and pulled it back from her face. 'I gave you the chance to tell me the night Jeopardy left here. You said nothing. My feelings meant too little to you. Oh Paradouze, why did I let myself love either of you?'

Lucien knew he should reach out to comfort her but could not bear the thought of touching her. He regarded her as if she was a strange animal, giving tongue in a bestial language. I am becoming like him, he thought, too like him. Not real. Not entirely here in the world. I should feel something. I should *care*. He knew that in a short while Amber would beg him to hold her, and that he'd comply. The wound would scab over once more, simply to fester inside. It was up to him to sterilise the injury, the words were his to utter, but he guarded them jealously. He knew he would never tell Amber any of the things she wanted to know. He would deprive her, and she would suffer.

No one seemed unaffected by Jeopardy's flight. Lucien wondered whether this was because his action had brought the truth of the Ixmaritians' position in the household, in society, into sharp focus: they were slaves, pampered pets, objects that were owned. Only Jeopardy had had the courage or lunacy to snatch back his freedom. The cost might well be death or privation, but there was dignity in his escape, in his sacrifice of physical comfort. Lucien also realised that, no matter how the others in the house, from Mandru and Nehushtah down to the most menial scullion, had scorned Jeopardy in the past, berated his arrogance and despaired at his eccentricities, they had all been fascinated by him. He had been a beautiful icon in their lives, forgiven his faults because, in some esoteric way, he fulfilled a lack in them. His presence had been a vital elixir; without him, the house seemed drab, the routines pointless.

Lucien perceived instinctively that although Mandru had provided men to help the Church militia scour the countryside for Jeopardy, he had little real heart for the search. Lucien paid close attention to what Mandru said and discerned a subtext to the remarks he made about Jeopardy. He realised that Mandru, too, was experiencing a sense of relief that Jeopardy had gone. It was almost as if there had been something corrupt about him, something distasteful. He had affected everyone like a sickness. They had not realised how he'd penetrated their lives until he removed his presence. Now, everyone was waiting for the fever to break, for the sickness and delirium to leave the walls of the house, for life to continue much as it had before.

Amber felt physically ill and cursed herself for her weakness. Her limbs ached, and she felt continually nauseous. Despite medication, she could not perform the Vibrancy. Lucien could offer little consolation. It seemed as if the spaces between the points of reference in his life had become larger; he could see through the routines, the safe and familiar. He could discern the voids, the unanswered questions.

Time passed. The months moved on and Jeopardy was not found. Lucien heard that the local Church hierarchy, who had been called in by Mandru when Jeopardy first disappeared, had advised him to keep quiet about the matter. It would not proceed beyond his friends in the Church. An Ixmaritian absconding could have far-reaching repercussions. Mandru himself might invoke retribution from the Church for allowing Jeopardy to escape. His establishment might be investigated and the religious laxity of his household discovered. Penalties would be incurred, and Mandru's Church friends might be implicated. Everyone in Scarcement Chase was fond of Mandru and his wife, and enjoyed the relaxed evenings they spent at the house. They did not want to risk losing Mandru's lavish hospitality. Also, it was best that other Ixmaritians never got to hear about Jeopardy's escape. It might well encourage them to take the same action. A bishop who was a close friend of Mandru's came to talk to the staff and the remaining

Ixmaritians. The threat beneath his fatherly pleas for obedience and gentle words about faith was not ignored.

'Someone will die with Jeopardy's name upon their lips,' Amber said one day, some months after he'd disappeared. Lucien deplored her tendency to be over-dramatic.

'Well, it won't be either of us,' he replied sharply, and then became angry. Amber hadn't mentioned Jeopardy for nearly two weeks. Lucien had hoped the affair was over. 'He's gone. We should all forget him. He's only a man.'

Amber shook her head. 'No, he isn't.'

'I am sick of hearing about him.'

'How dare you,' Amber cried. 'You wave your privileges in my face. You deliberately understate the way things were between you and him. You mock me!'

'There were no privileges,' Lucien said angrily. 'You are mistaken. And I do not mock you.' He sighed. 'Amber, this is unhealthy. We must forget him.'

She laughed harshly. 'Unhealthy? Perceive from a distance, Lucien. Is there anything in this house that isn't?'

That night, Lucien dreamed. He dreamed that Jeopardy came to sit upon the end of his bed. 'Tell me why the person I love betrays my memory?' he said.

'And which person is this?' Lucien asked, sitting up in the bed.

'Yourself, of course. How your words hurt me, Lucien.'

'You've never loved anybody but yourself. You are a false dream. Go!' Lucien lay down again and put his head under the blankets. Wake up, he told himself, wake up!

'I am so alone,' came the voice of Jeopardy. 'My path is so hard, yet I am compelled to follow it. Oh, Lucien, how I yearn for your company!'

'You cannot be the person of my dreams,' Lucien said, still hiding. 'Not in real life. I have never met the man I dream about in real life.'

'Perhaps that is because he is the man I dream about too,' Jeopardy said, in a mournful voice. 'The man I would like to be, yet cannot. He exists within me, but is trapped there. I cannot free him, but you, Lucien, you—'

'No!' Lucien cried, and hurled himself from the bed. He ran towards the door, yanked it open, and fell out into the corridor beyond. All was silent and still. For a few moments, he lay curled up on the floor. My mind torments me, he thought. It feeds me lies, terrible, sad lies.

After a while, he dragged himself to his feet and went back into his room. It was empty of ghosts or desires. Before getting back into bed, he lit the lamp. He did not want to sleep again, but tiredness overcame him. Mercifully, the next phase of slumber was unhaunted by dreams of any kind.

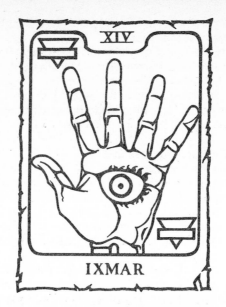

IXMAR

Delilah Latterkin was very tired. She had enjoyed the earlier parts of her journey with Trajan, even though they had often been hungry and cold. She did not concern herself greatly with physical comforts. To her, the light of a cold bright star in a black midsummer sky was as comforting as the cosiest of fires. The scent of dew-soaked grass was more intoxicating and famishing than that of newly baked bread or mulled wine. Trajan had approved of these traits, which he said were commendable in any human being although he did hasten to add that they were attributes shared by every Jeopardite he knew. Delilah's fascination with tales of the prophet had not waned, but she was beginning to weary of Trajan's constant praise of his lost comrades. They sounded like a dreary pious bunch. When she articulated this thought to Trajan, he remonstrated strongly.

'Dreary? No! To spend one night in a Jeopardite camp is to enjoy the true merriment of sound human company. None are so carefree and joyous as they.'

Delilah was unconvinced.

Sometimes, she thought about the Saltcats and what they had shown her. The time she had spent in the mill now seemed like a dream.

After they had left the vicinity of the mill, they had followed Greencover Course, an ancient causeway, which meandered beside the Tickpike as it tumbled west. South-west of the high moorlands and forests, other people became more plentiful upon the road, and settlements often had to be avoided. This made Delilah nervous. Trajan's afflictions had not been that much of an inconvenience in the lonely surround of the Mother's girdle, but now Delilah was aware of a flexing in his personality, a twitching of his senses, as if the scent of other people awoke strong, irresistible impulses within him. They foraged as much as they could from the countryside, stealing from fields, living off wild fruit and berries, but Delilah still longed to approach some homestead or village in order to buy proper food. It was an ongoing disagreement she had with her companion.

'Delilah, you do not understand,' Trajan said. 'We are in the land of the Ixmarites now. The people here are all staunch Ixmaritians. One conversation with you and they'd know you were not one of them. It would arouse too much suspicion.'

Crossroads and hilltops were now adorned with Ixmarite symbols. The hands and eyes of Ixmar reached out and stared from atop symbol-encrusted columns. Shrines clustered thickly along even the most lonely, unfrequented lane; statues of the god and his family watched sternly from every one.

One day, Trajan said to Delilah, 'We must travel by night.'

The tone of his voice unnerved her. 'But why, Trajan?' she asked quickly. 'Why now?'

He moaned and wrung his great hairy hands. 'The sun begins to prick me with his needles of fire,' he replied. 'The moon cackles behind my back. They are both waiting to unleash . . .' He could not continue.

Delilah felt defeated. She had been sure her presence had somehow influenced the dire course of Trajan's peculiarities, regulating them in some way. When she mentioned this, he reached out to touch her hair lightly.

'Ah, sweet maid, sweet darling maid, how I wish that were true.'

'You said it was,' she replied in the small voice of a child.

Trajan shook his head. 'I wanted to believe it, out there in the wilderness. Your presence was a balm to me; I only dreamed badly once. But I was deceiving myself. Only one person holds the reins to my curse, only one.'

'And are we approaching that person?'

Trajan looked uncertain, before answering, 'Yes, yes.'

Delilah had yet to test the power of whistling on Trajan, which the Saltcats had assured her would allow her to control him. A whistle seemed such a frail thing in comparison to the bulk of Trajan Sacripent.

There was perhaps another reason why it was advisable to travel under the banner of darkness. Delilah had never strayed far from Samberdell before and had imagined all of the world to be as sparsely populated as the land she had grown up in, yet now she discovered that not too distant from the higher ground a strange new society existed, one that burgeoned with people and activity. Not all of that activity was agreeable. She had been warned, of course, of the robbers and cutthroats that roamed the bare crags and pathways of the Toughtenny Crags, the child-stealing gypsies that roamed the flats. Her mother had even, on occasion, pointed out the curl of a gypsy camp fire in the distance, when they'd sat together on Bethany's Knoll. But these sinister characters had never intruded on Delilah's life; they were far away and mythical, like fairies or goblins. In the lower lands, things were very different.

'You have an open heart,' Trajan told her. 'You are an angel's child. But you must close that lovely heart, my pretty one. Keep your eyes to the stones and speak only when necessary.'

'Why is that, Trajan?'

'Have I not told you how Resenence Jeopardy has come to cleanse the world? Dark steam has seeped along the highways and into the towns – effluence of evil individuals, the Ixmarites with their hypocrisy and cruelty, the landowners who, driven by Ixmaritian creed, are starving for the fat of the people. This has warped the hearts of honest men and women. Here in the lowlands, Ixmarity's vigilance for heresy is keen. The people are afraid of the priests' threats and fear anyone who does not obey the Church.'

Delilah promised never to mention Mother Moistfoot's name in public. 'Do you know what angers me most about the Ixmarites, Trajan?' she said.

Trajan smiled. 'No. Tell me.'

She screwed up her face. 'Well, there are so many other gods apart from Ixmar. Why should everyone have to become an Ixmarite? My mother once said there are so many gods because not everyone has the same spiritual tastes. The Ixmarites would have us believe the other gods don't exist. I know that's not true, because I have felt the power of Mother Moistfoot myself. I have seen it.' She was thinking of the Saltcats.

'Ixmarity has little to do with gods,' Trajan remarked drily. 'It is only to do with power; corrupt men wanting power over other people. The religious aspect is just a blind, something for people to latch onto, so they don't feel so foolish succumbing to the Ixmarites.'

'Are people really so stupid?' Delilah asked. 'Can't they just ignore the Ixmarites?'

Trajan smiled sadly. 'The world is in a state of flux,' he said. 'But a changing time will come. Jeopardy is its herald, its archangel.'

'How can one man make any difference when people are so weak?' Delilah asked in exasperation.

'He is not simply one man,' Trajan said. 'He is himself and all of his followers. The following grows daily. It expands like a sunflower towards the sun.' Here Trajan frowned, having reminded himself of the solar power that afflicted him.

'I'm beginning to wonder whether we'll ever find him,' Delilah said, sighing. 'All we know is that we're heading in the right direction. Other than that, he could be anywhere.' She directed an accusing glance at Trajan. What am I to do with myself if and when I find this Jeopardy? she thought, and then smothered the thought quickly.

One evening, when Delilah woke up in her nest of grass beneath a tangle of concealing gorse, she noticed that many of her belongings were hanging from the thorns above. She woke Trajan immediately with a dismal cry, 'We are robbed, we are robbed!'

While they'd slept, someone had silently sorted through their bags. They had been carrying little food, but all of that was now missing. The money had also been taken.

Delilah felt desperate. She told Trajan that they needed to speak to people in order to glean information about where they should be travelling to. He disagreed, stating that instinct would lead him to Jeopardy. Delilah had no faith in Trajan's instincts. They were bound to be warped and unreliable because of his afflictions.

In moody silence, they tramped down a narrow, high-banked lane in the moonlight. At the first sign of humanity, she knew Trajan would gasp and bundle her into the forest on the left side of the path. Delilah's legs were raw from these frantic escapes, her stockings ruined, no more than a lacework of holes. Sometimes, she wished she could just run away from Trajan and throw herself upon the mercy of the first people she came across. Then he would look at her and smile in companionship, and Delilah would remember she was his only friend. She would reach for his hand and firmly push all rebellious thoughts from her mind.

They came to a steep hill where the lane swept down to a village. A board by the roadside informed them it was the settlement of Covendale. Looking down the road in the clear moonlight, Delilah could see that it was a small and tidy village, with a tiny marketplace and a single inn. Farms hemmed its boundary and ripening cornfields yawned up the sides of the hills that cupped the village, pushing back ancient deciduous forest that still crowned the hilltops. In some ways, it reminded her of Samberdell, even though in appearance it was very different. There were no woven walls to the village, no sky-shield, but there was a scent of witchery about the place that evoked memories of home.

Trajan uttered a few grumbling noises; he was always made uneasy by nodes of human habitation. He started examining the forest more closely for signs of pathways through the trees. Delilah sighed miserably. Soon, he would tell her they had to leave the road and scramble through undergrowth until they had passed the village. That meant they'd have to skirt the entire valley, which might take them most of the night. It was not a pleasing prospect.

'I want something to eat,' she announced.

Trajan indicated a field to their right with his thumb. 'Plump cabbages,' he said. 'Hop through the hedge and pluck a couple.'

'I don't want cabbages,' Delilah growled. 'Not raw. I'm sick of raw food.'

Trajan did not respond to her complaint.

They came to a crossroads which was marked in the centre by a wooden pole, topped with an Ixmarite symbol: the hand of Ixmar, with a round, peering eye in the centre of its palm. To Delilah, the eye looked perplexed. As she thought this, her skin shivered in a familiar way. It was as if a thread of female power had brushed her cheek. It was then that she realised she could not and would not steal from the people of Covendale.

'We'll have to leave the road now,' Trajan said gruffly, as Delilah had anticipated. 'We'll need something to eat before morning. Hop over the hedge, Delilah. There are turnips growing in the next field.'

Delilah shook her head stubbornly. 'No, I'm not going to.' She took a deep breath. 'Tomorrow, I'm going to go into the village. We'll not need to rob these people. I can feel it. Someone will feed us.'

Trajan put his hands on his hips. 'You will do no such thing, missy,' he declared.

'Why not?' Delilah asked. 'Just because you're older than I am, we always have to do what you want. I'm fed up with it. You may be older, but I don't believe you're wiser. Your afflictions have addled your brain, Trajan. You're far too suspicious of people.'

'Resenence Jeopardy taught me to be wary,' he said. 'There is a hooked blade hidden beneath every tongue.'

Delilah rolled her eyes in exasperation. 'My instincts tell me to go into the village, and that is exactly what I'll do.'

'Delilah!' Trajan thundered. His eyes were rolling, but the motion was clearly involuntary. His hands were flexing. Had she invoked his moon madness?

Delilah pursed her lips and began to whistle. Trajan hesitated. 'We are too near the town of Faneford,' he said. 'The Ixmarites have a local headquarters there, a garrison of Church militia. We should not linger in this area. It's possible Covendale shares the same function.'

'Can't you *feel* that it doesn't?'

'I feel only the pull of the moon,' Trajan replied stonily. 'That is all there is to feel.'

Delilah whistled another short refrain. 'Trajan, go up into the forest,' she said. 'I will dig up a couple of turnips for you, but tomorrow I'm going into Covendale.'

Early the following morning, Delilah set off towards the village with a jaunty step. Trajan had continued to voice complaints throughout the night, but they had petered away by dawn. Delilah had thoroughly worn down his objections by simply reiterating that she was going to do as she pleased. Her repeated whistling might also have had something to do with it.

'Give me a day,' she'd cried.

'A day!' Trajan had cried. 'Too long.'

'A day,' Delilah had repeated and whistled a refrain.

'No longer than that, or I'll come looking for you,' Trajan grumbled.

The village consisted of a central square, with four streets radiating away from it. Narrow lanes connected these streets so that, if viewed from above, the village resembled the design of a spider's web. Even though it was so early, there were plenty of people about, all of whom regarded Delilah with a curious eye as she passed. Nobody looked at her in a hostile manner. Still, bearing Trajan's advice in mind concerning strangers, Delilah kept her eyes downcast and her face solemn as she walked along. Once he had realised she was determined to carry out her plan, Trajan had advised her that inns were the best place to ask questions, seeing as hostellers were generally used to them.

The first establishment she came across was in the village square; a long, two-storeyed building crowned with heavy thatch and surrounded by ancient oak and chestnut trees. It was called the Cat and Bucket, although, looking at the picture swinging above the door, Delilah thought the bucket looked more like a great cooking pot. The cat held a spoon, grinned widely to reveal long white fangs, and wore a wide-brimmed pointed hat. Delilah warmed to this image instantly; she saw humour there and the white fangs spoke to her of protection rather than malice. A name was painted on the lintel in curling silver script: Pluffie Ratheripe.

The front door of the building was wide open, and held in that position by a black boulder. Delilah stood on the stone threshold and leaned forward. The door gave direct access to a large saloon. Inside, the inn was very dark and Delilah could see very little. She could discern only the glint of brass and glass behind the counter. The air smelled strongly of wood smoke as if a fire had been blowing back into the room down the chimney, and also of ale. She could hear a clock ticking, the slowest ticking she had ever heard. Slowly, she advanced into the room. Ancient beams supported the ceiling, and seemed to bow with the weight of the upper storey. The floor was of unpolished black tile. All of the windows were of thick, dark-green glass. 'Hello?' she said, in a soft voice. There didn't seem to be anyone around. She yawned widely. She realised she felt very tired, and sat down on a hard, shiny wooden chair near one of the windows, to decide what to do next.

The clock seemed to tick slower and slower. Delilah blinked. Her eyes felt gritty. She could barely keep awake. She hadn't realised she'd actually closed her eyes and begun to doze until a scraping noise shook her back to wakefulness. Blinking, she saw what she thought was the severed head of a youth lying on the floor a short distance in front of her. Its eyes, which were of a very unusual pale green, were staring right at her beneath a thatch of coarse yellow hair. Delilah couldn't prevent a sound of shock and revulsion escaping her lips. She jumped to her feet. It was then she realised that the head was actually poking up out of the entrance to the beer cellar, which was just inside the door.

'What are you doing here?' demanded the boy. He climbed up into the room.

Delilah wasn't sure how to respond. Had she really expected benevolent patronage from the people of this village? She had no money; she could buy nothing, not even a shred of information. She was a stranger in rags. Why should anyone be moved to help her? She resembled too much the sort of person she herself would take pains to avoid. She felt she looked like a thief.

The boy was securing the hatch that covered the cellar entrance. He was a tall and thin individual, and did not seem at all friendly. Delilah began to wish she'd just filched from the fields as usual.

'Well?' demanded the boy, hands on hip. Upright, he was very tall, and somehow stiff, like a scarecrow. 'What do you want? Are you a vagabond's lass? If so, be off. We've nothing for you here.'

Delilah took offence at the remark, mainly because it was so near the truth. 'I need work,' she announced, standing up. 'As the inn is the heart of any community, this seemed a good place to begin looking.'

The boy smiled without warmth. 'You need work, yet I find you snoring. That is hardly encouraging. Well, there's no work here and, more to the point, no charity.'

'I did not expect . . .' She sighed. She had no idea how to behave so that someone would offer work. It was, she reflected, far easier to steal. 'Look,' she said, 'I am in rather a predicament. My money was stolen, and I'm hungry. I'll do anything to earn a meal.' The boy was ugly, she decided, like a puppet made out of bones and parchment.

'Traveller, are you?' The boy narrowed his eyes. From the sarcasm in his voice, it was clear that he mistrusted her.

'Yes, I am travelling,' Delilah replied, trying to sound dignified.

'Well, you'll find no work around here,' the boy said. 'Try Faneford, but I expect you know that.'

Delilah was sick of his rudeness. She couldn't understand his attitude. Hadn't she been polite? 'Well, thank you for the information,' she said in a sharp tone. 'I'm sorry to have disturbed you.' With that, she walked to the door with her head held high, half expecting the boy to call her back.

'Anyone who steals from our fields will not live to enjoy their spoils,' he said.

Delilah wheeled round. 'I am not a thief!' she shouted. Absurdly, she did not feel she was lying.

Her loud denial summoned others from the deeper reaches of the building. A tall, scraggy woman loomed from the shadows behind the counter. She was drying her hands on a rag. 'Grackle, what is all this?' she demanded. 'What have we here? Is it trouble, is it, on such a fine day?' A teenage girl held up the curtain behind her, peering round it.

'This girl wants work, Mother,' said the boy and cast a significant glance at the woman, who caught it in her eyes and tossed it back, just as significantly. 'She is a traveller.'

'Oh,' said the mother, and addressed Delilah after a brief inspection of her face and clothes. 'I am Pluffie Ratheripe, proprietor of this establishment.' She put the rag down on the counter and enquired, quite pleasantly, 'Young to be on the road alone, aren't you?'

'I am not alone,' Delilah said.

'Your companions are outside?' Delilah could tell the woman thought she'd been sent in because she was the youngest, the one most likely to invoke pity in a stranger's heart.

'No,' she said. 'I am travelling with one other. A man. He has to wait

207

outside the village. He is cursed. I cannot bring him near anyone. It's too dangerous.' Speaking the truth seemed to soothe her, give her confidence.

'And you have come here to Covendale because of this curse?'

Delilah shook her head. 'No, we are taking the less frequented roads, and Covendale was simply before us. It is true that our destination involves the lifting of this curse, yes, but we do not even know where that is yet. We are looking for someone.'

Pluffie Ratheripe smiled. 'Perhaps you'll find them here.'

'I doubt it,' said Delilah. 'Is there nothing I can do to earn a loaf? I am very hungry, and so is my companion. We've eaten nothing but bitter roots and cabbages for two days.'

'I'm afraid I haven't any work for you here,' the innkeeper replied, 'but I can at least give you a bowl of broth.'

'That is very kind of you, madam.'

'Not at all. There's a pot been on the range since last evening. What's left would only go to the pig.' She turned to the girl. 'Bring out a ladleful, Imphee.' And then to Delilah, 'It'll be barely warm, mind.'

'That does not matter. I'm so grateful.'

Delilah sat down again by the window and the girl Imphee brought her a bowl of lukewarm soup which had a thick layer of cooling grease on its surface. Still, it was savoury and nourishing. Delilah gulped it down greedily. Poor Trajan, sitting alone beyond the village, his belly gurgling in the undergrowth, she thought. Imphee hovered about while Delilah ate, prowling between the dark wood tables, touching them with her fingertips, regarding Delilah sideways through slitted eyes. She was obviously the lanky boy's sister. The family resemblance was strong; long nose, ashy coarse hair, big hands. Imphee had very clear skin and the same pale green eyes as her brother. Unlike Grackle, she did not seem ugly to Delilah. Not pretty either, but interesting to look at.

'You don't have to worry,' Imphee said, coming to whisk Delilah's bowl away as soon as she'd put down her spoon. 'Mother will find work for you somewhere in the village.'

'That is very good of her,' Delilah said. 'And rather different from the way your brother treated me.'

Imphee shrugged. 'You mustn't mind him.'

'I cannot thank you enough.'

'It is plain you are not . . . a problem,' Imphee continued, and then smiled to reveal long, rather crooked teeth.

Delilah smiled back. 'How do you know? As it happens, my friend Trajan could be seen as something of a problem. He carries disease by day and murder in his blood by night.'

Imphee pulled a sympathetic face. 'An irksome companion, I would imagine,' she said. Delilah was quite surprised she accepted the information with no more reaction than that.

'Not really. Everything has been all right until recently.'

Imphee sat down. 'Tell me your story,' she said. 'That is, if you don't mind. From your face, I can see you have had adventures.'

Delilah decided there'd be little harm in telling the girl about how she had met Trajan, and what he had done in Samberdell. Imphee sat listening with an open mouth, gruesome delight shining in her eyes. She made sympathetic noises as Delilah described the privations of her journey. 'There must be something very special about this Trajan for you to want to travel with him,' she said. 'Forgiveness is a cardinal virtue, of course, but I personally would not be able to bear the company of someone who'd killed my family.'

'Well, it is difficult to explain,' Delilah said. Now that she had related her story aloud, in detail, she was quite astounded herself by the way in which she'd blithely taken up Trajan's company. What exactly was she doing with him? He was a murderer. For the first time, she felt a terrible pang of grief for her dead mother. 'I should hate him, I know, or at least not be able to stand being near him.' She frowned. 'It is to do with this Jeopardy person . . .' It was then that she realised she had omitted completely the story about the Saltcats. How odd that she should forget so important an event, yet when she opened her mouth to speak, no sound came out. She saw the face of Resenence Jeopardy beneath the water of the mill pool; the image was superimposed over Imphee's face. The hallucination, for all its intensity, was very brief. Delilah blinked and it was gone.

'You will be lucky to find Resenence Jeopardy now,' Imphee said, a curious expression on her face. She had evidently noticed Delilah's distraction.

'You know of him, then?'

'Who doesn't?' She grinned. 'The Ixmarites have hounded him and his people out of Gallimaufry. They say there was a massacre and many were killed. The following has split up now, for safety. In Ixmarite territory, it is not wise to advertise an adherence to Jeopardy's creed.'

'I hardly know what that is,' Delilah said. 'Trajan knows all about it. He's desperate to get back to his friends. Only Jeopardy can control his afflictions.'

Imphee pulled a face of disbelief. 'Your friend Trajan obviously believes that, which is what must make it true. Personally, I think there are others who could cure his calamities, but from what you've said, I doubt anyone could sway his faith to accommodate such a relief.'

'I have considered this myself,' Delilah said thoughtfully. 'To be honest with you, I am concerned about how we will travel at all now. Trajan seemed so tranquil in the higher country. Now I am afraid he will be ripping and infecting willy-nilly.'

'Has the time come, perhaps, for you to part company with him?' Imphee enquired delicately, clearly not sure whether her question transcended the bounds of propriety. She added quickly, 'Delilah, I have known you only a very short time, yet I can tell already that Covendale would be an ideal place for you, and you would be ideal for Covendale. Why not stay here awhile? Forget the trail of Resenence Jeopardy. Most think he will be dead soon anyway, if he isn't already. Why risk the wrath of the Ixmarites? They do such dreadful things . . .' Imphee cast down her eyes. 'To defy their rule, a person has to be discreet. Jeopardy is not discreet. From what I've heard, he is insane.'

Delilah considered. To be free from the anxiety of Trajan's company, to have security again: was this what she wanted? In all likelihood Resenence Jeopardy would be killed by the Ixmarites. As she had thought before, he was only one man, and now it seemed his following was fragmenting. And yet, she could not forget the image in the mill pool – that sacred face. Could she bear to live and grow old in the sanctuary of Covendale without ever seeing that face in the flesh, alive or dead? She couldn't give up the shred of hope that Jeopardy was all that Trajan claimed he was. Should she be tempted from her path? She felt sure that the Saltcats, in their opaque way, had encouraged her to follow Jeopardy. And yet . . . And yet . . . Delilah sighed and rubbed her face. She felt so tired, confused as to what was dream, desire, bemusement or commitment.

Imphee reached out and touched Delilah's hands. 'At least think about what I've suggested,' she said gently.

Delilah looked up at her and smiled weakly. 'Yes, I shall think about it. I need to think a lot. It seems I haven't done much of that recently.'

'Imph!' a male voice called from behind the curtain. Imphee glanced round impatiently.

'What?'

'Here!'

Making a grumbling noise, Imphee stood up. 'Excuse me a moment,' she said. 'I'll bring you some vanilla tea, if you like.'

Delilah nodded. 'Yes, I'd like that. Thank you.'

Imphee hurried behind the curtain and presently the sound of a low, hissing argument could be heard. Delilah strained to listen, but could not discern the actual words. Then she heard Imphee yelp and Grackle's voice cried, 'Hold your claws, sister!'

'Hold them? Indeed I will. In your face!'

The curtain shuddered as struggling bodies lurched against it from the other side. Delilah half stood up, wondering whether she should intervene. Then, she heard the mother's voice. 'Stop it! Stop it!' And the sound of two resounding slaps. Silence. Then urgent whispering. Finally, Imphee said, in a sullen tone, 'All right. *All right!*' And the curtain was lifted. Imphee came marching back into the room, a flush straining her pale cheeks, her arms folded. She halted by Delilah's table, glanced back once over her shoulder. Her mother appeared from behind the curtain and also folded her arms.

'I am at fault,' Imphee began in a strangled voice.

'How?' Delilah asked, mystified.

Imphee took a deep breath. 'I have no right to try and alter your path,' she said. 'No right to attempt to influence you in your decisions. There is something you should perhaps know.'

'Yes?' Delilah felt a flutter of consternation.

Imphee looked back at her mother. 'I am going against my instincts,' she said.

Pluffie Ratheripe shrugged. 'It is your place to tell her. I agree with your brother.'

'Oh, very well.' Imphee turned back to Delilah. 'There are two Jeopardites . . . staying here,' she said. 'Perhaps you should talk to them.'

'Really?' Delilah felt surprised, even a little frightened. Until this moment, her quest had been mostly unreal. Now reality came to her in the form of strangers. She wasn't sure she could cope with this alone. Perhaps Trajan . . . ?

Pluffie came forward into the room. 'They have to be careful hereabouts, with Faneford being so close,' she said. 'Please respect the secret nature of the information we have given you. Not all of us in Covendale approve or condone the Jeopardites' behaviour, because it brings danger to innocents. However, my son overheard your story, and feels you should at least be allowed to make up your own mind, be given more facts.' She eyed her daughter firmly. 'The fact that you have been led here, by whatever means, the fact that you were compelled to seek Resenence Jeopardy out, shows that he must be an important figure in your destiny. We cannot, and should not, stand in your way.'

'Er . . . thank you.' Delilah was bemused by the behaviour of the innkeeper and her family. Why make such a fuss? It made little sense to her.

'Inshave and Nebuline will undoubtedly be down in the private dining room come sundown,' Pluffie said. 'If you would like it, an introduction could be made.'

Delilah frowned. 'I wish I could have Trajan with me. I am unsure what to say, in all truth.'

'Given the nature of your companion's afflictions, his presence might be hazardous to the people of Covendale,' Pluffie said. 'However, the poor man must not suffer. I'll make up a breakfast for you to take to him after you've seen the Jeopardites.'

'Why are you helping me in this way?' Delilah asked. 'I must confess to being rather confused.'

'Resenence Jeopardy may, or may not, be the world's saviour,' said the innkeeper. 'None of us here knows if he is or not, but we cannot risk occluding the path of something great and beneficial. He is *something*, that's for sure. He does not follow our ways, which naturally we feel are the correct ways, but we may well be in the wrong. Jeopardy makes things happen. For a girl to experience what you experienced suggests events of importance. This cannot be ignored. I would not want a regression placed upon my life's reckoning by mistake.'

'Oh . . .'

'Now, sit here awhile. Imphee will bring you the tea she promised. If you like, she and Grackle can take you to the Sheen later. Sheen Meadow is a lovely spot, soothing to all the senses.' She smiled and departed.

The vanilla tea refreshed Delilah's spirits immeasurably. Sparing only a brief thought for Trajan crouched somewhere among the berries awaiting her return, she agreed to accompany the Ratheripes to the place Pluffie had called Sheen Meadow.

'It is where we celebrate,' Imphee said.

'Celebrate what?' Delilah asked.

Imphee cast a sidelong glance at her brother. 'Oh . . . seasonal things.'

'You mean religious festivals? Like the rituals of Mother Moistfoot?'

Both Ratheripes continued to exhibit guarded expressions. Delilah became impatient with their air of secrecy. 'Well, show it to me then,' she said.

The River Sheen rolled lazily, in ancient curves, through the cow-browsed sward of Sheen Meadow. Delilah immediately took the atmosphere of extreme age that permeated the spot; the elderly oak trees clustered in circles, the standing stones with their skirts of longer grass. Peace reigned in the meadow, sentinelled only by hovering larks. Fat, glossy roan cows lipped the lush verdure apathetically, their black-tasselled tails swinging against the afternoon flies. 'So beautiful,' Delilah said, holding out her arms and turning a few circles.

'It is the right place for you,' Imphee said. Her brother grinned.

'Why are you so anxious to have me here?' Delilah enquired, plucking a stem of grass to chew.

Imphee shrugged. 'No sinister reason,' she replied. 'We have many travellers passing through on their way to Faneford and the west. I take to none

of them like I've taken to you. There was something I recognised in you.'
She delivered a penetrating glance. 'Also, because I've taken to you so
quickly, I'm concerned about your future. The future of the Jeopardites
seems bleak.'

'They bring it upon themselves,' Grackle remarked. 'After all, we have
little trouble.'

Imphee glanced at him sharply. 'Well . . .'

There was an uncomfortable silence.

'So tell me about the Jeopardites staying at the Cat and Bucket,' Delilah
said. 'What are they doing here? Trajan led me to believe the group travel
together.'

'No longer,' Imphee said. 'Here, let's sit under the willows and cool our
feet in the Sheen.'

The three of them made themselves comfortable on the red soil banks of
the river and took off their boots and stockings. Delilah was ashamed at
how filthy her feet were, but neither Grackle or Imphee appeared to notice.

'The Jeopardites are a strange crew,' Imphee said, dipping her toes into
the slowly moving water. Black catfish could be seen beneath the clear
surface. Delilah hoped they wouldn't bite.

'Trajan has told me much about them,' Delilah said, 'but I suspect his
view may be biased. He describes them as a high-spirited and sociable
bunch.'

Grackle pulled a face. 'Then Nebuline and Inshave must be anomalies,'
he said.

Imphee nodded. 'Indeed. Nebuline Midnoon is the most morose creature
I have ever met, and she tries so hard to be that way. It is a fact that there
are several factions of Jeopardites. The ones that our guests belong to dress
only in black and paint their faces black and white, their lips a brilliant red.
One would imagine that such people would adopt a less outrageous mode of
dress to hide their identities, but not Nebuline and Inshave. Oh no.'

'Our grandmother nearly had a convulsion the first time she came across
Nebuline on the stairs,' Grackle said. 'She thought she'd been approached
by a revenant.'

'A what?' Delilah asked.

'A vampire's acolyte, walking dead,' Imphee explained. 'Nebuline never
smiles and I believe she sucks in her cheeks to appear thinner of face. Her
kind are interested greatly in death and all things dark, and are attracted to
Jeopardy because he communes with spirits. Still, Nebuline and Inshave
have money – plenty of it – so we don't complain.'

'Money? I'd have thought the Jeopardites would have been beggared.'

Grackle laughed. 'A joke! Only the sons and daughters of the rich are
drawn to Jeopardy's banner. It is a fact.'

Imphee frowned. 'You are too cynical, Grack,' she said. 'I'm sure Nebuline and Inshave aren't typical of their kind.'

Grackle shrugged. 'I doubt we'll ever find out.'

'Have you met many Jeopardites?' Delilah asked.

Imphee shook her head. 'No. A few months ago, some people came
through looking for the cult, but they hardly count as legitimate members.
Nebuline and Inshave are the first, although I suspect more will follow, once
the Ixmarites get to work. We've heard the Ixmarite oppression has become
harder further west since the ecclesiarch Wilfish Implexion had certain of
his decrees of authority passed by the Council of Ten in Gallimaufry. He

won't tolerate any transgression of Ixmaritian code and seeks to better his position in his Church. He does this by mass burnings of heretics and dissidents, I believe.' She shuddered. 'And we fear the fingers of Ixmarity are stretching eastwards, even to our little hollow.'

'But what have you to fear?' Delilah enquired.

'Covendale is not Ixmaritian. It never has been,' Imphee replied.

'But you must have an Ixmaritian church here, surely?'

'Yes,' Imphee answered warily. 'We do, but the priest is one of ours.'

'You mean he transgresses the Ixmarite code?' Delilah could hardly believe it. Although the priest in Samberdell had been tolerant, he would never have betrayed his faith himself.

'Our community is small,' Imphee said. 'We all know one another, and few Church officials pass through. Still, we are aware that this situation can't continue indefinitely. We just hope we get enough warning, should the Church begin to suspect us. We know its retaliation would be swift and brutal. Jeopardy has made it doubly suspicious and jumpy.'

Delilah shuddered in the warm afternoon. She could not imagine such a fell shadow falling over these rested hills. Across the river, she could see a lone figure in a long, flapping coat pacing around the field as if measuring something out. It was a tall, well-built man, whose head shone bald in the sunshine, but for a burst of long plaits and tails hanging from the top of his head. He appeared to be arguing with himself.

'What a strange man,' she remarked, pointing and laughing.

Imphee smiled faintly. 'That is Anvil Quizzinglass,' she said.

'What is he doing? Is he mad? Why is he staring at the ground like that and taking such big steps? Why the emphatic hand gestures and exasperated head-tossing, as if he is accompanied by someone who disagrees with him?'

'He is not mad,' said Grackle. 'He is merely fulfilling one of his functions.' And that was all either of the Ratheripes would speak on the subject.

When they returned to the Cat and Bucket, Pluffie Ratheripe was waiting with a smile and good news for Delilah. 'As luck would have it, a prominent personage of our community is looking for someone to clean her house,' she said. 'This would be a task of some weeks' duration, I should imagine, owing to the fact the job has not been done for several years.'

Delilah was not sure whether she should commit herself to so lengthy and employment. 'Who is this woman?' she asked.

'Her name is Mistress Wispish Ploverpage,' Pluffie said, in a tone that suggested the name should mean something.

'What does she do?'

'She is a woman of power, that is all I'll say for now,' Pluffie replied. 'Here, come and have a slice of pie before you meet our guests.'

By sundown, a number of people had come to drink in the bar of the Cat and Bucket, and Delilah helped out by ragging off spilled beer from the tables and gathering tankards. This was a job she quite enjoyed, owing to the fact that she was given much attention by the patrons and even had coins pressed into her palm by older members of the community. She was returning to the sluice room with an armful of washing up when Pluffie came and beckoned her into the corridor. 'The Jeopardites have come downstairs to dine,' she said. 'I have mentioned you to Inshave and he has agreed to speak to you.'

Delilah reached to brush strings of hair from her eyes with the back of her arm. She deposited the tankards in the large sink and rubbed her hands

213

on the apron Imphee had lent her. 'Shall I finish these first?'

Pluffie shook her head. 'No, no. You should go now, before they change their minds. They are, or can be, difficult customers.'

'Well, if it's any bother, I'll—'

'Come! Come!' Pluffie headed off down the corridor and Delilah was forced to follow.

The Cat and Bucket had a small private dining room for overnight guests at the back of the building, overlooking the yard. It contained only three tables, one of which, nearest the window, was spread with a sparkling white cloth and laid with cutlery. Two people were sitting there, in the light of a single candle. It was almost too dim to eat a meal, Delilah thought. Pluffie seemed to guess her thoughts and whispered, 'They are unfond of bright light, you see.' She ostentatiously cleared her throat. 'Master Macassar, Mistress Midnoon.' White faces turned towards them. Pluffie gripped Delilah's shoulders and pushed her forwards. 'Ahem, this is the young lady I told you about. The one looking for Resenence Jeopardy.'

At these words, Nebuline Midnoon hissed and half rose from her seat. 'What? You dare to reveal our presence to strangers?'

'Forgive me, mistress,' Pluffie continued doggedly, 'but I did have a word with Master Macassar earlier today when he came downstairs for another bottle of red wine. I was led to believe it would be quite in order for me to bring young Delilah to see you.'

'Well, it is certainly not quite in order!' Nebuline rasped. 'What were you thinking of, Inshave?'

The young man at the table dabbed his mouth with a napkin and shrugged in embarrassment. Delilah could tell he did not care much either way. He was painfully thin and sepulchrally white of face, dressed in black as the Ratheripes had described, his hair a furious thatch of inky feathery locks. Nebuline could easily have been his twin, but for the fact that her hair was lank about her face, hanging past her waist like a black silk veil. Her body was boyish in composition, with barely a bulge for breast or hip, swathed in a simple yet elegant gown of fine black linen. Her face was pretty but mean about the mouth. Delilah felt immediately wary of her.

'It will not, my velvet raven, do much harm to speak to the girl,' Inshave said in an affected voice. 'She is but a babe.'

Nebuline snarled emphatically. 'The Ixmarites are not beyond employing babies as spies!'

'I am not a spy for the Ixmarites,' Delilah said. 'I am travelling with Trajan Sacripent.' She hoped the name would mean something to the Jeopardites.

Nebuline frowned. 'Who?'

'A man . . . he is one of you. He became estranged from the group. He has a strange sickness and killed everyone in my village but myself. We are looking for Resenence Jeopardy.'

'I have never heard of this Sacripent person,' Nebuline declared. 'Have you?'

Inshave shook his head. 'He can be nobody of importance,' he said. 'You see, girl, we are of the inner circle of Jeopardy. We are of the elite. We know *everyone* of importance.'

Trajan, too, had claimed closeness with Jeopardy. Had he misled her? He certainly did not share the style or appearance of these two followers.

Delilah shrugged helplessly. 'We need to find the prophet,' she said. 'Only he can cure Trajan's afflictions. Please help me. If you know where Jeopardy is, tell me. You cannot imagine the difficulty we are in.'

'You are wasting your time,' Nebuline said, with a narrow smile. 'Jeopardy is not recruiting at present. We too have our difficulties, which is why the group is fragmenting for the time being. We have strategies to concoct for the future.'

'Do you know where Jeopardy is?' Delilah asked.

The two exchanged a covert glance. 'Of course,' Nebuline answered, 'but unfortunately we cannot divulge that information. It is too dangerous; we can trust nobody.'

Delilah walked purposefully across to their table. Up close, she could see the flakiness of Nebuline's white make-up. 'Please, it is very important. Trajan is dangerous and I cannot control him.'

'Jeopardy has worries of his own,' Nebuline snapped. 'A sick or deranged man is not his problem.'

A tide of anger coursed through Delilah's body. She had been spared a terrible death. Hidden knowledge had been revealed to her by the Saltcats. She was meant to find Resenence Jeopardy. Yet these two simpering humbugs were obstructing her. How could she extract information from them? It was obvious, from Nebuline's cold eyes, that she would not be forthcoming. Inshave's eyes were on his plate. That might be the way, then. But not here, not now. Delilah sighed and backed away.

'I understand,' she said. 'In your position, I would be as reticent, and in Jeopardy's position I would want my loyal followers to behave as such. But I can only swear to you that I mean your prophet no harm. My companion and I are heading south-west. If you were me, would you head that way?'

Inshave looked up quickly, and appeared about to speak, but Nebuline silenced him with a lethal stare. 'You can travel whichever way you want,' she answered. 'If Jeopardy wants you to find him, you will.' She picked up a silver fork and fingered its tines. 'Can I give a fairer answer than that?'

'No, mistress,' Delilah answered demurely. 'I thank you.'

Nebuline gestured carelessly with her hand. 'No need,' she said.

Delilah retreated and, with Pluffie, who had waited for her by the door, gratefully left the room. Outside, she sighed, her shoulders drooping in disappointment. Pluffie made a strangled sound which might have signalled disapproval. 'They came from the south-west,' she said.

'Pardon?' Delilah blinked up at her stern face.

'You heard. Come along now, there's pots to wipe and your friend must be hungry out there in the woods. Grackle can walk you to the edge of the village. These are strange times. It is best that a woman does not walk about alone at night.'

'I did not greatly take to your visiting Jeopardites,' Delilah said to Grackle Ratheripe as he walked her to near where Trajan was hiding.

'They have their ways, we have ours,' he replied enigmatically, swinging the basket of food his mother had made up on his arm.

'And what are your ways exactly?' Delilah enquired. 'You and Imphee are very secretive, your mother too. You are not Ixmaritian, so what are you?'

'We are not secretive,' Grackle said, 'not really, just careful. It seems that

215

everyone who does not share the Ixmaritian creed walks a dangerous course at present. We prefer not to advertise our beliefs, an idea you would do well to emulate as you travel.'

'I am not used to people in great numbers,' Delilah said glumly. 'This is all very confusing to me. At home, we had Ixmarites and Domino priests as well as our own witches and wizzakers. Nothing was secret. This suspicion and fear of danger is all very strange.'

'Well, you are a long way from home,' Grackle said. 'A little carefulness does no harm to anybody. Here, we have reached the crossroads. Where is your friend hiding?'

'You had better wait here,' Delilah said. 'The moon waxes gravid and his mood can be unpredictable. I'll be as quick as I can.'

Trajan was fretful when Delilah found him. 'Where have you been?' he demanded. 'Twice I decided to leave, but fear kept me under the roots of this tree. How could you keep me in terror like this?'

'Trajan, I'm sorry. I've made friends, who will help us. I have a job—'

'A job? How long are you planning to stay here?'

'We need funds,' Delilah said patiently. 'We cannot keep stealing from people. I have told my friends about you, and hope to find you somewhere secure to stay for a while so that I can earn some money.'

'Lock me in a room?' Trajan asked miserably. 'It will do no good. The moon enriches my muscles with terrible strength. Iron could not hold me against Her will!'

Delilah sighed. 'Well, your own fear held you here this evening. Trust me, Trajan. You said yourself you cannot risk entering a densely populated area, yet our necessity drives us to the very places you should avoid.' She paused. 'I've met two Jeopardites at the inn.'

Trajan's face lit up. 'Have you? Then we must be near to Jeopardy himself.'

Delilah loathed to disappoint him. 'I don't think so,' she said. 'It appears the cult is in trouble. The Ixmarites have broken them up. These people in Covendale know where Jeopardy is, I think, but they won't tell me.'

'That is because they are wary,' Trajan said, still beaming. 'What are their names? I might know them. Perhaps I could risk speaking to them – from a distance.'

'They do not know you, Trajan,' Delilah said. 'I asked. Their names are Nebuline Midnoon and Inshave Macassar. They say they are of Jeopardy's elite inner circle.'

Trajan frowned. 'Then they must be recent additions to the group,' he said. 'I can't say I've heard of them either.'

'Oh well.' Delilah squeezed Trajan's shoulder. 'Eat your food. How do you feel?'

Trajan sighed. 'Lonely,' he said.

MAGIK

Mistress Wispish Ploverpage lived in a high narrow house on the northern edge of the village. Hers was the only residence at the end of a long, narrow, twisting lane that was hemmed on either side by tall hedges of holly, punctuated by heavy ancient oaks. On the left, small hedged fields held flocks of sheep, while on the right an arm of the ancient forest crept right to the fringes of the hedge.

Delilah walked up the lane with Imphee Ratheripe hanging on her right arm. Pluffie Ratheripe marched ahead of them, wearing a smart bonnet decorated with red wax fruit and silk poppies. From the Ratheripes' air of nervous expectation, Delilah could only deduce that Mistress Ploverpage was indeed a person of rank and authority. She hoped the woman would not be too severe. Neither of the Ratheripe women responded favourably to questions concerning Mistress Ploverpage, but Delilah imagined she must be a rich woman living alone, perhaps someone concerned with the running of the village. The chimneys of the house could be seen from the end of the lane, which spoke of wealth. But if this was the case, why hadn't Mistress Ploverpage any servants to do her cleaning for her? The situation didn't really make much sense to Delilah, and she hoped she wasn't acting unwisely by allowing the Ratheripes to take control of her like this.

They came to a high wicket gate set in a socket of dense laurel. Pluffie paused with her hand upon the rusted latch. 'Answer succinctly any questions the mistress might put to you,' she advised Delilah, 'but ask no questions of your own.'

'My intention is to work, not ask questions,' Delilah said.

With a satisfied nod, Pluffie opened the gate, which screamed as if in alarm, and led the girls up the path. Delilah was amazed by the garden: hollyhocks, thorn-apple and ornamental thistles loomed over the rain-bleached, blue-gravel path. Ivy grew all over the house, and even over some of the windows. In places, mats of creeper lolled drooping towards the ground, as if someone had ripped it away from the panes. Looking at the state of the windows – her mother had taught her long ago that you could tell much from the cleanliness of a woman's windows – Delilah decided

Mistress Ploverpage must be very old and probably very eccentric, which was why she didn't want servants around. Still, there was evidence that the garden was tended, even if it was rather overrun by the more dominant plants.

The front door, of twisted wooden panels, stood ajar. Pluffie knocked three times and entered the house, the girls following.

Delilah's heart sank when she saw the hallway. The floor was of stout oak planks, the stairs a grand sweep of oak to the first-floor gallery. The walls, too, were panelled in wood. However, it seemed that no one had applied wax to the wood for many years. Dust mantled everything; the floor was sticky underfoot. Stained windows above the stairs were dull with grime.

'As you can see,' Imphee confided in a whisper, 'there is much work to be done.'

Delilah thought it would take her an entire season to clean the hall alone, never mind the rest of the house. Perhaps the other rooms weren't as neglected. She began to think of ways in which she could get Trajan to help her. His awkward afflictions aside, she could do with an extra pair of hands.

'My lady?' Pluffie called out. Her voice was swallowed by the stillness of the house. There was no response, but it seemed the house had heard the call. There was an air of cautious expectation.

'Perhaps she's in the garden,' Delilah suggested, walking over to examine a series of small cupboards, little more than boxes, on one of the walls. All the cupboards were open, revealing their contents. In one was a collection of coloured stones, in another a heap of dusty, dismembered dragonflies. Other boxes contained such bizarre things as desiccated dead mice, plaited hanks of mouldy corn, stuffed lizards, the shell of an enormous spider, and the legs and claws of birds. Delilah drew away in distaste. Some of the boxes smelled highly disagreeable. She was regretting, with every passing moment, her decision to accept the job.

'My lady!' Pluffie called again. Delilah thought she detected a note of unease in the woman's voice.

The sound of a door opening came from the gallery. It was followed by silence, and then the quick scamper of feet, such as a child might make. Delilah heard, or thought she heard, a faint, mischievous giggle.

'Pluffie?' Someone leaned over the banisters overhead. Delilah looked up and saw a veil of pinky-red hair framing a small, pixie-like face.

A child, she thought. A child?

Pluffie curtsied and said, 'Lady Wispish, we have brought the girl. Delilah Latterkin. The girl to clean for you.'

'So soon?' declared the creature drooping from the gallery. 'Has time passed so quickly?'

'Indeed it has, my lady,' Pluffie said, in a voice one might use with a fractious infant. 'The cleaning time has come.'

Wispish Ploverpage emitted a loud sigh that swept around the lofty environs of the hall. She ran to the stairs in a maelstrom of bright hair, trailing a fluttering robe of vivid red and purple silk adorned with indigo fringes. She seemed like a small coruscating hummingbird in the dark, silent gloom of the house. She fluttered to a halt before Delilah and took the girl's hands in her own. She was more or less the same height as Delilah, but from close quarters it was possible to see that Mistress Ploverpage was not a child. Still, she appeared to be a very young woman, perhaps somewhere between the ages of eighteen and twenty-one. To Delilah, she looked imp-

218

ishly inhuman, and she wondered whether Wispish Ploverpage claimed a measure of hewkin blood.

Wispish gave Delilah's had a firm shake. Her hands were like little paws, hot and dry. 'And who is it that looked into your eyes and left that presence there?' she asked, with a smile.

Delilah shrugged awkwardly. She felt very large and clumsy beside Mistress Ploverpage, despite the fact they were very much of a size. Her first thought was of the Saltcats; her second of Resenence Jeopardy. 'I don't know,' she said lamely.

Wispish gave her hands another brief shaking, and released them. 'Well now, Mistress Ratheripe, you have found me a flower, a blood-kissed flower, for which I thank you. I could offer you tea, but my creatures have spoken against that today. Perhaps tomorrow. Soon we shall see.' She paused.

'Do not apologise,' Pluffie said. 'I understand perfectly.'

Wispish nodded vaguely. 'Ah, I hear Anvil's step in the fern behind the house. I think it would be better if he didn't see you at this moment; it could change a whole host of tomorrows, I promise you. Design is a wicked business.'

'We shall take our leave of you, then,' Pluffie said, and put her hand upon Delilah's shoulder. 'Take care,' she said. 'Perhaps we shall see you again soon.'

'But what about Trajan?' Delilah asked. She felt she should have broached this subject before. 'I can't leave him out in the woods alone for . . . well, for as long as it will take me to clean this house.' She glanced dismally around the hall.

Pluffie looked slightly discomfited, as if she wished Delilah had not mentioned Trajan in front of Wispish Ploverpage.

'It is careless to leave men in the woods,' Wispish said. 'Better to gather them in, in case they forget they are human.'

'Perhaps you had better explain about your friend,' Imphee suggested.

'Oh, later, later,' Wispish said, with a smiling frown, shaking her hair.

'But—' Delilah noticed Pluffie giving her a discreet signal; she held her tongue.

'Until later,' Pluffie said, bowing her head to Wispish Ploverpage. 'Come along, Imphee.'

They walked out of the door, and Delilah watched the bright silk flowers bobbing on Pluffie's hat until she disappeared from sight through the gate. It was like friendship walking out of her life. She sighed and turned round. If anything, the hall seemed gloomier and filthier than before. 'Where would you like me to start?' she asked.

Wispish was still staring through the open door, a thoughtful expression on her pointed face. 'Hmm? Oh, with a cup of cinnamon tea and a story. Come upstairs.' She scampered away, floating up the stairs like a scrap of gaily coloured rag. Delilah began to walk up after her, but after a few seconds was alarmed to find she had not passed beyond the third step. How strange! She was convinced she'd mounted at least a dozen. Wispish was waiting for her on the gallery. 'Run!' she called, leaning over the banister. 'It is the only way.'

Delilah increased her pace, and the stairs seemed to fly by. In fact, she was not convinced her feet even touched the treads. One moment, she was standing at the bottom, the next she was beside Wispish on the gallery.

'That felt very odd,' Delilah said weakly. She felt quite dizzy.

'Mmm, a precaution,' Wispish explained. 'When I am alone, I spend all of my time upstairs, and don't like people intruding. Once, a man came to investigate my house – not an Ixmarite, for I have other traps for them – and I was so engrossed in my thoughts, he was stuck on the stairs for several days! Anvil found the poor creature; he was nearly dead of thirst.' She hooked a hand through one of Delilah's elbows. 'Come, see my room.'

'She must be a witch,' Delilah thought, allowing herself to be led along the gallery, her head aswim. 'She weaves enchantments.'

Judging from the clutter in the room, Wispish Ploverpage appeared to spend all her time there. It was a large room on the first floor, with heavy chenille curtains of faded crimson and purple to disguise the rather stained and crumbling walls. The floor was covered in tapestried rugs and enormous silk cushions, in jewel colours. A single broad table against the wall was heaped with books and plates, articles of clothing and small glass vases, which presumably contained cosmetics and toiletries. Along one wall was an array of glass tanks, which contained an abundance of emerald-green lizards. But the main feature of the room was that it was full of cages, each with a single occupant – birds of every size and hue. A thousand songs seemed to fill the air, every one different, but all in harmony. Delilah felt her dizziness increase as she stepped over the threshold. How could anyone converse in such a din? She saw Mistress Ploverpage's mouth moving and assumed she must be speaking, but could only raise her hands in a helpless gesture of incomprehension. Wispish pursed her mouth and shook her fingers. Instantly, the room was silent. Every cage had mysteriously become covered with a dark blue cloth.

'You are a witch,' Delilah said.

Wispish shrugged. 'Not a word I'd use,' she said. 'I prefer to think of myself as a designer, a designer of life, of reality. It is merely a matter of belief. So, what brings you to Covendale?'

'I am on a journey,' Delilah explained, sitting down on the cushion Wispish indicated to her. 'I am looking for a man; a prophet who is also a sorcerer.'

Wispish threw another shawl over her shoulders – this one scarlet with gold fringes – and sat down opposite her guest. A fat ginger cat slunk through the cushions and crawled onto her lap. Wispish plunged tiny, thin fingers into its fur.

'Who isn't?' she replied, frowning. 'If I met a woman who wasn't looking for a man with those qualities, I would know I'd met an imbecile. Tea?' She lifted a rug by her side to reveal a tray set with steaming teapot, milk and cups.

Delilah nodded. 'This man is . . . different.'

'All men are different,' Wispish remarked, pouring the tea. 'What I would like to know is what led you to seek him out. I can learn far more hearing about you than the man himself. Tell me the history you think you have, the one you can recall.'

Delilah frowned. 'I don't think I understand you. The history I can recall? Are there others?'

Wispish nodded. 'Of course there are. Tell me what you remember.'

As Delilah spoke the words that wove her own story, she found a sense of unreality creeping over her. It was like reciting a fairy tale she had learned by heart; a memory of a memory. It no longer seemed real. She could describe in detail the smells and sounds of Samberdell as it died, but it was as if she'd only read the description somewhere. Her own sensations were dim. Wispish listened carefully, stroking her cat all the while. Delilah wanted to tell her about the Saltcats, and was afraid she would not be able to speak, but there was no lock on her tongue in Wispish's presence.

'I know these women,' Wispish said.

'Have you been to the mill pool?' Delilah asked.

'No. What I mean is, I know them as types. You were privileged; you wove your story well at that point.'

'I seemed to have little control,' Delilah said.

'Nonsense, we create our own histories from one step to the next,' Wispish said. 'Still, I am concerned for you. You are pursuing an illusion. I wonder what the Saltcats had in mind for you. I cannot believe they are interested in Jeopardy. Why should they be? He is a mote compared to them.'

Delilah was quite surprised by Wispish's remark. 'His followers think him a great man.'

Wispish sighed. 'They would. Foolish lambs. One thing that is a constant source of perplexity to me is the way people have to attach themselves to beliefs. They turn a thing that should be music and light into clay. Beliefs should mutate daily, otherwise the history becomes warped. Ixmarity is the product of such clay. Jeopardy, too. He is nothing; a posturing and arrogant self-absorbed buffoon! He likes the sound of his own voice far too much; he has been imprisoned by his belief in himself that he is special.'

'I have to find him,' Delilah said in a low voice. She dared not look Wispish in the eye.

'His face interests you,' she remarked. 'I have heard of his beauty. I have seen it too.'

'You've met him?'

'No. I don't have to. His image is caught in the eyes of his followers. I see him now in you.'

Delilah looked down.

'And of course you have to find him.' Wispish laughed. 'You have decided that, and it is not my place to interfere. Anvil – my partner – and I observe his career with great interest, but from a distance. It will all end in blood and smoke, I'm sure. A wise girl would watch from the boundary of his influence.'

'I will bear your advice in mind,' Delilah said.

'Your friend Trajan must come to the house tonight,' Wispish decided. 'Anvil can fetch him.'

'But his afflictions—'

Wispish waved this objection away. 'Anvil believes in nothing, including curses, if curse it is. Therefore they cannot affect him adversely. Personally, I think this Trajan has created these afflictions to make himself more interesting, but it is difficult to judge without having met him. Most of the Jeopardites are like that; boring people with an innate need for character.' She smiled. 'However, I do not view you as such.'

'You inspire a strange kind of hope and confidence within me, Mistress Ploverpage,' Delilah said.

Wispish made a playful, girlish gesture. 'Good. I hate to see you wasting your time, but I suppose there must be some purpose in this folly.' She put her hands upon her knees and then scrambled to her feet. 'Well, as is the custom, we must set you to work. I hope cleaning is not a labour you find tedious, otherwise I shall have to feel sorry about inflicting it upon you.'

221

'I will not find the work tedious,' Delilah said, 'although I am concerned about how long the task will take me. Could Trajan not assist me?'

Wispish frowned. 'Oh dear me, no. That would never do. My neighbours would be most upset. It'd be against their custom, you see, and I do all that I can to abide by their traditions.'

'What custom is this?'

'A custom of belief,' Wispish answered.

'Are you the priestess of this community?' Delilah asked, hoping that wasn't too probing a question.

Wispish shook her head. 'No, in some ways I am a captive of Covendale, in others its inspiration and its lifeblood. Later, I might explain. It is a story to tell in darkness, after the consumption of a good meal and considerable quantities of liquor. Anyway, to return to your work. You will need to finish the job by midsummer morn.'

Delilah had lost track of time wandering the hills and forests. 'And when is that?'

'In ten days,' Wispish answered.

Ten days! Delilah thought woefully of the size of the house, its utter decrepitude. Still, perhaps all Wispish would require of her was a bit of sweeping and dusting; she did not appear to place too much regard upon tidiness.

'You can start in the kitchen, which is the heart of the house,' Wispish said.

Delilah followed her out of the room. 'Must I run downstairs?' she asked.

Wispish grinned at her. 'Not unless you want to.' With that, she lifted her fringes and skirts and scampered down the gallery towards the stairs.

In the hallway, the square of light framed by the door was occluded by the tall figure of a man who stood with legs apart, his hands on his hips. Delilah felt he had been waiting for them to come downstairs. She recognised him as being the person she'd seen pacing Sheen Meadow the day before, whom the Ratheripes had told her was Anvil Quizzinglass.

'Anvil!' Wispish exclaimed. She ran up to embrace the man in an affectionate manner. 'Look here, we have a girl. She has been sent to clean our house.'

Anvil Quizzinglass regarded Delilah thoughtfully. His attention seemed held elsewhere. After a few moments, he twitched his shoulder and ducked his head to the side, with the remark, 'It is all nonsense! She seems perfectly human to me!'

'Excuse me?' murmured Delilah.

Wispish uttered a short cry of impatience and began tugging Anvil's ropes of hair. A swarm of small creatures, half lizard, half rodent, burst chittering from his plaits and tails to run wildly across his bare head, apparently uttering cries of consternation.

'Enough, skitterlings!' Wispish said. 'You must not insult our guest and employee.' The small creatures uttered a consonous moan of regret before burrowing back into the roots of Anvil's locks. He gave a twitch of discomfort, and then smiled widely.

'Welcome,' he said, his eyes sparkling in a manner that spoke of wicked and irresistible secrets about to be revealed.

At Wispish's instruction, Delilah told Anvil about Trajan and where he could be found. As Wispish had predicted, Anvil exhibited no concern whatsoever for Trajan's tempers or infectious blights. Delilah stared at him in wonder.

'I am confused,' she admitted, 'for I have seen the dire effects of Trajan's curse myself. How is it that you can be immune, simply because you refuse to believe in the afflictions? I hardly think my dead family and neighbours gave the possibility of disease a thought when Trajan burst into our community. Consequently, I fail to understand how it could have affected them, if belief in the condition is what causes it to work.'

'The matter is indeed complex,' Anvil agreed. 'Later, I will attempt to enlighten you.'

'Trajan himself will no doubt be interested,' Delilah said.

Anvil assured her that she could count on her companion being safely installed in the house after sundown. Then, with a twirling gesture of his right arm, he departed into the depths of the house, singing a ribald tune as he did so.

'Dear man,' Wispish exclaimed, her eyes misty, and then collected herself. 'Now, the kitchen.'

The kitchen was, as Delilah suspected it would be, messy in the extreme. It was a huge, low-ceilinged room, dark because the windows were filthy. Black pots were heaped in a stained and cracked sink, all coated with mature grease and the remains of meals. All the crockery had somehow melded into one sticky pile; it had been dumped on the wide kitchen table.

'Some of the plates will break when you clean them,' Wispish said, showing no shame whatsoever for the state of her house. 'But that is unavoidable.'

Delilah looked around herself with despair. Surely it would take her half a day to clean the windows alone; the kitchen needed at least two days' work on it in her estimation, and it was but one room in the house. Wispish noticed her consternation and laid a reassuring hand upon her arm.

'Don't worry,' she said brightly, 'when you clean the heart, you are well on the way to cleaning the whole.'

Delilah smiled weakly.

She spent the whole day in the kitchen, with only the minimum of pauses, during which she leaned dazedly against the sink to inspect the small impact her labours appeared to have had on the mess. At sundown, Wispish tripped into the room. She spun round on her feet a few times in order to appraise Delilah's handiwork, but made no comment on it.

'Come and rest now,' she said, curling an arm round Delilah's shoulders and leading her from the room. 'You have done enough for one day.'

Delilah sighed. 'It is a task, to be sure,' she said wearily, a polite understatement, in her opinion. Only a small glimmer of relief had been provided by the discovery that at least the house had a water heating system – which growled below in the cellars. This had made the work somewhat less arduous but nevertheless all Delilah had managed to achieve that day was clearance of the washing-up. All the cupboards had been filthy and would need scrubbing before she could put anything away. Miserably, she had simply hung a few clean pots up above the range and had stacked everything else on the table, which she had managed to scrub down.

'Forget the drudgery of it all,' Wispish cried cheerfully as they mounted the stairs at a trot. 'This evening we shall have a fabulously sumptuous meal together.' The remark made Delilah's heart sink even further. The last thing she wanted to do was begin the next day with more pot-scouring.

'I am unconvinced your friend will be safe from Trajan Sacripent,' she said gloomily.

'No need for concern,' Wispish replied.

'But even should Mr Quizzinglass be immune to his crotchets, there is a danger Trajan will attack anyone else they might meet on their way here.'

Wispish shook her head. 'Anvil knows the quietest tracks,' she said. 'Please do not worry.'

Anvil brought Trajan directly to Wispish's private room. All the bird cages were covered and the room was lit by dozens of candles. Anvil himself was a big man, but he appeared dwarfed by the bulk of Trajan, who stood quivering and rolling his eyes like a great frightened, or partially enraged, bear. He looked at Delilah with an expression that seemed to signify she had betrayed him in some way. She found that she was not pleased to see him. His beard and hair were matted with twigs and leaves, his clothes were muddy and he smelled distinctly unsavoury, filling the room with a powerful sour odour that spoke of human dirt and fear. Still, although his hands twitched, he did not appear about to launch an attack upon anybody.

'Greetings, Master Sacripent,' Wispish said, rising from the cushions. 'Please make yourself comfortable while I fetch some refreshment.' She disappeared into an adjoining room through a curtain and returned almost instantly with a tray heaped with covered dishes. These she placed upon the table which had been cleared of mess. Delilah presumed there must be another kitchen on the premises, seeing as Wispish had not prepared any food downstairs. She hoped it was in better condition than the one she'd just left.

While Wispish flitted back and forth, carrying more dishes and tureens into the room, Anvil pulled aside another curtain, which Delilah had presumed covered a window, to reveal an alcove where three enormous flagons of ale sweated upon a stone shelf. Eventually, all was ready and Wispish summoned Delilah and Trajan to the table.

'Don't you have any servants?' Delilah asked as she sat down.

Wispish shook her head. 'No, they are often sour, and besides, what would I need them for?' She helped herself to a ladleful of leeks steamed in spices. Delilah could not think of an answer.

Trajan had not yet spoken to Delilah, and despite the fact that she stared at him across the table, did not even look in her direction. Delilah considered his behaviour puerile. Hadn't she brought him to comfort and a hot meal? Wasn't he in company unaffected by his condition, which meant he could relax? She watched him as he helped himself daintily to generous portions of food, deciding that she would not be the one to break their silence.

'So, you believe you carry a curse upon your head,' Wispish said, biting into a patty of spiced meat. 'How long have you carried it?'

Trajan gave her a sidelong glance. 'Since childhood,' he said.

'How inconvenient,' Wispish declared. 'In that case, you are lucky to have survived to maturity. I would have thought someone would have ended the nuisance of you before now.'

Trajan lowered his eyes. 'It has become worse over the years. As a young boy, I offended a strange woman who lived alone in the forest with her son. I was always big for my age, and confess with shame I often abused my size. I bullied the child of the forest woman, pushed him into water, made him fall from trees, forced him to commit dangerous and unreasonable dares. Eventually, the lady came to the yard of my parents' house and screeched out her revenge. She cursed me. For years, the curse manifested in no worse way than to pollute my sleep. I dreamed continually of death and decay. I didn't have a decent night's rest from the moment the curse was uttered, which turned me into a fretful, sour creature. Then, as adulthood stole upon me, I began to realise the dreams. At first, the plague was weak, and only made people who came into contact with me feel tired and depressed. At night, I became irritable in the extreme and often caused fights in local hostelries. Then, as time advanced, people whom I worked with or visited during the day began to fall ill; they vomited and voided with uncontrollable frenzy. Gradually, people associated these bouts of sickness with proximity to me. Healers examined me cautiously, but it was evident I did not suffer from the malady I passed on to others. My family were exhausted by constant sickness, so I was forced to move out of my home and live alone. While the infectiousness strengthened, so did my night-time tantrums. Eventually, I killed a man.'

'And how long ago was this hag-ridden climax reached?' Anvil asked. He had a smile upon his face, as if he did not believe what Trajan was saying.

'Just before I joined the Cult of Jeopardy,' Trajan said.

'That would seem to be a great coincidence,' Anvil said. He twitched suddenly, and Delilah thought she could see tiny pricks of light, which might be reflected from little eyes, glinting among the heavy plaits that fell over his shoulder.

'You said you could explain how Trajan's curse affects people,' Delilah said.

Anvil made an expansive gesture with his hands. 'All I can explain is how it doesn't affect me, or Wispish, or perhaps even you.' He leaned forward to expound upon this, frowning and slapping his head as high-pitched squeaks emanated from his hair. 'I feel that being affected by other people's curses – which some might say reside only in the minds of those who carry them – is simply a symptom of the way the world is. It seems to be human nature to have no autonomy, to relinquish hard-earned independence at the least excuse, to possess no confidence or faith in oneself. I believe that people fear being powerful which, if only they could know it, is an innate condition of humanity.' He shrugged. 'I accept my own brilliance as a living creature; none can affect me. Wispish feels the same, as do many others. This Jeopardy character is probably one of them.'

'My curse is very real,' Trajan cried. 'This theorising makes no sense. Tell it to a person coughing out his life after a spore of my plague has touched him!'

Anvil paused to lift a skitterling from his collar by one of its puny limbs. He examined it as it hung, wriggling and protesting, from his fingers. 'I do not dispute the reality of the condition, only people's inability to protect themselves.' He flicked the skitterling back onto his head, where it ran shrieking to the sanctuary of his hair. 'I find it hard to sympathise with deliberate victims.'

Delilah, thinking of her dead mother and friends, thought that remark was grossly unfair. 'What are those things running about over your head and nesting in your hair?' she demanded bluntly, pointing. 'Are they part of a curse?'

Anvil laughed politely. 'Not at all. They are my messengers and advisers.

Would you like one?' He reached up, as if to withdraw a skitterling from his scalp.

Delilah shuddered, chastened because she had not scored a point. 'No thank you!'

Wispish laughed in a shrill manner and then grinned at Trajan. 'You must tell us how you met your saviour, the great Jeopardy,' she said. 'What did he do to you?'

Trajan straightened his spine and jutted out his chin. 'I can remember it as if it were yesterday. I had been living rough for several months, ostracised by my family after I'd attacked my grandmother, and scorned by my friends after I'd made them all ill. As I travelled to escape the pain in my heart, the symptoms of the curse intensified. I was a danger to all I met. My only respite came in the early evening, when day turns towards night, because both afflictions are at their weakest then. One day, I came across a crowd of people unexpectedly, gathered at a crossroads. My instinct was to hide, but my attention was caught by the man who stood on an old monument in the middle of the crossroads. It was Resenence Jeopardy. I listened to his words, and though I could understand little of what he said, somehow his voice soothed me.

He saw me in the crowd. I was aware of the attention of his eyes; they were as yellow as a wolf's. He pointed at me and uttered a few unintelligible words. Then he leapt down from the monument and strode towards me. I cowered away from him, trying to explain the dangers of too close an approach. Jeopardy only shook his head. "I see your despair," he said. "In my presence, in the company of my followers, you are healed." He laid his hands upon my eyes. Moments later, a number of his company came to lift me to my feet, for I had fallen as he'd touched me. They hugged me and pronounced themselves my brothers and sisters. Suddenly, I belonged somewhere again and could experience the warmth of love. As long as I was with the Jeopardites, the curse did not manifest once.' He shook his head sadly, clearly mourning the loss of his companions.

'Unfortunate stipulations upon the cure,' Wispish said to Anvil, and then smiled in rather an acid fashion at Trajan. 'A more generous, or more powerful, healer would have lifted the curse completely.'

'You do not understand,' Trajan said in a surly voice. 'My afflictions are spiritual more than physical.'

Wispish laughed. 'Rats' testicles bulging from a bag!' she exclaimed. 'I hardly think your victims would have particularly spiritual thoughts in mind as they writhe and bleed to extinction.'

Delilah saw Trajan's face colour round his beard. She hoped Wispish and Anvil wouldn't provoke him too much. 'I was safe with Resenence Jeopardy,' he said mulishly.

'So how did you come to lose him?' Anvil asked.

Delilah knew that Trajan did not like to talk about that. She herself had never been able to drag the details out of him, other than that he blamed himself.

'It was the fault of the Ixmarites,' Trajan said, which was certainly a new thread to the hidden story.

Anvil and Wispish exchanged a glance. 'Is that so?'

'Why, yes. I was guarding the path. My people should have come back for me . . .' For a moment, there was the ghost of anger in Trajan's voice, then he sighed. 'They would have come back for me, but it was too late, too

226

difficult.' He shrugged. 'It's no matter. I tore the Ixies who were following us limb from limb once the moon rose.'

Wispish grinned and effected a theatrical shudder. 'How careless of Master Jeopardy to leave such a potent weapon as yourself lying around.'

'And, it might be added, how irresponsible,' Anvil said, brushing a rogue skitterling back behind his ear.

'You do not understand,' Trajan said. 'It was not Resenence's fault. He did not know I'd been left behind. He was being hounded by the Ixmarites. All was confusion.'

'Did not know, or did not care, I wonder,' Anvil said.

Trajan clenched his fists and spoke in a strained voice. 'It pains me to hear you cast doubt upon his integrity.'

'Perhaps we are unfair on you,' Wispish remarked, 'for we do not share your zeal. Come now, commit this fare to your belly. We should be enjoying ourselves.'

After everyone had eaten and drunk to their fill, the party slumped down upon the cushions once more. At Delilah's request, Wispish explained how she had come to live in Covendale, and what her function was there. As Delilah had suspected, Wispish's blood was not completely human. At least, Wispish's mother had claimed she'd been seduced by an ardent hewkin, once it became evident to her community that she was with child. 'We lived on the fringes of Haling Heart,' Wispish said. 'It is a forest that heaves with all manner of peculiar life, driven there, I suspect, by the Ixmarites.' When Wispish had reached her teens, she became victim to an irrepressible desire to travel. 'It was my father's blood, she said. 'It was never happy staying in one place. I had to obey its surges.' Eventually, her wanderings led her to Covendale.

She had not planned to stay, but she arrived at an unfortunate time. The Covendalers, being a witching community, were presided over by a Lady of magical prowess who acted as mentor and spiritual guide. Wispish went into the Cat and Bucket in order to refresh herself. Inside, drinking ale, was aged Dame Bleadie, who was Covendale's Lady at that time. When she caught sight of Wispish, she rose abruptly from her seat with a squawk, knocked over her ale, pointed a rigid finger at the surprised newcomer, and keeled over dead. The inn's customers looked on in stunned surprise, and then hurried forward to surround Wispish.

'Frankly, I was terrified,' Wispish confessed. 'I thought they meant to do me harm, but that was not the case. Apparently, Dame Bleadie had been sick for months and had been complaining that she had lived too long and now wanted only to die in peace. The Covendalers would not hear of that; she had to find a successor before she could depart her life. Consequently, poor Bleadie had been kept alive with potions and magical inducements. The moment she saw me, she lost no time in passing over the burden of her authority.' Wispish sighed. 'So, now I am here, and my father's blood, satisfied for being recognised, allows my feet a respite. It is not too bad a life. I preside over festivals, I fashion cantrips and spells, I give advice when it's asked for. In return, all my wants are catered for.' She smiled at Anvil. 'And I bewitched myself a mate when the right one came along. Now, we work together.'

'The Covendalers seem to provide cleaning staff on an infrequent basis,' Delilah could not help pointing out.

Wispish shrugged. 'Ah, that is easy to explain. Through the purging of

227

my abode, I experience a surge of vitality and youth. I think I should point out that I have lived in Covendale for fifty years. I am intrinsically bonded to this house.'

'Would you grow old and die if you left it, then?' Delilah asked.

'Who can tell?' Wispish replied. 'I have never thought to test the matter.'

The following morning, just after dawn, Delilah experienced a strange awakening. Late the previous night, Wispish had installed her in a small comfortable room a couple of doors away from her own chamber. As she was unused to drinking large quantities of liquor, Delilah had fallen asleep very quickly and had slept the wooden sleep of the drunken. However, just after sunrise, she was literally shaken awake. At first, upon opening her eyes, she was convinced that someone had physically touched her, but then she realised that the building itself was in motion. From below came the sound of something crashing to the ground.

Delilah scrambled out of bed and lurched over to the window. Her head swam with more than the effects of the previous night's drinking. As she peered through the glass, she realised that the tremor had passed. Outside all was still, and the world seemed wrapped in an eerie silence. Delilah noticed that there was a long crack in the tiles of the yard below, from which a yellowish steam emerged. 'It was an earthquake,' she thought muzzily, and felt suddenly very sleepy again. She staggered back to her bed and snuggled under the quilts once more, soon to be embraced by a lighter sleep than before, which was filled with a succession of brief disquieting dreams of being lost and threatened.

A few hours later, Delilah woke up again, feeling considerably less dizzy than when the earth tremor had troubled her sleep. She washed herself at the toilet stand in the corner of the room, and used some of the subtly scented powders and creams Wispish had left there for her use. Then, she left her room and went to find Trajan. She knew which room had been allocated to him, and hoped to discuss his cool behaviour towards her the night before, which had not been resolved by the time they'd gone to bed.

His room, however, was empty, the bed neatly made. Perhaps Anvil had taken him out with him.

Wispish's room was also empty of human presences, but a tray had been left on the table containing a plate of bread rolls, a dish of creamy butter curls and a saucer of rich blackberry conserve. A jug of fresh, cold milk stood on the shelf in the alcove. Knowing instinctively that the breakfast had been left for her, Delilah ate and drank her fill. Then, feeling much refreshed, she went downstairs to recommence work.

In the kitchen, she was surprised to discover she had obviously achieved more than she'd imagined the previous day. The shelves of the cupboards were still rather grubby, but all the working surfaces were clean, and the range did not appear half as grease-encrusted as she'd thought. She filled some pails with hot water at the sink, and opened the cupboard beneath to extract the last bag of cleaning grit. She would have to speak to Wispish about purchasing some more. The two bags she'd used so far had been ancient and mouse-nibbled, the grit inside almost solid through damp. It seemed, however that her mistress anticipated her requirements: pushed to the back of the cupboard were over half a dozen new packets of grit. Delilah was surprised that Wispish had thought to address such a mundane issue as the replenishment of cleaning supplies; she seemed scatty and vague in the extreme. With renewed optimism, Delilah set to work.

By lunchtime she had nearly finished in the kitchen. The cleaning grit seemed to be of a superior blend to the one she'd used the previous day, because the accumulation of oily grime succumbed to the wisp and bristle of her cleaning utensils without much of a fight. Feeling bored of her surroundings, and yet rather pleased with the fruits of her labours, she decided to stop work for a while. She left the kitchen and ran up the stairs, to see whether Wispish or anyone else was about. If not, perhaps some lunch had been left out for her.

The moment Delilah set foot over Wispish's threshold, every bird in the room suddenly began to shriek as if in panic and senselessly threw themselves against the bars of their cages. Their shrill cries did not sound like bird calls. To Delilah, the strident cacophony sounded like the terrified screams of thousands of human beings in pain, heard from a distance. She pressed her hands over her ears, the effect of which was simply to clarify the screams in her head. She heard laments and cries, a multitude of souls bemoaning circumstances of privation and despair, grieving their losses and torments with soul-deep horror. The birds continued to hurl their fragile bodies at the cage bars, dislodging feathers which flew into the room. Delilah wished that Wispish would come. What if the birds all killed themselves? She stumbled backwards to the door and gratefully escaped into the corridor. The moment the door closed she could hear nothing at all.

'How very peculiar,' she thought, followed quickly by the realisation that a person should never be surprised by what they might encounter in a witch's boudoir.

As she reached the bottom of the stairs and the passageway that led to the kitchen, Delilah heard a comforting noise that spoke plainly of human activity. Something was being moved on the kitchen table. Hurrying along the passage and into the kitchen Delilah was surprised to discover Grackle Ratheripe nosing through the crockery on the table.

'What are you doing here?' she demanded. 'How did you get in?' She realised she had been more shaken by the episode with the birds than she'd thought. Her voice sounded shaky, and far too sharp. She was really quite relieved to see Grackle standing there.

'I came to see you,' Grackle replied, and then added, 'My mother sent me.' He swept a bow. 'I apologise for invading your premises, Mistress Latterkin, but I came in, as people generally do, through the back door.'

'It was locked,' Delilah said, pointing at the door. The previous day, she had tried to open it herself, but the bolts and locks had been so rusty she hadn't been able to move it.

Grackle shrugged. 'Well, it's open now.' He looked round the kitchen, his hands on his hips, nodding appreciatively. 'My, what a job you've done on this place.'

'Well, it'll do,' Delilah said modestly. She didn't think she'd done all that wonderful a job. And yet, as she glanced round the room, she was surprised by the improvement. It would not be an exaggeration to say that the place appeared newly decorated, even though she hadn't taken so much as a rag to the walls. Pots gleamed, windows sparkled; there was even a scent of lemon in the air. Had Wispish turned her hand to the job in the night?

'Are you hungry?' Grackle asked. 'Mother has sent you a basket.' He gestured to a covered pannier standing by the door.

'Yes, I'm starving.' Delilah went to explore Pluffie's offerings. 'Would you like some?'

Grackle dragged a chair away from the table and sat down. 'Yes, why not?'

Delilah found a number of parcels in the basket, which she unwrapped. One contained slices of ham, another a jar of pickles, while in a third she discovered some freshly buttered hunks of new bread. Her mouth began to water.

'Can I have one of these?' Grackle asked.

Delilah looked up. He was pointing towards a bowl of ripe, red apples. 'Didn't you bring them?' she asked.

He shook his head.

Delilah shrugged. 'Help yourself.' She knew the apples had not been there before she'd gone upstairs.

'Well, the final preparations are under way for Queen's Fete,' Grackle said, biting into an apple.

'Which queen is this?' Delilah asked. King Aristocete's wife, Shumah, had expired from a cachexy the year before. News of the death had been brought to every corner of the land, even Samberdell, by heralds on black horses, clothed in dark sackcloth, their heads shaved and smeared with ashes.

'The Queen of the Land, of course,' Grackle replied. 'Will you come to the fete?'

'We don't have a queen.' Delilah said. 'She died last year.'

Grackle grinned. 'This one never dies. She is the consort of the Harvest King. Will you come or not? I'd be happy to escort you.'

'I'll probably be too busy,' Delilah said. She felt disposed to be awkward, even though she realised she was pleased Grackle had asked her to the fete. She'd already decided he was not as ugly as she'd first thought.

'Oh, your work will be done by then,' Grackle replied airily. 'You must come. I might be moved to give you a midsummer kiss!'

Delilah grimaced. 'Is that supposed to encourage me?' she enquired primly. 'I prefer to decide myself whom I might kiss, and when.'

'Then I'll await your command,' Grackle said, flinging out his arms. He helped himself to some of the food.

Delilah decided to change the subject. 'Did you notice the earthquake this morning?'

Grackle laughed. 'What earthquake? I felt nothing.'

'Well, there was one,' Delilah snapped. 'Very early, just after dawn. I expect you slept through it.'

Grackle shook his head. 'Mother had Imph and me out of bed well before dawn this morning,' he said. 'None of us noticed the earth shaking.'

'Well, it must have affected only a small area then,' Delilah said peevishly.

'Perhaps you were dreaming,' Grackle suggested.

'I wasn't.'

They ate in silence for a while.

'If only you could help me here,' Delilah said, 'then I might feel sure the work will be finished by midsummer.' She sighed. 'As it is, I don't know. I think your mother and Wispish Ploverpage overestimate my abilities, and my stamina.'

Grackle grinned. 'Have faith,' he said. 'That alone will be more use to you than a thousand helping hands.'

After Grackle had left, Delilah started work again. She wondered whether she should have told him about the birds in Wispish's room, but decided she would probably have got a reaction similar to the one provoked by her earthquake story. Perhaps she should mention it to Wispish later.

By the late afternoon Delilah had worked her way along the corridor that led from the kitchen, polishing and sweeping as she went, and had now reached the entrance hall. She felt light-headed, almost as if she was dreaming. The work seemed so effortless; the more she did, the easier it became. As she swept leaves out of the hall into the garden, she wondered whether some sorcerous agency was at work. It seemed impossible she could have achieved so much in such a short time. The ceiling of the hall was so high above her head, she'd thought she'd have to use ladders to reach them, but a long-handled felt duster had been sufficient to remove all traces of sticky dirt. She was bewildered and astounded, but was not complaining.

She propped the broom against the door frame, and her shoulders began to prickle, as if she was being watched. She turned swiftly, and saw that Wispish was crouched on the newel post at the bottom of the stairs, as motionless as an exotic carving. Scarlet rags hung down from her gaily coloured skirt, wafting slowly in the breeze from the door.

'You made me jump,' Delilah exclaimed.

Wispish did not apologise. 'You are doing well,' she said.

Delilah nodded. 'Too well,' she replied. 'And I'm sure I have you to thank for the unseen help.'

Wispish shrugged. 'This work is the product of your own energy,' she answered enigmatically.

Delilah picked up a duster and gently began to wipe ancient stains from a marble table near the door. 'Why was I picked to do this job? Was it through a process similar to how you became Lady of the village?'

Wispish hopped down off the newel post and skipped towards her. 'No, it was coincidence,' she said. 'You just happened to be in the right place at the right time.'

Delilah nodded, unconvinced.

'You're not unhappy, are you?' Wispish asked.

'No, not at all. I feel rather confused, that's all. I went into your room today, at lunchtime, and your birds behaved in a very peculiar way.'

'Oh?' said Wispish. She darted off to one of her cupboards and extracted a wizened bird claw which she proceeded to examine with apparent extreme concentration.

'Yes. When I walked in, they all went mad, and the noise they made . . . It was dreadful.'

Wispish afforded Delilah a strange, slit-eyed glance over her shoulder. 'My birds are sensitive creatures,' she said. 'They tend to absorb any emanations people give off.'

'I wasn't emanating anything.'

Wispish shrugged. 'I suppose anything could have upset them.'

'Like the earth tremor this morning?'

Wispish raised her eyebrows. 'Oh, was there one?'

Delilah sighed impatiently. She sensed an impenetrable wall between herself and any information Wispish might be able to give. 'Your yard was cracked by it,' she said doggedly.

231

Wispish raised her slim shoulders in another insouciant shrug. 'I haven't noticed it,' she said, 'but then again, I haven't exactly looked very hard.'

'I doubt you'll find anything now. The Ratheripes didn't notice the earthquake either. I'm beginning to wonder whether Grackle was right, and I dreamed it all.'

'Have you seen Grackle Ratheripe today?'

Delilah nodded, feeling absurdly guilty. Was she allowed to have visitors in this house? 'Yes, he called in with some lunch from his mother.'

Wispish replaced the bird claw. 'How kind of Pluffie.'

'He told me about the Queen's Fete,' Delilah said. She hesitated, and then plunged into another question that had just occurred to her. 'Is there any connection between the fete and your house-cleaning?'

'The Covendalers adhere to a very ancient religious tradition,' Wispish replied. 'Many of its customs have been eroded over the centuries, but Queen's Fete is one of the two major festivals that remain in their calendar. The other is celebrated at midwinter and is known as King's Wake. The fete is very simple, just a fair and a bonfire, not much else. As a rule, my house-cleaning tends to coincide with midsummer, yes. It's probably to do with the weather. Nothing so miserable as being up to your elbows in suds on a cold day!'

'To be honest, Wispish, I've not had to get my hands that dirty,' Delilah said. 'The house seems to clean itself.'

Wispish smiled. 'Well, isn't that convenient.'

It was obvious Wispish was not going to be forthcoming with explanations. Delilah had the distinct impression that although, from the Covendaler's point of view, Wispish was an essential part of the coming celebration, she herself was detached from it. She did not seem part of the ancient traditions of the village, but something more recent, something different. How was it that Wispish could move through the world so blithely when she was obviously not Ixmaritian, while Delilah, fearing detection, had to avoid Ixmarites and behave discreetly. It was clear Wispish had no knowledge of discretion. How did she and Anvil protect themselves? How did they remain invisible to the Ixmarites when they were so extraordinary? Wispish reminded Delilah of the Saltcats but, if anything, she seemed even more unusual. Delilah couldn't help feeling a little frightened of her, even though she was always friendly. Wispish was small and she was fey, but Delilah could tell that really she was incredibly strong, both physically and mentally. There was a whisper of threat beneath her airy, feather-brained manner.

'Where's Trajan?' Delilah asked, anticipating more evasion. 'He's not in his room.'

'Anvil took him out,' Wispish replied. 'He had business in Hissock's Wood. Your friend will be quite safe, and so will everybody else. Anvil will make sure of that.' Wispish darted towards the front doors and threw them wide. 'Come, defy your mops and dusters for a while. The sun hangs lazy. Let's fritter away the rest of this mild afternoon lying in the poppy fields beyond the garden wall.' With that, she leapt into the sunlight, and Delilah followed.

Wilfish Implexion paced up and down the high-ceilinged Council chamber of the town hall of Faneford, which had become yet another of his temporary headquarters. Beneath a high stage at one end of the room, a long, highly polished council table held the remains of his lunch and also a deep metal tray containing instruments of torture. A torturer stood nearby, cleaning his fingernails with a sharp iron spike. In the centre of the room, a man crouched on the bare stone floor.

'Now, let us go through your story again,' Implexion said patiently. A week or so ago, the man's daughter had said something suspicious to her teacher at Faneford's Church school.

'We're going to dance with the Summer Lady,' she'd said.

The teacher, alert for profanity among her charges, had questioned the child further. Where, and with whom, would this dance take place?

'With Aunty Hannah, in the fields. We dance in the moonlight.'

Further questioning had produced disturbing information concerning the girl's relatives. Celebrations regularly took place out of doors, apparently. And although religious in tone, they were obviously not Ixmaritian. The relatives lived in Covendale. It was known the villagers had an annual summer fair, but the Ixmaritian priest appointed to the parish had never reported anything profane about that. Was it possible he was unaware what was going on?

The Church had been informed and, as Wilfish Implexion and his inquisitors happened to be nearby, the ecclesiarch had been sent for. This was a spot of favour-currying on the part of the Faneford Church officials. They knew Implexion enjoyed uncovering blasphemous conspiracies, in the hope of gleaning further information about the Jeopardites, and was grateful for anyone who shoved a heretic beneath his nose.

The accused man, abject beneath the ecclesiarch's cold scrutiny, would now be regretting initiating his young daughter into his pagan ways. How foolish to trust the loose, indiscriminate tongue of a child, Implexion thought. Children had no concept of secrecy, unless the secrets were those they invented themselves, or they were threatened with physical abuse should they reveal the truth. No doubt the heathen tradition had been maintained for generations within the man's family, only to be revealed now by an innocent child. Implexion had listened to the feeble excuse of how his daughter had merely been talking of a time the previous summer, after the fair, when her aunt had taken her for an evening walk outside Covendale. Nursery songs had been sung, old songs. They meant nothing. The child had a vivid imagination. She made things up.

Implexion had listened to all this patiently before remarking, 'The girl spoke of many people taking part in the dance. She even mentioned some of their names, and that she had been taken to Covendale for the summer dance by you and your wife every year for as long as she could remember.'

'She is making up stories,' the man insisted. 'We are good people. We go to church. Ask anybody.'

Implexion's people had visited the man at his place of work, and had discreetly taken him into custody. As yet, not even his family suspected their filthy practices had been uncovered. And Implexion knew it was important they did not find out. He wanted to catch the witches of Covendale red-handed. When the local officials had suggested the Covendale priest should be interviewed, Implexion had disagreed. Incompetent, unvigilant priests were not unknown within the Church, but there was also the possibility, however distasteful, that the man was fully aware of what was happening. Some inappropriate loyalty to his flock might have prevented him from reporting what he knew, or else, more distasteful still, he was involved in the pagan practices himself. Implexion wanted to wait and see. He did not want to risk alerting the community by sending for the priest. The local Church officials had been embarrassed when Implexion had asked them why they hadn't thought to investigate the midsummer fair before. Weren't they aware of the significant dates on the pagan calendar?

'We are always invited to attend,' one official had said. 'We did not think there was any harm in it.' Implexion could see from the man's expression he was beginning to doubt whether inviting the ecclesiarch to investigate the situation had been a good idea.

'Then you've neglected your duties,' Implexion had said with relish, unable to resist making the man feel worse. 'It is your function to be continually vigilant for heresy. Procedures are too sloppy out here in the country. It is appalling. These pagans should have been rooted out decades ago.'

'It will not happen again,' the man had said, bowing low.

'It certainly won't,' Implexion had agreed.

The man on the floor was still burbling about his daughter's supposed fantasies. Fool!

'Rosario, the hooks,' Implexion ordered blandly.

The torturer sniffed and began sorting noisily through the instruments on the tray. The accused man gave a small whimper.

Implexion loomed over him. 'Have you seen an expert with hooks at work?' he enquired delicately. 'The exquisite pain they can conjure in human flesh is almost artistic.'

The man put his hands over his face, and Implexion allowed him a few moments' despairing panic. Then he kicked him on the thigh.

'The midsummer fair in Covendale is a pagan celebration, isn't it?' Implexion said. 'Admit it to me. That's all I need to know. Admit it, and you will be allowed to take retreat in an Ixmaritian Reflection Cloister and recant your pagan ways. Admit it, and you'll keep your eyes. Admit it, and your family, your women, will keep . . .' he shrugged, 'whatever I choose to take. Keep silent and, well, it would be dreadful, wouldn't it?'

The man crouched even lower, until his head virtually touched his knees. His hair fell forward to touch the floor. Implexion felt a pang clutch at his heart, almost as if a hook had been inserted into the pulsing muscle, and jerked sharply. The man before him, his face hidden, his luxuriant hair spilling forward, reminded him so strongly of the false prophet Resenence Jeopardy. Oh, to have that lunatic before him now! If only it *was* Jeopardy kneeling there, at the mercy of the Church.

The air in the hall seemed to condense, the light to become darker. The scent of burning filled Implexion's nostrils. He felt as if he'd stepped into a different season.

Resenence Jeopardy lay huddled on the floor before his feet. The prophet's clothes were ripped, revealing starved flesh that was marked by whip and brand. His face was hidden. Implexion could hardly breathe. He felt profoundly excited. He wanted to lean down and yank that hidden face up by the hair.

'I have you now, trickster,' he said, under his breath.

The torturer moved forward eagerly.

Implexion took a deep breath and addressed the prostrate form in front of him. 'You have five seconds to tell me what I want to know,' he said. 'On the count of five, Rosario will begin to wield his hooks. We shall go on from there.'

Jeopardy did not look up. He neither moved nor spoke. Implexion wondered how long he'd be able to resist the compulsion to put his hands into that thick, ragged hair, to pull the prophet's face up to his own. He wanted to see the fear in Jeopardy's eyes. 'One.'

The torturer knew his cue. He held four gleaming, viciously barbed metal hooks, slim as needles, up to the light that fell in narrow bars through the high windows.

'Two.' Implexion's excitement mounted. Soon, the hooks would slide into Jeopardy's flesh, into his eyes, his groin, his mouth. Soon, the blood would come, and the sounds, the beautiful sounds.

'Three.' What would happen should the prophet decide to speak? Implexion would have to delay the torment. He wasn't sure he wanted that.

'Four.' *Look at me, Jeopardy, look at me. Look upon my face. See what you have done to me!* Now at last, Implexion was in control. *He* was not writhing at *Jeopardy's* feet. The hooks were not hanging over *his* flesh.

'Five.' The hall was utterly silent, as if there was no world outside. Implexion turned his back on the prisoner and glanced at Rosario. 'Proceed,' he said gently.

There was a noise of scuffling. Rosario was strong. No one could resist him. Implexion closed his eyes, clenched his fists. He held his breath, felt a tingling in his flesh. Then the sounds came. Sounds as lovely as the most angelic choir. The beautiful voice of the prophet raised in agony and fear. Implexion felt faint. He could die at this moment from the beauty of it. Soon, he would turn round. He would see Jeopardy's eyes turning red with blood and pain. He could drink the blood if he wished to.

'Oh, mercy! Stop! Stop! I'll tell you! I'll tell you!'

Wilfish Implexion was almost physically sick. Something wrenched inside him, the ground heaved beneath his feet. Sound came crashing back. The noise of humanity outside, the sobbing behind him. He wheeled round quickly. The prisoner was lying face down on the floor. Rosario had stepped back. His work had made little mess, just a few spots of blood on the floorboards, although the prisoner had soiled himself in his terror. A high reek of urine polluted the air, but there was no stink of blood. Rosario was holding only two hooks.

Implexion virtually bounded across the room and yanked the prisoner's head up by his hair. The face was ugly. It had no chin, thick lips. Not beautiful at all. Resenence Jeopardy had escaped him again. Some drab peasant, half blinded, one eye ruined, his mouth seeping blood, shuddered on the floor where only moments ago Jeopardy had been within his power.

He turned away, rubbed his face. His voice, when he spoke, sounded weaker than usual to his ears. 'So tell me what you know,' he said.

Behind him, the prisoner gasped. 'I will! I will ! Only don't hurt me any more.'

Implexion made a curt gesture with one hand. 'Just get on with it.' He was aware of Rosario staring at him intently. Had he noticed anything unusual about his manner?

'It's true. The fair at Covendale is a disguised midsummer rite to the goddess,' blathered the prisoner.

Implexion's head had begun to throb with pain. He rubbed his temples, hardly able to speak. But the question had to be asked. It was his duty. 'And where exactly will this abomination take place?'

'Sheen Meadow in Covendale. By the river. Tomorrow night.'

The ecclesiarch sighed heavily. He looked at the man on the floor. Disgusting! If he'd been handsome, Implexion might have spared him now. Might have. I am too tired, he thought. I need to rest. Too little sleep. Insidious dreams.

The two other men in the room were waiting for his order; one in dread, one in anticipation. Implexion no longer cared about it. He felt drained, disappointed, exhausted.

Turning smartly on his heel, he walked briskly from the hall. It took him every grain of strength he had to accomplish it, but he would not betray his condition to either prisoner or torturer. At the door, he paused, although he did not look round. 'Have them hanged, Rosario. Him and his women.'

The prisoner's fading wail followed him down the hall and out into the sunlight. It was the cry of a dog, not an angel.

By midsummer morn, Wispish Ploverpage's house was as clean and sparkling as if its construction had only recently been completed. Delilah was not sure how she'd managed to scour it so thoroughly, and could remember barely half the time she'd been engaged in doing it. Still, the job was done, Wispish had given her a heavy purse of money, and soon she and Trajan could be on their way. They would travel south-west, the direction from which the Jeopardites had come. Travelling might be difficult now, with so many people around, but she'd just have to take things day by day and hope that they came across Resenence Jeopardy before Trajan laid waste to anything or anybody.

Trajan had been kept occupied by Anvil Quizzinglass. At first, Delilah had believed he had simply accompanied Anvil on his mysterious forays into the wood, but then Wispish had taken her to see how Anvil kept Trajan harmless.

There was a huge old barn behind the house in which Anvil kept a wide circle of empty wooden casks. Trajan was induced to stand in the middle of this circle while Anvil ran round it, beating the casks with sticks. During this procedure, Trajan stood passive and slack-jawed, as if in a trance.

'What is Anvil doing?' Delilah asked in a puzzled voice.

'Binding the curse,' Wispish answered, biting into an apple she'd produced from the pocket of her woollen coat. 'It could take days.'

'I thought Anvil didn't believe in the curse,' Delilah pointed out suspiciously.

Wispish shrugged. 'But Trajan does.'

'Anvil must have a lot of stamina to keep that up for days,' Delilah said. She could see he was dripping with sweat, his face manic and savage as he pounded round the circle.

'He has that all right,' Wispish said.

Although Trajan said very little to Delilah, she could tell he did not like Wispish or Anvil. She asked him if he minded about Anvil taking him out to the barn every day. Was it uncomfortable?

Trajan had shaken his head. 'No. But it is a waste of his time,' he added.

'Then why go along with it?'

'I seem to have no choice,' Trajan said with a shudder. 'These people are weird. I suspect their motives. They might be illusionists.'

'They are sorcerers, Trajan,' Delilah corrected sharply. 'Like Jeopardy. They are full of magic.'

'They are not like Jeopardy,' Trajan answered. 'They are clever and they are keen. They manipulate minds, but I'm not sure what else.'

Sensing his immovability on the subject, Delilah had let it drop.

Today, midsummer day, the Queen's Fete would take place. Grackle Ratheripe arrived at Wispish's house just before noon. Delilah, wearing a dress of nubbed purple silk that Wispish had given her for the occasion, bravely took the arm that Grackle offered her and accompanied him down the lane towards the Meadow. Wispish had already departed the house, presumably to assume the role of Fete Queen for the day.

The north side of Sheen Meadow was now covered in yellow pavilions that were festooned with orange streamers, which fluttered madly in a warm breeze. Stalls heaped with produce were ranged between the tents. At the centre of the Fair, in the place deemed exactly suitable by Anvil, was an enormous bonfire. Anvil had spent two days supervising its construction. Grackle explained that entertainments could be found within the pavilions: contortionists, tregetours, mummers. All of Covendale seemed to be there, wearing their best clothes and their widest smiles. Every hand seemed to be gripping clay cups of elderflower wine and, perhaps as a consequence, the atmosphere was one of jollity and abandon. Even the token Ixmarite priest was in attendance, his austere habit draped with a blue shawl, a young girl on each arm.

Delilah was immediately infected by the carefree spirit. Trajan had been left behind in Wispish's house; today, she could not worry about him or his afflictions. She felt as light as a feather as Grackle led her from stall to stall. He bought her a candied fruit and bright blue ribbons for her hair. They watched some thin, trembling dogs walking on coloured balls, encouraged in their balancing by a young girl dressed as a harlequin. When the performance finished, the little dogs ran towards the crowd, wagging their tails and holding small, open boxes in their mouths, into which people threw coins.

Delilah thought she saw Anvil and Wispish a few times in the distance, distinctive shapes amid the crowd, but she and Grackle never caught up with them. She noticed some strange, skinny people mingling among the villagers, noticeable because of their wild black hair and dull yellow, layered clothes. They were somewhat smaller in stature than the Covendalers.

'Who are they?' she asked Grackle, pointing.

'Travellers, like yourself, I expect,' he replied.

'So many of them?' Delilah said scornfully. 'I think they must be hewkins, come to Witness the rites of humans. Perhaps they are kin of Wispish Ploverpage.'

'In that case, do not meet their eyes.' He grinned at her. 'They might spirit you away!'

Presently, they met up with Imphee and Pluffie, who were stationed behind a long table, dispensing ales and flower wines. Delilah was pleased to see them again and stayed to help with the refreshments for an hour or so. Then she, Imphee and Grackle wandered off to drink wine beside the Sheen, and eat a late lunch. The afternoon passed lazily and pleasantly.

At sundown the villagers wheeled out a huge wooden construction into the meadow. Imphee told Delilah it was a representation of the Queen of

237

the Land. Although it certainly resembled a female shape, Delilah was unimpressed by the workmanship, which to her seemed crude and unfinished.

'Your Queen of the Land must be a relative of Mother Moistfoot,' she said. 'A field goddess, perhaps.'

'Hush!' Imphee hissed. 'Are you mad? To talk of goddesses, other than the relatives of Ixmar, is heresy, and you never know who might be nearby with waggling ears. Outsiders sometimes come to these events, but to them this day is no more than a jolly pageant, an excuse for merriment.'

'Is that why the model is so rough?' Delilah asked in a low voice. 'So that the Ixmarites won't realise it's supposed to be a goddess?'

'We conduct our festivals with an alert eye and our ears cocked,' Imphee replied. 'The Church believes our community to be devoutly Ixmaritian. Our priest helps with the disguise – may the Lady bless him – but the Ixmarites are unpredictable. Sometimes they seem to scare themselves into believing the most innocent communal events can somehow affect their power. They see heresy everywhere and will make an example of a community. Arrests are made, accusations levelled, executions carried out.'

'If the risks are so great, why have an effigy of the goddess at all?'

'We try to retain some dignity,' Imphee answered. 'We invite the Church officials at Faneford over to the fair every year, but they never come. However, the invitation has always been enough to secure our freedom for the day.'

Delilah sighed and took another drink of wine. She could not help thinking the Covendalers were overly cautious. Why should the Ixmarites care about their little village fair? What difference did it make to the great god Ixmar and his followers? None whatsoever.

As dusk came down, Delilah went to stand alone beside the river. The fire had been lit and the wooden figure of Summer's Queen was a monstrous silhouette against it. People had begun to dance timorously round the flames and the wiry, black-haired people, who Delilah thought might be hewkins, had brought out instruments and now blew upon flutes and banged tambourines. The hewkin maids sang in high, eerie, warbling voices, clicking their long fingernails like castanets.

Ever since her conversation with Imphee, Delilah thought she perceived a measure of reserve about the celebration. As the effects of the wine misted up her head, she began to feel very much apart from the proceedings. A vague depression hovered around her. Had she allowed Trajan Sacripent to delude her? Resenence Jeopardy could not be the wonderful being Trajan had made him out to be. People in Covendale jeered at his name, and the two Jeopardites she had met seemed shallow, posturing people. She could see Nebuline and Inshave now, hovering on the edge of the crowd, sombre and unsmiling, mindful of their appearance.

Sighing, Delilah walked off into a clump of willows. Her family was dead, her home was gone. She'd flown in a spume of madness out into the wilderness with a lunatic and now did not know where she was, or what she should do. Perhaps Imphee was right. Perhaps she should stay in Covendale. With time, it was possible she wouldn't feel so distanced from the people here. She liked Wispish and Anvil and the Ratheripes. Life would be simple here, and yet . . . She did not feel that it would fulfil her for very long. 'What do I want?' Delilah wondered aloud. 'I wish I knew.'

'Such sadness!' came a voice from overhead. Delilah made a sound of surprise and jumped backwards. The willow branches rustled above her and someone jumped down to land in a crouch in front of her.

'Grackle!' she cried. 'Were you spying on me?'

'Not I,' he replied. 'You wandered to the foot of my eyrie, from where I was watching the dancing, only to disturb me with your mournful reveries.'

'It was not my intention,' Delilah said. 'I thought I was alone here.'

Grackle put his head on one side. 'Why are you feeling sorry for yourself? Haven't you enjoyed the fair today?'

Delilah did not want to explain, feeling she couldn't cope with Grackle's tendency to ridicule everything. She made a dismissive gesture with her hands and walked towards the fringe of willow branches.

'Not so soon,' Grackle said and took hold of her arms from behind.

'Let me go,' Delilah said, and pulled away. She ran out of the willows and up along the river bank. She could hear Grackle following her, and started to laugh. Soon, she might let him catch her to see what would happen. The night was warm on her skin, the air perfumed with the smell of burning wood and cooking meat. Music from the fair was thin yet sweet. Delilah felt reckless and delirious. Looking back over her shoulder, she could see Grackle's long limbs flailing behind her; he too was laughing so much he could barely run. Delilah swerved away from the river bank and headed towards the village. The grass was lush and damp against her ankles; field voles rustled from her path. 'I could run the whole night through,' Delilah thought. She gazed up at the cloudless sky, threw up her arms, and remembered the pool of the Saltcats. She came to a halt and let Grackle pant and scramble up behind her.

'Kiss me,' she thought, closing her eyes, 'because I have never been kissed.'

Grackle very tenderly put his hands on her hair and then stepped away from her. Delilah turned round. He swept a bow.

'Madam, on this rare night of summer, I entreat your favour,' he said.

'Oh? What favour?' She laced her hands in front of her.

'The favour of your eyes, so sweet and dark, your pretty lips so fit for bruising.'

Delilah laughed. 'But I feel nervous of doing so. What would follow?'

'All that is natural on the Queen's night,' he replied, twirling round in a little dance.

Delilah clapped her hands. 'Aha! An answer such as might be given by a trickster!'

'You have all my attention,' said Grackle. 'This is a spell of binding. Force my eyes to look away from you.'

'With my hands?'

'No, your voice.'

'Ah, that is easy. Look at that.' Delilah pointed past his shoulder.

Grackle shook his head and grinned. 'Not so simple, my lady. I will not look.'

'Hmm.' Delilah cupped her chin thoughtfully in one hand. 'Then perhaps you will look up at the sky with me. There is a shooting star there.'

Grackle would not look away from her. Then Delilah frowned, apparently in perplexity.

'Well,' he said, 'what feeble enticement are you thinking up now?'

Delilah pointed behind him. 'Who are they?' she asked, in a hushed voice.

Grackle shook his head. 'You've already tried that one,' he said. 'It won't work.'

'But you must look!' Delilah said with urgency. 'There is a great company of riders approaching.'

Grackle laughed. 'A pathetic attempt. I can hear nothing, and one would presume such an enormous company would make some noise.'

'I can hear them,' murmured Delilah. 'Listen. Can't you hear the hooves and harness?'

Grackle only started howling like a maddened animal and danced around Delilah in a circle, never once taking his eyes from hers. He began dipping and diving, flapping his hands like a bird.

'No!' Delilah said. 'Grackle, something is happening! I feel it. *Grackle!*'

She was not attempting to trick him. How could she make him see? Couldn't he feel the earth tremble, couldn't he hear the jangle of harness, the thud of hooves? She could see about two dozen enormous dark horses galloping towards them, their riders cowled and hunched down in their saddles. She knew immediately that they were not part of the entertainment. The mere sight of them terrified her. She had to escape. If Grackle insisted on ignoring her warning, then she would run away without him. Grackle attempted to hinder her departure, grabbing her round the waist and attempting to throw her up into the air. Delilah beat at him with her hands.

'You are blind and deaf,' she screamed. 'Let me go!' The horses were almost upon them. They would be run down, crushed into the soil. Even as she struggled and screamed, her vision went black, and she was enveloped by an icy coldness.

'They are passing right through me!' she cried, sobbing in terror. 'Oh Mother, they have touched me with cold!'

Her obvious distress at last penetrated Grackle's festive mood. 'Delilah?' he said, gently lowering her to her feet. She stood gasping and shuddering, barely able to stand. Her hair hung over her eyes. She lifted a listless hand and pointed over Grackle's shoulders.

'They come again,' she murmured. 'They are coming for us again!' The blackness had passed from Delilah's sight; the air was warm around her once more, but she could see, on the road from the village, the same company of riders, only this time, they were further away.

Grackle, who had realised the game was over, looked round. He gasped and stiffened with apprehension. 'By the Queen's toes!' he exclaimed, suddenly pushing Delilah ahead of him. 'Run!'

'Who are they?' she asked, stumbling beside him.

'Ixmarites!' Grackle cried. 'Run! We must warn everyone. From the look of them, they are not here to sup wines and enjoy the dancing.'

It was like being back in Samberdell: the grinding inevitability of it all, the sudden despair, the bewilderment. Delilah and Grackle charged across the meadow, but the horses could gallop so much faster than they could run. Delilah heard a voice shout, 'Halt!' and her instinct was to obey, but Grackle would not let her stop. When they were within shouting distance of the fair, Grackle opened his mouth to yell out an alarm, but before he could make a sound, he was lifted off his feet, propelled forward a few feet, and landed on his face on the grass, his legs and arms splayed out. One of the riders had hurled a lance which had taken Grackle through the spine.

Delilah could not scream. She was thinking, 'I must not die now. What is happening? This is madness! Why should these people want to kill me, or

240

anyone? I must not die now.' Her legs seemed to be working independently of her mind, pumping in a blur, although the lights of the fair did not appear to be getting any closer. At any moment, she expected to feel the impact of a lance in her back.

By this time, the Covendalers had noticed the approach of the Ixmarites and had begun to gather together in confusion. Delilah felt something whistle past her head; the lance she had expected. 'No, no, not me!' Was someone shouting her name? She reached out with desperate arms towards the crowd of people silhouetted against the light of the bonfire; they seemed so far away. Then the ground was rushing towards her and the air was knocked from her lungs. She was aware of a great pounding sound and, even though she was gasping for breath, she instinctively curled herself into a tight ball as the horses went over her. Screams and shouting filled the night.

'I will lie here,' she thought. 'They must think I'm dead. I'll lie here until it's all over. Oh goddess, protect me!' She had never felt so frightened in her life, not even when Trajan Sacripent had been lunging towards her with a raised axe.

Then she heard her name being shouted behind her. 'Delilah! Delilah!'

She was aware that someone, or something, was pounding towards her, and that it knew her name. She prayed wildly to Mother Moistfoot, wishing she had stronger words to form the prayer. Help me, save me, do something! Had the Ixmarites come for her? Had they somehow learned of her search for Jeopardy and come to punish her? She was seized in strong hands and thrown bodily into the air. Clawing and snarling with sheer lust for survival, Delilah attempted to free herself. She uttered curses she'd never spoken before.

'Stop this!' boomed a voice.

She recognised it instantly, even though it was badly distorted.

'Trajan!' A wave of intense relief flowed over her. She relaxed into his arms. 'Thank the Mother! Oh, Trajan!' She attempted to hug him, but Trajan was in no mood for tender emotion.

'They have harmed you!' he roared, his fingers digging into her body.

'No,' Delilah assured him. 'I'm all right. We must—'

With a harrowing howl, Trajan began to run towards the mêlée, Delilah still in his arms.

'Trajan, no!' Delilah cried in an agonised voice.

'They have harmed my sweet angel!'

'No, we must escape, run the other way! Oh Trajan, please!' She tried to beat at his chest with her fists. She could see that his beard was flecked with foam and that his eyes were rolling madly.

'Your spirit called to me in the rooms of the witch's house,' he moaned. 'I felt the black cloud pass over. I followed your call.'

'Then hear me now,' she begged. 'Don't do this, Trajan. Please. We'll be killed. There are too many of them.'

Trajan ignored all of her please. In a last attempt for control, Delilah tried to purse her lips to whistle, but it seemed her mouth was stretched into a grimace of terror. She could not manage it. Around them, Ixmarites on horseback were attempting to whip the Covendalers into a manageable bunch. Delilah could see that some people were lying motionless on the field, which had been churned to mud by the horses' hooves.

'You there!' a black uniformed shape called to Trajan. 'In line!'

Trajan growled and, after a brief pause, dropped Delilah sharply onto the ground. She crawled onto hand and knees in time to see Trajan haul the man from his horse. With seemingly little effort, Trajan wrenched the head from the man's body. Then, throwing the separate parts aside, he lumbered forward, huge fists flexing with a desire to rend and tear. Everything was in confusion: Covendalers were attempting to fight or flee, Ixmarites were attacking and herding anything that moved. Ignoring the wounds he received, Trajan marched purposefully through a gang of Ixmarites in order to unhorse and mangle them. Other Ixmarites were gathering to repel the menace.

Delilah had crawled over to one of the pavilions and now huddled among the guy ropes, numb with panic. What can I do? she wondered, entering a pocket of calm in her own mind. Do I run or lie still? Trajan will be killed! I will be alone! Oh goddess, if the Covendalers are all murdered too, I'll have nobody left, no one at all! What shall I do?

Tortured by such thoughts, Delilah nearly fainted with shock when somebody dropped down beside her. She covered her face with her hands, awaiting a blow, or rough hands that would haul her to her feet, but no such cruel treatment occurred. Delilah became aware of a strong scent of cloves, and a female voice said, 'Your friend fights well, with true spirit.'

Delilah peeked through her fingers and saw the bleached face of the Jeopardite woman, Nebuline. There was a grim smile on her face, and she did not appear to be in the least bit frightened. 'Ah, how I love the aroma of death,' she declared, as if in explanation. There was a streak of mud, or blood, on her face. Delilah could not speak.

'Well,' said Nebuline prodding her in the ribs with a sharp finger. 'Call the berserker back. We must leave.'

'What?' Delilah's voice was feeble.

'You heard. Have a little more mettle, girl! It is clear this superb weapon must be returned to Resenence immediately. Look out!'

She placed a firm hand over Delilah's head and forced it down as a missile whizzed overhead. 'There is little time. I can't be doing with this Ixmarite muddle. Now, where is Inshave? Hiding beneath a rock, I expect. Follow me, girl.'

'No,' Delilah hissed. 'I'm not moving. It's too—'

'Nonsense!' Nebuline interrupted. 'If we stay here, we'll be carted off in chains, or burned alive. Look sharp, missy. Don't you want to greet the sun again? Trust me and follow me. I'm used to this sort of thing.'

Nebuline began bellying off across the grass like an enormous black snake. Her body seemed so flat, it reminded Delilah of a stealthy she-cat stalking a mouse. Delilah only hesitated a moment. Nebuline had seemed so confident, and an offer of friendship from anybody was welcome at that moment. Taking one quick glance round the pavilion, she dropped onto her belly and followed the Jeopardite. Even though she had no liking for Nebuline, she could not help but be impressed by the women's courage and level-headedness.

Nebuline crawled through the fence of Sheen Meadow and dragged Delilah after her. They lay for a few moments in the ditch beside the road beyond, Nebuline holding Delilah firmly in her hard, skinny arms.

'Let me catch my breath,' Nebuline said. 'My, what a senseless fuss. But what should we expect from Ixies? Fools and boneheads that they are. The Covendalers are giving a good account of themselves. I don't suppose that was expected, otherwise there would be more Ixies here. Still, that's to our advantage.'

'Why are they doing this?' Delilah asked, in a gulping voice. 'Why are they killing people?' She was glad Nebuline was holding her, even though the embrace was far from comfortable; she couldn't stop shaking.

Nebuline snorted. 'The usual reason: sheer paranoia. Around this time, all the communities adhering to the old ways will be celebrating midsummer in one way or another. If the local Church officials get sufficiently annoyed by that – and I feel it depends on their general mood – they decide to make an example of one of the villages. Most of the settlements around here are larger than Covendale, which would make the task more difficult, or else they are too small to be worth bothering with. It is Covendale's misfortune to be the right size.'

'But Imphee said they'd had no trouble before.'

'Tah!' spat Nebuline. 'That is false security. The only way they could have guaranteed their hides would have been to raise an Ixmaritian church on the soil of Sheen Meadow and to worship the birth of Ixmar's daughter, Panphyla, at midsummer. Many people do that.' She shrugged. 'Any goddess is goddess enough, to some.'

'It's so monstrously unjust,' Delilah cried. 'Who here in Covendale hurts anybody else? I don't understand the utter stupidity of this attack.'

'Well, understand it you must, to survive in the world,' Nebuline said coldly. 'We had to. It will be a long time before the Ixies are crushed, but it will happen eventually. Conditions get much worse, much more difficult, further south.'

'I would have been better off staying in Samberdell,' Delilah said bitterly. 'Even though everyone was dead.'

'Don't fool yourself,' Nebuline retorted. 'Wherever you come from will not be overlooked by the Ixies for long. Now, we must think of a way to reclaim your friend before he's hacked to bits, and then get away.'

'How many times have you had to do this?' Delilah asked.

Nebuline made a noncommittal sound. 'I've lost count.' She let go of Delilah and peered through the weeds against the fence. 'Well I never! I do believe that is the ecclesiarch Implexion himself preening upon that black horse over there.'

'The horses are all black,' Delilah said.

'Implexion's is blacker than most,' Nebuline said with a slightly offended sniff.

'Who is he?' Delilah asked, also peering through the weeds. She thought she could identify the man Nebuline meant. He seemed to stand out from his colleagues, as if he possessed a greater power than they did. It was impossible, at this distance, to distinguish his features.

'He is the Archimage's right hand and Jeopardy's bane,' Nebuline explained. 'He's mainly responsible for our persecution. He is obsessed by Jeopardy. Some say his ardour to capture our Beloved One rivals that of the most lovelorn suitor.' She laughed and then frowned. 'I wonder if he's here because of Inshave and me. I wonder if he knows about us. Oh, it is irrelevant. Where's that beefy friend of yours? Ah, I see him.'

'Can we call to him?' Delilah asked lamely.

Nebuline grinned, 'I doubt whether a shout will summon him. He seems too engrossed in his activities. My, that was a fearsome blow! Perhaps we will have to leave him behind after all. Our safety is the prime concern.'

243

Delilah crawled forward to see what was happening. As far as she could make out, an intense battle was raging on Sheen Meadow. The Covendalers were clearly not going to give up easily. She saw a child with a stout stick beating at the legs of an Ixmarite mounted on horseback. She saw women using ale cups as missiles, crouched behind the cover of half-tumbled pavilions. Trajan was easy to spot; an insane giant lurching across the field, a severed head held in one hand.

'I'm not sure if this will work,' Delilah said, and put her fingers in her mouth. She shrilled a piercing whistle, three times, and then ducked down again.

'That would call the dead,' Nebuline said. 'Let's hope the madman heeds it.'

'It is a special call,' Delilah told her. 'My only way of controlling him, but I'm not too confident of its reliability.'

'Oh well, we must hope for the best,' Nebuline said matter-of-factly. 'Try it again.'

'Won't the Ixmarites follow Trajan if he hears the call?' Delilah said. 'We risk exposing ourselves.'

Nebuline nodded. 'True.' She examined their surroundings. 'It is fortunate Inshave and I made a thorough study of the area when we arrived. We anticipated something like this occurring. Now, what we must do is wriggle our way down this ditch towards the hills. We should be safe there.'

'And leave Trajan behind?'

'For now. You'll simply have to repeat the whistle at suitable intervals and hope it has an effect. Come along. We have no time to waste.'

Delilah was unconvinced the plan would work, but there was little alternative. She was angry with Trajan's mindless stupidity and felt that, in some ways, he deserved his fate. They could have been far away by now if only he'd listened to her. Crawling on elbows and knees, she followed Nebuline's wiggling behind down the ditch. Eventually, they reached the end of the ditch and a crossroads. Here, Nebuline knelt up and looked around. All seemed quiet. The southern horizon was a tumble of gentle, forest-clad hills.

'That way,' Nebuline said. 'We must cross the road, and go through the fields, sticking to the spinneys and hedgerows. We should be all right this far from Covendale. Now, utter a whistle or two before we head off.'

'What about your companion, Inshave?' Delilah asked. 'Are you going to abandon him?'

Nebuline laughed. 'Abandon him? Ha! No luck would be so pure. He'll have high-tailed it to a safe location before the first whip was cracked. He'll find me later. He always does, which is why we're still together, I suppose. Now, whistle away, little maid. We have to be in those hills by sunrise.'

Nebuline would not let Delilah rest all night, other than to pause sporadically in order to whistle to Trajan. They scurried along in a crouch from hedge to hedge, tree to tree, until Delilah's whole body was aching unbearably. She had become gripped by a harrowing despair. Was she doomed to remain in Nebuline's company until they found Jeopardy? Was everyone else dead? What about Wispish and Anvil? She could not bear to think of what might have happened to them. And she had no way of knowing whether Trajan had been able to follow her, or whether he himself was being followed. Nebuline seemed unconcerned about their situation, other

244

than to complain that her clothes and hair had been ruined.

By the time the sun rose, they were well into the hills and there were no signs of pursuit. Nebuline decided they could risk walking upright again, and even took Delilah's hand in her own pale, cold paw as they climbed the narrow, stony paths. Conversation was confined to orders being given by Nebuline. Delilah had lapsed into a grief-stricken silence. Everything she owned, which admittedly wasn't much, had been left in Covendale. All she had to wear was the silk party dress. She didn't have even a single coin. The sight of poor Grackle hurtling through the air, pierced by the lance, kept replaying itself before her mind's eye. At the time, she'd been numbed by shock, but now, trudging along in a pre-dawn chill, it was horrifyingly vivid in her memory.

They scrambled up a loose stone path between limestone crags. Vegetation was sparse in this area; wispy grass and weathered gorse. As they passed beneath the bare branches of a dead thorn tree, something whistled through the air between them. Nebuline hissed and crouched before throwing Delilah aside.

'So, you're not dead again.' Inshave leapt down from behind the tree, as elegant and unmarked as if he'd spent an hour at toilet.

'No thanks to your protection!' Nebuline spat, seemingly unsurprised at having come across Inshave so soon. 'Jump back to your perch, fool, and guard the path with your darts. We await the arrival of a large hairy man, but let no others pass.'

'What if some of the villagers are with him?' Delilah protested, rubbing her arms through her torn sleeves. She had grazed herself badly when Nebuline had thrown her down.

'None of them will escape,' Nebuline said. 'Get up, little maid! I will be surprised if gentle Inshave has not equipped himself with a fat bag of food. We will find his hoard and refresh ourselves.'

Trajan found them in the early evening. He was cut about the face and arms, but otherwise seemed unharmed. Delilah had already warned the Jeopardites about Trajan's afflictions, so they made him keep his distance, although this twilit time between day and night was the safest for people to be near him. Still, it was best to take precautions. He crouched miserably on a rock some distance away from where Delilah sat with Nebuline, just as miserably. Across this safe space, Trajan related what had happened after Nebuline and Delilah had fled.

The Ixmarites had taken him prisoner through sheer force of their numbers, and their concentrating on him had effectively allowed many of the Covendalers to flee the scene. The ecclesiarch Implexion had been intrigued by Trajan's strength and resilience, and had ordered him to be bound, not killed, so that he could be taken to the nearest Ixmarite centre for interrogation. Trajan, in the grip of the moon's full madness, could only struggle in furious helplessness against his bonds. The ecclesiarch had then departed swiftly on horseback with his torturer, Rosario, which was perhaps unfortunate in the light of what happened the following morning.

'One strange incident penetrated my delirium,' Trajan said. 'As I watched, I saw Anvil Quizzinglass and Wispish Ploverpage limned against the flames of the bonfire.

'Ecclesiarch Implexion cried out: "Bring me the witches!" and his minions closed in. Anvil and Wispish were forced back against the fire. It was terrible! There was no escape for them; their capture seemed imminent. Then, the strangest thing occurred. They simply looked at one another and joined hands. With a joyful cry, they leapt up and backwards into the furnace heart of the flames. They must have been incinerated instantly, and yet, through the bloody film across my eyes, it seemed I saw two rags spiralling up among the sparks of the fire; two black rags or else two ragged birds.'

'They can't be dead,' Delilah said miserably. 'They *can't* be!'

'I'm not sure they are,' Trajan said.

At dawn, Trajan's moon rage left him and in the quiet before the sun truly rose, he sensed the insidious creep of the plague steal back into his bones. It began as a strange, barely perceptible crackling in his fibres, which made his muscles flex uncontrollably. Then, it was as if his veins became filled with liquid fire. Heat emanated from his skin, which he knew contained the spores of the plague. When the Ixmarite in command of the militia came to examine him, Trajan spat straight in the man's face, knowing full well that by doing that, the plague would be spread among the Ixmarites.

'And also among their prisoners,' Nebuline observed, interrupting Trajan's narrative.

Trajan gave her a hard, unloving glance. 'Lady, when spread by persons other than myself, it seems the infection has only a short time in which to disperse, living only a few days. It is true that innocents might be affected, but their sentence was death for heresy in any case, and even the plague kills more kindly than the flame or the torturer's pit. It was an unavoidable consequence.' He looked at Delilah. 'All night long, I heard the silver whistle of your lips trilling out to me, spinning a trail for me to follow in the air. I waited.'

'Did you see Pluffie or Imphee?' Delilah asked, dreading the answer. 'Were they captured with you?'

Trajan shrugged. 'I don't know. I didn't see them.'

After they had breakfasted, the Ixmarites had chained all their prisoners into a line in order to lead them to Faneford and the Heretic's Hold. Trajan took care to spit upon any Ixmarite who passed within range, knowing that the plague would take hold much more quickly that way. Sure enough, a scant hour after they had left Covendale, the Ixmarite commander climbed down from his horse to vomit, claiming he felt faint. Fairly soon, enough of the Ixmarites had tumbled from their horses for Trajan to break his chain and escape without much fear of pursuit. A few arrows were fired, some of which found their target, but they were as gnat bites to the huge man.

'You are magnificent,' Nebuline told Trajan when he'd finished his story. 'A strong weapon we can turn against the pestilent Ixies and their followers. We shall return you to Resenence Jeopardy as you desire.'

Trajan uttered a sound of outrage. 'Lady, you cannot mean such a thing!' he exclaimed. 'I am appalled by what I am, and I am horrified that you, a fellow Jeopardite, could even consider my afflictions being used as a weapon. It is against all that Jeopardy stands for.'

'I don't think so,' Nebuline said sulkily.

'I seek Jeopardy for him to tame this curse,' Trajan said. 'I want only to be rid of it.'

'Mmm,' murmured Nebuline. 'No matter. We shall be on our way. Look sharpish girl, there's no need for a face like that. Soon, the light of Jeopardy shall enhance your features for eternity.'

XVI

EXORCISM

Perpetuis Sleeve waited in his Chamber of Office for Salaquin and Nehush-tah Mandru to be shown into the room. A clerk shuffled papers at a desk nearby. Soon, he would take notes. Sleeve was looking forward to this meeting and was glad Wilfish Implexion hadn't got to hear about it, other-wise he would have insisted on being present. The ecclesiarch knew the report concerning Mandru's household existed, of course, but Sleeve had managed to keep the time of the Mandrus' visit to Gallimaufry a secret. It had taken some doing, some shuffling of staff, to divert the vigilant ears and eyes of Implexion's little band of informers. The ecclesiarch would be given an opportunity to interrogate the Mandrus, but all in good time.

The information concerning Resenence Jeopardy and his erstwhile con-nection with the House of Mandru had come to light quite accidentally. It had stemmed, perhaps almost too coincidentally, from another of Implexion's innovative ideas, this one apparently harmless to human life. He had initiated an audit of Ixmaritians who'd been sold to rich householders throughout the land. An impromptu inspection by Gallimaufric Church auditors had taken place in Shanariah some months previously. All house-holders had been required to allow the inspectors to examine their Ixmariti-ans and the premises used for religious purposes within their establishments.

Suspicions had been aroused on a number of counts in the household of Salaquin Mandru. The Ixmaritians in residence had appeared somehow insolent and undisciplined. Their clothing had been inappropriate, and the chapel of the house had appeared virtually derelict. The head of the house-hold had also been clearly discomfited by the unexpected arrival of the inspectors. When the Ixmaritians had been lined up for examination, the number present did not tally with Mandru's account with the Church. There were two Ixmaritians less than he had paid for. Only the fact that the academies identified their sales by allocated numbers rather than names prevented the inspectors from being alerted from the start about what had happened.

Mandru had initially attempted to get round the apparent shortfall by substituting two servant boys in the line for inspection, but of course they did not carry the appropriate brandings and had quickly been revealed as fakes. When questioned, Mandru had produced the excuse that the two missing Ixmaritians were away with his wife in Ixibatae. The inspectors were not deceived. Church officials were called in from the city, a search warrant was produced, and Mandru's wife was found hiding on the premises. Two Ixmaritians were missing and unaccounted for. Had they died from natural causes, accident or suicide, then the bodies would have been sent back to the Church for proper disposal. That left four possibilities: the Ixmaritians had died unlawfully; they had been resold illegally without the Church having received its commission; they'd been pensioned off without the Church having been informed (a minor transgression; in which case, why would Mandru go to such lengths to attempt concealment?); or, unthinkably, the Ixmaritians concerned had absconded. It had all been very embarrassing. Salaquin Mandru was a respected and influential man. He had friends high in the Church. But he would not tell the auditors what had happened to his Ixmaritians.

'Prosecute me!' he'd shouted. 'I'll pay whatever you ask. I can afford it. Or do you mean to imprison me?'

The auditors had been nonplussed. They knew a man of Mandru's stature could not be arrested and imprisoned like a commoner. Then Mandru's wife had spoken out.

'You know why he will not speak?' she said. 'One of them escaped us, duped us, betrayed our trust. We were so good to him too, ungrateful wretch! He has brought us disgrace! And you will know his name. You will know it well. He was Resenence Jeopardy.'

The news was sent to Gallimaufry at once; no further questions were asked.

Sleeve had let the Mandrus sweat for a while by not summoning them to Gallimaufry immediately. And now he kept them waiting in his outer office. They'd been there for over an hour. Long enough.

Sleeve signalled to his clerk, who rang a handbell, thus advising the receptionist outside that the Archimage was ready to receive his visitors. A small repast of exquisite foods had been prepared and lay on covered trays on a table by the door. Sleeve wanted the Mandrus to feel intimidated, but not threatened. They had been reminded of his displeasure by the long wait, but now he wanted them to talk to him freely, something they would be unlikely to do in Implexion's presence. What had Jeopardy been like as an Ixmaritian? The idea seemed inconceivable. The Archimage looked forward to hearing the Mandrus' answer to that question.

Nehushtah Mandru stalked into the room before her husband, brushing past the receptionist who was attempting to announce her. Sleeve suppressed a grimace of distaste. He mistrusted Ixibatabians; they seemed corrupt, too voluptuous. Nehushtah sat down, without being invited to, on a chair before Sleeve's desk, draping herself and her expensive robes sinuously over the cushions. Sleeve did not stand up to greet her. Mandru came in behind, his face tight and wary. He performed a stiff genuflexion of respect. Sleeve looked up at him and smiled, gesturing towards the other seat.

'I am glad you came,' he said. 'I have been looking forward to meeting you.'

Nehushtah made a small sound that might have been a disparaging snort, but Mandru cleared his throat to cover it and said, 'I am deeply embarrassed by this situation, Your Sacredness. You cannot imagine—'

Sleeve waved his remarks aside. 'I have not summoned you here to deliver a reprimand, or accuse you of transgression. I simply want to talk to you about the man who once lived in your house. Resenence Jeopardy.'

Nehushtah made another angry sound, this time louder. 'We have plenty to say on that score!'

'No doubt,' Sleeve said gently but in a cool tone. 'First, let me say a few things from the Church's point of view. You can imagine that it was a shock to us to learn of Jeopardy's connection with Ixmarity. Also, very soon after the revelation had sunk in, I found myself wondering why the academy of Exparlance, whom we have since discovered trained Jeopardy, never thought to advertise the fact that he was brought up there.' The fact that someone connected with the Church had also seen fit to keep information back clearly soothed and reassured Salaquin Mandru, as Sleeve had anticipated it would.

'Jeopardy has that effect,' Nehushtah exclaimed. 'He corrupts people.'

Looking at Nehushtah, Sleeve wondered what her definition of corruption entailed. 'Quite. I think we have all established that Resenence Jeopardy is an unusual man.' He didn't mention that the administrators of Exparlance simply hadn't made the connection between their erstwhile student and the prophet. They were rather an insular institution.

'He made bad things happen in our house,' Nehushtah continued, leaning forward in her seat.

'Such as?'

'My wife exaggerates,' Mandru interjected. 'Resenence was an eccentric character, and other members of our household considered him to be unstable. The fact is, several years ago, his bizarre behaviour worsened, he shut himself away from the rest of us and subsequently fled the house. It was thought he had run away in order to kill himself. There had been . . . emotional troubles. A triangle of some kind. A woman, two men. Jeopardy was involved.'

'Yes, and he murdered poor Lucien!' Nehushtah cried.

'Excuse me?' Sleeve said.

Mandru sighed. 'The other Ixmaritian who disappeared. Lucien had gone into the city with my wife. She sent him on an errand and he never returned to her.'

'Jeopardy killed him,' Nehushtah insisted.

'We have no proof of that,' Mandru reminded her.

'It is obvious.' Nehushtah turned in her seat to face her husband. 'It happened about the time that evil scoundrel began making his seditious speeches in public. Too much of a coincidence. Lucien would never have run away. Never! He was a loyal, gentle boy. Resenence Jeopardy must have hated him. He had Lucien killed.'

'This is an interesting development,' Sleeve said, 'and one which we must discuss later. However, for the time being, I'm more interested in finding out more about Jeopardy himself. Were there any signs of his . . . *leadership* qualities while he was in residence at your estate?'

Mandru sighed. 'People either loved Resenence or hated him. He was compelling to look at, and a superb vibrancer. But he was arrogant and cold. I suppose he had the potential, even then, for what he has since become. Sometimes, I think he was born in the wrong place, into the wrong life.' He smiled. 'The Church should have perhaps recognised his qualities earlier and had him placed in a more suitable position. Resenence Jeopardy is not one of the sheep, but one of the wolves. A subordinate station never rested easy with him.'

'A commendable theory, but alas it is too late to act upon it,' Sleeve remarked. 'You know that miracles have been accredited to the man. Have you anything to say about that?'

'He was always bad magic,' Nehushtah said. 'When he left us, the house became plagued with strange phenomena.' She went on to list some of them.

Sleeve listened with mounting anxiety. Nehushtah obviously exaggerated and he discounted much of what she said, but when Mandru corroborated the bulk of his wife's unlikely testimony, he became very disturbed. Resenence Jeopardy clearly did have power. Sleeve realised that Implexion's fears concerning the prophet might not be as paranoid as he'd thought.

At the end of their narrative, Sleeve motioned to the clerk to serve the refreshments. Mandru wiped his lips with his fingers. They appeared cracked, inflamed, almost, Sleeve thought, as if talk of Jeopardy had injured his mouth. That was nonsense, of course. Still, the Mandrus no longer appeared defensive; they looked haunted. They had invoked something – a memory.

'To be honest with you, I was glad when Jeopardy disappeared,' Mandru said, accepting a plate of sweetmeats from the clerk. 'Everyone seemed anxious to hush the affair up, forget it. Of course, we should have informed the Church office. It was foolish of me to imagine Jeopardy's escape would never be discovered. And we should also have informed you of Lucien's disappearance, but it was as if, by keeping silent, we kept Jeopardy, or some unspecified threat, from our threshold.'

'Why were you relieved when Jeopardy left the house?' Sleeve asked abruptly.

Mandru squirmed uncomfortably in his chair. 'It sounds ridiculous. I'm ashamed to say it . . .'

'Please, go on. It might be important – useful to us.'

'Well, when Resenence was there, it was as if I did not have true control of my household. He had the power, he always had it. Of course, I confessed this to no one at the time, and in fact only really realised it myself once he'd gone. A weight lifted from my heart, and from the house. It was uncanny. He was unlike any other Ixmaritian I've ever met. He was unbowed, untamed, feral.'

'And he manipulated you utterly,' added Nehushtah, who had been uncharacteristically quiet for a few minutes. 'It sickened me. He was never loyal to you. He said the right words and, no doubt, touched the right spots, but I believe now he was always planning his escape.'

'It is easy to say that with hindsight.' Mandru snapped.

'You were the one who let him use you, not me,' Nehushtah retorted. 'He always had to have people adoring him. Or hating him. It didn't matter which. The strength of the emotion was all that mattered to him.'

Mandru glowered silently at his wife. His cheekbones were inflamed with spots of colour. Sleeve's heart went out to the man. He cleared his throat pointedly. 'What's done is done. We know Resenence Jeopardy has an ability to manipulate people.' He smiled reassuringly at Mandru. 'Even strong people like yourself. You must not feel ashamed of that.' Sleeve thought briefly of Implexion. Was it possible his obsession with the prophet had somehow been encouraged by Jeopardy from afar? No, surely not. And yet the strength of Implexion's feelings seemed irrational at times, they overwhelmed his common sense.

Sleeve leaned back in his seat, sipping from a cup of hot tisane. 'Now,' he said, signalling for his clerk to take up the pen once more. 'Tell me about the other one, the one called Lucien.'

Rain had come to Gallimaufry, and Bessie Anywhither had constructed a canopy on her roof garden so that she and her family could still enjoy sitting out. It was late afternoon, and Walterkin and Lucien were beneath the canopy. A single candle burned between them, its flame weak and easily shivered by the cool air from outside. Walterkin was telling Lucien a fable.

'There is a legend,' he said, 'of a man who could hear what others could not; he could hear voices. Often, he would say to his companions, "Listen to this silvery lilt, these words of deadly beauty" and his friends would have to point out that they could not hear anything at all.'

Lucien perceived a parallel in the story with some of the tales he'd told of Resenence Jeopardy. He felt impelled to interrupt. 'The man might have heard the voices of spirits, or he might simply have been mad. In the end, is there any difference?'

'Allow me to finish the story,' Walterkin said. 'Eventually, the voices lured this man away from his home with their elusive promises. He followed the call and no one ever saw him again. Now, did he follow his own madness into eternity or was he privileged by a visitation of a mystical kind?'

'The answer to that depends on how the story ends,' Lucien said. 'Did he ever catch up with the voices? Did he learn anything of value or interest from them?'

'Unfortunately, there is no satisfactory conclusion to the legend,' Walterkin said regretfully, 'I recited it simply to illustrate a point. Were you lured from the House of Mandru or did you just follow your own fancies?'

Lucien smiled. 'You're leaping ahead of me,' he said. 'I have yet to disclose how and why I left Mandru's household.'

Walterkin shrugged. 'Your narrative seems to be leading to a single point. Or perhaps you will surprise me.'

'I might accomplish both,' Lucien said. 'As I said, we were not allowed to roam outside the estate alone, even though escape did not cross our minds. We led a comparatively pampered life and by running away would forfeit our pension. I think we were supervised for our own protection.'

'And you had no yearning to follow Jeopardy out into the world? You didn't miss him?' Walterkin smiled slyly.

Lucien shook his head, and reached forward to dip his fingertips in the molten wax that had pooled beneath the flame of the candle. 'I was relieved he had gone, and that is no lie.'

If he'd not had Amber as solace, Lucien might have felt differently about Jeopardy's departure from his life, but as the days passed it became easier to convince himself that his relationship with Resenence had been nothing but a physical release, a manifestation of lust. He was concerned by the way Amber was sinking into a lovelorn decline; weight was falling from her body at an alarming rate, and she had assumed a morbid, haunted look. For some reason, she had started to blame herself for Jeopardy's departure and spent most of her time in Lucien's company analysing the past. She wanted to mull over all she could remember Jeopardy having said to her, and interpret the meaning of every glance he had given her, every gesture.

'We must find the answer to the puzzle,' she said. 'The reason why he had to run away.'

It was obvious to Lucien that Jeopardy had never confided in Amber at all, but he felt no urge to enlighten her with what little he knew. Eventually, he became impatient with her obsession.

'I have other things to think about,' he said.

'Like what?' Amber spat back.

'The Lady Nehushtah, for example.'

'There is no problem there,' Amber grumbled. 'She adores you.'

It appeared that whatever carnal cravings Nehushtah had harboured for Lucien had been gratified by a single experience, because she did not summon him to her bedchamber again. Lucien, however, constantly dreaded that she would. She demanded his presence in her salon every afternoon as if nothing had happened between them. Lucien had cringed with embarrassment the first time he'd faced her after their brief intimacy, but she appeared ignorant of his discomfort and showed no awkwardness. In her opinion, Lucien had simply been absorbed into her select entourage. It was obvious that, even had she known of Lucien's discomfiture, she would not have been able to understand it.

One morning she sent a message via Kamariah that she wanted Lucien to accompany her into Shanariah. A party of Ixmarite bishops were coming to stay at the house for a few days, which provided an ample excuse for Nehushtah to sally forth into the city and spend inordinate amounts of her husband's money on some new fabric, which she would have made up into robes and gowns for the occasion.

Lucien had hoped to take part in the Vibrancies that were being put together for the Ixmarites' entertainment and uplifting – he was guaranteed a prominent part in any piece since his performance with Jeopardy – but Nehushtah's word was not to be contested. She looked upon Lucien as one of her pets now, which meant he effectively had to put any thought of serious work behind him. As part of Nehushtah's little group, he could perform only for her pleasure. Most people in the house regarded this as a privilege, but Lucien was bored with the endless afternoons in Nehushtah's smoke-filled chamber. Sometimes he thought wistfully of his previous position and decided that for all its junior status, he missed the freedom he'd enjoyed as a nonentity and the amount of time he'd been able to spend alone.

There was no excitement in his heart as he followed Kamariah to the Lady's rooms. He had no interest in visiting the city.

Nehushtah was waiting for him, already choosing between a selection of outdoor coats of thick, silky furs. 'Lucien, I can tell you have an artistic eye,' she said. 'You can help me choose my fabrics. You may even select a bolt of cloth for yourself, and I'll have one of my girls make up a tunic and leggings for you. How about a new sash too?'

'My lady, because of your generosity I already have all the clothes I need,' he replied. 'But, if it pleases you, I will choose a bolt of cloth.' By that time, he knew which responses gratified her most.

Nehushtah nodded in satisfaction. 'We shall depart after we have taken a light lunch.'

Only two house guards accompanied them into the textile quarter of the city. Nehushtah and Lucien rode in an open carriage which was covered by a diaphanous tent of gold-threaded fine linen. Little gilded bells adorned the poles at each quarter and tinkled as the carriage descended the hill. It was a warm day and Nehushtah carried a fan made of enormous feathers, dyed purple and crimson. She covered her face in the Ixibatabian fashion, which reminded Lucien of the days when he'd worn a mask himself. He would never have believed he would have been able to face strangers and open spaces with a bare face, and yet to be masked now would have been irritating in the extreme.

'Stop here!' Nehushtah called. The carriage rolled to a halt outside a grand warehouse that boasted a large shop at the front. Only rich people could afford to buy the splendid cloth that was woven here. It was called Rooklacks; the name was emblazoned in gilded lettering above the door. Nehushtah flapped her hand at Lucien to command his assistance as she descended from the carriage. With a swish of her furs, she swept in through the double doors of the shop. The guards followed discreetly; Nehushtah didn't seem to notice they were there.

Inside, the shop was dark yet highly polished. Fabrics glinted enticingly on high shelves; huge rolls revealed a wanton flap of colour like dancing girls raising their skirts to display their thighs. Shop assistants flocked to Nehushtah's presence as if they scented her affluence. Nearly a head and shoulders taller than anyone else present, Nehushtah unwound the veil from her face and worded a haughty enquiry. Immediately, lesser minions of the establishment were sent to swarm up ladders to carry down the lolling bales for her inspection. Nehushtah presided over the coruscating spills with a critical eye, demanding that this roll and that should be partially unwound for her. Crushed velvets of jewel-like hues, shimmering satins and sulky, heavy silks tumbled across the counters. Lucien couldn't summon any interest in the fabulous materials. The thought of how Amber would coo and exclaim over them made him smile. She would have appreciated this excursion far more than he could. What a pity Nehushtah hadn't chosen her company.

'Lucien, what do you think of this?' Nehushtah asked, fingering a bolt of black velvet that, when turned in the light, showed a glimmer of old gold.

'Beautiful, my lady. It would compliment you well, and the splendour of the fabric would be more than enhanced by your loveliness.'

'Mmm. I thought so too,' Nehushtah said. 'I suspect this is imported cloth. Am I right?'

'Madam,' gushed the chief assistant, 'you are quite correct. This is cloth of the rarest value, woven in the mountain silk farms high above the Ixibatabian city of Soleis. None compares in richness of texture or brilliance of hue.'

Nehushtah nodded. 'I thought as much. My people know the way of weaving far more than any other race.'

'Oh, I agree absolutely,' said the shop assistant.

'Well, I'll have some of that,' Nehushtah said, gliding on to the next counter where more luxurious fabrics were displayed for her appraisal. Lucien was beginning to tire of the procedure. As far as he was concerned, pointing at random would have been just as efficient, since all the fabrics were so costly. After an hour or so, as Nehushtah demanded yet rarer silks to be brought from the deepest recesses of the warehouse, he decided it would not matter to his mistress if he sat down upon a chair near the door. She had changed her mind so many times about the fabrics, and had asked his opinion so often, his head was aching. He thought with regret of the exercise courts back at the house and how, with Nehushtah absent for the afternoon, he could have spent hours there practising movements; it was the only way he could relax. Nehushtah noticed his posture.

'Lucien, do not sulk,' she said. 'You may choose your own fabric in a minute or two.' She pursed her mouth and addressed the shop assistant. 'He is a vibrancer, you know, and they have very active dispositions. I suspect he needs some exercise.'

The assistant nodded sagely. 'They always have to be on the move, don't they,' he said. 'What a lovely boy, madam. He is a credit to you.'

'Mmm,' said Nehushtah. 'Lucien, why don't you walk around outside for a while.' She lifted the silk purse which hung from her wrist in a tangle of black tassels. 'Here, take a few coins. Buy me a sherbet. I am thirsty.'

Lucien hesitated at this command, for in his experience it was highly irregular for one of Mandru's Ixmaritians to wander about the city alone. Had Nehushtah forgotten her husband's directives? If he made a move to pass the door, the guards would surely bar his way.

'Lucien, why are you staring at me like a great fish?' Nehushtah declared. 'Be off with you, but don't be too long. I need to visit Madam Malinda's before we return home.'

Wordlessly, Lucien took the coins she offered and walked out into the street. The guards never even turned their heads, and he realised there must be more advantages to being one of Nehushtah's favourites than he had imagined.

Most of the buildings in the street housed cloth merchants and weavers, but there were one or two small booths nestling between them that sold refreshments. Lucien had never been out alone in the city before and leaned against the wall of the shop, wondering whether he was going to feel dizzy or frightened. After a few moments, he still felt completely normal, so assumed it was safe for him to venture down the street. Nobody looked at him with suspicion or scorn, and he sauntered along with a jaunty step, as if he walked the streets of Shanariah every day. I could get used to this, Lucien thought. He even smiled and nodded at a beggar girl, who only spat at him because he did not toss her a coin.

Unfortunately, his first taste of freedom seemed destined to be brief, for after only a hundred yards or so, he came across a refreshment booth. He looked in the window for a few minutes, as if making up his mind concerning the selection of confections which were displayed in tissue paper and silks amid a vast nest of chocolate shavings. Eventually, he realised he could not put off his errand for any longer and went inside.

A squat youth behind the counter pulled a face when Lucien requested a sherbet.

'No, sorry, no sherbets today,' he said.

'Oh?' Lucien replied, confused. 'But there is a sign outside—'

'I know, I know, but the ice vendor hasn't turned up. Some say he lost his entire stock because one of his sons built a fire in the ice house last night. A nuisance, for we have a brisk trade in sherbets this time of year, but—' he shrugged, '—unless you have ice yourself there is nothing to be done about the situation.'

'I've been sent to buy a sherbet for my mistress,' Lucien explained, 'and I don't want to disappoint her. Could you recommend anywhere else around here where I could buy one?'

The youth gave another shrug. 'You could try Totterpins' on the Harbourwards,' he said. 'They are pricey in comparison to ourselves, but at least they have their own icehouse. Other than that, all the local traders use Miglings for their ice. You'll have to venture further across the city otherwise.'

Is it far to the Harbourwards?' Lucien enquired. 'Could you give me directions?'

'It's a few minutes' walk, but a fairly straight one,' the youth replied. 'Turn right at the end of this street and keep walking till you see the signs.'

Lucien thanked the youth and left the shop. Outside, he wondered whether he should return to Rooklacks and inform Nehushtah of the delay, but decided against it. Attention to trifling matters often annoyed her; she admired initiative in her favourites. Anyway, hadn't the youth told Lucien it wasn't that far to Harbourwards? Nehushtah was probably so engrossed in her purchases she wouldn't notice how long he was away, and if he ran, the errand would take even less time.

Greenskirt Avenue, at the end of the street, was very busy. Lucien had to push his way through the crowds browsing along the roadside textile markets. Further down, the avenue widened into a square with four roads leading off it. Here, it was virtually impossible to wriggle through the thickly clustered bodies at all. Everyone appeared to be looking at something, and he could hear shouting voices up ahead.

'What's going on?' he asked a man standing next to him.

'Orators,' was the reply.

'Orating about what?' Lucien demanded impatiently. 'Are the crowds always this bad?'

The man shrugged. 'New to the city, are you?'

'Tourist,' Lucien answered swiftly.

The man nodded. 'Well, this is a speaker's square and usually they're a tedious bunch, but there's a good one on today.'

'What do they speak about?' Lucien asked. 'What could possibly be this interesting?'

'Life, love, religion – that sort of thing,' replied the man.

Lucien rolled his eyes in exasperation. 'I've heard more than enough on those subjects to last me a lifetime.' He frowned. 'This is a nuisance. I'm trying to get to Harbourwards. Is there no other way to reach it?'

The man laughed. 'There're plenty of ways, but why miss such a spectacle?'

'I'm on urgent business,' Lucien said importantly.

'Well, it's up to you,' said the man, 'but as you're a visitor to Shanariah, you should listen to this speaker while you can. Later, you might find it a talking point. He won't be around for long, that's for sure.'

'Why's that?' Lucien asked, alerted by the man's tone.

'Let's just say he does not discuss the Ixmarites in the most complimentary of fashions. In fact, he berates them at every turn. I've heard him speak three times now.'

'Really?' Lucien's interest was pricked by that in spite of himself. He was in awe of anyone who could maledict Ixmar in one of His strongest cities.

'Yes,' the man continued. 'He speaks a strange creed, for there is no talk of gods at all, yet his words definitely hold a religious reek. He says what others think but dare not voice. You must admit that's a new approach.'

'What exactly does he talk about, then?' Lucien was beginning to feel uneasy.

'Freedom,' said the man. 'Look, don't stand here listening to me. Listen to him! Perhaps you'll be more entertained than you thought.'

'I might. Thank you.' Lucien nodded a goodbye and began to edge his way forwards through the crowd. People were reluctant to let him pass and made indignant noises as he pushed them, apparently resenting anything distracting their attention from the man bellowing and exhorting somewhere up ahead. At this distance, the words were virtually incomprehensible, Lucien did not pay them much attention. The voice sounded hoarse and ragged with a frenzied edge; the voice of a fanatic.

As he struggled forward, Lucien was aware that time was slipping by and soon Nehushtah might start to worry about his absence. He did not want to risk upsetting her because she might never let him out of her sight again. Perhaps he should abandon the search and return to the shop. Still, he was enjoying his freedom. Far from being frightened by the crowds, he liked the way he was so totally invisible among them. His behaviour meant nothing to anybody. Within reason, he could do anything he liked, and go anywhere he liked. There was no one to stop him, no one to restrict his movements. He felt a stab of envy for the house guards who could wander the city whenever they pleased in their off-duty hours. He was determined now to remain in Nehushtah's favour because then there might be more excursions like this to enjoy.

The people ahead of him were confounding all his efforts to reach the other side of the square. He decided he would have to abandon the search for Harbourwards and return to Rooklacks. Perhaps he could buy Nehushtah a simple fruit juice from one of the booths in the street on the way back.

As he was about to turn round, a woman behind him jerked forward, and almost knocked him off his feet, crying, 'Oh master! Master!' People near the woman looked at her in surprise and amusement. She began clawing at Lucien and anyone else who blocked her path to the front of the crowd. Lucien realised he was very near the front himself.

Encouraged by the screaming woman, the crowd surged forward against him, carrying him along in its relentless tide. Lucien cursed aloud, pushing with all his strength against the pressing bodies, but to no avail. The crowd had condensed; there did not seem to be a hair's width between each person. He became aware of the tension in the air, an intense feeling of restrained emotion about to burst free. It was futile to try and fight his way back now. All he could do was scramble forward and hope to escape to the side so that he could follow the edge of the square back to Greenskirt Avenue.

The man bellowing at the crowd was standing on a raised dais. Lucien did not look up at him until he'd won free of the jostling bodies. He seemed to pop from the crushing ranks into the small space between dais and crowd. It was then he took a look at the speaker. His heart nearly stopped, and for a second his vision went black. The speaker was Resenence Jeopardy.

'. . . have power, all of you!' Jeopardy was saying, prowling up and down the stage. 'You have the power to make anything you believe in become real.'

'Tell that to my friend!' a heckler called from the front of the crowd. 'His house just burned down!' People laughed at the remark.

'Possessions mean nothing,' Jeopardy said. 'Perhaps there is a lesson to be learned in losing one's home to a fire. Perhaps it shows that the bricks and mortar mean more than the life that's lived within them. To be really free, you have to shun material things.'

256

Lucien watched in stupefied dismay.

'Say something about the Church!' someone called. Again, more laughter.

Jeopardy grinned and spat on the dais. The crowd roared in delight or horror; it was difficult to tell.

Lucien could not remember falling, but suddenly he found himself on hands and knees among a forest of trampling feet. Somehow he'd been shunted backwards into the crowd. For a moment or two he stayed where he was, trying to convince himself his eyes and ears had deceived him. That could not be Resenence Jeopardy up there. If Jeopardy had fled the House of Mandru, surely he'd have had the sense to flee the city too. Only an imbecile would be so stupid as to risk making public appearances when they were an escaped Ixmaritian. Anyone from the house could have seen him – off-duty staff, friends of Mandru who'd seen Jeopardy perform. No, Lucien decided. That man must just look like Res, that's all. Still, he was afraid to stand up.

A woman leaned down to him. She grabbed him by the upper arms and tried to drag him to his feet.

'Leave me!' Lucien hissed, but she didn't appear to hear him.

'He sees!' she told everyone around them. 'He is one of them! Oh, the boy sees. Take him forward.'

'No!' Lucien attempted to pull away, but a dozen hands suddenly grabbed at his clothing. If it was Resenence Jeopardy up on the dais, the last thing he wanted was to be carried into his presence. His terror was eclipsed by pure anger. How dare they manhandle him!

'Do not struggle, boy,' someone said to him, cupping his face with damp hands. 'Let the prophet touch you. We saw how his voice affected you. We saw you shine and fall.'

'No, I didn't!' Lucien cried feebly. 'Let me go!' His protests were ignored.

Just as it seemed inevitable that he would be propelled, supine, into Jeopardy's presence, the cries of the crowd and the speaker's voice were drowned by a harsh blare of alarm clarions. There was a moment of utter confusion; the crowd fell suddenly silent and Lucien could hear the unmistakable clamour of iron-shod hooves on the cobbles of the square. Then, he was dropped unceremoniously on the ground.

'Ixmar save him, it's a Church patrol,' someone moaned.

'He'll be arrested,' another cried. Lucien scrambled onto his hands and knees; his tunic had been pulled up to his shoulders. He was being kicked as people clambered over him in a sudden panic to leave the square. Lucien protected his head as best he could, all thoughts of Nehushtah's refreshment and the sudden reappearance of Resenence Jeopardy driven from his mind. It was lucky he'd been so near the front of the crowd, for soon the frenzied feet had all passed by and over him. He knelt up, panting, and pulled his tunic back into place. For a second or two, there was no one between him and the dais ahead. The speaker was being coerced down from the dais by two ragamuffin companions who looked like gypsies, while the Ixmarites attempted to ride through the crowd to block their escape. Lucien realised he had not been mistaken. Although bedraggled and unshaven and barely recognisable, the man on the dais was unquestionably Resenence Jeopardy.

As this positive recognition settled in Lucien's mind, Jeopardy suddenly jerked and pulled away from his companions. He turned and looked Lucien right in the eye. His face seemed to rush towards Lucien until it appeared to hang only a few inches from his face. Jeopardy's mouth moved. Lucien heard no sound, but he recognised the shape of his name. Then, refusing to let him linger any longer, Jeopardy's companions dragged him off down a sidestreet at a run. Horses pounded forward, but a surge of bodies had somehow filled the avenue of Jeopardy's escape. Lucien struggled painfully to his feet. It seemed his mind had switched off. He had no idea what to do next.

'Can you smell burning?' Walterkin asked.

Lucien looked up at him, dazed. Painfully, he pulled his mind back to the present. 'No,' he said. 'I can't smell burning.'

'Perhaps it's because I know,' Walterkin said mysteriously.

'Know what?'

'That there's an immolation being conducted at the east gate.'

'An immolation of what?'

'Heretics.'

'You are wrong, they don't burn heretics any more.'

'They burn dead ones.'

Lucien shuddered. 'Let's go inside. I don't want to smell that.'

DELUSION

'Javelot, you've become a very mournful companion,' Cleo said. The pair had been riding for two hours, away from The Haunt in a southerly direction. Dauntless had been silent the whole time; he had not even grunted in response to Cleo's remarks. This had happened before when they'd had a disagreement, but a female instinct warned Cleo that something new was amiss with her companion. 'Are you angry because I insisted we stay for breakfast?' she asked, and prodded him in the ribs with her fingers. 'Oh, come on. This silence is intolerable. I won't have it!'

Dauntless made a sound of distress. How could he tell her what he'd seen the night before, the malevolent ghost-child who'd prophesied his death? He still hoped it had been a meaningless hallucination, but fear of somehow helping the prediction become truth by voicing it aloud held his tongue. In some ways, he longed to turn to Cleo for reassurance. He knew that she would try to explain it away, make him feel better. She would chide him for his foolishness perhaps, but she would exorcise the ghost.

'Daunt, what's wrong?' Cleo asked again.

He couldn't tell her. 'Before I came upon you by the stream, my life had become a meaningless twist of blank time. Since we met, however, a more sinister breath has come to befuddle my life's tedious path.' It was all he could say on the matter. He half hoped Cleo would intuit what he really meant.

'You're blaming me because you're depressed!' Cleo said, taking his remarks at face value. 'You must have been lonely before, paladin. You should be grateful for my company.'

Her tone had its usual effect. Irritation swamped him. 'Your reckless behaviour has endangered my life,' he retorted. 'Am I supposed to be grateful for that?'

'Oh, don't be ridiculous,' Cleo scoffed. 'We've had some adventures, that's all. And what else is a paladin good for? You are too cautious Javelot. Nothing I've done or suggested has caused us any lasting harm.'

'Hmph,' responded Dauntless, 'if that is the case, I suspect it owes more to accident than design. You live up to your name, Cleo Sinister. I cannot

259

imagine how I ever allowed myself to become involved in your eccentric life.'

Cleo's irritation gave way to anger. 'You don't have to be involved with me at all!' she yelled, aware even as she spoke that if he decided to abandon her, the journey south would become much more arduous. Contralto was no nimble steed, but at least the horse afforded transport and Cleo had to admit she did not relish the prospect of travelling alone again, however morose her current companion might be.

'Don't think I haven't thought about it,' Dauntless replied. 'Only my sense of chivalry prevents me from tipping you from Contralto's back and galloping off at speed.'

'Daunt,' Cleo said, in a more soothing tone, 'don't let's argue. We are two lonely souls abroad in the world, and we have found each other. And, I can't help feeling your complaints about me are based upon your deep-rooted pessimism more than actual events.'

Dauntless grunted, apparently mollified by her softer approach. 'I would feel happier if you would follow my advice more often,' he said. 'When we come across strange houses in the woods, and I express misgivings, please heed my words. I am sure we escaped dire trouble by the narrowest of margins back there.'

'Perhaps you are right,' Cleo conceded, gritting her teeth behind his back. 'I shall pay more attention. Now, will you please cheer up?'

In the mid-afternoon, they came across a modest white-walled shrine nestling among the trees, which had become less looming and oppressive. This was altogether a younger and less menacing part of the forest, which perhaps indicated they were near the edge of it.

'I do not believe it,' Dauntless exclaimed, reining in Contralto.

'Believe what?' Cleo asked. 'That place looks religious to me.' Like all residents of the Burrows, she harboured a deep mistrust of organised religions.

'And so it is,' Dauntless declared. 'You see those cupped hands carved upon the lintel? That tells us that this is a fane of True Valiance himself. What fortune!'

He jumped down from the horse, suffused with a sense of relief. Here was a place to exorcise the malign ghosts of The Haunt. Just by seeing the fane, he felt better.

Cleo observed him dubiously. 'Do we need to pause here, Daunt?' she asked.

He turned to her with beaming face. 'We shall be welcomed here,' he said. 'Have no doubt of it, and the welcome will not be tainted by peculiar habits or professions. If I'm not mistaken, the fane will be attended by Sisters of Valiance, gentle virgins whose voices will be as honey in our ears.'

Cleo had never met any gentle virgins and suspected she would not enjoy the experience now; especially since the virgins concerned were going to be of a pious disposition. 'But we have supplies and water enough,' she argued. 'Surely we should be concentrating on leaving the forest rather than prolonging our stay here.'

Dauntless gave her an irritated glance. 'Cleo, trust me. If there's one thing I would welcome now, it's spiritual refreshment. You too would benefit from the company of such modest and honest maidens as we shall no doubt find within. Perhaps some of their goodness will rub off on you.'

Cleo hissed at him.

'Do not mistake my meaning,' he said, raising his hands to her. 'I realise it's not your fault you have the character you do, but the fault of your upbringing in insalubrious surroundings and the obviously suspect character of your estranged husband.'

'There was nothing wrong with Wakelate's character,' Cleo objected, astounded that the way she was moved to defend him. 'He never harmed me, or even raised his voice . . .' She pulled a rueful face. 'Lately, I wonder why I ever questioned my life with him.'

'It was because he cold-bloodedly murdered a child who was dear to you,' Dauntless bluntly reminded her, and then added gently, 'In your place, I would not let myself forget that.'

Cleo sighed and slid down off the horse. 'Very well. Let's go inside this place and meet your gentle virgins, then.'

The entrance hall of the fane was shadowy and smelled of antiseptic incense, an aroma that badgered the senses rather than beguiled them. Cleo pulled a sour face. 'It smells like a sickroom,' she said. Dauntless made no response but ventured towards the inner door. Almost as if she had been lying in wait beyond, a woman glided out to meet him. This must be one of the gentle virgins, Cleo thought. The woman was young and dressed completely in white. Her head and neck were constrained by a tight and stiff-looking wimple, covered by a long veil. Her features were plain and without expression, her hands hidden in her sleeves. She inclined her head and Dauntless executed a grand bow.

'Sister,' he said, 'I am a paladin of True Valiance. My name is Dauntless Javelot. I am escorting this lady to the south, but beg that you allow us to pause in our journey here, in order that I might take advantage of your spiritual offices.'

The woman flicked a cold, fish-eyed glance at Cleo but then adopted a smile. 'I am Sister Pankodine,' she said. 'My sisters and I live a simple life here, but we will gladly share what little we have.'

'That really isn't necessary,' Cleo said. 'We have plenty of supplies.'

The woman ignored her. With a thin white hand she indicated the way inside to Dauntless. Cleo followed them, her heart racked with instinctive misgivings.

Sister Pankodine serviced the fane with two others, Sisters Umling and Despera. All three were named after Valiance martyrs, girls who had refused marriage and consequently had their tongues, eyes, breasts or feet removed, prior to grisly deaths by burning or slow blood-letting. It seemed they believed themselves wedded to True Valiance himself and as his wives had devoted themselves to his service, uttering the holy passions that, as a husband, he adored above all else. Cleo hated their sanctimonious manners at once, and viewed what she considered to be their perversion with utter distaste. She worshipped no god, but held life itself in high regard. To her, wedding oneself to an abstract ideal, shutting oneself away from the world and conserving one's chastity for a lifetime seemed absurd in the extreme. It denied life.

The visitors were offered a bath in the spring behind the fane. 'You will pollute our waters,' said Sister Pankodine with downcast eyes, 'but we would be most gratified if you would take advantage of our offer.'

'And do we drink this water afterwards?' Cleo asked, alert for pranks.

The sister shook her head. 'Today's pitchers have already been taken, but tomorrow I and my sisters must drink from the spring. We shall drink your soil to remind ourselves of the foulness of this world.'

'Why not take a few more pitchers from the spring now for us to wash in?' Cleo asked. 'That way your spring remains clean.'

Sister Pankodine knotted her hands beneath her chin and gazed upwards. 'That would be selfish of us,' she said. 'We cannot think of our own comfort, at any time.'

Cleo decided she must urinate in the water, to gratify the sisters' urge for self-torture even further. She allowed Dauntless to take his bath first.

While he immersed himself, Cleo joined the three sisters in a plain room, barely more than a cell, which was furnished with just two hard benches where the women sat embroidering a cloth.

'This must be a strange life,' she said, aware how her jovial tone disrupted the atmosphere of the room.

The sisters looked up at her and one spoke. 'Strange? No. It is as we have chosen.' Her miserable smile implied pity for Cleo's unenlightened mind.

'You must have endured sad lives before to choose this one, though,' Cleo continued.

The sisters smiled indulgently. 'I am inclined to agree with you,' one said, 'although you may not when I tell you we came from good families and lacked for nothing.'

'What influenced your choice, then?' Cleo asked, quite interested in spite of herself. 'Was it a call, a compunction to follow the idea of True Valiance as a man? Was it that you could not get his image from your mind, that you desired to love him and he to love you? How did the call come to you?'

The virgins flushed at her questions. 'Nothing so direct,' Sister Pankodine said. 'In my case, the decision came as a simple ray of light into my mind. I never perceive True Valiance as a man. My marriage to him is of a high and pure nature. I sought to escape the base instincts of the flesh.' All three sisters directed a glance at Cleo that seemed to imply they believed her to be a wanton perpetrator of such base instincts. Still, they did not look at her with repugnance, merely a sincere kind of pity, which Cleo found even more offensive. She stood up, sighed, and walked to the barred window of the cell. Outside, she could see Dauntless in the spring pool, naked but hidden from the waist down by the gently foaming water. His body was lean and wiry, his dark hair clinging to his shoulders. He is not without attractions, Cleo thought, a pity he is such a bore.

She turned round. The sisters were engrossed in their embroidery, apparently unaware that a naked man was visible from their window. She was tempted to call one to her side to witness her response, but decided she couldn't be bothered.

The sisters invited their guests to partake of a simple meal with them. Cleo had taken a hurried bath in the spring pool and was now hungry, but she did not view the plate of boiled, unsalted greens put before her with any great appetite. A goblet of wine was also offered, but its contents were so watered down as to be less palatable than plain water itself. The sisters had given Dauntless and Cleo a fork each but ate their own meals with instruments that were almost impossible to manoeuvre: simple sticks of polished metal, maybe six inches long and thin as a child's finger. Cleo watched with fascination as the virgins dextrously ultilised the sticks to flick minute strings of green vegetables into their mouths. She and Dauntless had finished eating long before the sisters were halfway through their meals.

'What unusual cutlery,' Cleo said, into a silence broken only by the sisters' discreet mastication and swallowing. 'Is it a local tradition?'

Sister Pankodine dabbed her lips with a napkin. 'No, it is a tradition of our Order. To appreciate fully the gift of sustenance from our beloved Husband, the act of feeding ourselves must necessarily be protracted and arduous. Otherwise, we might take his gift for granted.'

Cleo couldn't resist laughing out loud. 'You are indeed slaves to your husband's whims,' she said. 'I could never behave as such, and my husband was a man of flesh and blood, not just a make-believe name!'

At this remark, Sister Umling gave a mew of distress and rose to her feet, staring above the heads of the others. 'Oh, my beloved, forgive me! I had an impious thought.' she cried, wringing her habit between her hands. 'When our guest spoke, I desired to retaliate in anger. I desired to push her face into her plate!'

'Sister, you should not judge the benighted,' Sister Pankodine exclaimed, her face a mask of censure.

'Oh sisters mine, absolve me,' groaned Sister Umling. 'Mortify the sinning thought from my mind.'

'Rise, Despera,' Sister Pankodine ordered.

Sister Despera fastidiously dabbed her mouth with her napkin and rose slowly to her feet, followed by Sister Pankodine.

'Accept our sacrifice,' Sister Pankodine murmured.

Cleo watched in horrified fascination as Sisters Despera and Pankodine fell upon their companion, dragged her to the ground and kicked her senseless, all the while crying, 'Oh, beloved sister, dear one and true, through our love we will help absolve your impiety.'

Cleo uttered a shocked protest, which was ignored, and glanced at Dauntless in alarm. He had averted his eyes and was paying far too much attention to his empty plate. After a while, Sister Umling was left writhing and groaning on the ground and the other two sisters resumed their meals. Sister Pankodine gave Cleo a sweet smile. Cleo nearly vomited back her greens.

'We forgive you your ignorance,' Sister Pankodine said, 'and realise it is hard for unenlightened minds to comprehend the glory of our estate, but rest assured that True Valiance is no symbol of myth.' Her eyes lit up with a weird inner light. 'He is as real to us as you are; more so. Few have felt his presence so emphatically as we.'

Sister Umling crawled painfully back into her seat, mouthing silent prayers.

Cleo could not repress a shudder.

Dauntless made plain his intention to spend a night in the fane, a revelation which did not please Cleo at all.

'So, Madam Moan, who only yesterday complained of the discomforts of sleeping in the open, you yearn for the forest floor as a bed, do you?'

'I just don't want to stay here,' Cleo cried. 'These women are insane. You saw what happened during the meal.'

Dauntless looked away. 'Cleo, as Sister Pankodine rightly pointed out, you cannot comprehend their way of life, therefore you are not well placed to make judgments upon it.'

Cleo growled in response.

She was given a hard board to sleep on in a tiny stone cell, with a single coarse blanket for warmth. She imagined the accommodation in the debtors' gaol at Scaraby could be no worse. Sister Pankodine led her to the room and gave her a small stub of candle so that she at least had a little light in which to undress.

'You will find a pamphlet of maiden's prayers on the windowsill,' Sister Pankodine said, without much conviction in her voice that Cleo would avail herself of it.

'Thank you,' Cleo said stiffly, 'but my prayers are all directed to life, not ideas. There we differ, and that's the end of it.'

Sister Pankodine inclined her head with a tight smile and left the room.

Even though the season was summer, it was cold in the room. Cleo removed only her boots and lay down fully dressed on the board beneath the blanket. Still, the hour was early and sleep evaded her. She knew that Dauntless intended to spend the whole night before the Altar of Devotions, seeking spiritual sustenance from his god. She suspected he would greet the day with renewed vigour and be mostly unbearable as a travelling companion.

Cleo sighed and, to pass the time, took down the pamphlet from the windowsill. She scanned a few pages before throwing it down in disgust. Such sickly sweet sentiment! Such claptrap! She learned that True Valiance had died protecting the chastity of a group of maidens. According to the text, the maidens had lived together, enjoying a simple life and seemly pursuits, only to be pestered by the attentions of the sons of a neighbouring estate. True Valiance had been a paladin of an older chivalric order, the Knights of Allegiance, and as luck would have it was passing the maidens' abode at the precise time when the neighbours were about to press their suits in an unequivocal manner. A slight and slender youth, Valiance had galloped his horse into the garden where the rape was taking place, waving his sword heroically. Unfortunately, as is often the case with martyrs, he was overwhelmed by the burly neighbours and while they perpetrated the rape upon him instead, the maidens managed to escape, thereafter to form the Order of True Valiance and enlist the sons of noble houses to its banner. Valiance himself died of his injuries after the thwarted neighbours assaulted him with weapons other than those that nature had provided. Or so went the legend.

'So, they made a god out of a wimp,' Cleo thought. 'It's all too stupid to contemplate.'

With such thoughts, she turned on her side and closed her eyes.

Some time in the middle of the night, she was awoken by a sound that had died away by the time she'd reached full consciousness. She sat up on the board, aware of how much her body was aching, and strained her ears to listen. Again, it came. A moan, the sound of a man in pain. As far as Cleo knew, there was only one man at the fane – her so-called protector, Dauntless. Quickly she cast off the blanket and pulled on her boots. The candle had long burned out, so she had no light to guide her way. Outside her cell, the corridor was in darkness. The smooth white walls emitted a spectral glow; there was no moon. Now, the noise was unmistakable, and Cleo thought she recognised Dauntless's tone in the cries. What was he doing to himself? Cleo wondered. Or were the sisters inflicting some peculiar torment on him? She crept towards the sound.

The Chamber of the Mysteries, wherein the altar was housed, lay behind a closed door. Cleo pressed her ear against it and assured herself the sound of Dauntless's distress came from within. Then she heard another sound, and that was unmistakably female. What was going on? Cleo opened the door as quietly as possible. The room was lit by torches hung upon the walls. Dauntless was hanging face down over the altar while a slight, naked female stood with her back to the door.

'What are you doing?' Cleo cried and instantly the woman turned round with a snarl. Cleo realised it was Sister Pankodine and that until that moment she had been attached to Dauntless by means of the false phallus she was wearing strapped to her groin. Cleo didn't know whether to laugh or scream, but at that moment something lunged through the air and kicked her in the side of the head. Knocked to the floor, she saw that it was another of the sisters who had attacked her.

'Defiler! Whore!' cried Sister Umling, her face distorted by large bruises and torn lips. She came towards Cleo with fingers outstretched.

'What is this?' Cleo cried. 'Are you all mad? Dauntless, stop them! You're supposed to be my protector.'

Dauntless made no move. All Cleo could see of him was his raised rump and dangling legs. His feet were twitching feebly. As Sisters Umling and Despera stalked towards her in a crouch from either side, Sister Pankodine advanced frontally with an arrogant swagger. It occurred to Cleo she had interrupted some ritual interpretation of the Valiance legend and that Sister Pankodine must currently have the persona of one of the despoilers. She raised a hand and pointed at Cleo.

'Seize her!' It did not take much imagination for Cleo to guess what might happen to her should the sisters take her prisoner. With Burrows agility and Burrows instinct for survival she ran forward, pushed Sister Pankodine hard and ripped one of the torches from the wall. She waved it about wildly in the hope of striking one of the sisters. Sparks flew everywhere.

'Get back!' Cleo roared. 'Back or I'll bake your backsides!'

Sisters Umling and Despera hesitated and glanced at Pankodine for instruction.

'She is but one,' Sister Pankodine sneered. 'Take her!'

The other two sisters lunged forward and Cleo struck out deftly with the torch, causing them to yelp and fall. The air filled with the scent of singed flesh. Sister Pankodine narrowed her eyes, as if she realised she was faced with a creature whose instinct for survival undoubtedly outranked all others. Cleo grinned; she felt completely in control. These women were feeble actresses; they'd never known a true fight.

'Come on, then,' she urged cheerfully, gesturing with the hand that did not hold the torch. Neither Sister Despera nor Sister Umling seemed eager to renew their attack. Behind them, Dauntless lurched unsteadily to his feet. Sister Pankodine turned briefly to observe him and then, biting her lip, turned back to Cleo.

'You are truly shriven, sir paladin,' she said in a stiff monotone. 'I suggest you take your ward and leave the fane immediately.'

An embarrassed silence filled the room. Dauntless slunk forward, retrieving discarded garments from where they lay in a pile behind the altar. Cleo grasped the torch with both hands.

'This creature is a hell-cat,' Sister Pankodine said, surprisingly retaining her dignity despite her ungainly accoutrements. 'I want her removed from our sacred premises at once.'

Dauntless said nothing but moved towards the door. With one final threatening thrust of the torch, Cleo followed him, walking backwards in case of sneak attack.

'Seek your pagan mountebank!' Pankodine screeched, obviously having been informed of Cleo's search by Dauntless. 'You'll get no more than you deserve.'

Cleo pulled the door shut with a slam. Then she began to laugh hysterically. Dauntless trudged painfully down the corridor.

'Our horse is stabled to the side of the fane,' he said. 'Go there.'

Cleo took the torch with her. Outside, the night was vigilant and still. The spring bubbled to itself in a secretive voice. After a few moments, Dauntless came out of the building with their bags and saddled the horse. Neither he nor Cleo spoke a word to one another. In silence, they mounted the horse and trotted out onto the road, heading south.

By morning, they had reached the edge of the forest.

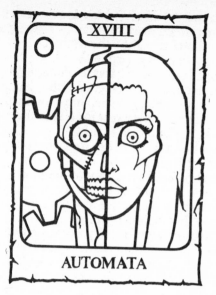

AUTOMATA

Inanna Grisaille was still being difficult with her lover, Wilfish Implexion. He was beginning to tire of it. It wasn't that she nagged him, or indeed voiced any of her thoughts, but her eyes were too knowing for his liking. They held the expression of a woman who suspected she had a rival in love. This annoyed the ecclesiarch because he never looked at other women. Too much trouble. If he took a new lover, he would have to train her to his needs. Such things bored him.

Implexion and Inanna were having dinner with one of the ecclesiarch's colleagues, another militia man, and his mistress. The dinner was held in a candlelit, heavily curtained room at Inanna's house, where opulent appointments reflected the light seductively and heavy Ixibatabian perfume burned upon a dish of smouldering coals. Conversation was muted, the low, musical laughter of the women cultured and beguiling. The wine was strong, the tamara weed freshly pressed. The room was entirely the province of the mistress of a powerful man. After the meal, talk had turned, as it generally did at social gatherings nowadays, to the Jeopardites.

'I would like to bed that beautiful prophet,' announced the companion of Implexion's colleague.

Implexion winced and glanced at Inanna to share his amusement with her. She was not smiling, but merely staring at him speculatively over a cup of wine. The candlelight suited her; she looked lovely. Implexion looked away and smiled insincerely at the other woman.

'You mean for a quick fumble with Jeopardy you'd give up your jewels, your lovely house and Danric's lavish donations to your coffers?' he enquired lightly.

The woman frowned. 'Not at all. I'd have it all. I am a woman of influence. I have everything I want or need.' She laughed, and waved her wine cup beneath her companion's nose to indicate she needed a refill. In Implexion's opinion, she'd had far too much already. In Danric's place, he'd have taken her home by now. Drunken women were so unattractive.

'I believe Jeopardy stipulates the surrender of all wealth before he beds any woman,' Implexion said. 'Surrender of all wealth to him, that is.'

'No bedroom bounce is worth that,' cried the woman.

'Indeed not,' Inanna added drily.

'He is so attractive though,' sighed the woman.

'Have you seen him, then?' Implexion asked.

The woman laughed. 'Of course. I was in Shanariah last year and made my servants keep their ears and eyes open concerning Jeopardite appearances. I used to attend them in a covered chaise, and I swear the prophet could see right through the curtains. He stared at me all the time.'

'I think that's unlikely,' Implexion said.

'Why? We all know he has a weakness for rich women.'

'You overrate your attractions.'

Danric cleared his throat noisily in embarrassment.

'Well, I . . .' the woman spluttered, clearly quite shocked. Her neck and the exposed part of her chest above her revealing gown had gone pink.

'More wine anyone?' Inanna's cool voice enquired into the silence.

Later, after the guests had left, there was a sullen silence in the bedroom, which Implexion did not feel inclined to break because he sensed Inanna wanted him to and that undesirable revelations would follow. She'd watched him climb into bed, and he could tell she was bursting with the need to speak her mind. After a short while, during which she was obviously wrestling with her conscience, she climbed in beside him and said only, 'I am worried about you, Wilf.'

He drew in his breath to speak, but she'd placed gentle fingers over his mouth.

'Listen to me. I don't want to hear anything you might say. We've known each other a long time, and I am aware there is much of your personality I have never seen, but what I know of you I love, in my own way. I try not to make demands upon you, but nowadays that is very hard for me. I can see what you're doing to yourself. It's like there's a fire inside you, burning you up, drying you out. Your eyes are always feverish. I know that look, Wilf. It used to be reserved for me alone. I've grown to be afraid of certain names, and I'm begging you to think hard about why you're thinking the way you are, and doing the things you're doing. Please, trust me, and trust my judgment. I am very frightened.'

She turned away and leaned over to douse the flame in the lamp on the beside table. The canopy over the bed seemed full of whispers. The moon-light watched. Implexion listened to the beat of his heart. It drowned out the whispers above him. He felt light-headed, energised, and very much alive.

He realised what Inanna was implying. The trouble was, she didn't understand his feelings. She couldn't. They were so complex. He could appreciate why his interest in Resenence Jeopardy could be interpreted as infatuation. He had long ago admitted to himself that the prophet obsessed him, but he did not agree with Inanna's assessment of the nature of the obsession. No, he and Jeopardy were following an apocalyptic trail. It was preordained, and it had nothing to do with desire. He was sure of that. Jeopardy had been placed in his path to test his faith and his strength. Inanna was on the verge of becoming an impediment to the resolution of his objective. Very soon, he would begin to put a distance between them. He felt that the empathy they'd once enjoyed had faltered, their relationship had run its course.

Implexion lay in the dark, thinking about Resenence Jeopardy. It seemed the only time he was allowed the peace to do that, to analyse his thoughts, was when he was in bed. He remembered the day when he'd first seen the prophet. It must have been five or six years ago now. He had been commanding his own arm of the Ixmaritian militia by then, stationed in Shanariah, and his unit had been directed to break up a public gathering in one of the city squares. There had been talk around the barracks for some weeks about a harebrained fool who'd started making speeches around the Harbourwards that were plainly heresy. It would only be a matter of time before he was taken into custody and persuaded against his blasphemous ways.

Remembering, Implexion wondered whether he'd experienced any sense of presentiment as he'd mounted his horse and led his men out into the city. He felt as if he should have done, but could only recall the event from when he'd arrived at the edge of the square.

There had been so many people, far more than was usual for such performances. And the air of excitement, even hysteria, had been totally new. Lunatics often stood up to speak in such places, badgering the crowds of tourists, hawkers and shoppers with their outlandish and mistaken beliefs. Generally, they were ignored by the Church, being thought harmless and pathetic, but there were rumours about the man speaking today. He was different. He had power, charisma. He seemed sane.

Implexion had not believed any of it, but as he'd ridden in among the people, he had seen, across a sea of heads, the person addressing the crowd: a lean, almost scrawny, figure in ragged clothes with wild unkempt hair. But such a face! It radiated power, courage, strength. When Implexion caught sight of that face, he had experienced an intensely significant moment of recognition. He was honest enough to face the fact that the path of his life had divided in front of him then. Down one route, he'd have galloped to Jeopardy's side and without question become part of his movement. But Implexion had followed the other path, the one that was expected of him, that he expected of himself. He'd suppressed his irrational feelings and had hit out in anger. The crowd had been brutally dispersed, but not before Jeopardy had escaped. It had set the pattern for everything that had happened since.

Now, in the dark, Implexion dared to wonder what his life would have been like if he'd obeyed the dangerous compulsion he'd briefly experienced and had followed the prophet. Could he really have abandoned all he believed in so easily? If so, why? How could Jeopardy manipulate a mind as strong as his own? That was Jeopardy's secret, the one Implexion wanted so desperately to prise from him. For a brief moment in Shanariah, his faith had wavered. Jeopardy had done that. It was frightening and part of the reason why the prophet should be destroyed, but it was fascinating too.

'Ixmar, stand by me,' Implexion prayed. 'Let me do Your duty.'

The day dawned drizzling and grey. Lucien offered to go into the town for Bessie, and Walterkin asked to accompany him.

Later, in one of the little cafés that dotted the side streets of Gallimaufry, they sat together drinking strong, milky coffee. Bags of vegetables were stowed beneath their table. They'd been talking about inconsequential things – Walterkin's father, people walking past the café. For perhaps the first time in Walterkin's company, Lucien had not been thinking about himself. But then, following a brief, comfortable silence, Walterkin said, 'So you ran away from Nehushtah Mandru to follow the new prophet, then.'

Lucien almost felt disappointed. He had been glad to forget about his problems for a while. Still, the story had not yet ended. He could not abandon the exorcism when the ceremony was but half completed. He shook his head. 'Not at all. It wasn't like that.'

After Jeopardy had disappeared down a side street from the public square in Shanariah, Lucien simply stood staring after him. His mind felt utterly numb. Around him, people were fleeing in confusion as Ixmarite officials on horseback cantered towards them. Lucien's instinct was to follow Jeopardy. Why, he could not determine. Was it to ask questions, seek answers? Was it to pursue a repressed desire? Or was it something else? Lucien recognised the feeling in his heart: envy.

Unexpectedly, a horse reared up beside him and a short whip struck down, catching him on the side of the head. Lucien caught a glimpse of a hard, passionless face, framed in a black hood. The face of Ixmarity; mindless. 'Disperse!' yelled the man on the horse. 'Get moving!'

Lucien felt his mouth twist into a sneer. For some reason, he wanted to hold his ground. Then the whip struck down again, catching him on the shoulder. He staggered back, aware that the Ixmarite was about to dismount. Further violence seemed imminent. Why couldn't he run away? He wanted to, didn't he? He wanted to hurry back to Nehushtah and forget this bizarre episode. And yet there was an unfamiliar feeling building up inside him. He could not name it, but it made him half afraid, half exultant.

'You disobey Lord Ixmar!' declared the Ixmarite. Lucien could see that he was grinning.

'I have disobeyed no one,' Lucien said. 'I am on an errand.'

'You were told to move!' The Ixmarite jumped down nimbly from his horse. It was a heavy animal, its eyes rolled madly in its black head. Its rider produced a short truncheon from his belt. 'Heretic!' he said.

'No—'

'Leave the boy be!' a voice behind Lucien cried. 'He's simple. I'll take him home.' Lucien felt hands grip his arms from behind and straighten him up.

'Yours, is he?' sneered the Ixmarite.

'Yes. I apologise for his apparent disobedience. He's easily confused.'

Lucien remained silent and allowed himself to be led off swiftly down the square. He saw that he had been rescued by a short, skinny man of indeterminate age, who wore a leather skull-cap and a long brown leather coat. 'Just keep walking,' the man advised in a low voice. 'No fuss. It's not worth it. That was the commander Wilfish Implexion you were annoying. He is famous for, shall we say, his impatience.' He led Lucien down an alley to the left of the square, where tall buildings pressed close together overhead. Here, Lucien shook himself free.

'I have to get back,' he said. 'My mistress . . . I am late.' He made as if to run back the way they'd come, but his protector grabbed his arm.

'Hush now, attract no more attention,' he said. 'Do you want your head cracked open? The militia are jittery today. Only a fool would provoke them.'

'You don't understand,' Lucien said. 'I am in town with my mistress. I will be late. She will miss me. I'll be punished.'

The little man stared at Lucien intently for a moment or two. 'You mean you're a slave?' he asked, in apparent incredulity.

270

Lucien rubbed his face and considered his answer. 'Yes,' he said at last.

'I would not have thought it,' said the man. 'You don't seem the type. Slavery is a strange choice of life.'

'Not my choice,' Lucien said. 'It was decided for me a long time ago.'

The little man grinned. 'And now it seems destiny has put the reins into your hands. The choice now is yours. Return to your mistress or come with me and claim your freedom.'

Lucien looked at his rescuer in astonishment. 'Come with you? Why should I? Who are you?'

'I am Cartesian Blink,' he said, with a short bow. 'As for your other question, why shouldn't you come with me? Have you a better option? Personally, I have no interest in your future, but as a free man I feel honour bound to point out the beneficial realities of your situation.' He began to walk down the alley, his hands clasped behind his back, his head lowered, and Lucien followed.

'If I run away, I'll be tracked down and maimed,' he said.

Cartesian Blink nodded. 'That is a distinct possibility – if you happen to be very stupid.'

'But if every slave just ran away when they were out on an errand, there'd be no slaves at all,' Lucien said, exasperated. 'It just doesn't happen. We can't escape; slave-owners call in the Ixmarites to assist them.' Even as he said this, he was thinking of Jeopardy. He was confident enough to flaunt himself beneath the very noses of the Ixmarites and he had not been recaptured.

Cartesian gave Lucien a shrewd glance. 'Your remarks call for consideration. As to your first point, I agree, which makes me wonder why indeed there are slaves. It suggests a certain complicity on the part of the enslaved in the arrangement, wouldn't you say? Perhaps a complicity engendered by laziness, fear or ignorance. Who can tell? Each case must differ, of course, and be the result of its unique components. As to your fears about capture, look around you. Would you not say this city is huge? What is one slave, or even a hundred, in a place of such magnitude? Also, it helps if a potential runaway has influential friends.'

'Well, I have no friends,' Lucien said, but was aware that a savage excitement, a daring to believe escape was possible, had flared within him. 'I have no money, no family to support me, nothing. If I tried to get work, my brand would be noticed.'

'What brand?' Cartesian asked.

Lucien touched his thigh. 'Well, it's hidden, but it could be noticed.'

'What would you say if I offered you both friendship and shelter?'

Lucien considered. 'I would suspect your motives.'

Cartesian nodded. 'Well, there is little to suspect. The moment I saw you, I was convinced you were to be part of my future. Coincidence is not at work here, Cartesian, I told myself, but fate. Step in and prevent that poor creature from inviting a blow to the head!'

'So you are acting purely from instinct and a belief in fate?' Lucien couldn't help smiling. He did not believe it for one moment.

Cartesian pulled a sad face and sighed. 'I can see you are not convinced. Before I continue, perhaps I'd better explain that I am an inventor. Today, you find me in a bitter temper.'

Lucien did not think this was apparent. 'Why so?'

'Only half an hour ago, I was let down by a potential apprentice. The boy had seemed so promising, too. Now I have a vacancy that must be filled today, because I am a very busy man. The minute I saw you, I saw possibilities. There's an intelligent face, I thought. There are dextrous hands.'

'Are you suggesting I become your apprentice?'

Cartesian nodded. 'In return for a roof over your head, a bolt hole, I would expect you to do my menial work for me.'

'But that's absurd. You don't know me. I am not at all technically minded.'

'I am an astute judge of character and potential,' Cartesian argued. 'Do you want the job or not?'

Lucien was rather taken aback by the offer. 'It seems to me that, should I accept, I'd only be exchanging one form of slavery for another.'

'Harsh words,' said Cartesian mournfully. 'You should look at the situation from my perspective. Some return for my generosity is not unreasonable, surely? How about if I offered you a wage?'

'Am I really worth this effort?'

'Upon first inspection, yes. I am rarely wrong in my judgments, although I might change my mind upon closer acquaintance with your character.'

'I don't know,' Lucien said. 'My life is reasonably comfortable. I have no wish to become a dogsbody.'

'Dogsbody? By no means. You should not view things in that way. Look upon this as a new avenue, an opportunity for learning. A wise and cunning person could make all manner of wonderful things happen. Change is the catalyst, that's all. If you decide to descend into another rut, that's your problem. Change and risk are the condiments of life. Without them, the taste is bland and dull.'

Lucien stopped walking. He thought about Nehushtah waiting imperiously in the textile quarter for her sherbet and the return of her pet boy. He thought of the comforts of Mandru's house, his friends there, Amber. Did he care for Amber? There didn't seem to be any feeling inside him concerning her. 'And now,' he thought, 'I rarely have the solace of performing a true Vibrancy. I am no more than a lap dog.' In Mandru's house, his life was pointless. He had no autonomy, he was a decoration, nothing more. More to the point, Cartesian Blink had offered him a wage. Even with his meagre experience, Lucien was aware that without financial independence, freedom was impossible.

He wondered whether living the life of a runaway in the city would compare favourably with one afternoon's relative freedom. And yet, if Jeopardy possessed the courage and determination to take back his freedom, why couldn't he? With just a small amount of money he could travel, escape the city, become a person in his own right. With a jolt, Lucien wondered whether this was what he'd wanted all along, perhaps from the very moment he'd been incarcerated in Por Tanssie. Had he yearned for freedom, but not realised it? All his natural desires had been repressed by discipline imposed from without and within. It seemed unreal. Standing there, in a dark alley, with a strange little man who offered very little in the way of life enhancement, Lucien felt as if something was growing and blooming inside him, as if he was waking up

'I accept your offer,' he said. 'I might live to regret it, but at this moment I do not want to go back to where I came from. There have been significant events for me, too, this afternoon.'

Cartesian beamed in pleasure. 'I am glad you made this choice,' he replied, 'and not just for the reasons you might think.'

Shanariah had few dirty corners in which a criminal breed could hide, but there were poorer areas of the city where professionals of dubious nature were allowed a tenuous existence, as long as they did not cross certain boundaries of propriety or extravagance. The Ixmarites knew very well that the presence of thieves among the populace swayed people's favour towards those that supposedly protected them from such threats.

Cartesian Blink occupied two floors of a dingy, dilapidated house in the area known as the Steeps. It was close to the harbour and all the streets were of a vicious incline, hence the name. Despite the splendid views, the idea of toiling uphill to one's residence did not appeal to people who thought themselves genteel; only poor people, nonconformists, unsuccessful artists and the quasi-criminal occupied its treacherous slopes. At the very highest levels were the estates of the robber barons.

Lucien fitted fairly comfortably into Cartesian's household. There was a sullen, middle-aged woman named Ulain who cleaned and cooked, but apart from her Lucien was the only other human occupant. Cartesian often went out into the city on business he never cared to explain, so Lucien was left to his own devices most of the time. At first, he was nervous of venturing outside, expecting to come across ranks of Ixmarite officials intent on hunting him down. His dreams were filled with terrifying images of a furious Nehushtah bursting into his room and dragging him off to be flayed alive, all the while lamenting her disappointment in her favourite vibrancer. Lucien would wake up, gulping for air, alert for sounds of someone breaking in. After a few moments of lying awake in the dark, the gentle creaks of the house would lull his taut senses, and Lucien would laugh at his own fears. Cartesian Blink's house felt safe; it was an enclosed and secret world.

Cartesian was obsessed with mechanical devices and had sought to alleviate the drudgery of Ulain's duties by means of several labour-saving contraptions. Some of these worked quite well, although others were more likely to injure the user than assist them. Ulain was patient with Cartesian, and Lucien suspected she might be in love with him. She was not an attractive woman, being too thin and mean of face. She had also lost a lot of her hair to a childhood disease, which meant she always wore a scarf about her head. She was polite to Lucien but clearly had no inclination to befriend him.

Lucien's duties were simple. He had to tidy Cartesian's workrooms and make sure all his tools and components were kept in their appointed places. Occasionally, under Cartesian's direction, he would help construct one of the inventions, although it was never clear to Lucien what the machines were supposed to be used for. They had moving parts, devoured oil and water, but rarely seemed to produce any end result.

Sometimes, friends of Cartesian would come to the house while he was out, to use his workrooms. Lucien would show them where everything was and keep an eye on them to make sure they didn't misplace or lose anything. Cartesian was very particular about things like that. His friends were all strange, furtive little men. They tended to treat Lucien as some kind of expert, which he did not bother to contest. Cartesian and his friends seemed complex and peculiar creatures, maelstroms of conflicting urges and emotions. Still, they did not abuse him, and on top of the modest yet not ungenerous wage Cartesian paid him, Lucien earned ample tips. All of this

273

money he hid beneath his mattress in a leather wallet.

In the evenings, other nondescript little men came to the house, but these individuals were always led to the upper storey by Cartesian himself, all parties speaking in urgent whispers. Lucien was intrigued by this behaviour and mentioned it to Ulain. She rolled her eyes as she wrung out a cloth which she'd had to wrest from the blindly grabbing mechanical arm attached to her bucket.

'Them and their toys,' she said. 'They're like kiddies, all of them.'

'Cartesian has toys upstairs?' Lucien had examined all the rooms in the house on the first occasion Cartesian had left him alone. Most of the rooms on the upper floor had been locked, but he'd had a feeling they'd been empty anyway.

Ulain nodded. 'Toys, yes. Master Blink and his friends are learned gentlemen, masters of hermetics and science. They have special toys.' And that was all she'd say on the matter.

Lucien had tried all the handles of the upper rooms again, but they'd still been locked. At one room, however, his attempts at entry seemed to provoke a response from within – a rustling, sighing sound. Following this, Lucien had confronted Cartesian and asked him what was hidden inside the rooms. He'd expected excuses and lies, but Cartesian merely handed him a set of keys and told him to look for himself.

'I must admit, I didn't think you were that interested in my inventions,' he said. 'Still, if you want to see, by all means do. But please don't touch anything. Some of the mechanisms are delicate.'

Lucien was almost disappointed by this frank admission. He looked through all the rooms, one by one, and found most of them to be full of packing cases. He opened one or two, but whatever devices Cartesian was storing there were all dismantled. In the last but one room of the upper corridor, he opened the door onto what appeared to be a lady's boudoir. Curtains were drawn against the afternoon light and the room was mostly in rust-coloured shadow. As he entered, something stirred on the enormous canopied bed set against the right wall.

'Excuse me,' Lucien said, believing he'd come upon the chamber of another occupant of the building. Then it occurred to him to wonder why Cartesian would lock them in. As he looked at the bed, a set of shapes sat up slowly on it. He saw three young women, clad only in corsets and stockings, their hair loose round their shoulders, their dark eyes large in their pale faces. They regarded him in watchful silence, in the manner of cats or serpents. Lucien departed quickly, but neglected to lock the door.

Cartesian was out on business, so Lucien left the keys on the kitchen table. He wondered whether he should mention the young women to Ulain, but because of his suspicions concerning her affections for Cartesian, and her unpredictable moods, he decided against it. Later, one of Cartesian's friends, an earnest young scholar of undistinguished features, named Ormicle, came to use Cartesian's workshops. Lucien pitied Ormicle. His brain was undoubtedly huge and crammed with astounding knowledge, but he was unable to communicate effectively with others, and was thus a silent watcher of the world. The machines he dreamed up were virtually impossible to build in solid materials as they were so delicate and insubstantial. He talked in an embarrassed whisper about catching dreams and thoughts, giving them form. In Lucien's opinion, the most difficult dream to realise was the one that involved the building of his machines.

As Lucien fetched the tools Ormicle asked for, there was a cry from Ulain, apparently coming from the kitchen.

'Is she hurt?' Ormicle had asked in dismay.

Another cry came, and another, and the unmistakable sound of assault by broom.

'Perhaps we had better see,' Lucien said.

In the kitchen, they found a desperate Ulain cornered by the three young women from upstairs. Ulain's headscarf had come adrift, and her sparse hair was sticking up in all directions, as if in terror. She was striking out at the still, silent women with the broom.

'Oh!' exclaimed Ormicle in a mild voice. 'However has this happened?' With surprising confidence, he marched forward and took the broom from Ulain's hands. She stared at him with panicked eyes. 'It's . . . it's all right,' he said, with the shade of a stutter.

'Who are they?' Lucien asked. At the sound of his voice, all three of the strange women turned towards him. He could see at once they were not creatures of flesh and blood. Their skins were of pale silk, their faces artfully painted, their eyes of glass, fringed by unnaturally long lashes.

'Cartesian's automata,' Ormicle told him, running his fingers through his hair. 'Oh dear, I don't know all their commands. How shall we return them to their room? I'm not sure they'd allow us to carry them.'

'Automata?' Lucien asked in incredulity. He approached one of the women and reached to touch her face. She was much shorter than he was; an exquisite, somewhat malevolent doll. When he touched her, her jaw dropped open to display perfect porcelain teeth and a wet red tongue. 'Are they without will?'

Ormicle made a huffing sound. 'That is difficult to ascertain. They are constructions, yes, but the manner in which they were contrived involved certain . . . oh, perhaps I'd better not say. Still, they are, by and large, unearthly creatures.'

'They came for me!' Ulain cried, still cringing against the cooking range. 'They are evil revenants!'

'No,' Ormicle said patiently. 'They would not have attacked you, Ulain. I suspect they were merely curious.'

'Are they ever dangerous?' Lucien asked.

'Not that I'm aware of,' Ormicle said. He took hold of one of the automata's arms and attempted to lead her from the room. She appeared rooted to the spot and opened her mouth to hiss, although she made no violent move.

'Let me help,' Lucien said and added his strength to Ormicle's. The automaton, however, was immovable.

'She is very strong,' Lucien said, 'and obviously quite heavy.'

Ormicle nodded dismally. None of the automata would consent to leave the room, apparently quite happy to stand in the middle of the kitchen, staring round themselves. Eventually, they were coaxed into chairs. Their movements were unnatural, but not noticeably mechanical.

'It's his witchings,' Ulain declared. She had recovered her composure enough to help guide the automata to their seats. 'I knew nothing good would ever come of his meddlings. These terrible creatures have no souls, no hearts.'

275

'Actually, they do have hearts of a sort,' Ormicle said. He became more voluble when speaking of subjects of a scientific nature. 'In some respects, they are entirely animal.'

'Do they have blood?' Lucien asked.

'Not precisely, but their frames are lubricated by a network resembling crude veins and arteries, containing fluid. Parts of their bodies are moist. Ahem.' He put a closed fist against his mouth.

'Abominations!' hissed Ulain.

'Can they speak?' Lucien enquired.

'If they can, they choose not to demonstrate the ability,' Ormicle answered. 'Cartesian would know.'

At that moment, Cartesian arrived home. He expressed consternation that his automata were downstairs, sitting round the kitchen table, but he was not a man of bad temper and did not get irate.

'I think it is my fault,' Lucien said. 'I looked in their room earlier, and I must have forgotten to lock the door.'

'Oh well,' Cartesian said. 'No harm done, although I don't like them roaming about. If they got out on the street, they would end up being destroyed in one way or another.' He adopted a commanding stance. 'Chasteless, Impiety and Inveritude!' They stood up and advanced towards him. 'Back to your nest, my pretties.' He gestured towards the stairs with his arm and the automata obediently obeyed him. He followed them out of the room and closed the door behind him. Neither Lucien nor Ormicle had the spirit to continue working and spent the rest of the day until suppertime drinking tea with Ulain in the kitchen – her fright had made her more friendly than usual. The incident had done much to unite all three of them. Lucien not only felt easier in Ulain's company from that day forward, but also felt he had breached some defence or barricade of shyness with Ormicle.

Caught up as he was in his strange new life, Lucien had much to occupy his mind. The incident in the square, when Cartesian had found him was never mentioned again, and Lucien shrank, for reasons he could not pinpoint, from showing any interest in the fanatical speaker who had caused the disturbance that day. But at night he was tormented by thoughts of Jeopardy speaking in public in Shanariah, risking not only recognition as an escaped Ixmaritian, recapture and its inevitable dire consequence, but also the wrath of the Ixmarites for his outspoken ideas. What had possessed Jeopardy to leave Mandru and come down to the city like this? Was he really mad? Lucien wondered, too, how his own disappearance had been greeted by Mandru and his lady. Was there now a price on his own head? He wished he could find out. At one time, the only thing he'd lived for had been the Vibrancy; now, he barely bothered to practise. His previous life seemed no more real than a half-remembered dream; inconsequential and worthless. He spoke little to Cartesian about his previous existence, though he admitted knowing Jeopardy, and thankfully Cartesian asked no pointed questions.

Lucien had been living in the Steeps for about four months when Cartesian announced that it was time he ventured outside the house.

'Do I have to? I am quite happy here,' Lucien said. He was still terrified of being recognised.

'Yes, of course you have to,' Cartesian said with a smile. 'Lucien, if you allow this fear of the outside to overwhelm you, it will become a true handicap. If you are worried, dye your hair, wear an unusual hat.' He patted

Lucien's hand. 'Today, I suggest you accompany Ulain to market. You will no doubt feel safer with a companion, and Ulain is a spry old biddy. She'll be alert for those who might take too great or sinister an interest in you.'

Lucien conceded with no great enthusiasm.

Once he had overcome his initial fears however, he found he was very much stimulated by the bustle and activity of the city. Ulain never ventured much beyond the Steeps themselves, for they were skirted by markets and slaughterhouses, although sometimes she went down to the harbour to buy fresh fish from the fishermen's wives who had stalls along the sea front. Lucien began to enjoy accompanying her and, taking Cartesian's advice, persuaded her to take him to a steam-house, where one of the services was hair-drying. He had the colour black stripped from his hair and then had them apply a rich henna. He felt it altered his features considerably. In Mandru, he had always worn kohl round his eyes and his hair loose. Now, he affected no face paint, allowed his eyebrows to grow thickly once more and, whenever he was out, tied up his hair severely. Surely, no one but an intimate would recognise him now. After a while, he did not even quiver when walking past groups of Ixmarite officials, and eventually could walk out alone without fear.

He also began to spend a lot of time with Cartesian's automata. They intrigued him. At first, the thought of touching them frightened him; he did not trust them not to harm him. Still, he now knew that Cartesian and his friends had sex with them regularly, and nothing untoward had ever happened to them. He wanted to ask Cartesian about the procedure, out of curiosity, but shrank from doing so because it made him feel slightly ashamed. They were, after all, machines, and he felt that by using them to gratify his desires, he would be debasing himself in some way. They were very lovely creatures, though. Chasteless particularly he admired, for her silk skin was dyed a subtle olive hue and her hair was a thick and lustrous black. In her movements, he discerned a ghost of intelligence and consciousness and for this reason often spoke to her. She appeared to listen to what he said – stories of his past life, thoughts of Resenence Jeopardy. She would put her head on one side as he talked, while her sisters combed her hair with their fingers. There was no cunning caprice about her, which he'd come to expect from women. She seemed as open and innocent as a recently bloomed flower. She seemed full of tolerance and acceptance.

One day, Lucien said to her, 'If only you could talk to me. If only you were real!' His tone had been quite emphatic and, because the automata recoiled with such abruptness, he realised they must respond to tone of voice rather than actual words. Then, Chasteless leaned slowly forward, staring at him with her expressionless glass eyes. She reached up to touch his lips, her face close to his own. Looking into her eyes, Lucien could perceive tiny movements behind the glass, as of minute cogs and wheels, like the workings of a clock. Does she see me? he wondered. He knew very little about how much perception the creatures had. Her lips were rubbery, dyed a dark, brownish red like dried blood.

'You are so beautiful,' Lucien said. 'And that might well be because you do not have a human soul.'

Chasteless's mouth stretched, almost imperceptibly, into the semblance of a smile. She pressed her closed lips against his own, and he put his arms round her body which, like her lips, felt more rubbery than human flesh. He could sense hard metal mechanisms working within her limbs. With

277

inhuman strength, her arms closed about him and she drew him backwards, curling her legs round him. A sound came from within her body; a hiss, a low whine. She began to move rhythmically and lubricating fluid spilled from between her legs. Lucien did not want to believe that her apparent submission was merely a mechanical response to something he'd said or done. He felt that Chasteless was offering herself to console him in some way. There was no tension involved in making love to her, because he knew she expected nothing from him, nor could she make judgments or comparisons. As a result he felt he made love to her more expertly than he ever had to Amber. It was a pity she could not appreciate it, but then again, maybe she did.

Afterwards, Chasteless became quiet and still, as if all life had left her body. Lucien hastily got up from the bed. Impiety and Inveritude, who had been standing nearby, came forward and leaned over their sister, apparently to clean her mechanisms. Lucien was overcome with embarrassment and shame, and left the room. He never told Cartesian what had happened.

One day, a whim overcame him and he approached Cartesian in his study before lunch. 'Cartesian, you know I spend a lot of time with the automata,' he said.

Cartesian smiled up at him. 'I know. I feel they interest you more than real women.'

Lucien made no comment on that observation. 'Well, could I possibly take Chasteless into town with me today?'

Cartesian frowned, apparently puzzled. 'What for? She is hardly a garrulous companion and might attract unwanted interest.'

Lucien fidgeted uncomfortably. 'I know it must sound bizarre, but I would like to learn more about the extent of her perceptions. I want to monitor her reaction to a new environment.'

Cartesian nodded. 'Noble reasons,' he said. 'As a matter of fact, I have long been intending to test for the existence of consciousness or intelligence in my creations, but have lacked the time. Would you be willing to take this task on, Lucien?'

Lucien nodded quickly. 'Most definitely. I find it very interesting.'

'Well, I am gratified to discover you have interests in this direction,' Cartesian said. 'When I found you, all I'd been looking for was a competent assistant, but the more I become acquainted with you, the more I realise you are a very intelligent boy. It is an added bonus to your discovery.'

Lucien narrowed his eyes. He found Cartesian's remarks offensively patronising. 'I shall cover Chasteless's head with a veil, and she can wear a light but concealing summer coat. I don't think anyone will suspect what she is. At most, she'll appear an invalid, with her strange gait.'

'Your choice is wise,' Cartesian said. 'Of the three, I have always found Chasteless to be the most alert, but then she was the last one I made, and my expertise had increased by then.'

'How did you make them?' Lucien asked.

Cartesian looked away. 'Best you are not made aware of all the details yet,' he said hastily, 'but suffice to say, I needed help from a group of gentlemen to complete the work. Understandably, the Ixmarites take a dim view of automata, so it is most important their existence is not made public.'

'I understand,' Lucien said, disappointed Cartesian would not reveal more to him.

* * *

278

Chasteless stood motionless as Lucien dressed her in one of Ulain's frocks, borrowed for the occasion with quite a few grumbles. He put a wide-brimmed hat of pale green felt on her head, from which hung a long georgette veil. Ulain's best summer coat completed the disguise. Ulain watched with folded arms as Lucien dressed the automaton.

'Don't you bring them togs back with any rips or stains,' she said ominously.

'Don't worry,' Lucien said, and tied the ribbon of the hat under Chasteless's chin. 'We are going out,' he told her. 'You will see many new things. Won't you like that ? I know you're a curious creature.'

'Bah' spat Ulain. 'You're getting as mad as Blink, talking to that thing!'

Seemingly in response, the automaton emitted a sound through her mouth which sounded uncannily like a rude retort, but it might have been coincidence. Cartesian had instructed Lucien on how to shut Chasteless's mechanisms down, should she run rogue while out in the street.

'I don't think she will, but you can never be sure,' he said. 'She will copy your motions if you say the words "Like this", which should be precaution enough. However, if that does not suffice, insert a finger into either of her ears, hook it round the thread of gut you will find and pull hard. She will collapse, and then it's up to you to get her back here in one piece.'

Lucien walked down the stairs with Chasteless holding his arm. It was so hard to believe he was not accompanied by a living creature. He could not regard any of the automata as human, but they at least seemed to possess the intelligence of dogs or cats.

He decided to take her to the tourist quarter where there would be street entertainers for her to see. They hired a public carriage at the edge of the markets and rode quickly to Repansol Square. Lucien spoke to Chasteless the whole time, while she stared from the carriage without apparent interest at the passing scenery.

They alighted at Tipman's Corner, and became absorbed by the slowly moving crowd. Chasteless showed neither alarm nor curiosity, although one of her fingers twitched upon Lucien's arm. Wary of overwhelming her sensory mechanisms, Lucien led her into a quieter street, lined by quaint inns where people sat outside sampling the vast array of ales on sale. Chasteless walked with a stately tread of seemingly deliberate slowness, as demure as a maiden of high birth. Lucien sat her down at a table outside an inn where there were no other customers, and hailed the pot-boy to fetch him a tankard of Witfail Brew. 'Nod to me after I speak, like this,' Lucien said and nodded his head. Chasteless nodded, the movement slow and sinuous.

'It is a beautiful day,' he said and nodded as he spoke. Chasteless imitated the gesture.

'And the city is so full of foreigners.' Another nod was mimicked.

He went on to demonstrate a shake of the head, a gesture with the hands, a shift of position, all of which Chasteless copied exactly.

'Now,' he said. 'Will you deliver a response without the magic words?'

Chasteless obviously recognised the tone of his voice – a request – but seemed unsure how to react. She stared at him, apparently with tension, awaiting some command. 'Like . . . ?' Lucien said. The automaton jerked. He leaned back. Chasteless seemed about to copy the motion, but then raised her hand slightly in what might have been a dismissive gesture. Lucien laughed, and Chasteless turned her head away as if to examine the

279

passers-by. He was not sure whether he'd proved anything or not.

He was just about to leave the inn when a youth came running down the street. He was pressing pamphlets into the hands of all those seated outside the inns. Lucien took the paper that was thrust at him and the boy ran on, dropping a pamphlet into Chasteless's non-reacting hands.

'What is this?' Lucien asked, frowning at the paper, thereby failing to notice that Chasteless had nodded at him.

'Know your own truth!' proclaimed the pamphlet. 'Take back your freedom!' Something made the hairs rise on Lucien's neck.

'What is this?' The voice seemed to come from far away, as if it was an echo blown on the wind, little more than a whisper. Lucien looked up sharply. Had the question come from Chasteless?

'It's him,' Lucien said. Chasteless stared back at him through her veil. Lucien stood up. 'Come,' he said and held out his hand, a command Chasteless was already trained to obey.

The pamphlet directed all readers to converge in Teller's Place in ten minutes. An oratory was to be delivered that would surprise and confound.

When they reached Teller's Place, a small crowd had already gathered, jokingly asking each other questions about what was to come.

'I think I have seen this man before,' one woman said to Lucien. 'His performances were common at one time, but he's not been around for well over a year. Thought he'd been imprisoned or something. But no. He's back again. A strange one, but you can't help listening to him. It's a wonder the Ixmarites haven't taken his tongue by now.'

'Who is he?' Lucien asked.

The woman shook her head. 'Don't know his name, although I've heard him called the Mad Prophet.'

'He divines the future?'

The woman frowned. 'It seems so, but then again, I can't be sure. If he's a simple madman, well, it's still good entertainment!' She peered at Chasteless. 'Sir, your lady looks a trifle unwell, poor thing. It's probably the heat, you know. Why not take her to that bench over there in the shade.'

'Thank you,' Lucien said and hastily led Chasteless away.

'Would you like any help?' the woman asked. 'I could fetch a tumbler of water maybe, or a cordial . . .'

'No, thank you,' Lucien said over his shoulder, and quickly disappeared into the crowd.

Presently, a couple of warmers came to invoke the spirit of the gathering. They climbed up onto a rudely constructed stage and began marching back and forth, saying: 'Do you sense there is more to life than has been revealed to you? Do you want this knowledge? Do you want more power over your life? Do you want freedom of thought, and extension of intelligence?' Many in the crowd affably shouted affirmatives to these questions, obviously regulars to these occasions and familiar with the routine. By the time the warmers jumped down behind the stage, the crowd was quite excited. Lucien's heart had begun to beat hard and heavy in his chest.

'I am afraid,' he said to Chasteless. 'I wish I could make myself leave.'

Again came the ghostly whisper. 'What is this?' Chasteless's lips had not moved, but Lucien was convinced the words had come from her. He stared at her intently for a moment and then squeezed her arm. 'I should be giving you more attention at this moment,' he said. 'I should feel exultant because we have made a breakthrough, but there's something else on my mind that demands all my attention.' Chasteless gave no response. Lucien wondered why he had bothered trying to explain himself to her. She couldn't possibly understand.

Suddenly, the crowd fell silent, and a dark figure walked slowly out onto the stage. He was dressed almost in rags, his trousers held together by rough leather thongs, his shirt ripped and soiled. His face was unshaven, his eyes mad as a rabid dog's, the whites showing all round their dark centres. His hair was a matted mane, falling down over his chest. He brimmed with life, he thrummed with it, and this vitality flowed over the crowd in an irresistible flood.

'Greetings, sleepers,' said Resenence Jeopardy, and the crowd sighed, or drew in its breath. A few people whistled or made jeering noises. Lucien felt as if he would faint. He gripped Chasteless's arm with more force than a live woman would have endured.

'Look at you!' growled Jeopardy in a scathing tone, and folded his arms, tapping one foot against the stage.

'Look at *you*!' someone called back.

Jeopardy nodded, smiling, tongue in cheek. It was obvious he was enjoying himself. 'You are like the docile sheep that graze the hills beyond the city!' he cried.

Hecklers in the crowd mimicked the bleating of sheep.

'You drool and kick in a sheep-like slumber, passive victims of your unimaginative realities!' Jeopardy roared.

The same hecklers, mainly youths, made loud snoring noises, but the laughter from the crowd that had accompanied their interruptions was becoming strained.

Jeopardy walked up and down the stage, apparently deep in thought. Then he wheeled round and seemed to hang over the crowd from the stage. Lucien saw people visibly jump backwards in surprise.

'You're being trampled on, and you won't admit it!' Jeopardy snarled. 'No, you all lie there sleeping, even as the bones of your souls are crushed to powder. I say to you,' his voice rose in timbre to a mighty yell, '*wake up*!'

'Wake up! Wake up!' a heckler echoed, and a few brave souls responded with a laugh. But this time, Jeopardy did not smile at them. Now, he was serious and, obeying his unspoken command, the crowd fell silent.

'There is a time,' Jeopardy continued, in a softer tone, 'and it is a time not far removed, when the earth will shake itself free of sleepers. You will all vanish into chasms that will yawn beneath your houses. Unless,' he crouched down and his voice fell to a whisper, 'unless . . .' He sucked his lips for a few moments, staring at the splintery floor of the stage, and then stood up. 'Unless you can wake up, my friends,' he said in an affable tone. 'You restrict yourselves simply through your own fears, your own nightmares. Those are the only rules the oppressors have: that you believe in your fears.' It was obvious he was referring to the Ixmarites, although he was careful not to mention them by name.

A less subtle voice from the crowd interrupted his oration. 'Will surrendering my fear stop the cutting of a blade, or the tightening of a hangman's noose?'

Jeopardy seemed to seek out the questioner with unfailing eyes. 'Yes,' he said simply. 'Today, I believe it can.'

'Prove it, then!'

Jeopardy closed his eyes and shook his head with a sigh. '*I* can't; only you can do that. The trouble is we are born into a world that has already been designed for us. We are taught to believe that we should lead "good" lives in order to earn a good death, a pleasant afterlife. And what is a good life? In the eyes of those who make the laws, it is handing over your money to perpetuate the structures of oppression, kowtowing to imported deities that have no relevance, no message, no empathy with your cultural soul. So, you obey the injunction; you kiss the shrines, walk the path of life looking neither to left nor to right, in the hope it will lead you to celestial halls. That is good life. Every so-called law-abiding person in this land would agree. And yet . . .' Jeopardy sat down upon the stage. He had the attention of everyone present.

'Imagine you are a murderer, with a murderer's soul. To you, a good life would encompass regular killing. Your gods might well be very different from those the majority of people worship. Your gods might enjoin you to kill; that would be part of your devotion. The murderer kills regularly to please his deity. He lives what he perceives to be a good life. Then, he is caught for what the majority see as his crimes. He is tried and sentenced. Death. He can't understand it. He lived a good life, didn't he? Has his god deserted him? His captors are outraged. "Our gods abhor the needless taking of human life," they say. "You must be punished." It is a battle of gods. Or it appears to be. In fact, it is not. It is simply a battle of beliefs.'

He stood up, made a languid gesture with one hand. 'I don't believe in traditional gods,' he said. 'To be honest with you, I don't really believe in anything. Much has happened in my life to make me contest the existence of a hard reality. But sometimes I need to pray, sometimes I need to address a higher intelligence. We all have that need. So I create one for myself; I imagine its face, its body, its personality. I give it flesh and I pray to it. Oh, I can see you thinking, but this is heresy against the true gods. Think of this: the true gods were created by humans to fulfil a need. We outgrow our mortal parents, those people to whom we turned for reassurance, and as adults we invent divine parents. In times of crisis, terror and despair, we turn to them in prayer and cry, "Please, help us!" And sometimes, depending on the strength of our faith, we are comforted. Even miracles might occur.

'The gods are necessary for our mental health perhaps, but we should not imagine they exist independently of ourselves. If we receive comfort from our prayers, or our dilemmas are magically, miraculously, swept away, it is our belief in ourselves, the selves that energise the prayers, that has created the miracle. What I am saying is that you have the power to administer your own life. You do not need a set of laws imposed from outside, from others. You should wake up to this great possibility and reclaim your freedom. Do not fear the threat of death, because death itself is merely a transformation. Flesh is transient, yes, but if we believe that all that exists beyond this life is what others prescribe for us, are we not condemning ourselves to their immutable reality? I say to you: wake up and become the designers of your own being, in this life and beyond.'

Jeopardy let his words resound in the minds of the crowd. He spoke so convincingly, Lucien thought, but then he always had. His presence carried the words, his physical beauty framed them. But what drove Jeopardy to say these things in public? Why did he care what other people believed in? It seemed he existed beyond the law. He scorned what he saw as oppression by the Ixmarites. And yet, by attempting to discredit the rule of Ixmarity, he was trying to supersede it surely, to impose his own views and laws. It seemed contradictory to what he was saying. Lucien wondered whether he should voice these questions. He felt someone should. But the last thing he wanted at that moment was for Jeopardy to recognise him.

The crowd remained silent, even the hecklers. It was as if they'd been stunned by Jeopardy's speech, but Lucien did not feel they had mindlessly accepted it. Neither, it appeared, did Jeopardy.

'Is it really so hard for you all to admit the possibility that some of what I say might actually *work*?' he said in an exasperated tone. 'Would you all rather doggedly believe that the others, the black-robed men of power, hold the ultimate truth? Why can't you just experiment with the ideas I've suggested? Let go of your restrictive beliefs if only for a second. For just one moment, experience total freedom!' The crowd still did not respond. It was as if they were waiting for more. Jeopardy frowned and rubbed his eyes wearily. 'There is no such thing as truth or untruth. There is simply being, and perception.' He smiled sadly. 'Am I wrong to force my own perception upon you?' He raked the crowd with lambent eyes.

It was as if he'd been reading Lucien's mind. Lucien felt a surge of shock course through his body. Around him, people were looking at one another, as if seeking cues, a leader.

Above them, Jeopardy waited. Never had Lucien seen him so radiant, so powerful, so painfully beautiful, and he felt that everyone else in the crowd must share these feelings. How could I fool myself I was glad you had left my life? he wondered. How could I forget how beautiful you were?

'If we wake,' said a voice from the crowd. 'What then? Tell us in real terms. What then?'

Jeopardy smiled. 'Greet the weapons of your oppressors with laughter, wither steel to water with unbelief.'

The crowd seemed to be waking up from a drugged sleep. It was beginning to murmur like a hive of bees.

'Tear down the churches!' someone cried.

'Smash the statues!'

'Liberate the crossroads of our land!' That last remark, Lucien thought, must be from a northerner. Those whose ancestors had worshipped in the old way often believed that Ixmarity controlled Gleberune because the roads were built upon lines of power. Nearly every crossroads sported an Ixmaritian monument and it was thought this blocked the natural power of the land.

Lucien made his own suggestion, but beneath his breath: 'Free the vibrancers.'

'Free the vibrancers!' Jeopardy yelled. Then he paused, as if confused. He searched the now noisy crowd with troubled eyes. 'Lock Ixmar in His Mansion!' he cried, the first direct remark he had made concerning Ixmarity. 'Dissolve the power of His sons! Unbelieve them! Make them . . .'

The sentence remained unfinished.

Suddenly, Jeopardy made a choking sound and jerked backwards, clutching his throat. He fell to his knees, coughing. The excited babble of the crowd rolled over into a murmur of consternation. What had happened? Was the prophet ill?

Then someone cried, 'He's been taken by a dart!'

Lucien blinked and saw that a line of red was seeping between Jeopardy's fingers where they clutched the wound, just above his collar bone.

A woman's voice cried, 'No!' A cry that was quickly echoed in every throat around her.

'Disperse! Disperse!' another voice yelled; the voice of authority. Looking round, Lucien could see that a squad of mounted Ixmaritian militia was flooding into Teller's Place, heralds yelling through horns to amplify their voices. Jeopardy was still slumped to his knees on the stage, while two of his companions bent over him, attempting to drag him to his feet. Jeopardy's filthy shirt was wet with dark blood.

'He is dying' Lucien thought. 'He is dead!' He gripped Chasteless's arm so hard, a living girl would have protested at the pain.

A line of grey-faced Ixmarites advanced on foot towards the stage. They held truncheons in both hands. Jeopardy's companions appeared bewildered as they watched the inexorable approach. They did not attempt to flee, staunch in their loyalty to their prophet.

The leading Ixmarite, riding behind a line of minions on a splendid black horse, announced, 'You are all under arrest!' He pointed with his whip at the stage. 'Submit, or suffer humiliation and pain!' His face wore the most frightening expression Lucien had ever seen, glacial, yet filled with a profound and cruel excitement.

A voice near Lucien's shoulder gasped in terror: 'Implexion!'

Lucien's flesh went cold. Over the last couple of years, Implexion had risen to prominence within the Church and had earned a reputation for brutality that inspired fear in every heart. Lucien knew he must escape Teller's Place immediately. The old fear of detection rose up within him like a frantic, flapping bird. He was convinced his former profession proclaimed itself from his bones to those who were trained to spot it.

All exits to the square were guarded by Ixmarite units who were allowing people through in single file. Lucien could see papers being exchanged between militia and civilians; fines, he presumed. Or perhaps names and addresses were being taken. The square was emptying. People wanted to get away as fast as they could. They would no doubt be making excuses to the Ixmarites, seeking forgiveness for daring to listen to the heretic. Lucien knew he should leave now; hurry back to Cartesian's house, get Chasteless to safety. And yet he dared not confront the Ixmarites. They would know him, he was sure.

On the stage, a line of Jeopardy's followers had picked up weapons. They had pulled packing cases in front of themselves to create a flimsy defence. The Ixmarites advanced slowly, as if Implexion wanted to savour this moment to the full.

A mounted Ixmarite trotted his horse over to where Lucien stood with Chasteless. The automaton had remained motionless, uttering no sound. 'If you're sensible, you'll leave now,' said the Ixmarite, scowling down from the saddle. 'The show's over. Why risk trouble?'

Lucien opened his mouth to respond, hoping some suitable words would come to him, but before he could say anything the man's jaw dropped open and his eyes glazed over. For a moment, Lucien thought he'd been hit by a knife or a dart, but he did not fall from his horse. His attention was held by whatever was happening behind Lucien's back. He turned round.

On the stage, Jeopardy had been helped to his feet. He stood up above the pathetic defences, his followers frozen in postures of anguished protection. He addressed Wilfish Implexion. 'I know you,' he said, and his voice

284

was as clear and ringing as a silver bell. 'I know you utterly, commander. We will have our day, our confrontation, but not yet.' He smiled. 'You will have to be patient.'

His words seemed to release a plague of panic among the Ixmarites. The line of advancing militia hesitated, their truncheons wavered. Teller's Place became full of a vague luminescence. What was happening? Lucien could hear a harsh, ragged voice issuing orders, but it was as if the Ixmarites were caught in stasis. Horses began to rear and scream. Riders were thrown, trampled underfoot.

Jeopardy's followers were clearly urging their prophet to make his escape. Lucien could hear their agonised voices entreating him to run. Jeopardy was bleeding from a point above his left collarbone. His followers' fluttering hands were stained red with his blood. Jeopardy himself appeared dazed and in pain, as if the effort of addressing Implexion had drained him completely of strength. He leaned heavily against his two companions as they began to help him down from the stage. Lucien felt a jolt within him, and experienced a strong urge to call out to Jeopardy's companions or go to assist them, but he forced himself to hold his tongue, make no move. What would be the point in letting Jeopardy know he was there? He was no more than a small part of his past, probably a forgotten part. Best to remain invisible – to both sides. Jeopardy was clearly a dangerous man to know.

Lucien became aware of Chasteless standing motionless and silent beside him. He looked at her expressionless face, barely visible through her veil.

'I love him,' he said. 'I have always loved him, I always will. I'll carry him to my grave.'

The automaton made no response. He had not expected her to.

Jeopardy was being led towards an alley behind the stage. Lucien felt trapped within a pocket of timelessness as, all around him, the Ixmarites tried to regain control of their horses, and their vicious leader sought to direct their attention to Jeopardy once more. It was not to be. Lucien could see that. Wilfish Implexion had disappeared from the perceptions of his men. All that remained of him was his echoing voice, and that was unintelligible. Jeopardy was escaping. He always would, until the moment he chose to die. And Lucien knew the time for that would come. It was part of the phenomenon that comprised the man.

'Goodbye,' Lucien thought, convinced this would be the last time he saw Jeopardy alive. But, even as he formed the thought, Jeopardy suddenly commanded his companions to halt. Painfully, he pulled away from them a little and turned round. His eyes met Lucien's like two hot coals striking a cold pool. Lucien felt the hiss of steam, of burning. He felt his face flame. Jeopardy's face was expressionless.

'Lucien,' he said. 'Follow me.'

And the pocket of timelessness opened. Lucien could walk through into Jeopardy's reality. There was no way he could resist it.

Jeopardy and his companions lived in the cellar of a house on the lower levels of the Steeps, not that far from where Cartesian Blink lived. All this time, Lucien had been so close to Jeopardy without realising it. The thought of that made him feel both hot and cold. Only two of Jeopardy's followers had remained to help him from Teller's Place. Despite their appearance, which was ragged to say the least, they possessed coins, and once they had left the alley they had managed to flag down a public conveyance, a wheeled

285

chair for four, drawn by two men in leather harness. Lucien was familiar with this form of transport; it was used mainly by tourists and generally cost too much for everyday use. Most of the chair-pullers lived in the Steeps too, and perhaps because of this they recognised members of their own kind in need, and without pausing stopped to assist. Jeopardy was bundled into the chair, supported by one of his companions. The other, barely more than a boy, would follow on foot. Lucien and Chasteless climbed in and sat opposite. Jeopardy said nothing, but leaned against his follower's shoulder, groaning softly. His companion was a woman, lean and dour-faced. She looked past Lucien as if he was not there, although, out of curiosity, her eyes strayed occasionally to Chasteless.

Lucien followed as unobtrusively as possible once they'd reached their destination. He felt Jeopardy's companion objected to his presence – in fact, he sensed a strong atmosphere of jealousy – but he did not intend to leave Jeopardy now. There were questions to be asked, the answers to which he'd been denied too long.

In the cellar, a band of fussing ragamuffins converged on Jeopardy in a murmuring throng, their hands flashing out nervously to touch him. 'Stand back!' cawed the woman who had accompanied him. 'And bring water.'

She led Jeopardy to a rickety chair, the sole seating in the room, which stood next to an ancient table that appeared to be covered in rags. Jeopardy made groans of protest as the woman forced him to sit down. A girl ran up with a stained and chipped enamelled dish filled with water. A rather grubby looking rag dangled from her arm, and a large roll of gauze was pressed against her body beneath her elbow. The dour-faced woman examined these articles with a downturned mouth, before taking them from the girl and arranging them in a line on the table. She dipped the cloth into the water and carefully wrung it out. Then, she barked an order at the curious onlookers, and dismissed them from the room. Reluctantly, looking back over their shoulders, as if hoping Jeopardy would countermand the woman's order, they filed from the cellar and disappeared into the dingy recesses beyond. The woman directed one sharp disapproving glance at Lucien – who had not assumed he was included in the dismissal – before ripping open Jeopardy's shirt and baring the wound. Lucien was horrified to see her spit onto the rag before she applied it to the injury.

Leaving Chasteless by the open door, Lucien walked purposefully over to the table. The woman glared at him once, before continuing with her task. Lucien could see that the bowl of water was already bright red with Jeopardy's blood. Jeopardy turned his head to look up at Lucien with bleary eyes. He smiled weakly, wincing as his companion probed his wound.

'I thought I felt your presence in the crowd,' he said. 'I dared not believe it. Lucien, it's good to see you. I knew you would not stay long at Mandru after I'd gone.'

'You should not speak,' the woman said sharply before Lucien could respond. 'You have lost much blood.'

Jeopardy frowned. 'Don't fuss, it is nothing. By tomorrow, it'll only be a scratch.'

'It is rather more than a scratch,' Lucien said, realising he was attempting to placate the woman. 'Are you mad, Res? What are you playing at?'

Jeopardy's weak smile broadened into a strained grin. 'Am I responsible for your freedom, Lucien?'

Lucien shrugged. 'Partly,' he said. 'You don't seem that surprised to see me.'

Jeopardy sighed, leaning back and closing his eyes. 'Of course I'm not. Why should I be? I caught sight of you in the city nearly two years ago.'

Lucien laughed harshly. 'Yet you never tried to find me.'

'Nor you me,' Jeopardy pointed out. 'Anyway, I knew that all I had to do was wait. You would come to me eventually.'

'You flatter yourself.'

'Not at all. Can't you remember? I told you we'd meet again once we'd parted.'

'Oh yes, was that the first pronouncement of the prophet?'

Jeopardy sighed. 'Lucien, don't be aggressive. Did you miss me?'

'Amber did,' Lucien replied, still rather sourly.

Jeopardy raised his brows, his eyes still closed. 'Poor Amber. I doubt whether I caused her any lasting harm.' He opened his eyes and looked at Lucien. 'Whereas you would certainly have possessed the power to do that. She must miss you more.'

Lucien squirmed uncomfortably. He hadn't so much as thought of Amber for months. 'I have cast that life off,' he said stiffly, feeling proud of the statement.

Jeopardy laughed, a ragged sound that degenerated into a cough.

'Keep still, will you!' snapped the woman as she attempted to wrap the bandage round Jeopardy's chest and neck.

'Brave little Lucien!' Jeopardy said.

Lucien leaned against the table and folded his arms. 'So, you have decided to become religious,' he said sarcastically.

Jeopardy ignored the remark. 'That's enough,' he said to the woman, pushing her hand away. The bandage was now secured. She protested a little before grumbling something incomprehensible and throwing the rag into the bowl, both of which she picked up. Jeopardy struggled upright in the chair. 'Leave us,' he said. The woman was clearly far from happy with that request and slammed the bowl down onto the table. Bloodied water slopped over the stained, dusty wood.

'Call me if you need me,' she said woodenly, and stalked from the room, giving Chasteless a wide berth.

Jeopardy didn't watch her go.

'How did you collect these people?' Lucien asked in a low voice.

Jeopardy shook his head. 'It's easy,' he replied. 'Let's not talk about them. I want to look at you, Lucien. Come closer.'

Lucien didn't move. 'You can see me well enough.' He laughed coldly. 'Well, am I supposed to think that you are all you hinted you were?'

'Did I *hint*, Lucien?' Jeopardy smiled warmly. Lucien suddenly recalled Jeopardy had often smiled, yet in his memory he'd remembered him as dour and humourless.

'All the time,' he replied. 'I thought you were just bored with your life, or bored with yourself. You just wanted everyone to think you were different from them.'

'Is that so unreasonable? Why should I want to be the same as everyone else? Do you?'

Lucien stood upright. 'Oh, stop that, Res! Stop the games. I don't know what I'm doing here, or what you're doing with your life! It seems insane.

287

You gained freedom only to risk losing it, to risk losing your life. What's the point?'

Jeopardy pulled a rueful face. 'How fiery you've become,' he said. 'You seem to have grown up a lot in a short time.'

'Don't patronise me! You're not that much older than I am.'

Jeopardy raised a hand weakly. 'I was always much older than you, Lucien. You know that's the truth. At Mandru, I alone was able to see your potential.'

Lucien laughed. 'Oh really?'

'Yes, really. Do you know how many Ixmaritians have escaped over the past twenty years? Five. Or at least, only five are known about. Three of those were recaptured. We are the other two, Lucien. Don't you see how significant that is? Even though you appeared to be a prim, well-behaved little Por Tanssie puppet, I knew you would leave Mandru. I could see it so clearly. And I didn't flatter myself it would be because of me. It was what interested me in you, Luce, more than your prowess as a vibrancer, which after all means nothing. Have you danced since you escaped captivity?'

Lucien shook his head.

'There you see. At one time, it was your sole reason for existence, the only thing that gave you shape and form in the world. Now . . .?' Jeopardy paused, and then spoke as if to himself. 'Why don't more of them run away? It's not that difficult.'

'It would be if more people tried it,' Lucien said. 'We were trusted. I was trusted so much Nehushtah brought me into the city with her and sent me off alone on an errand. I never went back.'

'That woman is a monster.'

'I agree. Anyway, tell me of your own escape. Where did you go?'

Jeopardy shrugged carefully, favouring his injured side. 'I climbed over the wall of the estate and ran west across Scarcement Chase. I swapped my clothes with some shepherds, ripped and muddied the garments they gave me, and entered Shanariah from the north, through the Beggars' Gate. An Ixmarite priest gave me a bowl of fish soup.' He grinned. 'I loved it! I touched my brow and thanked the man with a stutter. He put his hands on my head and blessed me. Can you believe it?'

'Yes,' Lucien laughed. 'What then?'

'Well, I couldn't dance to make money, in case someone realised what I was, and I knew no one in the city I could go to for shelter, so at first I joined the beggar community. It was depressing. I had thought people like that would be mad philosophers or visionaries, but in truth they were just hopeless creatures without energy of any kind. One day, I was offered a swig of a cruel liquor they drink all the time, and getting intoxicated, began to berate them. I really enjoyed it, poured out all my impatience with the world. Passers-by gathered to listen, and a man and a woman threw me coins. I realised I had stumbled upon the seeds of a new profession. I hated the Ixmarites and had always wanted to undermine them, and believed I might be able to do that in a small way now that I was free. But then I woke up – one of many awakenings – and realised I had the power to draw people to me. Every time I spoke in public, people would flock to listen and I would earn money. But eventually, it became more than that. People actually wanted to follow me. They said they felt they'd come home when they listened to me. I spoke a language they had forgotten but which I reminded them about. In my presence, they felt strong and free. That was when I knew I could be used, and could use myself, as a catalyst to create a movement that would contest the Ixmarites' absolute rule. At the most, all we hope for is that we can induce people to ask themselves questions. If we can make things difficult for the Ixmarites, that's enough. At the moment, most of those who've joined me are Steeps people. We've been out and about in the land this past year, testing the ground, as it were. Soon, we intend to get out there again and cause some havoc. We are nobody's slaves, we are free.'

Had Jeopardy wanted this all along? Lucien wondered. It seemed too . . . organised for him somehow. Perhaps Jeopardy had changed more than he could guess. 'Do you make a lot of money from it, then?' Lucien asked. Looking round the cellar, he couldn't believe that he did.

'Some,' Jeopardy replied. 'Enough to feed us all, and to buy a little essential equipment for the task.'

'I am impressed – I think,' Lucien said.

'So enough about me for the present. What is your story? You left Nehushtah, and . . . ?'

Lucien shrugged. He hadn't expected Jeopardy to ask him about himself; that was certainly a fresh attribute. 'I met a man named Cartesian Blink, and I work for him. He is an inventor. We live near here. It is a quiet life, but one that I enjoy.'

'Lucky coincidence, meeting such a man,' Jeopardy said. His eyes were laughing. Lucien dared not meet them.

'Well, it was, I suppose,' he said awkwardly.

Jeopardy shook his head, sighed, and then glanced up at Lucien with wide eyes. 'You were lovely, you still are. I dreamed of you a lot after I left, you know. You haunted me.'

Lucien felt a stab of anger. He wasn't sure why Jeopardy's words should affect him like that. 'Don't try to fool me, Res!' he snapped. 'You were only ever aware of yourself. I was just a mirror, like Amber was. You liked to see yourself in other people's eyes, become more real to yourself through their love for you.'

Jeopardy shook his head. 'That's not true.' He sighed. 'All I can say is that, at Mandru, I felt as if I could only communicate with you through a metal screen. Nothing was real there. The people were but puppets, simulacra, automata. How could anyone interact realistically in that environment?' He indicated his surroundings. 'This is real life, Lucien. It was too comfortable at Mandru. We need to experience danger in order to feel fully alive.'

Lucien smiled. 'I agree to a certain extent. However, I can't help feeling you're taking it a bit too far.'

Jeopardy shrugged slowly, his face creasing in pain. 'I like to annoy the Ixmarites. They took my youth, so I'm taking a small revenge. Ultimately, it's probably harmless. I'm not stupid. I know it will take more than the words of one man to motivate a populace into taking action. Still, there is always the possibility.' He smiled. 'I intend to try, anyway.'

Lucien shook his head in disbelief. 'How long do you think you can get away with this? It's senseless. You do more than annoy the Ixmarites, Res. You've attracted the attention of Wilfish Implexion, and he won't rest until you're dead! Haven't you heard about him, the atrocities he commits in Ixmar's name? To him, a heretic is sport, an animal to be hunted down and killed. If he wasn't an Ixmarite, he'd probably be a murderer. On top of that, he has ambition, and is respected greatly by the Church hierarchy.

I've heard people, joke that Implexion gets promoted every month, and its probably not so far from the truth. He'll attain a high position in the Church, everyone says so. Every day, it will become harder for you to escape capture.' He narrowed his eyes. 'Unless . . .' He approached the chair. 'I myself have seen you evade Implexion's militia twice. On both occasions, the odds against that were overwhelming. I don't even know what I saw today in Teller's Place. It was unreal. A mass hallucination? How did you do that?'

Jeopardy laughed. 'What are you saying, Lucien? I thought you believed me to be nothing more than a self-inflated fool. Are you saying you believe me to have *power*?'

'I don't know. I'm just asking you a question. Will you answer it or not?'

'I simply believe in myself,' Jeopardy answered. 'In moments of crisis, this faith is at its strongest. I don't do anything that no one else is capable of.'

'That's hardly an answer,' Lucien said. 'Did you will the Ixmarites to disperse, or hex them?'

'I just wanted space,' Jeopardy said. He turned his head towards the door, as if searching for a reason to change the subject. 'You have a companion. How still she is, how silent.' He beckoned to Chasteless. 'Come here, friend of Lucien.'

Lucien laughed. 'You're less clairvoyant than I thought,' he remarked. 'Chasteless is not a living person.'

Jeopardy looked surprised, and the faintest gleam of anger glowed in his eyes. 'Oh? What do you mean?'

'Chasteless, come,' Lucien said, performing the summoning gestures Chasteless was trained to recognise. With a small jerk, she seemed to come to life and walked towards the table; a luminous thing of dreams in the dark of the cellar. Lucien drew her to his side and cast back her veil. 'Forget the puppet people at Mandru,' he said. 'This is a genuine automaton. Her name is Chasteless. She was built by the man I work for.'

'Come here,' Jeopardy said in wonderment to Chasteless. Lucien was about to command her, but before he could speak or gesture she began to advance, in an apparently cautious manner, towards Jeopardy's chair. 'What an exquisite thing!' he exclaimed, reaching out to touch her face. 'So pure, so devoid of sleep!'

'She was created by necromancy, or so I believe,' Lucien said coldly.

'Ah, I have heard of this. A construct inhabited by a human essence.'

'Then you know more about the process than I do,' Lucien said. 'Cartesian is very cagey about it.'

'It is quite simple,' Jeopardy said. 'If you create the right conditions, life will grow. Build an appropriate nesting box in your garden and birds will come to inhabit it. In this case, a machine was built that attracted a soul, the essence of consciousness, perhaps only a wandering memory, a mote of information. It is rather like when life is conceived in the body of a woman. Your mentor is obviously a very learned man.' He addressed the automaton. 'You're no doubt as embarrassing to the Ixmarites as I am, my dear. Your very existence refutes many of their dogmas, or are you a soul on leave from Ixmar's Celestial Mansion?'

'What is this?' Chasteless asked.

Jeopardy laughed. 'I suspect you refer to life.'

'She asks no other questions,' Lucien said, rather sullenly.

'Of course not,' Jeopardy said, 'not until her first is answered.' He struggled upright again in his seat and took Chasteless's hands in his own.

'Be careful,' Lucien said. 'Don't get blood on her skin. It might stain her irrevocably.'

Jeopardy ignored him. 'This,' he said, in a low voice, staring into the automaton's eyes, 'is a single drop of dew on the flesh of a rose, and in the breath of the rose is the rising of the sun. In the heart of the rose is a beat of blood. This is what *this* is. You can remember if you try.'

'It is,' said Chasteless. 'It is?'

'Yes,' said Jeopardy, nodding.

Chasteless hurriedly copied his gesture and then said, 'Where is this?'

'In space and time,' Jeopardy answered, 'but you needn't concern yourself with that. If it has no relevance to you, all the better.' He released her hands. She turned round and walked back to Lucien's side.

'She has never spoken like that before,' Lucien said in amazement.

Jeopardy shrugged and made a careless gesture with his right hand. 'Perhaps no one has listened hard enough,' he said, 'or perhaps she had no need to ask things before. Who knows? She is a work of genius. You are lucky to work for such a man as her creator.'

'I know,' Lucien said. 'He is very good to me. He convinced me to take hold of my freedom.'

'In another life, I would like to meet him,' Jeopardy said, 'but there is no room for such casual socialising in this one.'

'As always, you speak in mysteries,' Lucien said, sighing. 'You have changed less than I, Resenence.'

'I can see that,' Jeopardy said. He lapsed into a moody silence, which Lucien did not want to break. The cellar was lit only by a handful of guttering candles; Chasteless seemed to emit more light in comparison. Lucien studied the face of the man he thought he loved. It was easy to see Jeopardy was still obsessed with himself, although Lucien felt the expression of that obsession had changed. It had somehow become externalised.

Jeopardy seemed to become aware of Lucien's scrutiny, and returned his stare. Then he said. 'Lucien, help me up.'

Lucien was unsure whether he wanted to touch Jeopardy at this point, but could think of no reasonable excuse not to. Jeopardy took hold of Lucien's outstretched arms and slowly raised himself from the chair.

'You feel so light,' Lucien said. 'Do you feed yourself properly?'

'Others remind me to fuel my body from time to time,' Jeopardy admitted. 'Look, there is a pallet in the corner over there. I want to lie down. Help me get to it.'

Lucien half carried Jeopardy over to the thin, dirty mattress. Grunting, Jeopardy eased himself down, wincing and grimacing. Lucien watched him settle and then sat down beside him.

'Why are you living like this?' he asked bitterly.

'I've told you,' Jeopardy replied in a tired voice, eyes closed.

'Yes, you've told me, but it doesn't change the fact that soon the Ixmarites will kill you. Everyone thinks so.'

Jeopardy swallowed slowly, as if he was thirsty. Lucien saw his whiskery throat move convulsively. 'Perhaps,' Jeopardy said.

'Why do you feel driven to lecture people?' Lucien asked. 'Or make them change their lives? You have your freedom now. Why not leave Gleberune, escape the reach of Ixmarity? What makes you think your way is the right way?'

'So many questions,' Jeopardy replied. 'I do what I feel is right for me, Lucien. But there is no fundamentally right way to do anything. I know that better than anyone. As I said to you before, all I want is for people to ask themselves questions. The Ixmarites stole my life from me as a child. You have no idea what I went through. I was always a rebellious son to them, I always asked questions, and for that they punished me severely.'

'You never mentioned that,' Lucien interrupted. He realised his words sounded like an accusation. 'You should have told me. All the time you talked about yourself, you never mentioned that.'

Jeopardy sighed. 'Don't feel hurt about it, Lucien,' he said. 'It wasn't that I didn't trust you. Even now, it is difficult for me to talk about my childhood. There are no marks left upon my body, but sometimes I feel as if my mind is nothing but a mass of scar tissue.'

'Tell me about it now.'

'No. There is no point. All I want to do now is hit back at those who abused me, and if at the same time I can make people realise how they've been duped, all the better. It is probably my ego, but it is no lie when I say I have no vocation as such. Yes, I could flit away to another land, but my words, my experience, my suffering would mean nothing there. It is here in Gleberune that my life has meaning. Do you understand?'

'No,' Lucien said. 'I don't. I think you are mad.'

Jeopardy sighed heavily. 'Oh, be quiet, Lucien. It does not matter. Lie beside me.'

Lucien hesitated and then lay down and rested his head on Jeopardy's chest. 'I can't believe I'm with you now,' he said. 'I never thought I'd see you again.'

'I have missed you,' Jeopardy whispered. He seemed exhausted.

'I wish I could believe that.'

'It is true. I valued the sight of you.'

'You flatter me.'

Jeopardy sighed again. 'I've made you cynical,' he said. 'I'm sorry. If I could have given you the love you needed, I would have done, but I couldn't. And yet I do love you in my own way, Lucien. There is none like you.'

'And soon I shall wake up in my own bed at Cartesian's, and this will be just another dream,' Lucien said with a sad laugh. 'I had many like it, all sweet lies, all painfully real.'

'Kiss me, Lucien. I cannot move.' Jeopardy's voice was weak, and Lucien began to suspect he was more seriously injured than he'd admitted.

Jeopardy's coarse whiskers grated against Lucien's face. His breath was sour, his lips cracked. For one terrible moment, Lucien was convinced he was dying. 'Why are you doing this to yourself, Res?' he cried. 'It makes no sense! It's pointless.'

'Sleep with me, Lucien,' Jeopardy said. 'Just lie here and sleep with me. I need you to.'

'I could not sleep now.'

'You can. Please.'

Lucien sighed and lay down again. Jeopardy's heartbeat felt erratic against his cheek, and his skin was hot through his tattered shirt. Lucien gazed through slitted lids at the pale, motionless form of the automaton standing in the middle of the room. Occasionally, her body emitted a faint whirring sound. 'I will not sleep,' Lucien thought. 'I can't.' Within moments, he was no longer conscious.

292

When he awoke, Lucien could not remember where he was and had no idea how long he'd slept. A single candle burned with a weak flame on the table. 'Jeopardy!' Lucien thought, and turned quickly on the pallet. He was not really surprised to find he was alone. Sitting up on the mattress, he remembered Chasteless and called out for her. There was no response to his summons. Lucien leapt to his feet, his head reeling as if he'd been drinking or drugged, yet he hadn't eaten or drunk anything in Jeopardy's company. How long had he been here? Where was Chasteless? Had Jeopardy taken her?

Panicking, Lucien ran out through the door and searched the adjoining passages and cellars, but it was as if no one had ventured down into them for years. There was no sign of occupation. Eventually, realising he'd not only been abandoned but that he'd lost Cartesian's automaton, Lucien leaned against the splintering, damp wood of an ancient door lintel and wept. How could Jeopardy have said those things to him only to sneak off in the dark and steal Chasteless away?

'I found you, only to lose you again,' Lucien murmured to the darkness, 'but then maybe I didn't find you at all.'

He wiped his eyes with the back of a grubby hand and stared at the flickering candle on the table top. It seemed defiant somehow. Suddenly, Chasteless and Jeopardy materialised before him. Jeopardy was leading the automaton by one arm towards the door. Lucien leapt forward with a cry, but found he was alone. Whatever he had seen had been an illusion, yet he was sure it had been a vision of the truth, or at least one possible truth. He shivered and rubbed his arms, glancing fearfully round the dank room, a sense of unease stealing into his mind.

'Are you still here in some way?' he whispered. Darkness seemed to condense around the feeble flame of the candle. Fearing he might invoke some kind of response to his question, Lucien fled the cellar, scrambling frenziedly up a flight of wet stone steps into daylight. For a few moments, he stood panting in the open air, his heart beating convulsively in his chest, the skin on his neck and shoulder blades crawling with anxiety. A sudden movement made him yelp in alarm. Two small, vague shapes flitted past him from behind, as if following him out of the cellar. Lucien knew the warren of chambers had been empty when he'd searched them. He staggered back against the wall of the building behind him, an ancient tenement laced with rotting balconies. The vague shapes seemed to shimmer as if his vision was blurred before solidifying into what appeared to be two young children, dressed in white. Lucien began to laugh in relief. No doubt they had somehow burrowed through the walls from an adjacent cellar; they were so small, yet they were also so clean. The children regarded him sombrely for a few seconds before joining hands and running off down the lane. Lucien heard the ghost of their laughter.

Then, with a sense of heavy foreboding, he turned his steps towards the house of Cartesian Blink, in dread of his forthcoming confession.

IXX

ESCAPE

'Ah, have you ever known such blackness,' Nebuline Midnoon exclaimed. Her voice echoed off the lowering crags to either side. None of her companions deigned to comment on her remark. Somewhere above them, a thin new moon was eclipsed by the cliffs; the stars hung bright and cold overhead.

'I am cold,' Delilah said. 'I don't think I have ever been so cold.' All she had to wear was the now tattered purple silk dress Wispish had given her, although Inshave had lent her his spare jacket, which fortunately had a fleeced lining. Delilah's little pumps, which had been suitable footwear for sauntering through the fair at Covendale, were a positive hazard for hill-walking. Their thin soles skidded on every stone.

The day before, the benign rolling hills with their mantle of soft turf and purple heather had merged into the barren range of mountains that the Jeopardites explained were known as the Lamentarges.

'Each mountain has a soul,' Inshave said in a melodramatic voice, 'and every soul is black and cold, which influences the surroundings.' Both Jeopardites seemed quite at home in this inhospitable terrain. The party was heading directly south, which puzzled Delilah who'd thought they should be travelling more to the west.

'This is a safer route,' Nebuline said. 'Soon, we shall come to a gully leading west. In winter, it is flooded, but it should be quite traversable at the moment. The Ixmarites rarely venture along these paths because there is nothing for them to steal. Not even bandits live in these mountains. People do not travel here.'

'Why not?' Delilah asked, with misgiving.

'There are quicker ways to both the south and west,' Inshave said.

'No other reason?' Delilah asked.

Inshave shrugged. 'Well, there are legends of travellers disappearing and so on.'

'Are we safe?'

'Of course,' Nebuline said cheerfully. 'Anyway, we have your friend to protect us. Is he still following? It is so hard to see.'

Delilah could feel Trajan's presence behind them. She could tell he was musing placidly as he walked. He was carrying all the supplies on his back, at the Jeopardites' insistence. They claimed the weight would dampen his urge to attack in the evening and prevent him running to catch up with them and infect them during the day. The explanation seemed plausible, but Delilah suspected they really only wanted to avoid carrying anything themselves. The moon's influence was weak on Trajan at present, but Delilah still thought it would be safer for everyone if he kept his distance. Poor lonely Trajan, she thought, I hope we find Jeopardy soon.

When Nebuline and Inshave were not boasting of their intimacy with the prophet, relating tales of every small thing he had done in their presence, however trivial, they were constantly bickering between themselves. They contradicted each other continually. Nebuline would relate a Jeopardy tale, only for Inshave to remark that she had warped the details to show herself in a better light. His amended version favoured his own participation instead. This would provoke Nebuline's temper and she would declare that Inshave was jealous of Jeopardy's regard for her. Delilah became sick of their fawning admiration for the man. She imagined that Jeopardy would be bored by both of them. If not, she wondered whether she would be disappointed by Jeopardy when she finally met him. It filled her with apprehension. She was also worried about how long their supplies would last. Inshave and Nebuline both insisted they had scant appetites, yet they applied themselves with gusto to every meal, devouring rather more than was prudent, Delilah thought. She and Trajan were both very careful with the food, though it seemed their abstinence only gave the Jeopardites an excuse to eat twice as much. Feeling far from happy about her travelling companions, Delilah nevertheless used the opportunity to discover more about Jeopardy. Nebuline was not averse to giving information, although it always emerged from her mind wrapped up in a parcel of bragging.

'I come from the house of Midnoon; the village that falls under my father's rule is of the same name. I remember well the day that Jeopardy called me to his side. He and his people came through Midnoon in the winter, begging food and shelter. The village is not far from the city of Gallimaufry, which as you must know is an Ixmarite capital, therefore my family wisely adhere to Ixmarity's dogma. The villagers would have no truck with the Jeopardites, so they came right to the gates of Midnoon Hall instead to beg for food. My father was aghast at their arrogance. My brothers and I watched as the dogs chased them off our land. Later, we rode out to their meagre camp beyond the village. We thought perhaps they could tell fortunes. That was when I saw him.' Nebuline sighed.

'He spoke to us, questioned why we allowed the Ixmarites to dictate to us. My brothers became quite abusive, Beraldo even brought out his whip to cut Jeopardy's cheek for his insolence. Jeopardy told them they were like frightened children, hitting out at what they could not understand, or what they did not want to face. The whip left no mark on his skin. I looked at the poor wretches surrounding Jeopardy, their ragged clothes, their feet bound up in uncured furs against the frost. They had so little and yet . . . they seemed to glow. Their warmth came from the inside; the cold really did not bother them.

'When I returned to my father's house, I could not get Resenence Jeopardy from my mind, and of course he came to me in my dreams and made love to me. The next day, I stole as much money as I could from my father's study and rode back to the Jeopardite camp. They had departed, but half a day's ride found them again.'

'So you went to live in poverty,' Delilah said, casting a sideways glance at Nebuline's fine cloak and gown, her dainty yet enduring boots. 'It does not appear so.'

Nebuline made a careless gesture. 'Oh, Jeopardy knew I was unfit for rugged travel,' she said, 'as were many other young people that came to him from rich houses. From time to time we return home for funds.'

'I'm surprised your family allow you home after you stole so much,' Delilah said. The story didn't ring true to her.

'My father never noticed the theft,' Nebuline said with a shrug.

'And he allows you to run harum-scarum across the land with a vagabond prophet whom the Ixmarites regard as a heretic and a criminal? He must be lenient indeed!'

'It is easier for him to indulge me than to suffer the humiliation should I reveal my vocation to his neighbours and friends,' Nebuline said. 'Most believe I am away being educated. The first time I went home, I was scolded thoroughly of course, but by that time my family had already concocted an enormous lie about my disappearance. It matters so much to them what others think, and they were terrified that the gossips would tell everyone I'd fallen pregnant by a servant, or something. Anyway, it is of little consequence. Jeopardy himself is of noble birth, which somewhat mollifies my parents.'

'Why do you follow him?' Delilah asked. She could not help but imagine the anguish Nebuline's parents must feel about her lifestyle, and sympathised with them, despite their undoubtedly shallow, haughty personalities. 'What was it that impelled you to give up your comfortable life in that way?'

Nebuline shrugged. 'It is almost impossible to describe. Once he looks at you and marks you, there is little choice in the matter. It is he that chooses you, not the other way round. He obviously saw something special in me.'

'And what of his beliefs? Tell me about them.' Delilah was sure that, for most people, it must be Jeopardy's knowledge that drew them to him.

'To be honest, I understand barely a quarter of what he says.' Nebuline uttered a trilling laugh. 'I doubt anyone else understands more.'

'So what do you gain by being his follower, then, if you surrender the bulk of your wealth and attain little knowledge?'

Nebuline made an irritated sound. 'We are close to him, that is all. He accords me special attention; I talk to him every day when we're travelling together. That's enough.'

'It will not be enough for me,' Delilah said. She was quite convinced she would understand far more of Jeopardy's words than Nebuline did.

'People envy me,' Nebuline said wistfully. 'His cult is bigger than you imagine, Delilah. If it wasn't for the Ixmarites, Jeopardy would rule the world.'

Later, when they stopped for the night, Delilah went back to talk to Trajan. He had built himself a small fire underneath an overhang and was cooking some dried fish on a stick in its flames. She told him all that Nebuline had said to her.

'Trajan, it's almost as if you and she belong to different groups entirely,' she said. 'With her, there is no talk of adopting a new way of life, of finding freedom, of searching for a place to root. She seems obsessed with travelling around showing herself off in Jeopardy's company. There is no philosophy behind her faith.'

Trajan sighed. 'Sad to say, there are many like her, but she brings money to the following, which Jeopardy needs. We have to buy supplies and medicaments, canvas for our tents and fodder for our animals. Putting up with the squawking scions of rich men's estates is a small price to pay for that security.'

'I suppose so, but it feels uncomfortably immoral to me,' Delilah said.

Trajan grinned. 'And what do you know of morals, pretty maid, in your short life?'

'I know what feels right to me,' Delilah said hotly. 'I have heard much about Resenence Jeopardy since I began this journey, and all of it conflicts. I don't know what to believe. Is he a charlatan or a saviour, a clever scoundrel or a genuine wise man? It is impossible to guess.'

'Jeopardy would say he is all of those things,' Trajan said. 'He does not pretend to greatness.'

'I don't think that's true,' Delilah argued. 'He is obsessed with himself, and passes that obsession on to others.' She glanced up at Trajan. He was staring at the flames. 'Will you ever tell me the rest of your story?' she asked timidly.

'When the nightmare is over,' he answered. 'Not before. I fear the invocation of bad luck.'

She reached to touch his huge head. 'I'm glad you're with me,' she said.

He sighed. 'I destroyed your life, my darling child. How can you gaze at me with such affection?'

'I like you,' she replied simply. 'Anyway, the events in Samberdell were a hideous accident. It was not your fault; you were not in control. I do not blame you, I can't. I feel it was a necessary tragedy, one designed to propel me into the world. I am driven towards Resenence Jeopardy, Trajan. I cannot help it. And you are here to protect me.'

Trajan sighed again. 'Maybe I simply passed the infection to you,' he said. 'Not the plague, but my love of the man. Perhaps you were not immune to that. If I had not come to Samberdell, you might never have heard of Resenence Jeopardy.'

'But you did come, therefore it was meant to be. I'll hear no more words about it.'

Trajan smiled weakly and glanced to where Nebuline stood a short distance away, her pale fists clenched by her sides. 'The white-faced bitch watches us intently,' he said.

'Perhaps she covets your strip of fish,' Delilah replied. 'Oh, I hope she and Inshave lead us to Jeopardy soon. I am becoming very tired of their company!'

The following afternoon, the party came across the gully leading west, as the Jeopardites had predicted. It was clear they'd used this route before. The path underfoot was treacherous with small, sharp stones which shifted dangerously when they took the weight of a human body. Unrelenting wet black crags rose to either side, unblemished by any weed or shrub.

'It is not far now,' Inshave said. 'If we follow this path for a day, we shall come into the Low Laments Range, which is altogether a much more fertile area.'

Delilah was relieved to hear this. They had enough food remaining for perhaps two more meals. However, calamity followed Inshave's confident announcement, because the party were brought up short by a massive rock-fall across the path. A great smooth slab had split from the righthand cliff to wedge like an impenetrable door across the gully. It was unscalable. Inshave and Nebuline, however, did not appear very distressed by the obstruction.

'A small inconvenience,' Inshave said. 'We passed a northerly tributary a short way back. We'll simply have to retrace our steps and take a detour that way.'

'I didn't see any tributary,' Delilah said. 'Won't we risk getting lost?'

'Of course not,' Nebuline said briskly. 'Inshave has memorised a map of these mountains. He is a Jeopardite range-finder. You must learn to trust him. His instinct for direction is uncanny.'

Delilah was glad to learn the otherwise unremarkable Inshave possessed this asset, and wished she could have faith in its existence. Still, he soon proved he was right about the side path, although the reason Delilah had not noticed it when they'd passed it before was because it was barely more than a crack in the stone. Trajan would have to squeeze himself through. It was fortunate the bulky supplies bag was so depleted. The walls of this narrow chasm, which it was impossible to avoid touching, were veined with razor-like blades of slate where the rock had splintered. Delilah walked behind the others with Trajan who remarked that one reason why this route was not used much was because the slate mountains were so treacherous, and could crack at any time, spewing down a fatal rain of sharp shards that could behead a man before he realised he was in danger. 'Still, the bitch and her puppy are right,' Trajan said. 'The Ixmarites wouldn't attempt to follow us here. They would expect the mountains to exact their own toll for our passage.'

Here, where the body of the mountains pressed so close, Delilah could hear the wicked flexing of the rock, as if it cracked its bones in malevolent glee, marking time until it showered the helpless travellers with deadly blades. Nobody mentioned stopping for the night. Everyone was frightened, but did not speak their fears aloud, in case they intensified. Delilah hurried forward to catch up with Nebuline and Inshave. She wanted to keep an eye on the paths Inshave took.

Their terror of provoking a rock-fall was so great, they hardly spoke as they walked and Inshave gave only a low moan of relief when he discovered a wider path leading west. Gratefully, the travellers increased their pace and hurried along the new path. Suddenly the vista ahead opened up, the sharp cliffs leaned away and a magnificent sight was revealed. Crowned by the crescent moon, a vast soaring edifice reared into the sky ahead, rising up from the shore of a still, black lake. Delilah had never seen such a massive structure and could barely comprehend it. Stark towers loomed in ranks and a faint phosphorescence could be discerned in a few of the narrow windows, which perhaps indicated people actually lived there. Just ahead of the travellers, two enormous columns supported a great stone lintel that spanned the road. Carved into it were a coat of arms and the motto, 'Domain of Pliance'.

'What is this place, Inshave?' Nebuline demanded of her companion.

Inshave was standing with folded arms, staring up at the portal. 'I have no idea. It is not marked on any map I've seen.'

'Are its occupants malign, do you think?' Nebuline enquired.

'How should I know?' Inshave snapped. 'I do not possess the gift of prophecy.'

'Perhaps it would be best if we just hurried past,' Delilah said. Her feet were sore, she was thirsty and tired, but her desire to escape the Lamentarges overcame all thought of comfort or rest. She didn't think that whoever lived in the castle could possibly be friendly to strangers.

'Hmmm, I am in two minds,' Nebuline said. 'We certainly need to replenish our water supply if not our food, and it is possible we could buy both at the castle. What do you think, Inshave?'

'I think this,' he replied. 'The occupants undoubtedly monitor this road, and if they are hostile they will probably obstruct us should we attempt to pass through the portal. This concourse is obviously part of the estate. Therefore, I feel we have no choice but to request passage, and we'll just have to hope it is granted. Benefits other than that can only be a bonus.'

'There is also the possibility that the castle is deserted,' Nebuline said.

'But there are lights,' Delilah pointed out.

'Yes, but they are strange, sulphurous lights,' Nebuline said. 'They could easily be produced by luminous fungi or lichens that often adorn ancient damp structures. We shall just have to see.'

'I suggest you and I go up to the castle while Delilah waits here for Sacripent,' Inshave said to Nebuline.

'Leave me here alone?' Delilah said.

'Oh, don't be silly!' Nebuline snapped. 'Trajan is but a few minutes behind us, and I for one do not intend to hang around waiting for him to arrive. The moon is thin, but the atmosphere of this place is eldritch. He is bound to be feeling murderous tonight and I have no intention of provoking him. You alone control the brute, so you must wait for him to inform him of our actions. Then tell him to wait further back up the road while you attend our return.'

'Nebuline, I have the gravest misgivings about remaining here alone,' Delilah insisted, looking round herself with wild eyes.

'In that case, go back and meet Sacripent!' Nebuline said. 'But be sure to return to this spot shortly.'

'You could be away a long time.'

'Oh really!' Nebuline sighed impatiently. 'Have you no spirit at all? I'll hear no more of it! As Jeopardy says, fear is the greatest threat known to humanity. Overcome it, Delilah, or risk disappointing the great man himself. Are you ready, Inshave?'

Glumly, Delilah pressed herself against the portal, making sure she was completely in shadow, and watched the lean forms of the Jeopardites set off once more down the road. One thing she could say in their favour, they were brave individuals. She would not have dared approach Castle Pliance. She hoped their courage wasn't misplaced.

Presently, Trajan came trudging up the road. He too marvelled at the sight of the castle and seemed impressed that the Jeopardites had walked up to it.

'How long shall we wait?' Delilah asked. 'What if they don't come back? They might be killed or, if the castle is occupied by friendly people, decide not to bother coming to fetch us. That would be typical of them. Trajan, I hate this place. I want to run under the arch and keep running until these dismal mountains are behind us.'

'Do not fret, my pretty,' Trajan said gently. 'For all their aggravating ways, those two are Jeopardites. Contact with Jeopardy hones the senses. If they feel safe approaching the castle, they undoubtedly are safe.'

'I wish I could feel so confident.' Delilah sat down upon the cold, hard road. 'The house of Mistress Ploverpage seems such a long way away, in both space and time,' she said, sighing. 'Oh, Trajan, are all the Covendalers dead? What happened to Wispish and Anvil?'

'From what I saw, I should imagine those two are well able to take care of themselves,' Trajan said. 'As for the villagers, well, it is to be hoped the majority managed to escape the purge.'

'This is a sad world, Trajan,' Delilah said.

Trajan reached down and patted Delilah's head. 'Aye, sadness and pleasure in equal measure is the best we can achieve, but most often the sadness waxes stronger.'

He hunkered down beside Delilah and she leaned against him gratefully. The comfort was only brief because just then Trajan, who had been scanning the road ahead, spotted two figures coming towards them.

'Is it Nebuline and Inshave?' Delilah asked in a squeak.

'Could be,' Trajan responded, his voice strained. 'The sight of those two mere shadows on the road excites a dreadful killing lust within me. I must go now, Delilah!' With that, he ran in the opposite direction.

Delilah leapt to her feet and waved. At first, there was no response, but then one of them raised a languid hand in limp salute and Delilah recognised the mannerism as being unmistakably Inshave's.

Nebuline appeared quite excited, the nearest she could become to flushed of face.

'Well?' Delilah demanded as soon as the Jeopardites were near. 'Is the castle occupied?'

'I'd say!' Nebuline responded, putting one hand against her throat and rolling her eyes in delight.

'And they are friendly?'

Inshave and Nebuline exchanged a glance. 'Certainly not hostile,' Inshave said.

'A most intriguing gentleman,' Nebuline declared.

'Who? Does he live there alone?'

'Delilah, my dear, *do* calm down,' Nebuline said. 'The gentleman is the noble Lord Alagaunt Pliance. He is a solitary soul and, but for a few retainers, occupies the castle alone. I must admit I found much to intrigue me in his character, and it was a blessing to be received by so courtly a personage after having been immured in the company of peasants for so long.' Realising her enthusiasm had perhaps overcome her rather flimsy sense of propriety, Nebuline had the grace to look rather abashed after her last remark. Delilah chose to ignore it.

'So, are we allowed to pass through the Pliance estate?'

'More than that,' Nebuline said. 'Lord Pliance has invited us to partake of a splendid supper.'

'In that case, I'm surprised you came back for me,' Delilah remarked tartly. 'I wouldn't have thought you'd have wanted Lord Pliance to know about your peasant acquaintance.'

Nebuline smiled acidly. 'Actually, Lord Pliance's servants must have noticed our arrival. He specifically requested we should come back for you. I expect he is a lonely man who craves company and is curious about strangers. Now, run back to Sacripent, Delilah, and tell him to wait for us here until morning.'

'That seems rather unfair,' Delilah said.

'So? What else is to be done? If it wasn't for his afflictions . . . You must understand, it is hardly good manners to inflict such a brute as Sacripent on a generous host. He can feed himself on what is left in our baggage. Run smartly, girl, it would be impolite of us to keep Lord Pliance waiting.'

As she followed Nebuline and Inshave up to the castle, Delilah wondered what tale they had spun to Lord Pliance. Probably some romance about their being gentlefolk in distress, although how they'd explained why they'd been travelling through this forsaken land she could not guess.

I wouldn't be surprised, Delilah thought, if Nebuline doesn't want me to pretend to be her maid!

With other such uncharitable thoughts passing through her mind, Delilah passed under the great hanging spikes of a black iron portcullis and into the courtyard of Castle Pliance.

What a terrible gloomy place, she thought, and immediately wondered what kind of man could live here, so isolated from all that was warm and human in the world. A robed seneschal waited to take them into the castle, a man as gaunt and sombre as his surroundings. When he spoke, it sounded as if his throat was full of dust.

'Lord Pliance would be most humbly grateful,' he said to Nebuline 'if you would allow him to furnish you with the attentions of his body servants, so that you might bathe. After this refreshment, he hopes you will don the clean clothes he is all too eager to provide for you.'

'We most graciously accept,' Nebuline said.

The seneschal led them into a cavernous hall which was dominated by the most enormous staircase Delilah had ever seen or could hope to imagine. Columns ten feet thick lined the hall and disappeared into the gloom high above. Tapestries the size of rooms adorned the walls, depicting cheerless scenes of majestic funerals and dour weddings. At the foot of the stairs, Nebuline paused, clearly to consider something. The seneschal turned, an enquiring expression on his face.

'Sir, I think it might be appropriate if you could house our companion here, Miss Latterkin, in more modest quarters. She is unused to appointments such as these, and I am concerned she might unwittingly damage something.'

Delilah was aghast, though not wholly surprised, but she held her tongue, feeling it would be undignified to protest. The seneschal, however, fixed Nebuline with a steely eye.

'Please do not concern yourself with that,' he said. 'It is Lord Pliance's wish that *all* your party should be catered for to the best of his ability.'

'In that case,' Delilah put in, 'what about Trajan? Shouldn't he be brought up here as well?'

'Delilah!' Nebuline said sharply. 'That is quite enough! I have mentioned the matter already to Lord Pliance, and advised him we would keep Sacripent far away from the castle walls. You know full well the idea of bringing him up here is both impractical and thoughtless.'

'No it isn't,' Delilah answered mulishly. 'I could run back and fetch him, and then take him to a secluded stable, or some such place. He would do no harm there and could at least have a night's comfort in the hay. He's carried

301

your baggage all the way from Covendale, Nebuline. It's not right that he should suffer out there in the cold alone.'

'Delilah, I will have no more of this nonsense,' Nebuline began, but the seneschal interrupted her.

'Mistress Midnoon, the matter of Master Sacripent is already being attended to.'

'Is it?' said Nebuline in some surprise. 'I think you should know the man is a lunatic by moonlight and will attack any that approach him. By day, he spreads the spore of a virulent plague. Altogether, he is not exactly a congenial guest in any household.'

'The occupants of Castle Pliance are more than capable of dealing with the gentleman's night-time affliction. By day, we trust he will have the grace to remain hidden.' With these words, the seneschal turned on his heel and continued upstairs, beckoning with a long, bony hand. Nebuline refused to look at Delilah, and by that Delilah realised she had scored a point of some kind.

Two silent maids in black costume attended Delilah's toilet, which she took in a copper bath on the floor of the bedroom that had been allotted to her. She found the bedroom gloomy and oppressive and did not look forward to spending a night in it. She didn't much like the servants either. They had an unhealthy look about them, and a rather nasty smell that did not suggest unwashed flesh exactly but a strange musty odour reminiscent of old books or furniture.

She was dressed in a green velvet gown, far more beautiful than any item of clothing she'd ever possessed. When she looked in the mirror she hardly recognised herself.

Downstairs, she was greeted by the seneschal in the entrance hall, who conducted her into a fairly comfortable wood-panelled salon. Here, she was reunited with Nebuline and Inshave, who were also dressed in new clothes of their favourite colour, black. They were standing in front of an unexpectedly cheerful fire, burning in an ostentatious fireplace of dark green marble and blacked wrought iron. The light of the flames did much to soften the features of the portrait of a cruel-looking man hanging above the hearth. Thick candles on elaborately wrought iron floor-stands offered the only other light. A female servant, dressed in a dark, floor-length uniform, emerged noiselessly from the shadows by the door and offered Delilah a small glass of an aperitif. Delilah nodded politely and took the drink, which burned her throat but warmed her belly. Nebuline would not even look at her, but Inshave raised his glass in a welcoming salute.

'Behold, the little slattern is transformed into a comely princess!'

Nebuline flicked Delilah a quick, cold glance, but said nothing.

'I am not a slattern,' Delilah said, advancing into the room. She was incensed that Inshave should speak to her like that in front of the seneschal and the serving woman, both of whom would doubtlessly relate the incident to all the other staff in the castle. 'I might be of simpler birth than yourself, Master Macassar,' Delilah continued with what she hoped was dignity, 'but I count myself a polite and mannered girl. I, for example, would never deliberately insult another person just for sport.' She sipped delicately from her glass, hoping the rebuff had hit home. Inshave coughed out a single, cynical laugh and then nodded with raised brows, his mouth curled into a wry expression.

'Forgive me, my lady, I perhaps spoke too crudely.'

'Oh stop this trivia!' Nebuline exclaimed slamming down her glass on the high mantelpiece. 'Delilah, behave yourself tonight. I shall be most hurt if you embarrass me.'

Delilah was struggling to think of a suitable retort when a silky voice spoke behind her.

'Such radiant company! I am honoured beyond measure!'

Delilah turned round to view who had spoken but not before she noticed Nebuline wriggling in delight at the flattery. The man behind her was astonishingly tall, paler than either Nebuline or Inshave, if that was possible, and thin as a pole. Like the two Jeopardites, he obviously favoured black as a colour, for his clothes were of no other hue. He wore a ruffled black shirt and tight black trousers that had a silky sheen. Over this, a black velvet jacket, frogged at the cuffs and collar, completed his outfit, which was simple yet elegant. As if to demonstrate a quirk, he wore black lamb's-wool slippers on his feet. Delilah appraised him critically. She had to admit he had a fine jaw and magnificent brows, but his eyes were a shade too small for true beauty, his lips a trifle too thick, though well-modelled. His hair, which was greased flat to his head, was grey-streaked black and confined at the nape of his neck in a purple velvet ribbon, the only sign of flamboyance.

'Lord Pliance,' exclaimed Nebuline. 'We can't thank you enough for your hospitality.'

Lord Pliance closed his eyes and laughed softly. 'I feel I should be thanking you for presenting yourselves at my threshold. I lead too lonely a life in these weary crags.'

'Why do you live here, then?' Delilah asked.

'Delilah!' Nebuline warned menacingly, but Lord Pliance did not look as if he'd taken offence.

'Circumstances prevent me moving to a more convivial clime,' he said. 'It is a tragedy, but there is nothing to be done about it.'

'How terrible,' said Delilah. She could not think of a worse fate than being forced to live in this grim place. Nebuline made another angry noise, but Lord Pliance merely reached out a bony finger to touch Delilah's cheek.

'She has a warm heart, this little maid,' he said, smiling.

During supper, Delilah received much courteous attention from their host, by which she was extremely flattered, especially as she knew how much it vexed Nebuline. Lord Pliance had tucked her hand through the crook of his arm to lead her into the dining room, and had bent his head to her ear in order to tell her anecdotes about the paintings and tapestries hanging on the walls.

'That was the wedding of my great-grandmother Salome Anna Pliance. She wed her cousin Truman in order to keep the strain pure. See her gown? It came all the way from the bottom of the world, from a country that had no name where all the people have four arms and a naked tail . . .'

'Yours must be a very old family,' Delilah said as they passed through the enormous double doors of the dining room, Inshave and Nebuline following resentfully behind. She found she was having to hold her breath when Lord Pliance leaned close. He smelled so odd! A sugary, yet meaty smell.

'Indeed,' replied Lord Pliance, 'older than memory, older than time itself.' He sighed. 'Please, my friends, be seated.'

Four places had been laid at one end of a lengthy table. Silver candelabra shed light over the shining cutlery and sparkling glassware. Wholesome viands were transported from a dumb waiter at the end of the room and placed on the corner of table, where a cloth had been laid. Delilah sniffed in famished anticipation – sweet young beetroots in herb sauce, slices of goose meat dabbed with butter, mixed radish salad, fresh bread, cinnamon cheese. Her mouth watered. Where had all this fresh food come from? Did they grow it in the castle grounds? Lord Pliance was presented with a single plate covered with a silver lid.

'I hope my repast will not offend you,' he said, curling his fingers round the lid ring, 'but I am victim of an hereditary malfunction which means I may only consume uncooked meat.'

'How disagreeable,' Delilah exclaimed, prompting a severe glance from Nebuline. She had become ominously silent, perhaps trusting that Delilah would disgrace herself in some way, thus losing Lord Pliance's favour.

Lord Pliance sighed and, fastidiously placing the lid to one side, picked up a heavy knife and fork and began to cut the reeking slab of flesh on his plate into small squares.

As usual, Nebuline and Inshave ravenously devoured their food, and Delilah was so hungry she was beyond noticing Lord Pliance's nauseating meal, gratefully filling her plate and swiftly clearing it.

After supper, Lord Pliance suggested the company should retire to their chambers. 'It has been a pleasure to share my table with you,' he said. 'Regretfully, I will be unable to bid you farewell in the morning, as I shall be engaged in business from an early hour. However, please order as much as you need from my pantry to replenish your supplies. The clothes you are wearing, though unsuitable for travel, might be useful once you reach your destination. Please keep them. I have requested my staff to clean your own garments for you; they will be ready in the morning.' He smiled at Delilah. 'And for you, little maid, there is a new set of travelling clothes which I have taken the liberty of appropriating from my absent sister's wardrobe. You and she are of a size, and I hope you will approve of my choice.' He bowed. 'Good night to you all.'

Nebuline and Inshave looked rather disappointed that their host should be abandoning them so soon. Delilah supposed they'd been looking forward to spending a few hours in conversation with Lord Pliance before bedtime. She herself would have liked to hear more stories of his family.

'May I see Trajan before I go to bed?' she asked. Lord Pliance hesitated.

'You refer to your friend housed in the stables outside?'

She nodded. 'I don't want him to feel lonely,' she said. 'He is given to melancholy.'

'I can assure you he is comfortable and well-fed,' said Lord Pliance. 'By now, he is doubtless snoring away in contented sleep. I advise you to wait until morning before going outside.'

With that, he turned smartly on his heels and walked off down one of the corridors. Delilah was far from satisfied with his reply but dared not go to look for Trajan alone. Nebuline and Inshave, she knew, would be brave enough to do so, but she also knew that neither of them had an inclination to assist her. They did not care greatly about Trajan one way or the other. Now, all Delilah could look forward to was a long night in the gloomy chamber the seneschal had installed her in.

'Nebuline, would you like me to brush your hair before bedtime?' Delilah asked, hoping to delay the inevitable incarceration and deciding that even Nebuline's abrasive company was better than none.

'Certainly not,' Nebuline responded. 'You are not a servant, Delilah. You have reminded us of that fact often enough this evening.'

Miserably, Delilah went alone to her room and locked the door behind her.

Some time in the middle of the night, Delilah's worst fears were realised and she was woken up by a sound in the room. The candle she'd been left was burning low in its porcelain bowl, throwing out eerie shadows on the wall. The fire had practically burned out and emitted only a feeble red light.

'Is anyone there?' Delilah asked in a shaking voice, and then added with passion, 'Oh please do not harm me, for I have an important quest to fulfil. If I die, my spirit will wander in frustration and confusion, thwarted of its purpose!' Her words hung in the still air.

'Sometimes the path of one's life may change,' said a voice. She recognised the cultured tones of Lord Pliance. Although in some respects this gave her some relief, she wondered what he intended to do to her. Did he have rape on his mind, or something worse? She had locked herself in, which suggested Lord Pliance had used a secret entry into her room.

'Sir, what is it you want of me?' she asked as he emerged from the shadows into her line of sight. 'If you propose injury of some sort, please have a little consideration for my youth. Also, Trajan Sacripent, who sleeps outside in your stable, is attuned to signals of distress from me. At this moment, he will be waking up and fighting an urge to seek me out. Should my fear intensify, he will break down the doors of Castle Pliance to find me. I would not wish your property to be damaged, sir. Therefore, I beg you, set my mind at rest concerning your intentions.' She was quite proud of that little speech.

'Trajan Sacripent will not wake,' Lord Pliance said.

Delilah was convulsed by a horrid thrill. 'What have you done to him?' she cried.

'Nothing irreparable. He will sleep till morn and on waking might feel a little weak, nothing more. We were made aware of his afflictions, my dear, therefore we were forced to take precautions against them.'

Delilah wondered whether he was telling the truth or not. She dared not think she might be truly alone, without hope of aid. 'Sir, you have not answered my question. What do you want of me?'

Lord Pliance came further into the light of the candle. His eyes glowed almost as red as the embers in the grate. 'Lie back, my dear,' he said. 'I have no wish to hurt you.' He advanced towards the bed.

'What are you going to do?' The more Delilah looked at Lord Pliance, the less human he seemed in her eyes.

He sighed. 'It never fails to astound me when travellers such as you and your companions drop so willingly into my net. Were I in your position, travelling a wild and desperate land such as this, I would hurry past any dark, forbidding residences resembling Castle Pliance. Have you no imagination, child? What did you expect to find in this awful place? I am a vampire. You should have recognised my setting.'

'I had no idea,' Delilah said. 'My education has been limited.'

Lord Pliance made an irritated sound and licked his lips. 'Well, whatever, your friends should have realised.'

'Have you visited their chambers?' Delilah asked timidly. She already guessed the answer.

305

'No. You are far more in keeping with the vision of my ideal victim, for which I must apologise. Surrender yourself, my dear. There is no respite from my advance.'

Delilah scrambled backwards up the pillows, her limbs curled up. 'Wait! Nebuline and Inshave would welcome a visit from you, I'm sure. They have a liking for things dank and deadly.'

'Bah!' exclaimed the vampire. 'And what pleasure would there be in that? I have already considered the pair of them and deduced that they are more predatory than myself. They would suck me dry!'

'I do not want to die,' Delilah said. 'You seemed such a courtly gentleman, sir. I cannot believe your behaviour now.'

'I know. I am ashamed of myself. However . . .' He loomed over her, a string of saliva hanging from his lip.

Delilah's first instinct was to pray to Mother Moistfoot, but what dominion could She have in such a barren land? The presence of the Lady moon seemed remote and uncaring. There was no goddess here to protect her; it was a shunned place. Then, an image shone into her mind: a mill pool, the moon shining on its surface, the face of a drowned man beneath. She felt a blade of warmth within her breast, as of the igniting of a flame. The vampire hissed in wonderment.

'What is this visage in your eyes?' he asked. 'Oh, you are like a deep pit and there are treasures hidden there. What is this face?'

'The face of my protector,' Delilah said. And in her mind, she forced the image of Resenence Jeopardy to open its eyes. There was a flash of silver. The vampire retreated a few paces.

'Put it away,' he said. 'This man looks into the hole where my soul once lived and scours its raw boundaries.'

'He can destroy you!' Delilah said, inspired. 'When Trajan cannot assist me, the spirit of Resenence Jeopardy flows in to take his place. He is invincible, sir. I advise you to change your plans.'

The vampire wiped his mouth with the back of his hand. His shoulders slumped. 'Pleasures are so few and far between in this place,' he said, with a sad sigh. 'You cannot understand. What seems foul to you is but life to me, and life is much denied me.'

'Well, I sympathise with you, sir, but I must look out for myself,' Delilah said. 'You have fresh meat to eat, so you are not starving. I believe the idea of feeding from me is an over-indulgence, and one which you can live without.'

'What a rare jewel you are,' declared Lord Pliance. 'So pure and uncorrupted. You are not afraid of me, are you?'

'Sir,' said Delilah, 'in truth I am very much afraid of you, but I have my faith to sustain me, and the source of that faith knows no fear.'

'Is he a spirit, this man you speak of? Is he dead?'

Delilah shook her head. 'No, we are all on our way to join him,' she said. 'He is a great prophet, who can free people from the prisons they have built for themselves.'

'I see no prison walls around you,' Lord Pliance remarked.

Delilah considered his words. 'I am not completely free, because I rely on others too much.' She glanced up at him. 'Like you do, I suppose.'

The vampire winced. 'I would not dare to consider I had much in common with yourself. I am more like your friend Trajan Sacripent: a victim of uncontrollable urges that strike by night, and often leave me weak with self-loathing.'

'Yes, I see the similarity,' Delilah agreed. 'Trajan believes Resenence Jeopardy can free him of his curse, however. His suffering is due to end.' An idea came to her. 'Lord Pliance, why don't you come with us to find the prophet? Perhaps he could free you from your afflictions too.'

Lord Pliance laughed. 'The only cure for me is destruction,' he said. 'And it would not take a prophet to accomplish that.'

'You could at least try talking to him,' Delilah said. 'You said yourself he could see deep within you, and that was only through the medium of my imagination.'

The vampire hesitated. 'I don't know . . .'

'Can you travel by day?'

'It is uncomfortable, but yes. In a shuttered carriage.'

'Well, there we are then. We could all ride in your carriage which would save a lot of time. There is doubtless a staunch steed in your stable that Trajan could ride behind us. You would be doing us a favour and at the same time you'd get to meet Jeopardy yourself.'

'Delilah, I am unsure whether I actually want to lose my affliction,' Lord Pliance said.

Delilah eyed him shrewdly. 'Then that, I suspect, is the greater part of your problem.'

XX

CROSSROADS

Although Cleo found it hard to admit it to herself, she had been shocked by Dauntless's behaviour in the fane of True Valiance. For this reason, she hadn't the heart to poke fun at him about it. She'd always viewed his strange piety with a kind of exasperated amusement. Now, she realised there were darker currents to his stream of belief. For nights after they had left the fane, she dreamed of the horrific yet ridiculous apparition of Sister Pankodine stalking towards her, giant fake phallus asway. She would wake in a sweat, a sour taste in her mouth, feeling utterly disgusted. She detected a new serenity in Dauntless, but he had become more distant from her. They hardly spoke.

The forest path they'd been following led to a great highway that crossed the land from Upper Twospar in the north to Gallimaufry further south. There was considerable traffic on the road, and they were able to beg meals at least once a day.

'You are pilgrims,' one woman said to them, nodding. She was a metal merchant on her way to the furnaces of Caldrick How, north-east of Gallimaufry. 'There seem to be many of you on the road at present, though few will admit to it.'

'Pilgrims of what?' Cleo asked carefully.

'If it's anything but Ixmarity, mouths remain sealed,' the woman said. 'It's a strange time. Soon, the season will roll onto autumn, yet the flavour of the air speaks of springtime. Sometimes, I smell fire and blood. Often, the earth shakes. Folk in secluded spots look haunted.' She sighed. 'Many people have gone mad, I feel. Further south, gibbets line the road, heavy with the meat of heretics. I, for one, kiss my seal of Ixmar and look the other way.'

'Have you heard of the prophet, Resenence Jeopardy?' Cleo asked.

The woman narrowed her eyes. 'I'd be blind, deaf and stupid if I hadn't!'

'Where is he? Do you know?'

'Is that a casual interest?'

Cleo shrugged.

The woman sighed and shook her head, making a noise that sounded like

'Eee-eee-eee' through her teeth. 'Girl, haven't I told you folks have gone mad? If you seek Jeopardy, do not speak of it. If you have anything else you could do, anything at all, do that instead. There are so many young people running away to dance after the prophet, and for what? An Ixmarite noose round the neck? Makes no sense to me. You can't fight something as powerful as the Church of Ixmar, and its sword-arm, Implexion. Jeopardy was a thorn between the ecclesiarchs' toes; now he's a forest of thorns ripping their flesh. They intend to hack him down, his followers with him.'

'He must be clever that they haven't caught him yet.'

'Sheer luck,' said the woman. 'His sands are running thin, believe me. He's careless and relies solely on audacity to get away with what he does. In my opinion, he kindles rebellion simply for the sport of it, from mischief. Is it a religion he's offering? I'm blessed if I know. He just makes people confused, and they become mad as revellers at a spring festival, intoxicated and stupid. But there will be a price to pay, and it will be more than the sore head common to all after the spring festival. Where have you come from, girl?'

'Scaraby,' Cleo said.

'And is life so bad there that you must leave it to follow Jeopardy's path to the grave?'

'No,' Cleo said. 'Life was not bad there at all. I was married . . .' She sighed. 'But . . . I am driven to seek out the prophet, I have no choice. There is more to it than that, but suffice to say I could not go back to Scaraby now if I tried. My feet would lead my protesting brain south to Gallimaufry, whatever.'

'They all say that,' the woman said, glumly. 'He's a sorcerer, that Jeopardy. I thank Ixmar his madness has not touched me.'

'Have you no idea where I can find him?' Cleo asked.

The woman grunted. 'It goes against the grain to give such potentially lethal information to anyone,' she said, 'but I gather Jeopardy doesn't stray much from the Gallimaufry area. His following has fragmented and the majority have fled north, but he and the most adept of his people continue to plague the Ixmarites, slinking in and out of the city like grey cats, inciting a few people before fading back into the shadows. They are alert for him, but have yet to catch him. He's slippery as oil.'

'Thank you for the information.'

The woman groaned and touched the rumps of her mules with a frayed stick. 'You'll not thank me, one day,' she said, 'but I'll spit for your safety with a benison.' She did so, at Cleo's feet. Then, jumping up onto her cart, she urged the mules into a trot and was soon too distant to be discerned.

'There, you see,' Dauntless said, who'd been observing the conversation without comment. 'You walk into peril. I shall deliver you to the Jeopardites and then make a smart retreat.'

'Where to?' Cleo asked sharply. 'To roam the forest once more?'

He made no reply, but his face became troubled.

At sundown, they came to a crossroads where a wide paved road from the east joined the highway they were travelling. Cleo was thirsty and foul-tempered; they'd not met anyone for leagues and their water carriers were empty. She ordered Dauntless to stop the horse and jumped down from its back to sit disconsolately on the steps of an Ixmaritian obelisk marking the centre of the crossroads. Beneath a carving of Panphyla, wooden road signs were attached to the stone.

'Is it much further to Gallimaufry?' Cleo asked, kicking one of the white ornamental boulders set on the steps.

Dauntless squinted at marks on the obelisk. 'Unfortunately, I cannot tell you. It would seem that Jeopardites have defaced the road signs with jargon of their creed.'

Cleo glanced behind her with a sigh. 'Oh look, Daunt, there is something approaching from the east.'

Dauntless peered up the road. 'You are right. It would appear to be a carriage of considerable size.'

'Let us hope its occupants are of a charitable disposition.'

Cleo went to stand by Dauntless to await the arrival of the carriage. As it drew nearer, she could see it was drawn by four black horses which were being driven at a steady canter. She raised her arms to salute the driver, but the carriage did not slow down. Resolutely, Cleo stepped into its path and waved wildly. It was only because Dauntless had the wit to leap forward and push her from its path that she was not run down.

'Well!' Cleo declared breathlessly, scrambling to her feet. 'So much for charity.'

'You are lucky my chivalry overcame my personal desires,' Dauntless said drily. 'Personally, I feel my life would have been enriched had I allowed the carriage to crush you flat.'

'I've had enough of you!' Cleo cried, stamping her feet. 'How dare you criticise me and look down on me. After what I saw in the fane of True Valiance! You are full of perverse lies. You're a weak and lamentable scrap of repugnance. Go away! Leave me now! I'll sit at this crossroads until someone else comes along. If it's Ixmar's demon sister Atavenom, I would not care. Anyone would be better than you. I hate you!'

Whereupon, Cleo sat down once more on the steps of the obelisk. She felt close to tears of sheer frustration and exhaustion but managed to control herself.

'Cleo—'

'No! Shut up! I don't want to hear your wheedling voice again. Go away.' Cleo put her hands over her ears. She felt panicked and numb at the same time. She wanted Dauntless to leave her, yet she was afraid of being alone. It seemed her life path had suddenly fallen away, revealing a depthless chasm. Could she leap the gap and survive?

'Very well,' Dauntless said. 'If that is truly how you feel, I shall go. Just remember how much time I've given you, and given freely.'

'I didn't ask you to,' Cleo said.

'You'd have probably died without me.'

'Well, we'll never know that, will we. I might just have gone home. You could be the one responsible for me persisting in this lunatic quest.'

'That is an outrageous accusation.'

'I don't care. Just—' A wild cry made Cleo shut her mouth. Galloping through the dusk, on the eastern road, was an enormous horse. Whoever rode it was yelling and screaming. It sounded as if a whole group of people were riding it.

Cleo stood up in alarm.

The horse thundered towards the obelisk, sending up shards of stone from the paved road. She had a glimpse of the snarling face of an immense bearded man and the smaller, pale face of a young girl behind him. Then the man seemed to fly through the air towards her, foam streaming from

his open mouth. Cleo screamed and backed against the obelisk. The girl
scrabbled for the horse's reins, attempting to whistle through her teeth in a
strange, frantic manner. Then the huge man blotted out the sight of both
horse and rider and Cleo saw the design of her own death in his eyes.

'Desist!' Dauntless cried and ran to Contralto – whose attempts to flee
were hindered by the reins becoming entangled with his hooves. Trying to
avoid being trodden on, Dauntless hastened to unsheathe his sword. 'Desist,
or I will strike!' He brandished his weapon in a menacing manner. The
huge man ignored him and continued his advance on Cleo.

'Don't move, mistress!' came the high voice of the girl on the horse. 'Be
still!' She whistled furiously, a shrill desperate sound. The man hesitated,
but then shook his head and continued forward. The whistle seemed to
peter out on the evening air, as if it was sucked away through time. The girl
made an anguished sound.

'Desist!' Dauntless ran up behind the man and hacked him with the
sword. The man grunted, blinked and then turned on Dauntless with a
vicious growl. He punched him under the ribs and sent him sailing high
into the air. It was then that the image of the ghostly child he'd seen in The
Haunt came back into Dauntless's mind.

While the madman slavered and snarled over Dauntless's recumbent
form, Cleo somehow found the strength to lift a heavy ornamental boulder
from beside the obelisk. She staggered up behind the wild man and slammed
the boulder down on the back of his neck. He crumpled to the side with a
whimper like a fretful baby. Cleo stood over him, gasping, aware that all
the muscles in her arms had been pulled and strained. There was a sharp,
silvery pain somewhere in her back. Her whole body seemed to have gone
into spasm. She was aware of the girl running past her to fuss over the fallen
madman. Dauntless was lying just beyond him, spread-eagled on the road.
Painfully, Cleo staggered towards him.

'Daunt?' she asked. His eyes were open, but a thin stream of blood was
seeping from the side of his mouth. 'Daunt, are you dead?'

The paladin coughed and groaned, and one of his legs moved jerkily.

'Thank Ixmar!' Cleo cried. 'I thought you were finished!' She knelt down
beside him. The sight of Dauntless so helpless kindled a nurturing sense
within her. For an instant, Inky's face flashed before her mind's eye. 'Can
you move, sit up?'

'Cleo . . .' the paladin said weakly. 'I am dying.'

'No! No, you're not!' Cleo said. 'You're all right now. I felled the lunatic
with a rock.'

Dauntless shook his head slowly. 'No, it has been prophesied to me. My
task is over. I deliver you to your fate.'

'Daunt, don't talk this way!'

'There is a cloaked figure waiting on the road behind you. All is misty
and dark . . .'

'It is just the twilight.'

'No. I see a light in the sky in the shape of Valiance's lance. I died in the
forest before I met you, Cleo Sinister. I can see it clearly now. My shade
persisted to bring you here. Now, it is over, and I welcome the release. All
was lost. All.'

'Dauntless! Don't talk such nonsense!' Cleo said severely. She took his
hands in her own. 'Let's forget our squabble. We'll rest here awhile and
then, perhaps tomorrow, we'll continue on to Gallimaufry. You can ride

Contralto; I'll walk. I don't mind. When we get there, we can find a physick. I could sell my poisons. Oh, Daunt, Daunt . . .' Cleo realised her exhortations were useless. Dauntless Javelot's eyes stared beyond her at a far point in the sky. He was dead.

'Don't leave me,' she said. 'I did not mean the things I said. Oh Daunt.' She fell upon his body and began to weep. The feelings inside her were strange, unfamiliar sensations. It felt as if all the fibres that held her together were coming apart. She felt like a torrent of fluid.

Delilah stared in horror at Trajan's prone body. Surely he couldn't be dead. She was aware that the slim black-haired woman was weeping over the other man, and knew that Trajan had succeeded in killing him. It was all her fault. Nebuline had urged her to ride with Trajan as a safety precaution, and they'd kept away from the road at first. But Gallimaufry was so close now, and the road at dusk had been so empty.

'Ride down from the gorse,' she'd said to Trajan. 'The road is empty. Let's gallop along it for a while.'

'I don't think we should,' Trajan had replied. He was irritable and kept rubbing his neck, presumably to scratch the small wound left by the attentions of Lord Pliance's staff at the castle many days before. It was healing very slowly. 'If we turn a corner and folk are there, I will not be responsible for my actions. Look at the spectre of the moon, how full she waxes. We should not risk it, Delilah.'

'Oh Trajan, I'm so tired. Lord Pliance's carriage must be many leagues ahead by now. We've difficult days ahead of us, when we reach the city. Speed our journey a little now. At the first sign of life, I'll order you from the road.'

In the event, her orders had meant very little to Trajan, they had not seemed to penetrate his lunacy at all. It was obvious that the persuasive power of her whistle had dwindled, exactly as the Saltcats had warned her. Now, a man was dead, and what of Trajan?

The weeping woman suddenly straightened up and turned to look at her.

'I am sorry,' Delilah said. 'My friend has a strange affliction that causes him to become violent at night.'

'So I see,' said the woman in a strange, monotonous voice. 'Is he dead?'

'I don't know.' Delilah knelt down and shook Trajan firmly. He uttered a groan. 'No. He is very strong. He once took a spear through the back and shrugged off the injury as if it was nothing.'

'And when he wakes he'll want to kill me, I suppose,' said the woman.

Delilah nodded. 'It would be best if you could go now,' she said. 'Can I help you with . . .' She could not bring herself to speak the words. What could she say to this grieving woman whose companion Trajan had slain? It was all too awful. She had no idea how to behave. The woman folded her arms and narrowed her eyes.

'I have some medicine in my saddle bag,' she said. 'It is renowned for calming lunatics, and can in fact mend their sad minds for ever. I think I should administer some to your friend, don't you?'

Delilah was wary. 'I think not,' she said. 'Best leave me to cope with this as best I can.'

'You mistrust me?' said the woman.

'I can't see any reason why you'd want to help us,' Delilah replied carefully, wondering whether she should fear this woman.

'I cannot blame you,' she said, and then smiled warmly. 'Still, what's done is done. There is no point in allowing further suffering.'

She seemed genuine, and there was also an unusual air about her that reminded Delilah strongly of the Saltcats. Was this another meeting of importance? Delilah looked up at her cautiously. Mother Moistfoot, speak to me, she prayed earnestly. Shall I trust her or not? 'You can really cure his affliction?' she asked hesitantly.

The woman nodded. 'Yes, I think so,' she said. 'I am a healer. My life is dedicated to helping others.'

'I am from the north,' Delilah ventured. 'There are many women like you there.'

'Then we have something in common,' the woman said. 'I too am from the north.'

Delilah felt that some kind of knowledge had passed between them, which she took to be a recognition of the goddess. 'In that case, I would be grateful for your help.'

The woman smiled sweetly, and went back to her horse. Presently, she returned carrying a leather sack from which she removed a corked glass vial wrapped in brown tissue paper. This she unwrapped and held up to the moon. Delilah could see it glowing crimson.

'What a pretty medicine,' she said. 'It's like a liquid jewel.'

'Yes, isn't it,' said the woman. 'Come, help me roll the man onto his back so we can administer a robust dose.'

Delilah complied. 'You can't imagine how much easier this will make things for us,' she said. 'Poor Trajan is afflicted by madness at night, and spreads a virulent plague by day. He is accursed, you see. We seek the prophet, Resenence Jeopardy, to heal him.'

'Do you indeed?' said the woman, gazing at Delilah with an expression of surprise. 'I have heard it is dangerous nowadays for people to speak of the prophet, especially so when they are seeking him.'

Delilah shrugged. 'I do not feel you are an Ixmarite,' she said.

'Well, you are right there,' said the woman. 'I'm certainly not that. Lift his head now, if you can. There, just a mouthful should suffice.'

Delilah laid Trajan's head back down and moved to wipe his lips, but the woman stayed her hand. 'No! The medicine has adverse affects on those who are not mad.'

'How long will it take to have an effect?' Delilah asked.

'Oh, a minute or two.' The woman stood up and took her bag back to the horse. She leapt into the saddle in a flurry of tattered red skirts. 'Well, I had better be off.'

Delilah couldn't help glancing at the dead man on the road. Did the woman intend just to leave him lying there? How bizarre! One moment she weeps over him in an agony of grief, the next she seems completely cheerful and heads off without a thought. How strange.

Suddenly Trajan gave a peculiar groan. 'Wait!' Delilah shouted to the woman. 'I think he wakes.'

'I doubt it,' she said, and her face twisted into a wicked, crooked grin. All semblance of kindness left her features. 'He'll never kill again, girl. The medicine I gave him was a mordant bane. He will be dead in two minutes.'

'No!' Delilah sprang to her feet and ran towards the woman's horse. A strange, unfamiliar emotion overcame her. For the first time in her life, she felt furiously violent. 'You bitch!' she cried. 'You deceived me in the

Mother's name! May Her Daughters have vengeance on you!' Her vision seemed eclipsed by a red fume. She wanted to inflict pain upon the evil woman, and clawed her hands to do so.

'Let go!' the woman cried, beating at Delilah's hands with her reins. Delilah's fingers were ripping at her skirts, trying to reach her flesh. 'The monster got no more than he deserved. He has just murdered a paladin of the Sacred Order of True Valiance. I had no choice but to avenge his death.'

'Then you are a murderer too!' Delilah screamed. 'And I shall avenge Trajan's death by killing you!'

The woman laughed. 'Don't be ridiculous. If I got down from Contralto now, I could knock you flat with one hand. Idiot! Be off with you. Be thankful I was gracious enough to spare you the same fate as your companion.'

Delilah suddenly felt overwhelmed with defeat. What was she doing trying to fight this woman? Trajan was dying on the road behind her, and she was attacking the only person who could help him. She gripped the horse's mane. 'I'm sorry,' she said desperately. 'I understand how you feel. But, despite what has happened, my friend is not an evil man. Please believe me. He is my protector. Without him, I shall be alone. Oh madam, if you have an ounce of sisterhood within you, and an antidote for your bane, have pity on me now and use it!'

'Your friend had no pity for Dauntless Javelot,' said the woman, 'Be off, or I'll ride the horse over you.'

At that moment, Trajan lurched unexpectedly to his feet. The woman's mouth dropped open in horror.

'Oh, I burn!' he roared. 'I burn with little white flames! Oh! Oh! It is the moon's seed! She devours her children! Oh!' He threw himself around in a rabid manner.

'Child, if you've any sense, you'll accept the only offer of help I'm prepared to give, and leap up behind me now,' said the woman, in a low voice. 'Some protector! The monster's bewitched. That was Tamper's Grue I gave him. No one can survive its effects.'

'Trajan is like no other man,' Delilah said with a sneer, 'and I won't leap up behind you!' She felt she had proved something, and turned to run towards her companion. 'Trajan, are you all right?'

'Ah, the fire, the fire!' he exclaimed. 'Is my flesh smoking? Is it? Does a moon steam rise from my body?'

'No, Trajan,' said Delilah. 'That woman over there fed you poison because you killed her friend. It is the poison in you.'

'No poison!' screamed Trajan. 'No! No poison! I feel the moon slip through my blood. I feel her white stream. Her hands are blessed now, cool as dew. She strips her curse from me.'

Suddenly, Trajan began to laugh. He fell on his knees to the road, and put his head in his hands, still laughing wildly. Then, his laughter turned to tears. He staggered to his feet once more and lurched towards the woman on the horse. She was trying to get it to move, but it seemed more interested in investigating the body of the dead man.

'Don't come near!' cried the woman in a terrified voice. She jumped down from the horse and began to run, but Trajan caught her in both his arms.

'Goddess!' he cried and lifted her high. Then he set her down slowly and sank to the road in front of her. 'You are She, aren't you?' he said. 'Oh, my lady, have I denied you? Do you forgive me?'

314

'He is obviously still mad,' said the woman in a shaking voice to Delilah, 'but the Tamper's Grue appears to have altered the madness somewhat.'

Trajan raised his head. 'I am no longer mad,' he said in a clear, musical voice. 'Whether you are witch or goddess, you have saved me.'

XXI

MYSTERY

'We are within sight of the end, aren't we?' Walterkin said to Lucien.

'The end of the story?' Lucien asked quizzically.

Walterkin shrugged. 'Just the end. You know that. When your story's done, you'll be looking for Jeopardy again, won't you?'

They had come back to the roof garden for what both of them knew was the final instalment. 'I'm not sure,' he said.

Walterkin smiled. 'You don't look so tired now. Telling the story has eased you, hasn't it? If only you could have told it to Jeopardy himself, eh?'

Lucien laughed bleakly. 'I would never tell him everything.'

'Perhaps he knows that,' Walterkin said. He leaned forward. 'So, speak.'

It would have been easier for Lucien had Cartesian Blink manifested his anger at the loss of his automaton, but when Lucien finally slunk into the house, sought Cartesian out and guiltily mumbled his news, Cartesian only sank into a melancholy silence. He nodded morosely, as if his worst expectations had been realised. Without delivering one word of reprimand or accusation, he disappeared into his study and shut the door. Lucien stood in the dark corridor, which was lit only by a begrimed blue skylight littered with skeletons of long-dead birds. He stared at the door for several minutes in helpless frustration. He wanted to justify himself, but it seemed Cartesian did not even require an explanation. Lucien knew that Cartesian had become very fond of him, and he was also conscious of how much he owed his employer. Without his encouragement and help, he would still be a slave in the House of Mandru. For the first time in his life, Lucien experienced the agonising shame of having greatly disappointed someone who was close to him, someone who had expected far more.

Sighing, he slouched into the kitchen where Ulain was making bread and, having no other ear, slumped down in a chair at the table and related the story to her. It was through Ulain that he made the startling discovery that he'd been missing from the house, not for a single night, but for over a day; Jeopardy had stolen that time from him.

'So you met an old friend who took you back to his place with the automaton,' Ulain said coolly, summarising the events. 'Did you get drunk?'

'No!' Lucien cried. 'I fell asleep.'

Ulain gave him a sceptical glance. 'Hmm, and while you're sleeping, *for over a day*, your friend runs off with the automaton.'

'Yes.'

'Well, in my opinion, it's no great loss, seeing as the creatures are abominations against nature,' Ulain said, pounding dough in a businesslike manner. 'Still, theft is a theft, and it's a poor friend who could do that.'

'I'm sure there is more to it than that,' Lucien said, but could not explain further. He doubted whether Ulain would sympathise with, or even understand, the complexities of his feelings for Jeopardy. Neither Cartesian nor Ulain had ever pressed him for details of his past, but Lucien had explained when he first arrived at Cartesian's house that Resenence Jeopardy was someone he'd known before, although he had not mentioned the extent of their relationship, nor the fact that he held any regard for him. Rather flippantly, he had told them Jeopardy had always been regarded as a trifle unhinged by others and that now his mind seemed to have descended into some private madness, the laws of which were known only to Jeopardy himself.

In the afternoon, Cartesian emerged from his study. He came into the kitchen where Lucien was still sitting, and where Ulain was now devoting herself to the preparation of heavy, rich cakes. Adopting a somewhat heroic stance at the head of the table, Cartesian pronounced that he blamed himself for Chasteless's loss, which made Lucien feel worse.

'No,' Cartesian said, raising a hand to stem Lucien's protestations. 'You cannot imagine how much Ulain and I suffered during your absence. Chasteless is a priceless creature, true, but you . . .' he fixed Lucien with a significant stare, 'are of even rarer value, to us.'

'We were that worried,' Ulain said hurriedly. 'There was such a to-do when Implexion tried to break up the prophet's meeting. We heard talk of sorcery, burning air and blood. We were terrified you'd got mixed up in it. We weren't all that wrong, were we? Still, we believed the Ixmarites had taken you.'

It was the first time Lucien had received the slightest intimation that Ulain cared about him. He wished he could be experiencing it in happier circumstances. 'If only they had taken me,' he replied, a sentiment that all three people in the room knew was a lie.

Ulain shook her head. 'Cartesian had his friends scouring the Steeps for you,' she said. 'Enquiries were made in hazardous quarters. We feared you were dead.'

'But happily, you are not,' Cartesian said with a sad smile, placing a hand on top of Lucien's head.

'I was foolish!' Lucien said, ducking away from Cartesian's hand. 'I should have brought Chasteless back here before pursuing my own wild jaunts. I should have thought!'

Cartesian sighed heavily. 'Well, what is done, is done. I hope the mad prophet treats Chasteless properly. She is a delicate and finely tuned instrument.'

'He has no right to treat her in any way at all!' Lucien exclaimed. 'He has stolen her! I still cannot believe he did it. I know Jeopardy had many faults, but I never considered him to be an outright thief!'

'Well, one of the beauties of the human creature is its limitless ability to surprise and confound,' Cartesian said wearily. 'We should not be too depressed.'

Lucien had never seen him so gloomy. 'We should perhaps report him to the Ixmarites,' he said, unconvincingly.

'And incur their penalties for necromancy? I think not.'

Lucien shrugged. 'I'm just so angry.'

'He made a fool of you, that's all,' Ulain said. 'You wouldn't betray him. I can see that in your eyes.'

Lucien was not grateful for this piece of perceptiveness.

'Impiety and Inveritude are behaving in a strange way,' Cartesian said hastily, as if to curtail a line of conversation he found uncomfortable or did not want to confront. 'They are almost listless and react slowly to my commands. It is as if they miss their sister already. I hope this does not presage a degenerative process.'

Lucien could not bear to think he might be responsible for the loss of all three automata. A daring idea came to him. 'Then there is only one recourse,' he said, defiantly. 'I shall have to find Chasteless and bring her back.'

Cartesian gave him a wise look. 'Go after your mad prophet, you mean? Trace him, hunt him down?'

'It should not be difficult,' Lucien said, averting his eyes from Cartesian's gaze. 'He has, after all, been very visible about the city.'

'But he has not been threatened with actual arrest before,' Cartesian pointed out. 'Do you really think he'll be so easy to find now?'

'I can only try,' Lucien said. 'It's the least I can do. In my defence, I can only say I had no reason to suspect duplicity on Resenence's part, but the blame must still lie with me.'

'I do not blame you,' Cartesian said. 'It is a sad accident, that's all. In your position, I might have acted the same.'

'Perhaps he wants you to find him,' Ulain said. She had divined more from the spaces in Lucien's narrative than he had realised. 'That could be why he took the automaton with him when he left. It sounds as if he's playing with you, including you in his mad world.'

'Well, that is a possibility,' Lucien said with admirable calm. 'And in order to return Chasteless to the house, I am prepared to play his game.'

'He might have left the city by now,' Cartesian said. 'Your search might be longer than you think.'

A certain tone in his voice alerted Lucien to the possibility that Cartesian might become difficult about his leaving the house. He had always insisted that Lucien was free and under no obligation to remain, but faced with the possibility that Lucien might abandon him, he was perhaps changing his mind. Lucien had never considered himself to be a particularly intuitive person, but now, looking at Cartesian, it was as if he could read the man's mind. He could see how Cartesian longed to forbid his departure, how he loved him, but that fear of rejection and ridicule would hold his tongue. Lucien did not know how he could suddenly be aware of these things, but he was also convinced that Cartesian would mourn him for a long time, after which a new boy would come to the house and become Cartesian's assistant. Lucien could even see this boy's face. He blinked and shook his head. Uncanny! Was he hallucinating? What had Jeopardy fed to him in that cellar and, more to the point, exactly when had he done it?

'What is it?' Cartesian asked. 'You look strange.'

'Nothing,' Lucien replied, and reached out to squeeze the man's hand.

'You have done so much for me. Don't ever think I take that for granted.'

Ulain delivered a knowing glance at them and tactfully took herself from the room.

Cartesian offered Lucien a shaky smile. 'Well, that certainly sounds like goodbye to me.'

Lucien longed to tell him the entire truth, but shrank from doing so. 'I have unfinished business,' he said.

'I can see that.' Cartesian sighed. 'I have felt it often.' He gave Lucien a sharp glance. 'Never compromise your safety. Be careful.'

Lucien nodded. 'I promise to do all that I can to bring Chasteless back.'

Cartesian shrugged. 'Oh, at the end of the day, she is only a sophisticated toy. Perhaps I should restart the project, improve upon my designs.'

'And what exactly are those designs?' Lucien asked.

Cartesian raised his brows. 'Let us just say that Chasteless and her sisters were conceived by half scientific, half magical means. They were built like machines, but empowered by sorcery. They might be more than they seem, or less. I'm afraid that I and my colleagues have, in some ways, abused the miracle of them by using them in the way we have. Perhaps this loss is the cost we have incurred for that.'

Lucien nodded. 'It's possible you could have done more to develop Chasteless's personality,' he said. 'I heard her say more to Resenence Jeopardy than either of us would have dreamed of.' He went on to explain what had happened in the cellar, and also what Jeopardy had told him about the process he believed had been used to build Chasteless.

Cartesian did not contest this explanation. He sighed and pulled a mournful face. 'I am beginning to wonder whether your friend in fact did the right thing by taking her away from us. Maybe, with this Jeopardy character, she will start to live a real life.'

'She does not belong to him,' Lucien said firmly. 'I will bring her back.'

'Maybe you shouldn't bother,' Cartesian said. 'Yes, the more I think about it, the less I think it's a good idea for you to go charging off into a possibly dangerous situation just to bring her back here. Let's forget it, Lucien. Together, we could build yet more fabulous wonders.'

Lucien lowered his eyes. 'I will bring her back,' he said.

Steeling his heart against his employer's obvious misgivings and reluctance to let him leave, Lucien crept out of the kitchen and set about packing some belongings, leaving Cartesian to stare miserably at Ulain's half-worked cake mixture. The money Lucien had saved since he'd lived at Cartesian's house could, if used prudently, last several months. He might even be able to afford to take lodgings, if necessary.

He spent the day tidying his room, deciding which small mementoes he should take with him, which to leave behind. Cartesian did not approach him, which was a relief. Lucien did not want to argue. He had made up his mind. Jeopardy would always be in his heart until he was either exorcised completely or some kind of stable relationship could be established. Lucien doubted that the latter was likely, but he would have to find that out for himself. He thought Ulain's suggestion that Jeopardy might have deliberately taken the automaton to encourage pursuit was a sound one. But then, why the games? If Jeopardy wanted him, why hadn't he just asked him outright to join him? Was this the way of a lunatic, a selfish manipulator, or a man in love?

'I have to find out,' Lucien told his reflection in the mirror. 'I can't stay here, thinking about it for ever. I have to find out.' His reflection looked sceptical.

In the morning Lucien bade farewell to Cartesian Blink. 'It may be that I'll be back by sunfall,' he said. 'If I pick up no clue to Jeopardy's whereabouts, I'll return here.'

Cartesian nodded miserably and embraced Lucien warmly. 'Take care,' he said.

Ulain kept her thoughts to herself and offered Lucien only a curt goodbye.

Out in the street, Lucien realised that even though neither of them had actually said it, both he and Cartesian were convinced that Jeopardy had already left Shanariah, and that the search for Chasteless would be long. Even though he'd spoken of returning home soon, Lucien felt in his bones that his steps would lead him far beyond the gates of the city. Cartesian had given him a sheaf of forged identification documents with the words, 'You might not need these, but take them anyway.'

Within an hour of leaving the house, Lucien was presenting them to Ixmarite officials at the East Gate. Before that, he'd returned to the cellar where Jeopardy and his people had been staying. It was still empty, but now that he was in a calmer frame of mind, he examined the underground rooms more carefully for clues, lighting candles to facilitate the search. In one room, he found a printing press and bales of pamphlets, which suggested Jeopardy and his followers had decamped in a hurry. They seemed to have taken everything else with them.

Above the cellars, single rooms were inhabited by entire families. Lucien made enquiries there and was given the information quite freely that Jeopardy's people had vacated their premises the night before. Lucien spoke at length to a teenage girl who had a baby in her arms and two young children at her feet. It was from her that Lucien heard, for the first time, the term 'Jeopardite'. It seemed Jeopardy's neighbours were all aware of his name. The girl said she had not been on intimate terms with the Jeopardites and that they had shunned most of her friendly overtures, but they'd never been impolite exactly.

'I think they were afraid, and wanted their privacy,' she said. 'But they never caused any trouble. I was coming back from the Eel and Shovel last night, very late, and met Elsynth. She was one of Jeopardy's girls. She was carrying stuff from the cellar and when I asked her what was happening, she told me they were all getting out of the city. She was in quite a state, poor thing. Personally, I don't think she wanted to leave, but one thing I did notice was that when that Jeopardy got his hooks into a person, he never let go. I don't think she had any choice in the matter.'

Lucien thanked her for the information and offered her a coin, which she accepted without shame.

'I'll tell you now,' she said, 'the Ixmarites'll find out where the Jeopardites were holed up, and will come asking the same questions you have. When that happens, I'll give them the same answers. I don't want any trouble; I have my kiddies to think of. If you're looking for Jeopardy, you'd best make haste, for I feel his days of freedom are numbered.'

'I don't suppose the girl Elsynth gave any clue as to where her people were going?' Lucien asked, without much hope.

'What I don't know, I can't repeat,' the girl replied. 'For that reason, I never asked. I bear no grudge against them, for all their peculiar ways.'

It seemed obvious to Lucien that Jeopardy would not have led his people out of Shanariah in one group, and it seemed unlikely they would have left on one of the main thoroughfares. To the north lay the House of Mandru and the estates of Mandru's friends. To the south lay the sea, and it would be expensive to hire passage abroad for a large group. East of Shanariah, Ixmaritian retreats, training centres and academies dotted the land; to the west lay the sprawling expanse of plain, forest and hills, studded with communities large and small, that comprised the bulk of the island realm. In Jeopardy's position, Lucien thought he would have headed west. It was possible that once Mandru's estate, and those of his friends, were passed, the group would spread north, but for a while they'd probably keep to the south of Gleberune. There were many large cities along the coast where it would be easy for a group of individuals to hide. Lucien only hoped that Jeopardy's apparent love of public display would leave enough of a trail for him to follow.

He set off on foot along the great western road, the King's Way, which hugged the coast. To his left, breakers curled upon the yellow shore; to the right, fields and vineyards meandered up to gentle hills, dotted with patches of forest. Occasionally, through the foliage, glimpses of the estates could be seen. Had Lucien paused long enough to make a thorough inspection, he would have seen the low, dove-grey mass of Mandru's house clinging to a far hillside. In the evening, its lights would be discernible from the road. Visible, too, was the sweet, high meadow where Amber Epipheny had seduced him. But Lucien did not want to dwell upon thoughts of the past. At roadside stalls, selling sea produce and the treasures of beach-combing, he made discreet enquiries as to whether anyone had noticed a group of people travelling with haste down the King's Way in the early hours of the morning. He thought that Jeopardy and his people would have used a more secret route, such as through the narrow hedged lanes a little further north, but he would lose nothing by asking. His enquiries, however, elicited no concrete information and, by sunfall, he entered the seaside town of Long Flag no wiser than when he'd departed Shanariah.

After securing lodgings for the night in a modest hostelry near the seafront, Lucien sat outside, beneath a canopy of spreading trees, and enjoyed the evening air, with only a flagon of ale for company.

The land seemed at peace and, lulled by the effects of alcohol, Lucien gave himself up to the sad, mad joy of love and loss. The night seemed exquisitely, painfully lovely. With half-closed eyes he watched patrons strolling into the inn and surrendered himself to a heaving sea of sensations and impressions. He felt as if he could taste and experience all the hopes and fears of the people who brushed past him, their guilty desires, their seething hurts. And from each sensation, there seemed to be a narrow, hard line edging forward into the future, which branched again and again, making a limitless treelike formation. He realised he was looking at a multitude of possible futures, and also that he was able to see something that others could not. The experience felt like a dream at first, an intoxicated fancy, but the thought that it might be real brought Lucien to full alertness with a jolt.

'What has happened to me?' he thought, and willed the strange impressions from his mind. It was like trying to close a door against a high wind. He narrowed his eyes into the dusk and whispered, 'You have done something to me, haven't you?' Seabirds uttered cackling cries from the shore, some distance from the inn. To an imaginative person, the cries could have sounded like laughter.

Lucien sighed and lounged back in his seat. His mind was empty now; the bizarre sensations had gone, as if plucked from his head. He blinked up into the eaves of the inn. What was he running towards? Should he turn back now?

'Too late,' he thought. 'Oh, far too late for that.'

Just as he was about to retire for the night, his mind tentatively at peace, his thoughts spiced by a trace of wistful melancholy, Lucien was alerted by the arrival of a noisy group of people at the inn. There were three men and four women, all dressed in expensive clothes, their hair elaborately coiffured. Lucien realised they could very easily be friends of Salaquin Mandru. They were talking in loud and excited voices of an event they had recently witnessed in the public square of the town.

'Girls in their underwear tumbling this way and that! A disgrace!' one woman declared, cooling herself with a round paper fan. There was wry amusement in her voice.

'And the way he spoke to us!' another woman remarked with glee. 'Almost insulting.'

'But such a speaker nonetheless,' a man added. 'It was worth the coin I tossed to him.'

Disregarding any risk of being recognised, Lucien jumped up from his seat and intercepted the group as they entered the saloon of the inn.

'Excuse me,' he said, 'but I couldn't help overhearing your conversation. I hope you'll excuse my impertinence, but would you mind explaining your remarks to me?' He gabbled on without waiting for a response, even though he was aware of the disapproving expressions on the faces of the men. The women simply looked intrigued. 'I am currently seeking a man who styles himself a prophet, by the name of Resenence Jeopardy. It wasn't him you just saw by any chance?'

'Well, the man we have just heard speak might well be a prophet,' one of the men said. 'But we were not given his name. Why do you seek him?'

'He is an old friend,' Lucien said, invoking sceptical glances from the group. 'Where might I find him?'

'Down yonder,' one of the women said, pointing with her fan, but one of her companions slapped down her hand.

'The man we saw was not a prophet, but an entertainer,' she said sharply, with a glinting, meaningful glance to her friend. 'He's done no harm.'

'Look, I don't . . .' Lucien shook his head. 'It doesn't matter. Thank you.' He bobbed a series of hasty bows before hurrying off in the direction the woman had pointed.

After a few minutes he reached the square, only to find a small crowd in the process of breaking up. A fire was burning in the centre of the square, where nuts and chicken legs were being roasted and sold by local traders. Two booths, set up nearby, were selling drinks. Several people were lingering to refresh themselves, chattering in groups around the stalls. Lucien slunk among them, asking questions. People seemed bemused rather than annoyed by his approach, and he soon discovered that the performance by the speaker and his troupe of entertainers had only recently been concluded, and that all the performers had left the square. No one knew where they had gone, or if they were staying in Long Flat. People commiserated with

322

Lucien that he had missed the spectacle and recommended that he should endeavour to catch any subsequent performances. He spent half the night wandering around the town asking questions, but if it had been the Jeopardites performing earlier in the evening, they had vanished without trace. That alone could be seen as a positive clue.

In the morning, he rose early, and set off along the King's Way with greater optimism. At noon, his feet left the main road and took him inland, along a narrower, less frequented route. It was an instinctive move, and one which he gave himself up to entirely. He was convinced that the fibres of his being were aware of Jeopardy's trail, and that he could trust his instincts to lead him in the right direction.

After an hour or so, he came to a village. He walked directly to the central green, where he found a group of people who were all talking excitedly about an event that had just occurred.

'It was like a carnival,' one woman declared, eager to share her enjoyment of the performance with Lucien. She told him that a motley band of entertainers had run through the village a few hours before, announcing that a spectacle would be performed on the green a short time later. As such events were rare in the village, people had gathered in curiosity to see what would occur. At first, a group of girls in scanty costume had tumbled onto the green and proceeded to perform a lively dance. They had been accompanied by droll musicians wearing costumes of fluttering, gaily coloured rags and ribbons.

'You should have seen the leading dancer!' Lucien's informer exclaimed. 'She was completely veiled, you couldn't see a thing, but, oh, the way she moved! It was so bizarre. It was as if she was asleep and dreaming the performance.'

Shortly after this, a man in a long, ragged coat had appeared and begun to speak to the crowd.

'He had a hectoring tone,' said the woman, 'but you know, it was hard to take offence. I'm sure I was insulted, but I felt curiosity rather than outrage. Isn't that peculiar? Others I've spoken to felt the same.'

From these remarks, Lucien was convinced the performers had been Resenence Jeopardy and his followers. Again, they appeared to have vanished scant moments before he'd arrived. Chasteless the veiled dancer?

'And that is the way things have gone ever since,' Lucien said to Walterkin. 'I have been led across the land, from town to village to city, through forests and over hills, following the tune of Jeopardy's dance. Many times I have wanted to abandon the search and return to Shanariah, but it is as if my feet are enchanted.'

He had reached the end of his story now, the story that he wanted to tell. There was so much he could have said of the adventures he'd had along the way, the strange people he'd met, the sad people, the awe-inspiring people. He could have told of the scars he'd received, the lovers he'd touched and fled from, the women who'd offered him their worlds, the men who'd wanted his. He could have spoken of a thousand landscapes that were one landscape, mutated only by light and season; of the smell of the land and the taste of the land, of fear, and joy, excitement and shame. He could have described longing and regret. It would have taken for ever. Ultimately, he had said all he had to. He had come to the house of Bessie Anywhither and, on the roof of that house, and in the corners of the city beyond, he had woven his tale for Bessie's son. Now, sitting across from Walterkin on the coloured rugs of the roof garden, he wondered what the boy's interest in him really signified. Often, Walterkin had acted weirdly or mystifyingly. Often, he had spoken with something other than the voice of a common child.

'And now,' Lucien said to him, 'don't you have something to tell me?'

Walterkin lowered his head, his pale blond hair falling over his face. He shook his head. 'Not I,' he said.

Lucien made an impatient sound, and pounded his knees with his fists.

'I only wanted to hear your story,' Walterkin said. 'I knew it would be interesting.'

Lucien rolled his eyes and made a plaintive sound. 'Then I have told everything for nothing! You have deceived me!'

'How? Did I promise you something in return?' Walterkin appeared genuinely perplexed. 'What do you want of me?'

Lucien shook his head and let his hands dangle between his knees. 'Nothing. I should have known better.' He laughed bleakly. 'I am for ever fixing omens on the world.'

Walterkin smiled shyly. 'So, what is your aim now, Lucien? What are you going to do?'

'My aim is to corner the Jeopardites on the west coast.' Lucien said, and then grinned. 'I don't know. As long as Jeopardy lives, I feel he will purposely avoid me. If he is killed, perhaps the enchantment will end, and I will be free to go wherever I choose.'

'If that happened, you might lose your gift,' Walterkin said sharply.

'What gift?'

'Your clear sight.'

Lucien shrugged. 'It has earned me my keep during the journey, which I think must be Res's way of apologising for leading me a lunatic dance across Gleberune. He gave me the sight, I have no doubt of that, but I've no idea how or why he gave it to me. Still, it would not grieve me to lose it.'

Walterkin made a scoffing sound. 'Oh? And how would you live then? Dance for your money, or whore for it?'

Lucien fixed Walterkin with an outraged stare. How dare he speak to him like that! He was only a boy. Walterkin stared back. 'I should punch your nose for that!' Lucien said.

Walterkin shrugged. 'I'm sorry. I just can't think what you'd do with your life without Jeopardy to inspire it. What else have you left?'

'A home in Shanariah, perhaps. Cartesian would have me back.' Lucien was not certain of that, despite the conviction he tried to put into his words. Once, in a vision, he'd seen the face of the boy who would replace him. And now, of course, at the age of twenty-seven he himself was no longer a boy. Should I be afraid? he thought. Am I seeking my own extinction?

He jumped to his feet and went to the edge of the roof. Without his search for Jeopardy, what would his life comprise? Where would I go? he thought. He had made many acquaintances upon his journey but few friends. If only he could foresee his own future. He turned and looked at Walterkin, who was staring fixedly at the rugs, chewing his thumbs.

'Maybe your stepfather could find me work,' Lucien suggested.

Walterkin glanced up at him. 'That would be a disappointing end to the story,' he said.

Lucien shrugged. 'Give me another one, then.'

Walterkin looked thoughtful for a few moments. 'There is a rumour in the street today,' he said at last.

Lucien was alerted by his tone, but decided not to show too much interest. He was aware that Walterkin liked to tease him. 'More rumours,' he said. 'There are always rumours.'

Walterkin nodded. 'I know. However, this one might interest you. This morning I was walking down Fancy Lane and an urchin came up through a hole in the cobbles. He looked very furtive, as if he was afraid, or was being pursued. I stopped to watch. He carried a sheaf of pamphlets between his teeth.'

'A Jeopardite!' Lucien couldn't help interrupting.

'Yes. The boy offered me a pamphlet, and I took it.'

'Is there to be a performance?' Lucien asked. 'Here, in Gallimaufry?' Surely, Jeopardy would never risk such a thing.

Walterkin shrugged. 'Well, the pamphlet was designed to attract a large crowd. It said that Resenence Jeopardy plans to make an address on the parade ground outside Gallimaufry.'

Lucien hurried over to where Walterkin sat and loomed over him. 'When?' he demanded.

Walterkin stood up and walked past Lucien to the edge of the roof. He paused in the exact place where Lucien had stood a moment before. 'How wide the sky is this afternoon,' he said, 'and how blue. It is like the skirt of a goddess spread out in the heavens. She has the sun in her lap.'

'Walterkin, when?' Lucien demanded. He dreaded the meeting had already taken place, and that Jeopardy had been arrested for his audacity and incarcerated, or worse.

Walterkin looked back over his shoulder. 'Can't you feel the time within you?' His voice sounded strange, faint yet resonant.

'No! Tell me.'

Walterkin turned round and faced Lucien. He chuckled. 'Goodbye, Lucien Earthlight!' Raising his arms high, the boy jumped backwards off the roof.

Lucien ran to the edge and looked down. It was no surprise to him that Walterkin was nowhere to be seen. He had spoken with Jeopardy's voice.

'It was you,' he whispered. 'It's been you all along . . .'

In his heart, he knew that the end, whatever it might be, was near.

XXII

STRANGER

They had nothing to bury Dauntless Javelot with. For a while, Cleo, Delilah and Trajan stood looking at the body, each immersed in their own thoughts.

Cleo could hardly articulate how she felt. She was unexpectedly sad to lose Dauntless's company, and mourned his death, and yet simultaneously she was aware of an enormous sense of optimism blooming within her. Evening still stained the sky crimson on the western horizon, and voluptuous purple clouds massed around the glow. Cleo could not help feeling as if the fire of it reached out to her in some way, with messages unspecified and vague. She had meant to murder Trajan Sacripent and yet, since the unexpected results of her attempted poisoning, there was a conviction within her that the event was somehow preordained, and that her cruel impulse was merely a necessary part of that. She remembered the conversation she had had with the ghost at Dratslinger's house. This must surely be what it had referred to, and how bizarre that she and the other travellers should have a common goal in seeking Resenence Jeopardy. There was no possibility of their ways diverging now. Something had bonded them; a sequence of events, a tragic play, a living myth.

Delilah, too, was feeling bemused and enveloped by a sense of imminence. Cleo Sinister was as singular and colourful a person as the vampire Lord Pliance and the erstwhile lunatic, Trajan Sacripent. It seemed only right to her that the paths of these bizarre personages should converge; it brought a flavour of legend to her search for Jeopardy. It seemed clear to her that a dramatic climax was building up, that temporary relationships of an intense nature should be forged, the ranks of chosen humanity closing in as they were drawn towards the ending of their search. She felt an overwhelming love for all concerned, even the caustic Nebuline. They would all need one another in the days to come, and who could tell what would happen once they'd found the prophet? Would they even survive the meeting? She still did not know in her own mind whether Jeopardy was a benign entity or a malign one, or merely an insignificance. What she did know was that something had to be done, or precipitated, to destroy the power of Ixmarity. She did not deceive herself that she had the ability to do that, or even that

326

her companions did, but if there were many, many more like them? A man lay dead at her feet; his face set in a calm and beatific repose. Trajan's last victim. Delilah picked a roadside flower and placed it on his lifeless brow.

Trajan himself felt like a man who had woken up to discover his son had committed wicked deeds. He could not identify personally with the individual who'd carried the curse of plague and murder. His joy at the exorcism of that curse made him feel quite numb; there was no gratitude for the dark-haired woman who'd unwittingly freed him, only a profound sense of relief, so huge and intrinsic to his destiny it was beyond words to describe. While he'd been cursed, he'd been aware of its presence continually; a tightness in his flesh, a tingling behind his eyes, sluggishness, sometimes breathlessness. Now he felt utterly free of that. He felt clean. And he could look at the child he had protected all the way from Samberdell with new eyes, uncoloured by the ravages of the curse. So grave she was, so lovely, a sweet virgin who'd been immune to the terrors of the beast. He put his hand upon her shoulder and she glanced up at him with a quick, tight smile.

'We can't leave this man lying here,' she said. 'But there is nowhere to bury him, and we have no tools.'

'I'll carry him into that spinney over there,' Trajan said, 'and we can cover him with leaves. The animals will take them away later, but a gesture is all we can afford. I feel we must make haste to Gallimaufry now.'

'Are you agreeable to that?' Delilah asked Cleo.

She nodded. 'Yes. Look. It seems as if there is hardly anything left of him now. As he died, he told me he believed death had come to him a long time ago. Perhaps he was right. Perhaps, by morning, there'll be nothing for the animals to scavenge.' She turned away and walked towards Dauntless's horse. 'You seem real enough,' she said.

As they rode through the night towards the city, each of them told their tale and by morning, their throats dry, their bodies hardly able to remain upright in their saddles, the grey walls of Gallimaufry could be seen through a low mist. Delilah cried out and pointed. The carriage of Lord Pliance was waiting for them a short way up the road. Delilah dismounted from the back of Trajan's horse and ran forward to tell its occupants that Trajan was no longer cursed.

'How did you propose to cope with your afflictions once you'd entered the city?' Cleo asked Trajan as they waited. 'It would have been impossible to avoid people.'

'I would have hidden beyond the walls until Delilah found the prophet,' Trajan answered curtly.

After a few moments, Delilah waved to Cleo and Trajan who urged their horses forward. As they approached, Cleo heard a nasal female voice from within the carriage enquire, 'Are you quite sure it is safe to have the brute near?'

'Oh yes,' Delilah answered earnestly. 'Please don't call him a brute now.'

Cleo was inclined to take an instant dislike to the owner of the nasal voice before she'd even met her, but she reminded herself of the strange events of the night, and that she should at the very least keep her feelings neutral concerning all the Jeopardites she met. However, she could not hold her tongue completely, and when Lord Pliance stepped daintily down from the carriage, she complained to him in forthright terms about the way his driver had nearly killed her the previous evening.

327

Lord Pliance slid towards her and took her hand, pressing it briefly to his lips. 'Dear lady, these are peculiar times, and the risk of pausing in one's path for a stranger, however lovely, is often a risk not worth taking.'

'Had you taken that risk, however, a companion of mine might still be alive,' she said.

'But Trajan would still be afflicted!' Delilah cried.

'There is good and bad in every situation,' Lord Pliance commented glibly. 'Would you care to sit in the carriage for the remainder of our journey, mistress? You look tired.'

'I am,' Cleo agreed. 'Very well, A late ride is better than no ride at all. Come, Delilah, we shall both take advantage of this offer.' She held out her hand. Delilah glanced at Trajan, who nodded at her, and then took hold of Cleo's fingers without hesitation. Cleo felt almost shocked, not just by her gesture, but by Delilah's swift and natural response. She squeezed the slim little hand and Delilah squeezed back. Together, they entered the carriage, which, after the driver had secured Cleo's horse to the rear, set off at a smart pace once more to the city.

A minor disturbance in one of the outer suburbs of the city, just within the walls where transport companies and livery stables were situated, meant that Lord Pliance's carriage had to make a detour. The sounds of shouting could be heard and a smell of burning drifted in the air. Delilah poked her head out of the carriage to see what the trouble was. There was a lot of black smoke, and part of the road ahead appeared to have collapsed. Ixmarite peacekeepers had thronged like black flies into the area, and were now diverting traffic away from the scene.

'What has happened?' Nebuline demanded.

'The road has collapsed,' Delilah replied. 'At least, it seems to have done.'

'They say Gallimaufry is built over a system of caves and underground tunnels,' Inshave said. 'Perhaps there has been subsidence.'

Nebuline rejected this idea. 'And they say also that the caves, of which there were in fact only a few, were all filled in before the first foundations of the city were laid.'

'I felt the earth tremble in Covendale,' Delilah said.

'Well, I've felt nothing like that here today,' Nebuline said. 'Anyway, we had better give the driver directions, Inshave. Before we make any investigation as to Jeopardy's whereabouts, we need to be comfortable.'

'Will we be staying near where Jeopardy is?' Delilah asked.

Nebuline flicked a glance towards Lord Pliance. 'No,' she said. 'We have travelled hard and, I feel, deserve some kind treatment.' She smiled at the vampire, who of course carried the purse.

The group found accommodation in a well-appointed hostelry near the harbour area. It was a site that catered mainly for tourists and devout Ixmaritian pilgrims who came to the holy city to worship in the cathedrals, take expeditionary walks around those of the nunneries and monasteries that were open to the public and spend inordinate amounts of coin on the mementoes and religious bric à brac. Gallimaufry was kept carefully free of all signs of Ixmarite oppression. Seeing the placid nuns strolling along the harbour front, gentle smiles on their faces, Delilah found it hard to believe their belief system was responsible for all the bodies she had seen hanging from gibbets along the eastern road, and the devastation that had been committed in Covendale. But then she remembered Samberdell's hard-hearted Ixmarite priest.

The city itself was gracious and well-proportioned with wide streets which were kept in good order by a plenitude of municipal workers who removed litter and polished the faces of roadside idols representing Ixmar and His Family.

Lord Pliance hired a private dining room and, after the group had taken the equivalent of a night's sleep, met with his companions for an early evening meal. As was the custom in Gallimaufry, inn residents were required to take part in a short Ixmaritian ritual, presided over by a peripatetic priest who supervised the harbour inns. The priest entered the dining room and took stock of its occupants with a chilling glance. Everyone obediently recited the litanies at the priest's prompting, and after he had departed, strangely dissatisfied though he could not specify to himself why, the visitors addressed their meal without mentioning the incident.

'Well, we are here now,' Delilah said lamely, as she toyed with her dessert. In the last few moments, the realisation that her journey was nearly over, and the dénouement imminent, had struck her with unexpected force. Her heart had begun to beat quickly. She felt very nervous.

'Yes,' Cleo agreed, and patted the back of Delilah's hand with her spoon. She addressed Nebuline. 'You are sure you can find the prophet?'

Nebuline would not look at her, but dabbed her mouth fastidiously with a napkin before speaking. 'If he is here, we shall find him.'

'If he is here?' Cleo said in alarm. 'I thought you knew that he was!'

'Mistress Sinister, I would never presume to know all of Jeopardy's movements,' Nebuline said. 'But I do know that his plans involve Gallimaufry in a major sense. We are all aware that he will not be able to function in the manner he has for much longer; therefore a new tactic will be adopted.'

'Which is?' Lord Pliance asked.

Nebuline smiled at him. 'I do not have the information,' she said.

'I thought you were one of Jeopardy's most trusted companions,' Trajan pointed out, with some sarcasm.

Nebuline coloured a little. 'I am, but some things he keeps utterly to himself.'

Cleo sighed. 'Well, I for one would like to know exactly what he hopes to achieve. I've followed the idea of the man across half the island, unsure of my own motives and even less sure of Jeopardy's. What is his purpose? What are his general plans? I would like to know these things before I meet him.'

Nebuline assumed an earnest expression. 'I hope I can answer your questions,' she said, with importance. 'But you must understand that Jeopardy means a different thing to every person who follows him. There is no general plan, no rule, no doctrine.'

'There must be,' Cleo said. 'There has to be something attractive about his philosophy, otherwise people wouldn't bother listening to him, never mind trailing after him with an Ixmarite spear aimed at their backs. What is this thing, this special property, that he has?'

'He speaks of freedom,' Inshave said. 'Freedom for the individual, freedom from oppression.'

'Sometimes he speaks of that,' Trajan said, in a slow voice. Nebuline and Inshave glanced at him sharply. Trajan raised his arms in a shrug. 'Well, you must admit, he speaks of freedom when he believes that is what his audience wants.'

'What else does he speak of?' Cleo asked.

'Whatever engages his attention at the time,' Trajan replied.

'You speak in a strangely irreverent manner for one who claims to adore the prophet,' Nebuline said stiffly.

Trajan shrugged again. 'Not at all. I speak only from experience because I, unlike many others, actually paid attention when Jeopardy spoke. I could work out no design to his speeches, no overall message. Sometimes, what he said contradicted an earlier philosophy entirely. I sought the pattern but failed to find it. One day, I was convinced the design would be made clear to me, which is why I followed him. I felt there was something important about him; I knew there was, but I could not work out exactly what it was. Some nights, I would lie beneath the moon and feel her impish progeny tug cruelly on my senses. I would lie there thinking that Jeopardy was fooling us all, that he laughed at us. Then I would think he was simply mad, a madman who believed his own lunatic theories. Then he would come walking soft-footed through the camp and pause behind my head. He would reach down and touch my brow and say, "Be at rest," and the moon imps would scurry back to their mother in terror. I would open my eyes and see his face and love him, and realise he was a singular, wonderful human being. He would smile and walk on. He loved us all . . .' Here Trajan frowned, as if an uncomfortable recollection had come to him.

'What is it?' Delilah asked.

Trajan shook his head. 'I was assured of his love and yet now that my mind is clear of taint, my memories are less opaque. I remember the past with a new clarity, and . . .' He rubbed his brow with agitated fingers. 'There is yet another contradiction.'

'What?' Delilah gripped Trajan's right arm.

'The day I became lost.' Trajan gently withdrew his arm from Delilah's hold and knitted his fists beneath his chin. He gazed above the heads of his companions, down the length of the table. 'Jeopardy had spoken in Scaleforth, a town north of the city of Overstrew. It is a rugged area and the season was cold. Word came to us that a group of Ixmarites, under the ecclesiarch Wilfish Implexion, intended to surprise us on our leaving the town. It was said he carried the branding irons and hoped to mark a few more Jeopardites, as well as deliver a chastisement to any previously branded individuals. Naturally, alerted before the event, Jeopardy cut short the visit to Scaleforth. There were about thirty of us with him on that trip, the bulk of our fellows being camped in safer territory among the Droom Heights further north. Through our own network, misinformation had been given that the majority of the Jeopardites were camped further to the east, among the Swinkbacks, so we expected the attack to come from that direction, supposing Implexion would think we'd retreat that way. However, Jeopardy knew his adversary was an intelligent man, and that other groups of Ixmarites might well surround the town, so he directed myself and a few others to guard the northern road.

'It was a narrow pass north out of Scaleforth, with high cliffs to either side. I and my companions concealed ourselves high among the rocks, and were armed with longbows and a good store of boulders. You have to understand that my affliction was in abeyance, for Jeopardy had recently touched me. Therefore, I had no reason to fear a brief estrangement from his side.' Trajan sighed and smiled wistfully. 'How full of power I felt, eager to break a few Ixmarite heads! We planned that if no pursuit was sighted by sundown, we would follow our fellows to Droom and safety. The Ixmarites

330

were better prepared than we guessed, however. An hour or so after we'd concealed ourselves, we were surprised from above. A terrible conflict ensued. We were far outnumbered and all my companions were killed, but for one other. Together, we managed to escape and head north into the territory we knew so well. We knew we would be followed, so veered away from the road to Droom, not wanting to put the whole camp in danger. I was beginning to feel the presence of my affliction once more and was anxious to return to Jeopardy.

'One night, my companion and I huddled together against bare rock, and decided we would hurry to Droom come morning. There'd been no sign of Ixmarites for over a day. In the middle of the night, however, we heard the sound of footsteps on the rock above us, and leapt out of hiding, brandishing our weapons, fearing attack. But it was Resenence Jeopardy himself whom we found there. He told us we should stay where we were for the time being and tossed us a bag of supplies. More than that, he would not say. Before he left, he touched me and said, "Wait for me, Trajan. I will come back. Wait here." Then, he was gone. We had no idea what had happened. So, we waited.' Trajan paused, but nobody broke the silence. He glanced at every face.

'Jeopardy never came back,' he said. 'The effect of his touch lasted over a week, but he never came back. On the tenth night, the moon took me and, insensible of reality, I killed my companion. Like a raging beast, I ran north, roaring all the time. In two days, I came upon the camp at Droom, but it was empty. Nothing was left. Nothing.' He looked at Delilah. 'I travelled onwards, north-east, following an instinct, a hope, a dream. The land was mercifully empty, but eventually, I came to Samberdell.'

'And found me,' Delilah said.

'And destroyed the whole community,' Trajan amended. 'The rest you know. I sought the hand of Resenence Jeopardy, but was given the poison of Cleo Sinister. Cleo's cure is permanent, I know. Jeopardy's cure is a wage for my fidelity. It was paid often, but without it . . .'

There was another short silence which was broken by Nebuline. 'You don't know what happened?' she said.

'Do you?' Trajan asked directly. 'Were you with him, then? Do you know why he didn't come back?'

'How long ago was this?' Nebuline asked, frowning.

Trajan shrugged. 'Two seasons.'

She shook her head. 'I was in Tagnacarti at that time. Inshave and I were with a few others, distributing pamphlets. I have no idea what happened. We saw Jeopardy only briefly a month or so ago. He did not mention it, and of course we had no reason to ask. Trajan, you know we are constantly harassed by Ixmarites. There could have been a good reason why Jeopardy did not return for you.'

Trajan nodded. 'There could be, certainly, but I would like to know the reason why he told us to stay where we were. He moved like a cat through the night. He could pass under the nose of an Ixmarite unnoticed. He could have come to me at any time. You see, I have a dilemma. Mistress Sinister unwittingly proved my affliction to be curable, which Jeopardy told me it was not.'

'I can't believe that,' Nebuline said. 'He would never come out with so rigid a remark.'

'Very well, perhaps I exaggerate. But he implied as much.'

'You wanted to see that in his words,' Nebuline said. 'It was your interpretation. You should know that.'

'Please, we cannot argue about this,' Lord Pliance said. He smiled at Cleo. 'Should I wish to be rid of my own peculiarities, it would seem I wouldn't be amiss consulting the lovely Mistress Sinister here and her bag of beguilements. Perhaps I do not need to meet this prophet after all.'

Cleo smiled thinly. 'I would not recommend experimentation with my banes. I know only their affects upon a normal human frame. I have no idea what they would do to an abnormal frame.'

The vampire shrugged. 'Oh well. That is a shame.'

'I suggest you all go out and enjoy the evening,' Nebuline said. 'Inshave and I will make enquiries in the right places, and shall meet you later at the Bat and Widow inn.' She gave them directions.

'Indeed,' Lord Pliance agreed. 'The night is beautiful and I would be honoured to escort Mistress Sinister on a walk around the harbour.' He rose, bowed gallantly and held out his arm. Cleo got out of her seat and dubiously accepted his offer. Delilah and Trajan followed them.

As they walked out of the inn, Delilah and Trajan hung back a little. 'Am I right in thinking you are in two minds about finding Resenence Jeopardy now?' Delilah asked.

'That is a sore question,' Trajan answered.

'You think he betrayed you, don't you?'

Trajan sighed. 'My faith has been shaken,' he said.

'Jeopardy is not all-powerful,' Delilah pointed out. 'He could not have known the effects of that bane upon you. Surely, if he had, he'd have told you of the cure.'

'As Mistress Ploverpage pointed out in Covendale, my curse was largely self-generated. I can accept that now, but for all that, it was still very real. I cannot explain why the poison worked that way on me. Perhaps Jeopardy could. I don't know. I feel I know very little now.'

Delilah's face had become solemn. 'You have infected me, Trajan, but with something other than disease,' she said quietly. 'I want to find Jeopardy. I have to now.'

They walked on in silence.

After an examination of the immediate vicinity and its amusements, the group sought out the Bat and Widow inn. It had apparently been a spot popular with Jeopardites in happier days. There was a large, flagged garden at the front, where a noisy crowd of patrons sat sampling the inn's best elixirs which had exotic names such as 'Maiden's Moan', 'Midnight Woe', 'Golden Claw'. Delilah and Cleo seated themselves at one of the wooden tables, while Trajan and Lord Pliance went indoors to purchase drinks. The inn was so busy, the men were soon lost in the crowd clustering at the bar.

'I hope Lord Pliance does not become victim to a desire to taste flesh,' Delilah said, trying to peer through the inn door.

Cleo shrugged. 'If he does, and trouble ensues, we'll pretend we don't know him. Oh, what a pleasant evening this is. I wish I could appreciate it. I have reached the end of my journey, yet my heart is so heavy.'

'I feel the same,'Delilah admitted. 'It's as if we're crouching beneath a swinging sword.'

Cleo nodded miserably and opened her mouth to speak, but at that moment someone intruded on their company and sat down opposite them at the table. It was a young man wearing a long, brown, hooded cloak which was thrown back to reveal a handsome grinning face.

'Excuse me,' Cleo said, 'that seat is taken. Our gentlemen companions are at this moment coming back to us with refreshment, and they might not take kindly to your intrusion.'

'Ladies, my intentions are honourable,' he said. 'Permit me to introduce myself. I am Speckless the Tregetour and for a small coin will amuse you with tricks and caprices.'

'We need no amusements,' Cleo said. 'Be off!'

'Everyone needs amusements,' the man rejoined, ignoring Cleo's last remark. 'Behold, a woman with bats in her hair is in sore need of happy entertainment.' Whereupon he reached out and, before Cleo could cringe away, took a squeaking, fluttering creature from her hair. Cleo emitted a small shriek and Speckless threw the bat up into the air, allowing it to flitter drunkenly away.

'Expect no money for that indelicacy,' she said, scraping her hair out of her eyes. 'I advise you to depart at once, for I intend to tell our companions you have molested us.'

Speckless the tregetour shrugged, a wry expression of disappointment on his face. 'I am saddened by your reaction,' he said. 'That trick usually summons a smile from clients of the Widow.'

'Well, we are not regular patrons,' Cleo said. There was something uncomfortably compelling about the tregetour's piercingly blue eyes.

'You are strangers, then,' the tregetour said. 'Pilgrims, perhaps?'

'Delilah.' Cleo stood up. 'Come, we are leaving.' She intended to go into the inn and find the others. The tregetour made her skin crawl.

'Wait,' he said, rising.

Cleo stared at him in a challenging manner.

'I bring news for you,' he said.

Cleo did not change her expression.

'Tonight, at the hour before midnight, there will be a gathering,' he said. 'I believe you might wish to attend.'

'You do not know us,' Cleo said. 'Therefore, you cannot know how we might like to amuse ourselves. Come along, Delilah.'

The tregetour jumped earnestly to his feet as Cleo attempted to drag Delilah towards the inn. 'The old parade ground outside Gallimaufry,' he called after them. 'Approach it through the Old Gardens of Queen Lallow.'

Cleo bared her teeth at him and hauled Delilah into the jostling crowd beyond the inn door, leaving the tregetour still standing by the table outside. Delilah was behaving in a peculiarly sluggish manner. Cleo had to speak to her sharply several times before she spotted Trajan's head looming above the crowd by the bar. Cleo gratefully clawed her way to them. Trajan and Lord Pliance had just been served and were on the point of returning to their companions, Trajan carrying a tray of brightly coloured drinks.

'There has been an incident,' Cleo announced, and hurriedly related what had happened. Nobody was really surprised that there was no sign of Speckless the tregetour when they returned to their table.

'Perhaps you should have questioned the scoundrel a little more, my dear,' Lord Pliance said in mild admonition. 'I think he must have been a Jeopardite.'

'But how did he know we were looking for Jeopardy?' Cleo demanded.

'Do we have it written across our heads?' She grimaced. 'I think it's more likely he was an Ixmaritian spy looking for Jeopardites who are foolish enough to betray themselves.

'Well, whoever he was, he's gone now,' Trajan said, putting the tray of drinks down on a table. 'We shall tell Nebuline and Inshave when they arrive, and then decide whether or not we should attend this gathering he spoke of.'

XXIII

DEATH

The Archimage was feeling unwell and had retired to his bedchamber early. Far from being comforted, as he usually was, by the heavily curtained room, Sleeve felt that tonight his chamber was oppressive, its air thick. An acolyte had lit a bowl of healing fumes, designed to assuage the roilings in Sleeve's belly, but they merely made his head ache and he extinguished them with a cup of water.

Sitting down in a brocaded chair next to the hearty fire his attendant, Marmick, had built a few hours earlier, Sleeve picked up the goblet of spiced wine that had been left for him in the hearth. He sipped meditatively, for he had much to think about, many plans to make. He could feel the envelope that lay in a pocket of his robe pressing against his thigh. It was a tool of potential, he knew that, but it had to be used wisely in order to produce the desired results. His day had been frustrating in the extreme. It appeared that the Ten were beginning to allow Implexion's subjective, emotional outbursts concerning the so-called prophet Jeopardy to sway their opinions.

Sleeve thought back to the meeting of the Ten that had been held that morning. Gadeon Slitling was an ecclesiarch whom Sleeve had always believed to be the most rational and sceptical of them all, sometimes to the point of familiar tirades against Resenence Jeopardy, Slitling had been moved to stand and address his colleagues.

'I am sick of hearing of the prophet's supposed exploits,' he exclaimed. 'I agree with the Ecclesiarch Implexion that Jeopardy should be eradicated with all expediency, if for no other reason than this: too much of our time is being wasted listening to the honoured ecclesiarch's complaints about the man. It would benefit us all should the subject of his allegations be eliminated.'

Others had laughed at Slitling's remarks, but Implexion had smiled grimly, catching Sleeve's eye as if to say, 'One falls, the rest will follow.' Slitling's suggestion had been a joke, but Sleeve suspected that more than one of the nine ecclesiarchs had been made nervous by Implexion's nagging insistence that the Jeopardites should be wiped out. There had been a

335

peculiar atmosphere about the city this last week, an air of breathless expectation which suggested even to the least imaginative citizen that some kind of storm was about to break.

Sleeve was tired of disputing Implexion's exaggerated terms for the prophet. He had hoped that the ecclesiarch's obsession would burn itself out but, if anything, it seemed to be getting stronger. Sleeve's feelings of oppression had been worsened by the receipt of a report his agents had been compiling since the year before. Facts had been gathered concerning the Jeopardite movement, which Sleeve had hoped would demonstrate to the Ten that it was only a transient phenomenon. The report had not shown that, however. If Jeopardy's following was not exactly growing, it was somehow becoming more cohesive. True, at the moment it had fragmented because of Implexion's persistent harrying, but there were rumours flying around that Jeopardy intended to hold a mass meeting in the city very soon. The sheer audacity of that suggested he expected a robust turn-out, and should the Church attempt to interfere, violence might well ensue. Sleeve did not relish the thought of Jeopardites adopting guerrilla tactics.

Something else in the report had also worried him greatly. Despite a careful choice of words on the part of the reporter, the action of Implexion and his staff did not stand out in a very rosy light. It seemed they had been running riot throughout the land, supposedly to root out Jeopardy's supporters, but in the process leaving a trail of hanged and impaled bodies along the roads. Sleeve was concerned that innocents might well have suffered in the hysteria. When the Archimage had confronted Implexion with these facts in the Chamber, the ecclesiarch had merely shrugged.

'Sometimes unpleasant measures are necessary,' he argued, 'otherwise the populace would be scurrying back to northern ways. Through complacency, the Church would lose its hold on the souls of Gleberune. Is that what you want?'

'Of course not,' Sleeve replied scathingly. 'But neither do I wish responsibility for barbarous acts to be etched on my sepulchre! Some of your officers are going too far, Wilf.'

Implexion shook his head emphatically. 'Not at all. You forget that the bulk of this country's population are indigenous Runes. They are stubborn, stupid and innately pagan. It is our duty to protect Glebish civilisation. I don't think you'll find many complaints for my procedure in the south.' He stood up and faced the rest of the Ten with outspread arms. 'Without Glebish interference, this island would still be overrun with savage louts. Remember the history of Gleberune before the Glebish came: self-styled warrior kings battling over patches of scrub; disorder and cruelty. Weren't the Runes grateful for our assistance, then? They have short memories.'

'Jeopardy is from Glebish stock,' Sleeve pointed out.

Implexion made an irritated gesture and sat down. 'That is irrelevant.'

'You talk about the past as if it were yesterday,' Sleeve said in a careful voice. 'It is long past. We are not separate races any more, Wilf. There are no enemies out there.'

'You have not experienced life beyond the protection of the Church,' Implexion replied coldly. 'When did you last leave Gallimaufry and walk through the land? When did you last observe the people?'

'There are individuals who do that for me,' Sleeve said. 'The ones who count your gibbets and then halve the number before reporting back to me!'

'I only work with the sanction of the Ten,' Implexion said.

336

Gadeon Slitling interrupted. 'Heretics must be culled,' he said. 'As ecclesiarchs of Ixmar, we cannot allow ourselves the luxury of feeling squeamish about it.'

At that point, Sleeve had withdrawn from the discussion, letting it swirl around him. He felt that Implexion was losing self-control, which in turn made him uncontrollable within the Church. The more Sleeve thought about it, the more he was beginning to believe that there were two menaces at work within Gleberune: Jeopardy and Implexion himself. The time might yet come when he'd have to approach his staunchest allies in the Ten to convene a private meeting about the matter.

He thought about the letter that had been delivered to his office shortly before the meeting. He'd read it quickly, but what he'd seen there had been enough to interest him greatly. Now, he was prepared to sit back and let Implexion rant on. The raised eyebrows around the Chamber while Sleeve's clerk had read the report out loud had been revealing. Sleeve had made a mental note of whose expressions had been the most uncomfortable. He knew that Implexion would be awaiting an attack on him. The war zone had not yet been declared, but there had been much private marking of territorial boundaries. Sleeve was aware that Implexion considered him to be weak; he probably intimated his thoughts to the other ecclesiarchs whenever he got the opportunity. Once he'd thoroughly undermined Sleeve's credibility, he would make his move. Sleeve suspected that Implexion had an eye on the Archimage's throne itself.

Sleeve had been the first to leave the Chamber of Ten after the meeting, but the ecclesiarch had made a point of catching up with him in the wide, colonnaded corridor beyond. 'Your arguments are wearing thin, Perpetius,' he'd said. 'The opinion of the Ten is turning to me. I advise you to relent and give me your vote for crushing the Jeopardite menace.'

The gleam in his eyes was nothing less than fanatical. Sleeve observed him with distaste.

'I'll give my vote as and when I happen to agree with your suggestions,' he answered curtly, striding swiftly forward.

Implexion kept pace with him, laughing. It seemed he had no respect left for the Archimage at all.

Sleeve had halted then and turned on the ecclesiarch with a steely glare.

Implexion had attempted to hold his gaze, but then looked away. 'You can't afford to sit on the fence any longer,' he said, and marched off.

Sleeve had had the rest of the day to mull the matter over. He refused to let Implexion's outright rudeness discompose him. He needed to be firmly in control of his feelings, otherwise the adversary might gain an advantage. Still, the letter in his pocket was full of potential. After the meeting, he wrote a reply, sealed it, and had Marmick deliver it, for he trusted no one else as much. Something would have to be done about Implexion, and soon. The whole situation filled Sleeve with repugnance. He was annoyed with himself that he might have misjudged Jeopardy's power; he was furious that he hadn't recognised earlier the threat hidden in Implexion. He felt fairly sure the majority of the Ten would endorse his views, but it would still benefit his cause to utilise every shred of information that came his way.

Sleeve put down his cup in the hearth, and glanced at the clock on the mantelpiece. If he knew anything about it, his visitors would be on time.

Moments later, Marmick knocked on the door and, after a short pause, walked in. 'You have a visitor,' he said.

Sleeve looked up and nodded. 'Bring another cup of wine. No, bring an entire jug. But give us a few minutes alone first.'

Marmick bowed and retreated. Presently, the door opened again, and Sleeve rose from his chair. 'Good evening, madam,' he said. 'I am glad you were free to visit me at such short notice.'

Inanna Grisaille walked forward and took Sleeve's extended hand, pressed the Archimage's ring to her lips. 'I am honoured you requested my presence, Your Sacredness.'

'Please, sit down.' Sleeve seated himself once more and indicated a seat on the other side of the hearth. Inanna arranged herself gracefully and folded her hands in her lap, her spine erect.

She is a survivor, Sleeve thought. 'Well,' he said. 'I thank you for the note you sent me.' It was all the opening he was prepared to give her.

She nodded briefly. 'I trust you do not believe me to be some hysterical female,' she said. 'I am very concerned and, to be frank, feel there is no one but yourself I can trust. This matter must be handled discreetly.'

'I agree, and I am pleased you thought to consult me rather than any of the Ten. As it happens, I am totally in accord with your thoughts and have been worried about the situation myself for some time.'

'I fear that Wilf's . . . condition might become a . . . nuisance to others,' she said.

Sleeve could see the wariness in her eyes. She was testing him. 'You are talking, of course, of his animosity towards anyone who does not share his rather fervid views?'

She nodded. 'I think we understand one another.'

'Good. Well, I can assure you that a desire for Wilfish's good health is foremost in my mind. I too am concerned about his state of mind. It is obvious to those who are close to him that all is not well at present. I'm sure others have noticed his . . .' he risked a direct word, '. . . decline.'

'Indeed. That is my thought as well,' Inanna said. 'It is worrying to think the men under Wilf's command might also have noticed his distraction and are now speculating about it. This would not reflect well upon the Ten, and could also affect military discipline.'

'I commend your astuteness.' He paused and smiled wryly. 'You are well thought of in the Chamber, madam. In fact, I don't think it would be out of place to tell you that promotion might well be suggested in the near future. But of course this information is confidential.'

Inanna touched her throat and ducked her head. 'Your Sacredness, I am honoured. I must confess I have been wondering about my position recently, and whether my future is secure.'

'You need not worry on that score,' Sleeve said. 'Ah, here is Marmick with some fine mulled wine. Would you care to take a cup?'

'Thank you,' Inanna said. 'Just a small one.'

Marmick unobtrusively dispensed the refreshments, allowing Sleeve to observe his guest in silence. Her letter had intrigued him. She'd expressed concern for Implexion's health and had requested a confidential interview. He'd known right away that this must mean Inanna was worried about her own tenure. Perhaps she knew too much.

After Marmick had withdrawn, Sleeve and Inanna sipped their wine in silence for a few moments. A certain uneasiness had crept into the room, almost as if Inanna was regretting having come. Perhaps she feared the result of any disclosures she might make.

338

'Rest assured that, whatever you might tell me, I shall respect the confidential nature of this interview,' Sleeve said mildly. 'No matter how I might decide to use the information later.'

Inanna's head went up. 'I would prefer not to be implicated.'

'Naturally. I suggest you unburden yourself to me now.'

She hesitated. 'My position, after I have spoken, might be difficult. You know how Wilf is at the moment. If the information I have is of use to you, then he might suspect where it came from, whether my name is mentioned or not. I presume you intend to act quickly?'

Sleeve made a careless gesture with one hand. 'Please, don't worry. There are plenty of guest chambers in my apartments. I would be pleased to offer you accommodation here for a few days. If fur is to fly, you might as well keep your head down . . . to avoid being choked on it.' He smiled.

Inanna's responding smile was shaky. Obviously the metaphor was too much in accord with her fears. Did she really suspect Implexion might have her murdered? 'Your Sacredness, I am the mistress of a powerful man. I have known many women in my position and have seen what can happen when such women fall from favour. I do not wish to share the same fate.'

'You won't,' Sleeve said.

Inanna leaned forward. 'The situation has accelerated recently,' she said, 'but it was always at its worst at night . . .'

Inanna gave Sleeve much to think about. Her testimony proved beyond doubt that Implexion had lost his wits, There'd been no dramatic embellishments to her tale; she'd delivered the simple facts in a cool, efficient manner. She feared for both her position and her life, and the fact that Implexion seemed to have a vendetta against the Archimage gave her the information she needed to seek his aid. Despite her remaining fondness for Implexion, it was clear her betrayal of his secret rantings was necessary in order to protect herself. If Implexion's affection for her had remained constant, no doubt she would have held her tongue, no matter what he'd said about the Archimage. But he had become distant with her, suspicious. Over the last week, she'd often felt she was being watched.

Sleeve wondered how best to utilise what he'd heard. Despite the assurances he'd given Inanna, he might have to disclose his source of information to the Ten. Her good reputation would influence their reaction to his report.

A sharp knock on the door interrupted Sleeve's thoughts. 'What is it?' he demanded.

Marmick entered the room. 'Your Sacredness, you have *another* visitor.' His round eyes indicated he suspected something very interesting was afoot.

'Who?' Sleeve asked.

'Ecclesiarch Implexion, Your Sacredness.'

'Did he state his business?' Sleeve's voice was sharp. 'The hour is late.'

The boy shrugged. 'I'm sorry, he would not say, but he assured me it was urgent.'

Sleeve uttered a sound of irritation. 'Isn't it always! Very well, Marmick, show him in.'

'Shall I bring more refreshments?'

'No, and take the jug and cups away. Discreetly.'

Moments later, Wilfish Implexion marched into the room. He looked defensive, as if he expected antagonism or criticism. Sleeve greeted him with cordial politeness.

339

'Wilf,' he said. 'To what do I owe this pleasure?'

Implexion shook his head. 'I won't waste your time,' he said. 'The reason for my being here is this. Information has come to me that Resenence Jeopardy impudently plans to hold a large meeting tonight at the old parade ground. I am asking for your endorsement to surround the grounds with a sizeable force so that the nuisance can be put paid to once and for all.'

'So you still need my endorsement for that, eh?' Sleeve said.

Implexion shrugged. 'As a formality, yes, although the Ten could overrule your decision.'

'I am tired of this,' Sleeve said.

'We all are,' Implexion shot back. 'Well?'

'Do you intend to kill Jeopardy?'

'I'll do whatever is necessary.'

'Make a martyr of him?'

'We'll see.'

Sleeve smiled. 'He'll probably wriggle away from you again, Wilf, no matter how great your "sizeable force". How many times have you tried to net him?'

'In the past, we have attempted to maintain a fairly low profile. This time, I intend to throw everything I've got at the man. He will not escape, I promise you.'

Sleeve nodded thoughtfully. 'Very well.'

'What?' Implexion looked surprised.

Sleeve gestured languidly with one hand. 'I said, very well. Go ahead and gut Jeopardy if you want to, roast him, flay him alive. Do what you like. I don't care about the welfare of the prophet, and no longer intend to risk making enemies in the Chamber by speaking the voice of reason.'

Implexion did not bother to hide his surprise. 'Does this mean you now agree with my point of view?'

'It means you have my endorsement. Get on with whatever you have to do!'

Implexion bowed. 'I shall,' he said, and left without a further word.

Sleeve stared into the fire for a few moments. Implexion would not have come here unless he'd won the support of at least some of the other ecclesiarchs. Sleeve smiled to himself. Perhaps, by initiating this action, Implexion would force Jeopardy to retaliate. Come morning, the matter might be resolved and Sleeve would have to do nothing about the man himself.

He leaned back in his chair. It might take him a few weeks to regain the respect he had no doubt lost over this business, but he was confident he could handle it. 'Ixmar, we pursue our own interests in Your name,' he thought. 'But I doubt that You care.' He made a sacred gesture, in case his unspoken words had affronted the god. It was best not to be careless.

He stood up, thinking he would undress and go to bed with a selection of the Ixibatabian literature he had recently received. The room was nicely warm, and Marmick would bring him another hot drink. Sleeve stretched his limbs and padded towards the bed. Before he reached it, he noticed the curtains around it were shaking. Had his attendant come back into the room unseen to adjust the pillows? Sleeve pulled back the canopy, and recoiled in alarm. Several grubby young children were writhing around on his spotless lace counterpane, their filthy boots soiling the cloth. Sleeve uttered a cry of outrage and shock.

340

'Marmick!' he called, hoping his attendant was within hearing. The children glared up at him with pale faces. Sleeve reached forward to grab one of them in order to throw them from the room, but the children seemed to ripple forwards to meet him. One of them leapt up and bit his arm. 'Marmick!' Sleeve staggered backwards. The children had begun to laugh. They rolled around on the bed, hooting and pointing at him.

Aghast, Sleeve hurried towards the outer chamber. '*Marmick!*'

His attendant appeared in the doorway of the small kitchen, where he prepared drinks and small snacks for his master. 'Your Sacredness?' he said, wiping his hands on a towel.

'Marmick, there are filthy urchins crawling all over my bed!' Sleeve gasped.

'I beg your pardon?' Frowning, Marmick advanced towards the Archimage's bedroom.

'See for yourself!' Sleeve followed him. 'How could they have got in? Who are they?' He could still hear the children laughing. As Marmick approached the bed, Sleeve knew the boy would see nothing. The realisation hit him like a slap; he felt slightly sick. His pace slowed and he lingered in the outer chamber. He was not easily frightened, but he did not want to go back into his bedroom.

The sound of laughter had faded. Marmick's voice came through the open door. 'There is no one here!'

Sleeve leaned against the door frame. What had he just experienced? He could not even claim he'd been asleep and dreaming, because Implexion had only just left.

Marmick reappeared. 'You need an early night, Your Sacredness. You must have dropped off right after the ecclesiarch left.' His eyes spoke of loyalty and discretion.

Sleeve nodded. 'Yes, you are right . . .' He paused. 'Marmick, the fumes that were lit earlier this evening were a trifle heavy. I think the smell disagrees with me. Would you be so kind as to light a fire in one of the guest rooms in the adjoining apartment?'

Marmick appeared perplexed. 'If you wish it, Your Sacredness.'

'I do,' Sleeve said. 'I don't want any more disturbing dreams.'

Marmick hesitated, a thoughtful expression on his face.

'What is it?' Sleeve asked sharply.

The boy shook his head. 'Oh, nothing . . . Well, it's just that I had two novices working up here the other day, dusting down the cobwebs from the cornices, and they too spoke of having seen children scampering about the apartment. I thought they were attempting to fool me; they were cheeky creatures, who clearly envied my status. I ignored their stories.'

Sleeve raised his brows. 'What stories?'

Marmick looked uncomfortable. 'I hardly like to say. You will not enjoy hearing them.'

'Nevertheless, I would like to know.' Sleeve folded his arms.

'Well, you know what novices are like for dreaming up tales of ghosts and inexplicable events.' Marmick paused, frowning. 'I really don't think it's worth your attention.'

'Tell me,' Sleeve insisted softly.

Marmick squirmed. 'Well, it is ridiculous, but some people, over-imaginative people I might add, claim that the Archimagery is haunted.'

'By?'

341

Marmick gulped audibly. He looked as if he feared chastisement, and spoke hurriedly. 'The ghosts of Jeopardy's children, the ones that Lord Implexion had, well, you know.'

'Is that so?'

Marmick nodded miserably. 'I told you it was ridiculous . . . I'm sorry.'

Sleeve shook his head, and glanced briefly into his bedroom. It seemed too dark, too sinister. He was glad he wouldn't be sleeping in there tonight. 'Don't apologise,' he said. 'Emotions run high concerning this Jeopardy character. Who knows, the stories might be right.' He smiled to quell Marmick's expression of horror. 'Anyway, I feel we will have nothing more to worry about after tonight. Lord Implexion intends to wipe Master Jeopardy from the memory of Gleberune.'

The boy ducked his head. 'I am sure you are right, Your Sacredness. Would you like me to sit with you for an hour or two and read aloud?'

Sleeve reached out and touched Marmick's shoulder. 'That would be most agreeable,' he said, and closed the door to his bedroom.

Later, when he examined his arm, Sleeve found the marks of small teeth, but there was no pain. It was then that he realised he would have to witness, with his own eyes, what was to happen between Implexion and the prophet that night.

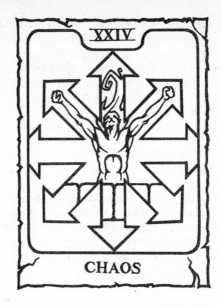

XXIV

CHAOS

The sun was sinking and Lucien Earthlight prowled the city. He was sure that if he walked for long enough, someone would press a pamphlet into his hand, telling him of Jeopardy's impending appearance. It was unthinkable that he should miss it.

No Jeopardites appeared to him, however; the streets he traversed all seemed unusually empty. Urgency and frustration gave way to a numb despair. Lucien walked like an automaton, his thoughts so confused and tangled they seemed like gibberish.

Eventually, as the shrine bells of the Devotional Way chimed out the advent of night, Lucien came to the gate leading into the Old Gardens of Queen Lallow. Beyond them, stated a plaque on the garden wall, lay the old parade ground. It was used nowadays mainly for official celebrations, but once the armies of the king had drilled up and down its length, preparing for battles with Ixibatae. Those days were over; now, truce reigned between the two island realms and the king of Gleberune bowed his head and his sceptre to the Grand Ecclesiarchs of Ixmar.

The tall, wooden gates were policed by two Ixmarite guards wearing ceremonial costume because many tourists passed that way. They paid no heed to Lucien as he passed between them.

Gallimaufry had at one time been the royal seat of Gleberune, although for sixty years the royal family had remained in Shanariah. The Old Gardens were arcane and eerie. Queen Lallow had had them designed specifically to re-create the fantasy lands of myth, described to her in tales by her Mathtarite nurse. Trees clustered thickly around the narrow pathways; sometimes the bemused walker would come out into a glade where a ruined tower would stand beside a still pool, and white deer would bound away into the dense undergrowth. It was still looked after by a regiment of gardeners, but this was not apparent from its appearance, for it looked as if the hand of husbandry had not touched it for a hundred years. Lucien had never visited the place before, and found it enchanting. The still air of antiquity reeked of romantic tragedy, of bewitchments and fell deeds. He paused in a glade where gravestones dotted the overgrown sward, their epitaphs written in a language he could not understand. Two mausoleums dominated the east and west ends of the glade, mostly covered by ivy. Lucien sat down within the portico of one of these and contemplated the graves. Ornamental death was a strange idea. He knew that nothing lay beneath the turf but Queen Lallow's childhood dreams. Perhaps they deserved a grave. Still, the atmosphere invoked by the scenery was truly that of a silent graveyard. Lucien felt invaded by its melancholy.

Presently, his thoughts were distracted by the arrival of a veiled woman. He noticed her walking slowly among the graves; hardly more than a shadow, her clothes of sombre black cloth. She seemed oblivious of his presence. Lucien thought she must be part of the scenery, perhaps employed by the Guild of Gardeners who cared for the place. Eventually, after weaving her way through the gravestones, she passed within a few feet of where Lucien sat, her long gown swishing through the grass. He did not expect her to pause or speak to him, but suddenly she stopped walking and stared at the ground. Lucien felt a chill pass through his body. Was it possible this secluded spot was haunted? Perhaps this was the shade of Queen Lallow herself. There was an unearthly quality to the figure. Then, the woman turned and came towards him. Her movements were halting as if she was in two minds whether to approach. Her face was invisible behind her veil.

'It is a beautiful evening,' Lucien said, in the vain hope the woman was both human and sane.

'Indeed,' she replied, in a faintly foreign accent which gave him some relief. The woman hesitated and then said, 'May I sit with you a while?'

Lucien laughed nervously. 'If your intentions are to enjoy the evening, or a little company, by all means.'

'What else could my intentions be?' she asked and sat down, arranging her long gown around her legs.

'You seem disturbingly a part of these surroundings,' Lucien said. 'For a moment, I thought you might be a ghost.'

The woman did not laugh or make any movement. Lucien wished he could see her face, and was tempted to reach out and throw back the veil, but some inner fear stayed his hand. Eventually, the woman sighed and said, 'Are you waiting here?'

'No,' Lucien replied. 'Why?'

'They say lovers use this spot. Are you looking for a lover?'

Lucien did not like the tone of that question. Was she about to proposition him? Then he thought of Jeopardy, and a needle of chill lanced his heart. 'I have not planned to meet anyone here,' he said. 'Your questions are searching, madam. Do you have any reason for asking them?'

The woman seemed to shudder and then turned on the seat almost violently. 'Oh Lucien, do you not know me?' she cried, and threw back the veil. Lucien flinched. The face was not human, not at all, though undeniably beautiful. The large eyes blinked.

'Chasteless!' Lucien gasped. 'Is it you?'

'Of course,' she replied.

'Chasteless, I have searched for you! What are you doing here? What happened to you? Why did you leave Shanariah without me?'

Chasteless shook her head. 'Too many questions,' she said. 'I cannot answer them all at once.'

'Did you know I'd be here?' Lucien asked.

She nodded, gazing at her gloved hands which lay loosely in her lap. '*He* knew. He always knows things. I was not supposed to show myself to you, but I could not help it. An impulse came. Oh, a strange feeling, but I am glad to see you. Is that not bizarre?' She reached out tentatively and touched his hands. 'You were kind to me before; you saw a thing within me that was life. Without you, I would be nothing. It was you that began the process. I remember you with fondness. Oh, your face is beautiful! You see, I can appreciate such things now.'

Lucien took her small hand in his own. Her smell of cured leather was partially eclipsed by a strong, sandalwood perfume. 'Has Resenence Jeopardy taught you all these things?' he asked. 'If so, he is a better teacher than I ever could have been. I am amazed. Imagine what Cartesian would think!'

But what she'd gained in intelligence she'd lost in other ways. Looking at her, Lucien could see that the ravages of time and life beyond the sanctuary of Cartesian's house had affected her appearance. The silk skin of her face was mottled, as if she'd been stained by rain, and there was a jagged rent on her brow that had apparently been stuck back down with glue. He wondered how the rest of her body was fairing. Did Jeopardy possess the knowledge to keep her mechanisms in trim? He supposed the evidence of her survival was enough to show he did.

'Are you all right?' he asked her. At the moment, he could think of nothing else to say.

Chasteless jerked her head up and nodded. 'Yes. I know I need a new skin – I felt you looking – but otherwise I'm fine. Jeopardy has friends all over the place. There is a woman we visit now and again who cares for my needs.'

Lucien shook his head. He could no longer look upon Chasteless as a mindless doll. How she had progressed since he'd last seen her! She was a much more convincing simulacre of a woman now. 'Cartesian was very upset when you left, and your sisters obviously missed you. Still, Cartesian did wonder whether being with Jeopardy might be the best thing for you.' He paused. 'Chasteless, why did you go with Jeopardy? Why have you stayed with him?'

'I had no choice,' she said. 'Not in the beginning. Now . . .' She shrugged. 'He has taught me so much, Lucien. I know now that I was once a living woman. I do not know the personality or face of that woman, or even how she died, but I do know that Cartesian somehow trapped her soul, put her into this machine. Res is helping me to remember myself, when I was human. I need to remember that so badly now, because I am aware of myself. I am a construct, a forced life.'

'You are no more a construct than I,' Lucien interrupted. 'I too was an automaton until I was forced to wake up.'

'It's not the same,' Chasteless said abruptly. 'Look at my hands.' She peeled off her gloves in agitation. Lucien winced. The silk sheath had all but worn away, revealing a peculiar network of leather and rubber tendons and artificial muscles. Transparent tubes pulsed with a transparent yellowish liquid. 'Jeopardy's friend cannot supply a quality skin,' she said. 'It wears away so quickly on my hands. I have to wear gloves all the time.' Her face could not give vent to human expressions and emotions, but Lucien could not help but believe there was confusion and helplessness in her eyes. 'I feel

I am a *woman*, Lucien, yet I also feel I am a monster. Consciousness has given me that.' A sighing sound escaped her throat; she shook her head slowly and put her gloves back on.

Lucien reached out to touch one of her hands. 'When you disappeared from Jeopardy's cellar in Shanariah, I began searching for you—'

'For me? Don't try to deceive me, Lucien. Res speaks of you sometimes. He says you've been following him. I am not stupid. I know there is some kind of bond between you and him. That is what impelled you to search for me – us.'

Lucien had to lower his eyes from her gaze. 'But I wouldn't have begun the search if he hadn't taken you. Now, my search is over. I have found you.' He squeezed her hand. 'Chasteless, let me take you back to Cartesian. He'd be able to help you, give you a new skin.'

Chasteless shook her head. 'Go back to Cartesian's house? No. I can't.'

'Why not? Won't Jeopardy let you leave him?'

Chasteless uttered a sad laugh. 'No, it isn't that. Jeopardy doesn't mind what I do. I have autonomy now. I simply don't want to go backwards, Lucien, not even to appease my vanity. If I went back, I am afraid I would lose all the awareness that has awoken within me. No, the only way for me is forwards, and I take that journey step by timorous step. If I am lucky, I will meet someone one day who has Cartesian's skills. Until then, I shall manage as best I can. I am a living woman, but I am a dead woman, too.' She looked away, into the shadows of the graveyard. Her voice, when she spoke again, was very distant. 'Sometimes, I fear the future. I don't know how long I have left to me on this earth.'

'Chasteless . . .' Lucien murmured helplessly.

'No,' Chasteless said firmly. She took her hand from his own and flexed her fingers. 'We will not talk of this. We have tonight to live through. Lucien, I have to take you somewhere. That is why I'm here.'

'Bait?'

'If you like.'

'So where will you take me?'

'To *him*,' she said, simply.

'For what purpose? More games? I am tired of it, Chasteless. I wish he would release me.'

'You don't mean any of that,' Chasteless said, standing up. 'You would not have followed him back and forth across the land otherwise.' She took a few steps into the shadows and beckoned with one hand. 'Come, Lucien. It is time. *Your* time. Can't you feel the earth shivering? Soon all will crack and spoil. The moon will turn her dark face towards us, and time will start again.'

'You talk with his voice,' Lucien said.

By sundown, Nebuline and Inshave had still not made an appearance at the Bat and Widow. 'Perhaps we should visit the place that scoundrel told you of,' Lord Pliance said to Cleo.

'And run into a glut of Ixmarite officials? I think not,' Cleo replied.

'There is nothing illegal about a group of tourists taking a walk round the Old Gardens,' Trajan said in a reasonable voice. 'It might not hurt to investigate.'

'But Nebuline and Inshave might return in our absence,' Cleo argued.

'I think the tregetour was genuine,' Delilah said. 'He had unusual eyes that, to me, were not the eyes of an Ixmaritian spy.'

'How would you know?' Cleo demanded in a cold voice.

Delilah shrugged. 'I just do.'

'You said nothing before.'

'I needed to think about it.' She had been very quiet while the others had talked over their drinks, mainly because she'd been thinking deeply about Speckless. He had initiated a memory within her that she could not place. Then, it had hit her. His eyes! His face! She remembered the mill pool. Speckless had not completely resembled the man she had seen beneath the water, but his eyes reminded her of the image she had invoked to repel Lord Pliance's advances. She might be wrong, but she felt in her heart she was not. Now, she dared to voice her thoughts. 'I think it was Resenence Jeopardy himself that came to our table.'

Everyone made noises of astonishment and denial, but both were short-lived.

'It is the sort of thing he would do,' Trajan said, and no one could refute his knowledge.

'Something is going to happen,' Delilah said. 'We must go the Old Gardens at once.'

No one contested her remark. The air around them shimmered with a sense of imminence.

To Delilah, stepping through the wall into the Old Gardens of Queen Lallow was like entering another world. She felt reverently humble in the presence of the ancient, gigantic oaks that were illuminated from beneath by flickering globes of gas light. The gardens seemed like a huge, dark forest that stretched into eternity, peopled by creatures who were strangers to the world outside; a timeless place of enchantment. The pathways were dark tunnels at the end of which anything might greet the unwary traveller. Cleo put her hands on Delilah's shoulders.

'It is very like the forest that Dauntless and I travelled through to get here,' she said. 'So old and haunted, as if the trees themselves are watching us and wondering how they might bewitch us from the path. I can imagine that people might get lost here for ever.'

Trajan laughed. 'Lost here? I doubt it. The gardens look bigger by night, but can be crossed in an hour. This is a place of illusion, Cleo, a folly built by a queen for her own amusement.' He strode forward along the path. 'This way. All paths lead to the other side.'

'Have you been here before, Trajan?' Delilah asked, skipping alongside him.

He nodded. 'Many times. Jeopardy loves the place. It appeals to him.'

Shortly, they came out into a clearing where a ruined temple overlooked a reed-fringed pond. 'The night is so clear,' Lord Pliance said, breathing deeply of the air. 'Ah, there is a majesty to nature that I miss among the peaks of Lamentarges.'

'I still don't know why you stay there,' Delilah said.

'Frequently, I become obsessed with myself and my solitude,' the vampire replied. 'When such melancholy comes upon me, there is no other place in which to exercise it. The setting of Castle Pliance lends itself entirely to an atmosphere of lonely torment.'

'What a miserable life,' Delilah said.

The vampire shrugged. 'Strange to say, I quite enjoy it. Still, I feel

347

refreshed by this excursion into a more fertile realm. And such romantic environs are completely right for a little dalliance of the flesh. Do you suppose we might come across a lone walker here whom I could delight in my inimitable way?'

Delilah laughed. 'I hope not!' Sometimes, Lord Pliance frightened her; she sensed the seriousness behind his humorous words, but she still admired the way he could make fun of himself and never took offence at what people said to him.

The group stood together beside the pool, taking in the wistful ambience of the place. To each it told a story.

To Cleo, it was a place where a young girl, perhaps a princess, had hidden from her cruel mother.

To Trajan, it was a place where a man had stood beside the pool contemplating the emptiness of his own life before he ended it.

To Lord Pliance, it was a place where red-lipped, pale-skinned nymphs concealed themselves among the reeds, waiting for a lone traveller to enter the glade so that they might tease him.

To Delilah, it was a place where something had waited an eternity for just this moment. 'What is that sound?' she asked.

'What sound?' Cleo demanded sharply.

Delilah lifted her head and peered at the treetops. 'It sounds like the beating of a vast wing,' she said softly, 'a wing as big as the sky.'

'It is the wind in the reeds,' Cleo said. 'How could you say such a thing, Delilah? Do you want to frighten us all?'

Delilah opened her mouth to apologise but at that moment the glade filled with a rill of music. It seemed to come from a single instrument, a flute of some kind, but its notes were piercing and full. A pale figure walked out of the trees on the other side of the pool and stood watching them, a double flute raised to its lips. The music stopped and the instrument was lowered. Silence reigned. Then, the figure was gone.

'A ghost!' Cleo said.

'A nymph?' Lord Pliance suggested hopefully.

'Probably a joke of Jeopardy's,' Trajan said. 'Come along. It's not far now.'

Inanna Grisaille stood tensely in the centre of the room that the Archimage had put at her disposal. Despite his assurances, she did not feel safe. The air around her rang with unheard sounds. Her skin prickled. She felt jumpy. A hurrying breeze that smelled of the sea fretted the curtains by the balcony.

Rubbing her arms, Inanna went outside. The western sky was a riot of bilious colours. There was a scent of rain in the air, a heaviness that presaged thunder. She knew that it could not be long before the matter of her lover and the prophet was resolved. No going back now. She felt sick, unsure of whether she had done the right thing going to the Archimage. She hadn't told him the entire truth about why she'd approached him. She hadn't mentioned the dreams that had been plaguing her, dreams of Resenence Jeopardy. She feared the prophet greatly now, not just because of what she felt he'd done to Implexion, but because of what he seemed to be doing to her. It was like a summoning, an insistent call. At night, when she awoke in the dark from feverish fantasies, she could hear his voice echoing in her room, a voice she had never heard in reality.

She must trust her instincts, the flexings of her belly, the beat of her blood. If she was at all responsible for what was to come, then so be it. She would survive.

A movement in the room behind her made her jump, but it was only Sleeve's attendant, Marmick. He was watching her from the shadows of the room.

'It's nearly midnight,' Inanna said, lamely. 'Why are you here again?' She feared something terrible had happened, something so bad she could not imagine it.

Marmick bobbed a respectful bow. 'Madam has not dressed for bed,' he said. 'Is there anything you require?'

Inanna shook her head. Her teeth were chattering. 'I only want the morning.' She smiled shakily. 'I doubt whether you can give that to me now.'

Marmick returned her smile. 'His Sacredness the Archimage asked me to look in on you,' he said. 'He too is finding it difficult to sleep.'

'Well, it is a strange night.'

'Indeed. So strange, in fact, that His Sacredness feels it is a night of particular significance.'

'Yes?' Inanna prompted.

'His Sacredness has decided it might be a good idea for you to accompany him to the old parade ground tonight, in order to witness certain events he feels sure will take place there.'

Inanna drew in her breath. Was something to happen so soon? 'I'm not sure I wish to become involved,' she said carefully. 'It could be dangerous.'

Marmick shrugged. 'Perhaps His Sacredness feels it would be safer should you remain close to him tonight.'

A moment of sheer panic cracked Inanna's habitual coolness. 'But I don't want to go!' she cried. 'I don't want to see!'

Marmick smiled blandly. 'Shall I fetch a wrap for you, madam?'

In the Old Gardens of Queen Lallow, Chasteless led Lucien to a small cottage among the trees where an automaton, designed to look like an old hermit, usually performed strange rituals within sight of anyone who passed the windows.

'So, you have found one of your own kind,' Lucien said jokingly when Chasteless told him what they would find within the cottage.

'No,' she said gravely. 'it is just a puppet.'

Lucien winced at his tactlessness.

Chasteless lifted the latch and opened the door, gesturing for Lucien to follow her inside. The cottage comprised only a single room, and the sparse furniture consisted of a table, cluttered with arcane paraphernalia, and a chair where the hermit automaton performed its functions. The automaton had been removed and lay upon the floor nearby; a sad wooden doll, writhing around, reaching for things that were no longer within its grasp.

Resenence Jeopardy sat in the chair, staring moodily at the table, drawing patterns in the dust with his fingers. He was unshaven, looked very tired, and his clothes were dusty. His hair, though longer than Lucien remembered it, appeared dry and faded. He was more beautiful than he'd ever been; a sad, somehow vulnerable figure sitting alone at the table. His face was that of a blameless boy, a face untouched by the ravages of experience. Another illusion? No. Lucien knew then that Resenence Jeopardy was intrinsically innocent; that was the danger of him. He did not look up immediately when Lucien entered the cottage.

Lucien felt faint. This could not be real. It was almost disappointing that he should finally come across Jeopardy so easily. It made him realise that had Jeopardy wanted it, the search could have continued for eternity.

'Lucien,' Jeopardy said and looked up. His eyes were a brilliant golden brown, the eyes of an angel. Lucien recoiled from the directness of his glance.

'Resenence,' he replied carefully. Jeopardy's raw attractiveness had kindled a wave of pure longing with him. He strove to suppress it. 'I can't say I ever thought this meeting would happen.'

'But it has,' Jeopardy said, and grinned. 'Do you know, seeing you standing there, it's as if the last four years have been but a single second. A moment ago, we were together in a cellar in Shanariah.'

'No, Res,' Lucien said, refusing to smile. 'That was indeed four years ago. You stole my employer's automaton. You betrayed me.'

'I did not steal her, I liberated her,' Jeopardy said. 'Look at her now, Lucien. Look at her.' Both of them observed Chasteless for a few moments. She turned away as if in embarrassment.

'I followed you to reclaim her,' Lucien said. 'You had no right to lure her away like that. Cartesian cared about her.'

'No living person can own another,' Jeopardy said coldly. 'It is an abomination. Chasteless is a woman; she thinks and feels. Your friend created her body, true, but she has developed a personality now, she is an individual.'

'But you cannot give her the help she needs to remain . . . healthy,' Lucien said. 'I've seen what's happened to her hands. Did you think about that when you induced her to run away with you?'

'Chasteless is aware of the hazards of being free,' Jeopardy replied. 'And we all hope that one day she'll find the help she needs. But it won't be at the hands of Cartesian Blink. Ask her, Lucien, ask her if she wants to return to an existence of mindless prostitution.'

Lucien sighed. 'I already know the answer to that.'

Jeopardy smiled. 'Anyway, you have not chased me back and forth across the land because of Chasteless,' he said bluntly. 'We both know it was a different obsession that pulled you to me.'

Lucien felt his face grow hot. 'You play with words,' he snapped. 'It was more a case of you pulling me after you!'

Jeopardy rolled his eyes. 'Oh, Lucien, Lucien, we are so entwined. We are one another, the same person.'

'That is nonsense. Don't try to get round me with clever words. They mean nothing.'

Jeopardy leaned forward. 'But it is the truth. I am a bizarre creature, Lucien. Only recently have I come to understand what I am. We have yearned for one another because we are just two parts of a sundered soul. The soul is big, so big. Perhaps it belongs to a fragmented god, and there may be good reason why it became fragmented. I don't know.'

Lucien interrupted Jeopardy's speech with a harsh laugh. 'Fragments of a god? What are you talking about? It was you who kept telling me there are no gods other than those we create ourselves.'

Jeopardy shrugged. 'But once they are created, they exist. Perhaps we invented ourselves.'

'This is too much!' Lucien cried in exasperation. 'I want to talk about why you have tormented me, why I feel the way I do. I want an exorcism, not more pointless games!'

Jeopardy's eyes had become glazed. He ignored Lucien's remarks. 'Some of my life seems clear to me, most of it is baffling and opaque.' He shook his head and sighed. 'Listen, there is a decision to be made tonight. I shall be making it very soon.' He directed a bare, appealing glance at Lucien. 'Whatever has happened in the past, I wanted you here with me tonight, Luce. I need you here.'

'We could have been together at any time if you'd allowed it.' Lucien snapped. 'My feelings mean nothing to you. I'm just a plaything to you.'

Jeopardy shook his head. 'No, no. We could not be together before this time. It would have changed things too much.'

Lucien slammed his fists on the table top. 'Oh, spare me all this mystical nonsense!' he cried 'Listen to me now. You are living in another world, Res. You tell other people to wake up all the time, but I think you need to open your own eyes first. I cannot express how I feel, standing here. You have haunted me from the moment I first met you. Haunted me, hurt me, plagued me . . . Seeking you became a quest, but all that exists now is the quest itself – the end has lost its meaning.'

Jeopardy laughed, but it sounded unconvincing. 'Lucien—'

'No, shut up! I haven't finished! Oh, you have talents, Res, I don't deny that. You can spin illusions of yourself in people's minds that don't exist in reality. Over the last few years, I've heard many tales about you. None of them sounded as if they were about the person I met in Mandru. Once, I wanted to tell you how I felt about you. Now, it seems an empty feeling. I love a man that looks like you, yes, but he does not exist. There is no possible conclusion to my search for him, just a fading away. Now I must face the shallow flimsiness of my dreams. I shall have to leave here and wonder where my life has gone.'

There was a brief silence. Then Jeopardy said, 'You are wrong, Lucien. You don't believe half of what you've just said.'

Lucien uttered an indignant snort. 'Stop playing, Res! Can't you see that face to face you have no hold over me? It's only when you're not there, when all I have is thoughts and desires, that your bewitchment waxes strong.'

'How I like to hear you trying to convince yourself,' Jeopardy said. 'You are so earnest, Lucien. Do you ever practise your precious Vibrancies now?'

'Do you?'

Jeopardy pulled a sour face. 'No. I want no more of Ixmar.'

'At Mandru, you worked yourself until it made you ill,' Lucien said. 'You were a perfectionist.'

'It was a role I played.'

'And what role are you playing now? What is the purpose of all this, Res? I don't think you really believe you're a prophet, or that you want to lead a spiritual revolution.'

'I might have changed more than you think.'

'I doubt it.' Lucien sighed and leaned against the table, his back to Jeopardy. He sensed Jeopardy's fingers reach out to touch him, he could feel the heat of his flesh, but the touch never came. He wanted to turn and ask Jeopardy to hold him. He needed that embrace now, the reassurance of it. In Jeopardy's arms, the past few years would mean nothing, could be

351

stripped away. Now, Lucien was mature enough to cope with him. In Mandru, he'd been too shy of rebuff, too eager to impress. Six years of tortured fantasising had embittered him and bruised him, but they had made him strong enough to take hold of the fiercest elements. In his dreams of Jeopardy, he had already imagined and lived through every possibility. Should he turn now? Should he? If he didn't, would Jeopardy make a move?

'There are people approaching,' Chasteless said, looking out of the window.

Jeopardy sighed, and Lucien felt the cold come back as his hand was drawn away. The moment was lost. 'Yes,' Jeopardy said, 'we must go to meet them.' He stood up. 'Lucien, will you do one more thing for me, one last thing?'

'I have never done anything for you,' Lucien said over his shoulder. 'so how can you ask me to do one thing more?'

Jeopardy ignored his comments. 'When we meet these people, say nothing. Whatever they might say, or I might say, remain silent. Can you give me your promise on that?'

Lucien shrugged. 'Why should I?'

'Because you will be entertained if you do. Because anything will happen, and your curiosity will not let you do anything to prevent that.'

'You are about to deceive these people in some way, I take it? Oh, very well.'

Jeopardy did not answer. He opened the door and went outside.

'Look!' Delilah raised a hand and pointed. Three people were coming towards them through the trees.

'It is the tregetour!' Cleo cried, grabbing hold of Lord Pliance's arm.

'That is not Resenence Jeopardy,' Trajan said.

'Are you sure?' Delilah asked.

'It is not him.'

The group advanced to meet the tregetour and his companions. Speckless bowed low as they halted before him. 'Greetings.' he said. 'You have come for the performance.'

'Can you take us to Jeopardy?' Delilah asked. In the dim gas light thrown up by the globes beneath the trees, it seemed to her that the tregetour's eyes were black, or very dark brown, not blue at all.

'I will take you to the parade ground,' the tregetour replied. 'Although you'd have found it yourselves in a few moments. The wall of the garden is just beyond this screen of beeches.'

He gestured for them to follow him, and after exchanging a few glances, they did so. Speckless's companions said not a word. One of them, a female, was completely veiled.

'We have travelled a long way to find the prophet,' Delilah said, hurrying to walk alongside the tregetour. 'Will we be able to speak to him personally?'

'It is a possibility,' Speckless replied. 'Why do you seek him?'

'It is a long story,' Delilah said, 'several long stories, as it happens. But, in short, the prophet intruded into our lives, although three of us have never met him before. We were compelled to find him. The big man is a Jeopardite. Do you know him? His name is Trajan Sacripent. He was seeking Jeopardy because he needed to be rid of a curse, but someone else has dispelled it for him. Now, he simply wants to know why Jeopardy abandoned him to his curse, for that is what happened.'

352

'You are a talkative girl,' said Speckless.

'Am I? You did ask me a question, and I was attempting to answer it as briefly as possible.'

The tregetour laughed. 'Here is the wall of the garden, and the door stands open. Pass through, my dear.'

Beyond the door lay the parade ground, a vast expanse of enormous marble tiles, most of them now cracked with age and mottled with lichen. It was surrounded completely by a tall colonnade, though many of the columns had broken. A wide road on the south side hugged the boundary of the gardens, leading back towards the city. This was the road upon which the soldiers would have marched in the days when the parade ground had had a military purpose. The ground was large enough to accommodate many thousands of people. In the centre was a huge plinth supporting the crumbling yet still impressive statue of a long-dead Glebish king: Meemon the Punctilious. A walkway round the upper edge of the plinth provided an area where army commanders had inspected their troops from above. The parade ground was full of a silent, shadowy horde who were milling around the plinth.

Lucien had expected Jeopardy to march forward and leap up onto the plinth, thus revealing who he was. However, he was still talking to the young girl they had met. Lucien felt the prickle of scrutiny and glanced aside to see that the girl's companions were watching him curiously. He turned away. Whatever Jeopardy was planning, he would let him get on with it.

'Is that where the prophet will appear?' Delilah asked the tregetour, pointing at the plinth.

'I would think so, wouldn't you?' Speckless replied. He turned to his male companion. 'What do you suppose, Lucien? Is that where Jeopardy will appear?'

'I am waiting for him to do so,' the young man said abruptly. Delilah was quite confused by the tone of his voice. He did not seem eager to see the prophet, yet must obviously be a Jeopardite himself.

'Then wait we all must,' Speckless declared.

Some distance from the tregetour, Cleo was standing close to the vampire, strangely comforted by his proximity, probably because she looked upon him as a predator who could perhaps be used in defence.

Lord Pliance sighed. 'So much flesh,' he said, shaking his head. 'And yet my appetite is far from stimulated. These followers of Jeopardy are an unpalatable bunch.'

'For that, I am grateful,' Cleo hissed. She peered at the crowd. There was something peculiar about them that she couldn't quite define. Suddenly, she gasped and grabbed Lord Pliance's arm.

'What is it?' he asked, alarmed.

'My husband!' Cleo groaned, ducking down. She thought she had glimpsed Wakelate's cadaverous, stooping shape a short distance ahead, his mournful face looking this way and that as if searching for someone.

Lord Pliance patted her hand. 'That is impossible, my dear. Why would he be here?'

'I saw him!' Cleo insisted. 'By Ixmar, he will kill me!'

The vampire attempted to reassure her, but Cleo broke away from his protective arm. She was considering running back into the gardens. Was it possible Wakelate had trailed her from Scaraby?

'See reason, Mistress Sinister,' said Lord Pliance severely. 'The sky holds a strange lour this evening. There is a flavour to the air that I feel can affect our perceptions. Look at the western horizon; the sun has long sunk yet the sky has a livid red tinge about it. The clouds are like black scars across the heavens.'

Cleo was in no mood to listen to the vampire's poetic descriptions. She scanned the crowd anxiously, hoping Lord Pliance was capable of leaping to her defence should her suspicions concerning Wakelate prove correct. The crowd was moving in somnolent slowness around her, their massed voices a low, sleepy murmur. Then, a small shape emerged from the shadowy mob. Cleo uttered a low-pitched oath, and shook Lord Pliance's arm. 'Look!' she hissed, pointing ahead.

'At what?' Lord Pliance asked politely.

'The child!' Cleo breathed. 'It is the child.'

In front of her, as real and solid as a person could be, stood Inky. He was gazing at her warily, the fingers of one hand stuffed into his mouth. Cleo took a step forward.

'Inky?'

The boy's face bloomed into a grin of recognition. Cleo swooped forward and enfolded the child in her arms. He was warm and tangible against her body; he smelled of coconut. 'Combs and beetles,' he announced. 'For tea!'

Cleo squeezed his small body. Wakelate had obviously not killed the boy after all; he must have given him a potion that mimicked the symptoms of death. The Salamancas had been fooled and she had abandoned her home for nothing! Now, Wakelate had brought Inky with him, to come and find her. She hoped he would forgive her, that both of them would forgive her.

Inky giggled in her ear and then squirmed away from her. 'Don't go!' Cleo called, standing up.

'Mistress Sinister,' called Lord Pliance. 'There is something greatly amiss. I see it now . . .'

Cleo ignored him. She was watching Inky, who had begun to push into the crowd ahead of him. She took a few steps towards him.

'Mistress Sinister,' repeated the vampire, more earnestly. 'My instincts tell me you should leave this place!'

Ahead of her, Inky paused and looked back. He held out a small, white hand, which Cleo lunged for. She heard Lord Pliance call her name again, shout out a garbled sentence, and then the crowd swallowed her up.

Delilah was still standing beside the tregetour and his companion, Trajan a short distance behind. 'We seem to be waiting a long time for Resenence Jeopardy to show himself,' she said.

Speckless glanced down at her. 'Hmm? Perhaps the prophet is waiting for exactly the right moment, and who are we to guess when that may be?'

Delilah sighed. 'These people wandering about are all quite strange.' She frowned. 'In fact, the more I think about it, they do not resemble a crowd at all, but simply a horde of individuals who happen to be occupying the same space.'

'I might be wrong, but I think you have just defined the word crowd,' the tregetour said quizzically.

'Look at them, though,' Delilah argued. 'Some of them are wearing bedroom slippers and have no coats. Others are dressed up as if to go to church.' She pointed. 'That woman is wearing only a dressing gown. She seems to be sleep-walking.'

The tregetour made an elegant gesture with one hand. 'Perhaps all are summoned to hear the prophet against their will.'

Delilah shook her head. 'No, it is something different.' She turned round and said, 'Trajan,' but the tregetour suddenly grabbed her arm. Delilah caught a brief glimpse of Trajan peering round the crowd, frowning, before Speckless insisted on directing her attention elsewhere. 'Look,' he said. 'Isn't that a male shape manifesting against the statue?'

Delilah peered above the shadowy heads of the milling crowd. The plinth appeared to be lit from beneath and threw a harsh radiance onto the person now leaning on the rail that circled the rim; he appeared to be waiting to be noticed.

'Yes,' Delilah said excitedly. 'It must be him!'

Throwing a quick glance back at Trajan, she began to push her way forward through the jostling bodies. At last! She would see the face of Resenence Jeopardy. She would look into his eyes, and they would be open for her. Something momentous would happen; the reason for her journey, her commitment to the idea of an unknown man, would be revealed to her.

'Res!' Lucien whispered hoarsely. 'What is going on? Who *is* that?' The figure on the plinth looked just like Jeopardy. Was it possible he looked *more* like Jeopardy than the person standing beside him? He looked back at the other man gazing down on the crowd. The unshaven face smiled slightly, long rags of hair fell down over his chest. Beside Lucien, Speckless the Tregetour was clean-shaven and neat, his hair combed, his clothes new and fragrant. He raised a finger to his lips and shook his head at Lucien's urgent questions.

Lucien was beginning to feel uneasy. The night had become close, as if a storm was creeping up from the sea. A sick, livid light gleamed on the western horizon. A breath of wind, cold as winter, sliced across the parade ground. Clouds massed up from the south.

The figure on the plinth leaned forward in a predatory manner. 'Friends!' he cried; around him, a dozen gas globes illuminated his face from beneath. Lucien peered intently ahead; there could be no mistake, the man on the plinth was Resenence Jeopardy. Those hands gripping the rail had once touched him intimately. That expression of amused cynicism was so familiar. It *was* Jeopardy. Lucien grabbed the arm of the man beside him. 'Res!' Speckless the Tregetour looked like a younger, less world-weary version of the man on the plinth. Yet he too was undeniably Resenence Jeopardy.

'Quiet, Lucien! he said. 'Pay attention.'

The crowd had fallen to silence, shuffling forward in a dense pack to surround the plinth in an impenetrable sea of flesh.

'Is this an illusion?' Lucien hissed. 'You have a twin? A double? Which is the real you? In the cottage, you were unkempt, tired. Now—'

'Lucien, you renege on your promise! Didn't I ask you not to bombard me with questions?'

'Only in front of those other people,' Lucien persisted, 'and they have gone now. I no longer have to keep silent.'

'Then I shall.'

Lucien looked round to try and find Chasteless, but she too seemed to have been engulfed by the crowd. People were still surging silently past

Lucien and the tregetour. Lucien was sure they were nothing like the usual curious onlookers who gathered around Jeopardy. His senses felt unreliable, as if he'd been chewing sleepbane. It was as if he was being engulfed within an amorphous mass of shadowy clouds.

'Where have these people come from?' he murmured, and shuddered. Speckless the Tregetour said nothing.

A line of darkness was advancing up the road from the city, spreading out to surround the parade ground as it reached the colonnade. At its head rode a company of Ixmarite marshals on horseback, led by Wilfish Implexion. They were followed by the entire Church militia resident in Gallimaufry at the time, augmented in numbers by members of the king's domestic guard.

Wilfish Implexion reined in his horse. His heart was beating fast; the air seemed hard to breathe, thick and rank upon the chest. He chewed a peppermint comfit to calm his stomach. He had never felt this nervous at the prospect of cornering Jeopardy before. Did these feelings of apprehension signify that, this time, his efforts would succeed? The previous night, he had dreamed of spitting Jeopardy on a sword; he had felt the flesh part beneath his blade. He had seen the blood.

Up ahead, the illumination around the plinth held the figure of a man in a web of radiance. From this distance, Implexion could not discern details, but by the churning of his guts, he knew the figure was Jeopardy.

One of the marshals urged his horse over to where Implexion's large, disciplined mount stood thoughtfully chewing its bit in the shadow of a massive, half-fallen column. 'He's pulled a fair crowd tonight, I'll give him that,' said the marshal. 'Biggest I've seen yet.'

'They all look bewitched,' Implexion said coldly. 'Fools!'

The marshal appeared sceptical. 'They are just curious,' he said, observing the ecclesiarch with an enquiring expression on his face. People had said for a long time that there was more to Implexion's hatred for the Jeopardites than met the eye. 'The people of Gallimaufry would never join Jeopardy's cult. They've probably got wind of our plans and hope to see a bit of action.' He paused and then added bluntly,' 'I have informed the men to take care when the order comes. We don't want unnecessary casualties.'

Implexion did not reply. His skin was crawling, as if a faint net of lightning were prickling from pore to pore. To him, anyone who gave Jeopardy a sympathetic ear was irretrievably tainted. The crowd before him filled him with disgust.

Perpetuis Sleeve and Inanna Grisaille sat in a covered carriage at the edge of the parade ground, screened from the militia's eyes by a line of elderly yew trees. Inanna stared at her hands, chewing the inside of her cheek nervously. Sleeve parted the carriage window-curtain with a gloved hand, peering out. Inanna made a small sound of protest.

'Madam?'

'I don't want to see,' she said, reaching up to rub her forehead. It was as if the world were about to be turned inside out. She was furious with Sleeve for forcing her to accompany him here. 'I feel strange. I don't want to be here. I've done what I can for you, given you information. Why have you forced this hideous spectacle on me?'

'Haven't you the slightest curiosity about the man your lover is obsessed with?' Sleeve noted how her face winced at his words.

'I have no lover,' she answered in a dull voice. 'And no curiosity. Obsessions can be contagious.'

'Superstition,' Sleeve said with a smile. 'You have already confronted the worst of your fears.' He leaned closer to the closed window. 'There is someone on the plinth of Meemon's statue. Is that the prophet, I wonder?'

Lucien watched with a rising sense of disorientation as the man on the plinth drew himself upright and glanced towards the edge of the parade ground. He seemed to watch something there for a few moments and then began to speak.

'Ah, my long-suffering friends,' he said. 'Are you waiting for a cataclysm?'

A murmur started up; not of consternation or excitement, but a flat, emotionless tide of sound: a reflex.

Jeopardy began to pace around the statue. 'Well,' he cried, 'it is with you now! Feel it! For you, the age of Ixmar is dead! You are free!'

The murmuring flowed softly across the parade ground.

'No more shall you swing from gibbets along the road!' Jeopardy shouted. 'No more shall your spirits be chained. No more shall Ixmar place his foot against the throats of your inner gods and goddesses. He must accept his defeat. The age of your gods has come, spawned from your free hearts. Call them from within you. People the air with their shimmering forms.'

Voices began to rise, in harmony with the rising howl of the wind. Lucien felt a few droplets of icy rain touch his cheek.

At the front of the crowd, Delilah's spirit rose within her. It seemed as if the prophet spoke to her alone. His eyes were as fierce as the image she had conjured of him, his face as beautiful as that of the drowned man beneath the mill pool. This must signify the beginning of her life. After hearing him speak, a hundred new shining paths would open up before her feet. Standing there, in a rain she could not feel, Delilah kept telling herself the search for Jeopardy had been worth the effort.

Cleo held Inky's shoulders firmly against her thighs. She would not let him go again. She knew now that he was the image of his father; radiant. The man pacing the rim of the plinth above her seemed to hold her soul in his eyes. From the moment she'd first seen him, the rest of the world had dimmed in Cleo's mind. She knew she would have to speak to him, have to experience his full attention, or die in the attempt. She wanted to tell him how since she'd cared for his son, she'd been driven to seek him out. She wanted to tell him she would do whatever he asked, knowing he would ask nothing of her. She wanted to feel his hands upon her brow, as Trajan had. He was so full of vitality and power, he seemed barely human, yet his eyes shone with human compassion. He would make love like a god, yet with the sweat and flesh of a man. Salt rain ran down Cleo's face. She wept the elements. Then she noticed Dauntless Javelot standing only a few feet away from her.

Wilfish Implexion lifted his arm in the signal to advance. Zigzags of light flickered across his vision; his head ached. He felt disassociated from reality, as if he'd just awoken from a deep sleep. Hooves clopped upon stone; an inexorable tide seethed in towards the crowd.

This time, Implexion thought, you will not get away. How bravely you bawl your audacious heresy. It will be short-lived, prophet! I will see you humbled. I will see you weep in weakness and fear. I will have you at my feet!

'Look!' Perpetuis Sleeve said. He reached out and pulled Inanna towards the carriage window. 'The crowd, they glow! I knew I was right to come. Something strange is happening. Something very strange.'

Inanna squirmed against the glass. She tried to close her eyes, but it was as if some inner, primitive part of her desired to look outside. She saw a boiling mass of light and activity upon the parade ground. She saw the silhouettes of the mounted militia, advancing. On the plinth, there was a pulsing core of brightness. She felt too cold, as if her life-force were being drained away. This was terrible.

'Let me go,' she croaked.

Sleeve opened the door to the carriage.

A low boom of distant thunder rolled across the sky. Cleo staggered on her feet, realising dimly that the world was no longer steady beneath her.

'Daunt!' she said.

The paladin turned his head towards her. He looked pale and dazed.

'We thought you were dead!' Cleo exclaimed. 'By Ix . . . oh, Daunt, we left you for dead!' She couldn't bear to think of him regaining consciousness alone, abandoned beneath a hasty cairn of twigs and leaves. She clutched Inky's shoulders with nerveless fingers, causing the boy to protest in pain.

Dauntless shook his head. It looked as if he was trying to speak, but could make no sound. He coughed, and a spatter of black dirt sprayed from his mouth.

Cleo felt her stomach turn. 'Daunt!'

The paladin coughed again. 'Cleo, leave this place,' he managed to croak in a soil-laden voice. 'The living are misplaced here.'

I am hallucinating, Cleo thought, the air is strange. With a strangled whine of anxiety, she pulled Inky against her more firmly. 'Where is my husband?' she said aloud to the busy air.

'Poisoner's wife,' said a whispery voice behind her. Cleo wheeled round to see the drooping figure of a woman in white standing there. The woman's lips were blue, her face parchment pale, her eye sockets bruised and swollen. Lina Salamanca.

It was then Cleo realised she was surrounded by a crowd of the dead, but still she did not let go of the child.

At the edge of the parade ground, Inanna Grisaille clung desperately to the ragged trunk of a yew tree, her gown already soaked by rain. Her face was pressed painfully against the rough bark. Beside her, Perpetuis Sleeve was standing upon a tapestried stool which his guards had produced from the back of the carriage. He had a good view of the proceedings. He was humming a tune to himself, and had removed his hat in order to make best use of a pair of spyglasses he had brought with him.

'It is the first time I have seen this Jeopardy,' he said, in awe. 'What a handsome fellow! I can see the attraction. A pity we have to sacrifice him to Implexion's obsession. Would you care to take a look, madam?' He offered Inanna the spyglasses, but she only moaned and pressed her face into the yew.

'No, I can see only too well.'

Sleeve sighed. 'I envy you your younger eyes. I wonder if Wilf will spit the prophet straightaway?' He sniffed. 'The night is young. Who knows, the prophet might trounce our friend and disappear again.'

'He won't.' Inanna murmured into the tree. She didn't want to look, but neither could she bear not to. She peered round the yew. *Oh Jeopardy, you are as lovely as a boy saint. I should hate you, but I can't. That is why I didn't want to come here. I was afraid I couldn't bear to watch you die, and I was right. I cannot watch either of you die.*

'What was that you said?' Sleeve enquired. 'Talk of death, is it? Ah, dear lady, you must overcome your squeamishness. This night is your triumph. Toast it with laughter and strength.' He grinned at her. 'Will you ask me for the prophet's head later? That would be amusing!'

Wilfish Implexion rode through the shuffling, whispering crowd which parted before his horse like mist dispelled by a strong breeze. The people looked insubstantial, plagued as he was by flickering vision. Pain hammered his head, and it was only by force of will he remained in his saddle. He was convinced that Jeopardy himself had caused the pain.

'Sorcerer, heretic,' he muttered under his breath. 'Fling your hexes at me! It will not change the outcome.'

Faces peered up at him as he rode by. Many wore ropes round their necks, as if to mock his holy function as executioner. Imp-faced children pulled jeering faces at him from behind the bodies of adults. The mage's speck was painted onto every small forehead; again, a mockery. Implexion's lips pulled back into a snarl. Soon, they would regret their arrogance.

The silent horde took no notice of the militia, other than to flow obediently in the direction they were herded, which was towards the plinth. Their attention could not be turned from Jeopardy. Their bizarrely passive behaviour suited Implexion well. It meant his men would not be distracted by people fighting or fleeing as Jeopardy was arrested. He sneered down at the apparently mindless gathering. Fools! How could they be so blind? Was it possible so many people could be hypnotised all at once by one man?

He could not hear Jeopardy's speech himself. The words were distorted and fragmented by the sour-smelling wind that hurried across the parade ground, driving a mass of boiling cloud across the sky.

Delilah was standing so close to Jeopardy, he could have reached down and touched her. Her eyes had filled up with water, and she had to blink continually in order to see the prophet clearly. She felt unsteady on her feet, as if the ground were flexing beneath her. It was becoming difficult to concentrate on what Jeopardy was saying. Sometimes, he seemed to be speaking in a foreign language. Then he looked right at her, and it was as if the two of them were suddenly alone in an empty, timeless void. All other sound but his voice died away.

'I came to a decision tonight,' he said.

'What decision?' she asked him. She knew the question was hers alone to ask.

Jeopardy shook his head. 'No words,' he said. 'But watch with me.'

And then the image of the drowned man was in her head, his motionless, sightless face looming towards her. The force of his physical beauty broke over her like a wave. He was inside her mind, and ideas and images were coming to her thick and fast.

I understand now, she thought.

A cold wind whipped her hair across her face. As suddenly as the experience had begun, it ended. The prophet's presence had fled from her mind. But he had left much behind him. As reality condensed around her, the thoughts he had planted within her slid away to a deep and hidden part of her mind.

Delilah felt dizzy, and could no longer focus on the man standing on the plinth. She felt it was someone else now, someone who wasn't Jeopardy at all. She became aware of the wind, the rain, the shuffling crowd. She was being pushed backwards, away from the plinth. Panic began to burn within her. Where was Trajan? Where were Cleo and Lord Pliance?

She saw a brief flash of vivid pinky-red through the dark, shadowy press of bodies. Instinctively, she moved towards it, clawing her way through dusty black coats and musty robes. 'Let me through!'

A hand grabbed her arm. Delilah struck out in panic and a voice said, 'Go back!' A face loomed towards her and Delilah nearly retched in terror when she recognised the features of Grackle Ratheripe, a Grackle who was without life, pallid and damp, wormy-looking. Delilah yelped in horror and renewed her attack on the obstructive crowd. Hands reached for her with sluggish insistence, faces loomed towards her and she recognised the dissolving features of friends from Samberdell, the priest, the witches, her mother.

'No!' Tears of terror and despair ran down Delilah's face. Everyone towered over her; she felt so small. Perhaps she could crawl her way out of the crowd, but to drop to the ground seemed unthinkable. She would only get trampled.

No one here is alive! she thought.

Was this what Jeopardy had lured her to? Was her life to be sucked from her by the hungry dead? What had happened to her companions? Had they been engulfed? Delilah felt her only hope was to reach the wall and the sanctuary of the Old Gardens beyond. She saw the flash of vivid colour again, and a familiar voice called, 'Run to me, Delilah! Run to me!

Small, childlike hands appeared in front of her, and a face poked through the jostling crowd to hang in the air, framed by pinky-red hair.

'Wispish!' Delilah cried.

'Yes, it's me.' Wispish's hands took hold of Delilah's own and pulled her forward. At her touch, warmth flowed back into Delilah's body. She hadn't realised how chilled she'd been.

'Are you dead?' Delilah asked, hanging back, even though the warmth of those hands seemed evidence enough that she was alive.

Wispish Ploverpage shook her head. 'Give some credit where it's due!' she exclaimed, and grinned. 'Half of Covendale is here, though. Delilah, what have you mixed yourself up in?'

'How did you get here?' Delilah demanded. 'Trajan thought you were dead. He saw you jump into the fire.' Wispish was dragging her forward, and Delilah was still not convinced she should allow that.

'Hush now, Lilah!' Wispish said grimly. 'Don't be afraid. I'm no ghoul, which is more than can be said for this lot! Later, I shall explain what happened to us. For now, we have more important matters than gossiping to attend to. I don't know what's afoot, but I think we'll be safer out of it.'

Wispish's insistent pushing and shoving brought them quickly to the edge of the crowd where they ran smack up against the line of slowly advancing Ixmarites. 'Let us through!' Wispish yelled. 'We are good folk out for a stroll, and find ourselves in the middle of this madness. The false prophet is a devil!'

360

To Delilah, the tall unsmiling line of men in black seemed inhuman, Wispish a mere scrap of living colour against them. They all carried long poles, and short swords hung at their hips, visible beneath their cloaks which were thrown back over their shoulders. It seemed inconceivable they would pay attention to Wispish's demands.

'Would you imprison honest women with this tainted bunch?' Wispish demanded, flinging back her hair.

One of the men stuck out a large, hard hand and pulled her through the line, Delilah following because she was hanging onto Wispish's arm.

'Make yourself scarce,' he said gruffly. 'But hurry.'

'We have no intention of lingering,' Wispish called. 'Come, Delilah, Anvil is waiting for me in the Old Gardens.'

And then the earth shook.

Cleo Sinister fell to her knees and pressed her face against Inky's body. 'I must be dreaming,' she thought. 'Please let me be dreaming.' Convulsively, her fingers gripped the child's clothes. She felt him put his small hands on her head.

'Cleo,' he said.

Cleo would not look up, even though she sensed the command in the child's voice.

'My mother died in a bed of grief,' he said. 'Your husband took his own life after you left.'

'No, don't tell me!' Cleo cried.

'But it is true,' Inky said. His voice was a small node of calm in the maelstrom of lumbering bodies and wind-lashed rain.

Cleo raised her head. She dared look at nothing but the child. 'And you?' she said.

Inky cupped her chin with his hands. 'I am following my father,' he said in a weirdly adult voice. 'Don't think of me as dead, but changed. Thank you for loving me, Cleo. I'll not forget you. I know you have come here to be part of something, and you were to be an important part, but my father has changed his mind about it. Still, you have not found him for nothing. You too are changed.'

'How?' Cleo asked. 'What will happen to me now?'

The child shrugged. 'You will find your way. You will find wonders in the world, because you create them. Now, you must go. There is no point in your remaining here. It is over.'

'What's over?' Cleo demanded. 'Inky, take me to your father. I have to meet him.'

Inky shook his head. 'No. It is no longer necessary for you.' He leaned forward and kissed her face. 'Goodbye, Cleo. Take care.'

'Don't leave me!' Cleo cried, reaching for the boy's arms. 'Not now!'

Inky shook his head. His hands dropped from her face and, even as she watched, he seemed to recede in her sight, as if he was being drawn down a long tunnel. As he faded, the ground beneath Cleo's feet began to shake.

'But what was the purpose?' Cleo yelled, staggering to remain upright. 'What was the thing I was supposed to be part of?' Thunder growled across the sky.

'A changing time.' Inky's mouth had not moved, but the voice was his. 'But it has come, regardless . . .' He had gone.

Cleo gave herself up miserably to the churning movement beneath her

361

and slumped to the ground. She could hear raindrops hammering against the slabs and felt their cold touch upon her back. She could smell damp grass. She wanted to weep, but could not summon the tears. Her mind, her heart, felt empty.

Around her, everything was breaking up into chaos as the ground heaved and the elements clashed. She looked up, searching for the man whose image had lured her away from home, but she could no longer see the man on the plinth. All was light and shadow and confusion. Insubstantial shapes reeled about her, scraps of rag upon the wind. 'Jeopardy!' she called, but her voice was blown away upon the wind.

The plinth was just ahead of Implexion now. Signalling to his immediate guard who promptly formed a circle of protection round his horse, Implexion dismounted and stared up at the man silhouetted against the statue of Meemon the Punctilious. He wanted to savour this moment before he made the arrest. In his mind, he was unsure whether he'd kill Jeopardy immediately or take him into custody for later execution. It was entrancing to have such a choice. Implexion noticed a couple of the marshals watching him with studied expressions. He coughed, dabbed his closed fist against his mouth and then briskly climbed the steps up the side of the plinth. Several Ixmarites followed behind.

Jeopardy seemed oblivious of Implexion's approach. He continued to rant at the crowd, although his words were nothing but a meaningless gibberish. Smugly Implexion realised the man was completely insane. He was no real threat to Ixmarity, never had been.

'Resenence Jeopardy!' Implexion cried into the wind. 'I arrest you in the name of Ixmar! Resist, and you risk injury.'

Finally, Jeopardy paused in his exhortation, his hands still held high, but he did not look at the ecclesiarch. 'On what charge?' he asked softly, his words strangely penetrating the noisy air.

'Absconding from an Ixmaritian post, heresy, public nuisance,' Implexion replied. 'I'm sure we can think of more.'

Jeopardy nodded and lowered his arms, turned round. Implexion could not stop himself from taking a step backwards. His hand shot to his sword pommel.

'I'm not going to attack you,' Jeopardy said in a clear, even voice. 'You are part of this.'

'Of what?' Implexion snapped. 'A gathering of imbeciles? Is *this* your great following, prophet?'

Jeopardy smiled gently. 'No, my dear ecclesiarch, this is *your* following. I summoned them for you.'

'What do you mean?'

'Look for yourself,' Jeopardy said, gesturing at the crowd. 'All these souls are attached to you. They should be. You are responsible for most of their deaths.' With these words, Jeopardy's face twisted into a savage leer, his eyes glowed silver. 'Every one of them carries your mark, Wilfish Implexion, the mark of death! My children are among them!'

Implexion resisted turning his head to examine the crowd, although his flesh had chilled. 'Jeopardy,' he said in a low voice. 'You are dead.' he drew his sword.

Jeopardy laughed. 'So, you intend to kill me too! You are a fool if you think that will help you. I am more than just a man. You cannot kill me.

You can only release me, as you released my children.'

Implexion heard a high-pitched giggle behind him. He would not take his eyes from Jeopardy's gaze. Small hands pawed at his trousers. He glanced down. A gang of children, each face malevolently intelligent. Their eyes shone with animal greed. Implexion froze. The children looked at one another and then silently joined hands in a circle round the ecclesiarch.

'Sorcery!' Implexion gasped. 'You are damned, prophet!' He tried to turn and call for assistance, but his muscles had frozen.

Jeopardy shook his head, folded his arms. 'Me, damned? No! You chose the wrong path, Wilfish. You could have been with me, which we both know is what you truly desired.'

'Never!' The pain in Implexion's head had become unendurable as the children circled round him. He could barely see. The earth felt as if it was churning beneath his feet.

Jeopardy shook his head again. 'Perhaps we were both wrong. I have no desire to become like you, none at all, and that is what could happen. It could happen so very easily. Therefore, I shall have to end what I've become.' He held out his arms to the ecclesiarch. 'Come and embrace me, brother, before the ending. It is time for us both to leave the stage.'

'Get back!' Implexion shrieked. 'Don't come near me! Don't!' The metal gleam of his sword seemed a feeble, fragile thing before the power in Jeopardy's eyes. The prophet threw back his head and screamed, a ringing cry that eclipsed all other sound, before throwing himself forward in a veil of billowing shadow. Implexion was engulfed in smoking air. The children danced, singing a nursery tune. Overhead, thunder growled, and the sound of it seemed to fill the world. The earth shrieked in response.

Watching Jeopardy standing up there on the plinth, yelling nonsense at the crowd, did not feel real to Lucien. All he could think of was the body he'd watched so many times in the exercise court at the House of Mandru, how it had flexed and turned before him, conjuring the first thorns of desire in his heart. It was almost impossible to believe he was now watching the same person. He felt that this uncanny night would never end, that he'd be compelled to stand there, spellbound by Jeopardy's voice, for the rest of his life. Even death would lend him no respite. He would stand there until he rotted, until his bones crumbled away, and still the dust of him would blow around the parade ground, enslaved by Jeopardy's will. Lucien had no energy to fight these thoughts. He felt incredibly tired, as if he hadn't slept once on the long, meandering journey from Shanariah.

Then the Ixmarites mounted the plinth, and Lucien knew there would be an ending. Of course. How could there not be? He recognised Implexion immediately, even from this distance, and the sight of him was like a sharp slap across the face. For a few moments, he was unable to breathe. What would Jeopardy do now? Would he defend himself, or allow Implexion to take him? Who *was* that standing on the plinth?

Lucien glanced around quickly, suddenly frightened, but Speckless the Tregetour, whoever or whatever he was, had vanished. Lucien also saw that he was no longer standing in the middle of a crowd. Behind him a sombre line of Ixmarite infantry was slowly marching his way. Self-preservation welled up within him. He did not want to suffer the same fate that was in store for Jeopardy's followers. His body became taut with the reckless desire to flee, which he knew he must control. He must think of a strategy.

But even before he had half formulated a suitable plan, he found himself stumbling forwards, towards the plinth.

'No!' Lucien screamed, in his head. 'I will not! I deny you!' Out loud he growled the name of his personal god, in the hag's croak of protection. 'Paradouze! Paradouze!'

In an instant, he found himself lying on his stomach on the smooth, ancient flags of the parade ground, only to be thrown onto his back moments later. Was this Jeopardy's doing, or the power of Paradouze's name uttered in desperation? Then he realized the ground itself was shaking; a low and angry groaning emanated from the earth. Lucien struggled onto hands and knees, noticing that behind him the line of Ixmarites had fallen into disarray. Now was his opportunity for escape, perhaps the only one. He lunged forwards, only to find he couldn't move. Someone had grabbed hold of his coat from behind. Snarling, Lucien wheeled round to strike out at whatever, or whoever, held him.

Lucien, don't!' A small figure shied away, hands up to its face. He saw it was Chasteless.

'Where did you go?' Lucien hissed and roughly grabbed her arm.

'I have been here all the time,' she said, shaking herself loose from his hold. 'Lucien, something terrible has happened.'

'I can see that,' Lucien said. 'I won't be part of it.' He glanced anxiously at the Ixmarites. 'I'm leaving while I still can.'

'I want to come with with you,' Chasteless said.

'And abandon your beloved prophet?'

'He is *your* beloved, not mine!' Chasteless replied sharply. 'Lucien, he has made his decision. Tonight, the path forked for him. He could either fulfil his ultimate potential or deny it. I think he chose the latter.' She looked at him bleakly. 'Lucien, I don't belong with the dead. I really don't. Why did he bring me here? Please, I want to come with you.'

Lucien couldn't help smiling. 'Then come,' he replied, and held out his hand.

Together they pushed their way through the floundering Ixmarites and ran towards the gates of the gardens, stumbling and reeling as the ground churned beneath their feet. A great crack opened in front of them Lucien leapt over it, Chasteless following less nimbly. She bumped against him, a heavy, solid mass. Eventually, after what seemed an endless nightmare of running on the spot, they threw themselves through the gates of the Old Gardens. Chasteless was propelled forward to land on her knees on the grass. Lucien turned round, arms flailing to keep himself upright. He looked back through the gates.

The parade ground was breaking up, great slabs cracking open. The misty black shapes of the crowd seemed to be swirling round like ink in water. Lucien watched in horror. 'They will all die!' he cried. 'The ground will swallow them. They are his followers. How could he let this happen?'

Chasteless lurched towards him, throwing herself heavily against his side. 'No, Lucien, they are already dead.'

'What? No!'

'It is true. There are no Gallimaufrians there, other than the militia. There are no Jeopardites. He sent them away. They are long gone. Those people out there are Implexion's victims, all of them.'

'But . . . but how?' Lucien's hands clutched his face. He felt sick.

'I don't know how,' Chasteless said quickly. 'He summoned them, that is all. It is his grand finale. His finish.'

Lucien stared at Chasteless in disbelief. 'What is he doing?' he murmured.

'Ending it,' she replied. 'It could go only one of two ways, and this is the way he has chosen.'

Lucien frowned. 'Then I must go to him,' he said slowly. 'He said he needed me.'

'No!' Chasteless cried, wrapping her strong arms round his body. 'Lucien, you mustn't! He has made his choice, or you made it for him. Don't you understand? Back there in the cottage, *you* had the power! He was yours for the taking. You could have decided the future, but you wouldn't let it happen. Now, he feels he has failed. Your part is over.'

Lucien uttered an anguished howl and made to throw himself through the gates, but before he could do so, a monstrous ripping sound filled the night as the plinth and the statue it supported cracked in half. A whirlwind of dust and debris boiled across the parade ground, tearing the crowd, who now seemed no more than insubstantial wisps of smoke, into tattered shreds. Through this maelstrom, Lucien saw a bright flash of metal as Implexion lunged forward to attack. Then, Jeopardy's shape seemed to expand, as if his clothes had transformed into enormous wings. An immense howl filled the sky that was half human shout and half elemental scream.

As Lucien watched in transfixed agony, the looming form that had been Resenence Jeopardy swooped down onto the ecclesiarch and enfolded him in a terminal embrace. Horses began to shriek in terror as the massive columns round the edge of the parade ground shook and fell. Dust rose high into the air as the remains of the plinth exploded. Jeopardy and Implexion disappeared, swallowed by the disintegrating rock. And then the rain came down like spears.

Inanna could only watch in helpless revulsion as her former lover mounted the plinth to confront the prophet. Even from the safe distance of the yew grove, she could see the confusion, madness – yes, and fear – on Implexion's face. Half of her wanted to run to his side and prevent whatever dreadful calamity was about to occur. The other half wanted to flee the parade ground and never look back. She felt she had the power to run across the sea in her longing to escape. Jeopardy was holding out his arms to Implexion now; Inanna's heart seemed to contract in her chest. The ecclesiarch's face was a mask of agony, an agony of both need and denial. Inanna knew in her bones that Implexion was about to die, and also that death would be no release for him. 'How helpless we are,' she thought, 'slaves to our senseless drives. But even slaves can find the courage to break free.'

The earth was shaking, and the great, ancient slabs of the parade ground were breaking up like chalk. Angry rain lashed down, and the yew trees groaned from the depth of their roots. Perpetuis Sleeve had been dislodged from his tapestried stool. He slipped his spyglasses back into his coat pocket and grabbed hold of Inanna's arm. 'I think we should step back into the road,' he said. 'The trees might fall. We've seen enough.' He did not seem overly concerned, even though a fearful soul might believe the world was about to end.

She let him lead her. 'Are you afraid?' she asked him.

'No. I feel quite elated actually. Why, are you afraid?'

She shook her head. 'Not that.'

Above them, the sky seemed to open up like a wound, and its gushing ichor was a mighty, elemental scream. Was that thunder?

No. The sword had struck home. At last.

XXV

CAROUSEL

Delilah lay on her back in the rubble. There was a weight across her legs. She could remember everything that had happened. It was strange, but she felt only peace inside her; no fear, no pain, no grief. Someone touched her face and she opened her eyes to a morning sky and the face of Trajan Sacripent, which was bloody and bruised. It looked as if his nose was broken.

'Trajan?'

'Don't move,' he said, and with tender strength removed the rocks from her legs. She turned her head and could see that Wispish was kneeling beside her, comfortingly real, her small face scratched, the skin round her nose caked with dried blood. Around them, the parade ground was littered with recumbent dark shapes – the bodies of Ixmarite militiamen. Many people walked among them carrying stretchers, others were administering to the injured. Yet there was a feeling that the catastrophe had happened many hours before.

'Where are Cleo and Lord Pliance?' Delilah asked, trying to rise. Her legs suddenly filled with a spasm of pain. She grabbed wildly for Wispish's torn coat. 'Where's Anvil?'

'Hush,' Wispish said. 'Lie still. Anvil will be here soon.'

Trajan had been staring at Wispish with mistrust. 'I saw the pair of you jump into the fire at Covendale,' he said. 'Yet you pop up here so conveniently, and without so much as a blemish! Are you illusionists or spirits? Why did you follow us?'

Wispish threw up her hands and rolled her eyes. 'Such probing questions! Anvil and I are not spirits, and the word "illusionist" is a feeble one to describe our talent. We followed you as soon as we could, because there was something intensely captivating about Delilah. We were intrigued as to why such a singular girl should be interested in the likes of Jeopardy, whom we believed to be a charlatan.'

'And what do you believe him to be now?' Delilah asked weakly.

Wispish wrinkled her nose. 'More than we imagined,' she said. 'Anyway,

367

he was an entertaining sight. You must stop wriggling about, Delilah! You have a broken bone.'

Trajan sighed and stroked Delilah's face. 'Wispish has spoken to one of the physicks. We must wait for him here.' He indicated one of the people who was attending to a groaning man, lying nearby.

'Can't you heal me?' Delilah said to Wispish, with a faint smile.

Wispish returned the smile, rather tightly. 'I am not at my most powerful at the moment,' she said. 'You'll be all right.'

'But the others . . .'

'We haven't seen them,' Trajan said. 'Now please be still.'

'The prophet is dead,' Delilah said.

Trajan hung his head. 'I'm not sure there ever was a prophet. Last night, I saw a host of lost spirits. I saw a dream. I saw a man obsessed. I don't know what I saw.'

'He had power,' Wispish said, 'but not the intelligence to use it. At least, that's my opinion.' She rubbed at her nose. 'Anvil would not come to watch. He's always wary of fanatics. He says that fanatical belief causes intelligence to die, but it can also be said that fanatical belief is an intelligence of death. What a strange night!'

Delilah sighed and closed her eyes. She smiled. 'I know something,' she said.

'Know what?' Trajan asked, reaching out to stroke her hair.

Delilah winced in pain. 'I thought there had to be a reason why we were looking for Jeopardy, some great purpose. Didn't we think we'd discover something, or be given something?'

Trajan made a bitter sound. 'We were wrong. *I* was wrong!'

Delilah shook her head slowly. 'No, neither of us was wrong. I understand now. It's something to do with what the Saltcats said to me. I misinterpreted it. There is no reason, no pattern. There never has been. There are just events, happenings. We learn from that, and what we learn is that there is no pattern.' She frowned. 'Jeopardy had the potential to create a great movement, something that would touch every heart in Gleberune, and perhaps beyond. But he realised that by doing that he would simply become the thing he hated most. He would crush the Ixmarites' power, yes, but he would attain it himself. He did not want that. We were to be part of it, Trajan, because all of us, Cleo, you and I, were somehow part of Resenence Jeopardy. He told me this.'

Trajan made a fretful noise and spoke to Wispish. 'She's speaking nonsense. She's fevered.'

'I don't think so,' Wispish replied.

Cleo woke up, with her clothes in disarray, somewhere in the heart of Queen Lallow's garden. At first, she thought she'd been attacked, but then remembered what had happened when the earthquake struck. Lord Pliance had come looming out of the flying smoke and debris and had grabbed hold of her garments. She remembered how he had slung her over his shoulders and, with lanky, long-legged strides, had fled the parade ground before too much damage had occurred. Still, Cleo had been buffeted by panicking people all around her, and had been virtually unconscious by the time the quake had finished and Lord Pliance had put her down. Strange, but the garden didn't seem to have been affected at all. Not even a twig had fallen from the great trees.

Cleo sighed and stretched out on the grass. Lord Pliance appeared beside her. He had torn a piece off his cloak which he'd soaked at a nearby pool, and now he gave it to her to suck.

'I'm sorry,' he said. 'Your journey was wasted. Your friend died for nothing.'

Cleo blinked up at him. 'What? Dauntless? Oh, he thought he was already dead, anyway.'

The vampire looked at her askance. 'You seem very flippant,' he said, 'for someone whose idol has just been stabbed to death and swallowed by the earth, and who has been involved in a major disaster!'

Cleo shrugged. 'Thank you for carrying me away from there.'

Lord Pliance sat down beside her and clasped his knees with loose hands. 'I must confess you ordinary folk confuse me,' he said. 'In your position, I would be maddened by grief, tormented by the fact that fate had cheated me of what I most desired.'

'I feel none of those things,' Cleo said. 'And in most ways my quest has been fulfilled.' She frowned. 'Indeed, I had no plans beyond seeing Jeopardy in the flesh, therefore I can hardly be disappointed. Still, I would have liked to touch him.'

'Madam Sinister,' said the vampire, 'if I did not know otherwise, I would now think you a rather unintelligent person.'

Cleo shook her head. 'Please, don't upset yourself. The truth is, if I'd paid more attention when the ghost spoke to me, I'd have realised by now that my true quest was meeting Trajan and Delilah.' She glanced at him sideways. 'And perhaps you.'

The vampire stared at her.

'When I think back,' Cleo went on, 'that ghost looked very much like Resenence Jeopardy. Perhaps it was him.'

'That's impossible,' Lord Pliance said. 'He wasn't dead then.'

'And Dauntless wasn't alive.' Cleo smiled. 'Ah, what a glorious morning.'

'Too glorious,' grumbled the vampire. 'If you don't mind, I'll just move back into the shade.'

Presently a figure came through the trees towards them. Cleo sat up. 'Speckless the Tregetour!' she said. 'You survived!'

'We share a common feature,' he said with a courtly bow. 'May I join you?'

'Please do.' Cleo patted the ground beside her and the tregetour sat down. 'Excuse my friend,' she said. 'He is a vampire and has little love of sunlight.'

The tregetour glanced round and smiled at Lord Pliance who stared grimly back at him.

'You appear to have lost your companions,' Cleo said, and then frowned. 'Oh no! Delilah and Trajan!' She swivelled round on the grass. 'Lord Pliance, we must look for them!'

'No need,' the tregetour said, laying a hand on her arm. 'They are quite safe.'

'You've seen them?'

He nodded. 'Yes.'

Cleo sighed. 'Good. Good. I feel tired. I do not want to walk just yet.' She contemplated the placid features of the tregetour. He was a supremely handsome man, his face intelligent and sensitive, his bones well-formed, his eyes wide-spaced. 'What will you do now?' she asked.

The tregetour raised his eyebrows. 'Excuse me?'

'Well, you are a Jeopardite, and Jeopardy is dead. Will you continue to do his work?'

The tregetour shrugged. 'When something dies, it is best to think of something new. I don't believe in tradition.'

'Oh. Well, that seems a shame. All that hard work Jeopardy did, all that gathering of souls. To be honest, I can't see what point he was trying to make. Did he know he was going to die?'

'People did call him a prophet,' said the tregetour, 'therefore we can safely assume he had an inkling.'

'All those people, though. They loved him. You'd think he'd have warned them being his follower would cause their deaths.'

'Mmm, well, nobody's perfect.'

'You don't seem that concerned.'

The tregetour leapt to his feet. 'Why should I be?' he asked. 'The morning is beautiful. The world moves on. Time spins a new web.' he stretched, and then smiled wryly at Cleo. 'The child was indeed beautiful,' he said.

'What?'

'If you've a mind, I could fulfil your wish. I could give you a replacement.'

'How dare you!' Cleo cried, divining the venal tone to the offer.

'Well, it was only a thought. Good day to you.' The tregetour walked off in a jaunty fashion through the trees. Cleo stared after him, dumbfounded for a few moments, then she stood up.

'Wait!' she cried. 'Wait!'

But there was no one there. The tregetour must have run off very quickly.

Epilogue

Gallimaufry is built upon a warren of caves and underground tunnels. It is not impossible that someone with a knowledge of the network, and the resources to undermine the weakest spots, could initiate severe subsidence in the city, and even choose which areas would be most affected.

Perpetuis Sleeve considers this as he surveys the wreckage of the Arch-imagery. It is preferable to believe in rational explanations for the devastation than to think Resenence Jeopardy might actually have possessed supernatural power.

As reports come in, it is clear that every Ixmaritian building, every church and shrine, every religious statue in the city, has collapsed. The effects might have spread even further afield, but this will not be ascertained until later. The casualties are numerous because most of the Ixmarites were asleep in their beds or else active on the parade ground when the disaster occurred. Marmick is dead, buried somewhere beneath the rubble of Sleeve's apartment. Seven of the Ten are dead; three spared because they were absent from their homes, at a gaming den in one of the less salubrious areas of Gallimaufry. All the documents and archives of Ixmarity have been destroyed.

Perpetuis Sleeve does not feel distraught. The sun is shining. The morning smells sweet. It is a new day. Many people will feel let down by Resenence Jeopardy now. A clever man could manipulate that situation, especially one from whom all adversity has been removed.

I have a choice, Sleeve thinks, as he strolls among the ruins of his garden. I could gather what remains of my staff around me and re-create the Church as it was before. Last night's disaster could conveniently be cited as evidence of Ixmar's displeasure with His children. Or, I could step forth to fashion a new Ixmarity, pursue a road which would lead to a fairer society, where there are no gibbets on the roadsides, and no fear of retribution. Ixmarity, in any form, will need an income, of course, but how much better if it is given willingly, through choice. What new industries can I dream up for a revived Ixmarity?

Sleeve smiles and looks around him. The wealth of Ixmarity is not its churches and archives, but its funds, which are safe in municipal banks, unaffected by the disaster. I could have a new title, he thinks, something less stiff and formal. An airier palace could be built that is more to my taste than that depressing old mausoleum which fell down. I could choose my own staff. Neoteric rituals could be devised, and new holy books would certainly have to be written; fresh and modern interpretations of outmoded creeds. The life of Resenence Jeopardy himself could be chronicled, showing him to be a catalyst of the New Age; a destructive but necessary force. In that way, even Jeopardy's sympathisers could be won over.

Already, Sleeve can visualise the park that could be built upon the old parade ground, an annex to the Old Gardens of Queen Lallow. He would call it Jeopardy Park, a monument to the mad prophet in the very place he died. There would be a statue, and a meditation bower. Icons could be on sale, and pamphlets, and . . . Sleeve sighs contentedly. The possibilities are limitless.

Yes, it is a good day. Sleeve salutes the sky. Jeopardy, wherever your spirit roams, I applaud you!

For Inanna, the choice is different. She is back in her house which has fortunately suffered no damage during the night, but seems cold and empty. It is as if she's been away for months. Clocks tick loudly, but other than that the rooms are filled only with silent accusation. Inanna will not let herself think of ghosts. Her hair hangs lankly about her face, and the skirt of her gown is badly ripped. She has not taken off her damp, soiled wrap, and is pacing from room to room, as if searching for something. In the bedroom, she finds it: the question.

Standing by the window, she glances back at the bed. She knows that she could easily slip off her clothes and ease herself between the sheets, give herself up to a spasm of anxiety. She could wait for the darkness and for the spectre of Resenence Jeopardy to come climbing over her balcony, battered and bloody, to demand her devotion, her sanity. It would be easy to do that, wouldn't it?

Or, she could shake herself free of the past, step out of this house and leave if for ever. She could find Perpetuis Sleeve and see if he still has a job for her. It is obvious his staff has been seriously reduced. He will need people like her. But is that what she wants?

Inanna sighs. They were solicitous at the parade ground this morning, the marshals sifting through the debris. Sleeve went among them to boost morale, while she walked to the gaping hole where the plinth had once stood. Men were in there, throwing out rocks.

'Have you found his body?' she asked.

Someone high-ranking looked up, pity all over his face. She is known to them all as Implexion's woman.

'No, my lady.'

The man clambered out of the hole and put his coat round her shoulders. She could not remember his face, even though he had shepherded her away, murmuring comforts. She'd been taken home, and deposited there, her escort considerate to the last. Then, he had hurried away in embarrassment, as if she was somehow tainted by Implexion's mania. The man did not know how right he was. He hadn't asked her whose body she'd meant.

'Even slaves can find the courage to free themselves!' she says aloud to the listening room.

After a moment, while the silence rings with the echo of her words, she takes off her ruined clothes and dresses herself in a clean outfit from her wardrobes. She puts her hands into the pockets of her coat and looks around the room, considering. Her glance skims over her dressing table where jewellery spills abundantly from open caskets and bottles of exotic perfumes are ranked before the mirror. She regards the open wardrobes that are crammed with the expensive clothes Implexion bought her.

No, there is nothing here she wants to take with her. She will walk into her new life unburdened, free, reborn.

Chasteless and Lucien Earthlight are walking back along the road to Shanariah. They have not said much for the past few hours, wanting only to put as much space between themselves and Gallimaufry as possible. Lucien does not want to think about what he has seen, or what he might be feeling, and instead concentrates on what he intends to say to Cartesian Blink when he and Chasteless arrive at his house. They will ask Cartesian to repair Chasteless, but he will not be allowed to reinstate her as a plaything for himself and his friends. If there is any argument about that, then Lucien and Chasteless will leave. In his mind, Lucien acts out the possible scenarios.

Suddenly Chasteless says, 'Look, Lucien, look at that pretty pavilion.'

At the side of the road, a tent has been set up, with a table out front. A group of half a dozen children or so are hanging around outside. One sits behind the table, apparently collecting money. A hastily scrawled sign reads: 'Magicks to be found within! Come, see the wonders!' Gaily coloured ribbons flutter from the top of the pavilion, gauzy veils flap in the morning breeze. Lucien experiences a shudder. One of the children looks very much like a younger version of Walterkin. What has happened to Walterkin?

'Can we look inside?' Chasteless asks, tugging on Lucien's arm.

'I don't think we should,' Lucien replies stiffly.

'Please, Lucien, we've had such a terrible time.' Chasteless is emphatic.

One of the children, apparently having observed their discussion, trots forward. 'The smallest coin you have will buy you entrance,' he says. 'You will not believe your eyes! Come inside.' He attempts to lead them towards the tent.

A thread of music emanates from among the folds of the pavilion. It speaks of a vast and magical landscape, of unimagined marvels, of soaring, sweet experiences. A perfume fills the air, the perfume of a thousand flowers, the salt perfume of the sea.

Lucien hesitates. It seems as if Chasteless, the boy, all the children behind him, the world itself, are waiting for his decision. He feels the touch of beloved hands upon his face. He senses a promise waiting to be fulfilled.

Now, or never.

Never.

Lucien takes Chasteless's elbow in his hand. He propels her forward. 'Not today,' he says to the child. 'Not ever.'

Soon, the pavilion is lost from view round a bend in the road. Lucien knows it will appear again, upon this journey and perhaps many times in the future. This time, he was strong enough to resist.

'I want the real world, Chasteless,' he says. She makes no response. When he glances down at her, she is walking stiffly by his side, a complicated and sophisticated machine. Maybe she will never speak again.

Lucien sighs. Shanariah is a long way off. Is his clear sight still with him? At some point, the road will turn to ashes beneath his feet.